THE COMPLETE
ANGEL CATBIRD™

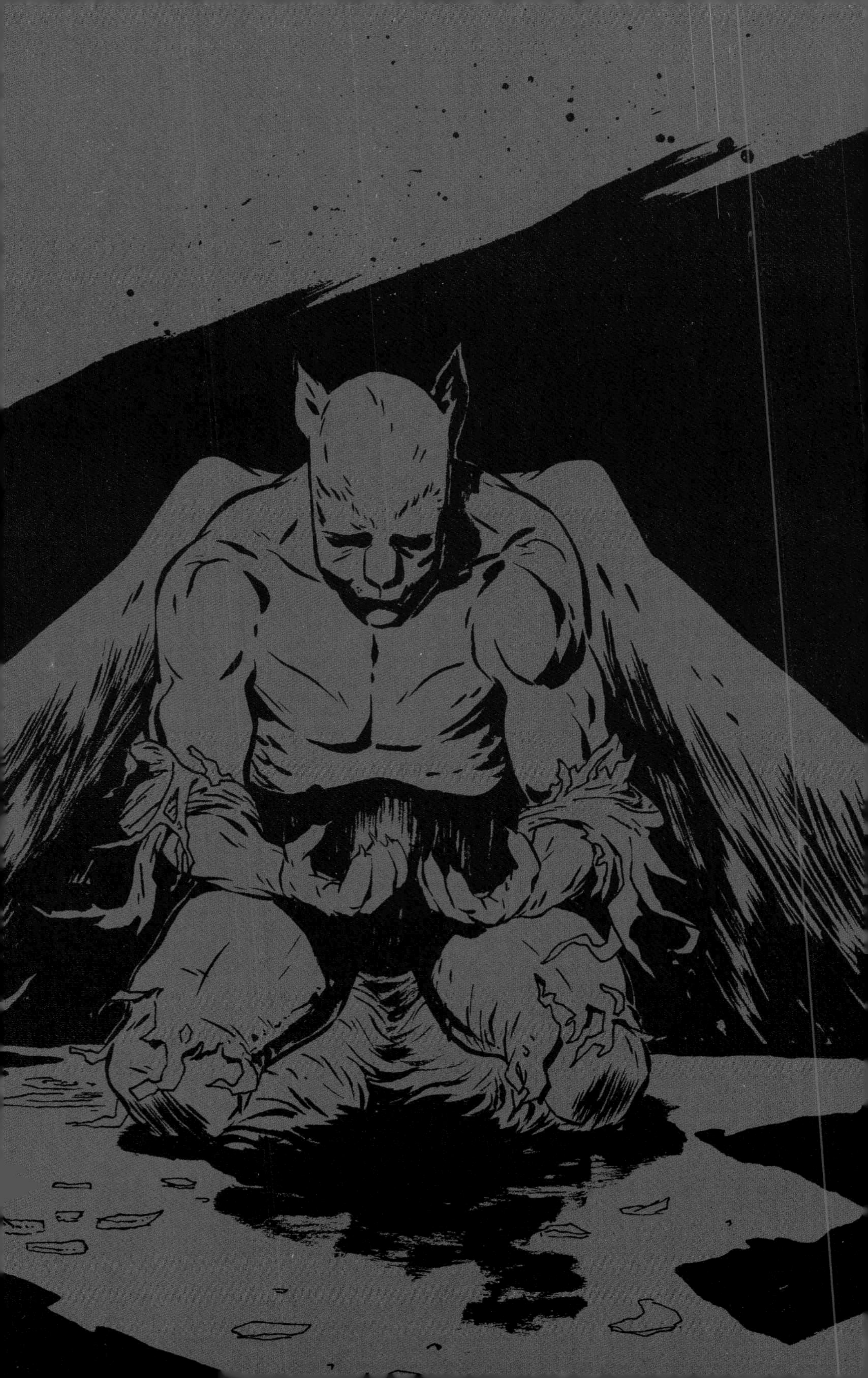

THE COMPLETE
ANGEL CATBIRD™

Story by MARGARET ATWOOD

Art by JOHNNIE CHRISTMAS

Colors by TAMRA BONVILLAIN

Letters by NATE PIEKOS OF BLAMBOT®

DARK HORSE BOOKS

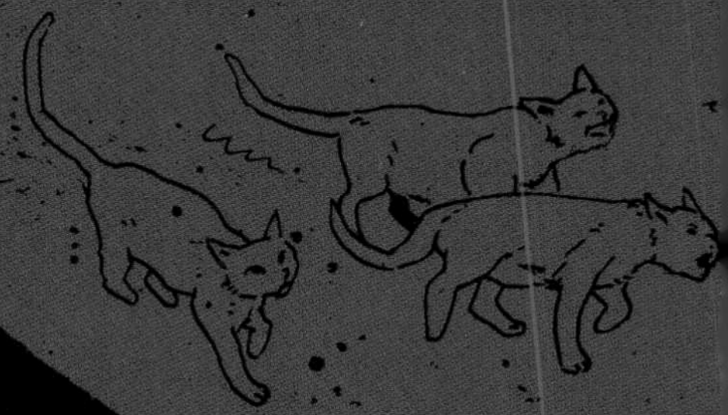

President and Publisher MIKE RICHARDSON

Editors DANIEL CHABON and HOPE NICHOLSON

Assistant Editors BRETT ISRAEL, CARDNER CLARK, and RACHEL ROBERTS

Designer SARAH TERRY

Digital Art Technician JOSIE CHRISTENSEN

Special Thanks to SARAH COOPER

Published by Dark Horse Books
A division of Dark Horse Comics, Inc.
10956 SE Main Street, Milwaukie, OR 97222

DarkHorse.com

To find a comic shop in your area, check out the Comic Shop Locator Service: comicshoplocator.com

First edition: October 2018 | ISBN 978-1-50670-456-2

10 9 8 7 6 5 4 3 2 1
Printed in China

Library of Congress Cataloging-in-Publication Data

Names: Atwood, Margaret, 1939- author. | Christmas, Johnnie, artist | Bonvillain, Tamra, colourist. | Piekos, Nate, letterer.
Title: The complete Angel Catbird / story by Margaret Atwood ; art by Johnnie Christmas ; colors by Tamra Bonvillain ; letters by Nate Piekos of Blambot.
Description: First edition. | Milwaukie, OR : Dark Horse Books, October 2018. | Summary: "A genetic engineer caught in the middle of a chemical accident all of a sudden finds himself with superhuman abilities. He takes on the identity of Angel Catbird and gets caught in the middle of a war between animal/human hybrids."-- Provided by publisher.
Identifiers: LCCN 2018016477 | ISBN 9781506704562 (paperback)
Subjects: LCSH: Graphic novels. | CYAC: Graphic novels. | Superheroes--Fiction. | Genetic engineering--Fiction. | Adventure and adventurers--Fiction. | BISAC: COMICS & GRAPHIC NOVELS / Superheroes. | COMICS & GRAPHIC NOVELS / Fantasy. | COMICS & GRAPHIC NOVELS / Science Fiction.
Classification: LCC PZ7.7.A896 Ank 2018 | DDC 741.5/973--dc23
LC record available at https://lccn.loc.gov/2018016477

MARGARET ATWOOD

INTRODUCTION

Some find it strange that a person known for her novels and poetry would take to writing comic books, especially comic books called *Angel Catbird*. Why is a nice literary old lady like me—an award-winning nice literary old lady—a nice literary old lady who should be resting on her laurels in her rocking chair, being dignified and iconic—why is such a nice old lady messing around with flying cat-owl superheroes and nightclubs for cat people, not to mention giant rat men? Strange.

But I myself don't find it very strange. I was born in 1939, and was thus of a reading age when the war ended and colour comics made a booming comeback. Not only did I read masses of comics in magazine form, I could encounter many of the same characters in the weekend newspapers, which had big spreads of colour comics. Some of the comics were funny—*Little Lulu*, *Li'l Abner*, *Mickey Mouse*, *Blondie*, and so forth—but some were serious—*Steve Canyon*, *Rip Kirby*, and the unfathomable *Mary Worth*. And some were superheroes: Batman, Captain Marvel, Wonder Woman, Superman, Plastic Man, the Green Lantern, the Human Torch, and their ilk. Some were even aimed at improving young minds: the *Classic Comics* series had an educational bent.

And some were just weird. In this last category I'd place *Mandrake the Magician*, *Little Orphan Annie*—in which nobody had eyes—and *Dick Tracy*: surrealist masterpieces, all of them, though somewhat disturbing for children. A criminal who could assume anyone's face, behind which he looked like melting Swiss cheese? It was alarmingly close to Salvador Dalí,

and kept me awake nights—as did Salvador Dalí, when I came across him years later.

Not only did I read all of these comics, I drew comics of my own. The earliest ones featured two flying rabbit superheroes, somewhat too jolly and fond of somersaults to be considered heavyweights. My older brother had a much larger stable of characters. They had more gravitas: they went in for large-scale warfare, whereas my own superheroes just fooled around with the odd bullet.

Along with the superhero rabbits I drew winged flying cats, many with balloons attached to them. I was obsessed with balloons, as no balloons were available during the war. So I'd seen pictures of them, but never the actual thing. It was similar with the cats: I wasn't allowed to have one because we were up in the Canadian forests a lot. How would the cat travel? Once there, wouldn't it run away and be eaten by mink? Very likely. So, for the first part of my life, my cats were flying dream cats.

Time passed, and both the balloons and the cats materialized in my real life. The balloons were a disappointment, liable as they were to burst and deflate; the cats were not. For over fifty years I was a dedicated cat person, with a few gaps here and there when I was a student. My cats were a pleasure, a comfort, and an aid to composition. The only reason I don't have one now is that I'm afraid of tripping on it. That, and of leaving it an orphan, so to speak.

As the 1940s changed into the 1950s and I became a teenager, the comic that preoccupied me the most was Walt Kelly's *Pogo*, which, with its cast of swamp critters combined with its satire of the McCarthy era's excesses, set a new benchmark: how to be entertainingly serious while also being seriously entertaining. Meanwhile I was continuing to draw, and to design the odd visual object—posters, for the silk-screen poster business I was running on the Ping-Pong table in the late fifties, and book covers, for my own first books, because that was cheaper than paying a pro.

In the seventies I drew a sort-of political strip called *Kanadian Kultchur Komix* for a magazine called, puzzlingly, *This Magazine*. I then took to drawing a yearly strip called *Book Tour Comix*, which I would send to my publishers at Christmas to make them feel guilty. (That didn't succeed.) It's no great coincidence that the narrator of my 1972 novel, *Surfacing*, is an illustrator, and that the narrator of my 1988 novel, *Cat's Eye*, is a figurative painter. We all have unlived lives. (Note that none of these narrators has ever been a ballet dancer. I did try ballet, briefly, but it made me dizzy.)

And I continued to read comics, watching the emergence of a new generation of psychologically complex characters with relationship problems (Spider-Man, who begat Wolverine, et cetera). Then came the emergence of graphic novels, with such now-classics as *Maus* and *Persepolis*: great-grandchildren of Pogo, whether they knew it or not.

Meanwhile I had become more and more immersed in the world of bird conservation. I now had a burden of guilt from my many years of cat companionship, for my cats had gone in and out of the house, busying themselves with their cat affairs, which included the killing of small animals and birds. These would turn up as gifts, placed thoughtfully either on my pillow instead of a chocolate, or on the front doormat, where I would slip on them. Sometimes it would not even be a whole animal. One of my cats donated only the gizzards.

From this collision between my comic-reading-and-writing self and the bird blood on my hands, Angel Catbird was born. I pondered him for several years, and even did some preliminary sketches. He would be a combination of cat, owl, and human being, and he would thus have an identity conflict—*do I save this baby robin, or do I eat it?* But he would be able to understand both sides of the question. He would be a walking, flying carnivore's dilemma.

But I realized that Angel Catbird would have to look better than the flying cats I'd drawn in my childhood—two-dimensional and wooden—and better also than my own later cartoons, which were fairly basic and lumpy. I wanted Angel Catbird to look sexy, like the superhero and noir comics I'd read in the forties. He would have to have muscles.

So I would need a coauthor. But how to find one? This wasn't a world of which I had much knowledge. Then up on my Twitter feed popped, one day, a possible answer. A person called Hope Nicholson was resurrecting one of the forgotten Canadian superheroes of the wartime 1940s and fundraising it via Kickstarter. Not only that, Hope lived in Toronto.

I put the case for *Angel Catbird* to her, we got together in a strange Russian-themed pub, and lo and behold, she came onboard and connected me not only with artist Johnnie Christmas, who could draw just the right kinds of muscles and also owl claws, but the publisher, Dark Horse Comics. The Dark Horse editor of the series is Daniel Chabon, who from his picture looks about fifteen. I have never met him, nor have I met Johnnie, nor the excellent colourist Tamra Bonvillain, but I am sure such a meeting will take place in the future.

All of these collaborators have been wonderful. What more could an illustrator manqué such as myself possibly ask for? What fun we have had! At least, I have had fun. Watching *Angel Catbird* come to life has been hugely engaging. There was, for instance, a long email debate about Angel's pants. He had to have pants of some kind. Feather pants, or what? And if feathers, what kind of feathers? And should these pants be underneath his human pants, and just sort of emerge? How should they manifest themselves? Questions would be asked, and we needed to have answers.

And what about Cate Leone, the love interest? Pictures of cat eyes flew back and forth through the ether, and at one point I found myself scanning and sending a costume sketch I had done. What would a girl who is also a cat wear while singing in a nightclub act? Boots with fur trim and claws on the toes? Blood-drop earrings?

Such questions occupy my waking hours. What sort of furniture should Count Catula—part bat, part cat, part vampire—have in his castle? Should some of it be upside down, considering the habits of bats? (Count Catula is important in his own right, for bats are in a lot of trouble worldwide.)

How to make a white Egyptian vulture look seductive? (You know what they eat, right?) Should Octopuss have a cat face and tentacle hair? Should Cate Leone have a rival for Angel Catbird's attentions—a part girl, part owl called AtheneOwl? I'm thinking yes. In her human form, does she work at Hooters, or is that a pun too far?

So. Like that.

There is, of course, a science-and-conservation side to this project: it is supplied by Nature Canada, who are not only contributing the statistics that can be found here and there in the book in the banners at the bottoms of the pages, but are also running a #SafeCatSafeBird outreach campaign to urge cat owners not to let their cats range unsupervised. The mortality figures for outdoor cats are shockingly high: they get bitten, hit by cars, eaten by foxes, and that's just the beginning. So, it's good for cats and good for birds to keep the cats safe, and in conditions in which they can't contribute to the millions of annual bird deaths attributed to cats. On CatsAndBirds.ca, cat owners can find resources to help them, and as we increase awareness, we can hope that there might be an uptick in the plummeting bird counts that are being recorded in so many places. It may also result in better conditions for stressed forests, since it is the migratory songbirds that weed insect pests out of the trees. Cats aren't the only factor in the decline of birds, of course—habitat loss, pesticides, and glass windows are all playing a part—but they're a big factor.

There used to be an elephant who came around to grade schools. He was called Elmer the Safety Elephant, and he gave advice on crossing streets safely and not getting run over. If your school had managed a year without a street accident, Elmer gave you a flag.

In my wildest dreams, Angel Catbird and Cate Leone, and maybe even Count Catula, would go around and give something or other—a flag, a trophy?—to schools that had gathered a certain number of safe-cat pledges. Who knows, maybe it will happen. Before we act, we imagine and wish, and I'm wishing and imagining a result like that. If it does happen, I'll be the first to climb into my boots with claws on the toes, or maybe sprout some wings, in aid of the cause.

Meanwhile, I hope you enjoy *Angel Catbird* as much as my partners and I have enjoyed creating it. It's been a hoot!

Or a meow.

Or both.

Margaret Atwood

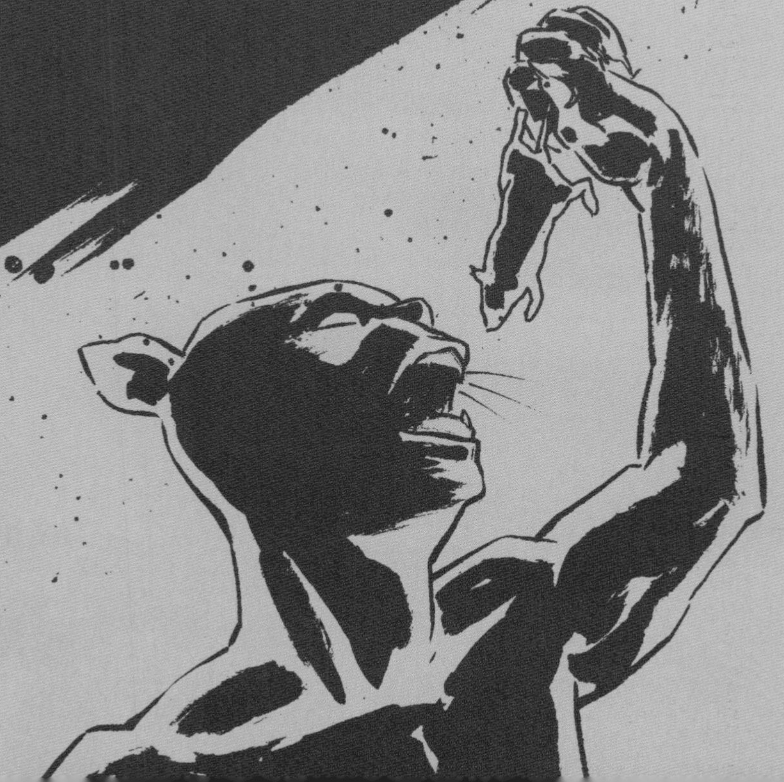

G. WILLOW WILSON

FOREWORD

Like all true Chimeras, the work of Margaret Atwood defies easy categorization. From the bleak dystopia of *The Handmaid's Tale*, which seems more relevant than ever in our era of newly restricted reproductive rights; to the sly surrealism of the *Oryx and Crake* trilogy, in which humankind reaps the whirlwind of hypercapitalism and ecological destruction; to the lush psychological drama of *Cat's Eye*, which throws the lessons of adolescence into painful relief, Atwood moves nimbly from subject to subject and from genre to genre. And like a Chimera, she seems to be fueled by some secret fire, one that makes her as dryly, mirthfully witty on Twitter as she is in the pages of the *Michigan Quarterly Review* or *Harper's Magazine*.

Most fiction writers alive today have been influenced by Atwood's work, whether they know it or not: by tackling the most pressing issues of each unfolding decade, she has achieved a kind of cultural ubiquity. I first picked up *The Handmaid's Tale* in the mid-1990s, when I was twelve or thirteen, which in retrospect is probably a bit too young to tackle that book. In the awkward grip of puberty, it read like a kind of body horror, a warning that there was no part of womanhood which could not be commodified. To encounter a novel like that in the banal, apolitical atmosphere of the nineties, when sexism and racism were "over" and strong viewpoints were seen as impolite, was an electric experience; it showed me that you could, in fact, address real-world issues in a meaningful way within the realm of fantasy and science fiction. Speculative fiction wasn't simply an escape; it was also an arrival.

Do Atwood's disparate creations have a unifying message? If they do, I think it might be tidily summed up as a simple directive: resist complacency. Resist it with whatever tools you have on hand—with wit, with humor, with irony, or with anger, but *resist* it, and do not apologize.

In *Angel Catbird*, we see that message at its most jubilantly pulpy. It is an unselfconscious romp through a world instantly recognizable both to fans of Silver Age comics and to the furriest corners of the Internet, a world in which the boundaries between human and animal blur and our most primitive instincts come into play. Like all great superheroes, Strig, the titular protagonist, is only momentarily alarmed by the onset of his strange powers: when you are given the ability to transform into a half-cat, half-owl, half-man (that's three halves), you must carpe that diem, and he does. *Angel Catbird* represents a side of Margaret Atwood we don't get to see very often: an unabashedly geeky side, one conversant in the tangled continuities of superhero comics and at home in fandom. The story is pure, distilled nerd catharsis, delivered by a literary legend.

Atwood's story is well served by coconspirator Johnnie Christmas, whose gleeful, kinetic art style pays homage to the era of Jack Kirby and Russ Manning, masters who peaked before the age of irony and to whom pulp was a kind of religion. If there is a joke, Christmas and Atwood are in on it together, and it makes for one heck of a read. There are puns, and then there are cat puns, and then there are Dracula cat puns, and then there are *visual* Dracula cat puns, and if you hung around for the end of that list, this is the kind of graphic novel you need on your bookshelf.

Meow.

G. Willow Wilson

KELLY SUE DeCONNICK

FOREWORD

A *foreword* is part of a book's *front matter*. It's usually written by someone other than the main author, and its purpose (these days, anyway) is more as a marketing aid than anything else. The idea is to get an esteemed person of some variety—an expert in a related field or perhaps a successful author of a similar book—to lend an air of credibility to the launch.

You see the problem, don't you?

The book you hold in your hands is by Margaret Atwood and Johnnie Christmas, with colors by Tamra Bonvillain. Christmas and Bonvillain may be new to you, but the Margaret Atwood in question is THE Margaret Atwood. Margaret Atwood of *The Handmaid's Tale*. Margaret Atwood of the MaddAddam Trilogy. Literary Grand Dame Margaret Atwood. Margaret Atwood: *Companion of the Order of Canada*. Unless this is, I dunno, the very first book you've ever read, chances are you've heard of her. Hell, if you're a woman of my generation, I'd lay odds you either have a *nolite te bastardes carborundorum* tattoo or you've seriously considered one. So, as proud as I am of my work and what I've accomplished as the author of *Captain Marvel*, *Bitch Planet*, and *Pretty Deadly*, there is no universe in which I have any credibility whatsoever to lend to MARGARET ATWOOD'S BOOK LAUNCH.

Then why am I here? Why are you reading this, and not jumping right into the further adventures of Angel Catbird? Because I'm con-stitutionally incapable of saying no to Margaret Atwood, is the short answer. But I'd like to justify my presence with something more useful than that. So what can I do?

As a comic book writer of some renown and a comic book *consumer* of thirty-plus years, it occurs to me that I might be able to offer you a little context. Some of you—perhaps even many of you—may have followed Ms. Atwood from her prose work to this medium. It may be new to you and maybe—maybe!—I can add to your

appreciation by filling you in on a little bit of our history. There are two areas I want to address: Golden Age Comics and Comics as Pedagogy.

GOLDEN AGE COMICS

Both in substance and style, *Angel Catbird* is a playful nod to the period of comics publishing from 1938 to 1955, referred to as the "Golden Age." Though the superhero genre had come to dominate the medium by the end of the Golden Age (and that rise is a significant part of how we define it), through most of the period, genres like horror, western, romance, war, and "funny animal" comics were equally popular. Atwood herself, in her introduction to the first *Angel Catbird* collection, cites Walt Kelly's talking-animal strip *Pogo* as an influence.

Pogo, which launched in 1941 in the premiere issue of Dell's creatively titled *Animal Comics*, is an unsurprising favorite for Atwood—like the woman and her work, it's both erudite and mischievous. Through the eyes of an "everyman possum," *Pogo* uses allegory to comment on human nature in a manner that reminds me of Greek mythology more than anything else. Sadly, it isn't remembered by as many people as it ought to be.

But back to the rise and rapid dominance of the superhero genre, which is what most of us think of when we think of the Golden Age. *Angel Catbird*, while full of *Pogo*-esque talking animals, is constructed primarily as a superhero tale. Though books of that genre in that period were mercifully devoid of relatable villains or devilish antiheroes—good was good, evil was evil, and the closest thing to moral ambiguity one encountered was a femme fatale torn between her attraction to the hero and the necessity of her plot against him (she wasn't *really* bad; she was just drawn that way)—Golden Age comics were also more sophisticated and sexier than the moralistic and goofy comics that followed in the Silver Age. This was, remember, before the Comics Code. (I don't have the time to get into that here, but if you're interested, I highly recommend *The Ten-Cent Plague: The Great Comic-Book Scare and How It Changed America* by David Hajdu.) Angel Catbird's feather booty shorts and sculpted nude torso would have been right at home among the virile heroes of the Golden Age.

Note that I am American and I write this overview from an American perspective. Atwood is Canadian. As it happens, this period was also a "Golden Age" for Canadian comics, since American comics were banned from import to Canada under WECA, or the War Exchange Conservation Act. During the six years the act was in effect, what came to be known as "Canadian Whites" (because they were printed in black and white) flourished. Titles such as *Triumph Comics* and *Better Comics* (which is almost as good a title as *Animal Comics*) unfortunately folded once WECA was lifted and their American counterparts flooded back into the market.

Americans: ruining Canadian comics since 1946. You're welcome.

COMICS AS PEDAGOGY

Comics are both multimodal and interactive.

"Multimodal" is a word academics use in a few different ways, but in this instance, Professor Ben Saunders, who heads the Comics Studies program at the University of Oregon, explained it to mean that comics "mix semiotic registers." Of course, that's so much more confusing than "multimodal" that Ben wrote "(ugh)" right after it in our correspondence on the matter. (Ben's a good egg.)

"Semiotic registers" basically means "ways of communicating." It's a little more complicated than that, but my search for understanding led me down a rabbit hole of mathematical language and Jungian approaches to literature and I want to spare you that folly. So, basically—just go with me on this—comics are multimodal because they communicate ideas using both written text (a series of symbols representing sounds, which, when "heard" together in your head, have meaning) and pictures (I'm not going to break down what pictures are and how they communicate meaning. I am also a good egg, see?). That two-pronged attack makes comics a very powerful way to engage the brain in story.

Comics are also *interactive*. What do I mean by that? Well, when you consume a movie or

television show, your role is passive—the pace is prescribed; you simply sit and take it in as it's served. With comics, the reader controls the pace. Even more than that, the reader's participation is *required* to fill in the action that happens between the panels—the space we call "the gutters." When we see a drawing of a woman ten feet from a door and then another picture of a woman's hand on a doorknob, something much more active than persistence of vision is required for our brains to understand that the lady from the first illustration walked to the door and raised her hand to open it—all in the gutter. You follow?

Combine multimodal and interactive and what you get is a storytelling medium that is so cognitively engaging as to be a powerful tool for education . . . or persuasion. *Angel Catbird* does both for bird conservation—educating us on the dangers of free-roaming cats, for example, and using statistics and suggestions to try to alter our behavior.

Comics have a long and fascinating history as a means of propaganda or persuasion. In World War II, the US Office of War Information published a comic called *The Nightmares of Lieutenant Ichi; or, Juan Posong Gives Ichi the Midnight Jitters* and distributed it throughout the Pacific theater to boost morale among the Filipinos and denigrate the occupying Japanese. In 1984, the CIA developed a comic and airdropped it over Grenada prior to the US invasion. I guess they viewed that book as successful, because in 1985 the CIA made another one for the Contras in Nicaragua! Think too of the fire-and-brimstone scare comics Jack Chick produced or, on a more pleasant note, *Martin Luther King and the Montgomery Story*, the comic that helped kick off nonviolent protest movements across the American South, and later, as far away as the Middle East.

Okay, so let's bring this home: I promised a bit of comics history to contextualize *Angel Catbird* and I think I've delivered, but there's one more idea I want to sneak in: in combining the traditions of Golden Age Comics and Comics as Pedagogy, Atwood has done something very modern: she's made a genre mash-up.

What was it I called her up there—erudite and mischievous? I stand by both.

Kelly Sue DeConnick
Portland, OR
2017

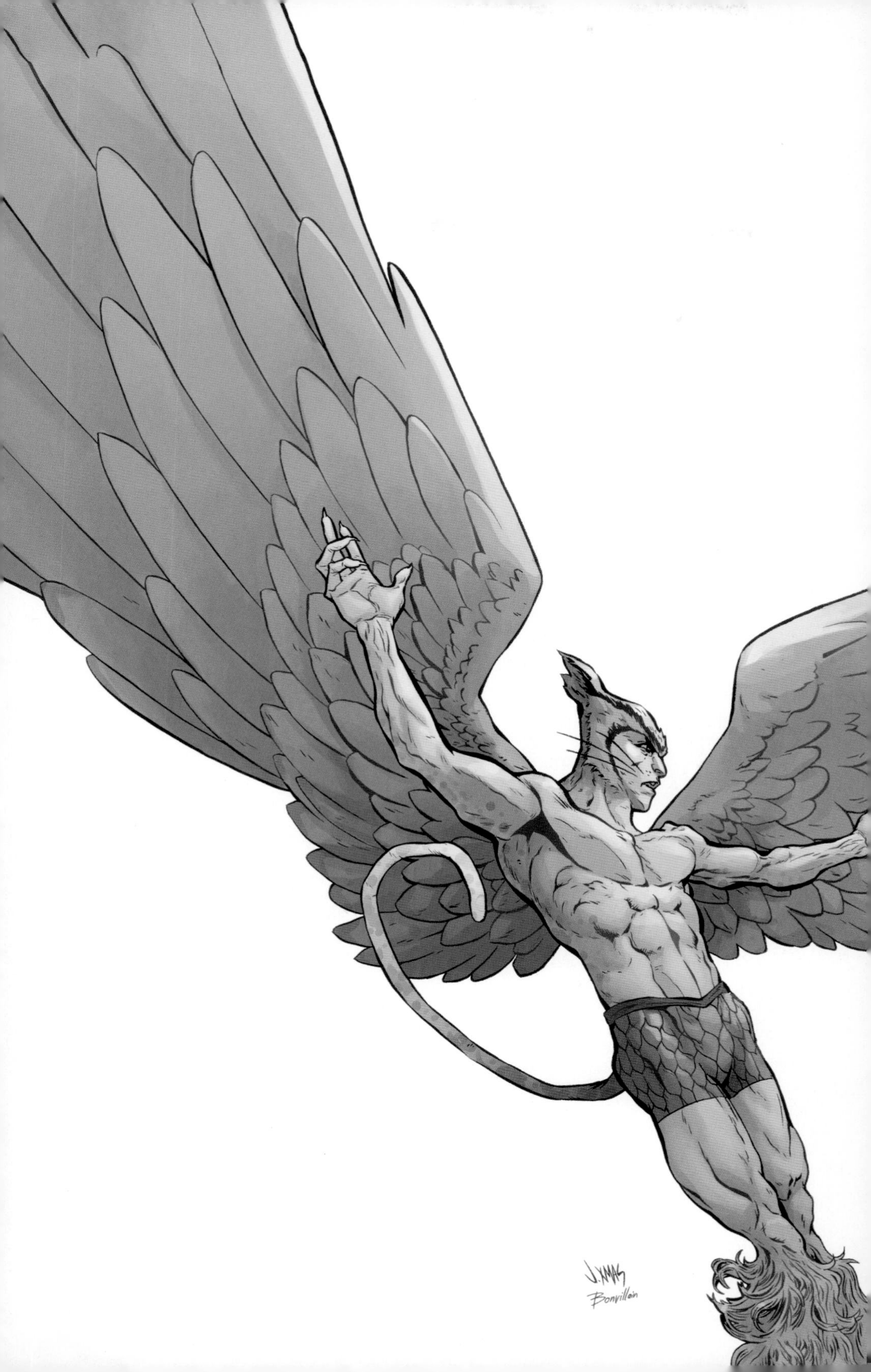
J.XMAS
Bonvillain

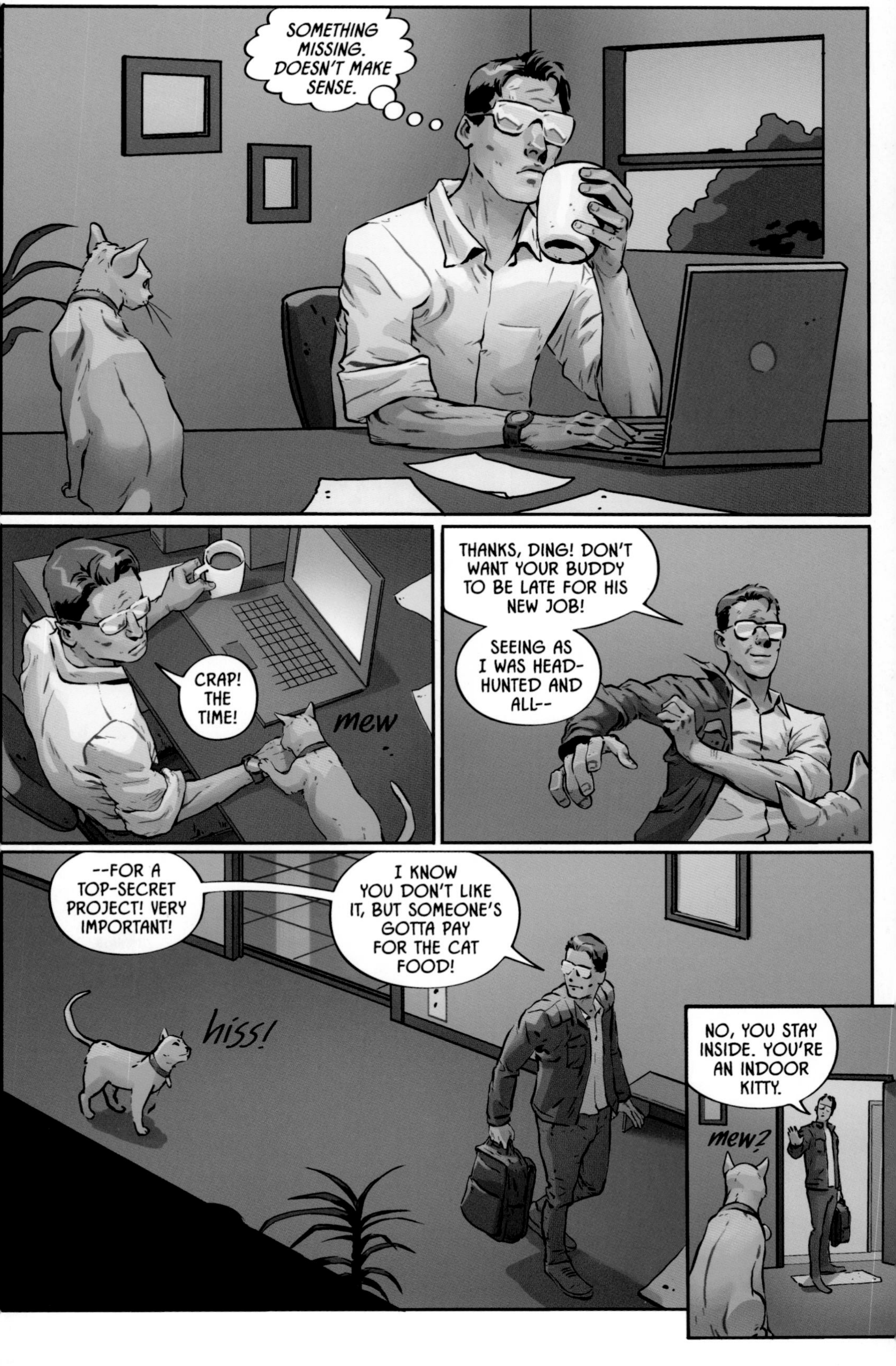
SOMETHING MISSING. DOESN'T MAKE SENSE.
CRAP! THE TIME!
mew
THANKS, DING! DON'T WANT YOUR BUDDY TO BE LATE FOR HIS NEW JOB!
SEEING AS I WAS HEAD-HUNTED AND ALL--
--FOR A TOP-SECRET PROJECT! VERY IMPORTANT!
I KNOW YOU DON'T LIKE IT, BUT SOMEONE'S GOTTA PAY FOR THE CAT FOOD!
hiss!
NO, YOU STAY INSIDE. YOU'RE AN INDOOR KITTY.
mew?

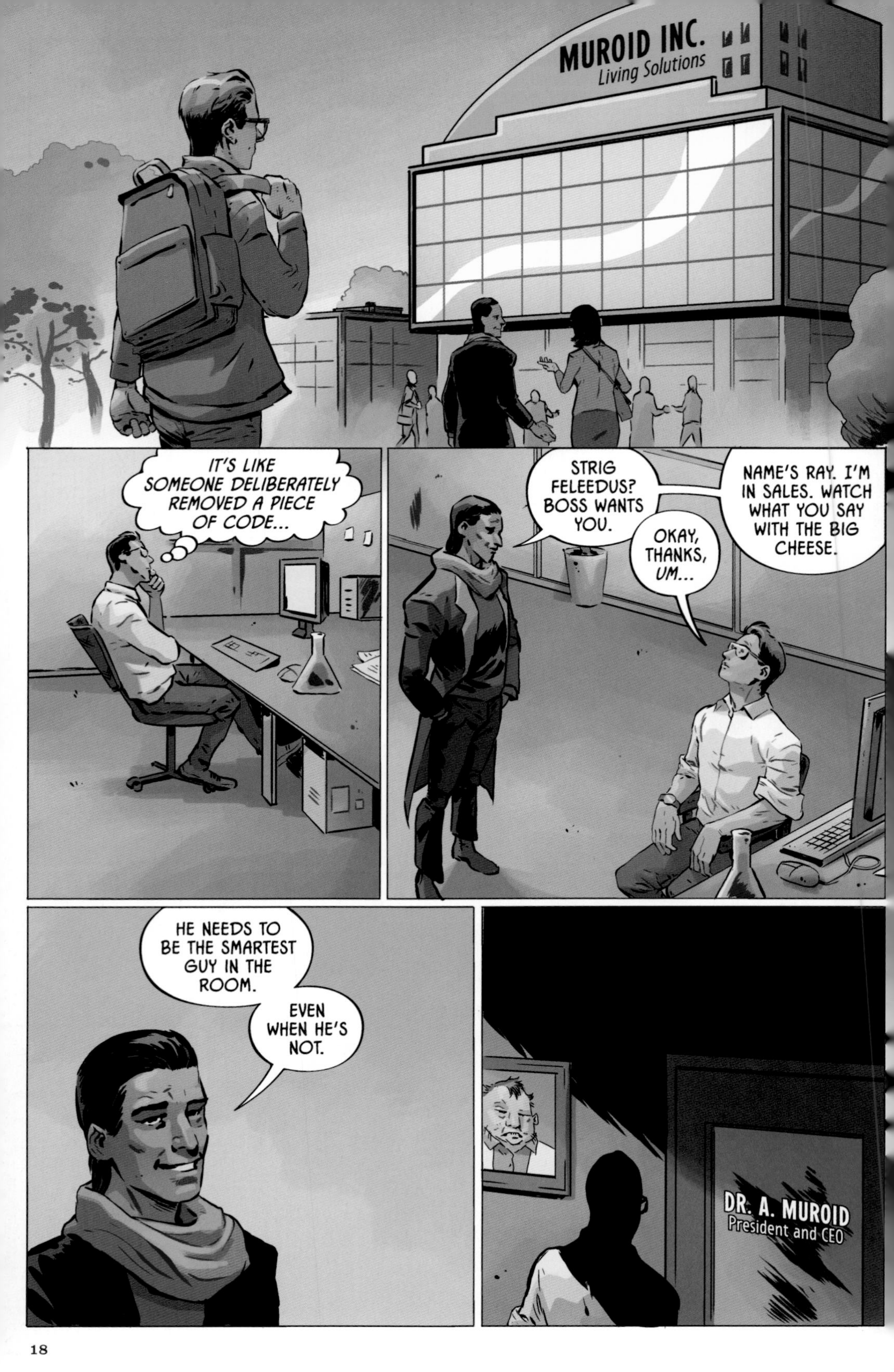
MUROID INC.
Living Solutions
IT'S LIKE SOMEONE DELIBERATELY REMOVED A PIECE OF CODE...
STRIG FELEEDUS? BOSS WANTS YOU.
OKAY, THANKS, UM...
NAME'S RAY. I'M IN SALES. WATCH WHAT YOU SAY WITH THE BIG CHEESE.
HE NEEDS TO BE THE SMARTEST GUY IN THE ROOM.
EVEN WHEN HE'S NOT.
DR. A. MUROID
President and CEO

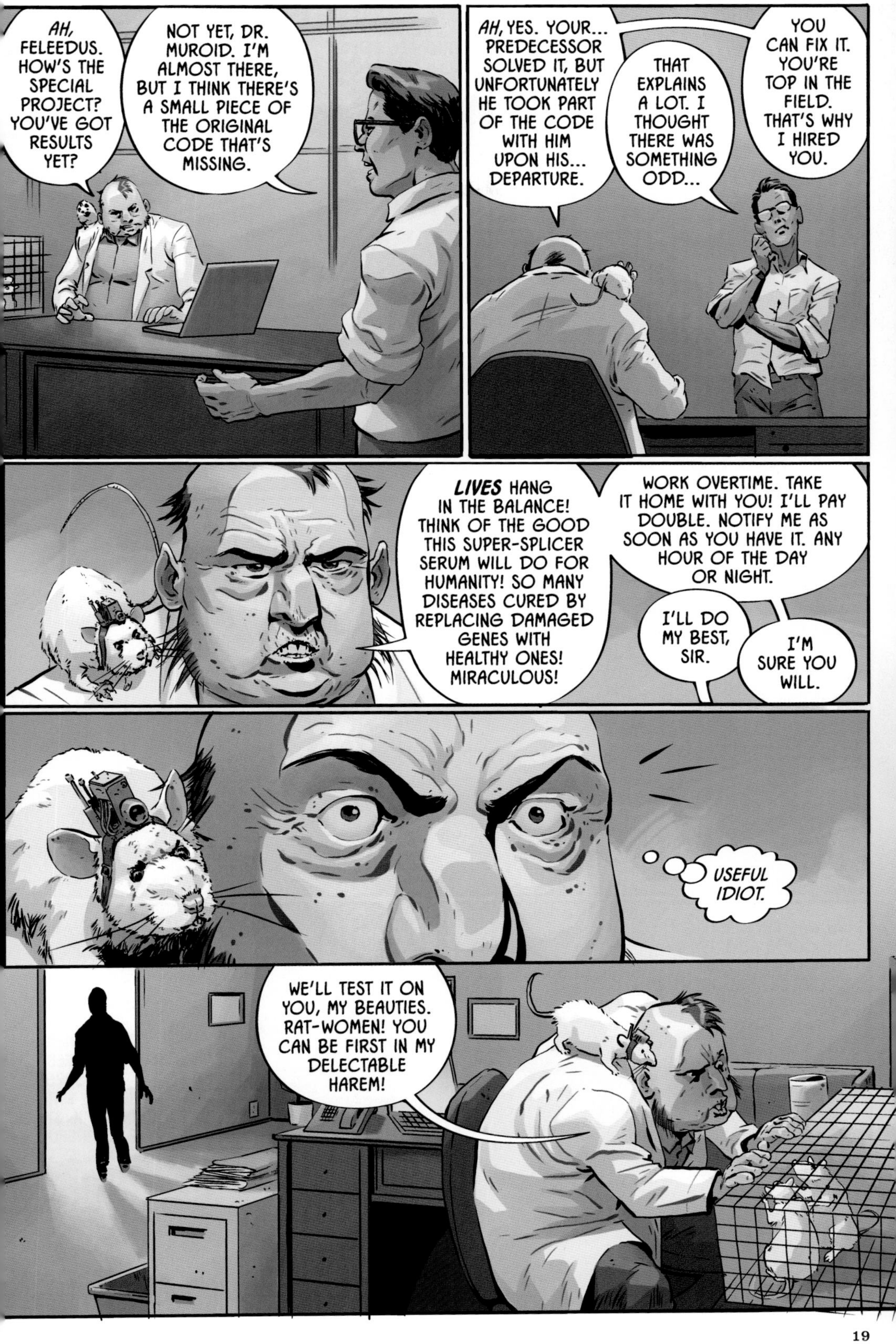
AH, FELEEDUS. HOW'S THE SPECIAL PROJECT? YOU'VE GOT RESULTS YET?
NOT YET, DR. MUROID. I'M ALMOST THERE, BUT I THINK THERE'S A SMALL PIECE OF THE ORIGINAL CODE THAT'S MISSING.
AH, YES. YOUR... PREDECESSOR SOLVED IT, BUT UNFORTUNATELY HE TOOK PART OF THE CODE WITH HIM UPON HIS... DEPARTURE.
THAT EXPLAINS A LOT. I THOUGHT THERE WAS SOMETHING ODD...
YOU CAN FIX IT. YOU'RE TOP IN THE FIELD. THAT'S WHY I HIRED YOU.
LIVES HANG IN THE BALANCE! THINK OF THE GOOD THIS SUPER-SPLICER SERUM WILL DO FOR HUMANITY! SO MANY DISEASES CURED BY REPLACING DAMAGED GENES WITH HEALTHY ONES! MIRACULOUS!
WORK OVERTIME. TAKE IT HOME WITH YOU! I'LL PAY DOUBLE. NOTIFY ME AS SOON AS YOU HAVE IT. ANY HOUR OF THE DAY OR NIGHT.
I'LL DO MY BEST, SIR.
I'M SURE YOU WILL.
USEFUL IDIOT.
WE'LL TEST IT ON YOU, MY BEAUTIES. RAT-WOMEN! YOU CAN BE FIRST IN MY DELECTABLE HAREM!

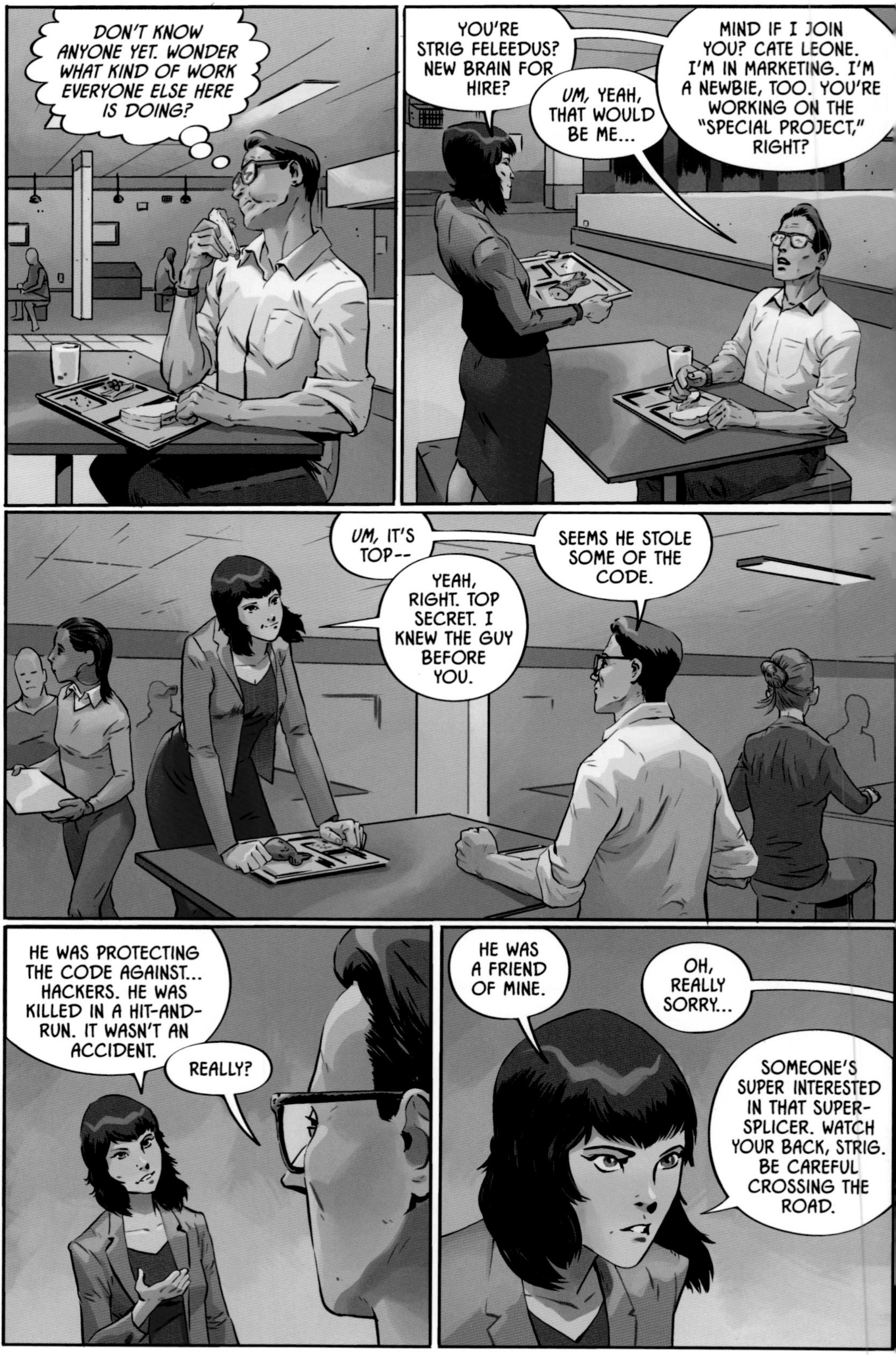
DON'T KNOW ANYONE YET. WONDER WHAT KIND OF WORK EVERYONE ELSE HERE IS DOING?
YOU'RE STRIG FELEEDUS? NEW BRAIN FOR HIRE?
UM, YEAH, THAT WOULD BE ME...
MIND IF I JOIN YOU? CATE LEONE. I'M IN MARKETING. I'M A NEWBIE, TOO. YOU'RE WORKING ON THE "SPECIAL PROJECT," RIGHT?
UM, IT'S TOP--
YEAH, RIGHT. TOP SECRET. I KNEW THE GUY BEFORE YOU.
SEEMS HE STOLE SOME OF THE CODE.
HE WAS PROTECTING THE CODE AGAINST... HACKERS. HE WAS KILLED IN A HIT-AND-RUN. IT WASN'T AN ACCIDENT.
REALLY?
HE WAS A FRIEND OF MINE.
OH, REALLY SORRY...
SOMEONE'S SUPER INTERESTED IN THAT SUPER-SPLICER. WATCH YOUR BACK, STRIG. BE CAREFUL CROSSING THE ROAD.

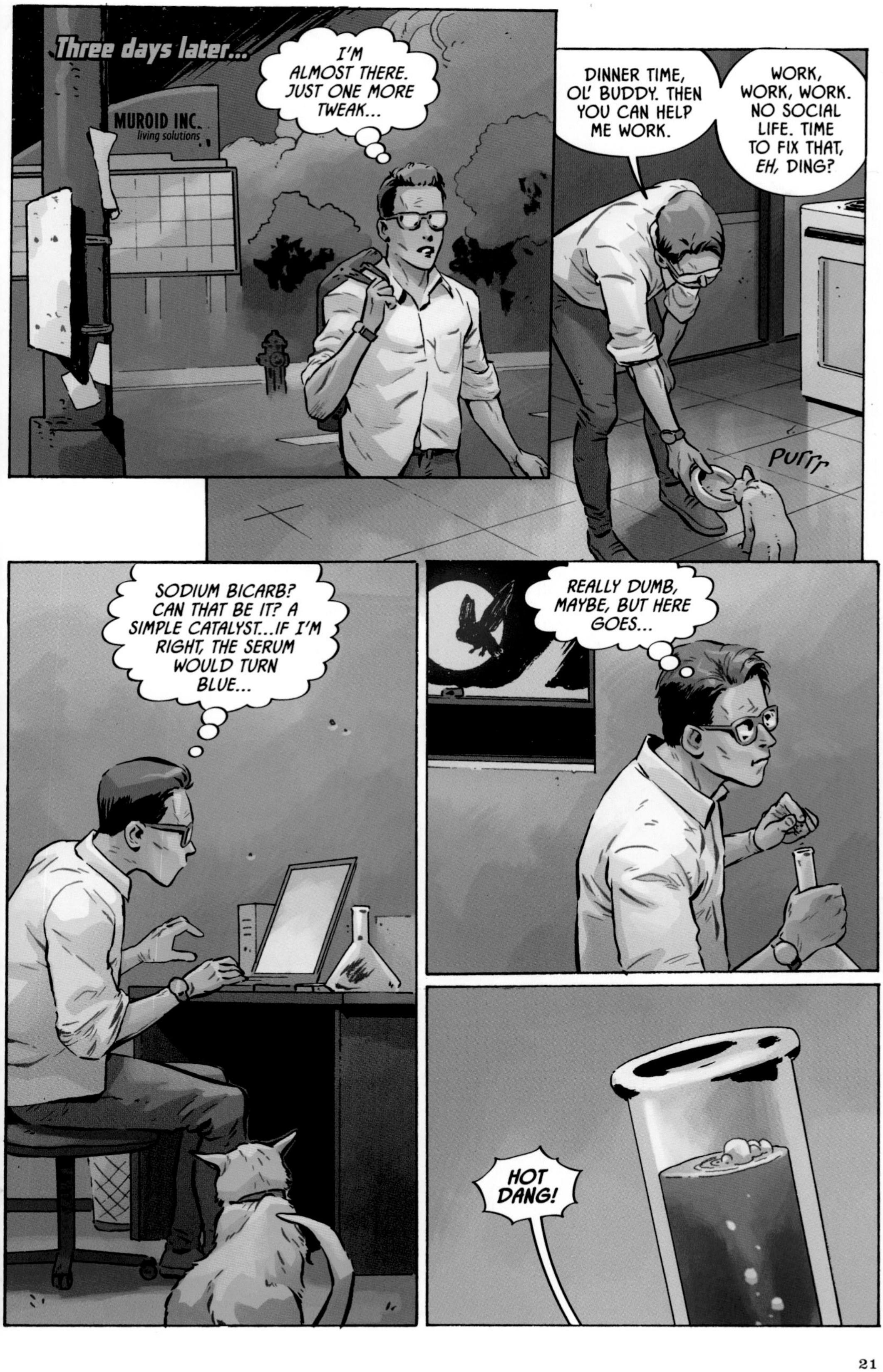
Three days later...
I'M ALMOST THERE. JUST ONE MORE TWEAK...
MUROID INC.
living solutions
DINNER TIME, OL' BUDDY. THEN YOU CAN HELP ME WORK.
WORK, WORK, WORK. NO SOCIAL LIFE. TIME TO FIX THAT, EH, DING?
Purrr
SODIUM BICARB? CAN THAT BE IT? A SIMPLE CATALYST...IF I'M RIGHT, THE SERUM WOULD TURN BLUE...
REALLY DUMB, MAYBE, BUT HERE GOES...
HOT DANG!

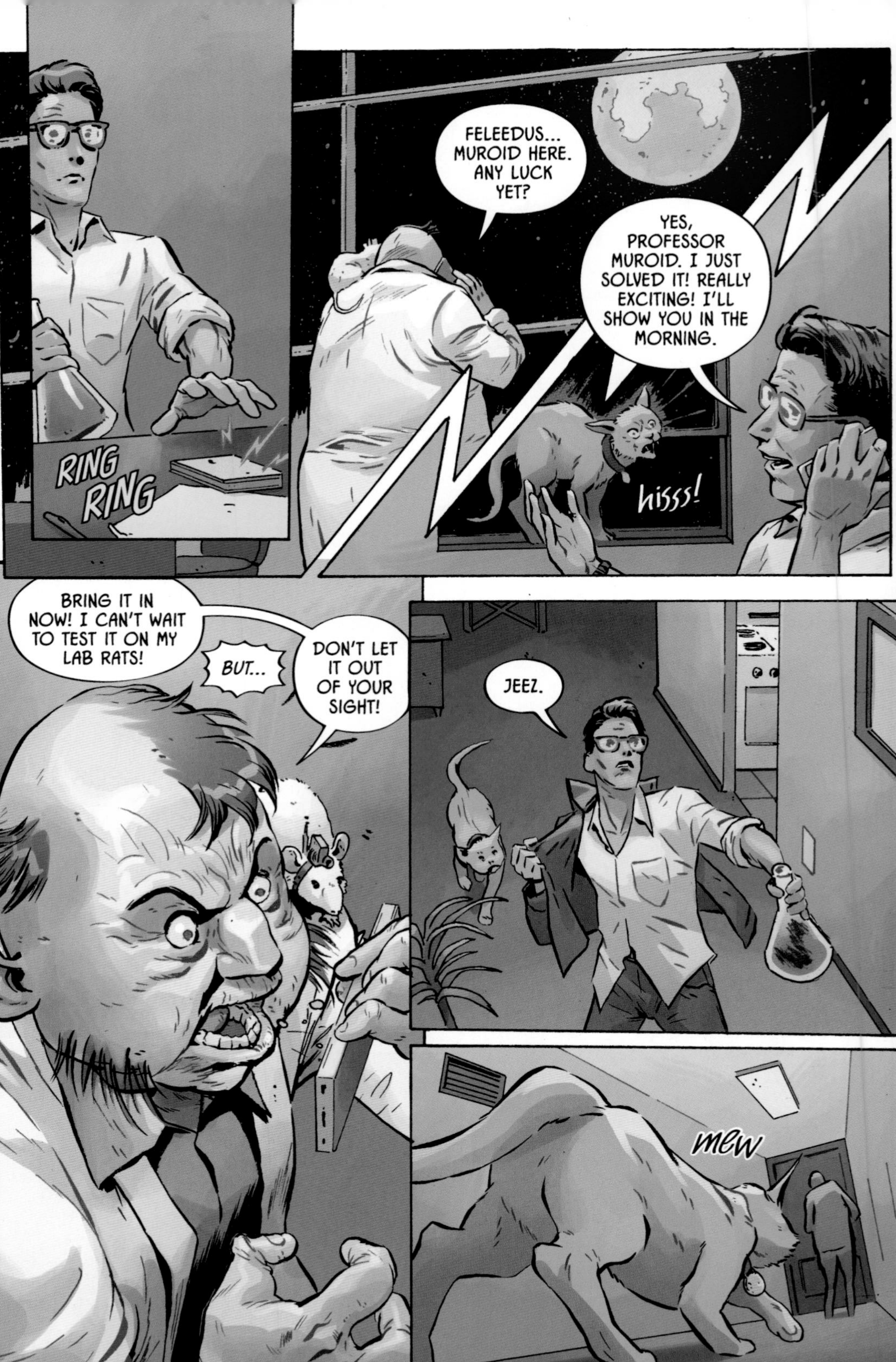
RING RING
FELEEDUS... MUROID HERE. ANY LUCK YET?
YES, PROFESSOR MUROID. I JUST SOLVED IT! REALLY EXCITING! I'LL SHOW YOU IN THE MORNING.
hisss!
BRING IT IN NOW! I CAN'T WAIT TO TEST IT ON MY LAB RATS!
BUT...
DON'T LET IT OUT OF YOUR SIGHT!
JEEZ.
mew

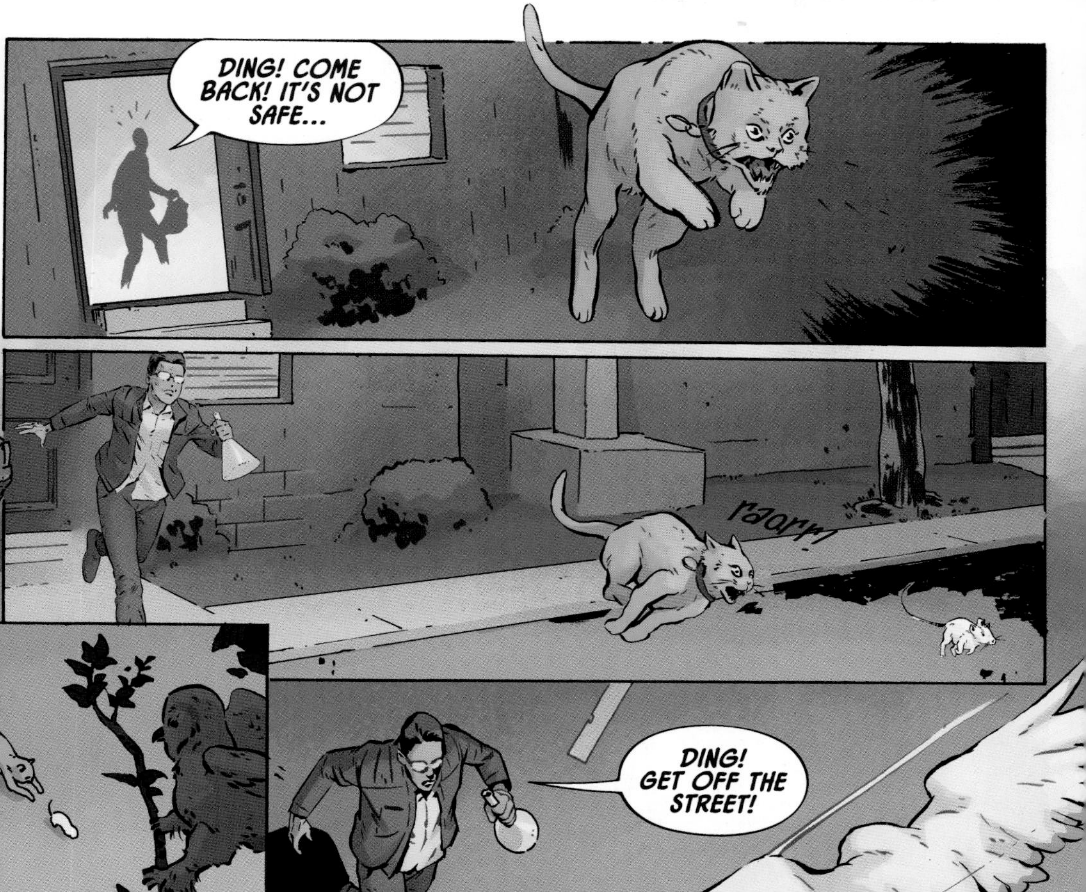
DING! COME BACK! IT'S NOT SAFE...
DING! GET OFF THE STREET!
SKREEEEEE

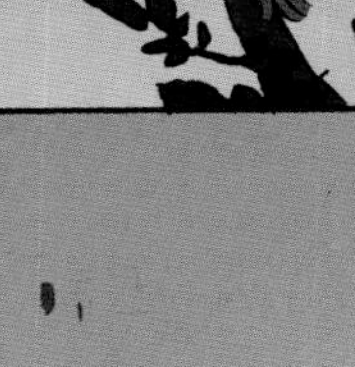

THERE LIES DANGER

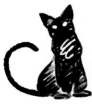

Outdoor cats live a fraction of the lifespan of indoor cats: as low as a third. They frequently get hit by cars and are at much higher risk of contracting diseases, getting lost, fighting with wildlife and other cats, poisoning, and parasites. www.catsandbirds.ca

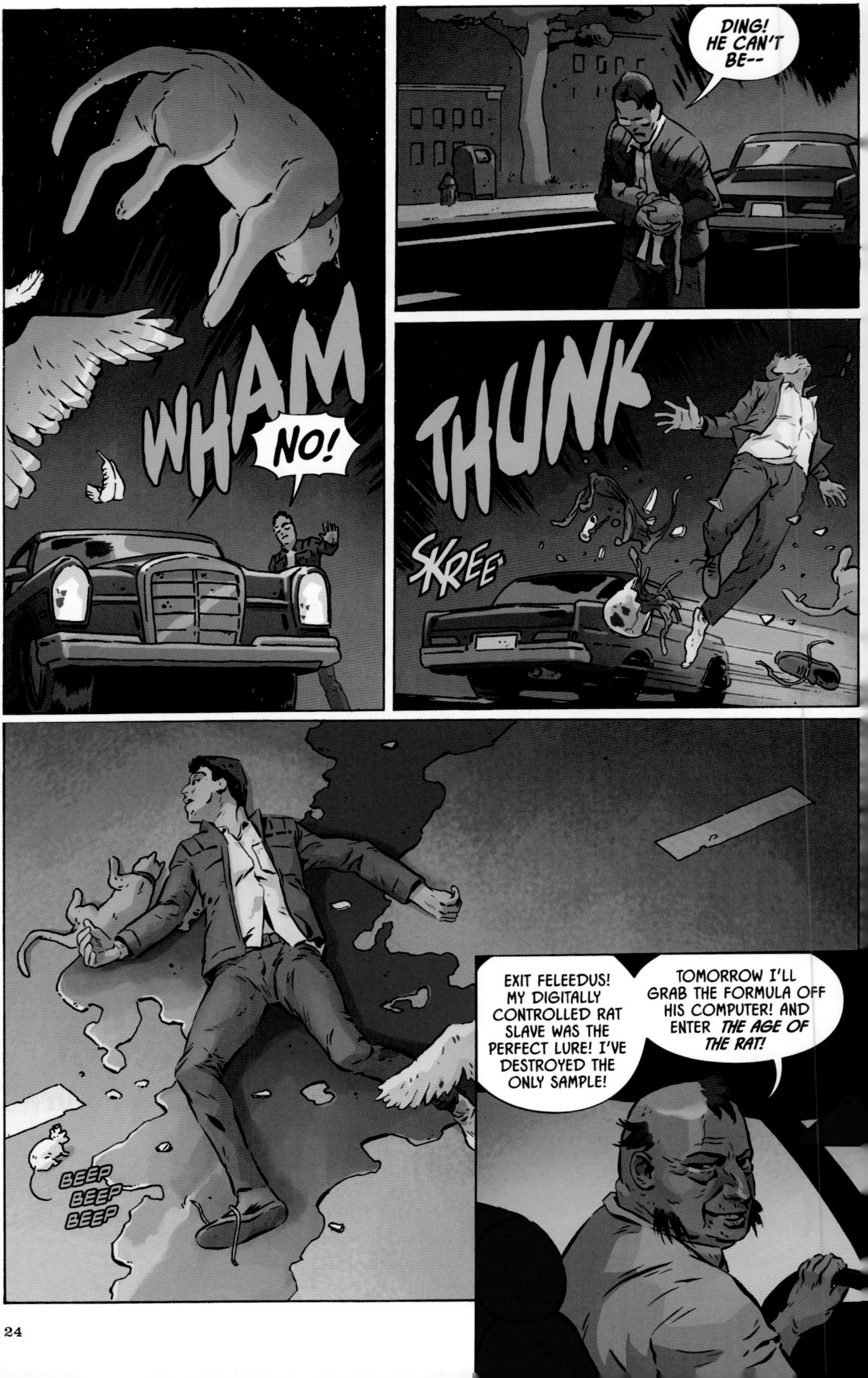

WHAM
NO!
DING! HE CAN'T BE--
THUNK
SKREE
BEEP BEEP BEEP
EXIT FELEEDUS! MY DIGITALLY CONTROLLED RAT SLAVE WAS THE PERFECT LURE! I'VE DESTROYED THE ONLY SAMPLE!
TOMORROW I'LL GRAB THE FORMULA OFF HIS COMPUTER! AND ENTER *THE AGE OF THE RAT!*

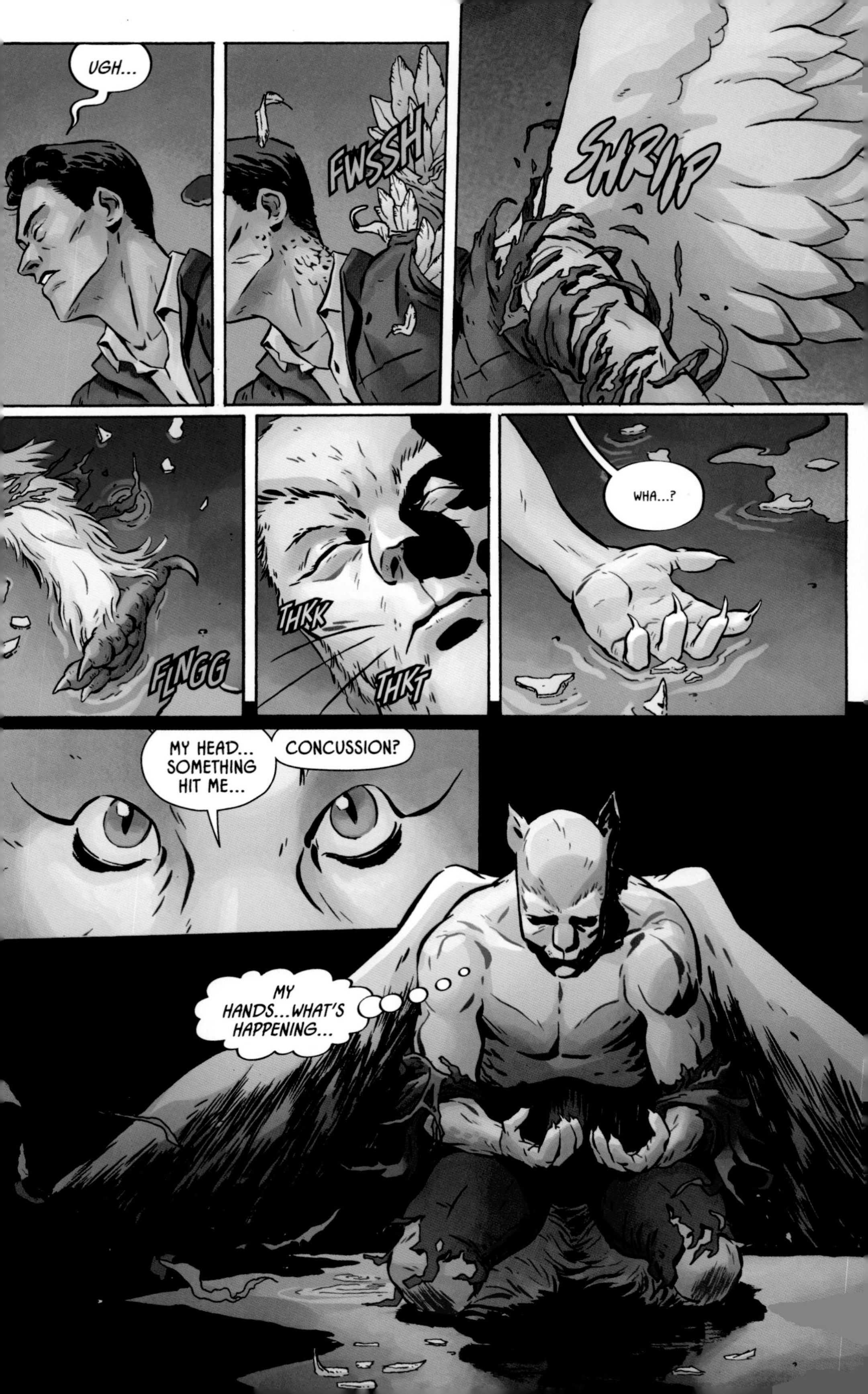
UGH...
FWSSH
SHRIP
FLNGG
THKK
THKT
WHA...?
MY HEAD... SOMETHING HIT ME...
CONCUSSION?
MY HANDS...WHAT'S HAPPENING...

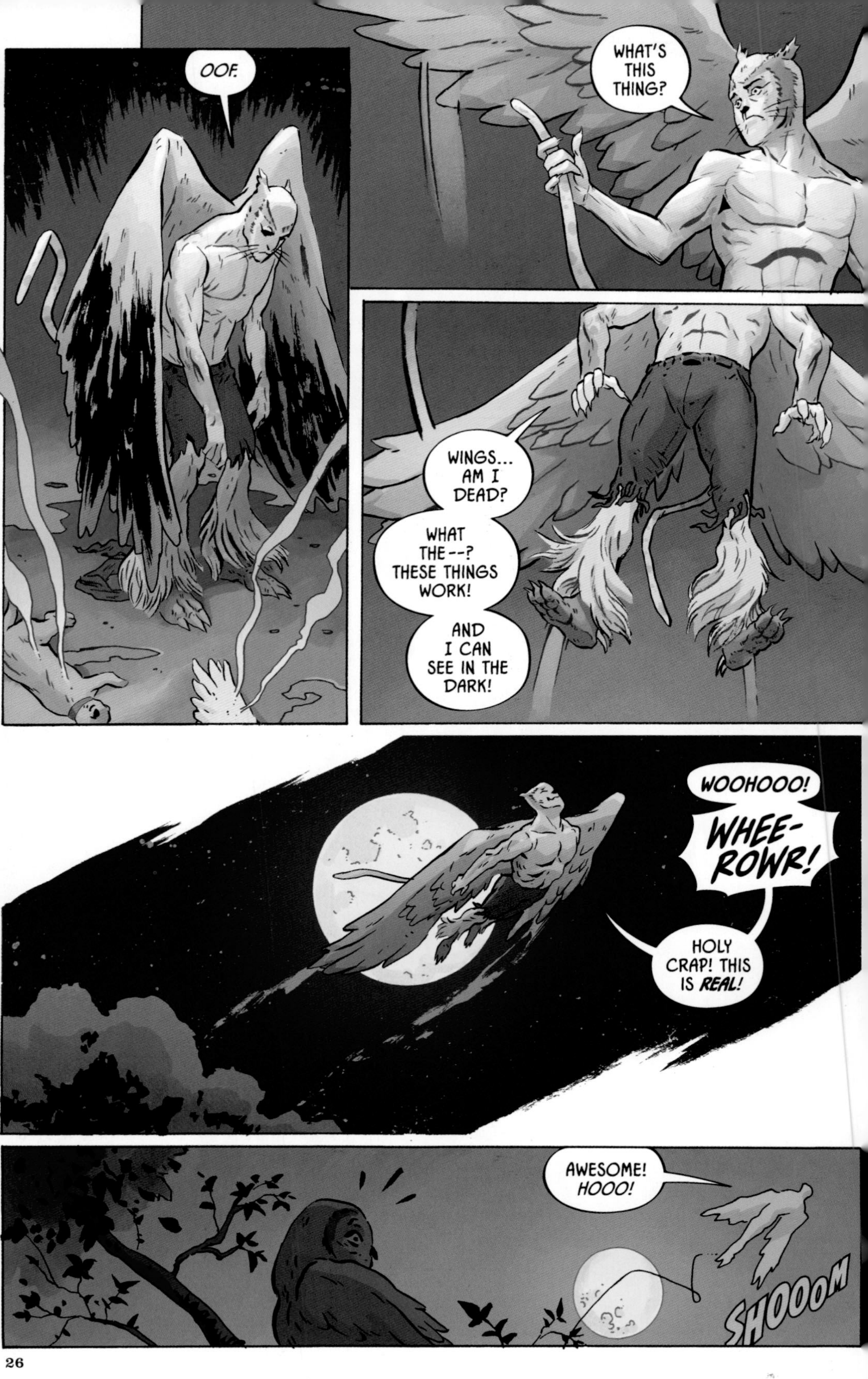
OOF.
WHAT'S THIS THING?
WINGS... AM I DEAD?
WHAT THE--? THESE THINGS WORK!
AND I CAN SEE IN THE DARK!
WOOHOOO!
WHEE-ROWR!
HOLY CRAP! THIS IS *REAL!*
AWESOME! HOOO!
SHOOOM

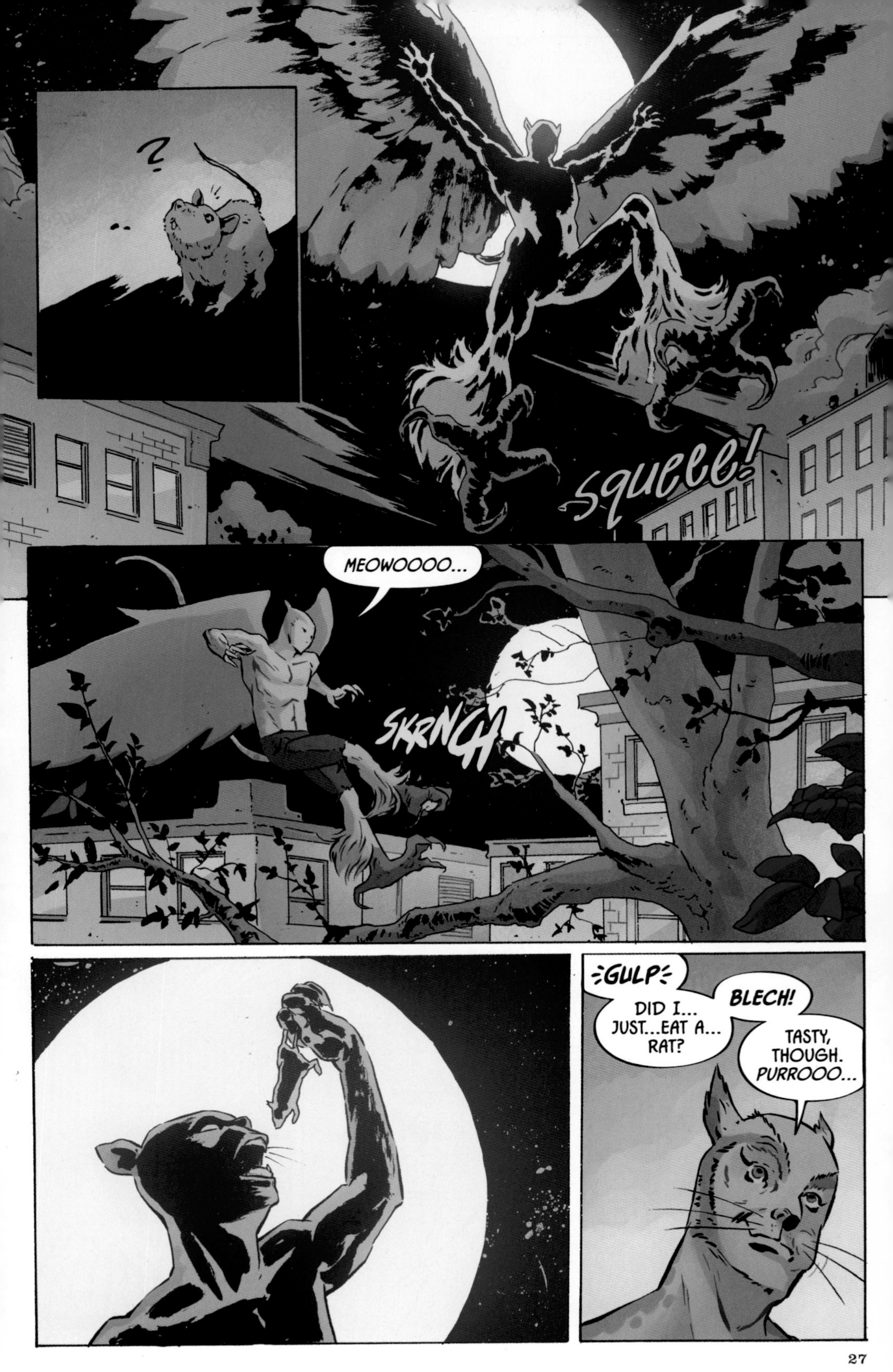
?
SQUEEE!
MEOWOOOO...
SKRNCH
GULP
DID I... JUST...EAT A... RAT?
BLECH!
TASTY, THOUGH. PURROOO...

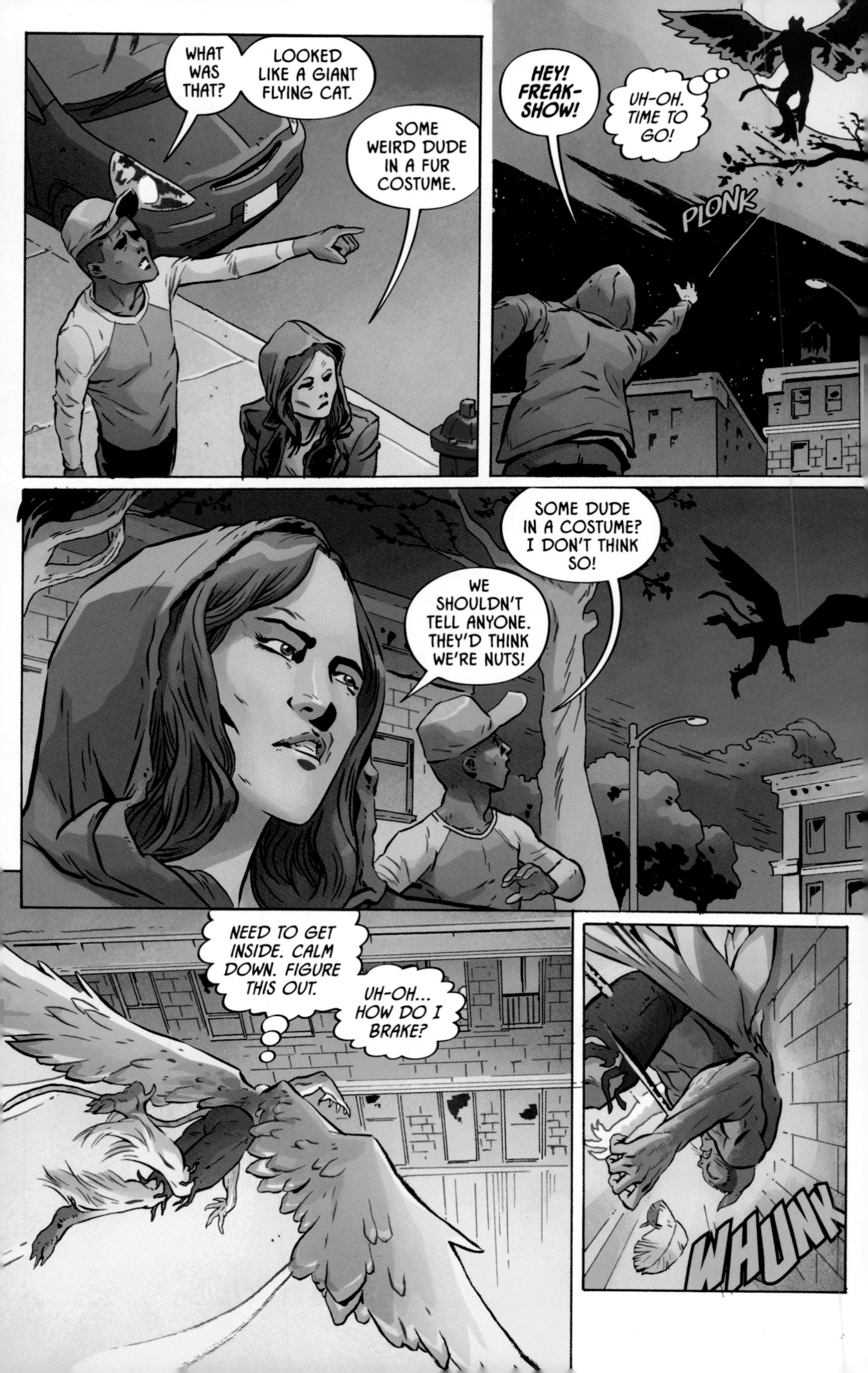
WHAT WAS THAT?
LOOKED LIKE A GIANT FLYING CAT.
SOME WEIRD DUDE IN A FUR COSTUME.
HEY! FREAK-SHOW!
UH-OH. TIME TO GO!
PLONK
SOME DUDE IN A COSTUME? I DON'T THINK SO!
WE SHOULDN'T TELL ANYONE. THEY'D THINK WE'RE NUTS!
NEED TO GET INSIDE. CALM DOWN. FIGURE THIS OUT.
UH-OH... HOW DO I BRAKE?
WHUNK

UGH...
THERE'S ANOTHER ONE. GOOD THING WE DO THIS AT NIGHT...
...IF PEOPLE KNEW HOW MANY CATS WERE DEAD IN THE STREET EVERY NIGHT, THEY'D BE YELLING.
WHAT WAS THAT?
FLYING? EATING A RAT? NO WAY!
SOME NIGHTMARE! BUT...
DING WAS RIGHT HERE...
DING?
DING

CATS AREN'T SO STREETWISE

Cars are a leading cause of sudden cat death, more so for young cats. In one study, 87% of trauma-related deaths were caused by cars. In the UK, an estimated 230,000 cats are hit each year. In the US, it's as high as 5.4 million. In Canada, about 200,000 cats die from car accidents every year.

www.catsandbirds.ca

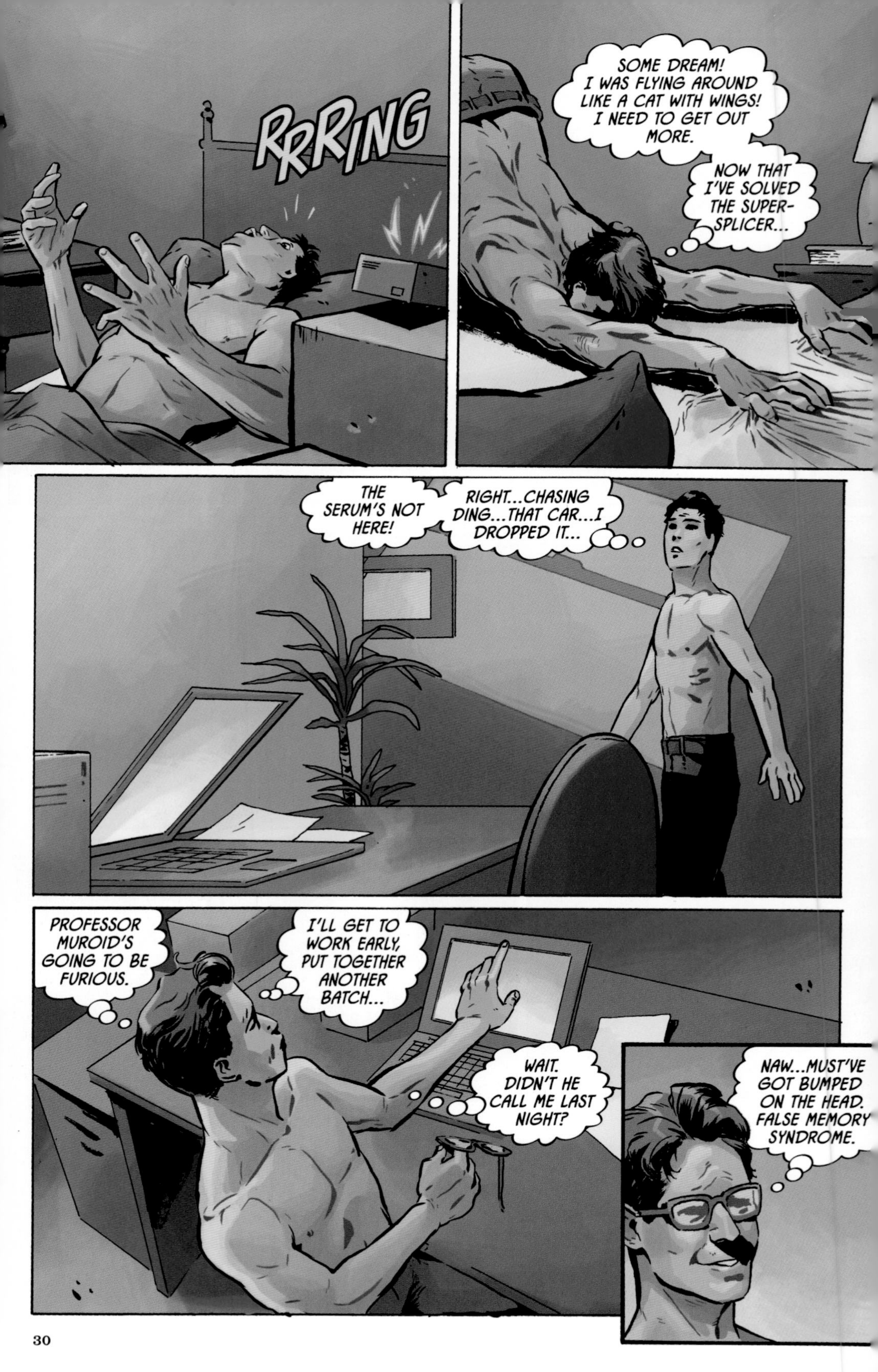
RRRING
SOME DREAM! I WAS FLYING AROUND LIKE A CAT WITH WINGS! I NEED TO GET OUT MORE.
NOW THAT I'VE SOLVED THE SUPER-SPLICER...
THE SERUM'S NOT HERE!
RIGHT...CHASING DING...THAT CAR...I DROPPED IT...
PROFESSOR MUROID'S GOING TO BE FURIOUS.
I'LL GET TO WORK EARLY, PUT TOGETHER ANOTHER BATCH...
WAIT. DIDN'T HE CALL ME LAST NIGHT?
NAW...MUST'VE GOT BUMPED ON THE HEAD. FALSE MEMORY SYNDROME.

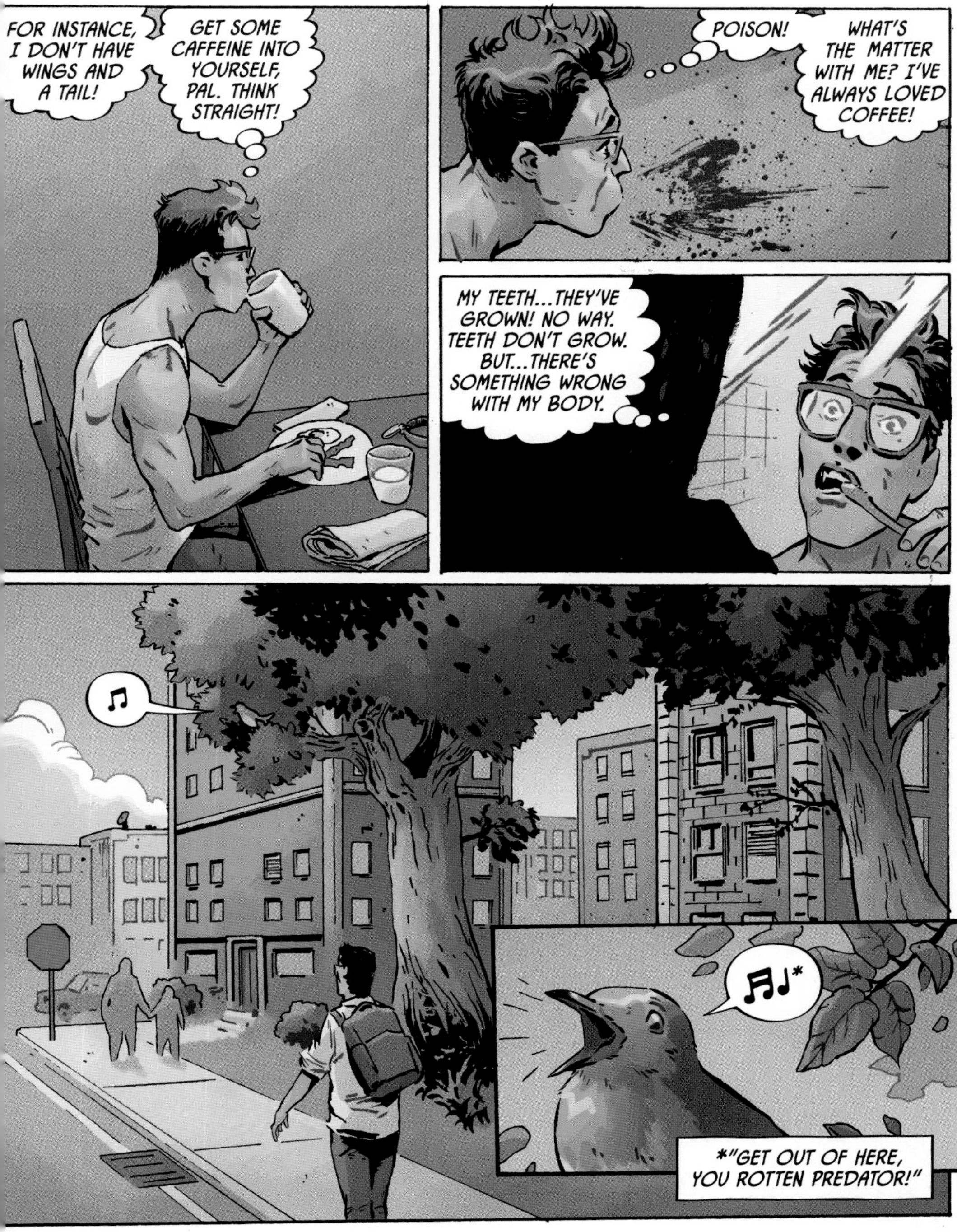
FOR INSTANCE, I DON'T HAVE WINGS AND A TAIL!
GET SOME CAFFEINE INTO YOURSELF, PAL. THINK STRAIGHT!
POISON!
WHAT'S THE MATTER WITH ME? I'VE ALWAYS LOVED COFFEE!
MY TEETH...THEY'VE GROWN! NO WAY. TEETH DON'T GROW. BUT...THERE'S SOMETHING WRONG WITH MY BODY.
♫
♬♩*
*"GET OUT OF HERE, YOU ROTTEN PREDATOR!"

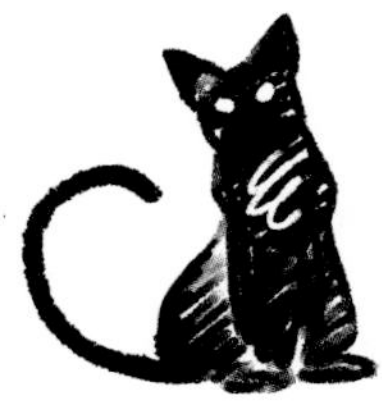

POISON, POISON, EVERYWHERE

Many human foods are toxic to cats: chocolate, coffee, onion, garlic, and tomato. Other poisons include common garden plants such as lilies, tulips, and begonias, as well as antifreeze, insecticides, and pesticides. Symptoms of poisoning include loss of appetite, vomiting, diarrhea, and loss of coordination. If your cat has eaten something toxic, contact a vet immediately.

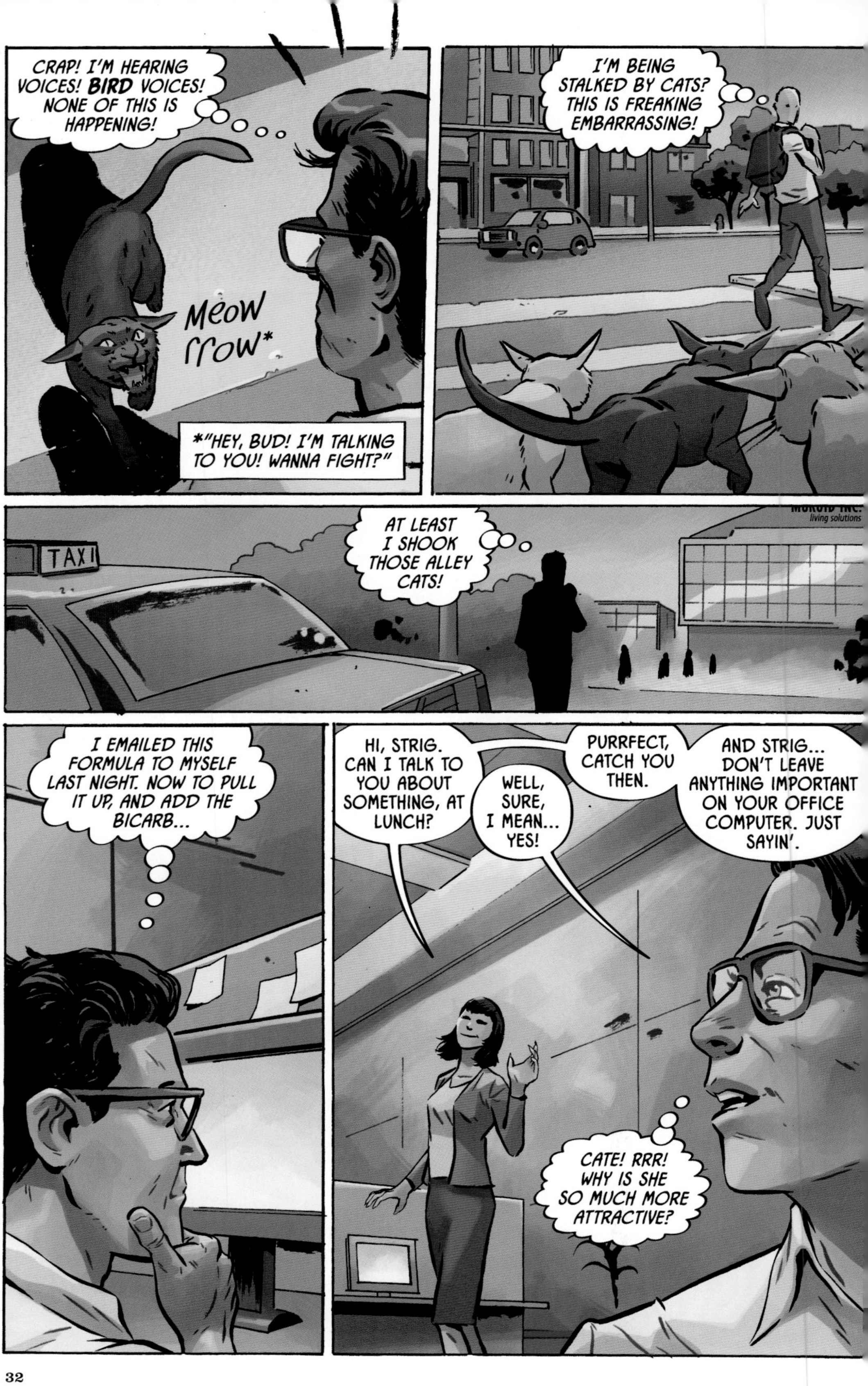
CRAP! I'M HEARING VOICES! BIRD VOICES! NONE OF THIS IS HAPPENING!
Meow rrow*
*"HEY, BUD! I'M TALKING TO YOU! WANNA FIGHT?"
I'M BEING STALKED BY CATS? THIS IS FREAKING EMBARRASSING!
TAXI
living solutions
AT LEAST I SHOOK THOSE ALLEY CATS!
I EMAILED THIS FORMULA TO MYSELF LAST NIGHT. NOW TO PULL IT UP, AND ADD THE BICARB...
HI, STRIG. CAN I TALK TO YOU ABOUT SOMETHING, AT LUNCH?
WELL, SURE, I MEAN... YES!
PURRFECT, CATCH YOU THEN.
AND STRIG... DON'T LEAVE ANYTHING IMPORTANT ON YOUR OFFICE COMPUTER. JUST SAYIN'.
CATE! RRR! WHY IS SHE SO MUCH MORE ATTRACTIVE?

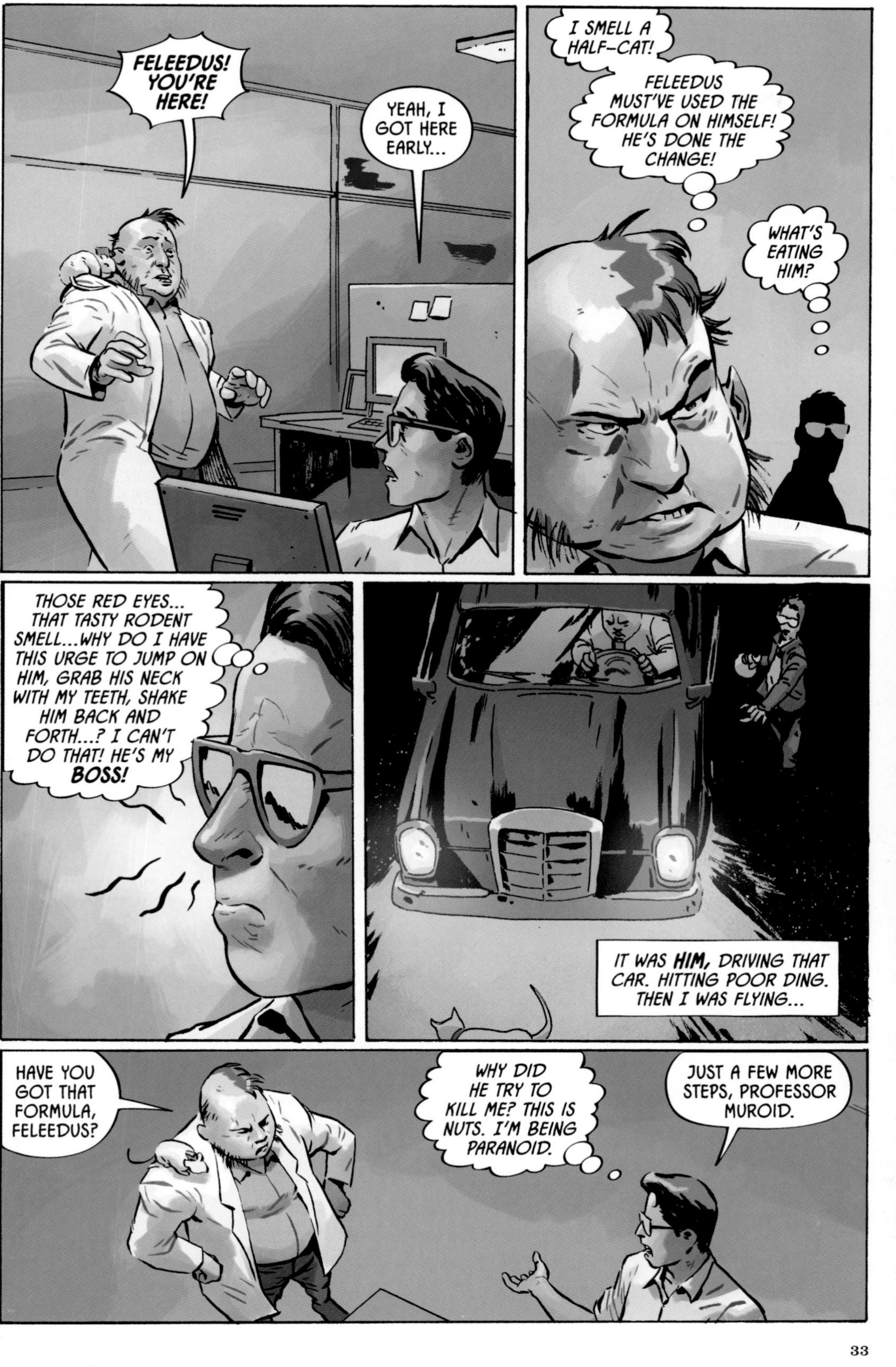

FELEEDUS! YOU'RE HERE!
YEAH, I GOT HERE EARLY...
I SMELL A HALF-CAT!
FELEEDUS MUST'VE USED THE FORMULA ON HIMSELF! HE'S DONE THE CHANGE!
WHAT'S EATING HIM?
THOSE RED EYES... THAT TASTY RODENT SMELL...WHY DO I HAVE THIS URGE TO JUMP ON HIM, GRAB HIS NECK WITH MY TEETH, SHAKE HIM BACK AND FORTH...? I CAN'T DO THAT! HE'S MY BOSS!
IT WAS HIM, DRIVING THAT CAR. HITTING POOR DING. THEN I WAS FLYING...
HAVE YOU GOT THAT FORMULA, FELEEDUS?
WHY DID HE TRY TO KILL ME? THIS IS NUTS. I'M BEING PARANOID.
JUST A FEW MORE STEPS, PROFESSOR MUROID.

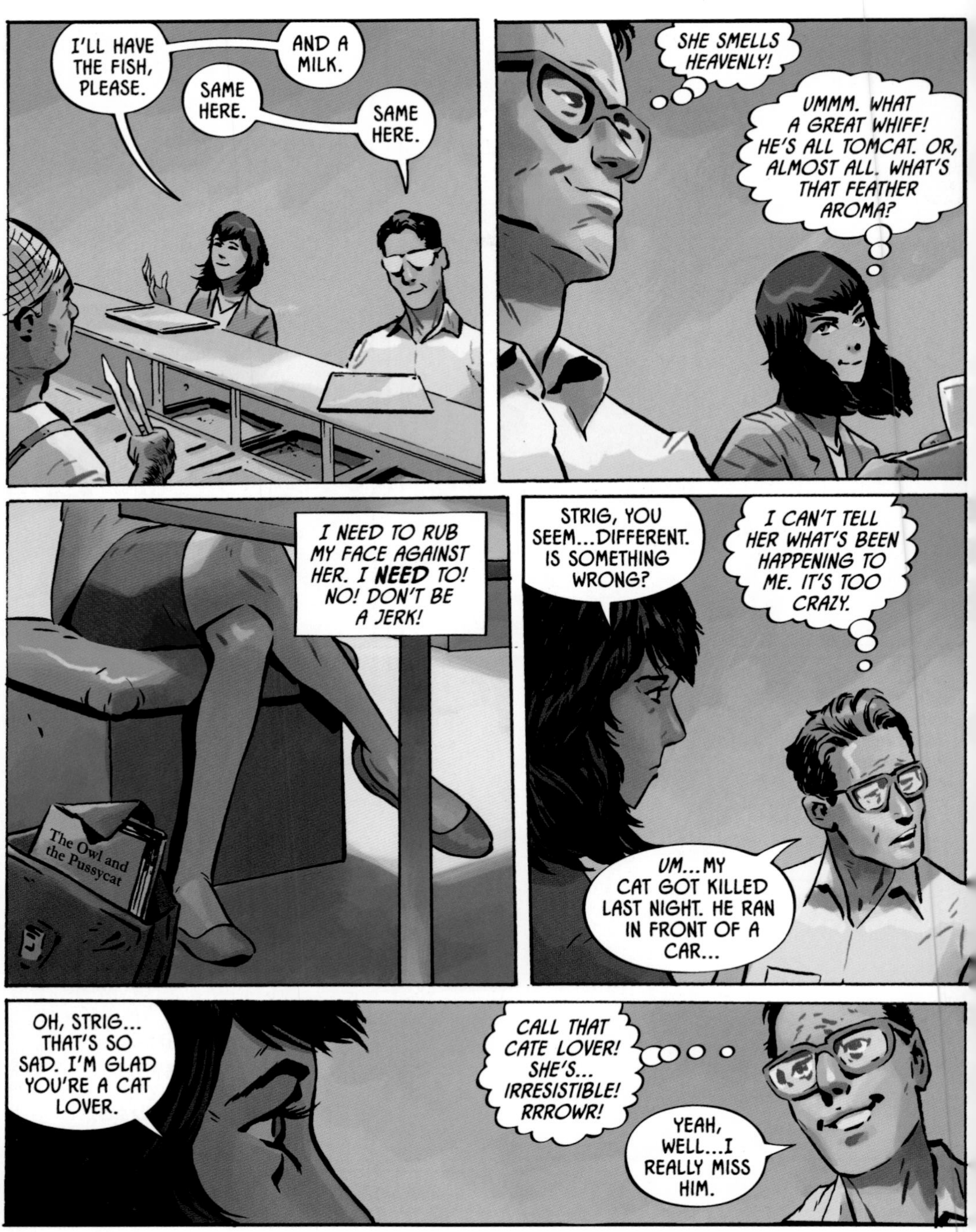
I'LL HAVE THE FISH, PLEASE.
AND A MILK.
SAME HERE.
SAME HERE.
SHE SMELLS HEAVENLY!
UMMM. WHAT A GREAT WHIFF! HE'S ALL TOMCAT. OR, ALMOST ALL. WHAT'S THAT FEATHER AROMA?
I NEED TO RUB MY FACE AGAINST HER. I **NEED** TO! NO! DON'T BE A JERK!
The Owl and the Pussycat
STRIG, YOU SEEM...DIFFERENT. IS SOMETHING WRONG?
I CAN'T TELL HER WHAT'S BEEN HAPPENING TO ME. IT'S TOO CRAZY.
UM...MY CAT GOT KILLED LAST NIGHT. HE RAN IN FRONT OF A CAR...
OH, STRIG... THAT'S SO SAD. I'M GLAD YOU'RE A CAT LOVER.
CALL THAT CATE LOVER! SHE'S... IRRESISTIBLE! RRROWR!
YEAH, WELL...I REALLY MISS HIM.

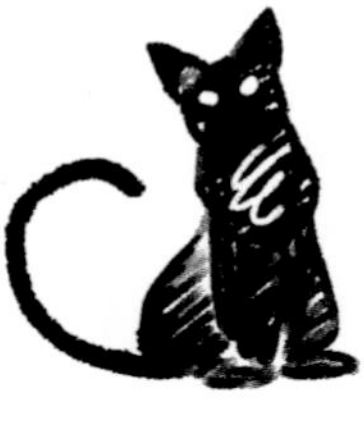

CATS SMELL WELL!

A cat's sense of smell is 14 times stronger than a human's, and it does a lot more than help them find mice—it helps them communicate with other cats. When your cat rubs up against you, she's using her glands to make a scent tattoo that says, "Mine!"

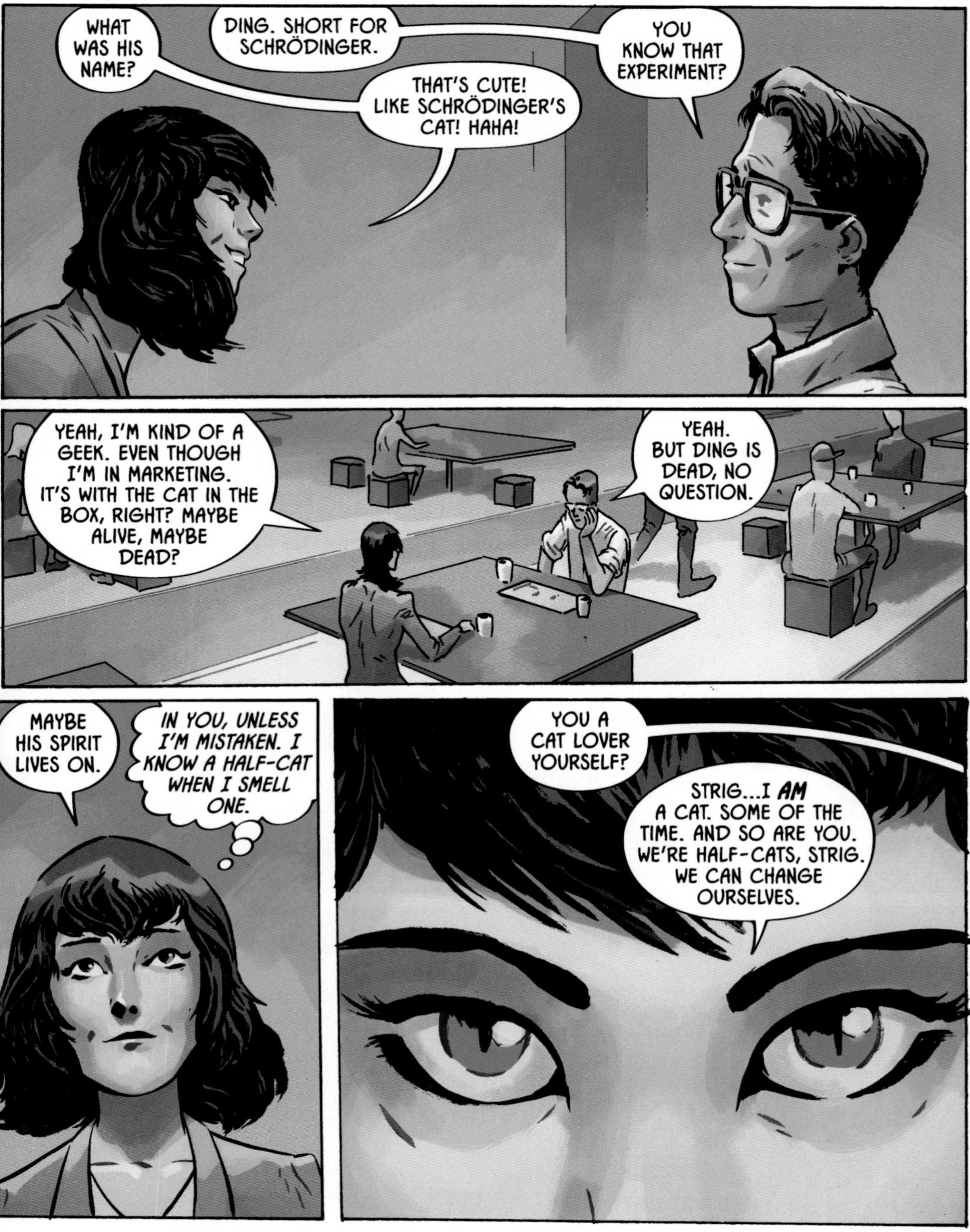
WHAT WAS HIS NAME?
DING. SHORT FOR SCHRÖDINGER.
THAT'S CUTE! LIKE SCHRÖDINGER'S CAT! HAHA!
YOU KNOW THAT EXPERIMENT?
YEAH, I'M KIND OF A GEEK. EVEN THOUGH I'M IN MARKETING. IT'S WITH THE CAT IN THE BOX, RIGHT? MAYBE ALIVE, MAYBE DEAD?
YEAH. BUT DING IS DEAD, NO QUESTION.
MAYBE HIS SPIRIT LIVES ON.
IN YOU, UNLESS I'M MISTAKEN. I KNOW A HALF-CAT WHEN I SMELL ONE.
YOU A CAT LOVER YOURSELF?
STRIG...I AM A CAT. SOME OF THE TIME. AND SO ARE YOU. WE'RE HALF-CATS, STRIG. WE CAN CHANGE OURSELVES.

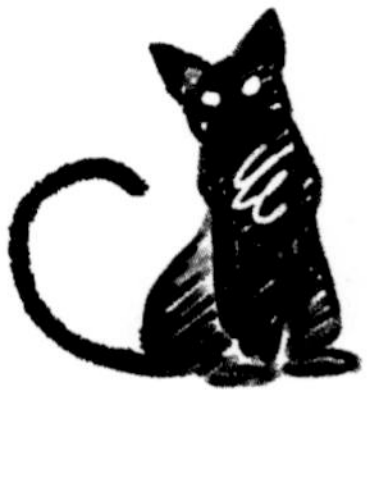

DEAD OR ALIVE?

Shelter statistics from the US, Canada, and the UK: 30% of lost dogs are returned to their owners, but only 5% of cats are. Sadly, many of those lost cats are probably dead, having been hit by a car or mauled by an animal. Identifying your cats with a microchip or tattoo increases their chances of being returned home. www.catsandbirds.ca

YOU ARE? I AM? I CAN?

YES. I CAN TELL. I'M NEVER WRONG.

BUT THERE'S SOMETHING ELSE ABOUT YOU. YOU'RE NOT ALL TOMCAT, RIGHT? THERE'S SOME BIRD THING GOING ON, TOO.

HOW CAN YOU TELL?

IT'S THE CAT NOSE. INFALLIBLE!

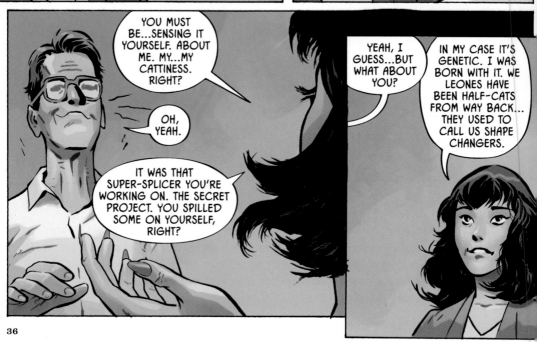

YOU MUST BE...SENSING IT YOURSELF. ABOUT ME. MY...MY CATTINESS. RIGHT?

OH, YEAH.

IT WAS THAT SUPER-SPLICER YOU'RE WORKING ON. THE SECRET PROJECT. YOU SPILLED SOME ON YOURSELF, RIGHT?

YEAH, I GUESS...BUT WHAT ABOUT YOU?

IN MY CASE IT'S GENETIC. I WAS BORN WITH IT. WE LEONES HAVE BEEN HALF-CATS FROM WAY BACK... THEY USED TO CALL US SHAPE CHANGERS.

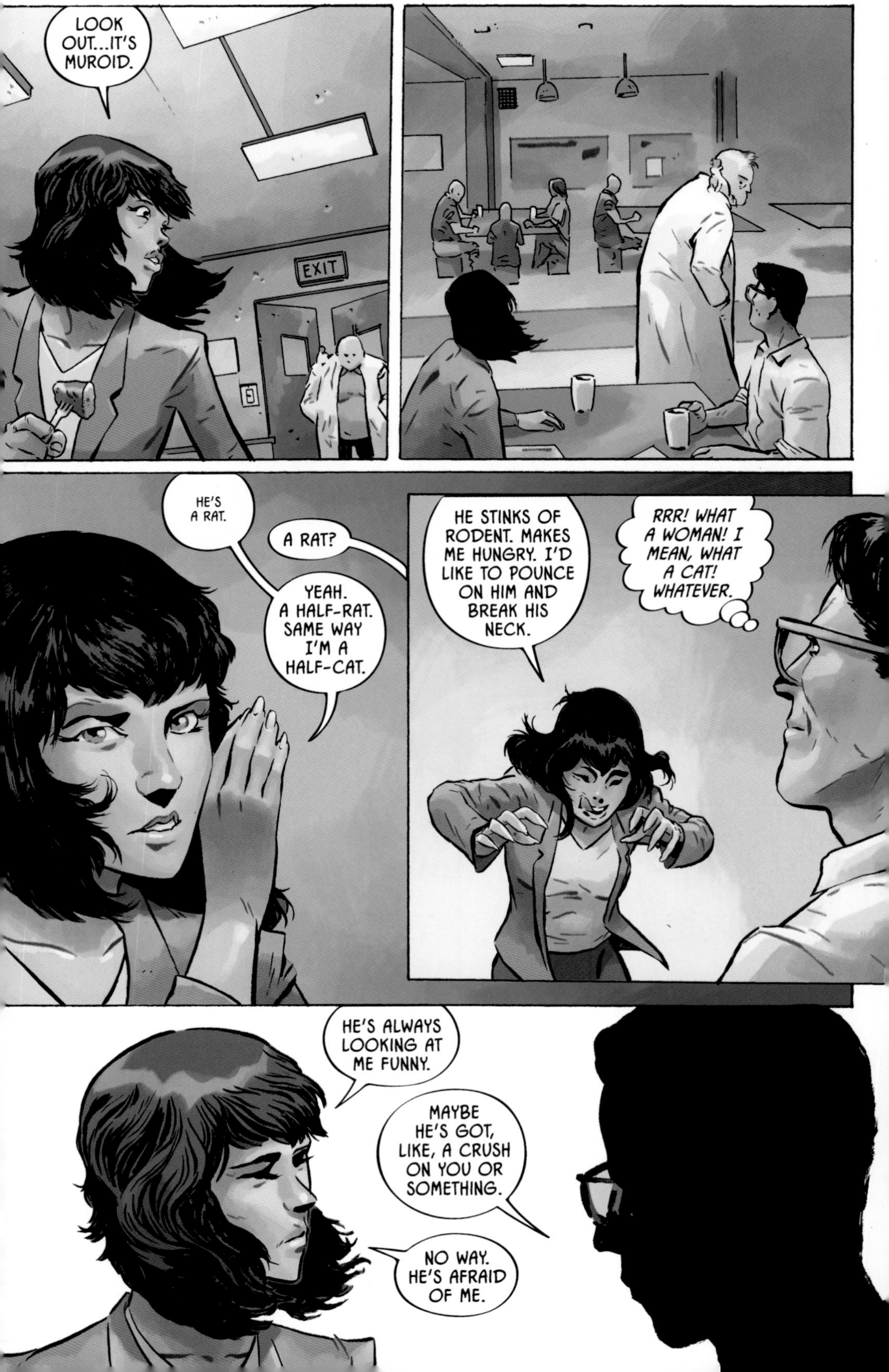
LOOK OUT...IT'S MUROID.
EXIT
HE'S A RAT.
A RAT?
YEAH. A HALF-RAT. SAME WAY I'M A HALF-CAT.
HE STINKS OF RODENT. MAKES ME HUNGRY. I'D LIKE TO POUNCE ON HIM AND BREAK HIS NECK.
RRR! WHAT A WOMAN! I MEAN, WHAT A CAT! WHATEVER.
HE'S ALWAYS LOOKING AT ME FUNNY.
MAYBE HE'S GOT, LIKE, A CRUSH ON YOU OR SOMETHING.
NO WAY. HE'S AFRAID OF ME.

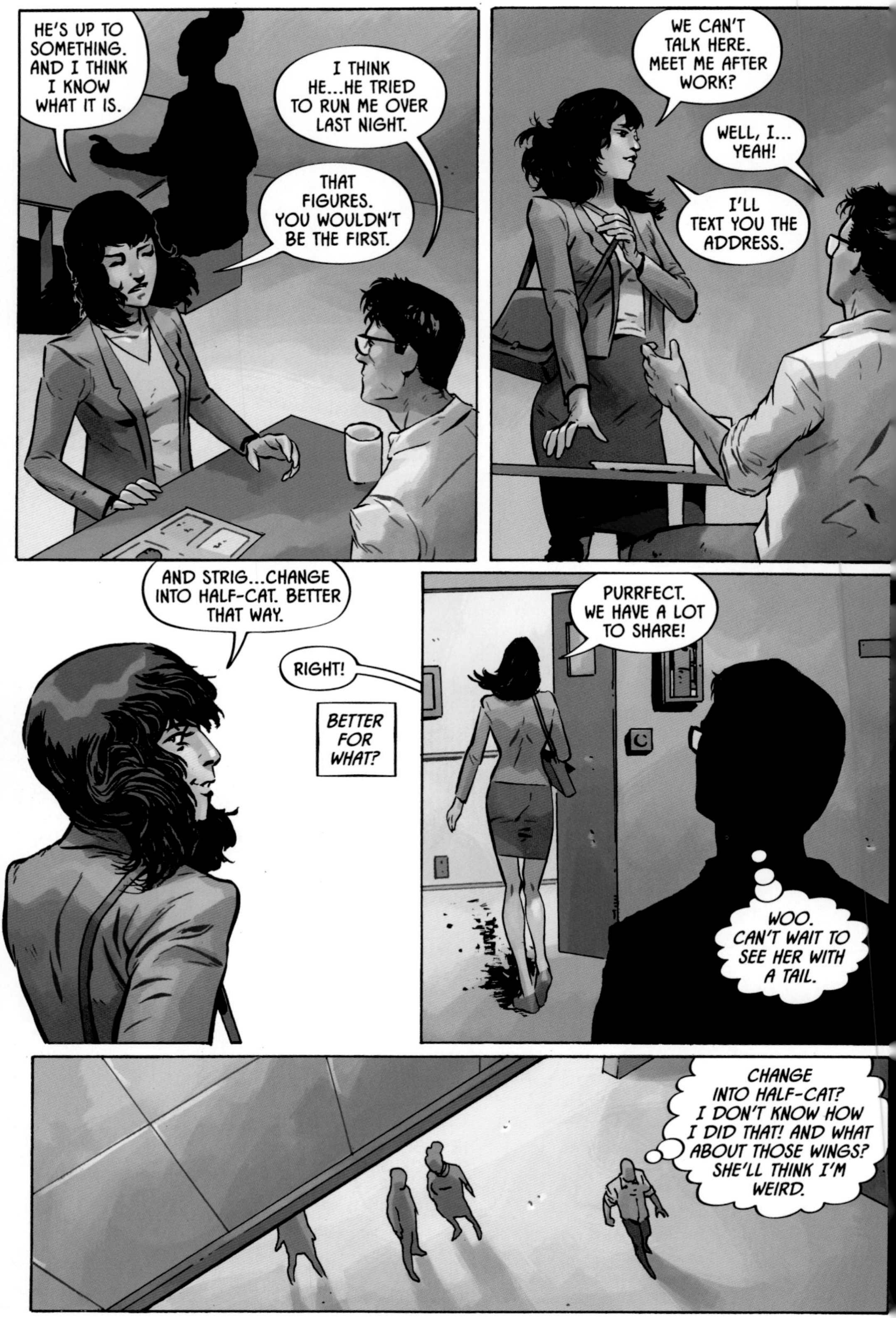
HE'S UP TO SOMETHING. AND I THINK I KNOW WHAT IT IS.
I THINK HE...HE TRIED TO RUN ME OVER LAST NIGHT.
THAT FIGURES. YOU WOULDN'T BE THE FIRST.
WE CAN'T TALK HERE. MEET ME AFTER WORK?
WELL, I... YEAH!
I'LL TEXT YOU THE ADDRESS.
AND STRIG...CHANGE INTO HALF-CAT. BETTER THAT WAY.
RIGHT!
BETTER FOR WHAT?
PURRFECT. WE HAVE A LOT TO SHARE!
WOO. CAN'T WAIT TO SEE HER WITH A TAIL.
CHANGE INTO HALF-CAT? I DON'T KNOW HOW I DID THAT! AND WHAT ABOUT THOSE WINGS? SHE'LL THINK I'M WEIRD.

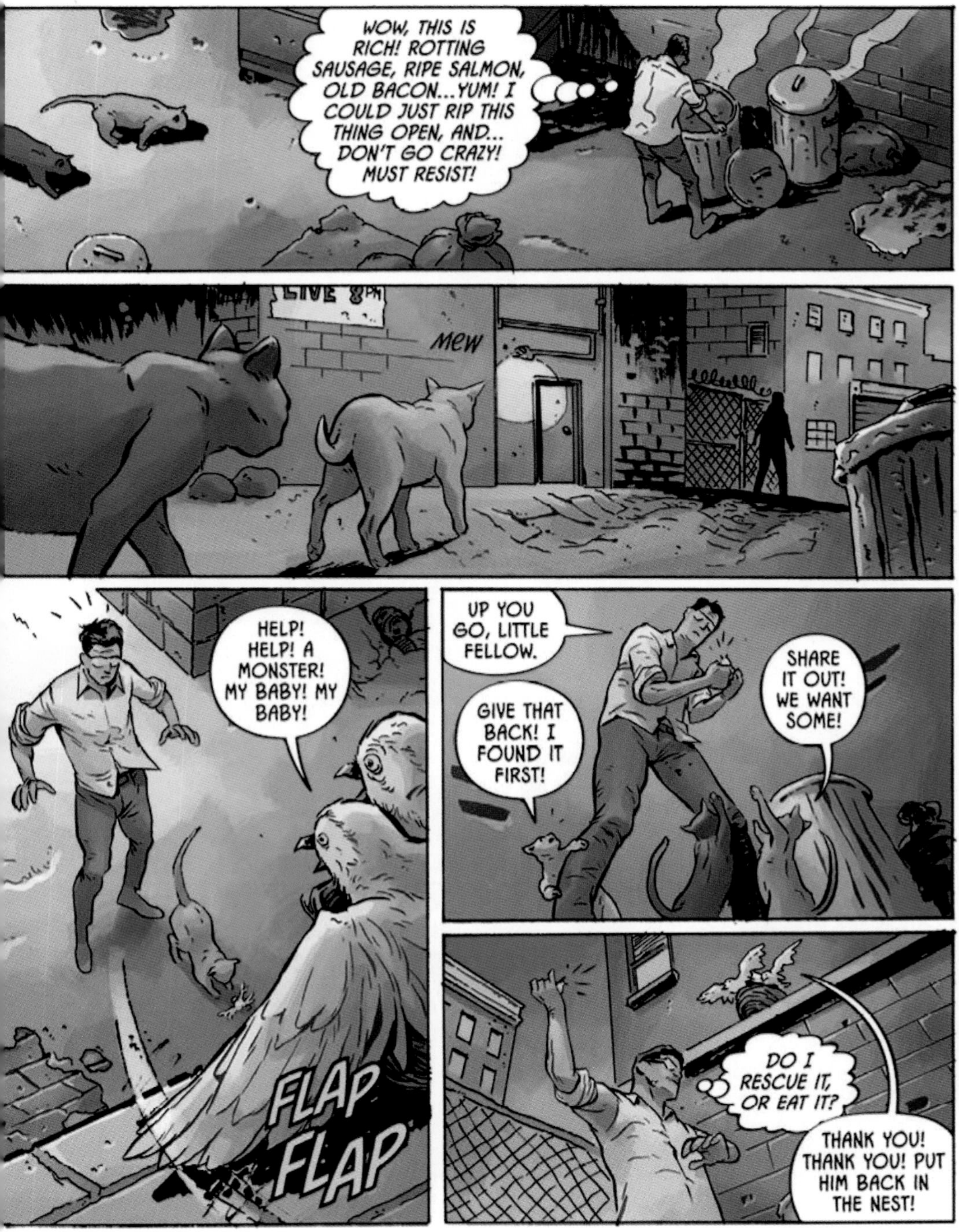
WOW, THIS IS RICH! ROTTING SAUSAGE, RIPE SALMON, OLD BACON...YUM! I COULD JUST RIP THIS THING OPEN, AND... DON'T GO CRAZY! MUST RESIST!
LIVE 8PM
MEW
HELP! HELP! A MONSTER! MY BABY! MY BABY!
FLAP
FLAP
UP YOU GO, LITTLE FELLOW.
GIVE THAT BACK! I FOUND IT FIRST!
SHARE IT OUT! WE WANT SOME!
DO I RESCUE IT, OR EAT IT?
THANK YOU! THANK YOU! PUT HIM BACK IN THE NEST!

CAT-BIRD MATH, Part I

Cats are estimated to kill 100-350 million birds a year in Canada. In the US, the figure is roughly 2.6 billion, and in the UK, about 55 million. Feral and stray cats are thought to be the cause of more than 60% of those estimated fatalities, despite the fact that their population is smaller than that of pet cats. Protect your cat—save birds! www.catsandbirds.ca

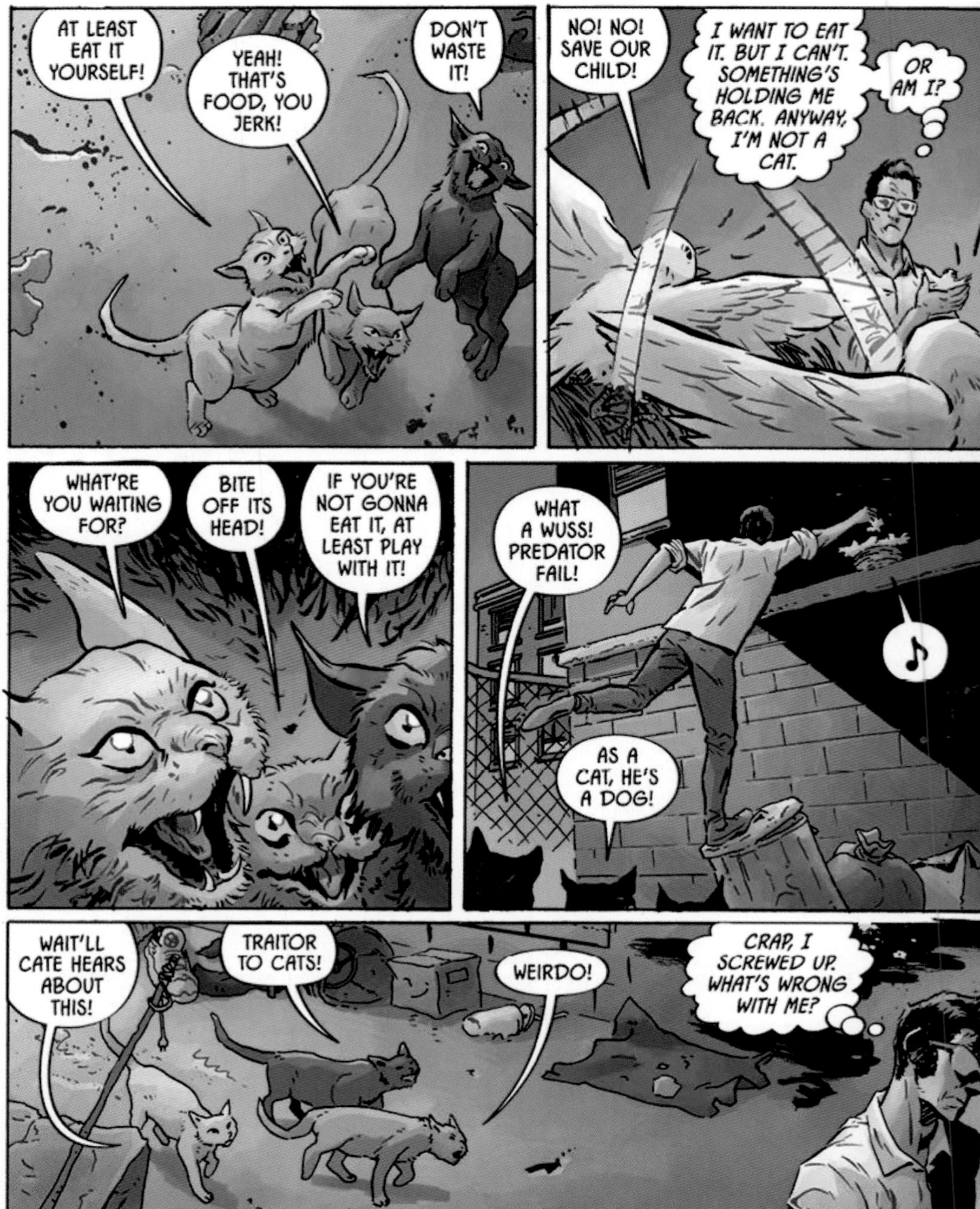
AT LEAST EAT IT YOURSELF!
YEAH! THAT'S FOOD, YOU JERK!
DON'T WASTE IT!
NO! NO! SAVE OUR CHILD!
I WANT TO EAT IT. BUT I CAN'T. SOMETHING'S HOLDING ME BACK. ANYWAY, I'M NOT A CAT.
OR AM I?
WHAT'RE YOU WAITING FOR?
BITE OFF ITS HEAD!
IF YOU'RE NOT GONNA EAT IT, AT LEAST PLAY WITH IT!
WHAT A WUSS! PREDATOR FAIL!
♪
AS A CAT, HE'S A DOG!
WAIT'LL CATE HEARS ABOUT THIS!
TRAITOR TO CATS!
WEIRDO!
CRAP, I SCREWED UP. WHAT'S WRONG WITH ME?

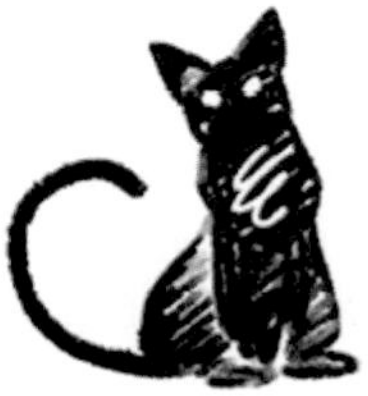

CAT-BIRD MATH, Part II

Pet cats kill fewer birds per cat than their feral cousins, but even well-fed pet cats still hunt. Canada's 10 million pet cats cause an estimated 38-133 million bird deaths each year. For pet cats, hunting is entertainment, providing stimulation and exercise. But play is an excellent substitute for hunting. Help your cat play!
www.catsandbirds.ca

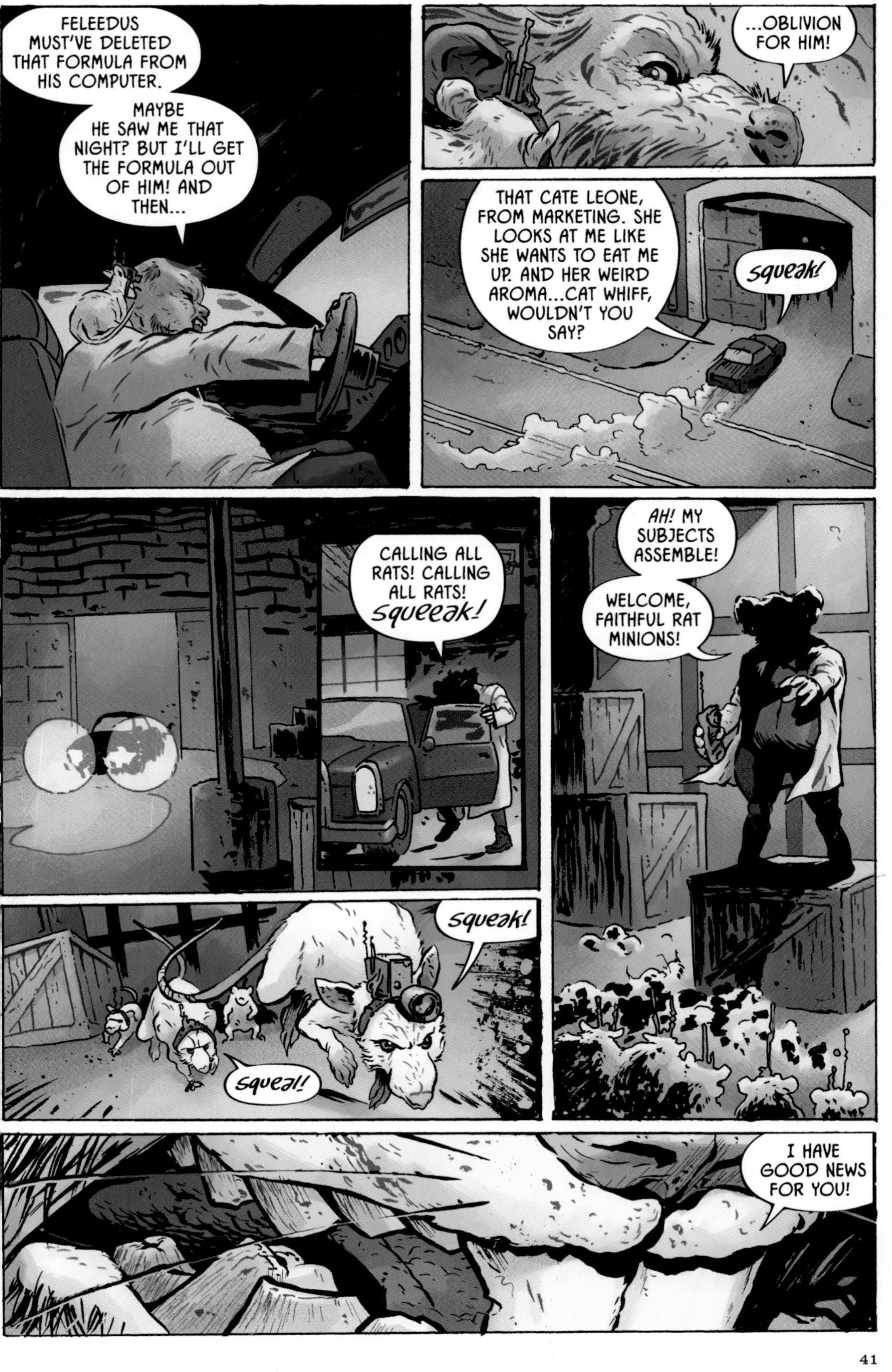

FELEEDUS MUST'VE DELETED THAT FORMULA FROM HIS COMPUTER.
MAYBE HE SAW ME THAT NIGHT? BUT I'LL GET THE FORMULA OUT OF HIM! AND THEN...
...OBLIVION FOR HIM!
THAT CATE LEONE, FROM MARKETING. SHE LOOKS AT ME LIKE SHE WANTS TO EAT ME UP. AND HER WEIRD AROMA...CAT WHIFF, WOULDN'T YOU SAY?
SQUEAK!
CALLING ALL RATS! CALLING ALL RATS! SQUEEAK!
AH! MY SUBJECTS ASSEMBLE!
WELCOME, FAITHFUL RAT MINIONS!
SQUEAK!
SQUEAL!
I HAVE GOOD NEWS FOR YOU!

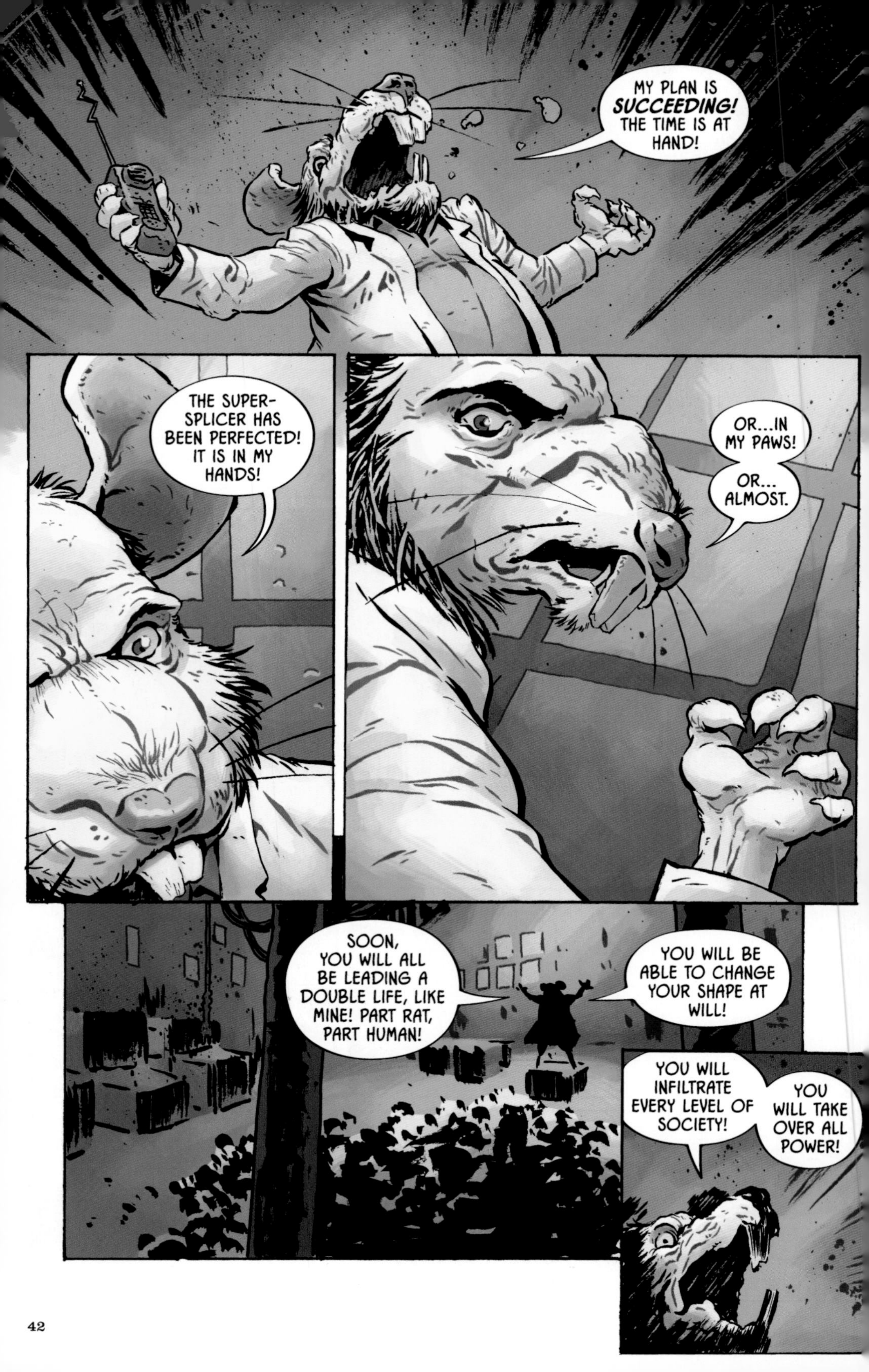
MY PLAN IS SUCCEEDING! THE TIME IS AT HAND!
THE SUPER-SPLICER HAS BEEN PERFECTED! IT IS IN MY HANDS!
OR...IN MY PAWS!
OR... ALMOST.
SOON, YOU WILL ALL BE LEADING A DOUBLE LIFE, LIKE MINE! PART RAT, PART HUMAN!
YOU WILL BE ABLE TO CHANGE YOUR SHAPE AT WILL!
YOU WILL INFILTRATE EVERY LEVEL OF SOCIETY!
YOU WILL TAKE OVER ALL POWER!

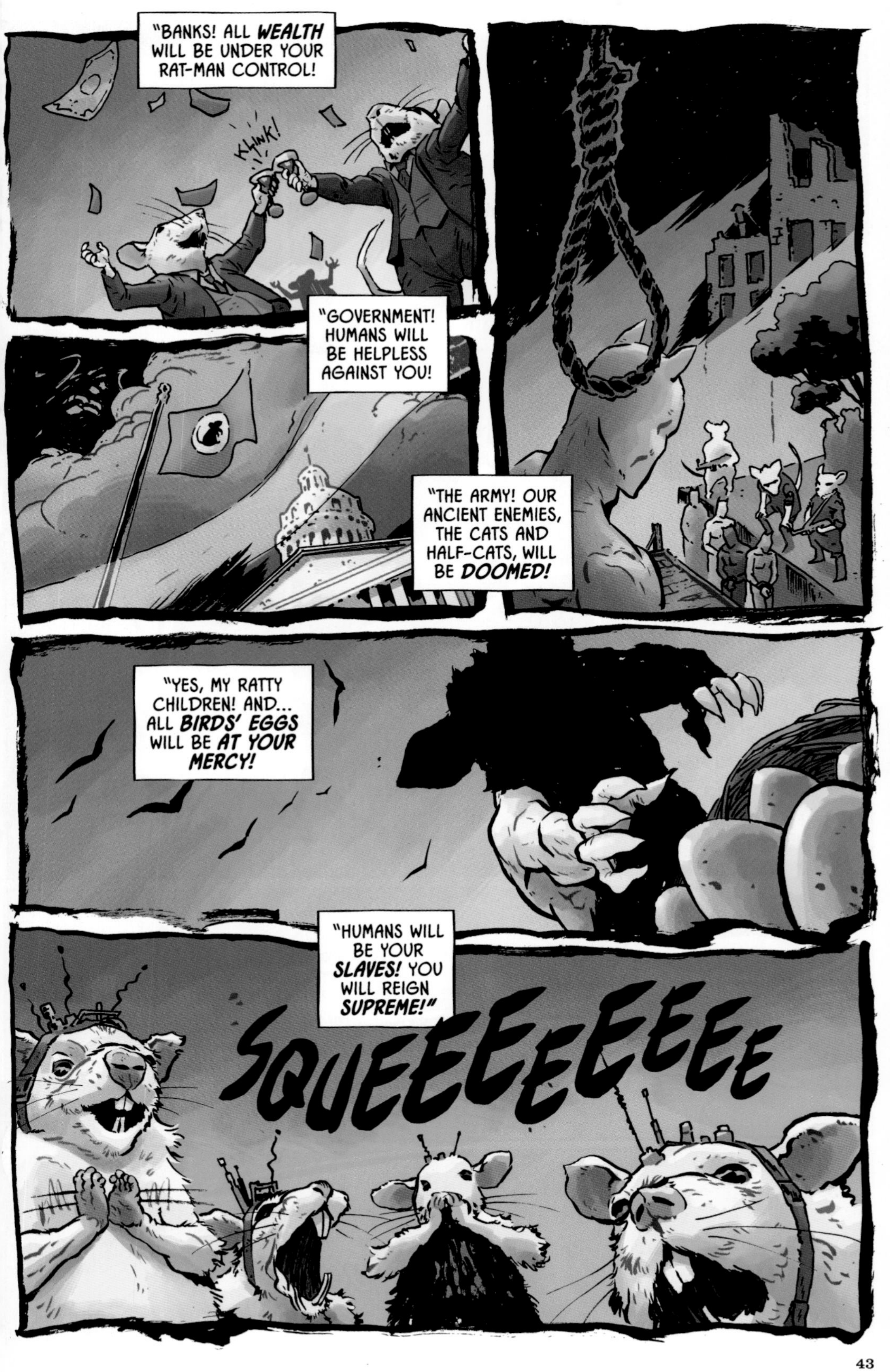
"BANKS! ALL WEALTH WILL BE UNDER YOUR RAT-MAN CONTROL!
KLINK!
"GOVERNMENT! HUMANS WILL BE HELPLESS AGAINST YOU!
"THE ARMY! OUR ANCIENT ENEMIES, THE CATS AND HALF-CATS, WILL BE DOOMED!
"YES, MY RATTY CHILDREN! AND... ALL BIRDS' EGGS WILL BE AT YOUR MERCY!
"HUMANS WILL BE YOUR SLAVES! YOU WILL REIGN SUPREME!"
SQUEEEEEEEEE

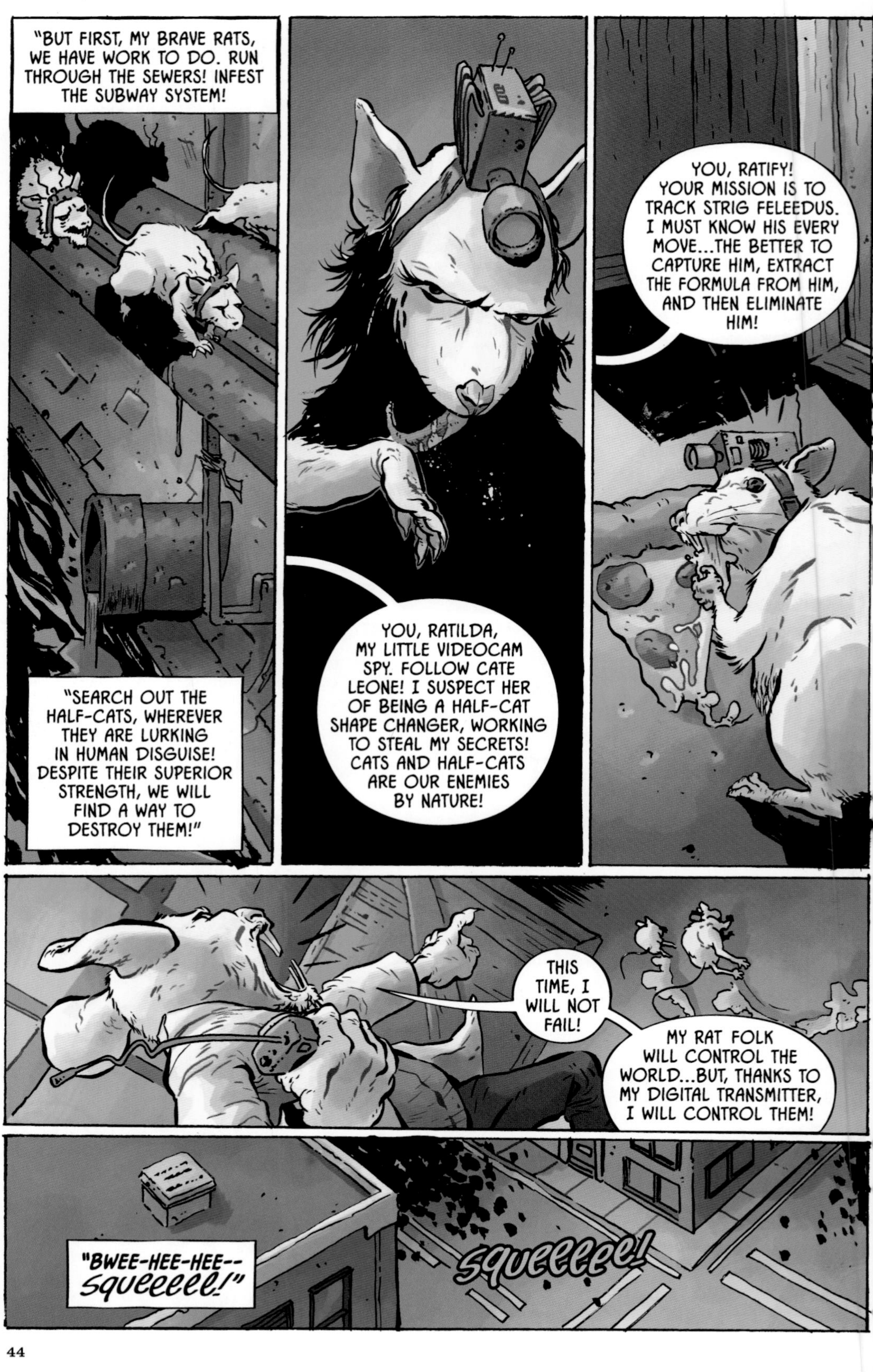
"BUT FIRST, MY BRAVE RATS, WE HAVE WORK TO DO. RUN THROUGH THE SEWERS! INFEST THE SUBWAY SYSTEM!
"SEARCH OUT THE HALF-CATS, WHEREVER THEY ARE LURKING IN HUMAN DISGUISE! DESPITE THEIR SUPERIOR STRENGTH, WE WILL FIND A WAY TO DESTROY THEM!"
YOU, RATILDA, MY LITTLE VIDEOCAM SPY. FOLLOW CATE LEONE! I SUSPECT HER OF BEING A HALF-CAT SHAPE CHANGER, WORKING TO STEAL MY SECRETS! CATS AND HALF-CATS ARE OUR ENEMIES BY NATURE!
YOU, RATIFY! YOUR MISSION IS TO TRACK STRIG FELEEDUS. I MUST KNOW HIS EVERY MOVE...THE BETTER TO CAPTURE HIM, EXTRACT THE FORMULA FROM HIM, AND THEN ELIMINATE HIM!
THIS TIME, I WILL NOT FAIL!
MY RAT FOLK WILL CONTROL THE WORLD...BUT, THANKS TO MY DIGITAL TRANSMITTER, I WILL CONTROL THEM!
"BWEE-HEE-HEE-- SQUEEEEL!"
SQUEEEEEE!

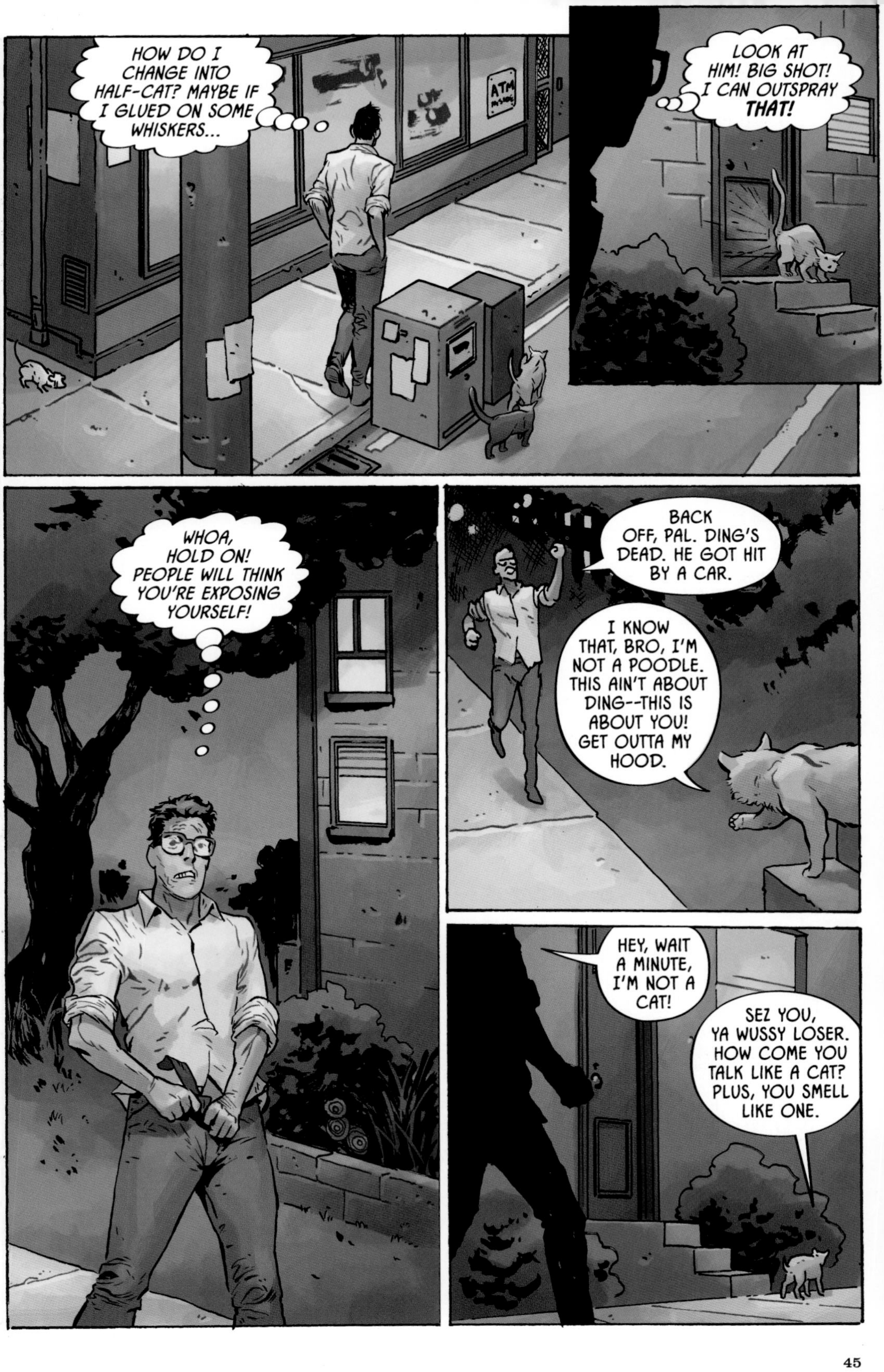
HOW DO I CHANGE INTO HALF-CAT? MAYBE IF I GLUED ON SOME WHISKERS...
ATM
LOOK AT HIM! BIG SHOT! I CAN OUTSPRAY **THAT!**
WHOA, HOLD ON! PEOPLE WILL THINK YOU'RE EXPOSING YOURSELF!
BACK OFF, PAL. DING'S DEAD. HE GOT HIT BY A CAR.
I KNOW THAT, BRO, I'M NOT A POODLE. THIS AIN'T ABOUT DING--THIS IS ABOUT YOU! GET OUTTA MY HOOD.
HEY, WAIT A MINUTE, I'M NOT A CAT!
SEZ YOU, YA WUSSY LOSER. HOW COME YOU TALK LIKE A CAT? PLUS, YOU SMELL LIKE ONE.

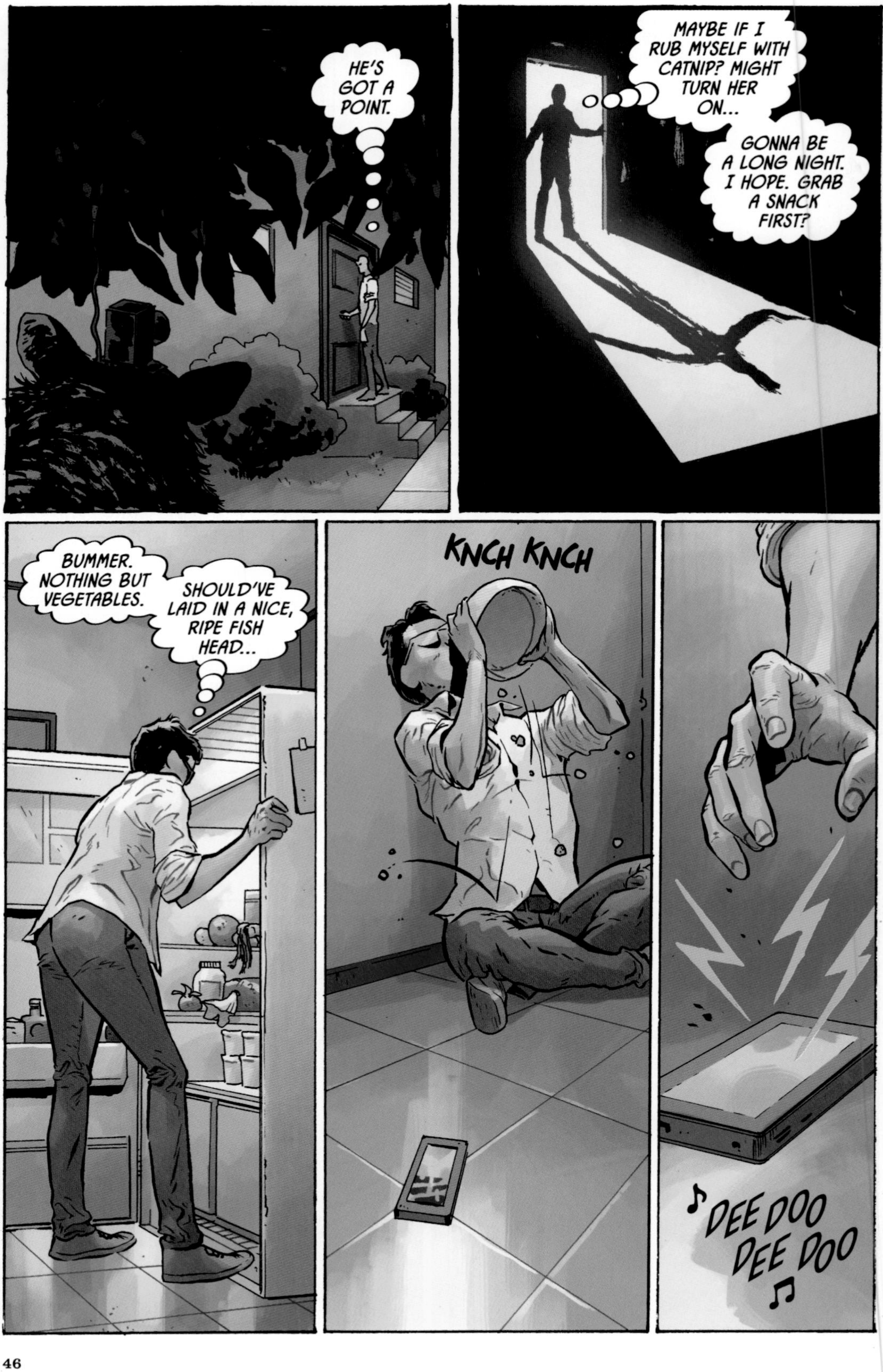
HE'S GOT A POINT.
MAYBE IF I RUB MYSELF WITH CATNIP? MIGHT TURN HER ON...
GONNA BE A LONG NIGHT. I HOPE. GRAB A SNACK FIRST?
BUMMER. NOTHING BUT VEGETABLES.
SHOULD'VE LAID IN A NICE, RIPE FISH HEAD...
KNCH KNCH
DEE DOO DEE DOO

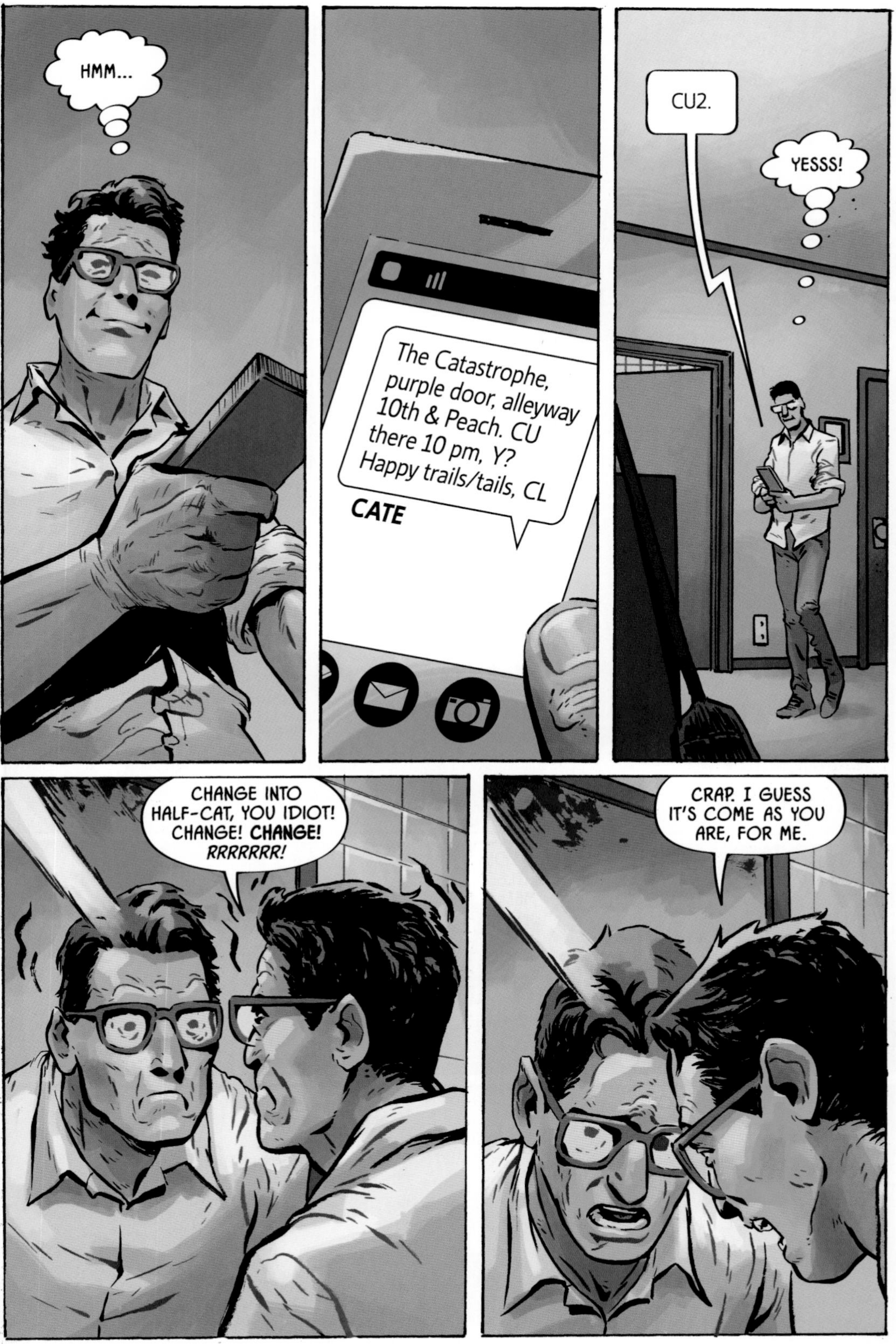
HMM...
The Catastrophe, purple door, alleyway 10th & Peach. CU there 10 pm, Y? Happy trails/tails, CL
CATE
CU2.
YESSS!
CHANGE INTO HALF-CAT, YOU IDIOT! CHANGE! **CHANGE!** *RRRRRRR!*
CRAP. I GUESS IT'S COME AS YOU ARE, FOR ME.

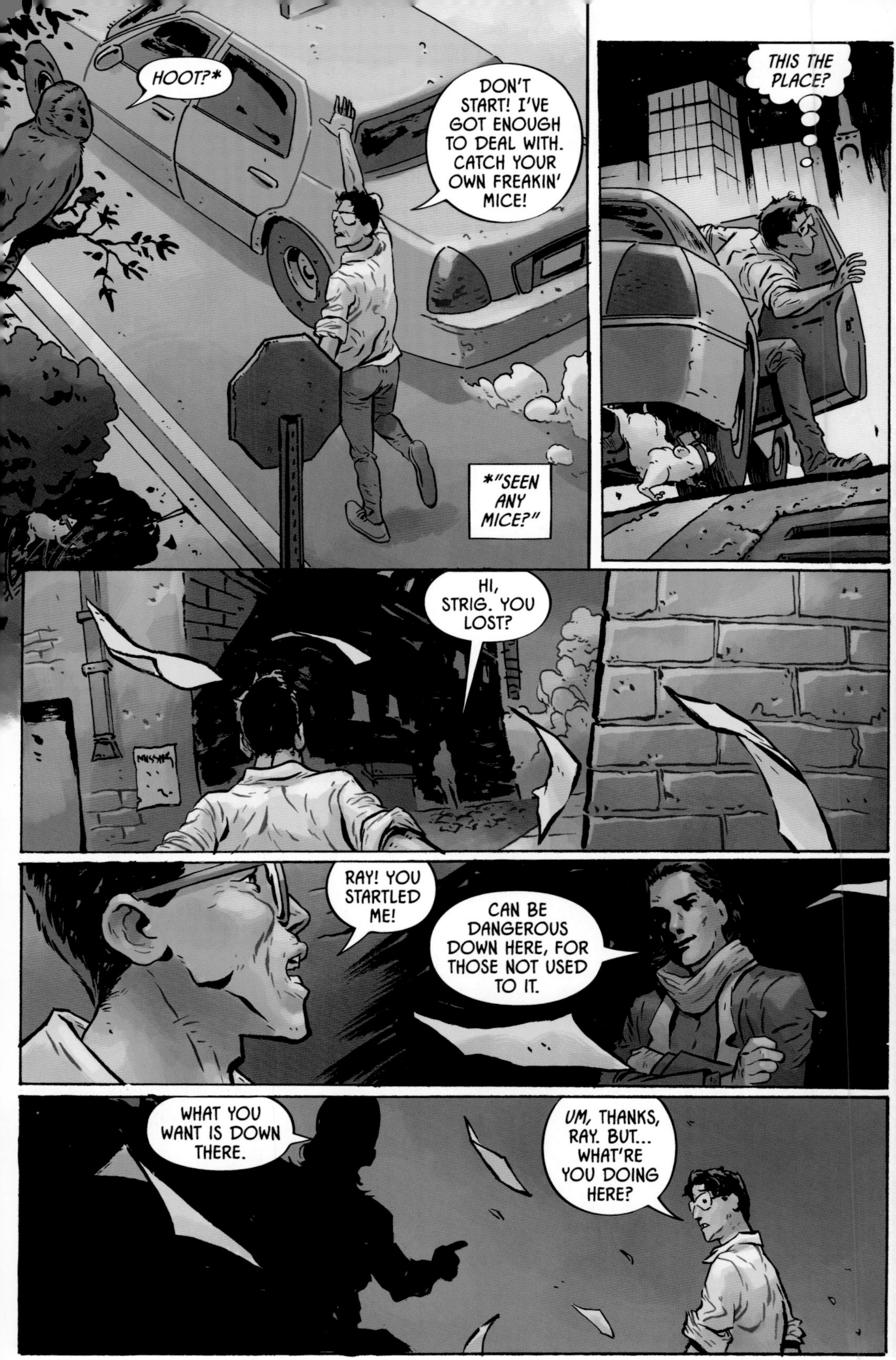
HOOT?*
DON'T START! I'VE GOT ENOUGH TO DEAL WITH. CATCH YOUR OWN FREAKIN' MICE!
*"SEEN ANY MICE?"
THIS THE PLACE?
HI, STRIG. YOU LOST?
RAY! YOU STARTLED ME!
CAN BE DANGEROUS DOWN HERE, FOR THOSE NOT USED TO IT.
WHAT YOU WANT IS DOWN THERE.
UM, THANKS, RAY. BUT... WHAT'RE YOU DOING HERE?

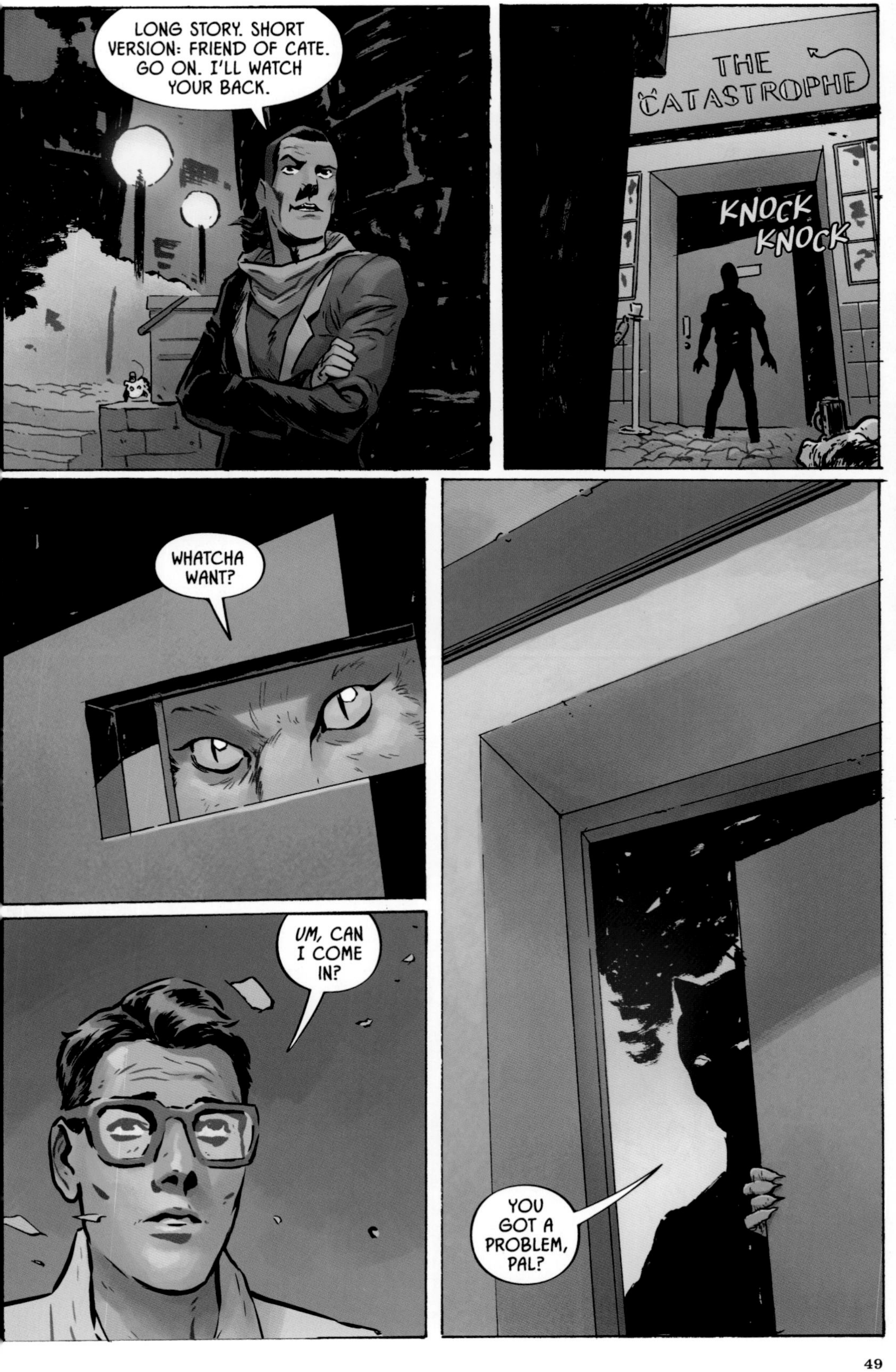

LONG STORY. SHORT VERSION: FRIEND OF CATE. GO ON. I'LL WATCH YOUR BACK.
THE CATASTROPHE
KNOCK KNOCK
WHATCHA WANT?
UM, CAN I COME IN?
YOU GOT A PROBLEM, PAL?

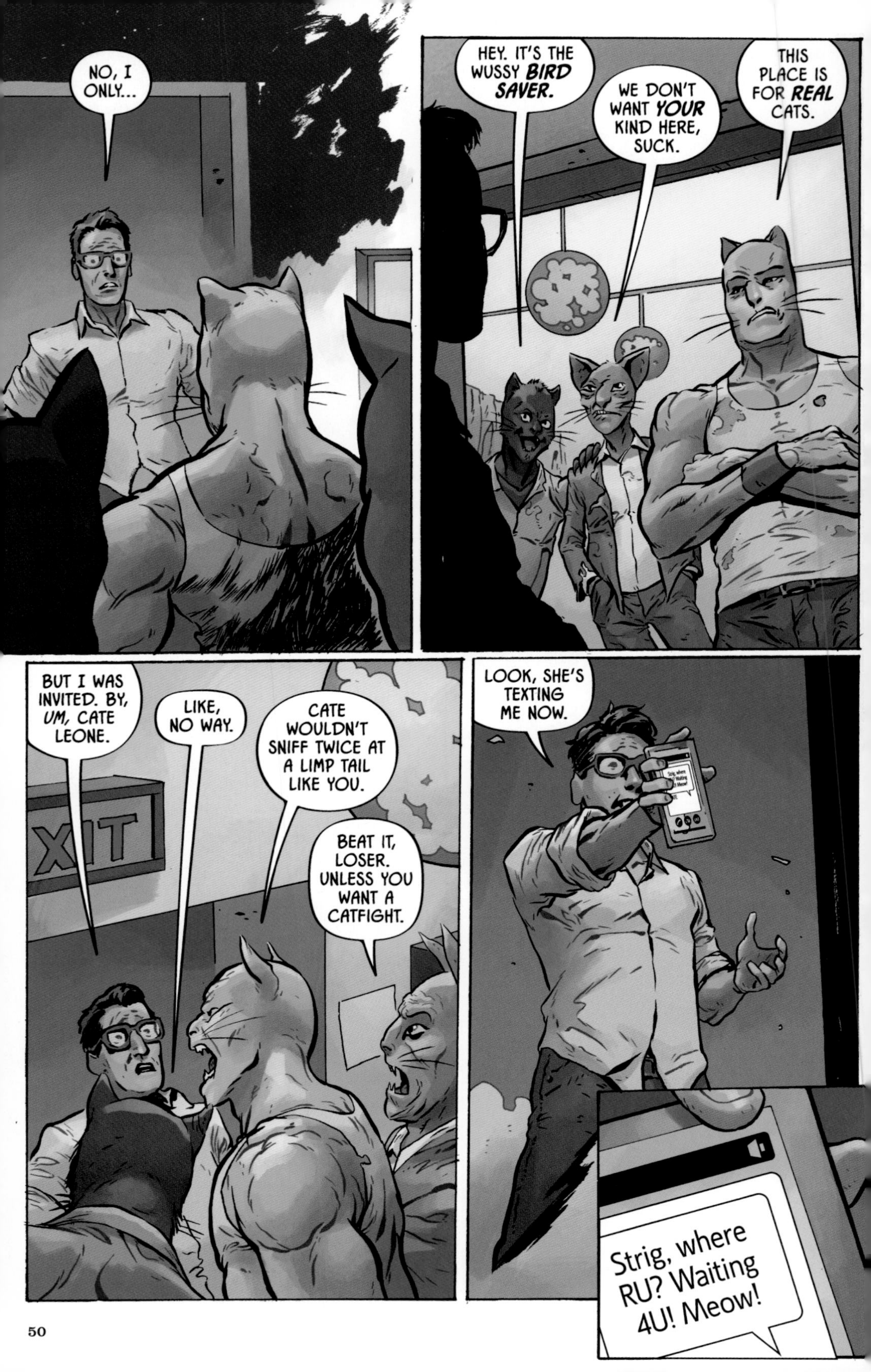
NO, I ONLY...
HEY. IT'S THE WUSSY **BIRD SAVER.**
WE DON'T WANT **YOUR** KIND HERE, SUCK.
THIS PLACE IS FOR **REAL** CATS.
BUT I WAS INVITED. BY, *UM,* CATE LEONE.
LIKE, NO WAY.
CATE WOULDN'T SNIFF TWICE AT A LIMP TAIL LIKE YOU.
BEAT IT, LOSER. UNLESS YOU WANT A CATFIGHT.
XIT
LOOK, SHE'S TEXTING ME NOW.
Strig, where RU? Waiting 4U! Meow!

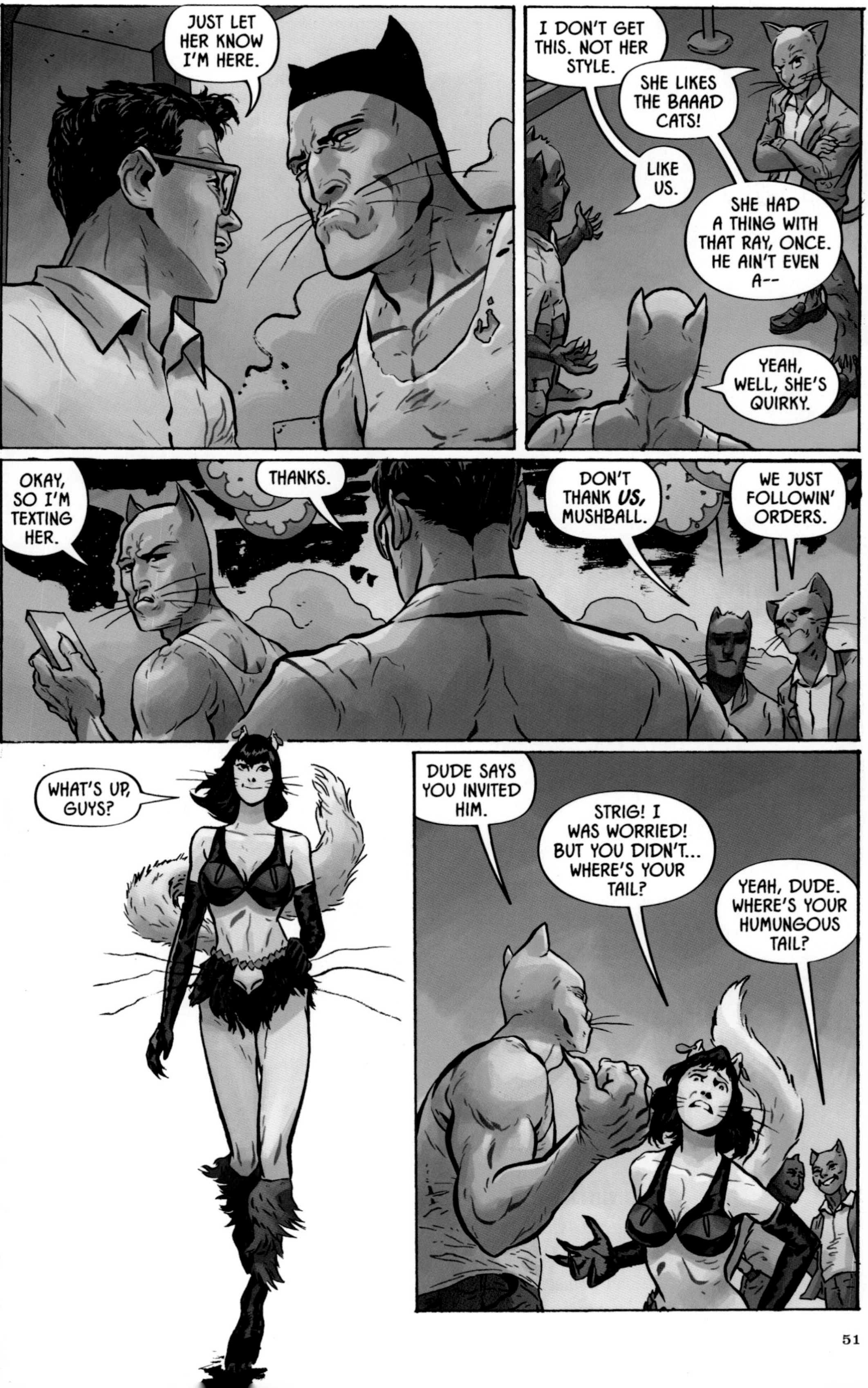
JUST LET HER KNOW I'M HERE.
I DON'T GET THIS. NOT HER STYLE.
SHE LIKES THE BAAAD CATS!
LIKE US.
SHE HAD A THING WITH THAT RAY, ONCE. HE AIN'T EVEN A--
YEAH, WELL, SHE'S QUIRKY.
OKAY, SO I'M TEXTING HER.
THANKS.
DON'T THANK US, MUSHBALL.
WE JUST FOLLOWIN' ORDERS.
WHAT'S UP, GUYS?
DUDE SAYS YOU INVITED HIM.
STRIG! I WAS WORRIED! BUT YOU DIDN'T... WHERE'S YOUR TAIL?
YEAH, DUDE. WHERE'S YOUR HUMUNGOUS TAIL?

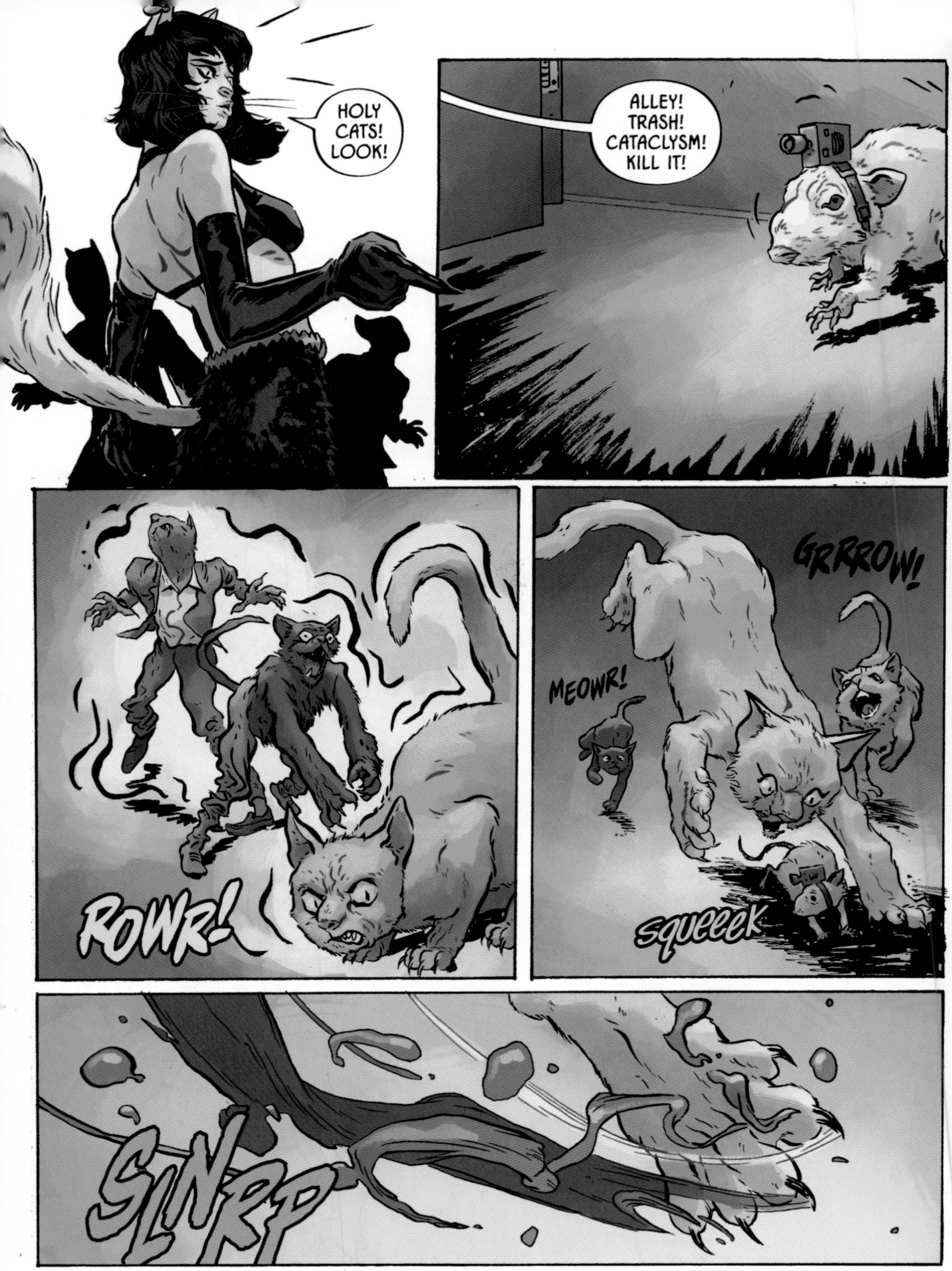
HOLY CATS! LOOK!
ALLEY! TRASH! CATACLYSM! KILL IT!
ROWR!
GRRROW!
MEOWR!
squeeek
SLNRP

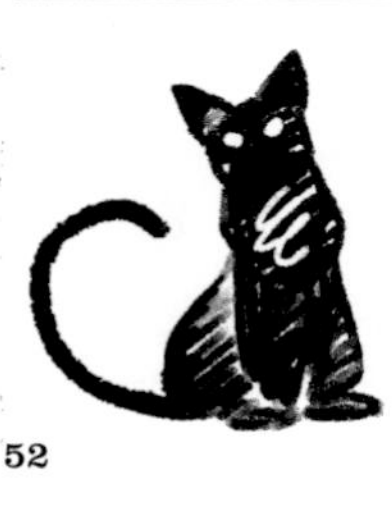

CATS ARE NATURAL HUNTERS

Hunting is a natural cat instinct. It's also "natural" for dogs to hunt cats, but we don't let them do it! Cats and dogs have been domesticated for thousands of years. They're pets, not wild animals.
www.catsandbirds.ca

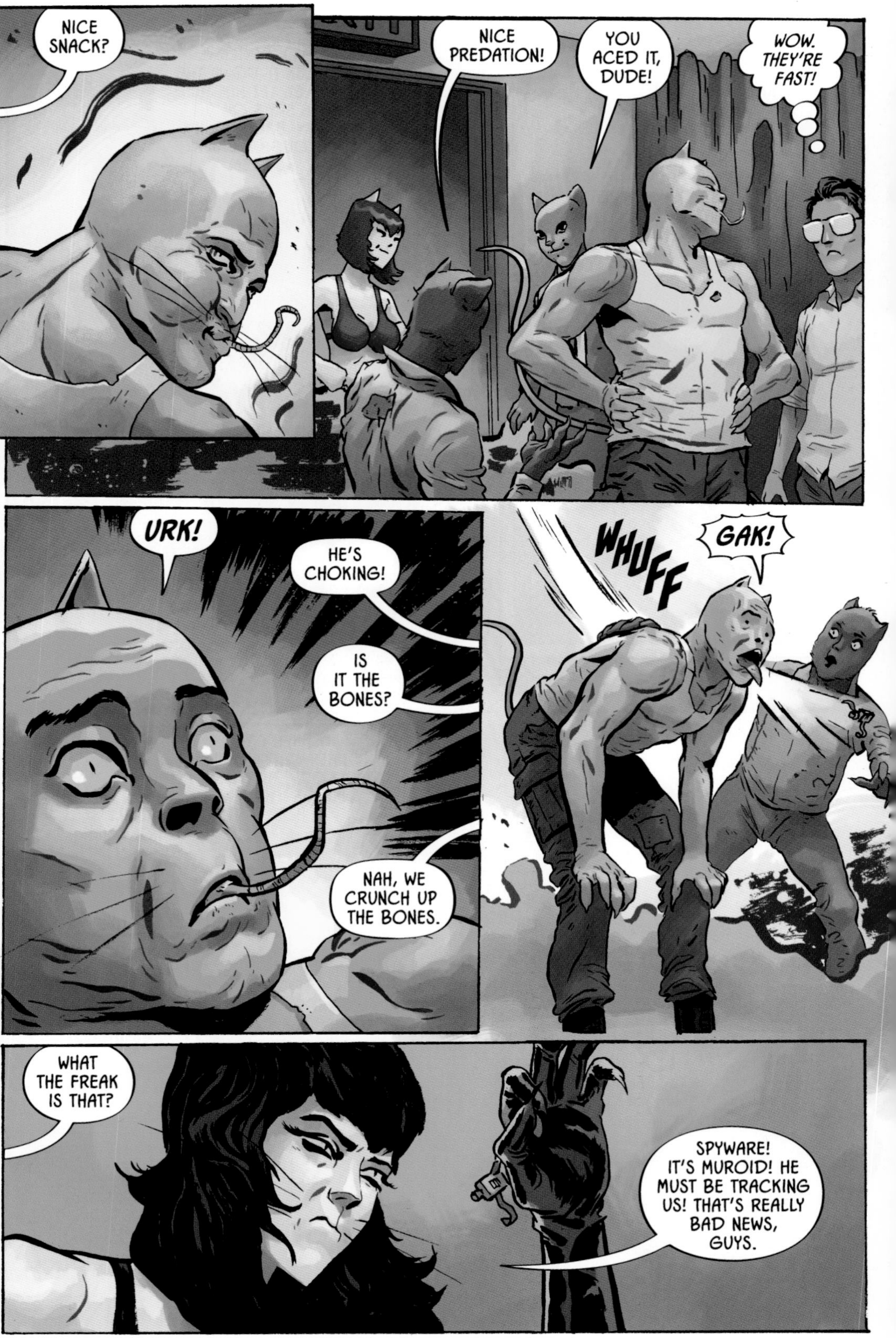
NICE SNACK?
NICE PREDATION!
YOU ACED IT, DUDE!
WOW. THEY'RE FAST!
URK!
HE'S CHOKING!
IS IT THE BONES?
NAH, WE CRUNCH UP THE BONES.
WHUFF
GAK!
WHAT THE FREAK IS THAT?
SPYWARE! IT'S MUROID! HE MUST BE TRACKING US! THAT'S REALLY BAD NEWS, GUYS.

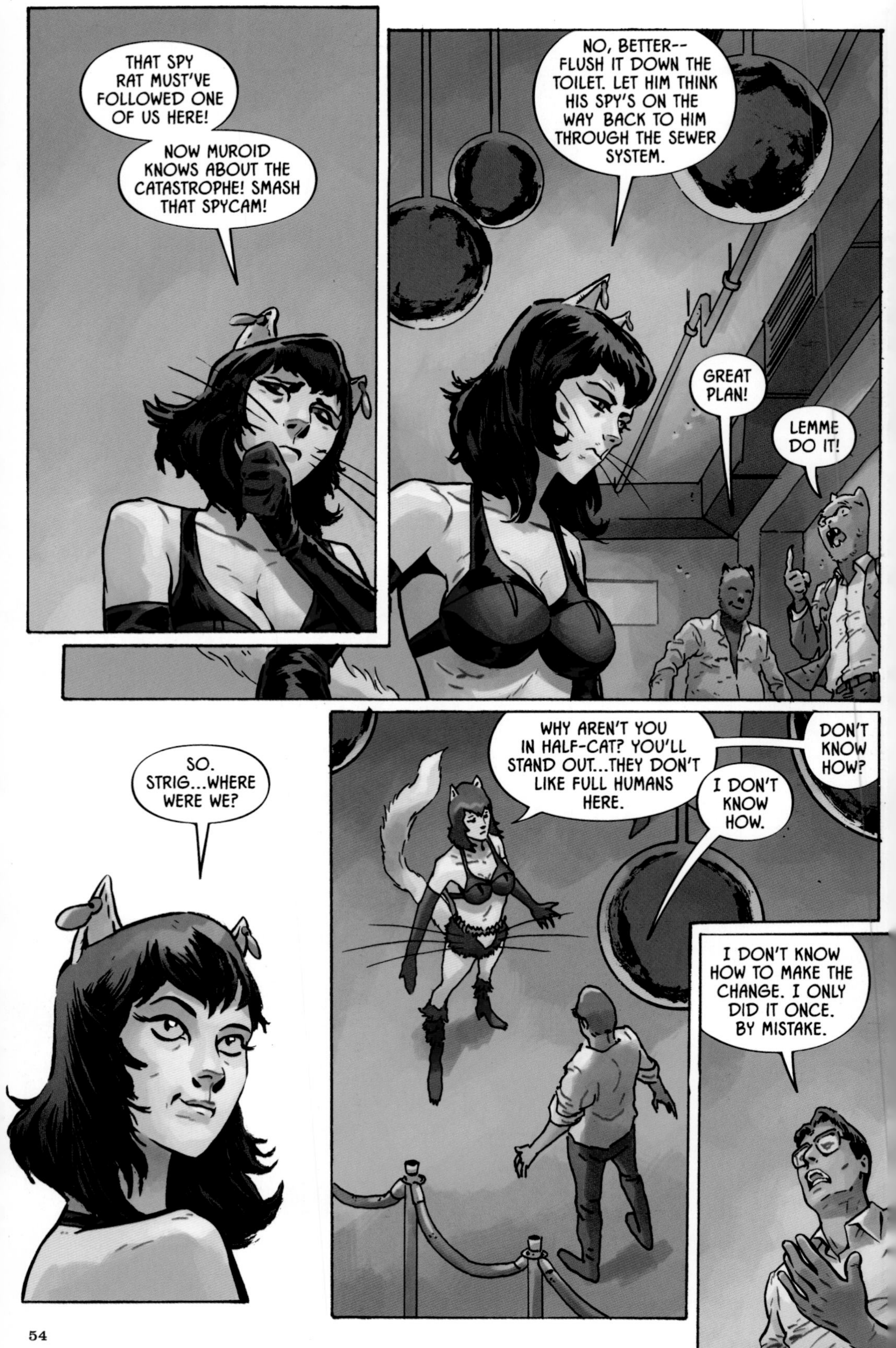
THAT SPY RAT MUST'VE FOLLOWED ONE OF US HERE!
NOW MUROID KNOWS ABOUT THE CATASTROPHE! SMASH THAT SPYCAM!
NO, BETTER-- FLUSH IT DOWN THE TOILET. LET HIM THINK HIS SPY'S ON THE WAY BACK TO HIM THROUGH THE SEWER SYSTEM.
GREAT PLAN!
LEMME DO IT!
SO. STRIG...WHERE WERE WE?
WHY AREN'T YOU IN HALF-CAT? YOU'LL STAND OUT...THEY DON'T LIKE FULL HUMANS HERE.
I DON'T KNOW HOW.
DON'T KNOW HOW?
I DON'T KNOW HOW TO MAKE THE CHANGE. I ONLY DID IT ONCE. BY MISTAKE.

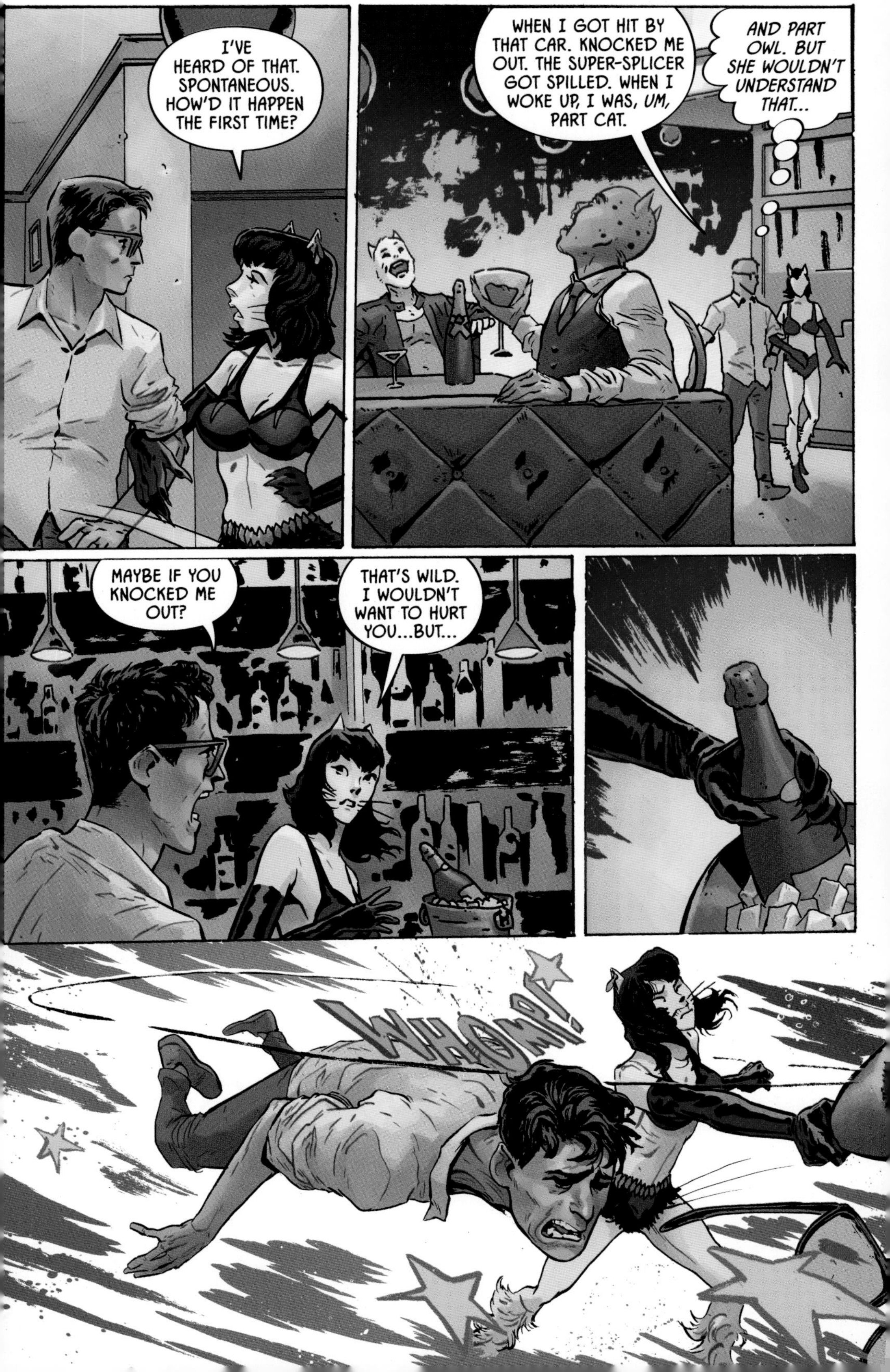
I'VE HEARD OF THAT. SPONTANEOUS. HOW'D IT HAPPEN THE FIRST TIME?
WHEN I GOT HIT BY THAT CAR. KNOCKED ME OUT. THE SUPER-SPLICER GOT SPILLED. WHEN I WOKE UP, I WAS, UM, PART CAT.
AND PART OWL. BUT SHE WOULDN'T UNDERSTAND THAT...
MAYBE IF YOU KNOCKED ME OUT?
THAT'S WILD. I WOULDN'T WANT TO HURT YOU...BUT...
WHOMP!

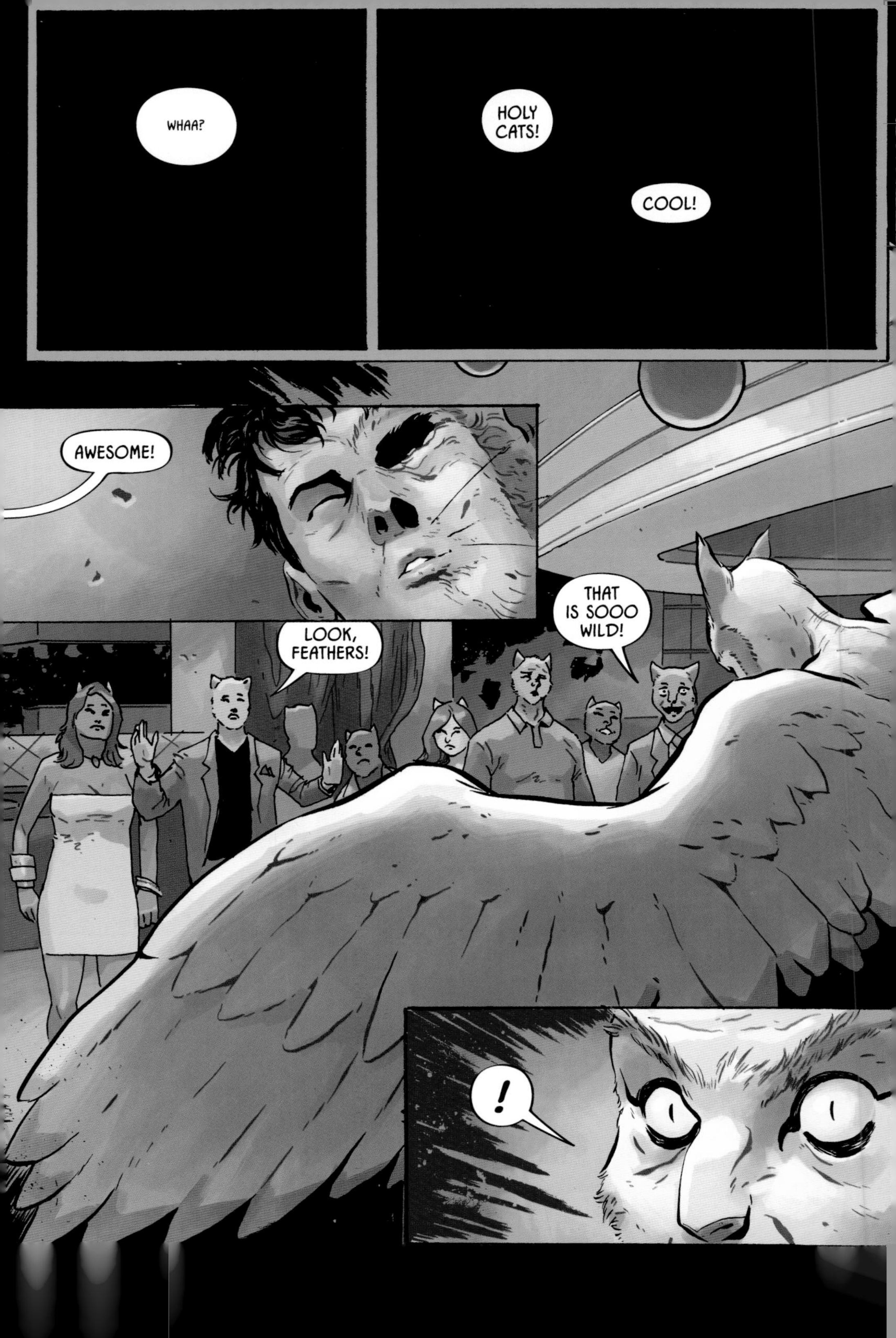
WHAA?
HOLY CATS!
COOL!
AWESOME!
LOOK, FEATHERS!
THAT IS SOOO WILD!
!

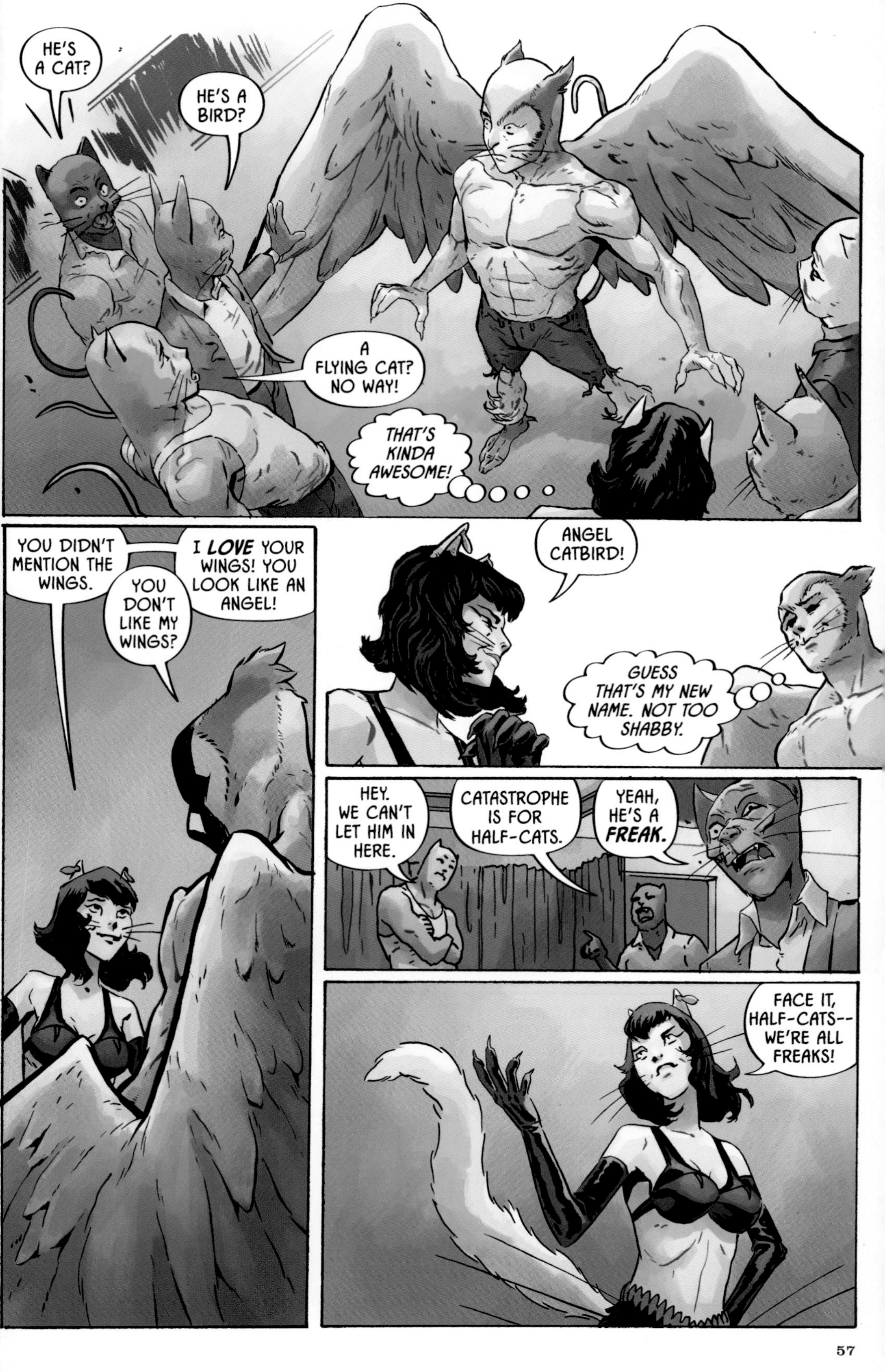
HE'S A CAT?
HE'S A BIRD?
A FLYING CAT? NO WAY!
THAT'S KINDA AWESOME!
YOU DIDN'T MENTION THE WINGS.
YOU DON'T LIKE MY WINGS?
I LOVE YOUR WINGS! YOU LOOK LIKE AN ANGEL!
ANGEL CATBIRD!
GUESS THAT'S MY NEW NAME. NOT TOO SHABBY.
HEY. WE CAN'T LET HIM IN HERE.
CATASTROPHE IS FOR HALF-CATS.
YEAH, HE'S A FREAK.
FACE IT, HALF-CATS-- WE'RE ALL FREAKS!

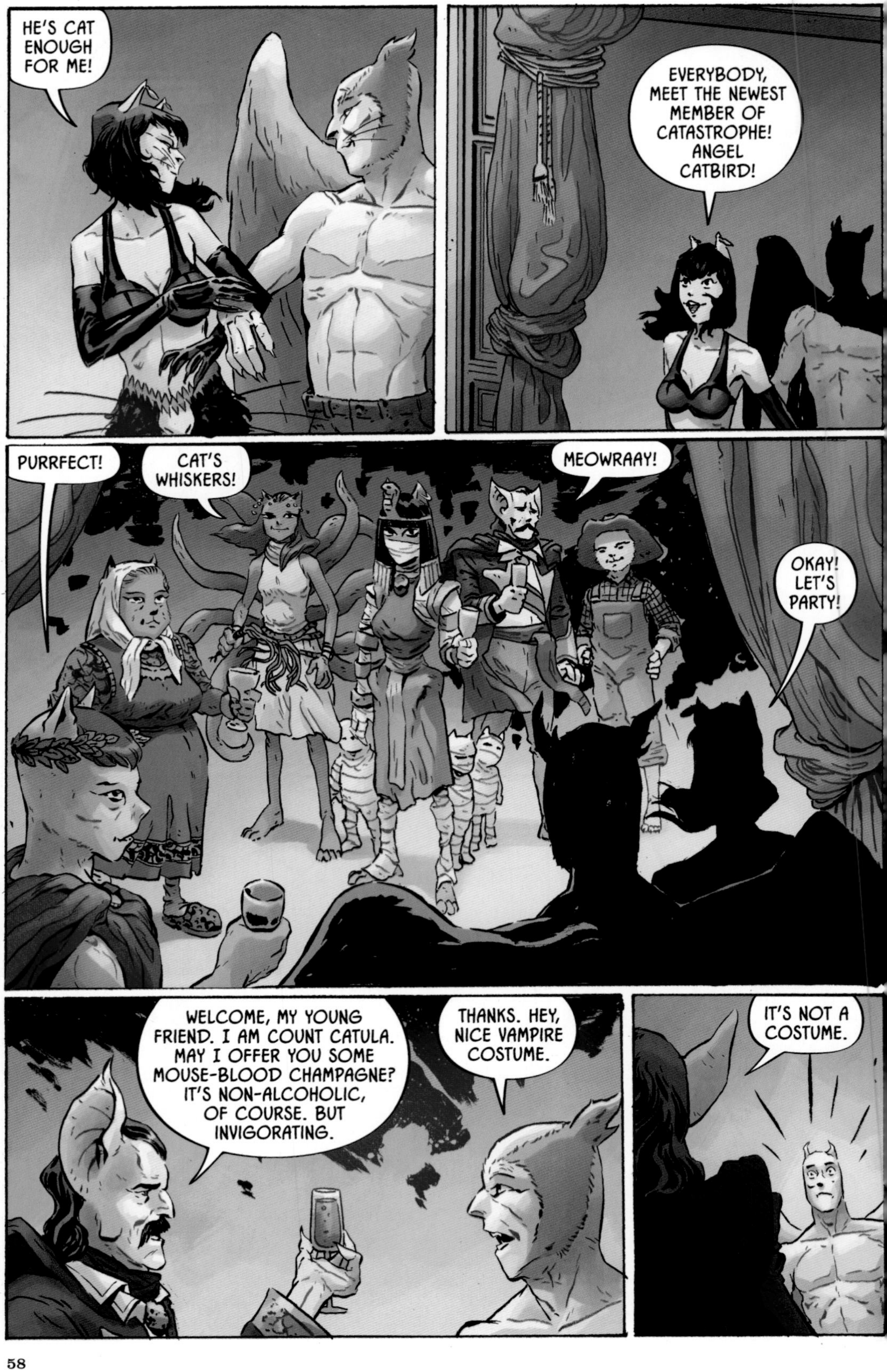

HE'S CAT ENOUGH FOR ME!
EVERYBODY, MEET THE NEWEST MEMBER OF CATASTROPHE! ANGEL CATBIRD!
PURRFECT!
CAT'S WHISKERS!
MEOWRAAY!
OKAY! LET'S PARTY!
WELCOME, MY YOUNG FRIEND. I AM COUNT CATULA. MAY I OFFER YOU SOME MOUSE-BLOOD CHAMPAGNE? IT'S NON-ALCOHOLIC, OF COURSE. BUT INVIGORATING.
THANKS. HEY, NICE VAMPIRE COSTUME.
IT'S NOT A COSTUME.

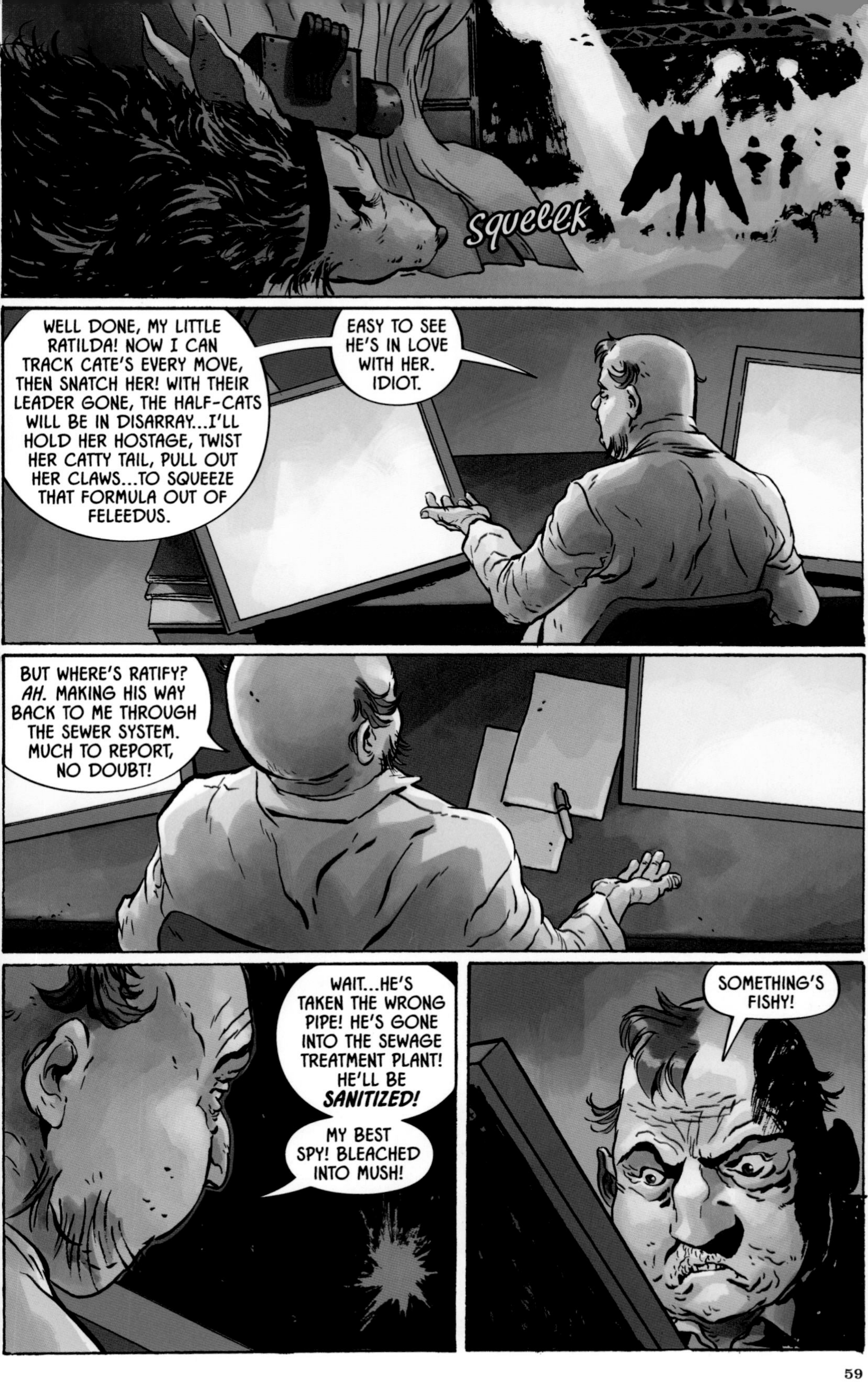

SQUEEEK
WELL DONE, MY LITTLE RATILDA! NOW I CAN TRACK CATE'S EVERY MOVE, THEN SNATCH HER! WITH THEIR LEADER GONE, THE HALF-CATS WILL BE IN DISARRAY...I'LL HOLD HER HOSTAGE, TWIST HER CATTY TAIL, PULL OUT HER CLAWS...TO SQUEEZE THAT FORMULA OUT OF FELEEDUS.
EASY TO SEE HE'S IN LOVE WITH HER. IDIOT.
BUT WHERE'S RATIFY? *AH.* MAKING HIS WAY BACK TO ME THROUGH THE SEWER SYSTEM. MUCH TO REPORT, NO DOUBT!
WAIT...HE'S TAKEN THE WRONG PIPE! HE'S GONE INTO THE SEWAGE TREATMENT PLANT! HE'LL BE ***SANITIZED!***
MY BEST SPY! BLEACHED INTO MUSH!
SOMETHING'S FISHY!

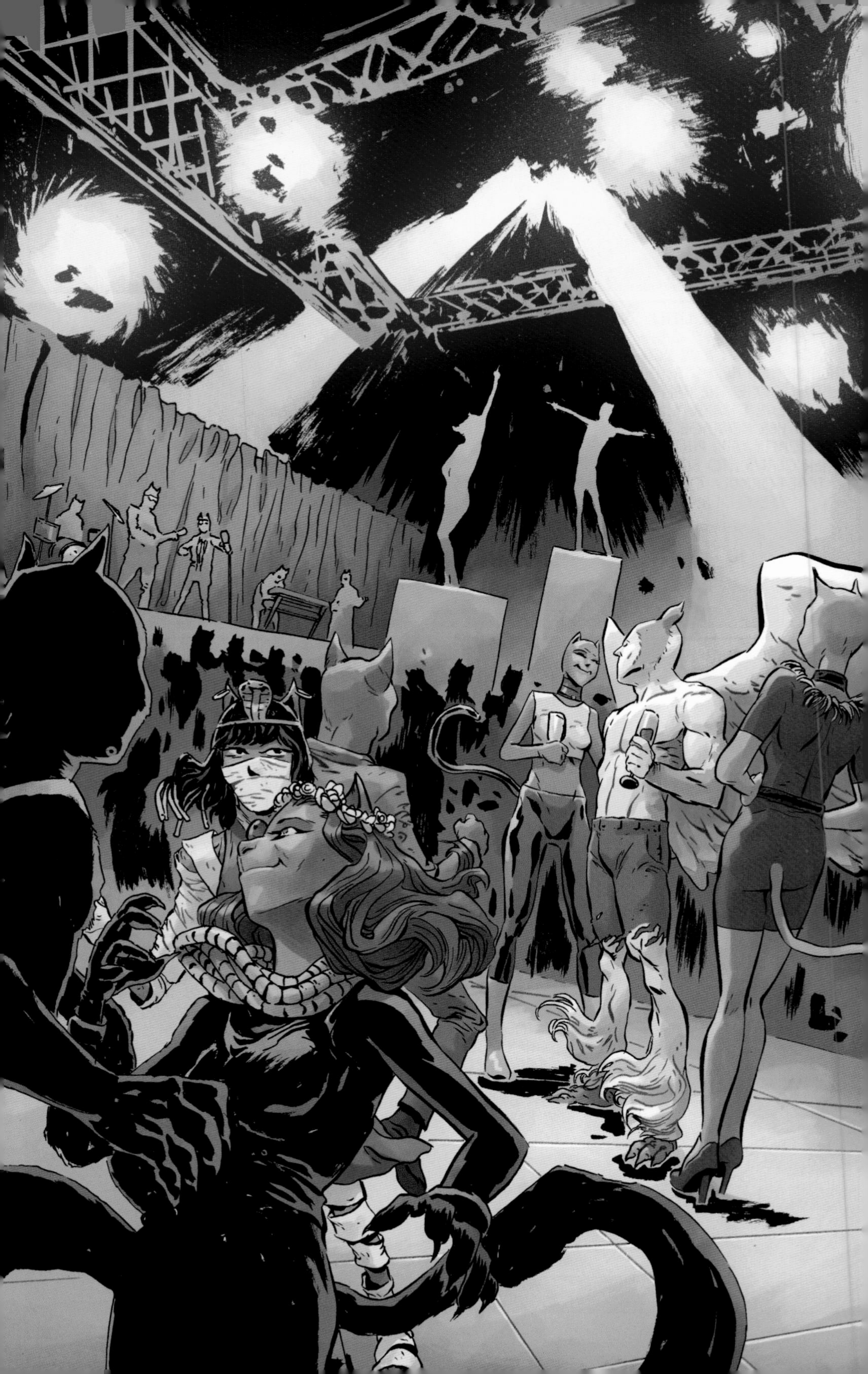

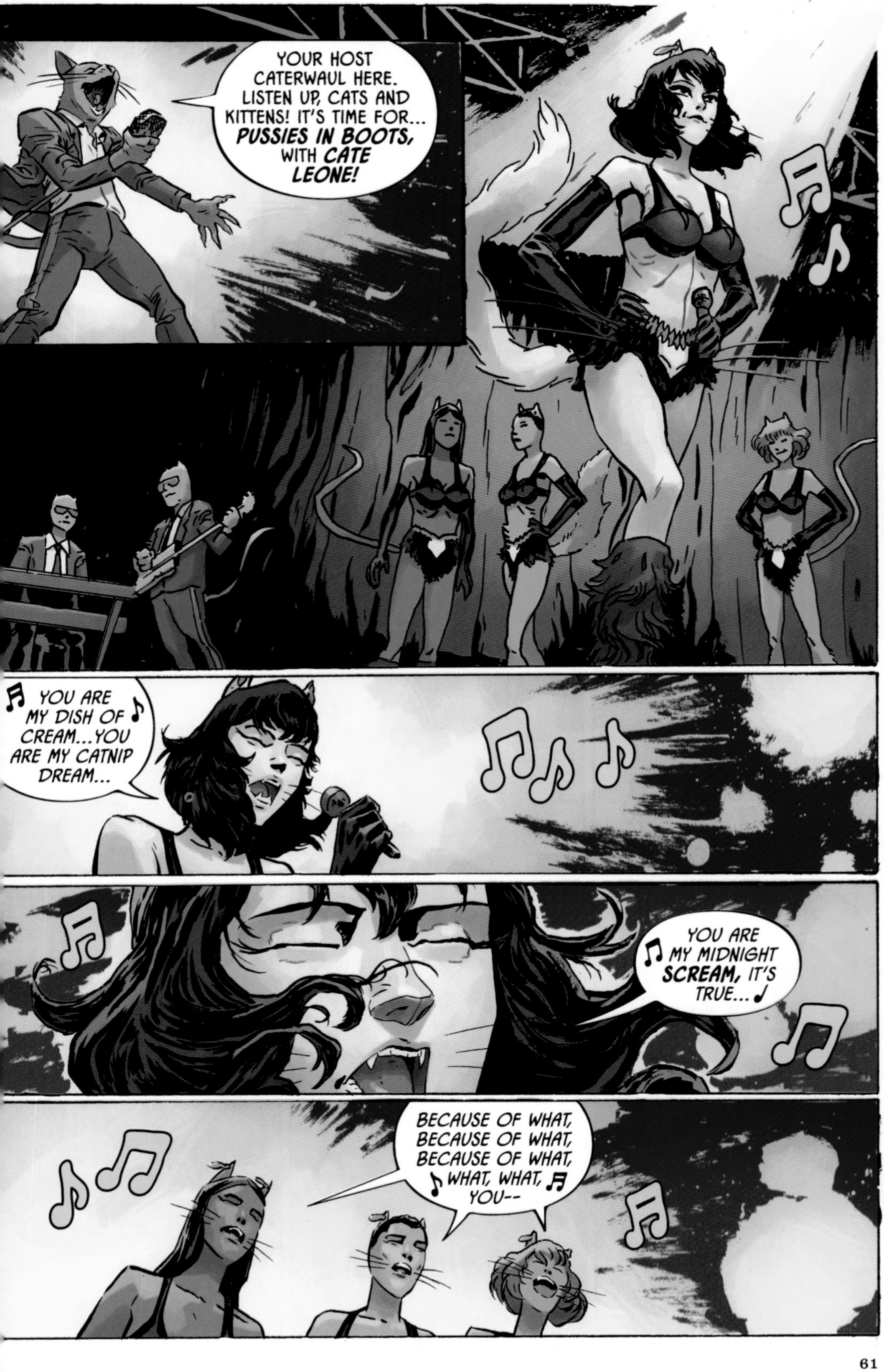
YOUR HOST CATERWAUL HERE. LISTEN UP, CATS AND KITTENS! IT'S TIME FOR... **PUSSIES IN BOOTS,** WITH **CATE LEONE!**
YOU ARE MY DISH OF CREAM...YOU ARE MY CATNIP DREAM...
YOU ARE MY MIDNIGHT **SCREAM,** IT'S TRUE...
BECAUSE OF WHAT, BECAUSE OF WHAT, BECAUSE OF WHAT, WHAT, WHAT, YOU--

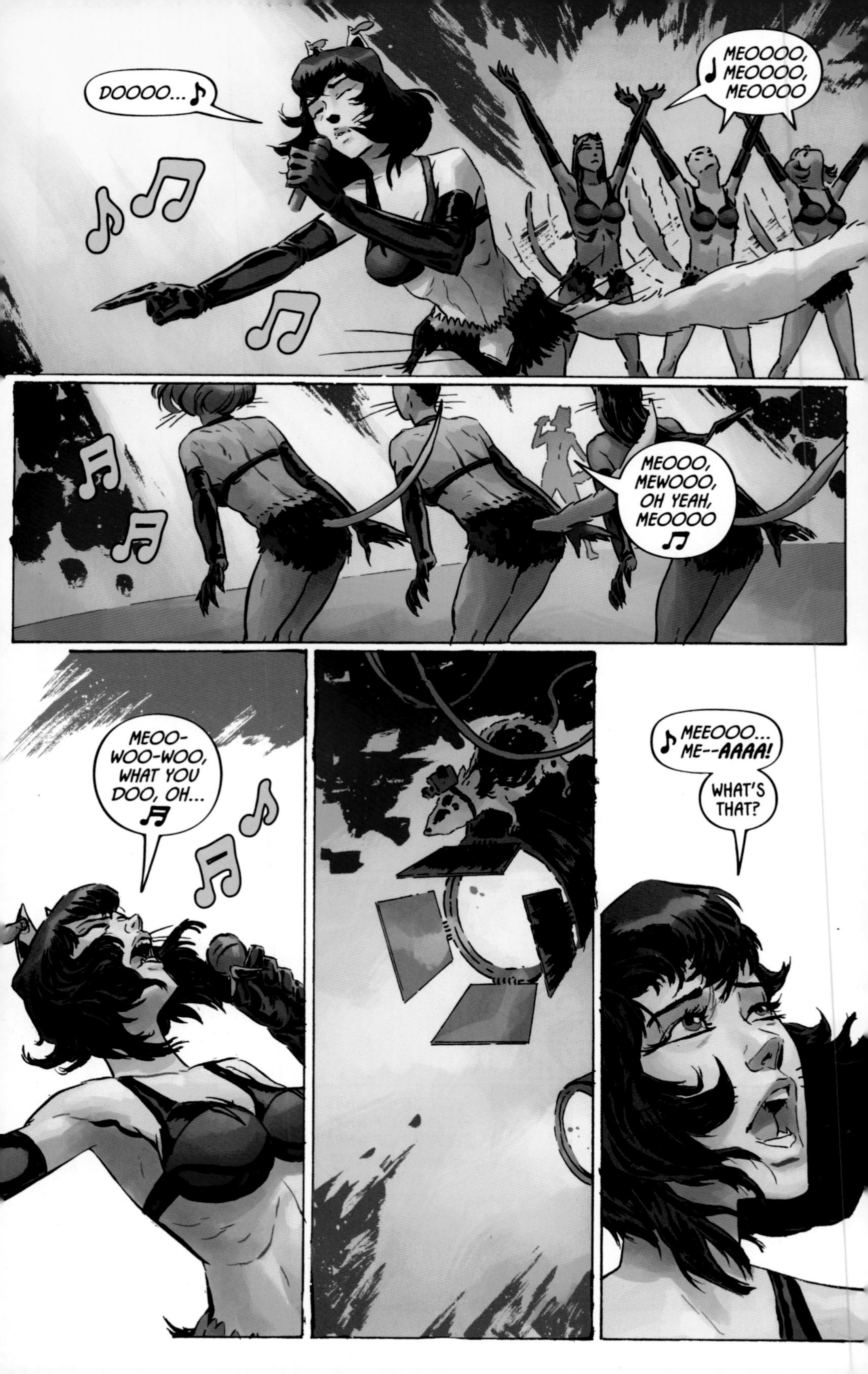
DOOOO...
MEOOOO, MEOOOO, MEOOOO
MEOOO, MEWOOO, OH YEAH, MEOOOO
MEOO-WOO-WOO, WHAT YOU DOO, OH...
MEEOOO... ME--AAAA!
WHAT'S THAT?

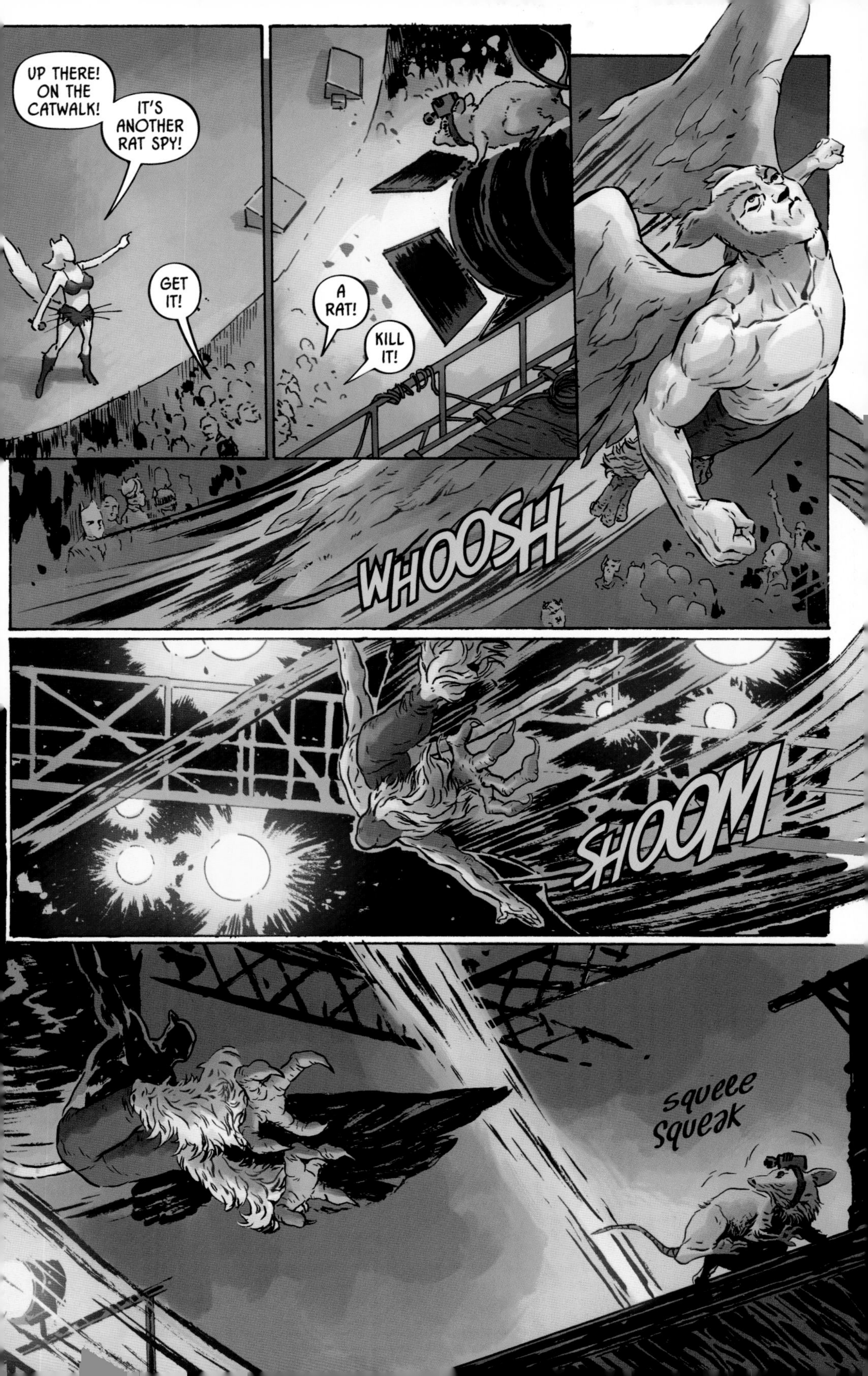
UP THERE! ON THE CATWALK!
IT'S ANOTHER RAT SPY!
GET IT!
A RAT!
KILL IT!
WHOOSH
SHOOM
squeee
Squeak

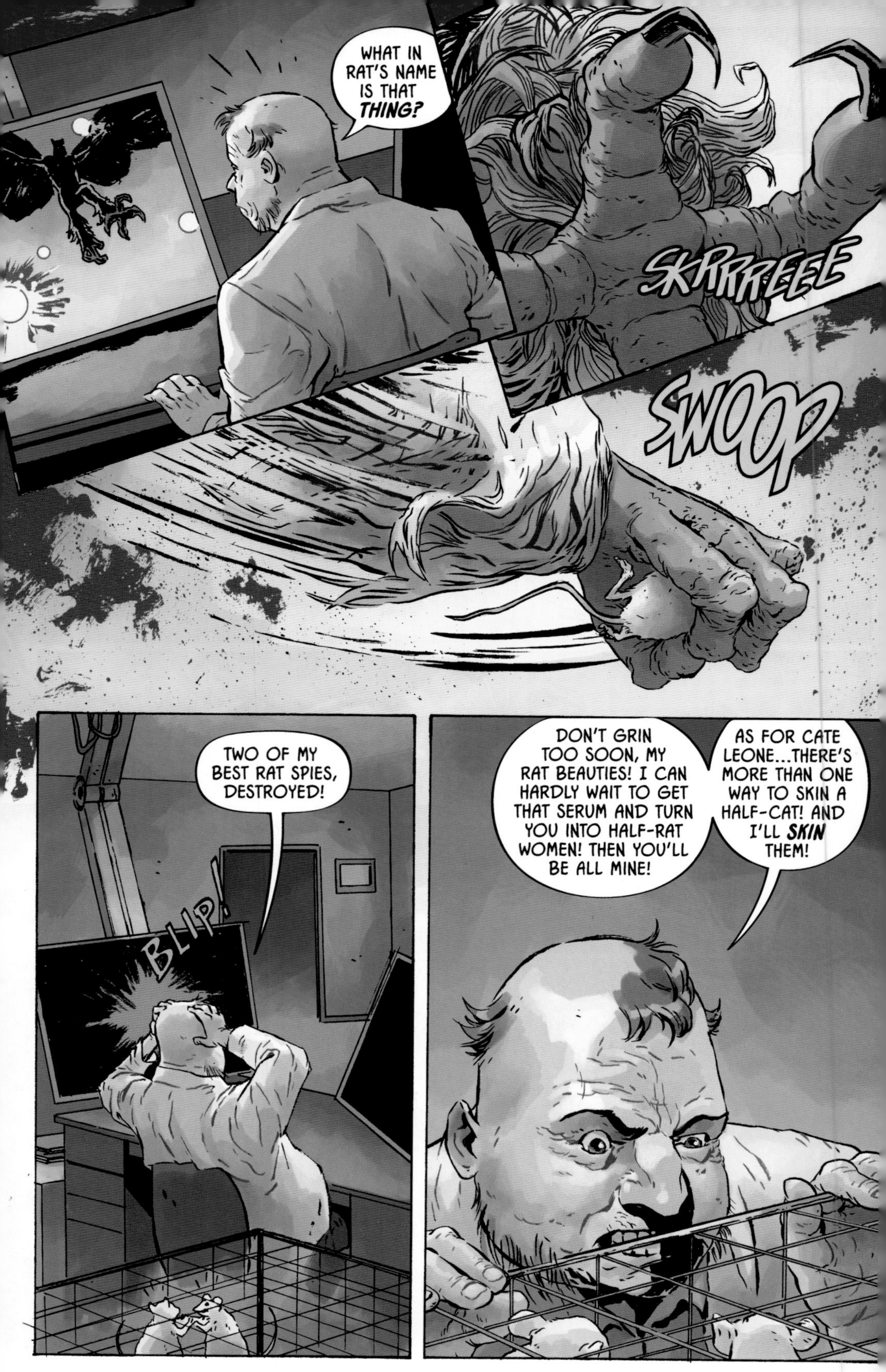

WHAT IN RAT'S NAME IS THAT *THING?*
SKRRREEEE
SWOOP
TWO OF MY BEST RAT SPIES, DESTROYED!
BLIP!
DON'T GRIN TOO SOON, MY RAT BEAUTIES! I CAN HARDLY WAIT TO GET THAT SERUM AND TURN YOU INTO HALF-RAT WOMEN! THEN YOU'LL BE ALL MINE!
AS FOR CATE LEONE...THERE'S MORE THAN ONE WAY TO SKIN A HALF-CAT! AND I'LL *SKIN* THEM!

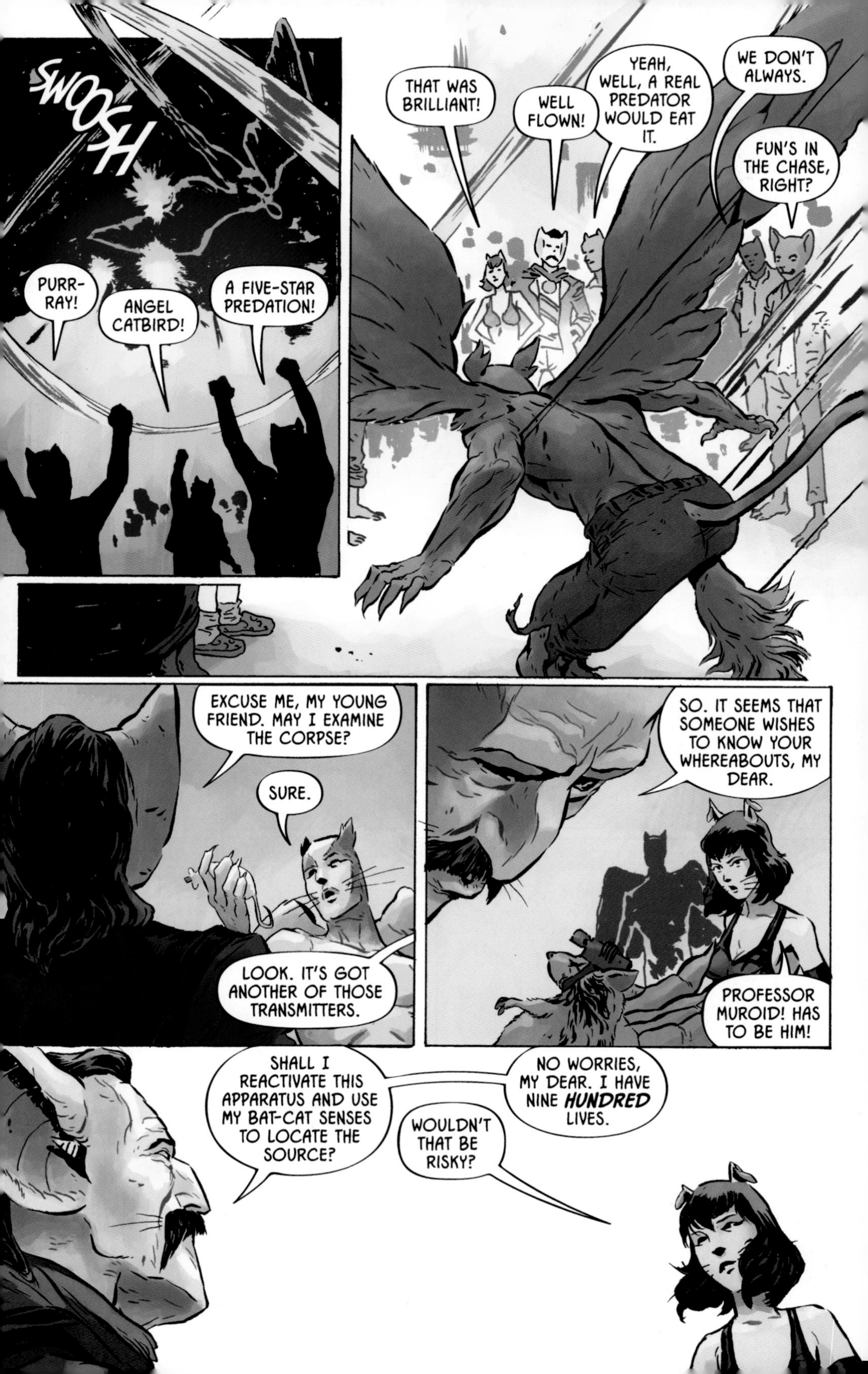
SWOOSH
PURR-RAY!
ANGEL CATBIRD!
A FIVE-STAR PREDATION!
THAT WAS BRILLIANT!
WELL FLOWN!
YEAH, WELL, A REAL PREDATOR WOULD EAT IT.
WE DON'T ALWAYS.
FUN'S IN THE CHASE, RIGHT?
EXCUSE ME, MY YOUNG FRIEND. MAY I EXAMINE THE CORPSE?
SURE.
LOOK. IT'S GOT ANOTHER OF THOSE TRANSMITTERS.
SO. IT SEEMS THAT SOMEONE WISHES TO KNOW YOUR WHEREABOUTS, MY DEAR.
PROFESSOR MUROID! HAS TO BE HIM!
SHALL I REACTIVATE THIS APPARATUS AND USE MY BAT-CAT SENSES TO LOCATE THE SOURCE?
WOULDN'T THAT BE RISKY?
NO WORRIES, MY DEAR. I HAVE NINE ***HUNDRED*** LIVES.

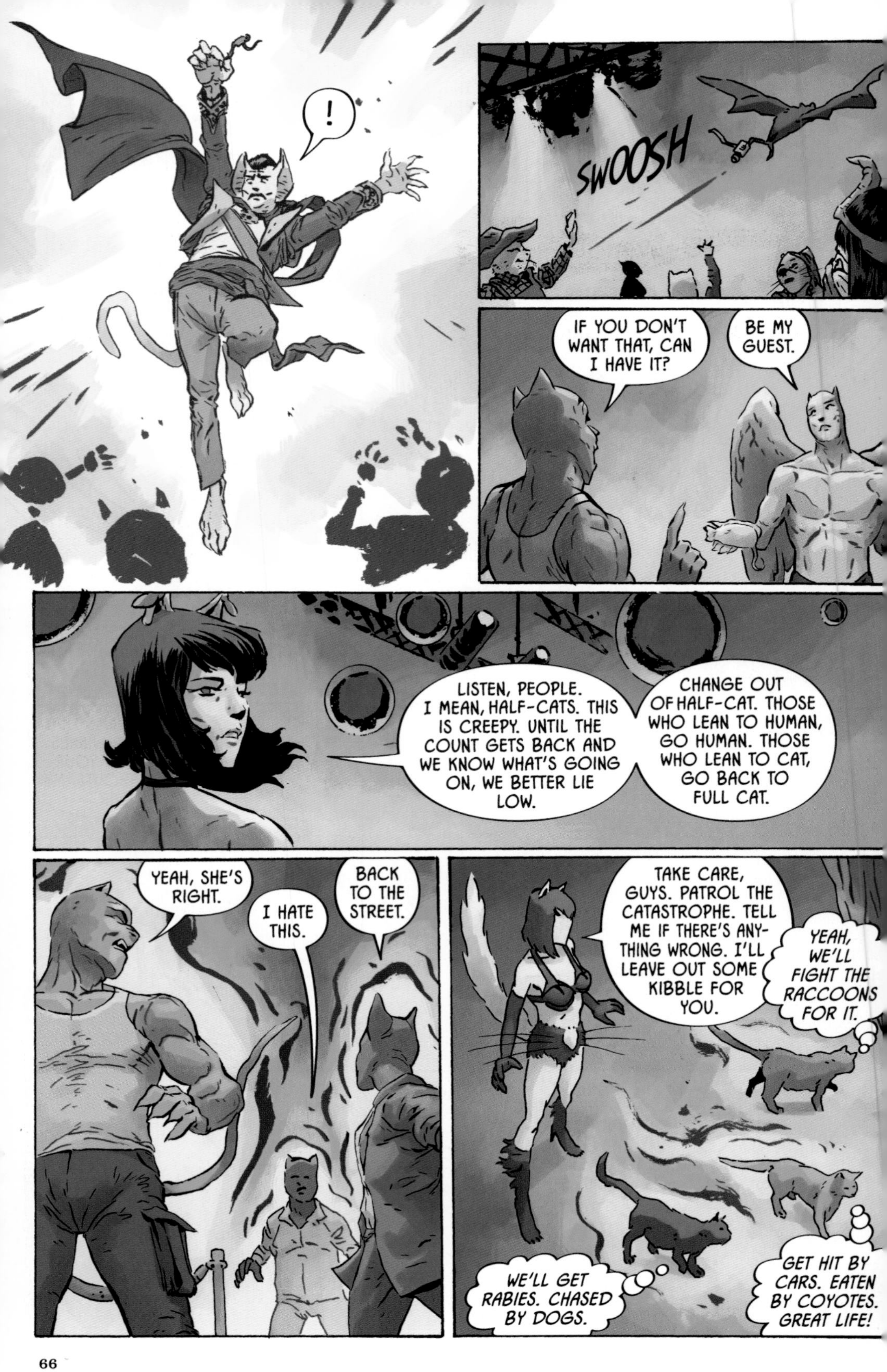
!
SWOOSH
IF YOU DON'T WANT THAT, CAN I HAVE IT?
BE MY GUEST.
LISTEN, PEOPLE. I MEAN, HALF-CATS. THIS IS CREEPY. UNTIL THE COUNT GETS BACK AND WE KNOW WHAT'S GOING ON, WE BETTER LIE LOW.
CHANGE OUT OF HALF-CAT. THOSE WHO LEAN TO HUMAN, GO HUMAN. THOSE WHO LEAN TO CAT, GO BACK TO FULL CAT.
YEAH, SHE'S RIGHT.
I HATE THIS.
BACK TO THE STREET.
TAKE CARE, GUYS. PATROL THE CATASTROPHE. TELL ME IF THERE'S ANY-THING WRONG. I'LL LEAVE OUT SOME KIBBLE FOR YOU.
YEAH, WE'LL FIGHT THE RACCOONS FOR IT.
WE'LL GET RABIES. CHASED BY DOGS.
GET HIT BY CARS. EATEN BY COYOTES. GREAT LIFE!

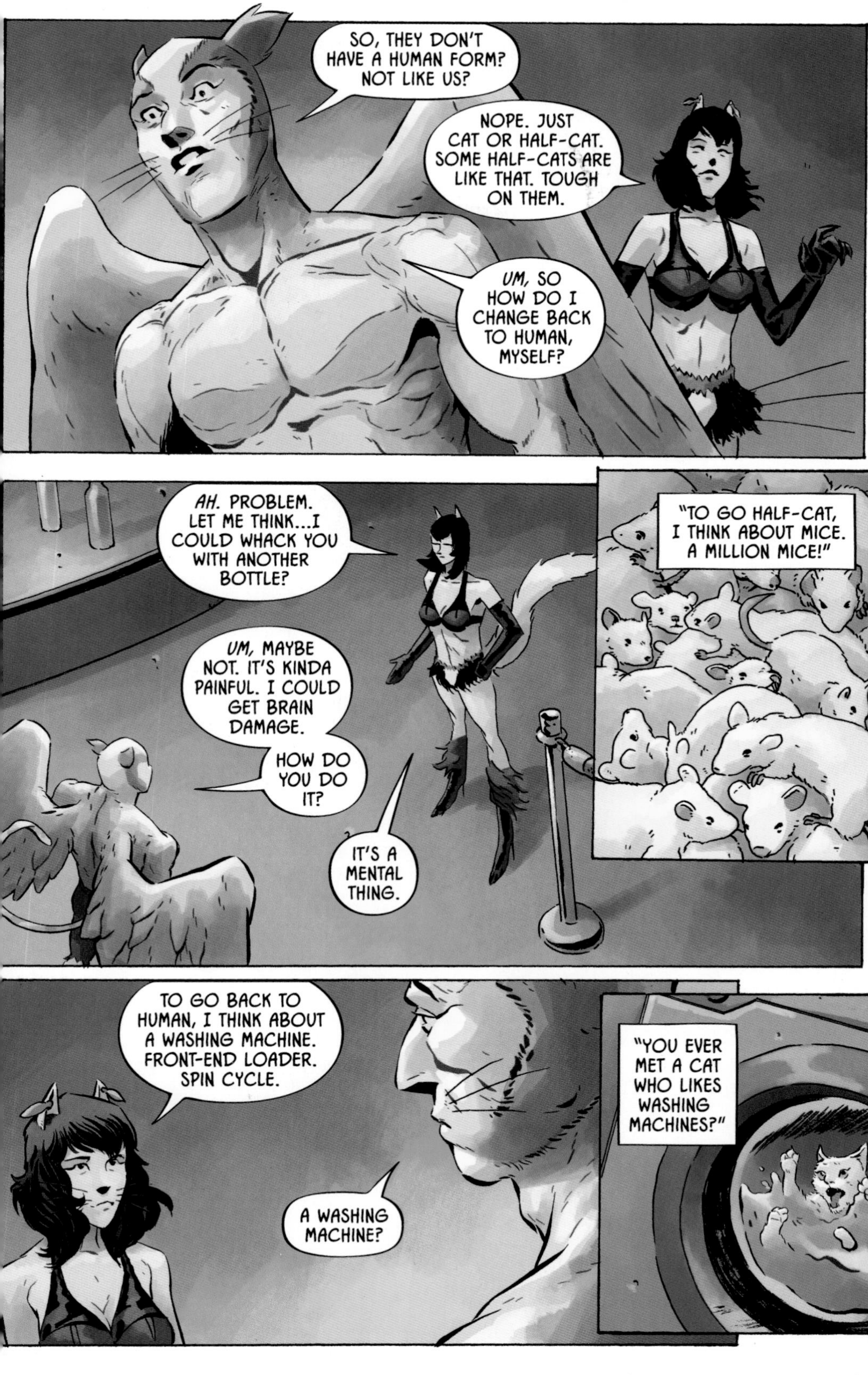
SO, THEY DON'T HAVE A HUMAN FORM? NOT LIKE US?
NOPE. JUST CAT OR HALF-CAT. SOME HALF-CATS ARE LIKE THAT. TOUGH ON THEM.
UM, SO HOW DO I CHANGE BACK TO HUMAN, MYSELF?
AH. PROBLEM. LET ME THINK...I COULD WHACK YOU WITH ANOTHER BOTTLE?
UM, MAYBE NOT. IT'S KINDA PAINFUL. I COULD GET BRAIN DAMAGE.
HOW DO YOU DO IT?
IT'S A MENTAL THING.
"TO GO HALF-CAT, I THINK ABOUT MICE. A MILLION MICE!"
TO GO BACK TO HUMAN, I THINK ABOUT A WASHING MACHINE. FRONT-END LOADER. SPIN CYCLE.
A WASHING MACHINE?
"YOU EVER MET A CAT WHO LIKES WASHING MACHINES?"

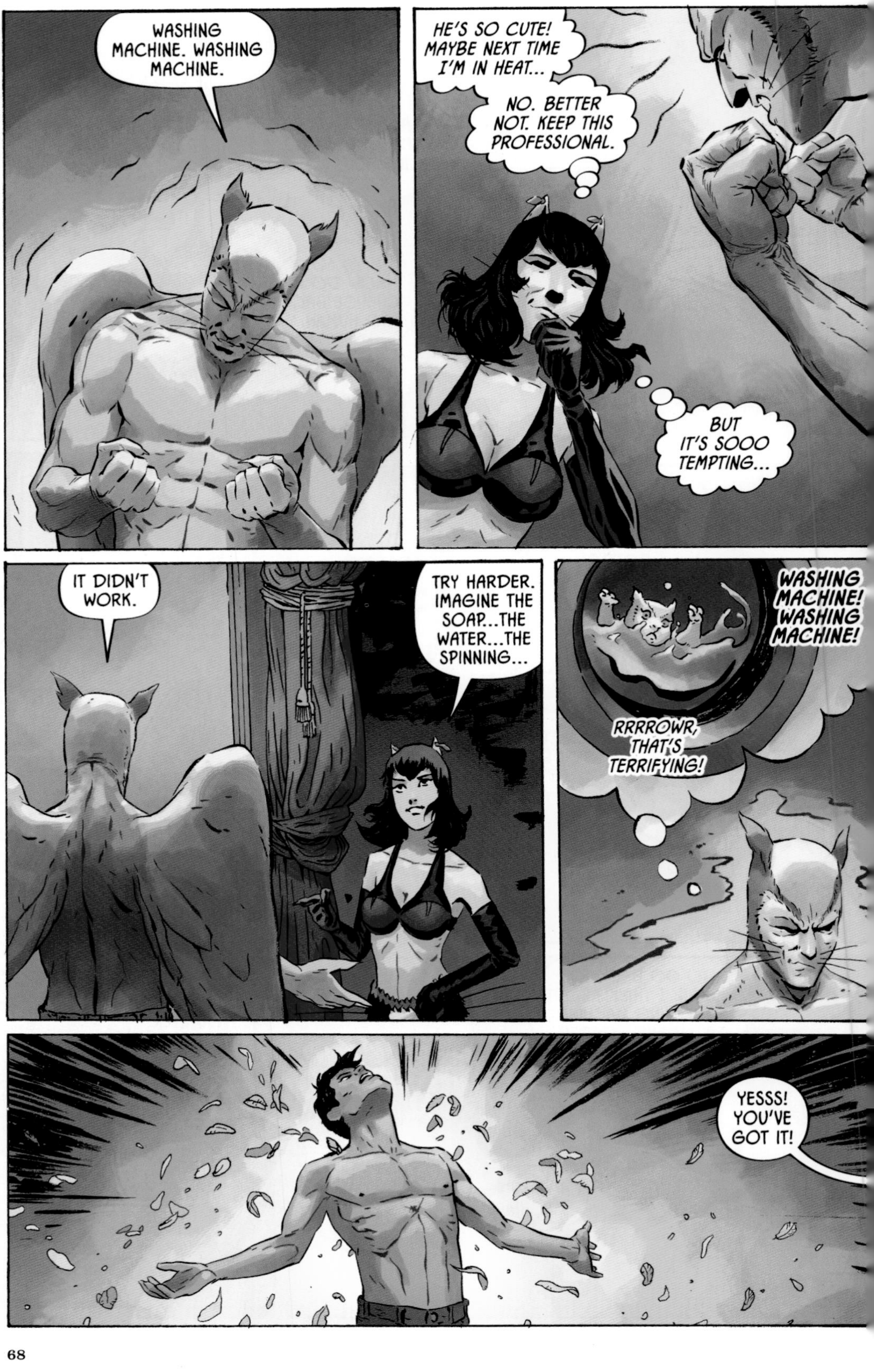
WASHING MACHINE. WASHING MACHINE.
HE'S SO CUTE! MAYBE NEXT TIME I'M IN HEAT...
NO. BETTER NOT. KEEP THIS PROFESSIONAL.
BUT IT'S SOOO TEMPTING...
IT DIDN'T WORK.
TRY HARDER. IMAGINE THE SOAP...THE WATER...THE SPINNING...
WASHING MACHINE! WASHING MACHINE!
RRRROWR, THAT'S TERRIFYING!
YESSS! YOU'VE GOT IT!

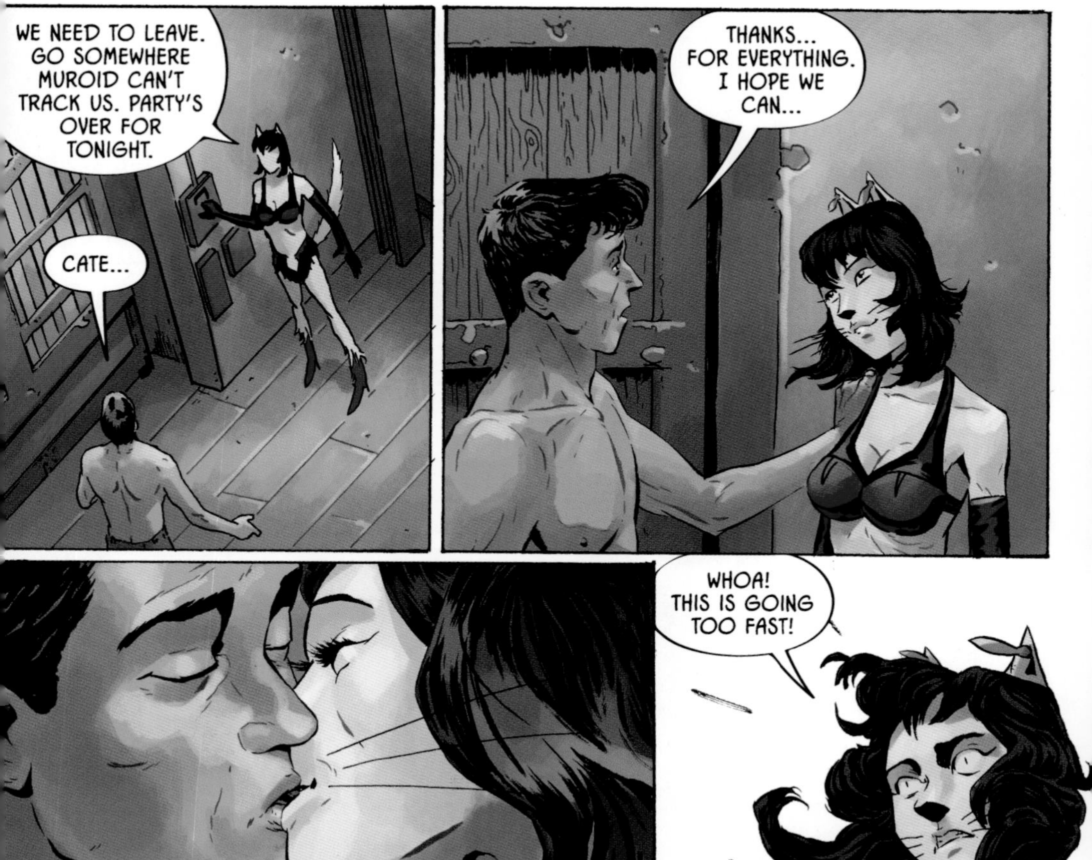
WE NEED TO LEAVE. GO SOMEWHERE MUROID CAN'T TRACK US. PARTY'S OVER FOR TONIGHT.
CATE...
THANKS... FOR EVERYTHING. I HOPE WE CAN...
smooch
WHOA! THIS IS GOING TOO FAST!
I NEED SOME SPACE. I'VE NEVER BEEN A ONE-CAT KITTEN.

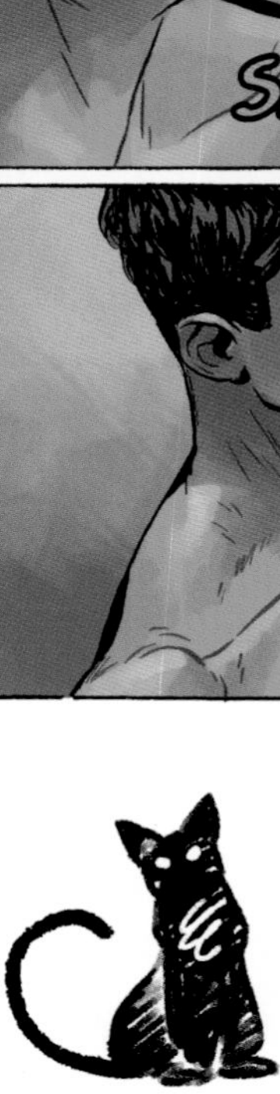

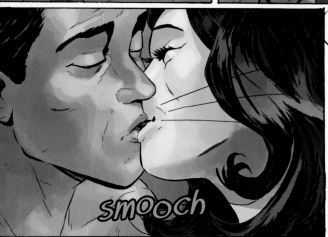

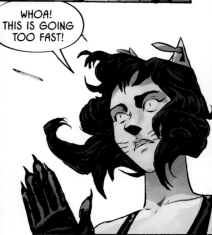

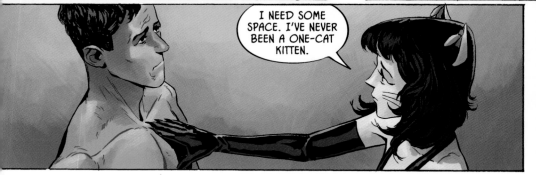

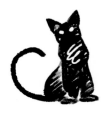

CAT-BIRD MATH, Part III

A female cat has an average of 1.4 litters per year, up to 3 in warm climates—with an average of 3 kittens per litter. At that rate, it takes only 3 1/2 years for your cat and her kittens to produce more than a thousand cats! Fix your cat! www.catsandbirds.ca

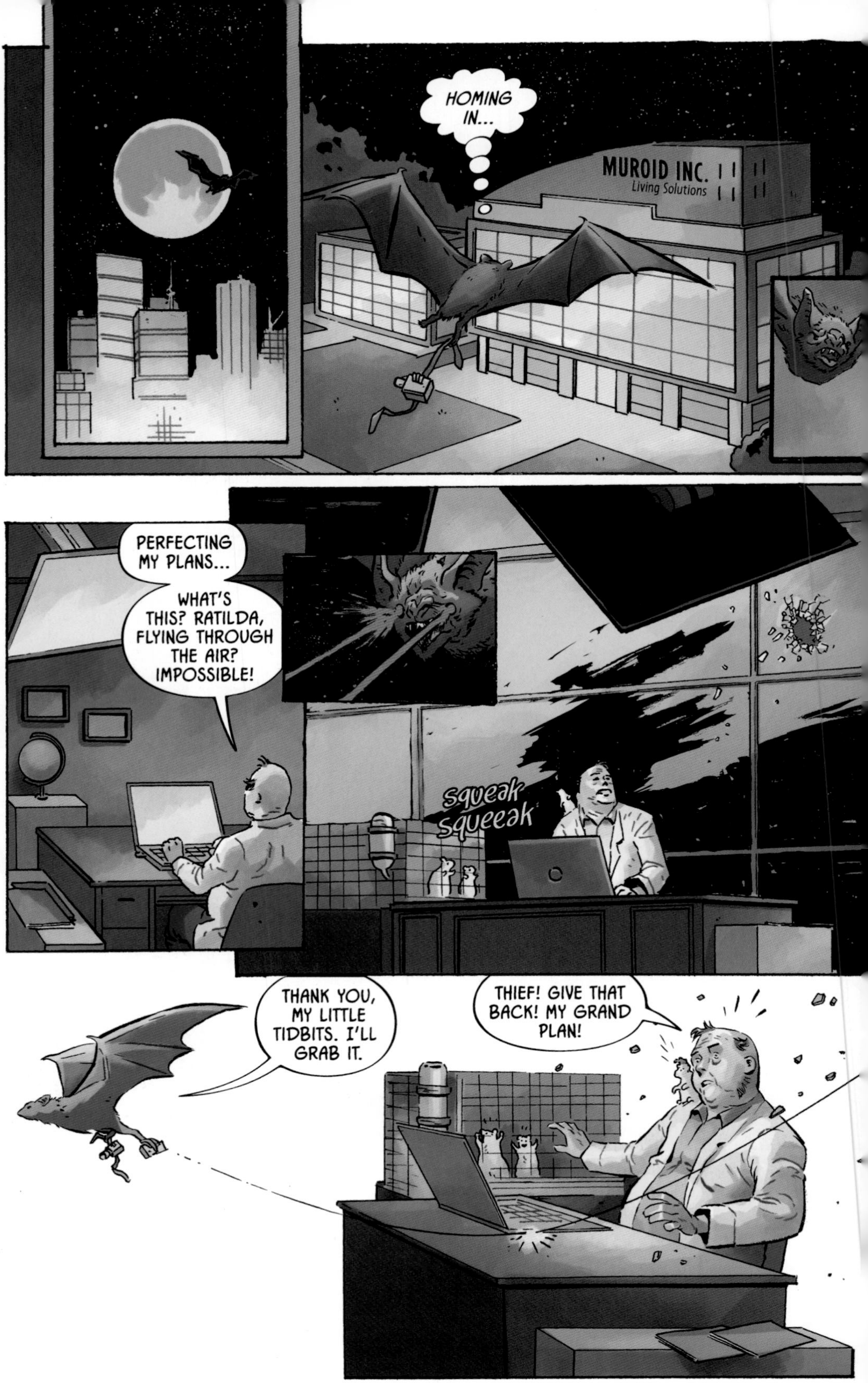
HOMING IN...
MUROID INC.
Living Solutions
PERFECTING MY PLANS...
WHAT'S THIS? RATILDA, FLYING THROUGH THE AIR? IMPOSSIBLE!
squeak squeeak
THANK YOU, MY LITTLE TIDBITS. I'LL GRAB IT.
THIEF! GIVE THAT BACK! MY GRAND PLAN!

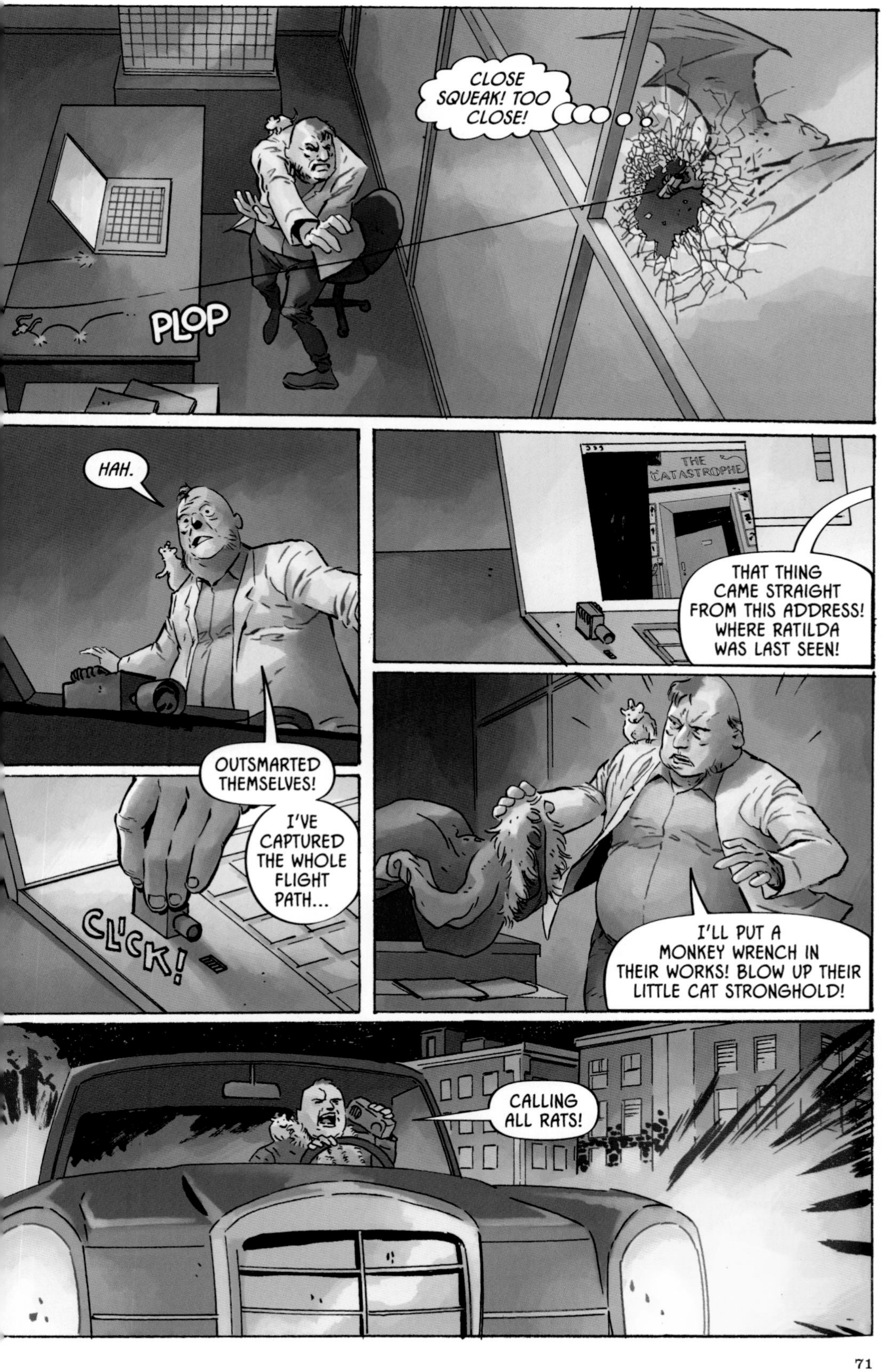
CLOSE SQUEAK! TOO CLOSE!
PLOP
HAH.
THAT THING CAME STRAIGHT FROM THIS ADDRESS! WHERE RATILDA WAS LAST SEEN!
THE CATASTROPHE
OUTSMARTED THEMSELVES!
I'VE CAPTURED THE WHOLE FLIGHT PATH...
CLICK!
I'LL PUT A MONKEY WRENCH IN THEIR WORKS! BLOW UP THEIR LITTLE CAT STRONGHOLD!
CALLING ALL RATS!

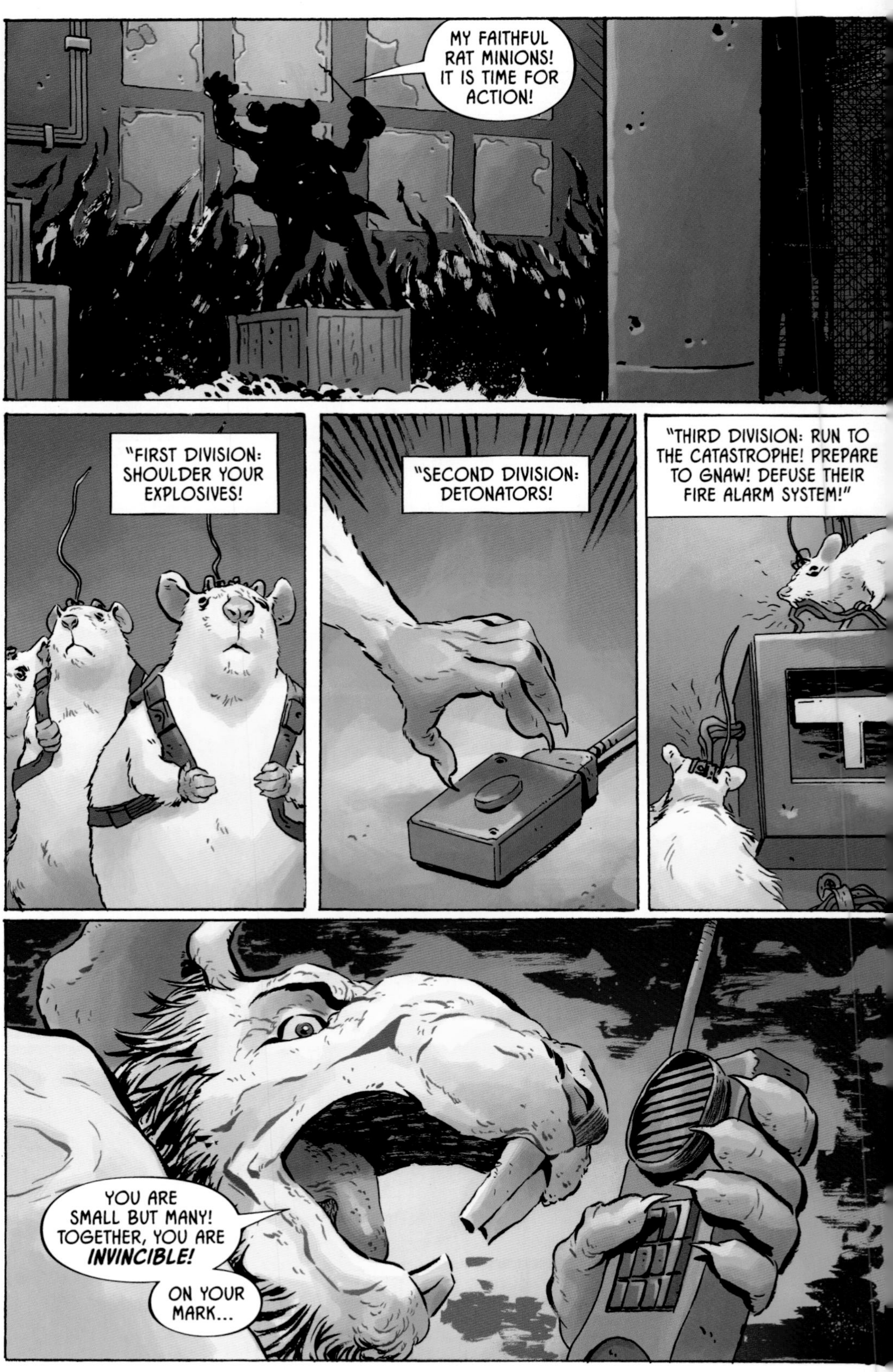
MY FAITHFUL RAT MINIONS! IT IS TIME FOR ACTION!
"FIRST DIVISION: SHOULDER YOUR EXPLOSIVES!
"SECOND DIVISION: DETONATORS!
"THIRD DIVISION: RUN TO THE CATASTROPHE! PREPARE TO GNAW! DEFUSE THEIR FIRE ALARM SYSTEM!"
YOU ARE SMALL BUT MANY! TOGETHER, YOU ARE *INVINCIBLE!*
ON YOUR MARK...

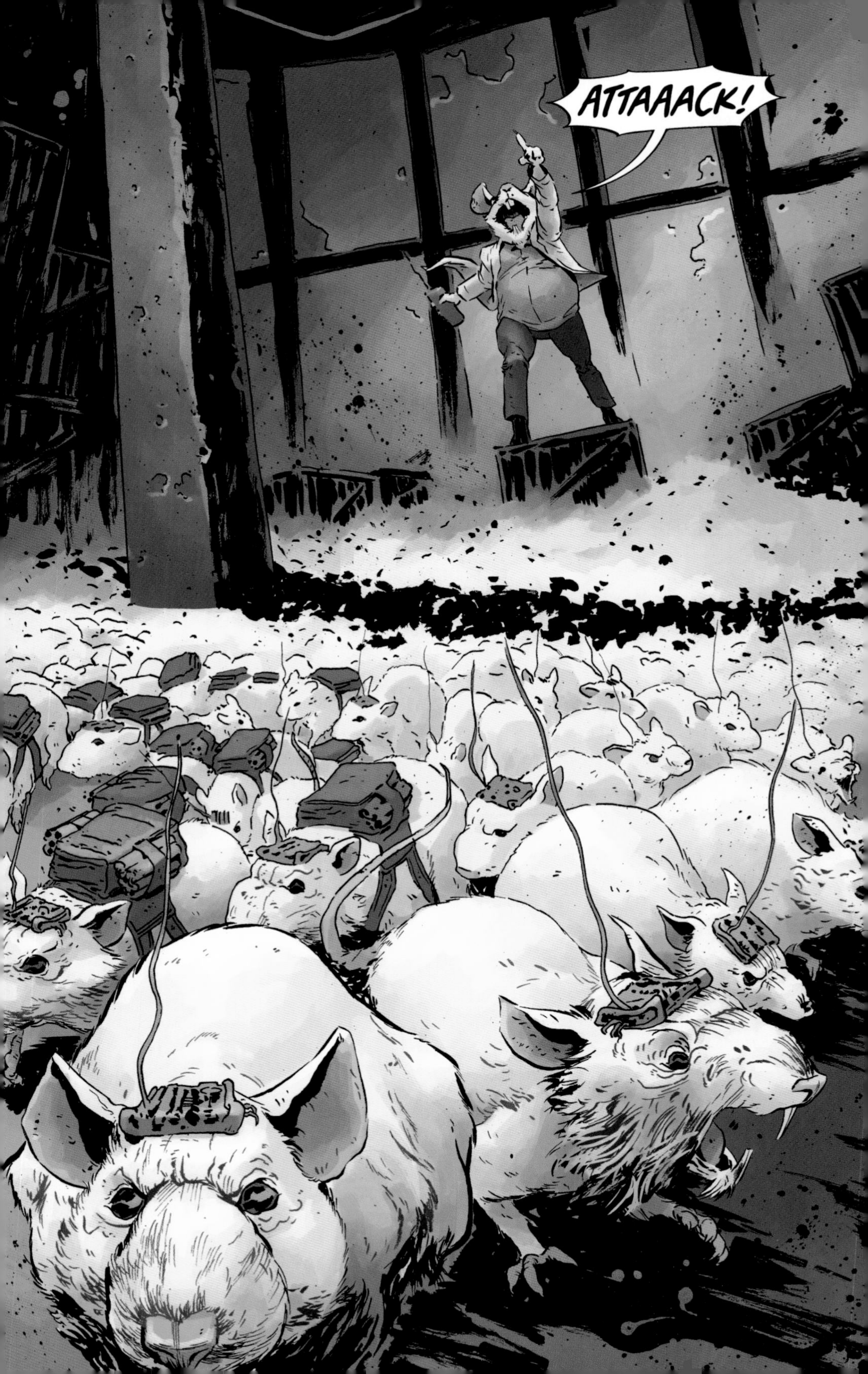
ATTAAACK!

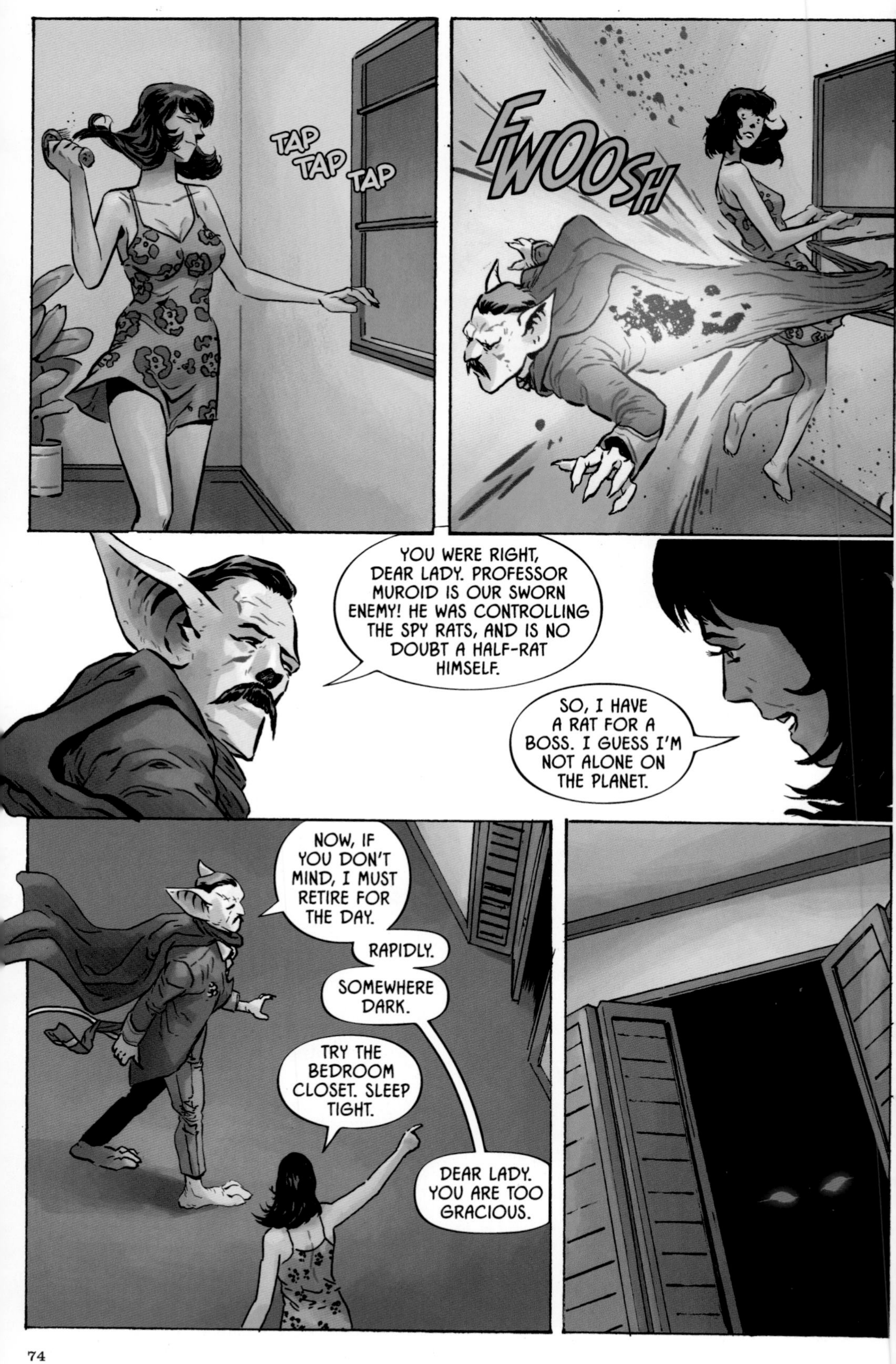
TAP TAP TAP
FWOOSH
YOU WERE RIGHT, DEAR LADY. PROFESSOR MUROID IS OUR SWORN ENEMY! HE WAS CONTROLLING THE SPY RATS, AND IS NO DOUBT A HALF-RAT HIMSELF.
SO, I HAVE A RAT FOR A BOSS. I GUESS I'M NOT ALONE ON THE PLANET.
NOW, IF YOU DON'T MIND, I MUST RETIRE FOR THE DAY.
RAPIDLY.
SOMEWHERE DARK.
TRY THE BEDROOM CLOSET. SLEEP TIGHT.
DEAR LADY. YOU ARE TOO GRACIOUS.

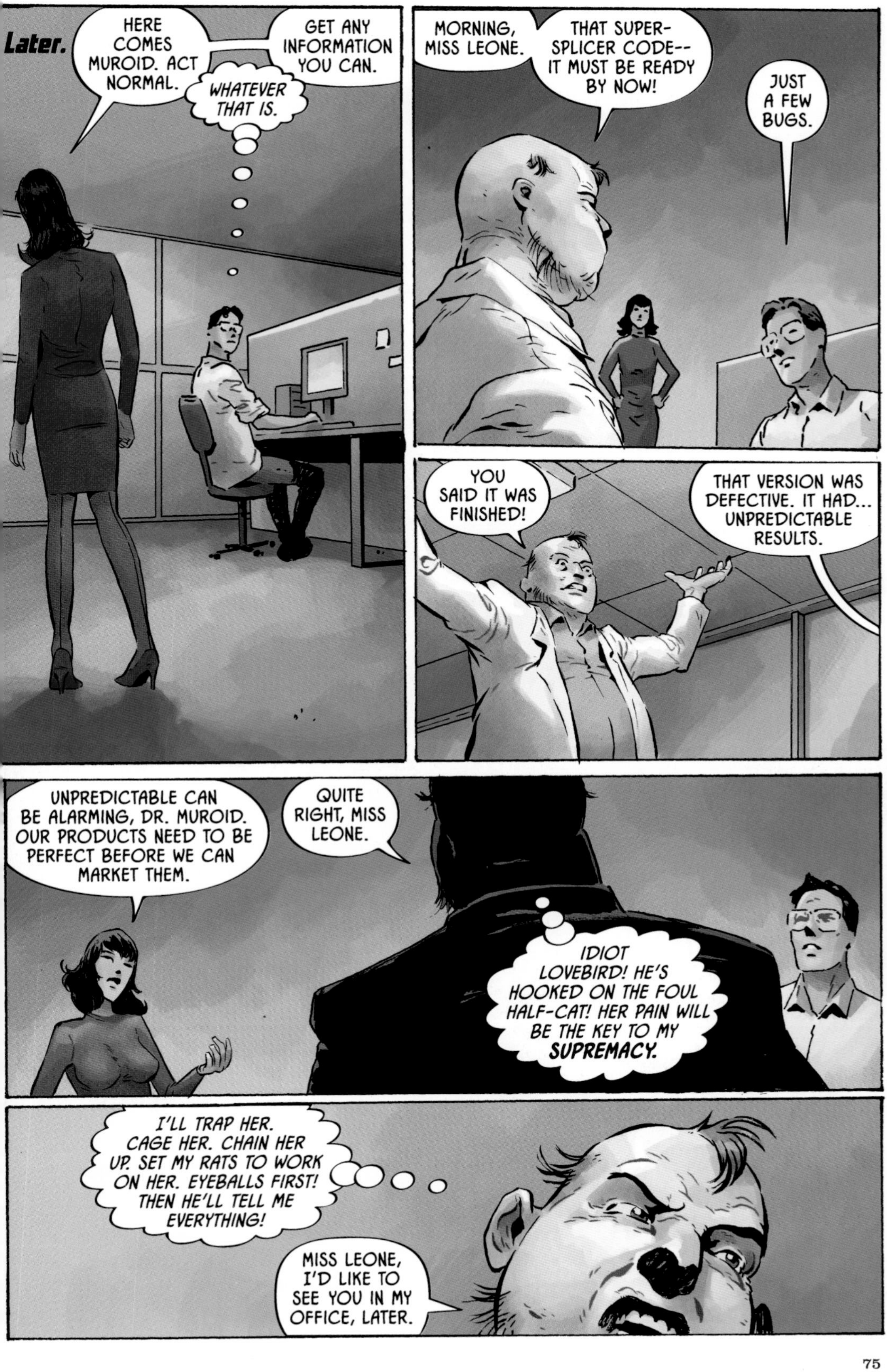
Later.
HERE COMES MUROID. ACT NORMAL.
GET ANY INFORMATION YOU CAN.
WHATEVER THAT IS.
MORNING, MISS LEONE.
THAT SUPER-SPLICER CODE-- IT MUST BE READY BY NOW!
JUST A FEW BUGS.
YOU SAID IT WAS FINISHED!
THAT VERSION WAS DEFECTIVE. IT HAD... UNPREDICTABLE RESULTS.
UNPREDICTABLE CAN BE ALARMING, DR. MUROID. OUR PRODUCTS NEED TO BE PERFECT BEFORE WE CAN MARKET THEM.
QUITE RIGHT, MISS LEONE.
IDIOT LOVEBIRD! HE'S HOOKED ON THE FOUL HALF-CAT! HER PAIN WILL BE THE KEY TO MY SUPREMACY.
I'LL TRAP HER. CAGE HER. CHAIN HER UP. SET MY RATS TO WORK ON HER. EYEBALLS FIRST! THEN HE'LL TELL ME EVERYTHING!
MISS LEONE, I'D LIKE TO SEE YOU IN MY OFFICE, LATER.

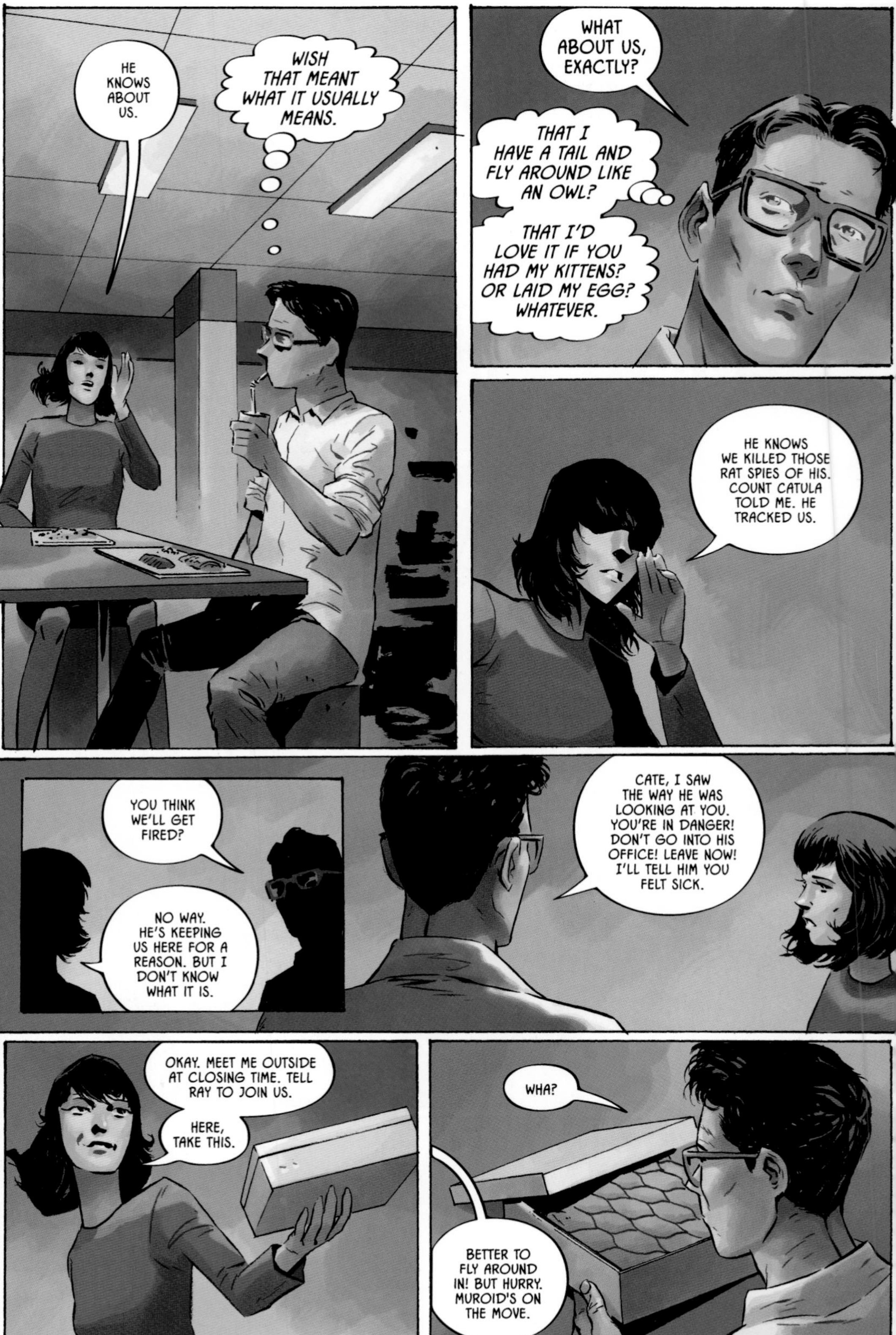

HE KNOWS ABOUT US.
WISH THAT MEANT WHAT IT USUALLY MEANS.
WHAT ABOUT US, EXACTLY?
THAT I HAVE A TAIL AND FLY AROUND LIKE AN OWL?
THAT I'D LOVE IT IF YOU HAD MY KITTENS? OR LAID MY EGG? WHATEVER.
HE KNOWS WE KILLED THOSE RAT SPIES OF HIS. COUNT CATULA TOLD ME. HE TRACKED US.
YOU THINK WE'LL GET FIRED?
NO WAY. HE'S KEEPING US HERE FOR A REASON. BUT I DON'T KNOW WHAT IT IS.
CATE, I SAW THE WAY HE WAS LOOKING AT YOU. YOU'RE IN DANGER! DON'T GO INTO HIS OFFICE! LEAVE NOW! I'LL TELL HIM YOU FELT SICK.
OKAY. MEET ME OUTSIDE AT CLOSING TIME. TELL RAY TO JOIN US.
HERE, TAKE THIS.
WHA?
BETTER TO FLY AROUND IN! BUT HURRY. MUROID'S ON THE MOVE.

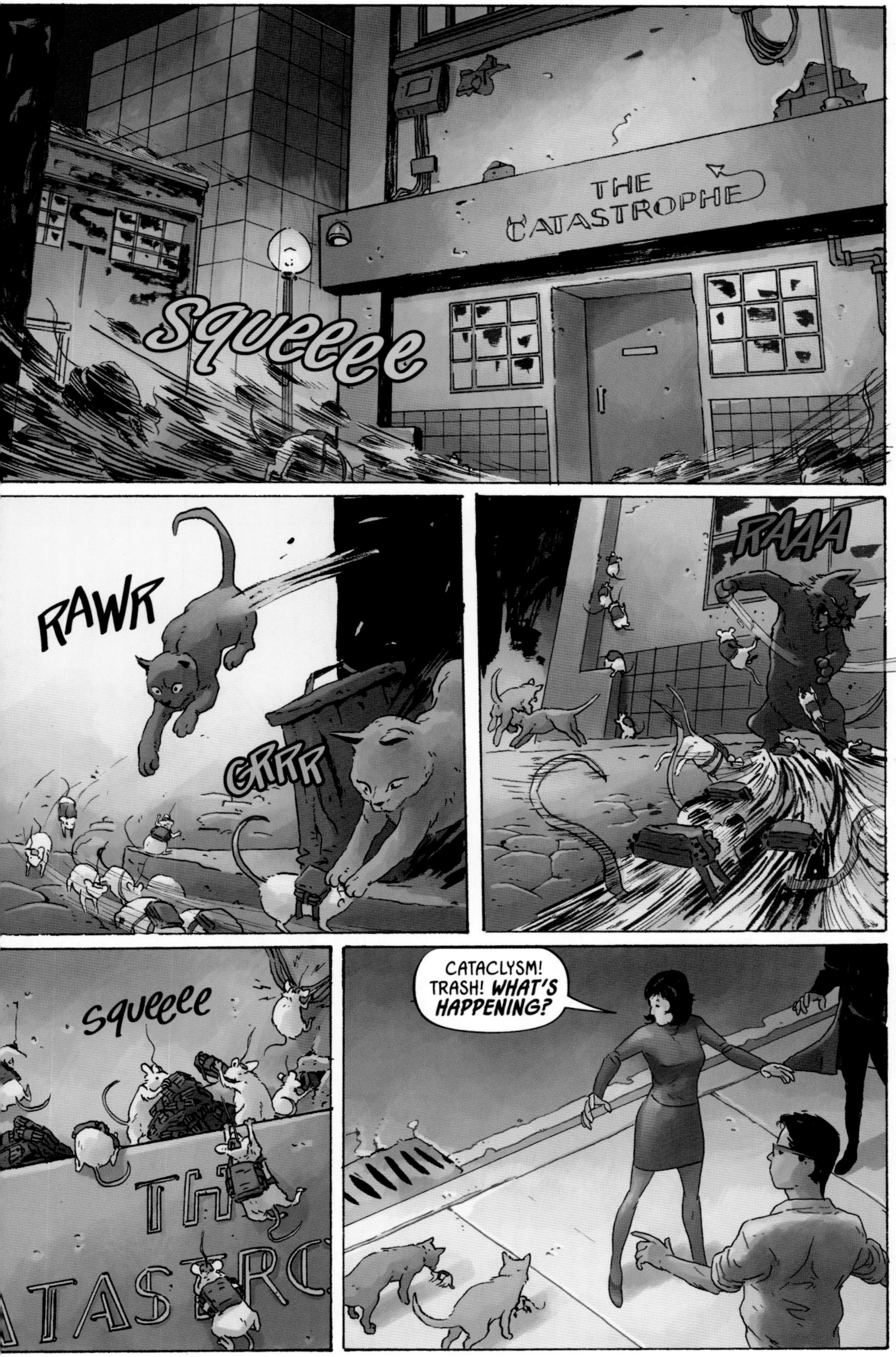
THE CATASTROPHE
Squeeee
RAWR
GRRR
RAAA
squeee
THE CATASTRO
CATACLYSM! TRASH! WHAT'S HAPPENING?

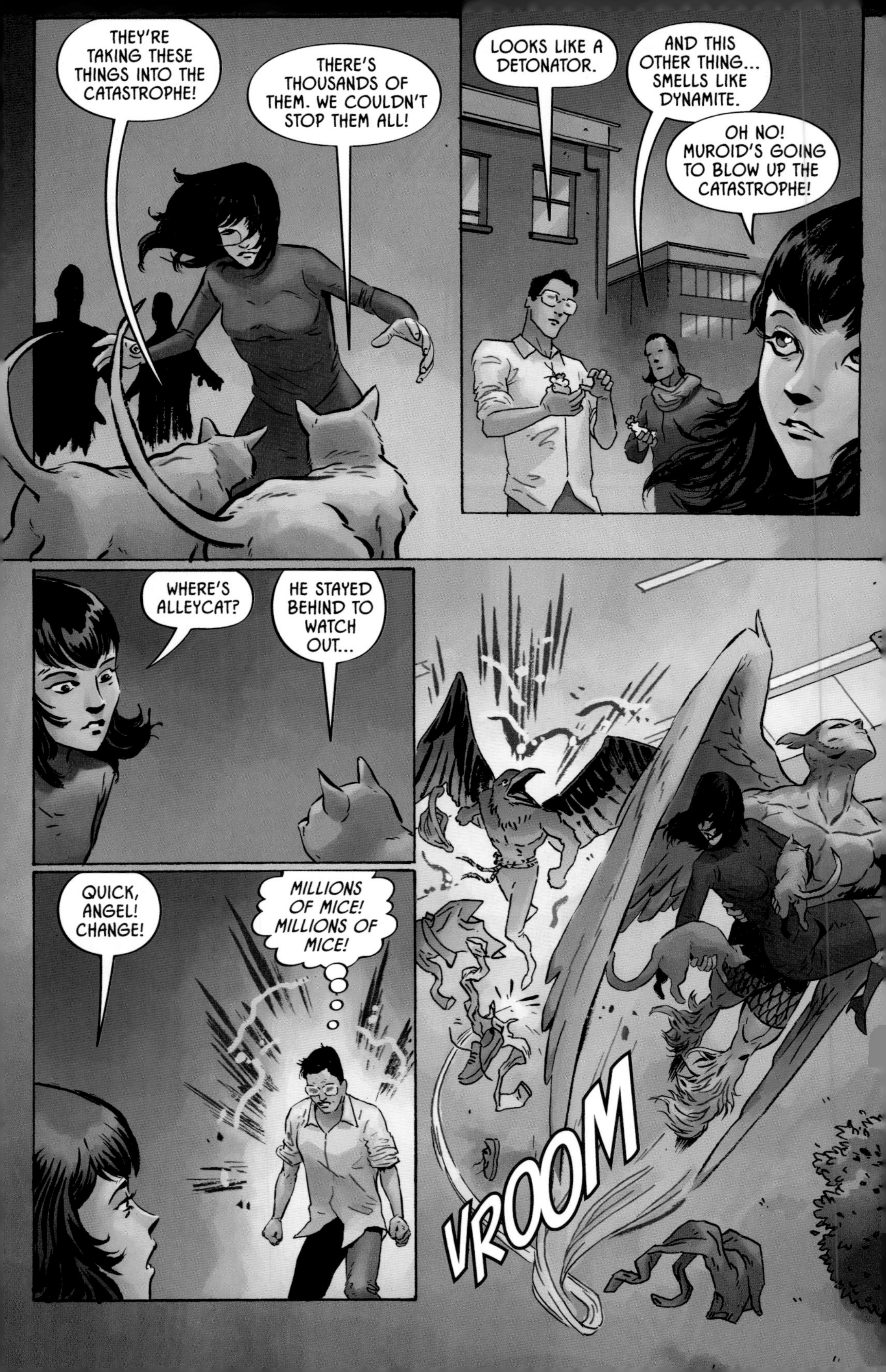
THEY'RE TAKING THESE THINGS INTO THE CATASTROPHE!
THERE'S THOUSANDS OF THEM. WE COULDN'T STOP THEM ALL!
LOOKS LIKE A DETONATOR.
AND THIS OTHER THING... SMELLS LIKE DYNAMITE.
OH NO! MUROID'S GOING TO BLOW UP THE CATASTROPHE!
WHERE'S ALLEYCAT?
HE STAYED BEHIND TO WATCH OUT...
QUICK, ANGEL! CHANGE!
MILLIONS OF MICE! MILLIONS OF MICE!
VROOM

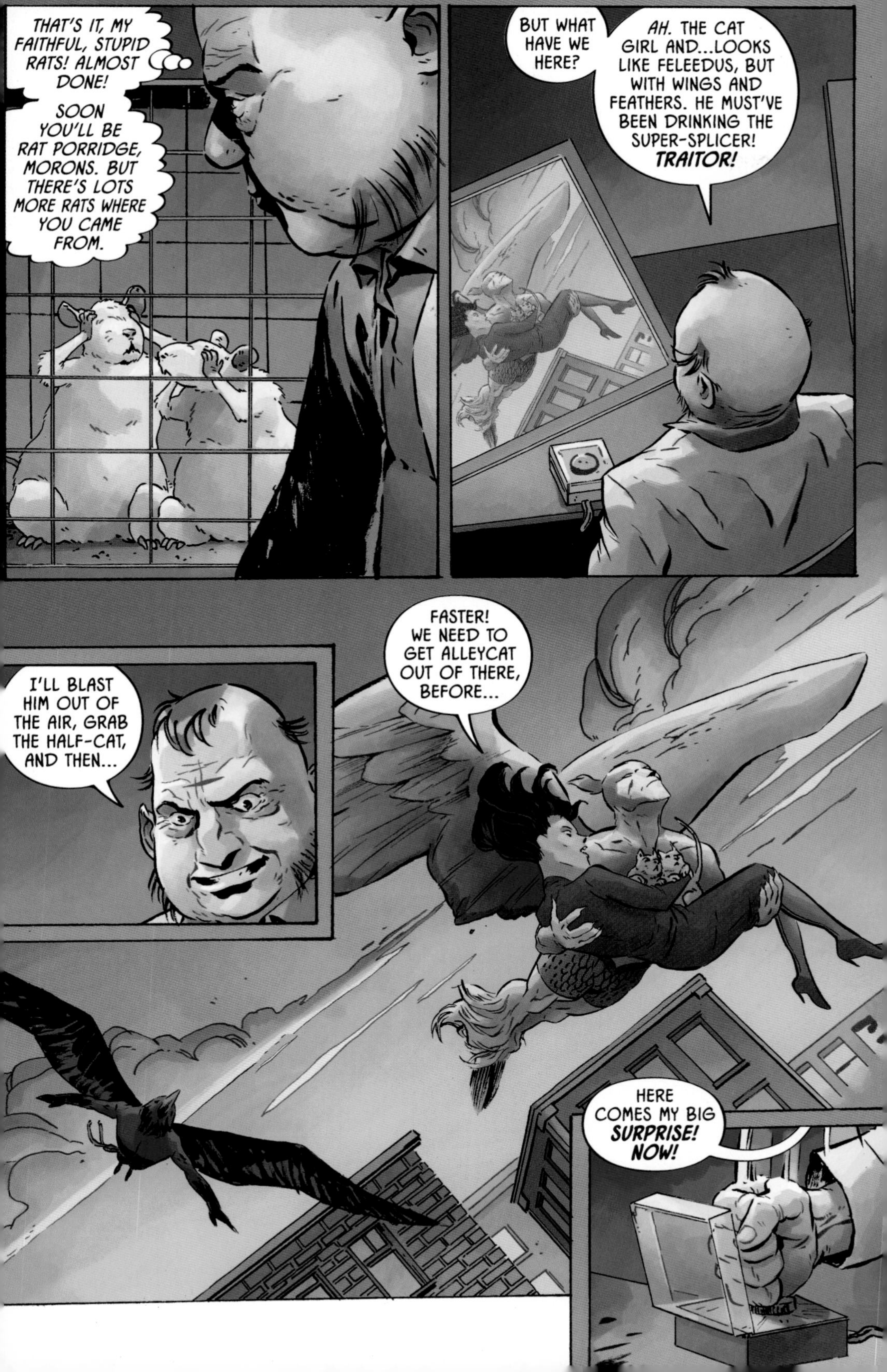
THAT'S IT, MY FAITHFUL, STUPID RATS! ALMOST DONE!
SOON YOU'LL BE RAT PORRIDGE, MORONS. BUT THERE'S LOTS MORE RATS WHERE YOU CAME FROM.
BUT WHAT HAVE WE HERE?
AH. THE CAT GIRL AND...LOOKS LIKE FELEEDUS, BUT WITH WINGS AND FEATHERS. HE MUST'VE BEEN DRINKING THE SUPER-SPLICER! TRAITOR!
I'LL BLAST HIM OUT OF THE AIR, GRAB THE HALF-CAT, AND THEN...
FASTER! WE NEED TO GET ALLEYCAT OUT OF THERE, BEFORE...
HERE COMES MY BIG SURPRISE! NOW!

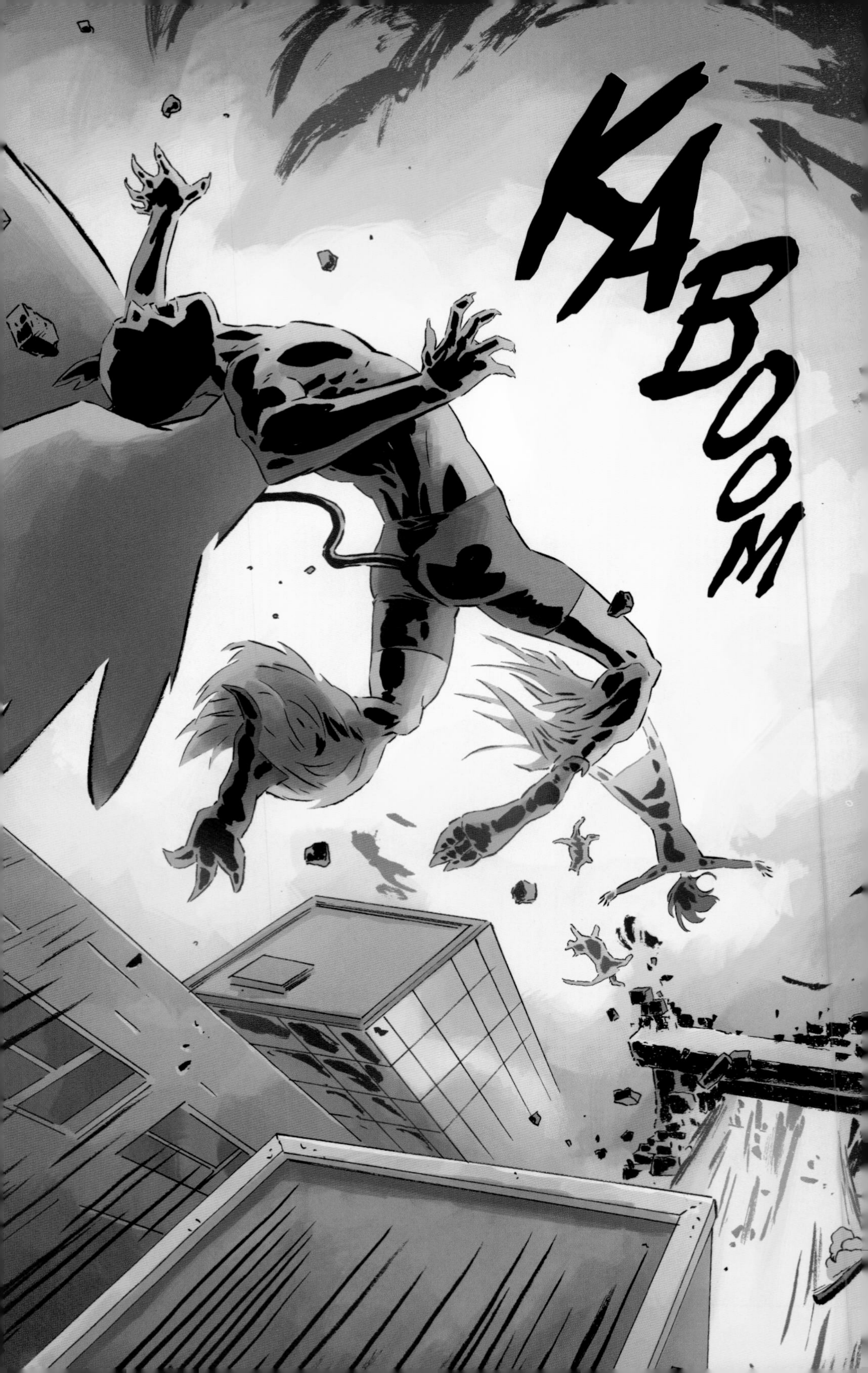
KABOOM

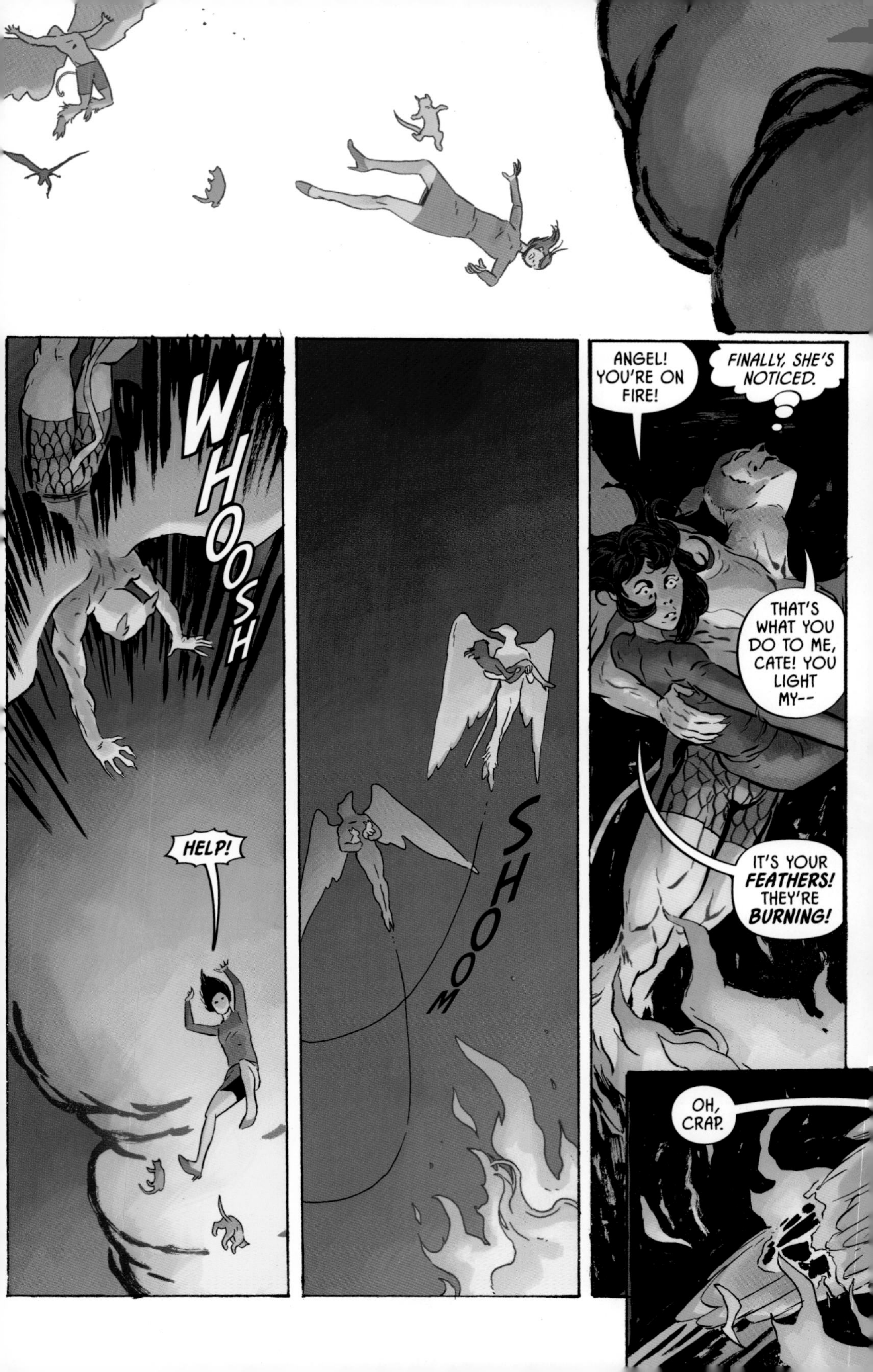
WHOOOSH
HELP!
SHOOOM
ANGEL! YOU'RE ON FIRE!
FINALLY, SHE'S NOTICED.
THAT'S WHAT YOU DO TO ME, CATE! YOU LIGHT MY--
IT'S YOUR FEATHERS! THEY'RE BURNING!
OH, CRAP.

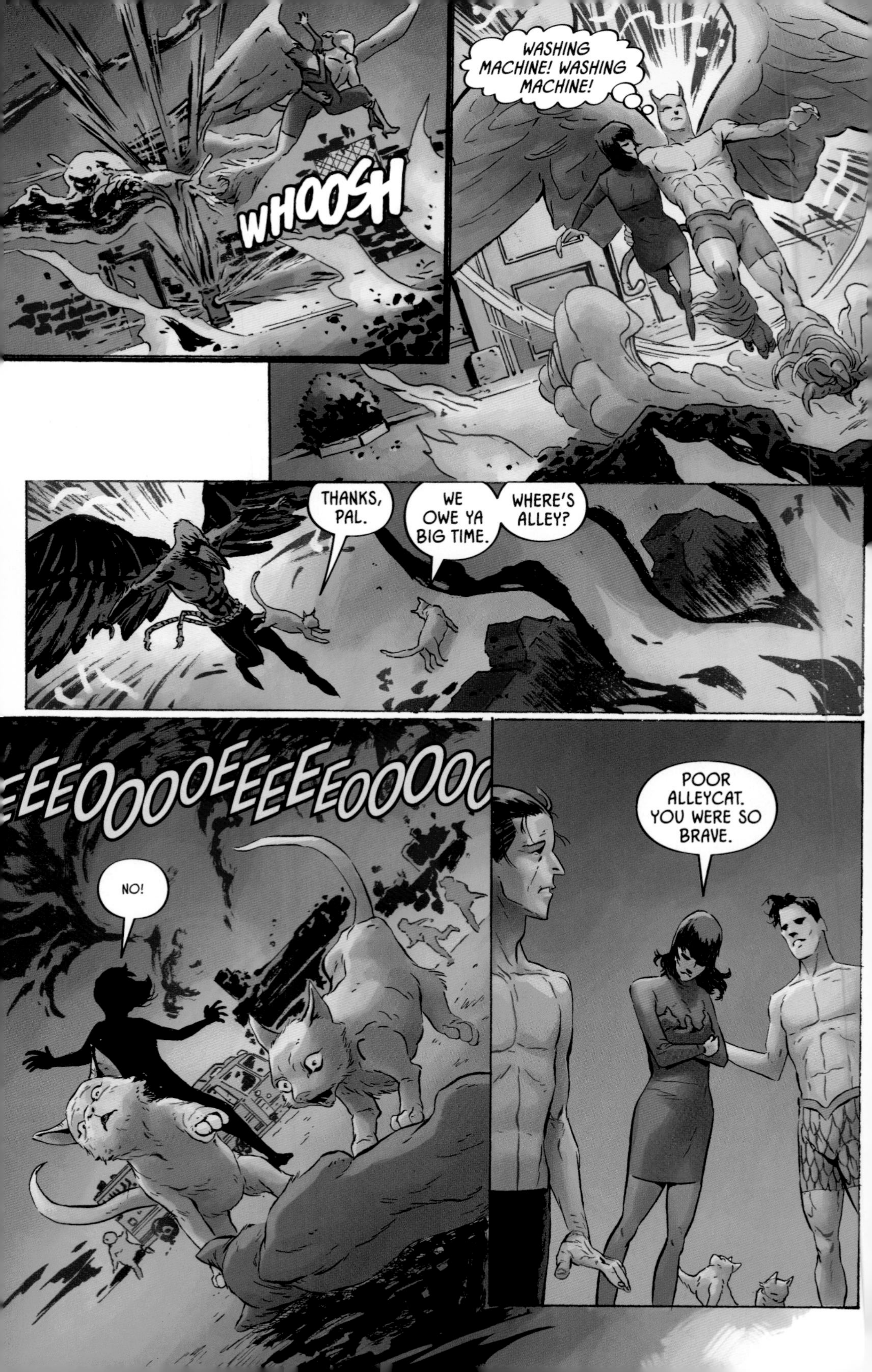
WHOOSH
WASHING MACHINE! WASHING MACHINE!
THANKS, PAL.
WE OWE YA BIG TIME.
WHERE'S ALLEY?
EEEOOOOEEEEEOOOOO
NO!
POOR ALLEYCAT. YOU WERE SO BRAVE.

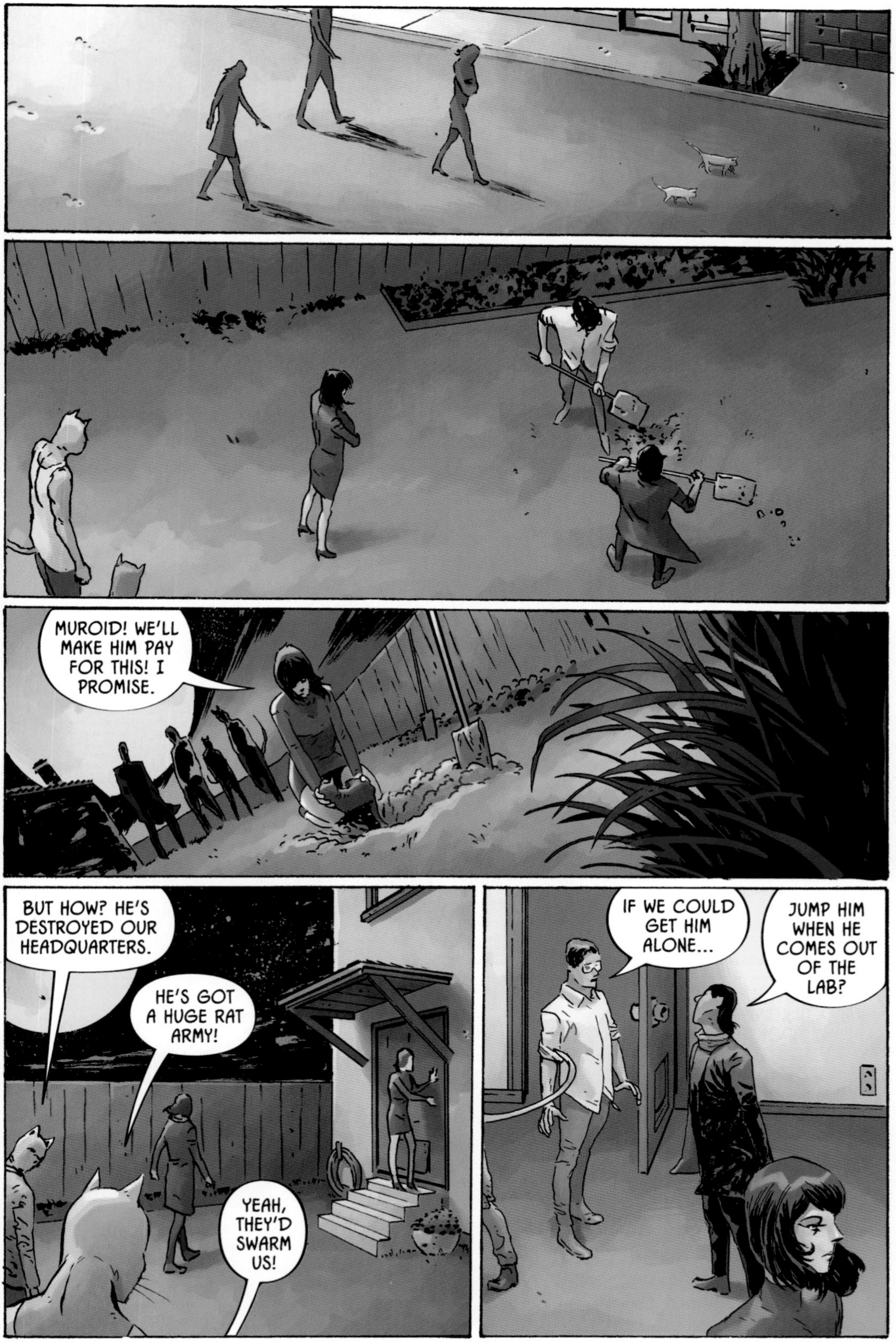

MUROID! WE'LL MAKE HIM PAY FOR THIS! I PROMISE.
BUT HOW? HE'S DESTROYED OUR HEADQUARTERS.
HE'S GOT A HUGE RAT ARMY!
YEAH, THEY'D SWARM US!
IF WE COULD GET HIM ALONE...
JUMP HIM WHEN HE COMES OUT OF THE LAB?

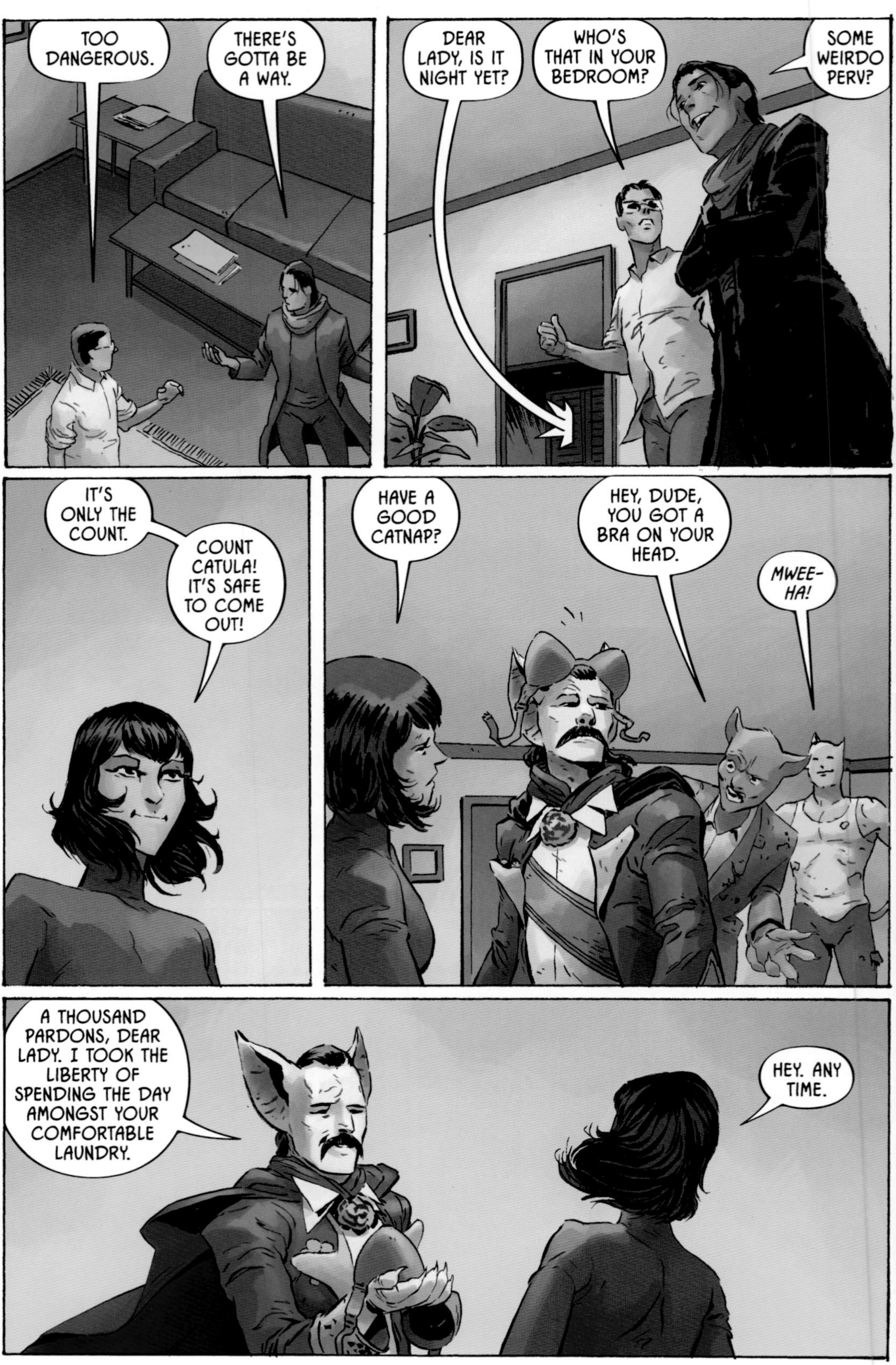
TOO DANGEROUS.
THERE'S GOTTA BE A WAY.
DEAR LADY, IS IT NIGHT YET?
WHO'S THAT IN YOUR BEDROOM?
SOME WEIRDO PERV?
IT'S ONLY THE COUNT.
COUNT CATULA! IT'S SAFE TO COME OUT!
HAVE A GOOD CATNAP?
HEY, DUDE, YOU GOT A BRA ON YOUR HEAD.
MWEE-HA!
A THOUSAND PARDONS, DEAR LADY. I TOOK THE LIBERTY OF SPENDING THE DAY AMONGST YOUR COMFORTABLE LAUNDRY.
HEY. ANY TIME.

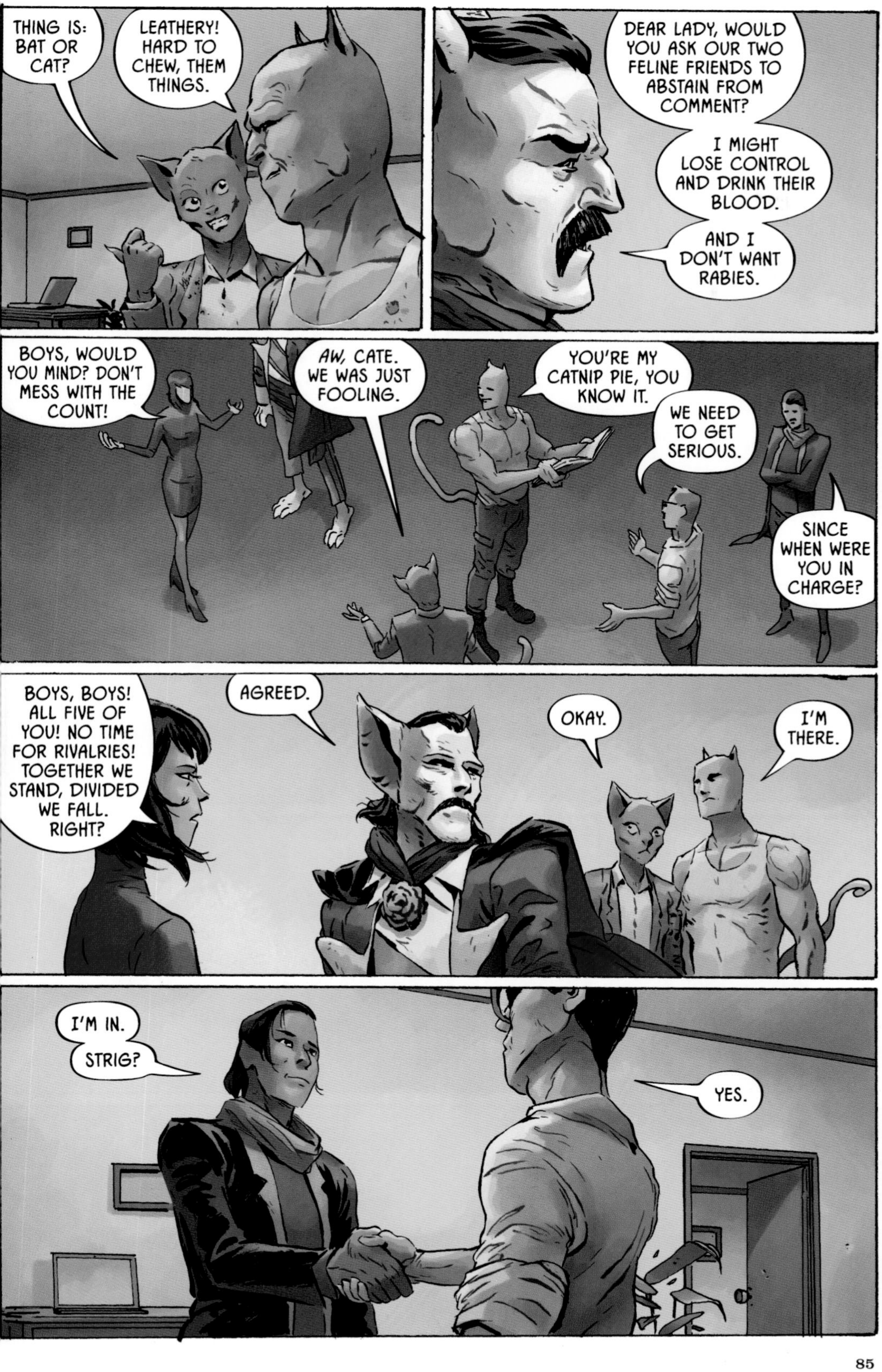
THING IS: BAT OR CAT?
LEATHERY! HARD TO CHEW, THEM THINGS.
DEAR LADY, WOULD YOU ASK OUR TWO FELINE FRIENDS TO ABSTAIN FROM COMMENT?
I MIGHT LOSE CONTROL AND DRINK THEIR BLOOD.
AND I DON'T WANT RABIES.
BOYS, WOULD YOU MIND? DON'T MESS WITH THE COUNT!
AW, CATE. WE WAS JUST FOOLING.
YOU'RE MY CATNIP PIE, YOU KNOW IT.
WE NEED TO GET SERIOUS.
SINCE WHEN WERE YOU IN CHARGE?
BOYS, BOYS! ALL FIVE OF YOU! NO TIME FOR RIVALRIES! TOGETHER WE STAND, DIVIDED WE FALL. RIGHT?
AGREED.
OKAY.
I'M THERE.
I'M IN.
STRIG?
YES.

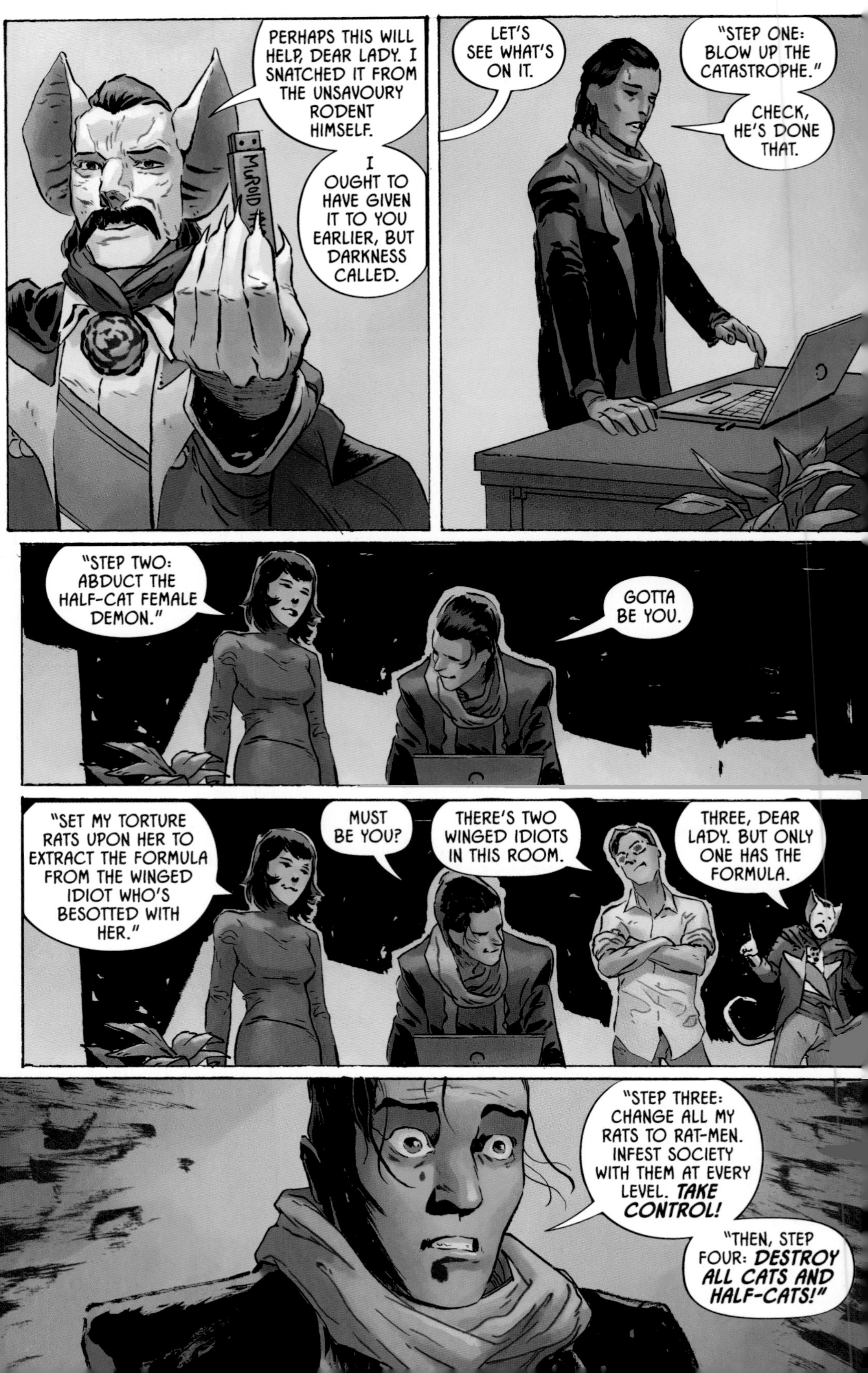
PERHAPS THIS WILL HELP, DEAR LADY. I SNATCHED IT FROM THE UNSAVOURY RODENT HIMSELF.
I OUGHT TO HAVE GIVEN IT TO YOU EARLIER, BUT DARKNESS CALLED.
MUROID
LET'S SEE WHAT'S ON IT.
"STEP ONE: BLOW UP THE CATASTROPHE."
CHECK, HE'S DONE THAT.
"STEP TWO: ABDUCT THE HALF-CAT FEMALE DEMON."
GOTTA BE YOU.
"SET MY TORTURE RATS UPON HER TO EXTRACT THE FORMULA FROM THE WINGED IDIOT WHO'S BESOTTED WITH HER."
MUST BE YOU?
THERE'S TWO WINGED IDIOTS IN THIS ROOM.
THREE, DEAR LADY. BUT ONLY ONE HAS THE FORMULA.
"STEP THREE: CHANGE ALL MY RATS TO RAT-MEN. INFEST SOCIETY WITH THEM AT EVERY LEVEL. TAKE CONTROL!
"THEN, STEP FOUR: DESTROY ALL CATS AND HALF-CATS!"

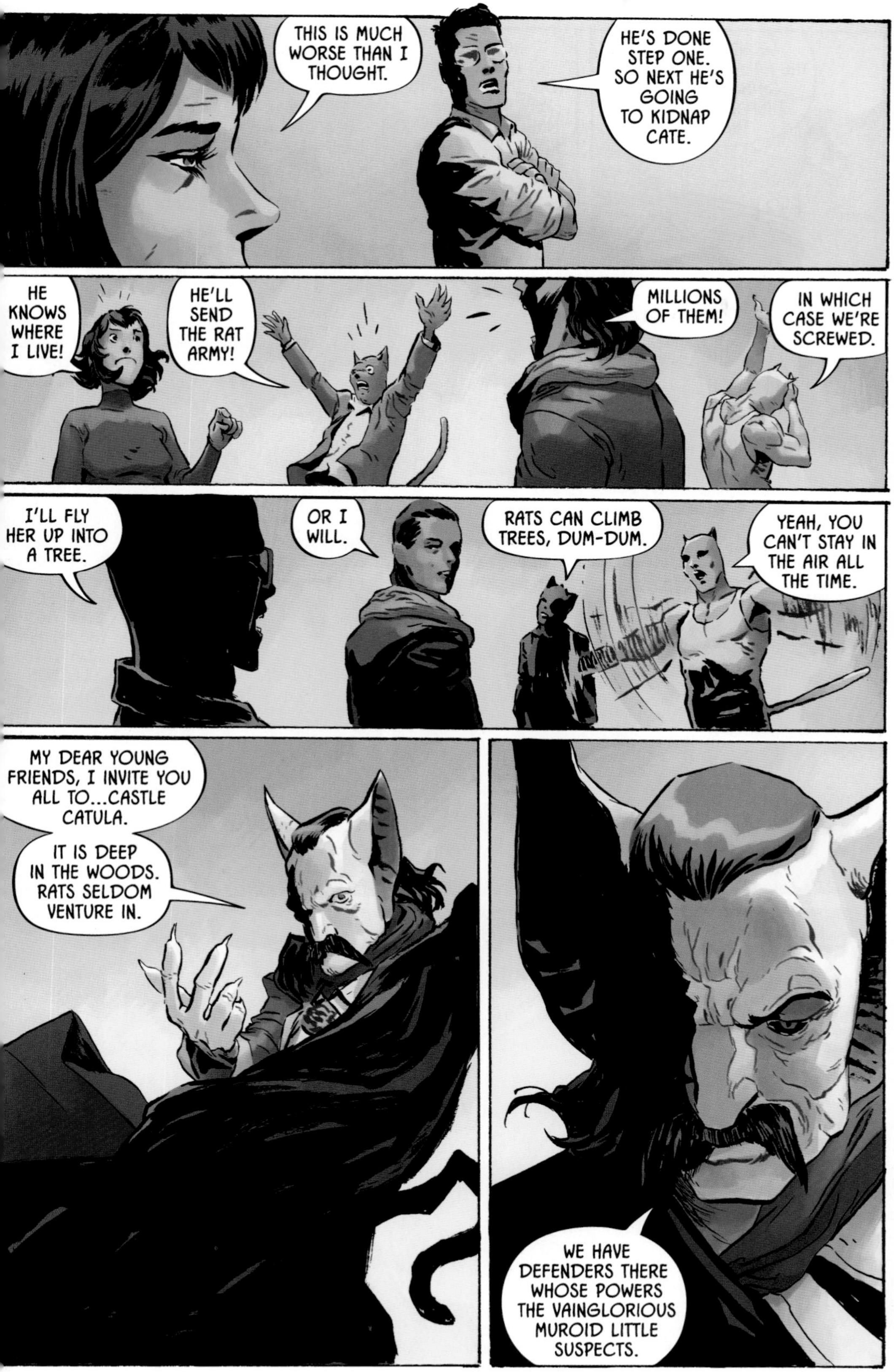

THIS IS MUCH WORSE THAN I THOUGHT.
HE'S DONE STEP ONE. SO NEXT HE'S GOING TO KIDNAP CATE.
HE KNOWS WHERE I LIVE!
HE'LL SEND THE RAT ARMY!
MILLIONS OF THEM!
IN WHICH CASE WE'RE SCREWED.
I'LL FLY HER UP INTO A TREE.
OR I WILL.
RATS CAN CLIMB TREES, DUM-DUM.
YEAH, YOU CAN'T STAY IN THE AIR ALL THE TIME.
MY DEAR YOUNG FRIENDS, I INVITE YOU ALL TO...CASTLE CATULA.
IT IS DEEP IN THE WOODS. RATS SELDOM VENTURE IN.
WE HAVE DEFENDERS THERE WHOSE POWERS THE VAINGLORIOUS MUROID LITTLE SUSPECTS.

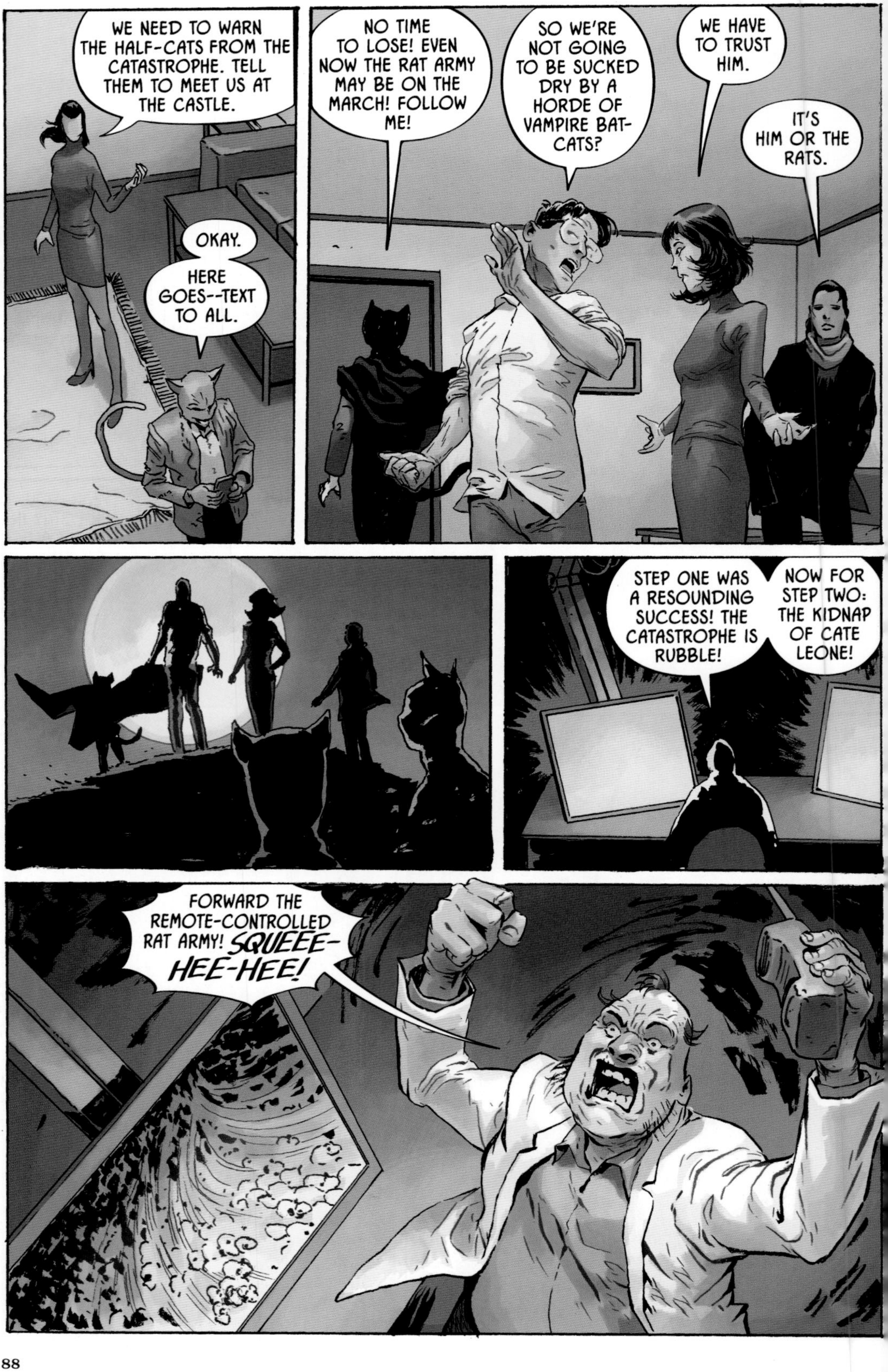
WE NEED TO WARN THE HALF-CATS FROM THE CATASTROPHE. TELL THEM TO MEET US AT THE CASTLE.
OKAY.
HERE GOES--TEXT TO ALL.
NO TIME TO LOSE! EVEN NOW THE RAT ARMY MAY BE ON THE MARCH! FOLLOW ME!
SO WE'RE NOT GOING TO BE SUCKED DRY BY A HORDE OF VAMPIRE BAT-CATS?
WE HAVE TO TRUST HIM.
IT'S HIM OR THE RATS.
STEP ONE WAS A RESOUNDING SUCCESS! THE CATASTROPHE IS RUBBLE!
NOW FOR STEP TWO: THE KIDNAP OF CATE LEONE!
FORWARD THE REMOTE-CONTROLLED RAT ARMY! SQUEEE-HEE-HEE!

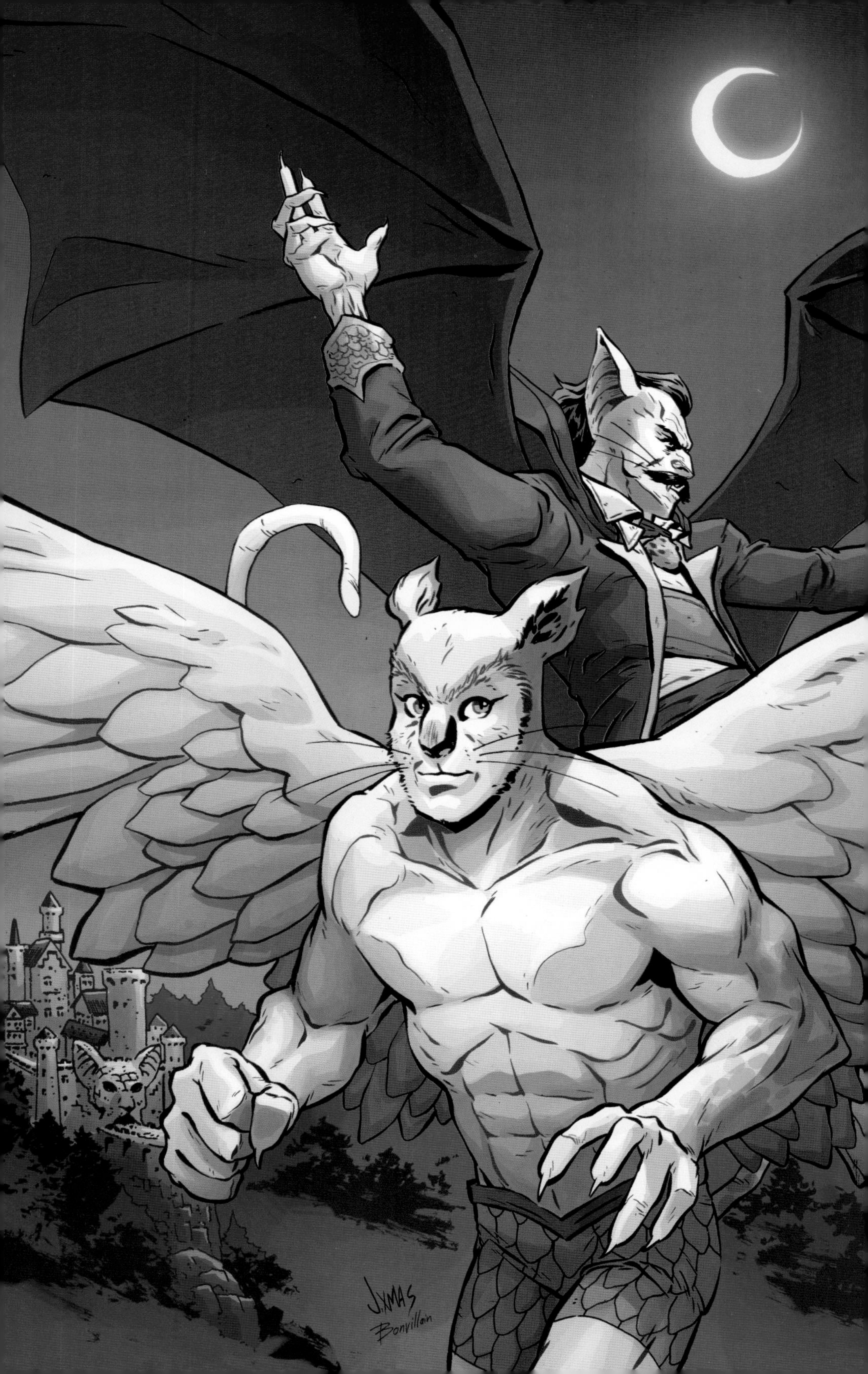
J.XMAS
Bonvillain

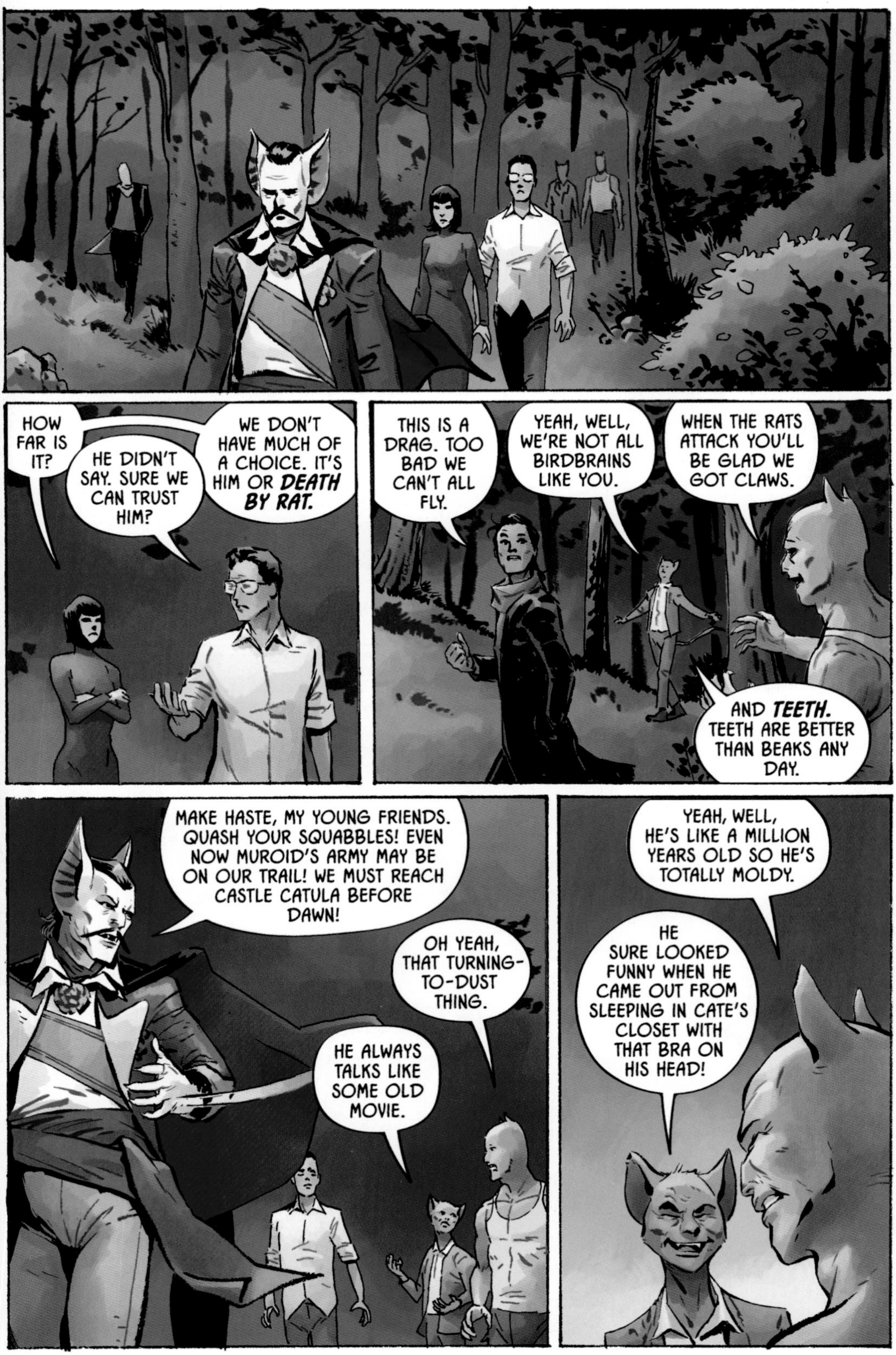
HOW FAR IS IT?
HE DIDN'T SAY. SURE WE CAN TRUST HIM?
WE DON'T HAVE MUCH OF A CHOICE. IT'S HIM OR DEATH BY RAT.
THIS IS A DRAG. TOO BAD WE CAN'T ALL FLY.
YEAH, WELL, WE'RE NOT ALL BIRDBRAINS LIKE YOU.
WHEN THE RATS ATTACK YOU'LL BE GLAD WE GOT CLAWS.
AND TEETH. TEETH ARE BETTER THAN BEAKS ANY DAY.
MAKE HASTE, MY YOUNG FRIENDS. QUASH YOUR SQUABBLES! EVEN NOW MUROID'S ARMY MAY BE ON OUR TRAIL! WE MUST REACH CASTLE CATULA BEFORE DAWN!
OH YEAH, THAT TURNING-TO-DUST THING.
HE ALWAYS TALKS LIKE SOME OLD MOVIE.
YEAH, WELL, HE'S LIKE A MILLION YEARS OLD SO HE'S TOTALLY MOLDY.
HE SURE LOOKED FUNNY WHEN HE CAME OUT FROM SLEEPING IN CATE'S CLOSET WITH THAT BRA ON HIS HEAD!

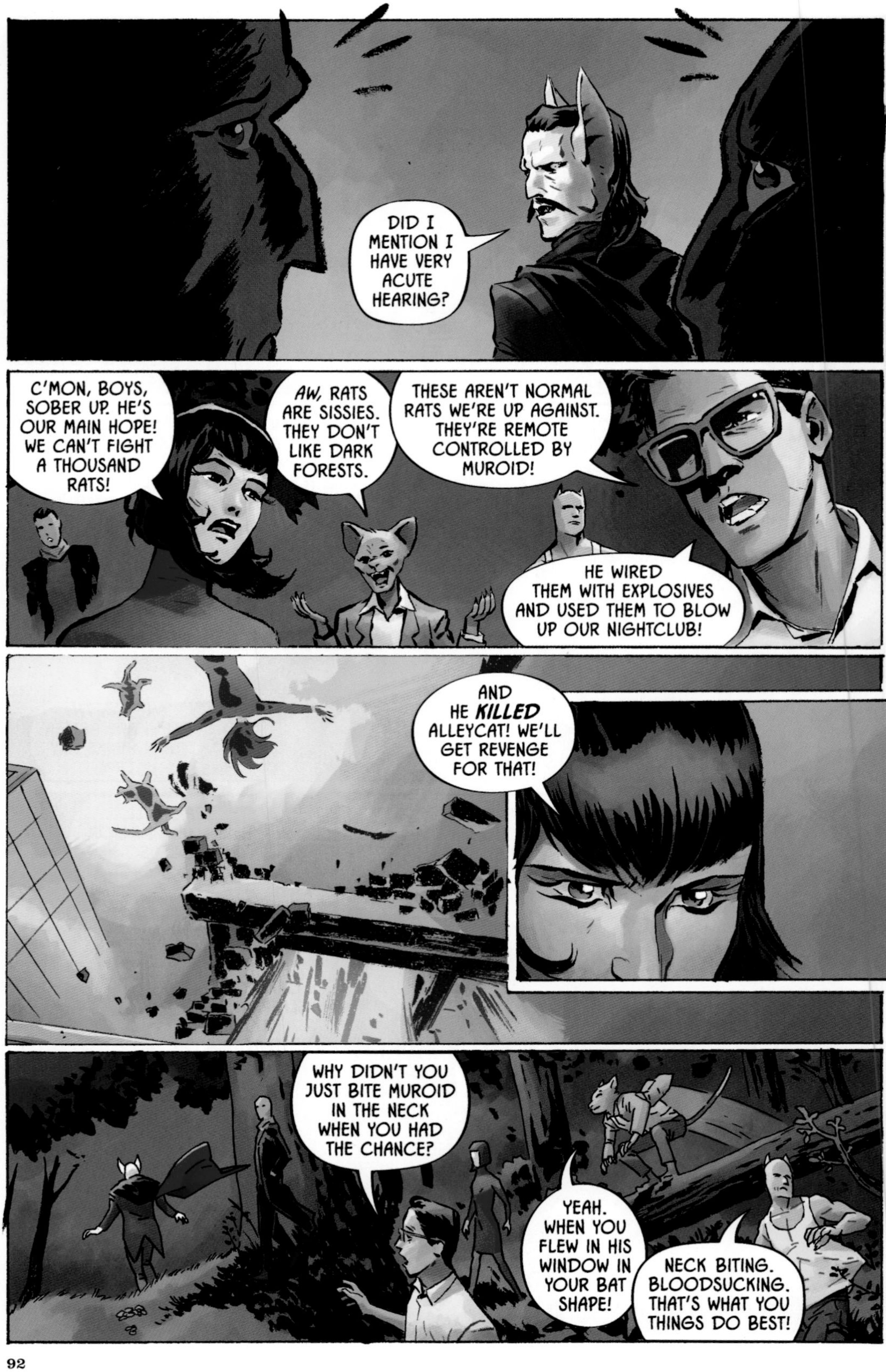
DID I MENTION I HAVE VERY ACUTE HEARING?
C'MON, BOYS, SOBER UP. HE'S OUR MAIN HOPE! WE CAN'T FIGHT A THOUSAND RATS!
AW, RATS ARE SISSIES. THEY DON'T LIKE DARK FORESTS.
THESE AREN'T NORMAL RATS WE'RE UP AGAINST. THEY'RE REMOTE CONTROLLED BY MUROID!
HE WIRED THEM WITH EXPLOSIVES AND USED THEM TO BLOW UP OUR NIGHTCLUB!
AND HE KILLED ALLEYCAT! WE'LL GET REVENGE FOR THAT!
WHY DIDN'T YOU JUST BITE MUROID IN THE NECK WHEN YOU HAD THE CHANCE?
YEAH. WHEN YOU FLEW IN HIS WINDOW IN YOUR BAT SHAPE!
NECK BITING. BLOODSUCKING. THAT'S WHAT YOU THINGS DO BEST!

MY DEAR YOUNG HALF-CAT. CONSIDER WHAT YOU SAY. FIRST, I HAVE STANDARDS. THE TASTE WOULD BE VILE!
IN ADDITION, BY IMBIBING MUTANT RAT-MAN BLOOD, I MYSELF RISKED BECOMING PART RAT--WITH HORRID CONSEQUENCES!
AND IF I PROCEEDED ALONG, AH, TRADITIONAL LINES, MUROID HIMSELF MIGHT HAVE JOINED THE UNDEAD.
THAT WOULD HAVE BEEN UNSPEAKABLE!
A VAMPIRE RAT-MAN! KINDA COOL.
WHAT ARE YOU SAYING? SICKENING! BLECH!
WELL MAY YOU SAY "BLECH," DEAR LADY. YOU ALWAYS EXPRESS YOURSELF SO DIRECTLY. WE ALL ADMIRE THAT IN YOU.
YOU CAN SAY THAT AGAIN...
SKRITCH SKRITCH
THUS I FOLLOWED THE PATH OF DISCRETION, AND MUROID IS REGRETTABLY STILL ALIVE. BUT WE MUST KEEP OUR FINAL GOAL FIRMLY IN VIEW.
CURTAINS FOR MUROID.
R.I.P.
EXIT RAT.
PAYBACK TIME.

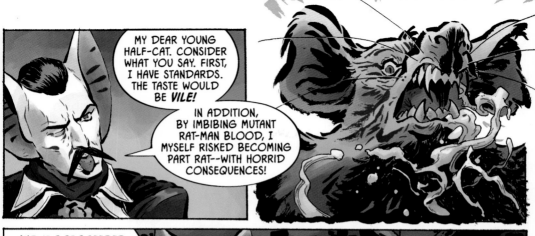

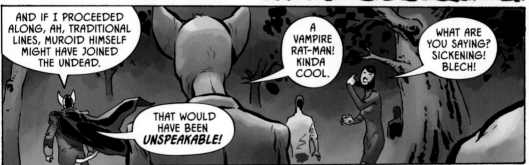

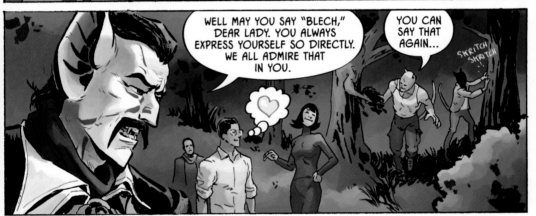

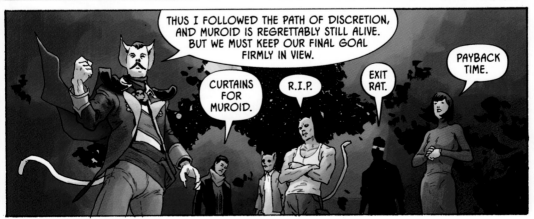

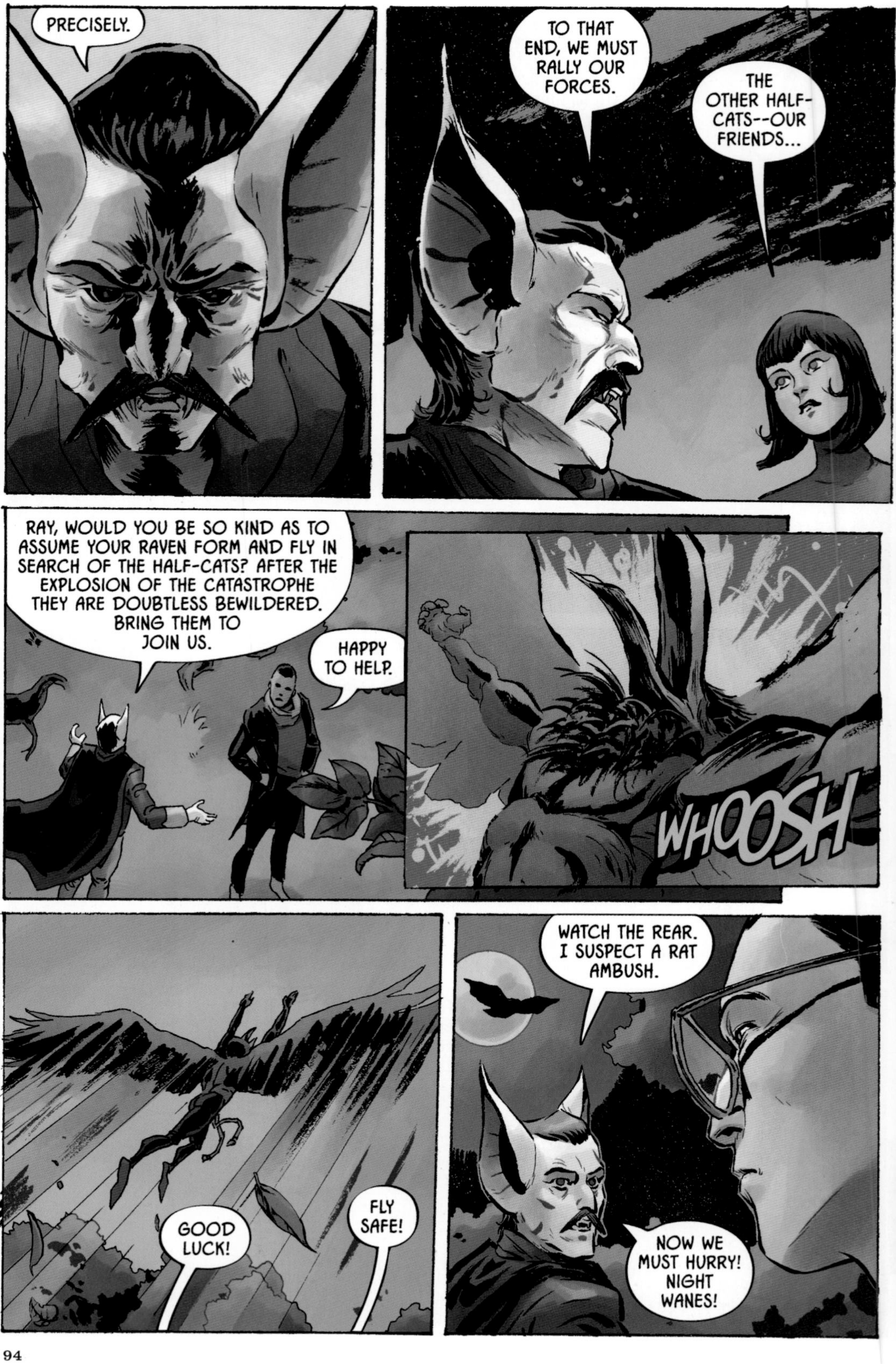
PRECISELY.
TO THAT END, WE MUST RALLY OUR FORCES.
THE OTHER HALF-CATS--OUR FRIENDS...
RAY, WOULD YOU BE SO KIND AS TO ASSUME YOUR RAVEN FORM AND FLY IN SEARCH OF THE HALF-CATS? AFTER THE EXPLOSION OF THE CATASTROPHE THEY ARE DOUBTLESS BEWILDERED. BRING THEM TO JOIN US.
HAPPY TO HELP.
WHOOSH
GOOD LUCK!
FLY SAFE!
WATCH THE REAR. I SUSPECT A RAT AMBUSH.
NOW WE MUST HURRY! NIGHT WANES!

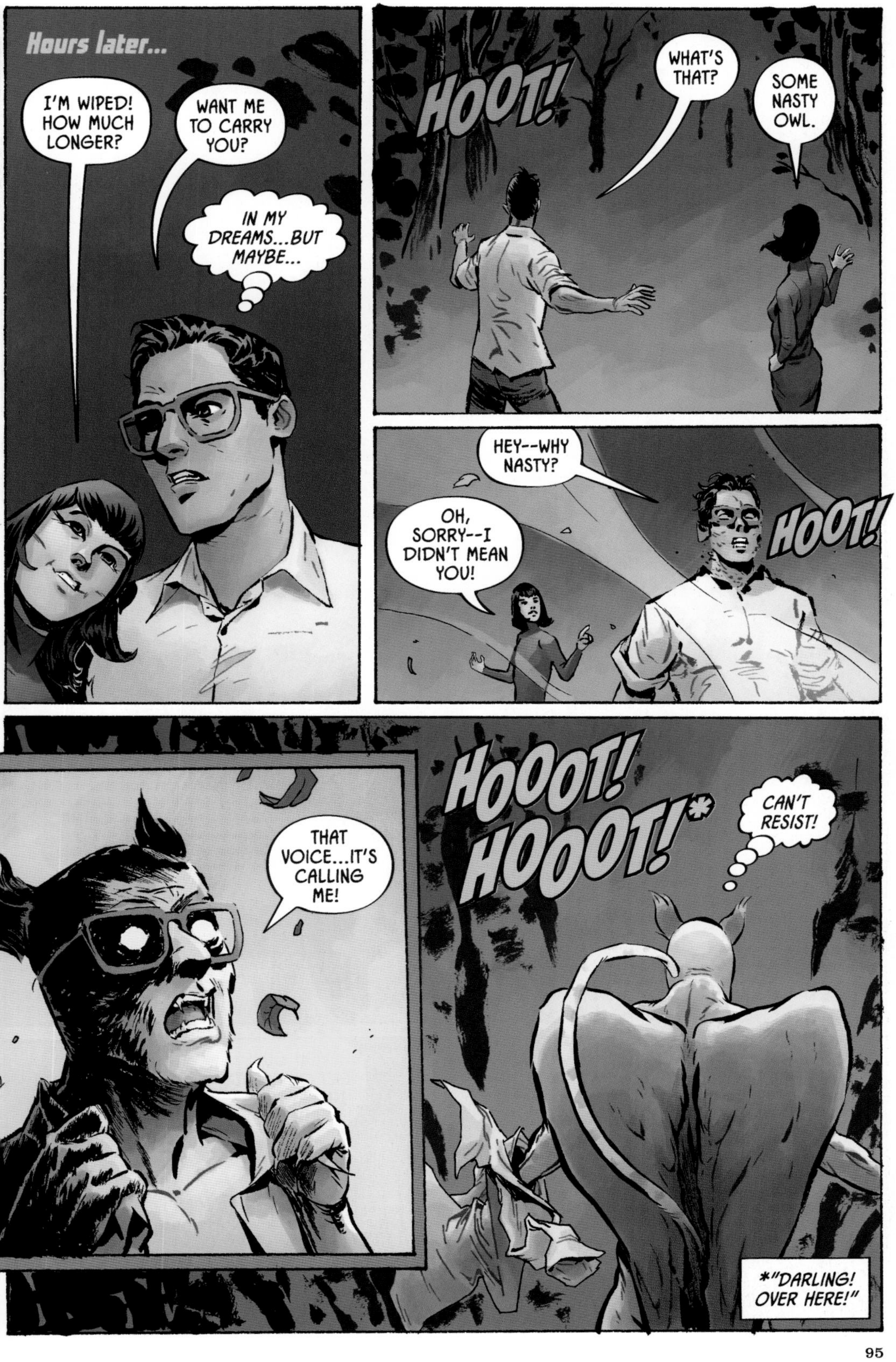
Hours later...
I'M WIPED! HOW MUCH LONGER?
WANT ME TO CARRY YOU?
IN MY DREAMS...BUT MAYBE...
HOOT!
WHAT'S THAT?
SOME NASTY OWL.
HEY--WHY NASTY?
OH, SORRY--I DIDN'T MEAN YOU!
HOOT!
THAT VOICE...IT'S CALLING ME!
HOOOT! HOOOT!*
CAN'T RESIST!
*"DARLING! OVER HERE!"

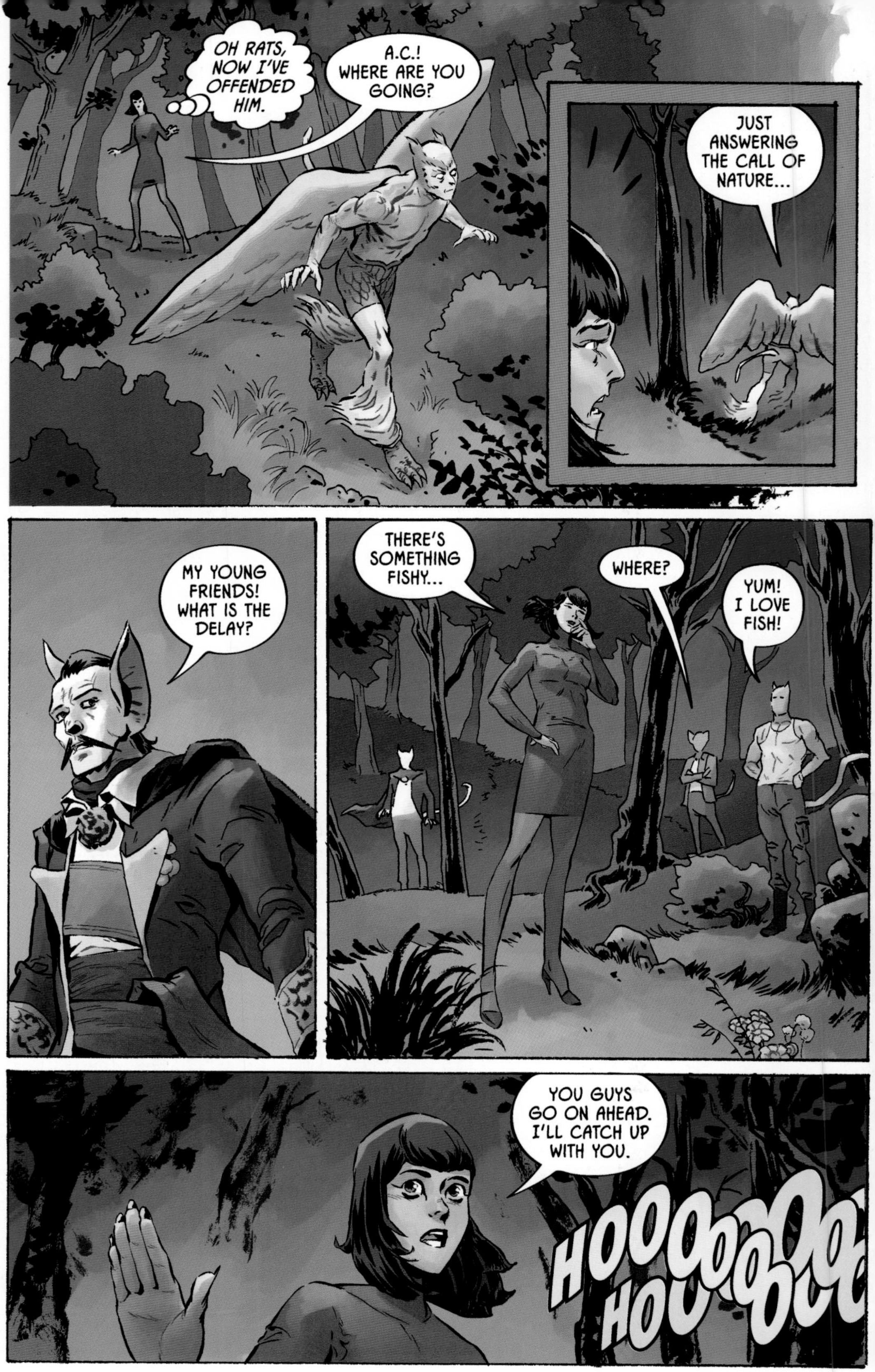
OH RATS, NOW I'VE OFFENDED HIM.
A.C.! WHERE ARE YOU GOING?
JUST ANSWERING THE CALL OF NATURE...
MY YOUNG FRIENDS! WHAT IS THE DELAY?
THERE'S SOMETHING FISHY...
WHERE?
YUM! I LOVE FISH!
YOU GUYS GO ON AHEAD. I'LL CATCH UP WITH YOU.
HOOOOOOO HOOOOOO

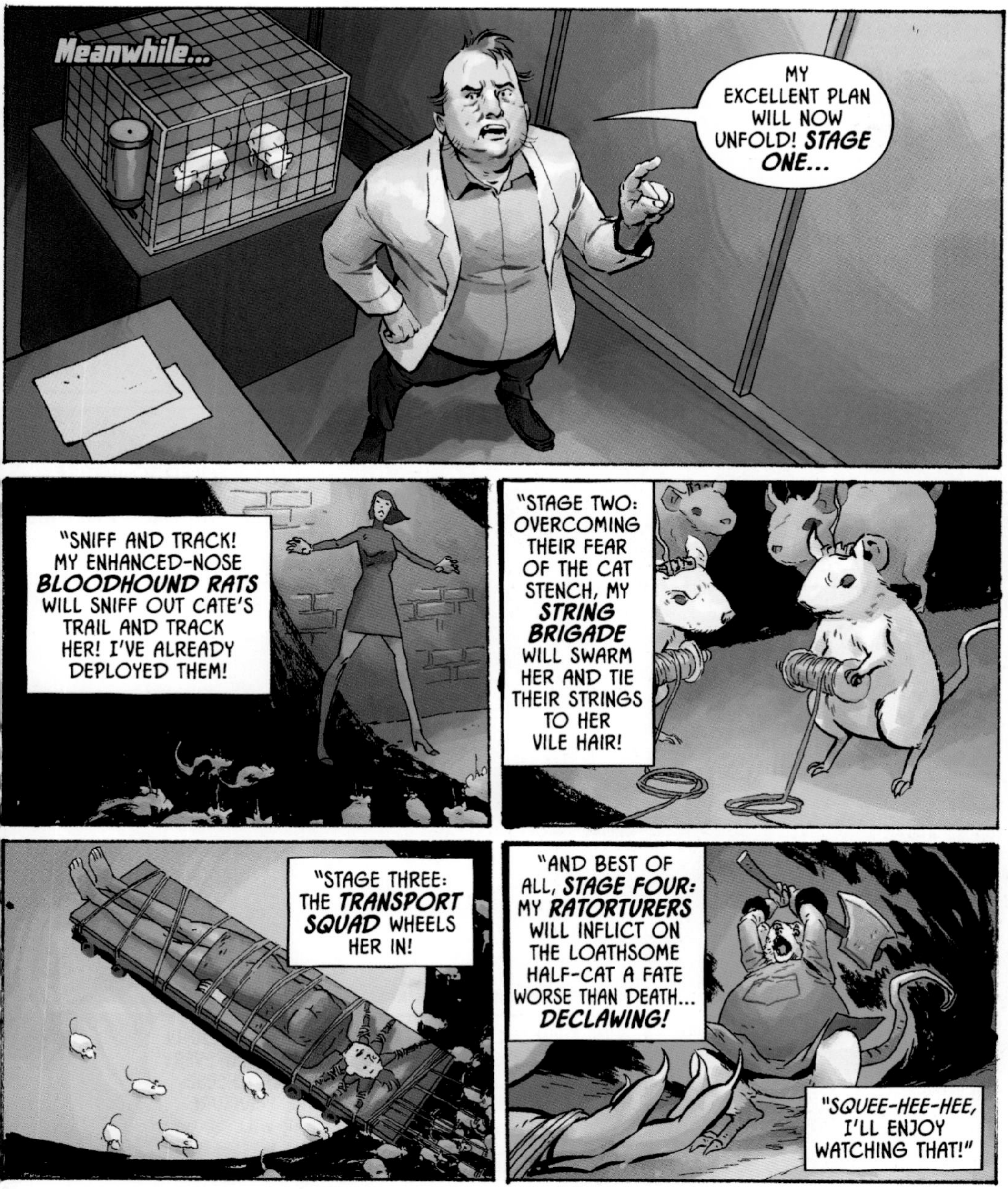
Meanwhile...
MY EXCELLENT PLAN WILL NOW UNFOLD! STAGE ONE...
"SNIFF AND TRACK! MY ENHANCED-NOSE BLOODHOUND RATS WILL SNIFF OUT CATE'S TRAIL AND TRACK HER! I'VE ALREADY DEPLOYED THEM!
"STAGE TWO: OVERCOMING THEIR FEAR OF THE CAT STENCH, MY STRING BRIGADE WILL SWARM HER AND TIE THEIR STRINGS TO HER VILE HAIR!
"STAGE THREE: THE TRANSPORT SQUAD WHEELS HER IN!
"AND BEST OF ALL, STAGE FOUR: MY RATORTURERS WILL INFLICT ON THE LOATHSOME HALF-CAT A FATE WORSE THAN DEATH... DECLAWING!
"SQUEE-HEE-HEE, I'LL ENJOY WATCHING THAT!"

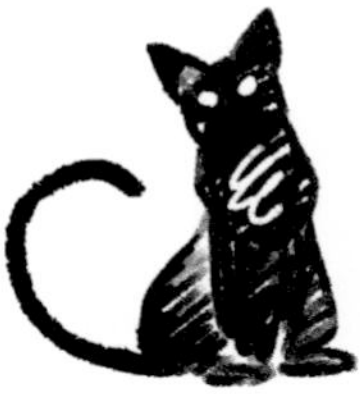

CATS NEED CLAWS

Declawing is a surgical procedure in which the last bones of a cat's toes, including the nail beds, are amputated. Scratching is a normal behavior for cats and serves several purposes. There are nonsurgical solutions to save your upholstery!
Read more at www.catsandbirds.ca

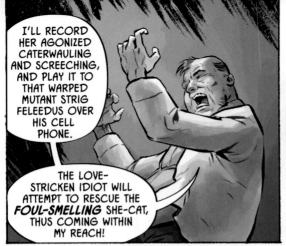

I'LL RECORD HER AGONIZED CATERWAULING AND SCREECHING, AND PLAY IT TO THAT WARPED MUTANT STRIG FELEEDUS OVER HIS CELL PHONE.

THE LOVE-STRICKEN IDIOT WILL ATTEMPT TO RESCUE THE *FOUL-SMELLING* SHE-CAT, THUS COMING WITHIN MY REACH!

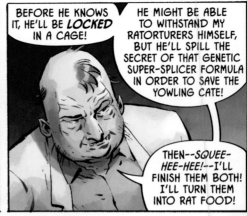

BEFORE HE KNOWS IT, HE'LL BE *LOCKED* IN A CAGE!

HE MIGHT BE ABLE TO WITHSTAND MY RATORTURERS HIMSELF, BUT HE'LL SPILL THE SECRET OF THAT GENETIC SUPER-SPLICER FORMULA IN ORDER TO SAVE THE YOWLING CATE!

THEN--*SQUEE-HEE-HEE!*--I'LL FINISH THEM BOTH! I'LL TURN THEM INTO RAT FOOD!

"AND THE WHOLE WORLD WILL SOON BE RAT-ATTRACTIVE! OURS FOR THE TAKING!"

AS FOR YOU, MY TREACHEROUS PETS, DON'T THINK I FAILED TO NOTICE YOUR COMMUNICATION WITH THAT RED-EYED BAT! ONCE I GET THE SUPER-SPLICER FORMULA, YOU'LL BE TRANSFORMED INTO TWO *RAT-A-LICIOUS* HOT RAT BABES IN NO TIME FLAT!

THEN I'LL PAY YOU BACK...I'LL KEEP YOU IN SLAVE COLLARS! YOU'LL CATER TO MY EVERY WHIM! OR ELSE! COVER ME WITH CHEESE SPREAD...NIBBLE IT OFF...THE PLEASURE WILL BE *MINE,* THE FEAR WILL BE YOURS!

THIS GUY IS NOT YOUR AVERAGE DREAMBOAT.

YOU THINK?

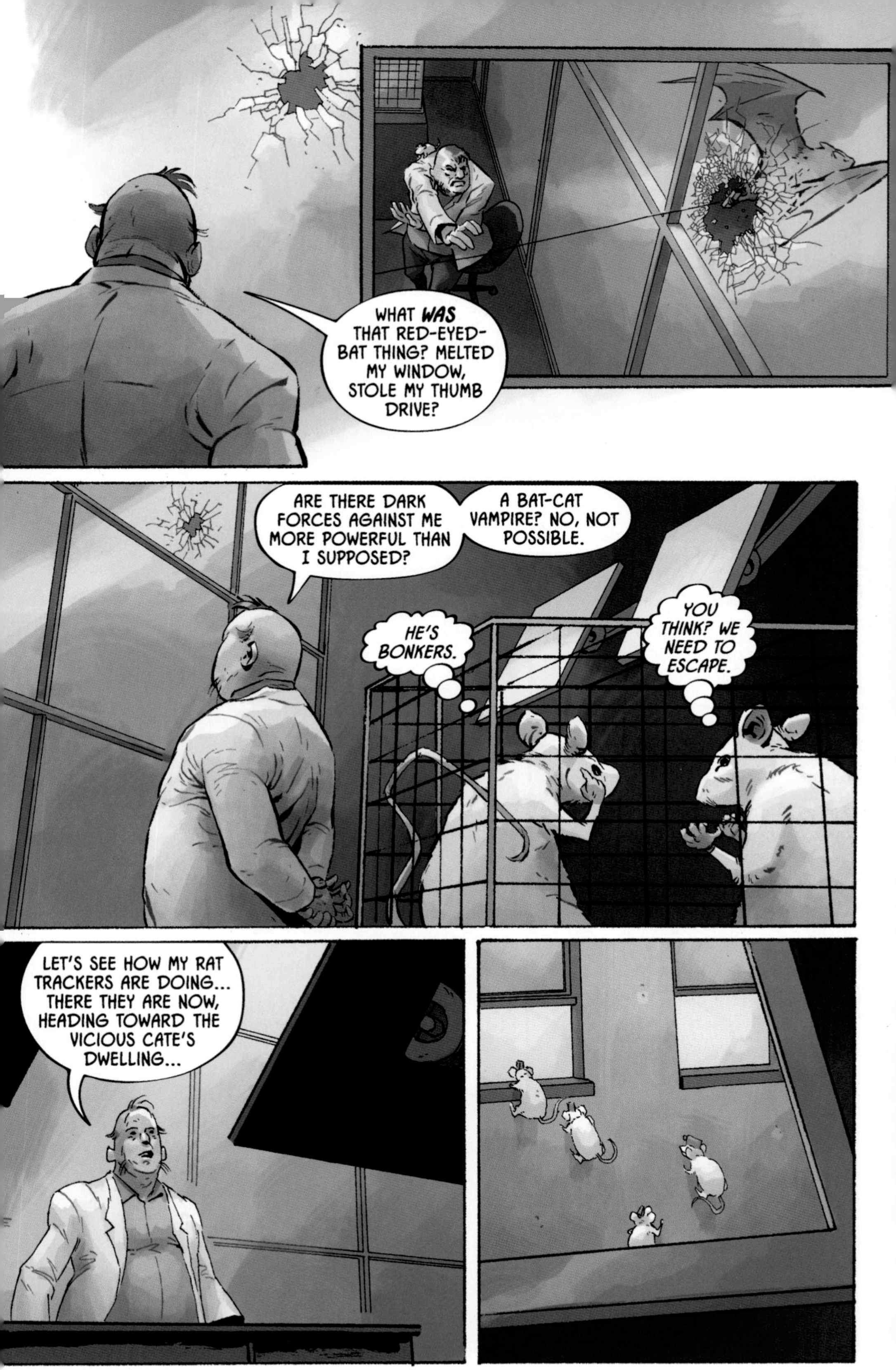
WHAT WAS THAT RED-EYED-BAT THING? MELTED MY WINDOW, STOLE MY THUMB DRIVE?
ARE THERE DARK FORCES AGAINST ME MORE POWERFUL THAN I SUPPOSED?
A BAT-CAT VAMPIRE? NO, NOT POSSIBLE.
HE'S BONKERS.
YOU THINK? WE NEED TO ESCAPE.
LET'S SEE HOW MY RAT TRACKERS ARE DOING... THERE THEY ARE NOW, HEADING TOWARD THE VICIOUS CATE'S DWELLING...

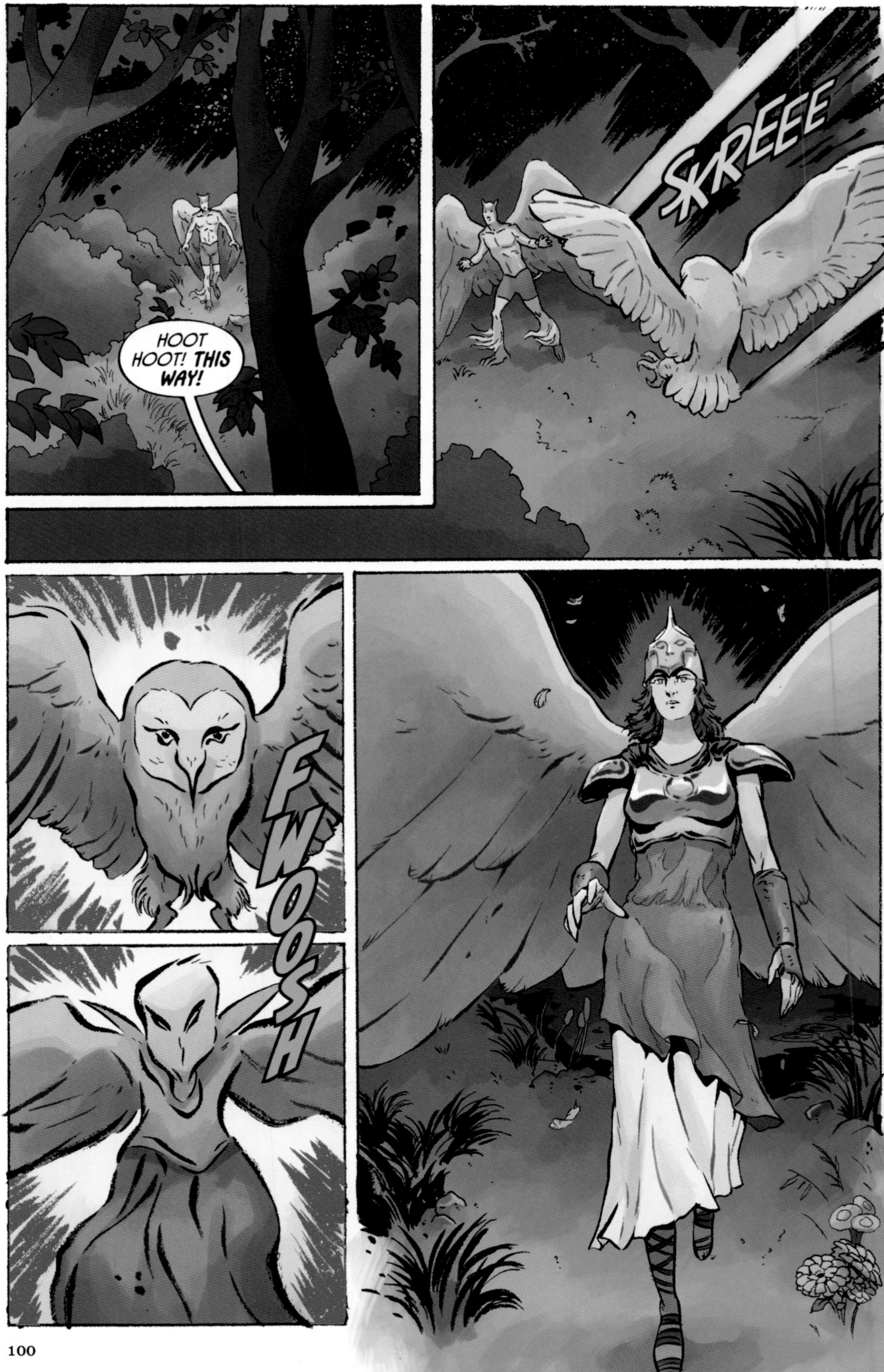
HOOT HOOT! THIS WAY!
SKREEE
FWOOSH

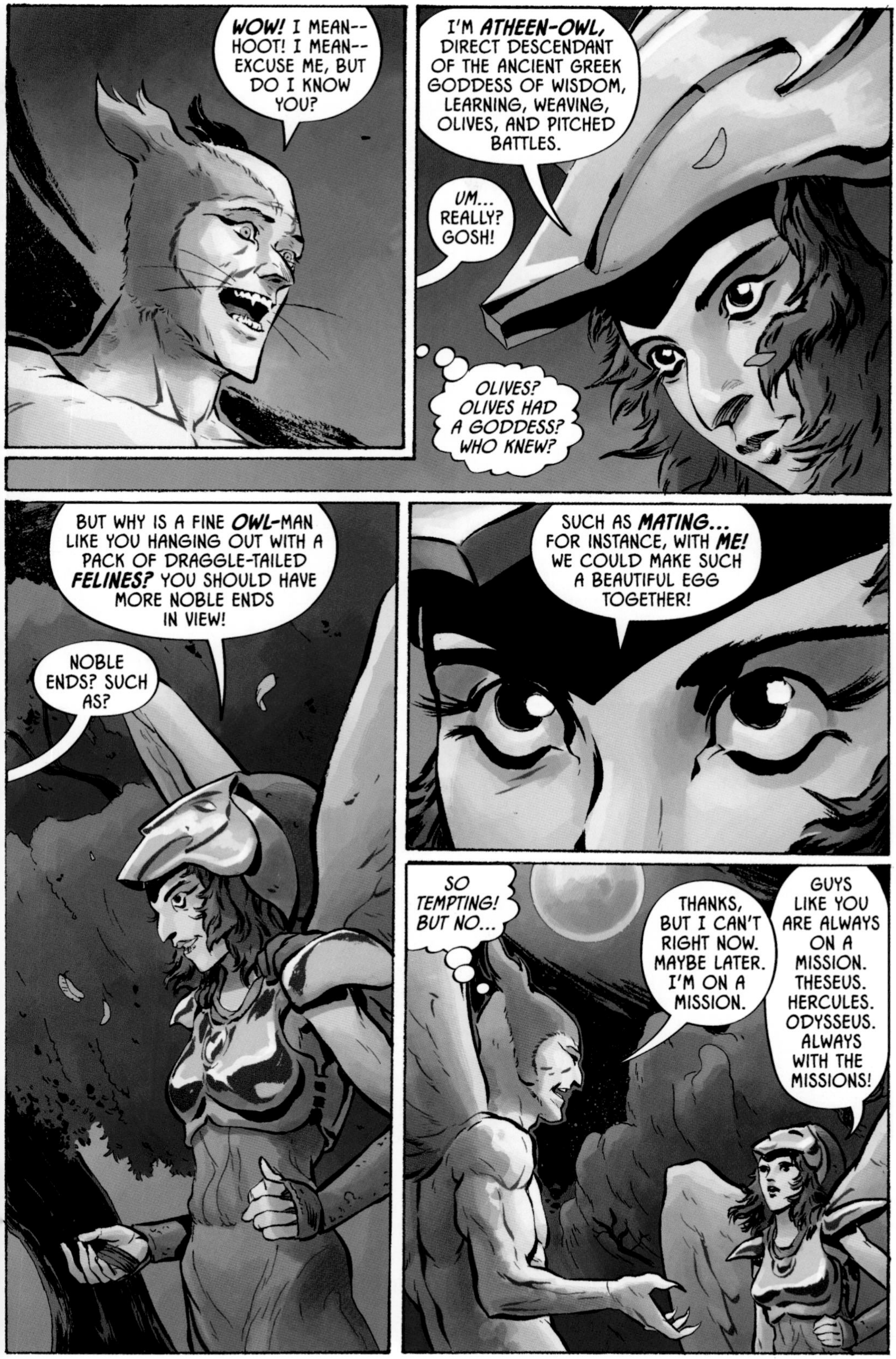
WOW! I MEAN-- HOOT! I MEAN-- EXCUSE ME, BUT DO I KNOW YOU?
I'M ATHEEN-OWL, DIRECT DESCENDANT OF THE ANCIENT GREEK GODDESS OF WISDOM, LEARNING, WEAVING, OLIVES, AND PITCHED BATTLES.
UM... REALLY? GOSH!
OLIVES? OLIVES HAD A GODDESS? WHO KNEW?
BUT WHY IS A FINE OWL-MAN LIKE YOU HANGING OUT WITH A PACK OF DRAGGLE-TAILED FELINES? YOU SHOULD HAVE MORE NOBLE ENDS IN VIEW!
NOBLE ENDS? SUCH AS?
SUCH AS MATING... FOR INSTANCE, WITH ME! WE COULD MAKE SUCH A BEAUTIFUL EGG TOGETHER!
SO TEMPTING! BUT NO...
THANKS, BUT I CAN'T RIGHT NOW. MAYBE LATER. I'M ON A MISSION.
GUYS LIKE YOU ARE ALWAYS ON A MISSION. THESEUS. HERCULES. ODYSSEUS. ALWAYS WITH THE MISSIONS!

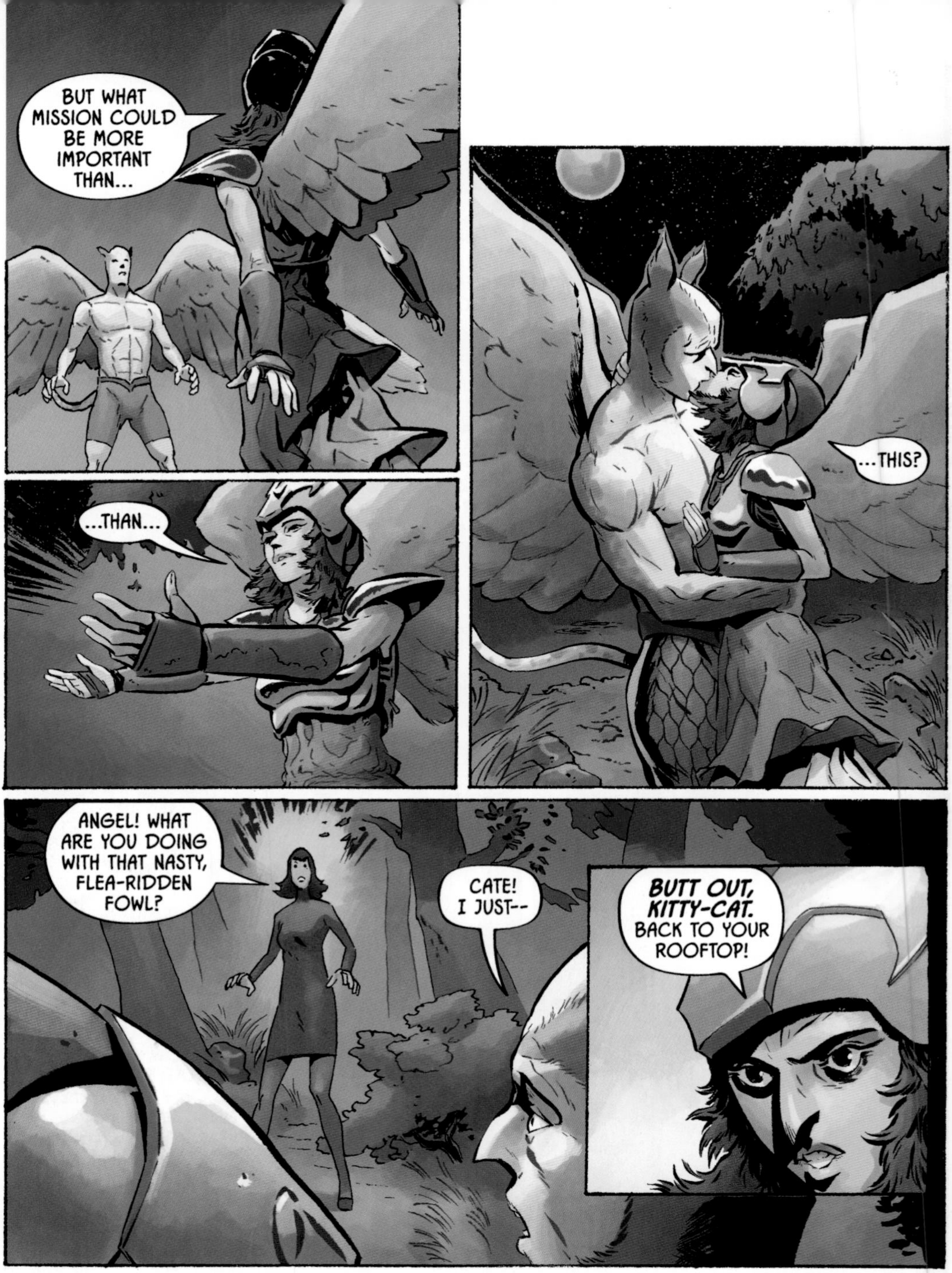
BUT WHAT MISSION COULD BE MORE IMPORTANT THAN...
...THAN...
...THIS?
ANGEL! WHAT ARE YOU DOING WITH THAT NASTY, FLEA-RIDDEN FOWL?
CATE! I JUST--
BUTT OUT, KITTY-CAT. BACK TO YOUR ROOFTOP!

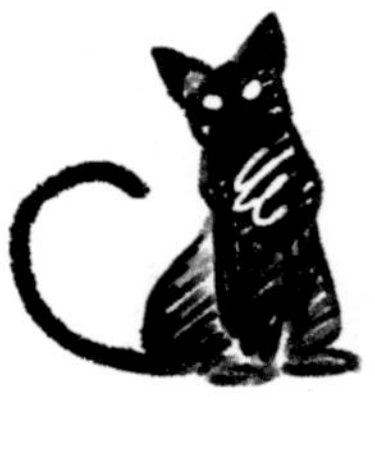

CATS IN THE CRADLE

Breeding season is a vulnerable time for birds. The eggs can get eaten and baby birds are very susceptible to predators. If young birds live long enough to leave the nest, they have no survival skills; they can't feed themselves yet, or fly well (if at all), or defend themselves.

Read more at www.catsandbirds.ca

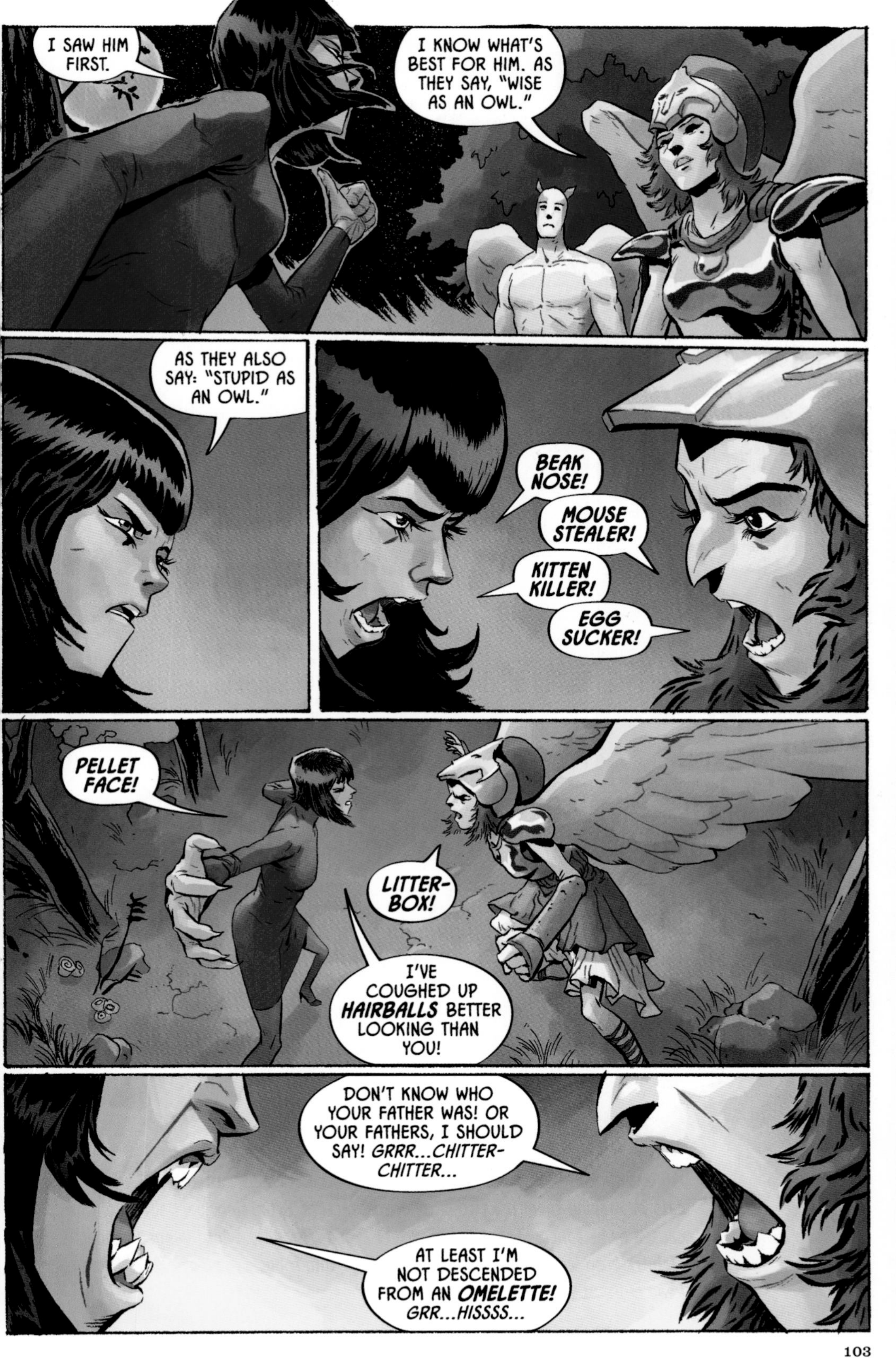
I SAW HIM FIRST.
I KNOW WHAT'S BEST FOR HIM. AS THEY SAY, "WISE AS AN OWL."
AS THEY ALSO SAY: "STUPID AS AN OWL."
BEAK NOSE!
MOUSE STEALER!
KITTEN KILLER!
EGG SUCKER!
PELLET FACE!
LITTER-BOX!
I'VE COUGHED UP HAIRBALLS BETTER LOOKING THAN YOU!
DON'T KNOW WHO YOUR FATHER WAS! OR YOUR FATHERS, I SHOULD SAY! GRRR...CHITTER-CHITTER...
AT LEAST I'M NOT DESCENDED FROM AN OMELETTE! GRR...HISSSS...

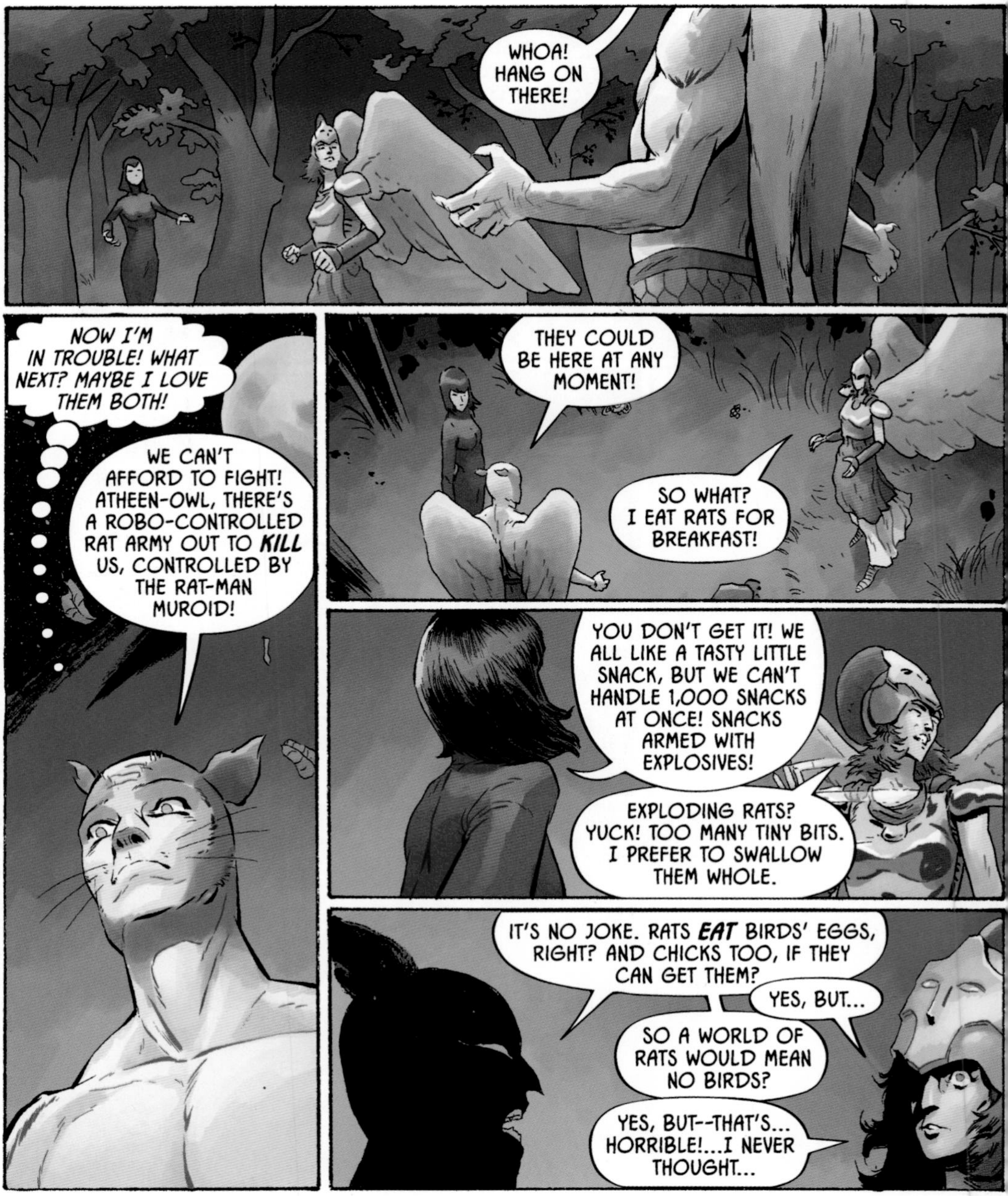
WHOA! HANG ON THERE!
NOW I'M IN TROUBLE! WHAT NEXT? MAYBE I LOVE THEM BOTH!
WE CAN'T AFFORD TO FIGHT! ATHEEN-OWL, THERE'S A ROBO-CONTROLLED RAT ARMY OUT TO KILL US, CONTROLLED BY THE RAT-MAN MUROID!
THEY COULD BE HERE AT ANY MOMENT!
SO WHAT? I EAT RATS FOR BREAKFAST!
YOU DON'T GET IT! WE ALL LIKE A TASTY LITTLE SNACK, BUT WE CAN'T HANDLE 1,000 SNACKS AT ONCE! SNACKS ARMED WITH EXPLOSIVES!
EXPLODING RATS? YUCK! TOO MANY TINY BITS. I PREFER TO SWALLOW THEM WHOLE.
IT'S NO JOKE. RATS EAT BIRDS' EGGS, RIGHT? AND CHICKS TOO, IF THEY CAN GET THEM?
YES, BUT...
SO A WORLD OF RATS WOULD MEAN NO BIRDS?
YES, BUT--THAT'S... HORRIBLE!...I NEVER THOUGHT...

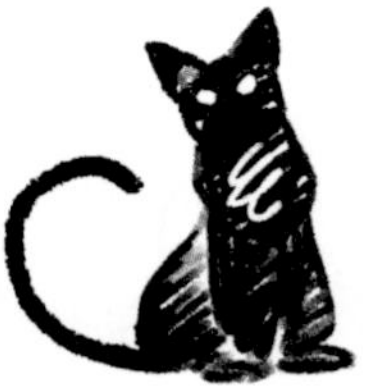

RATS AND CATS

140 bird species have gone extinct since AD 1500. Rats contributed to 41 extinctions and cats 34, making them the two most deadly factors. Extinctions partially or entirely caused by rats include species of lorikeet (Pacific Islands), white-winged sandpiper (Tahiti), bush wren and piopio (New Zealand), and robust white-eye (Lord Howe Island). Read more at www.birdlife.org and www.sciencedirect.com

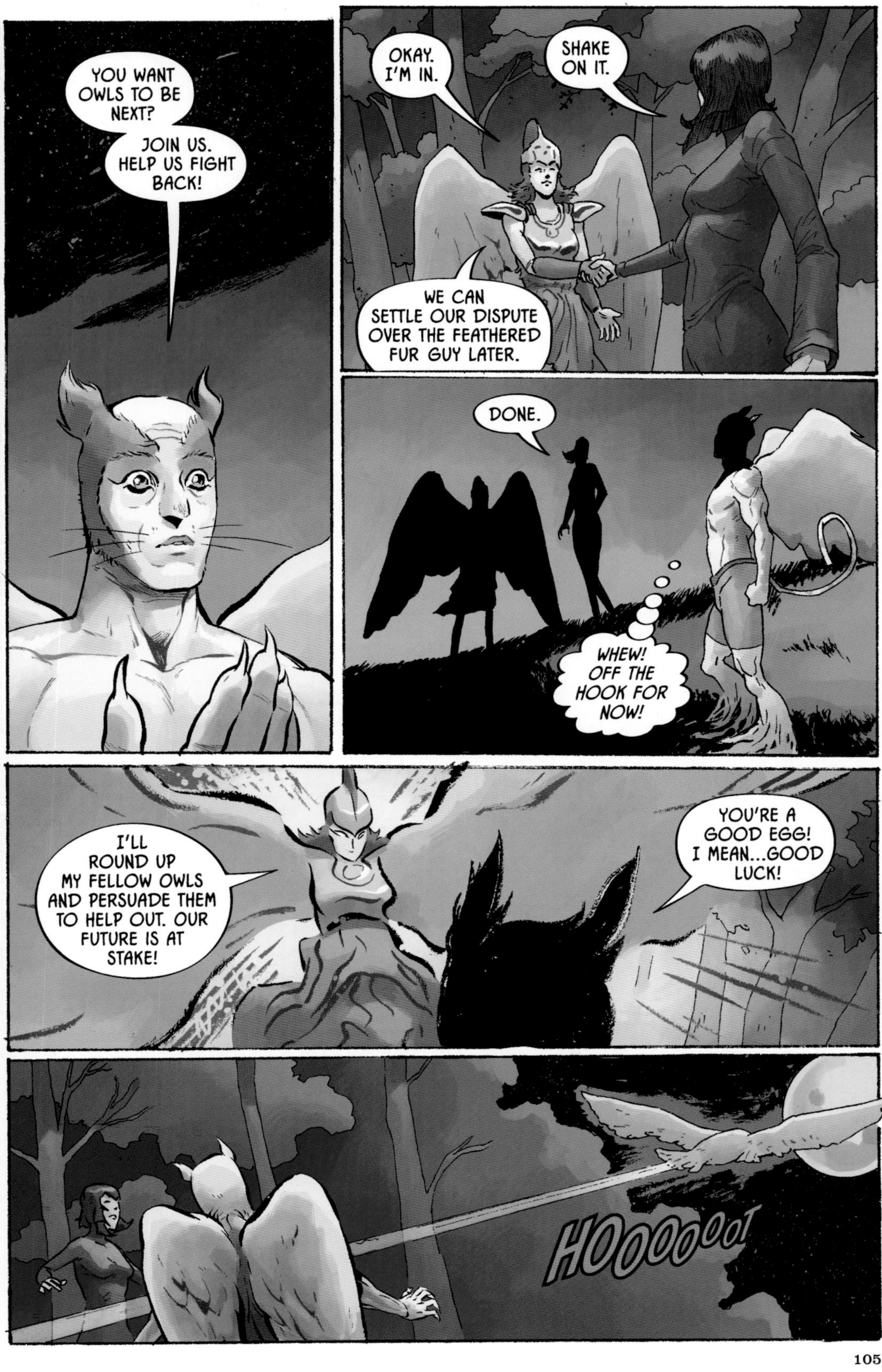
YOU WANT OWLS TO BE NEXT?
JOIN US. HELP US FIGHT BACK!
OKAY. I'M IN.
SHAKE ON IT.
WE CAN SETTLE OUR DISPUTE OVER THE FEATHERED FUR GUY LATER.
DONE.
WHEW! OFF THE HOOK FOR NOW!
I'LL ROUND UP MY FELLOW OWLS AND PERSUADE THEM TO HELP OUT. OUR FUTURE IS AT STAKE!
YOU'RE A GOOD EGG! I MEAN...GOOD LUCK!
HOOOOOOOT

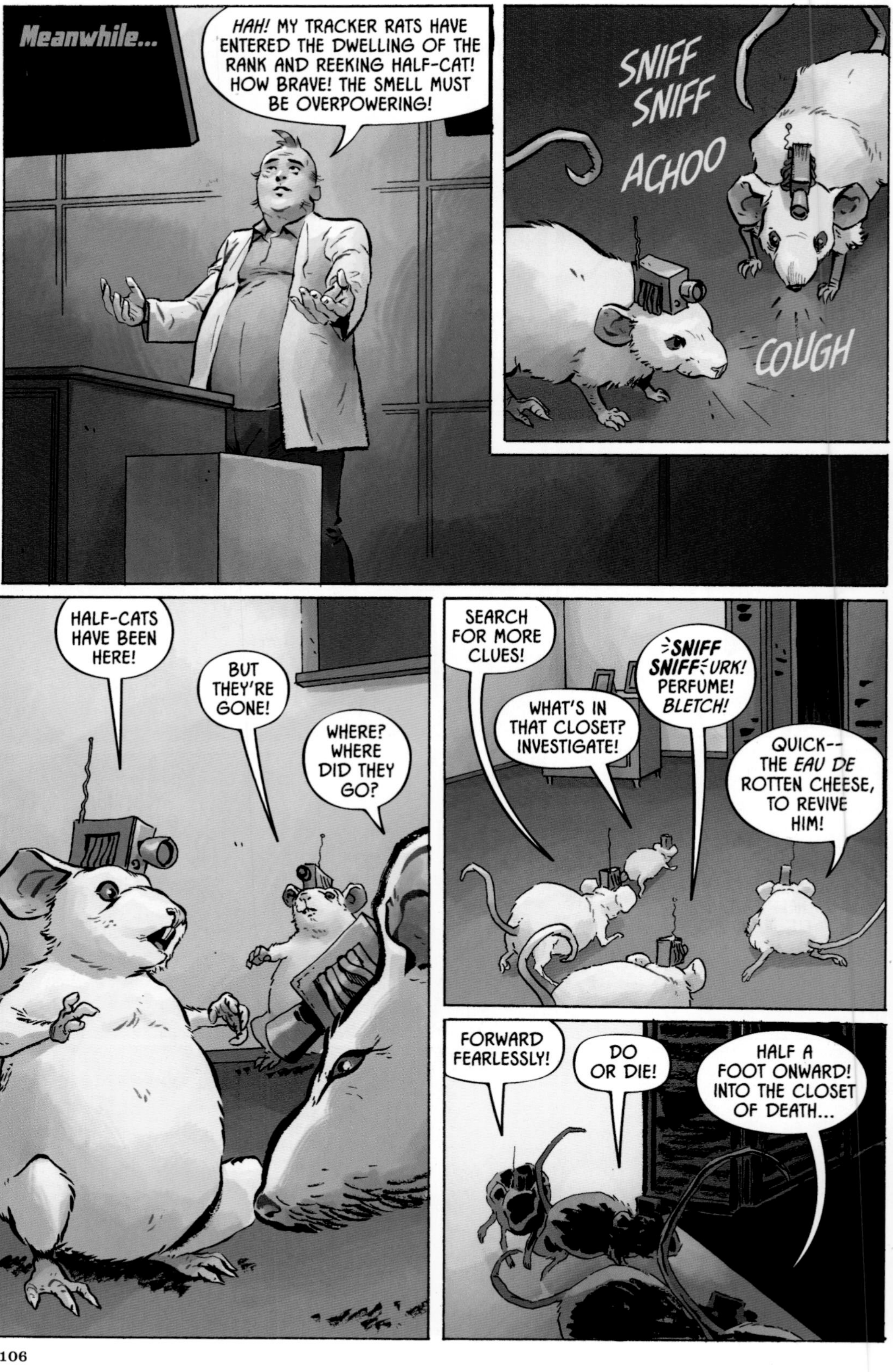
Meanwhile...
HAH! MY TRACKER RATS HAVE ENTERED THE DWELLING OF THE RANK AND REEKING HALF-CAT! HOW BRAVE! THE SMELL MUST BE OVERPOWERING!
SNIFF SNIFF
ACHOO
COUGH
HALF-CATS HAVE BEEN HERE!
BUT THEY'RE GONE!
WHERE? WHERE DID THEY GO?
SEARCH FOR MORE CLUES!
WHAT'S IN THAT CLOSET? INVESTIGATE!
SNIFF SNIFF URK! PERFUME! BLETCH!
QUICK-- THE EAU DE ROTTEN CHEESE, TO REVIVE HIM!
FORWARD FEARLESSLY!
DO OR DIE!
HALF A FOOT ONWARD! INTO THE CLOSET OF DEATH...

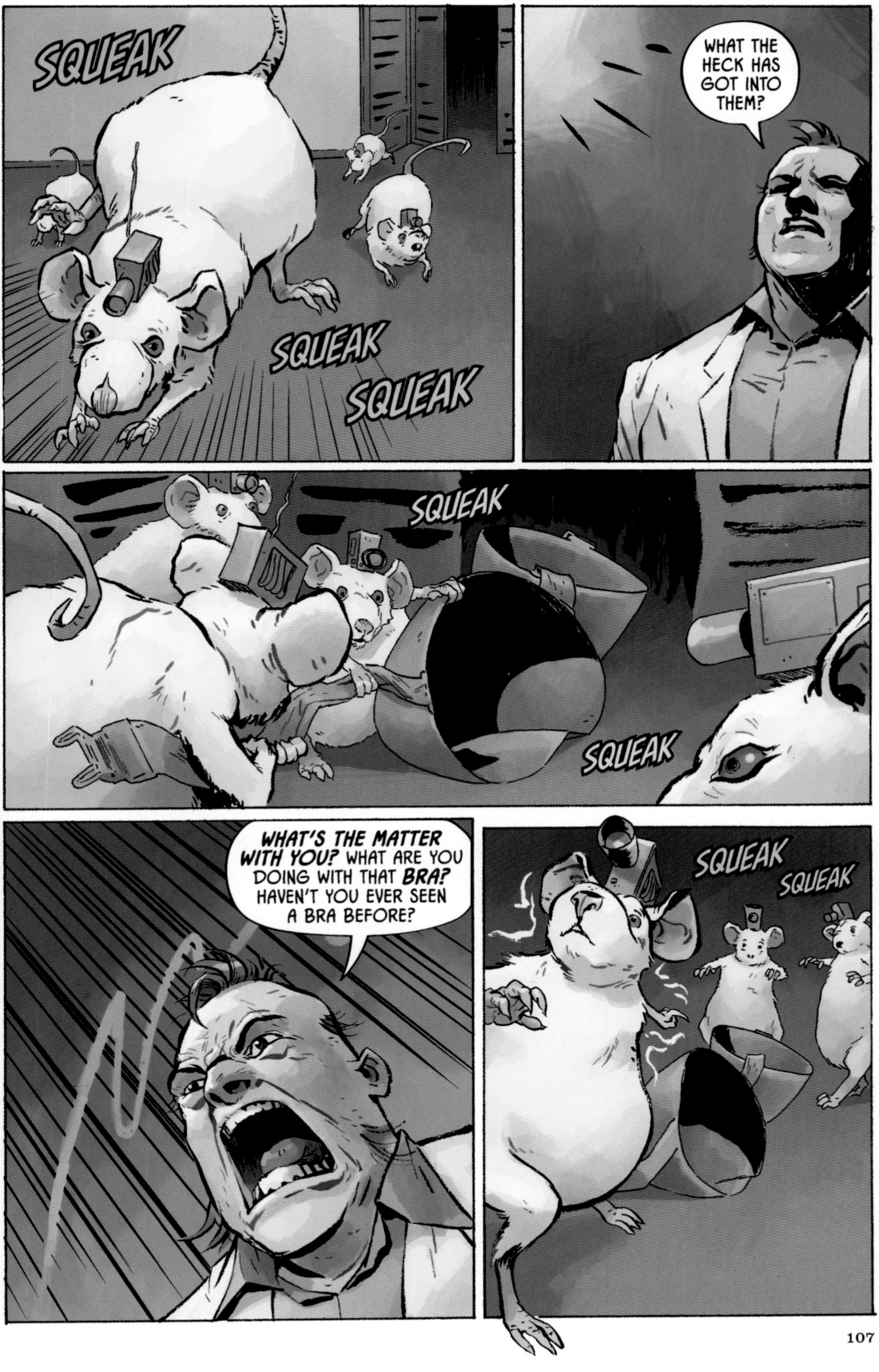
SQUEAK
SQUEAK
SQUEAK
WHAT THE HECK HAS GOT INTO THEM?
SQUEAK
SQUEAK
WHAT'S THE MATTER WITH YOU? WHAT ARE YOU DOING WITH THAT BRA? HAVEN'T YOU EVER SEEN A BRA BEFORE?
SQUEAK
SQUEAK

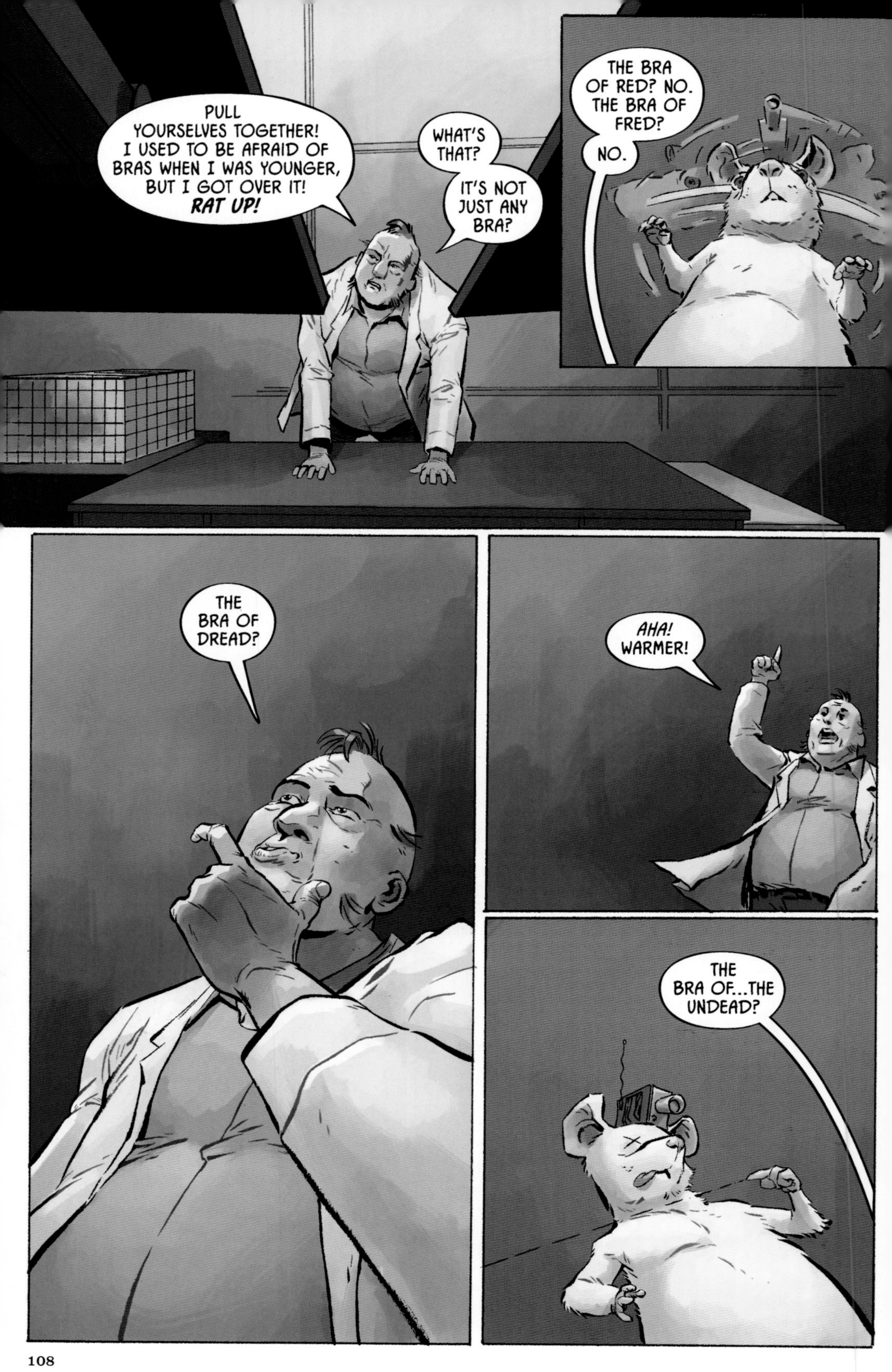
PULL YOURSELVES TOGETHER! I USED TO BE AFRAID OF BRAS WHEN I WAS YOUNGER, BUT I GOT OVER IT! ***RAT UP!***
WHAT'S THAT?
IT'S NOT JUST ANY BRA?
THE BRA OF RED? NO. THE BRA OF FRED?
NO.
THE BRA OF DREAD?
AHA! WARMER!
THE BRA OF...THE UNDEAD?

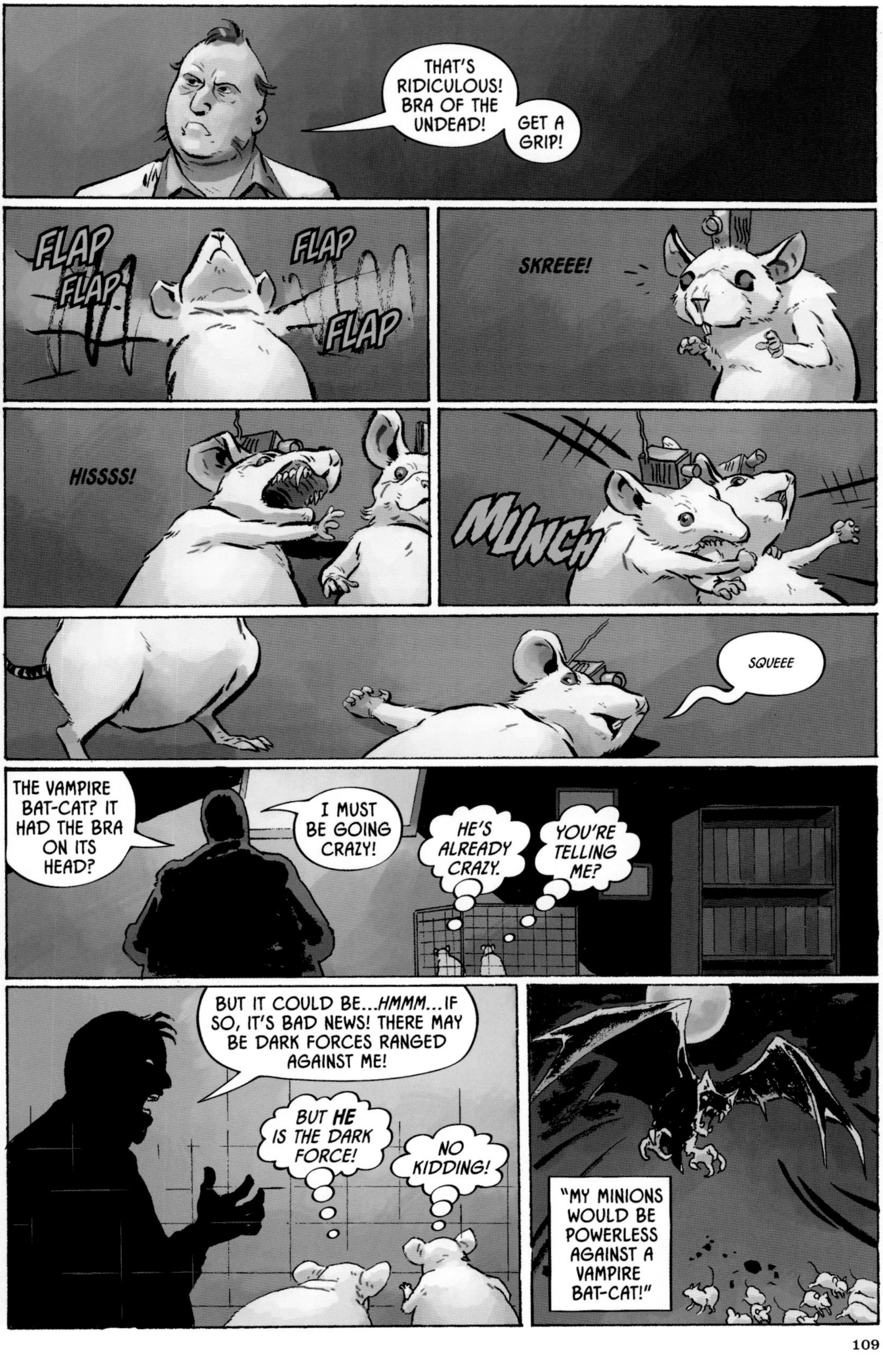
THAT'S RIDICULOUS! BRA OF THE UNDEAD!
GET A GRIP!
FLAP
FLAP
FLAP
FLAP
SKREEE!
HISSSS!
MUNCH
SQUEEE
THE VAMPIRE BAT-CAT? IT HAD THE BRA ON ITS HEAD?
I MUST BE GOING CRAZY!
HE'S ALREADY CRAZY.
YOU'RE TELLING ME?
BUT IT COULD BE...*HMMM*...IF SO, IT'S BAD NEWS! THERE MAY BE DARK FORCES RANGED AGAINST ME!
BUT **HE** IS THE DARK FORCE!
NO KIDDING!
"MY MINIONS WOULD BE POWERLESS AGAINST A VAMPIRE BAT-CAT!"

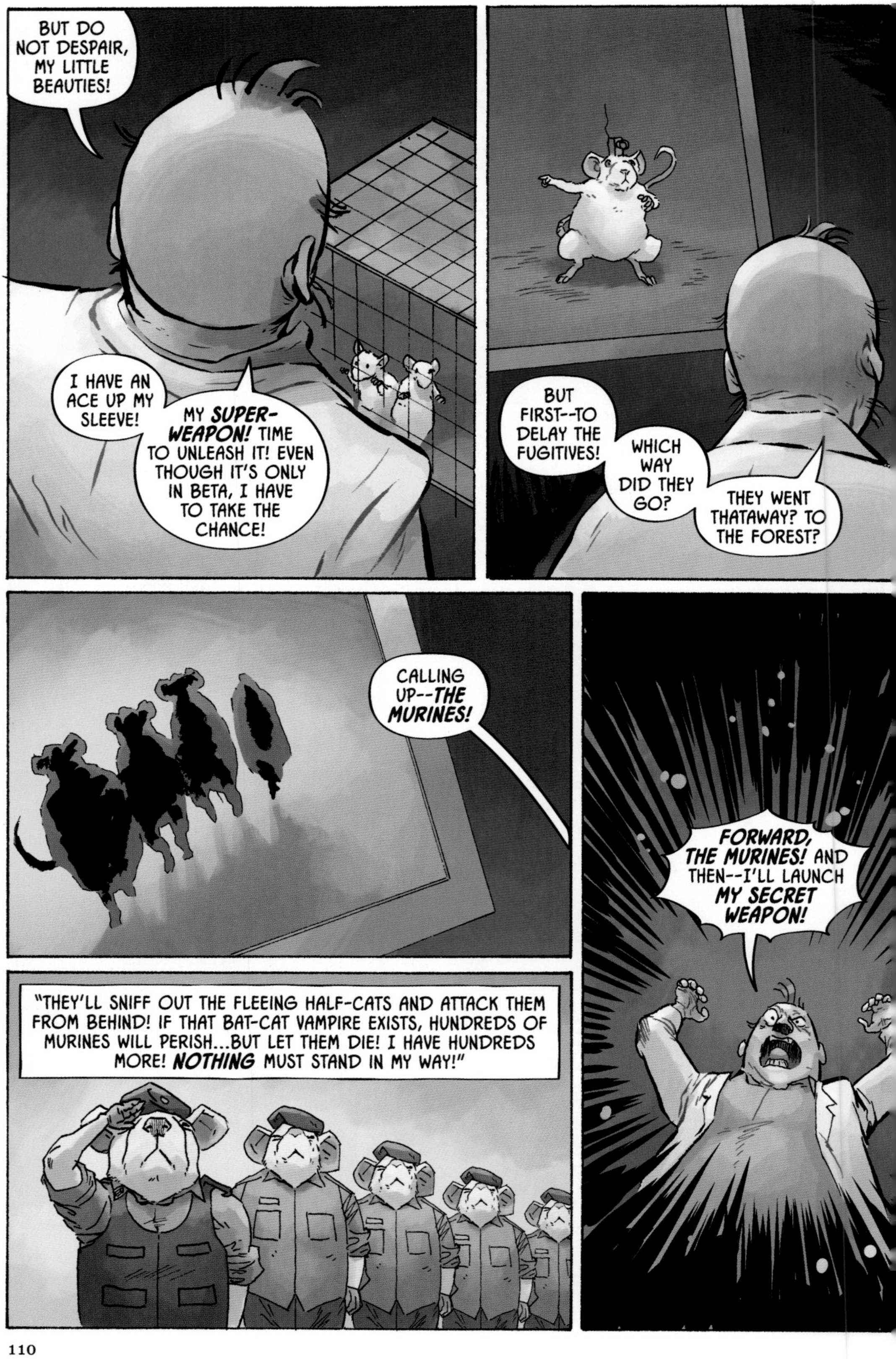
BUT DO NOT DESPAIR, MY LITTLE BEAUTIES!
I HAVE AN ACE UP MY SLEEVE!
MY ***SUPER-WEAPON!*** TIME TO UNLEASH IT! EVEN THOUGH IT'S ONLY IN BETA, I HAVE TO TAKE THE CHANCE!
BUT FIRST--TO DELAY THE FUGITIVES!
WHICH WAY DID THEY GO?
THEY WENT THATAWAY? TO THE FOREST?
CALLING UP--***THE MURINES!***
FORWARD, THE MURINES! AND THEN--I'LL LAUNCH ***MY SECRET WEAPON!***
"THEY'LL SNIFF OUT THE FLEEING HALF-CATS AND ATTACK THEM FROM BEHIND! IF THAT BAT-CAT VAMPIRE EXISTS, HUNDREDS OF MURINES WILL PERISH...BUT LET THEM DIE! I HAVE HUNDREDS MORE! ***NOTHING*** MUST STAND IN MY WAY!"

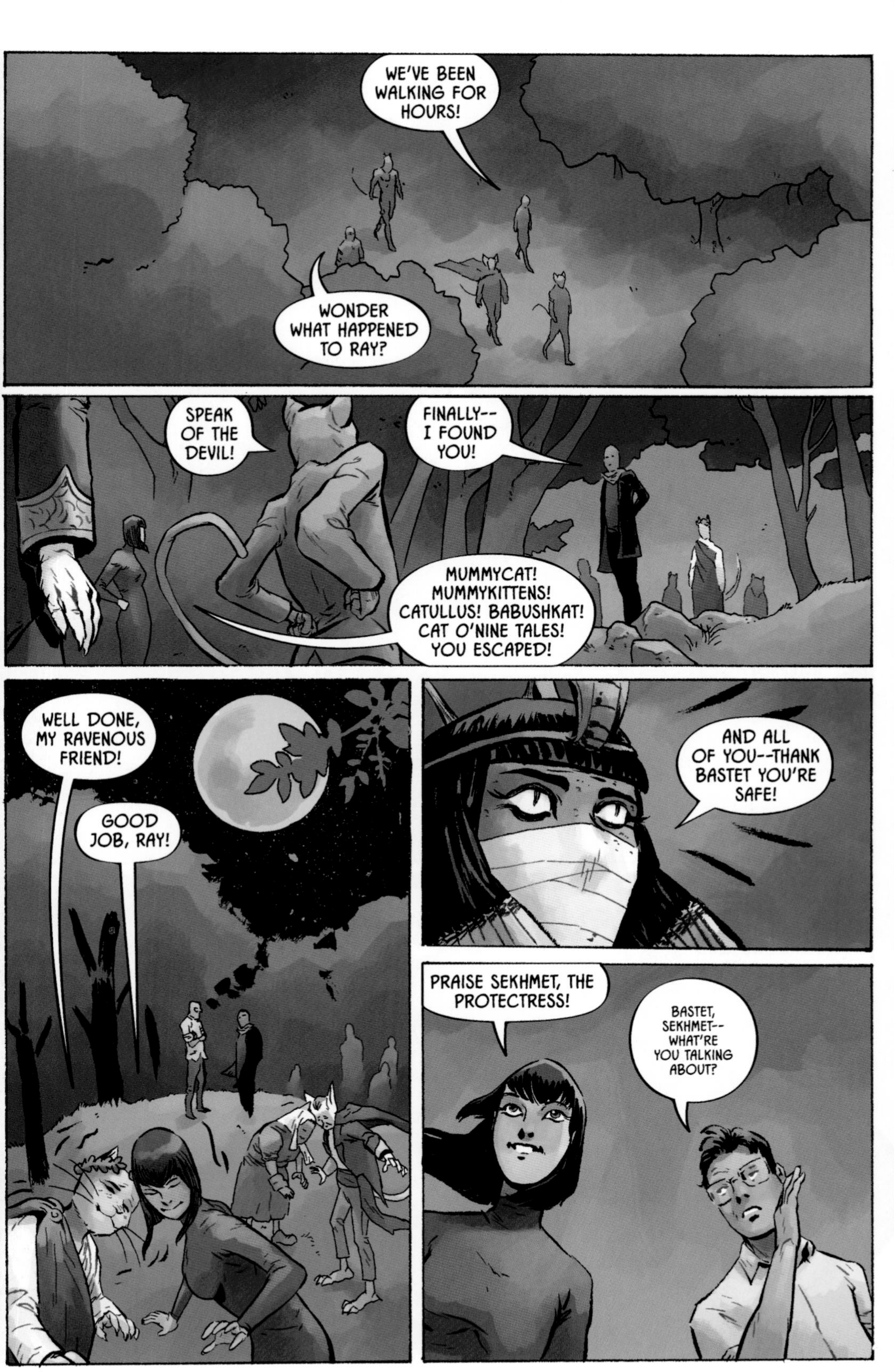
WE'VE BEEN WALKING FOR HOURS!
WONDER WHAT HAPPENED TO RAY?
SPEAK OF THE DEVIL!
FINALLY-- I FOUND YOU!
MUMMYCAT! MUMMYKITTENS! CATULLUS! BABUSHKAT! CAT O'NINE TALES! YOU ESCAPED!
WELL DONE, MY RAVENOUS FRIEND!
GOOD JOB, RAY!
AND ALL OF YOU--THANK BASTET YOU'RE SAFE!
PRAISE SEKHMET, THE PROTECTRESS!
BASTET, SEKHMET-- WHAT'RE YOU TALKING ABOUT?

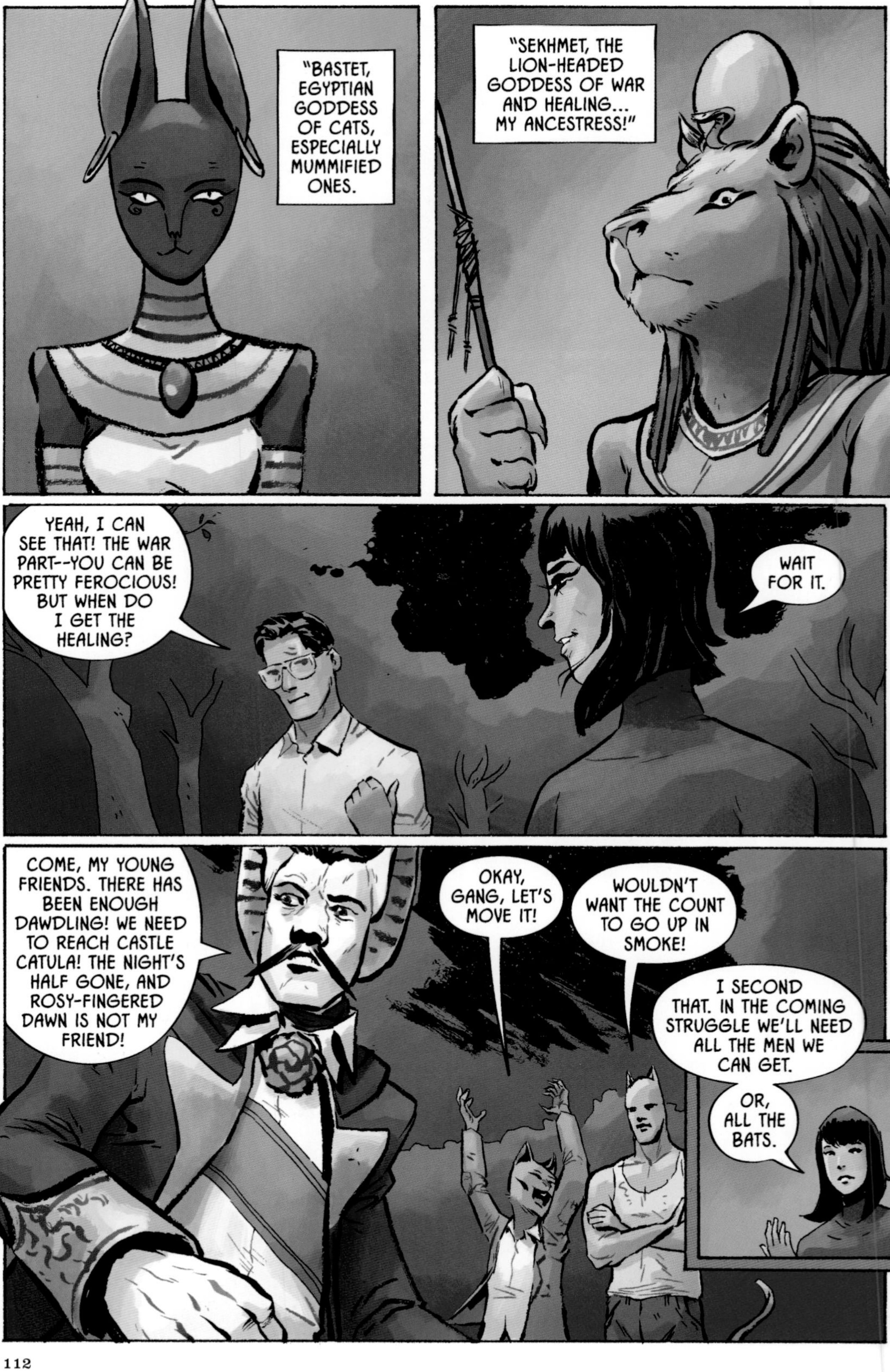
"BASTET, EGYPTIAN GODDESS OF CATS, ESPECIALLY MUMMIFIED ONES.
"SEKHMET, THE LION-HEADED GODDESS OF WAR AND HEALING... MY ANCESTRESS!"
YEAH, I CAN SEE THAT! THE WAR PART--YOU CAN BE PRETTY FEROCIOUS! BUT WHEN DO I GET THE HEALING?
WAIT FOR IT.
COME, MY YOUNG FRIENDS. THERE HAS BEEN ENOUGH DAWDLING! WE NEED TO REACH CASTLE CATULA! THE NIGHT'S HALF GONE, AND ROSY-FINGERED DAWN IS NOT MY FRIEND!
OKAY, GANG, LET'S MOVE IT!
WOULDN'T WANT THE COUNT TO GO UP IN SMOKE!
I SECOND THAT. IN THE COMING STRUGGLE WE'LL NEED ALL THE MEN WE CAN GET.
OR, ALL THE BATS.

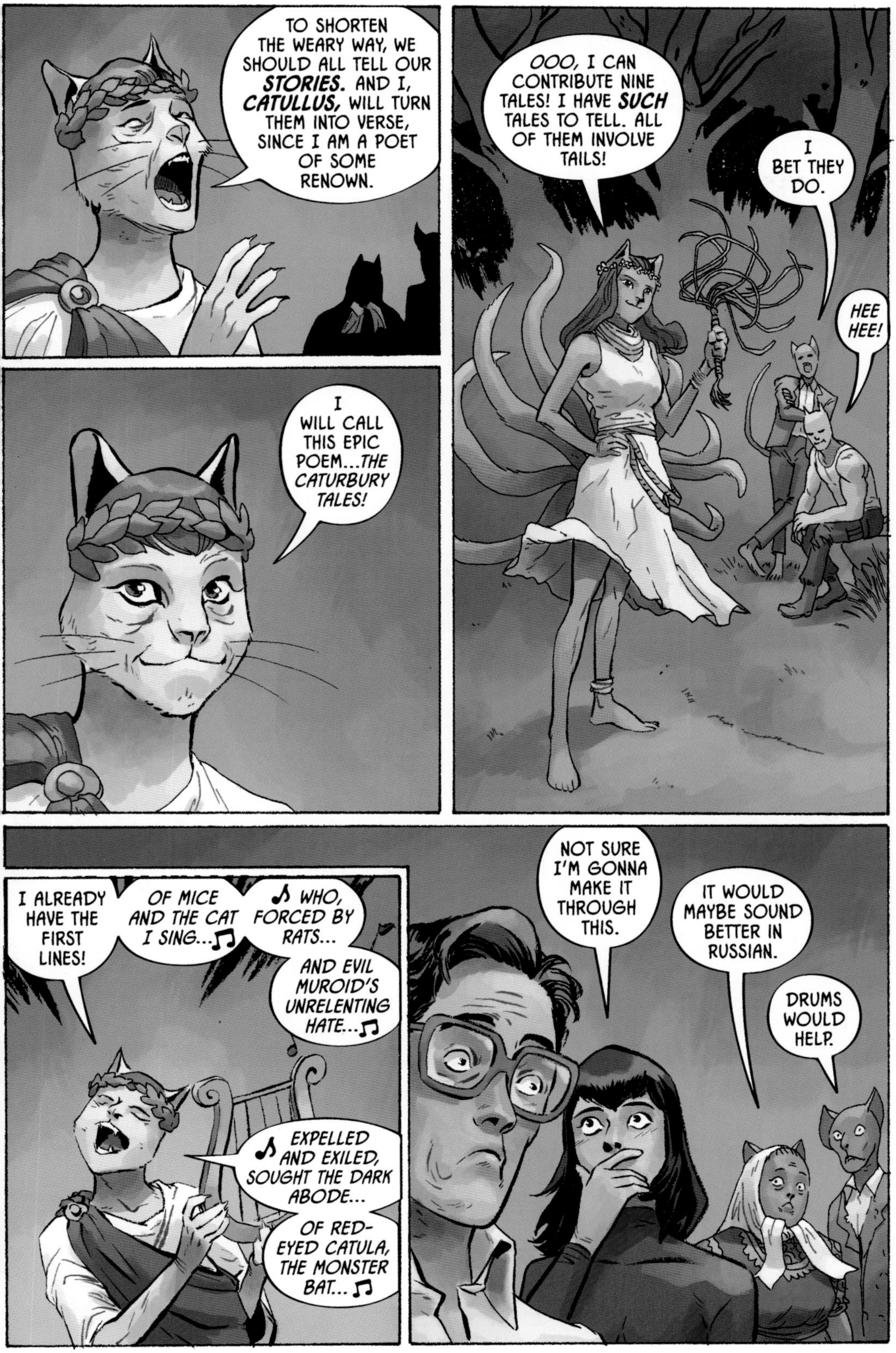
TO SHORTEN THE WEARY WAY, WE SHOULD ALL TELL OUR STORIES. AND I, CATULLUS, WILL TURN THEM INTO VERSE, SINCE I AM A POET OF SOME RENOWN.
I WILL CALL THIS EPIC POEM...THE CATURBURY TALES!
OOO, I CAN CONTRIBUTE NINE TALES! I HAVE SUCH TALES TO TELL. ALL OF THEM INVOLVE TAILS!
I BET THEY DO.
HEE HEE!
I ALREADY HAVE THE FIRST LINES!
OF MICE AND THE CAT I SING...♫
♪ WHO, FORCED BY RATS...
AND EVIL MUROID'S UNRELENTING HATE...♫
♪ EXPELLED AND EXILED, SOUGHT THE DARK ABODE...
OF RED-EYED CATULA, THE MONSTER BAT...♫
NOT SURE I'M GONNA MAKE IT THROUGH THIS.
IT WOULD MAYBE SOUND BETTER IN RUSSIAN.
DRUMS WOULD HELP.

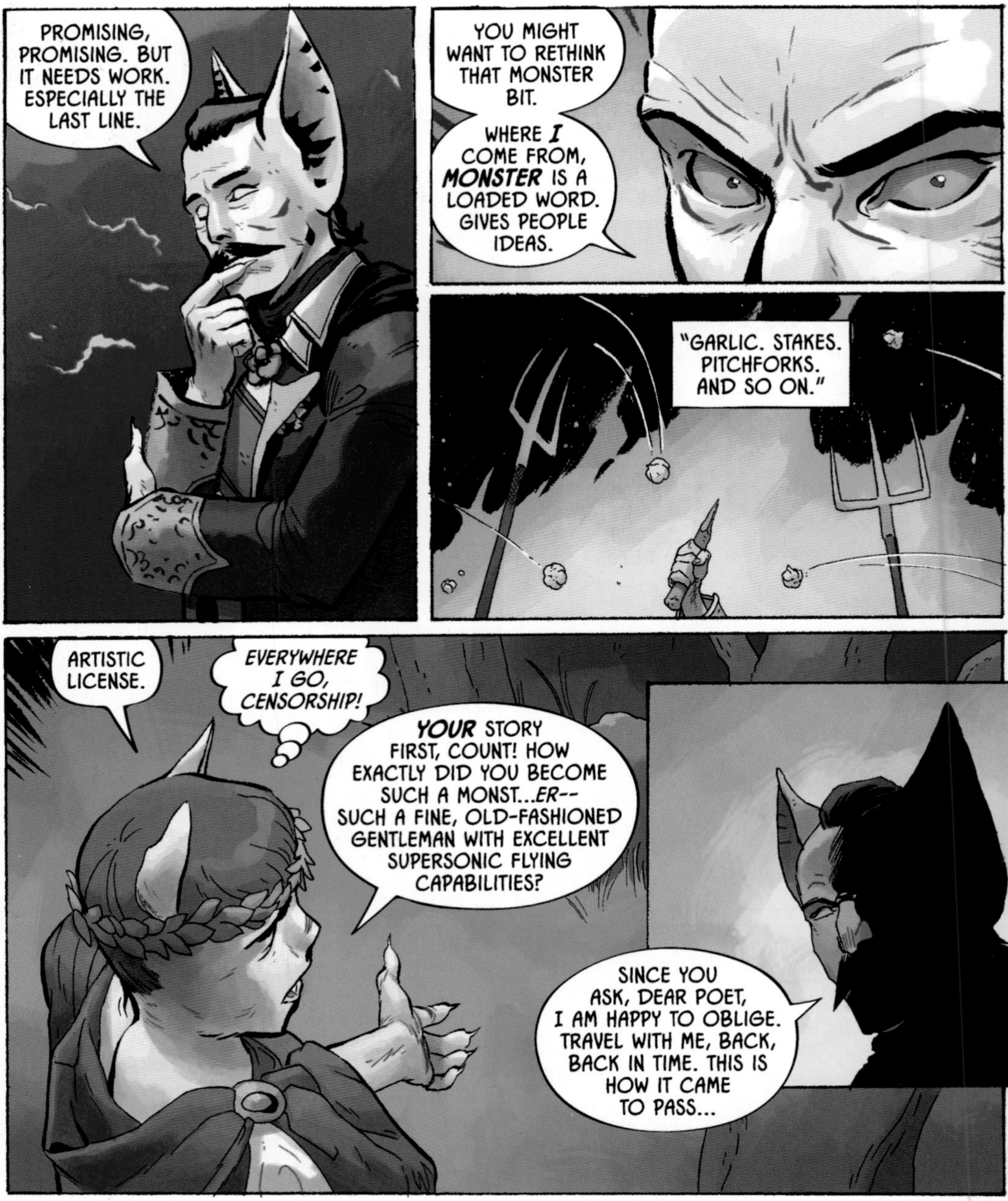
PROMISING, PROMISING. BUT IT NEEDS WORK. ESPECIALLY THE LAST LINE.
YOU MIGHT WANT TO RETHINK THAT MONSTER BIT.
WHERE *I* COME FROM, **MONSTER** IS A LOADED WORD. GIVES PEOPLE IDEAS.
"GARLIC. STAKES. PITCHFORKS. AND SO ON."
ARTISTIC LICENSE.
EVERYWHERE I GO, CENSORSHIP!
YOUR STORY FIRST, COUNT! HOW EXACTLY DID YOU BECOME SUCH A MONST...*ER*-- SUCH A FINE, OLD-FASHIONED GENTLEMAN WITH EXCELLENT SUPERSONIC FLYING CAPABILITIES?
SINCE YOU ASK, DEAR POET, I AM HAPPY TO OBLIGE. TRAVEL WITH ME, BACK, BACK IN TIME. THIS IS HOW IT CAME TO PASS...

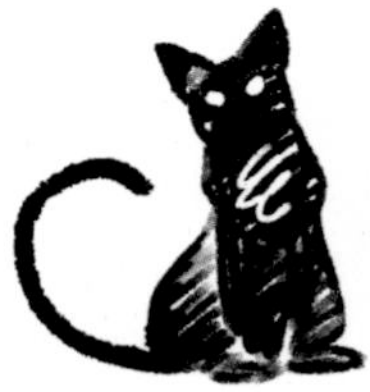

MONSTERS?

Cats are hunters, but they're not monsters—they're just doing what comes naturally. Cat owners are responsible for their pets' behavior, indoors and out, just as with dogs.
Read more at www.catsandbirds.ca

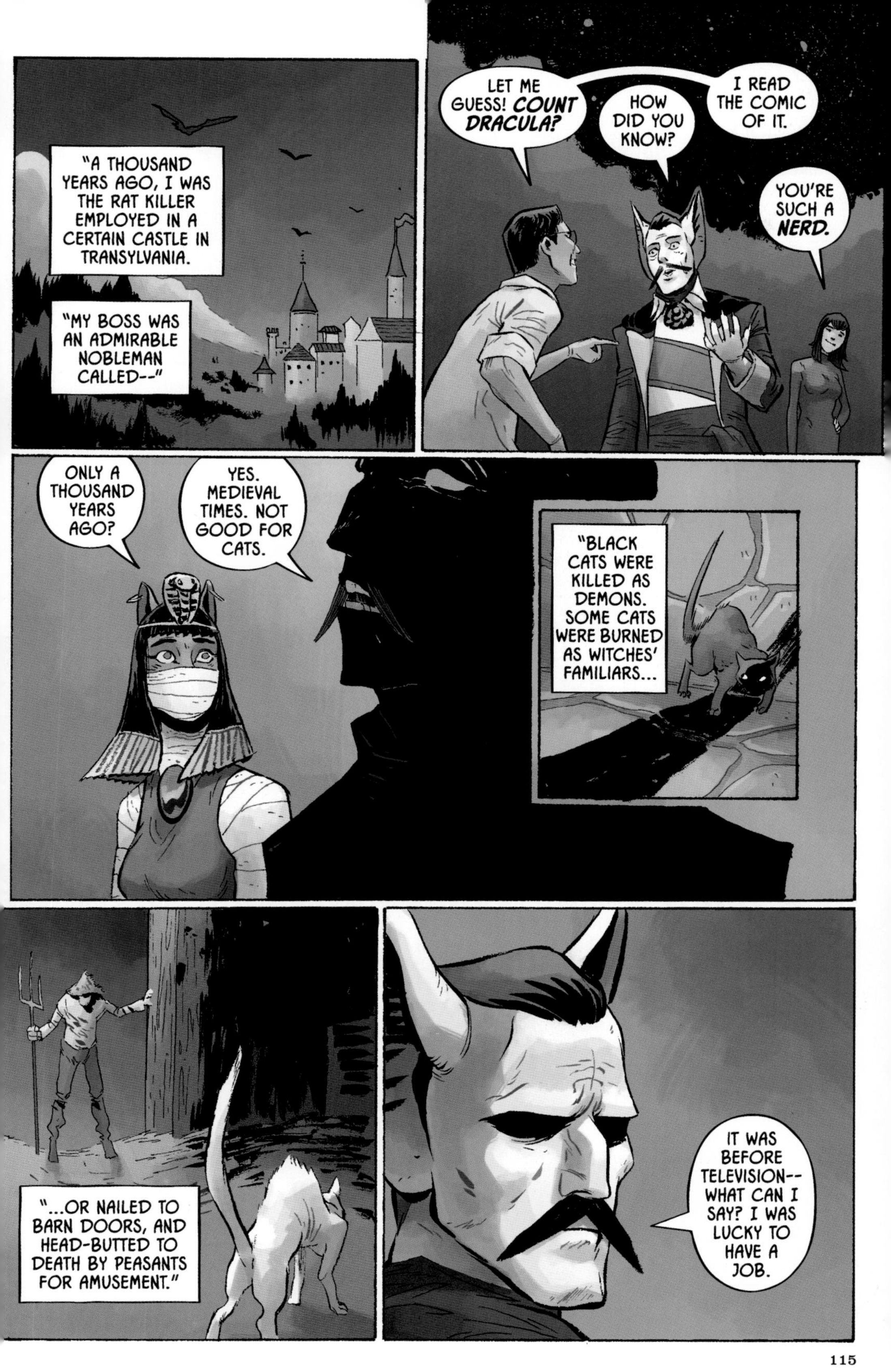
"A THOUSAND YEARS AGO, I WAS THE RAT KILLER EMPLOYED IN A CERTAIN CASTLE IN TRANSYLVANIA.
"MY BOSS WAS AN ADMIRABLE NOBLEMAN CALLED--"
LET ME GUESS! COUNT DRACULA?
HOW DID YOU KNOW?
I READ THE COMIC OF IT.
YOU'RE SUCH A NERD.
ONLY A THOUSAND YEARS AGO?
YES. MEDIEVAL TIMES. NOT GOOD FOR CATS.
"BLACK CATS WERE KILLED AS DEMONS. SOME CATS WERE BURNED AS WITCHES' FAMILIARS...
"...OR NAILED TO BARN DOORS, AND HEAD-BUTTED TO DEATH BY PEASANTS FOR AMUSEMENT."
IT WAS BEFORE TELEVISION-- WHAT CAN I SAY? I WAS LUCKY TO HAVE A JOB.

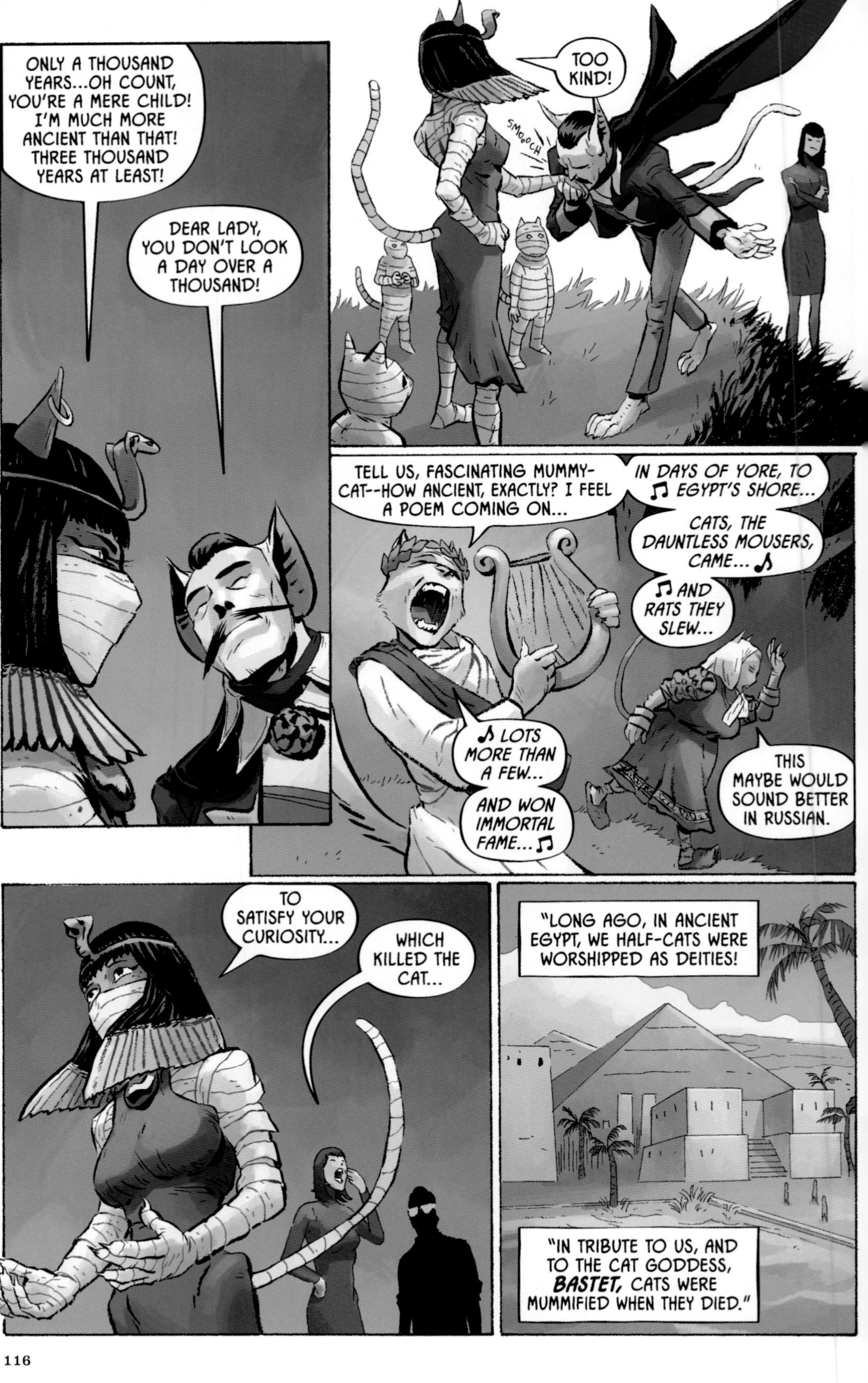
ONLY A THOUSAND YEARS...OH COUNT, YOU'RE A MERE CHILD! I'M MUCH MORE ANCIENT THAN THAT! THREE THOUSAND YEARS AT LEAST!
DEAR LADY, YOU DON'T LOOK A DAY OVER A THOUSAND!
TOO KIND!
SMOOOCH
TELL US, FASCINATING MUMMY-CAT--HOW ANCIENT, EXACTLY? I FEEL A POEM COMING ON...
IN DAYS OF YORE, TO ♫ EGYPT'S SHORE...
CATS, THE DAUNTLESS MOUSERS, CAME... ♪
♫ AND RATS THEY SLEW...
♪ LOTS MORE THAN A FEW...
AND WON IMMORTAL FAME... ♫
THIS MAYBE WOULD SOUND BETTER IN RUSSIAN.
TO SATISFY YOUR CURIOSITY...
WHICH KILLED THE CAT...
"LONG AGO, IN ANCIENT EGYPT, WE HALF-CATS WERE WORSHIPPED AS DEITIES!
"IN TRIBUTE TO US, AND TO THE CAT GODDESS, BASTET, CATS WERE MUMMIFIED WHEN THEY DIED."

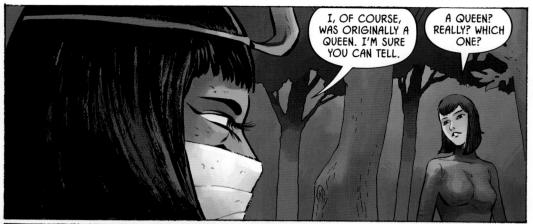

I, OF COURSE, WAS ORIGINALLY A QUEEN. I'M SURE YOU CAN TELL.

A QUEEN? REALLY? WHICH ONE?

"YOU'VE HEARD OF THE FAMOUS NEFERTITI?"

YES-- SO?

HER TOMB HAS NEVER BEEN FOUND. THAT'S BECAUSE I WAS NEVER ENTOMBED.

OR ENTOMBED FOR LONG. AS SUCH.

DEAR LADY, I KNOW THE FEELING.

TOMBS. SO CLAUSTROPHOBIC.

EXCUSE ME-- *YOU* ARE QUEEN NEFERTITI?

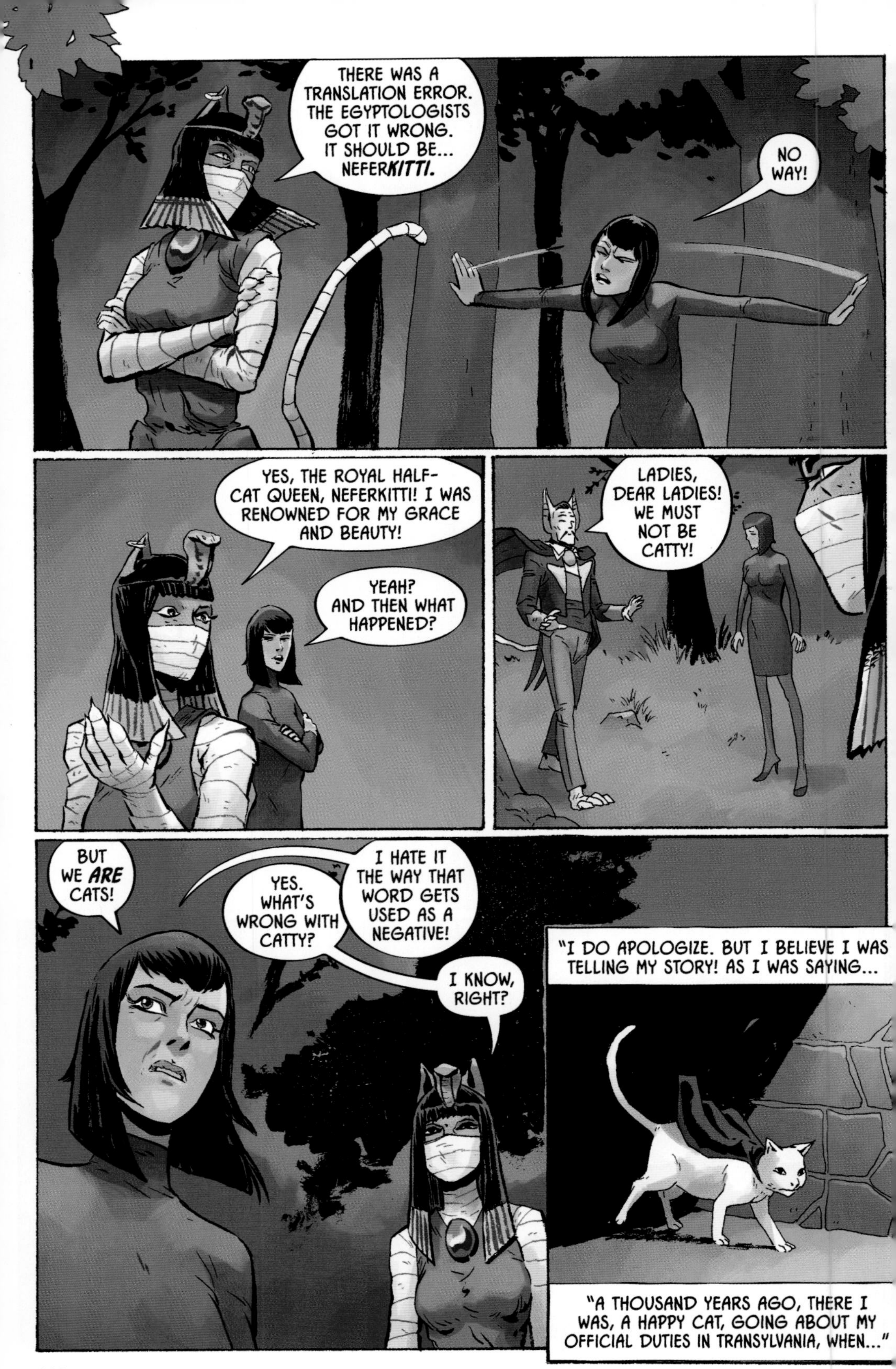
THERE WAS A TRANSLATION ERROR. THE EGYPTOLOGISTS GOT IT WRONG. IT SHOULD BE... NEFERKITTI.
NO WAY!
YES, THE ROYAL HALF-CAT QUEEN, NEFERKITTI! I WAS RENOWNED FOR MY GRACE AND BEAUTY!
YEAH? AND THEN WHAT HAPPENED?
LADIES, DEAR LADIES! WE MUST NOT BE CATTY!
BUT WE ARE CATS!
YES. WHAT'S WRONG WITH CATTY?
I HATE IT THE WAY THAT WORD GETS USED AS A NEGATIVE!
I KNOW, RIGHT?
"I DO APOLOGIZE. BUT I BELIEVE I WAS TELLING MY STORY! AS I WAS SAYING...
"A THOUSAND YEARS AGO, THERE I WAS, A HAPPY CAT, GOING ABOUT MY OFFICIAL DUTIES IN TRANSYLVANIA, WHEN..."

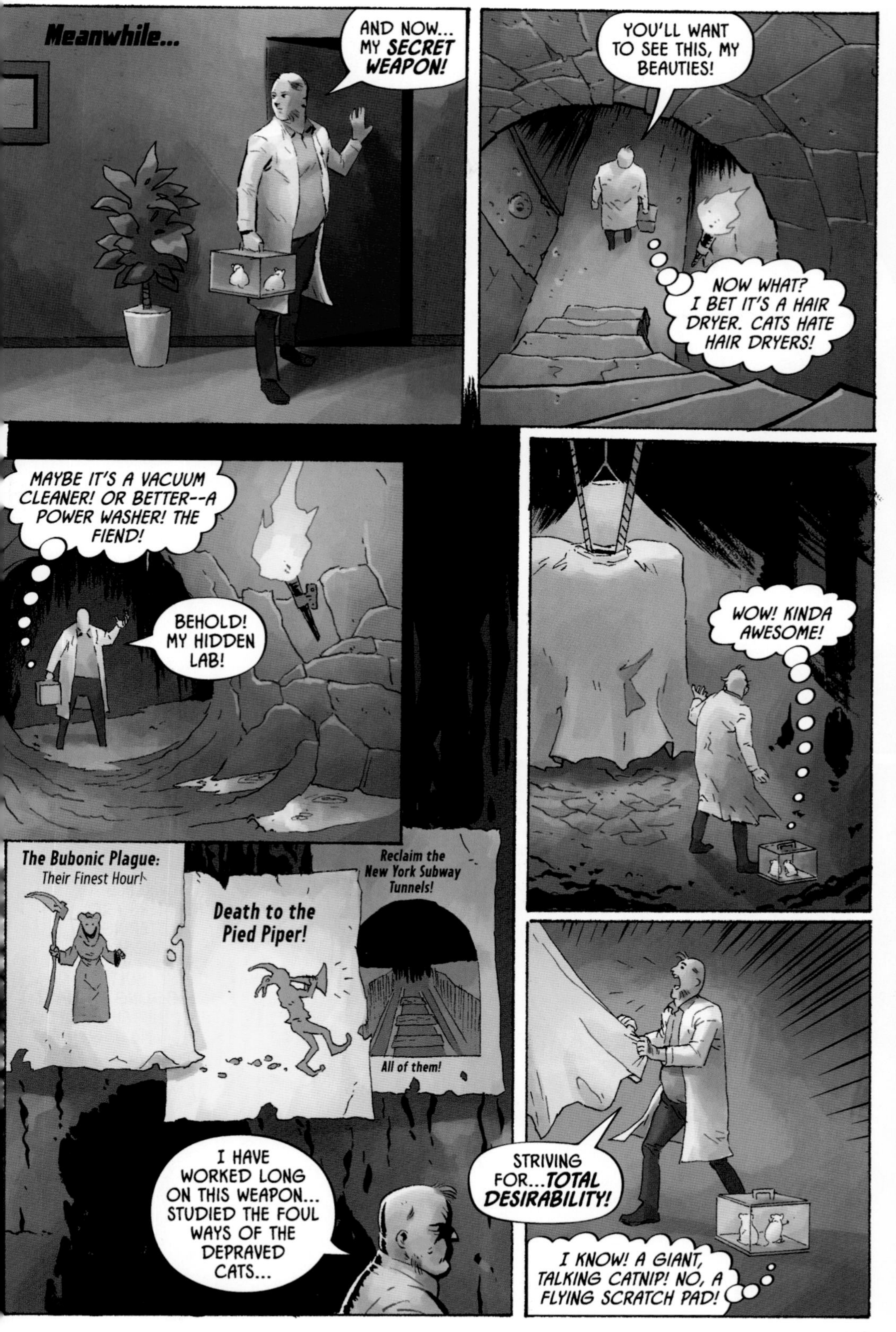

Meanwhile...
AND NOW... MY SECRET WEAPON!
YOU'LL WANT TO SEE THIS, MY BEAUTIES!
NOW WHAT? I BET IT'S A HAIR DRYER. CATS HATE HAIR DRYERS!
MAYBE IT'S A VACUUM CLEANER! OR BETTER--A POWER WASHER! THE FIEND!
BEHOLD! MY HIDDEN LAB!
WOW! KINDA AWESOME!
The Bubonic Plague: Their Finest Hour!
Death to the Pied Piper!
Reclaim the New York Subway Tunnels!
All of them!
I HAVE WORKED LONG ON THIS WEAPON... STUDIED THE FOUL WAYS OF THE DEPRAVED CATS...
STRIVING FOR...TOTAL DESIRABILITY!
I KNOW! A GIANT, TALKING CATNIP! NO, A FLYING SCRATCH PAD!

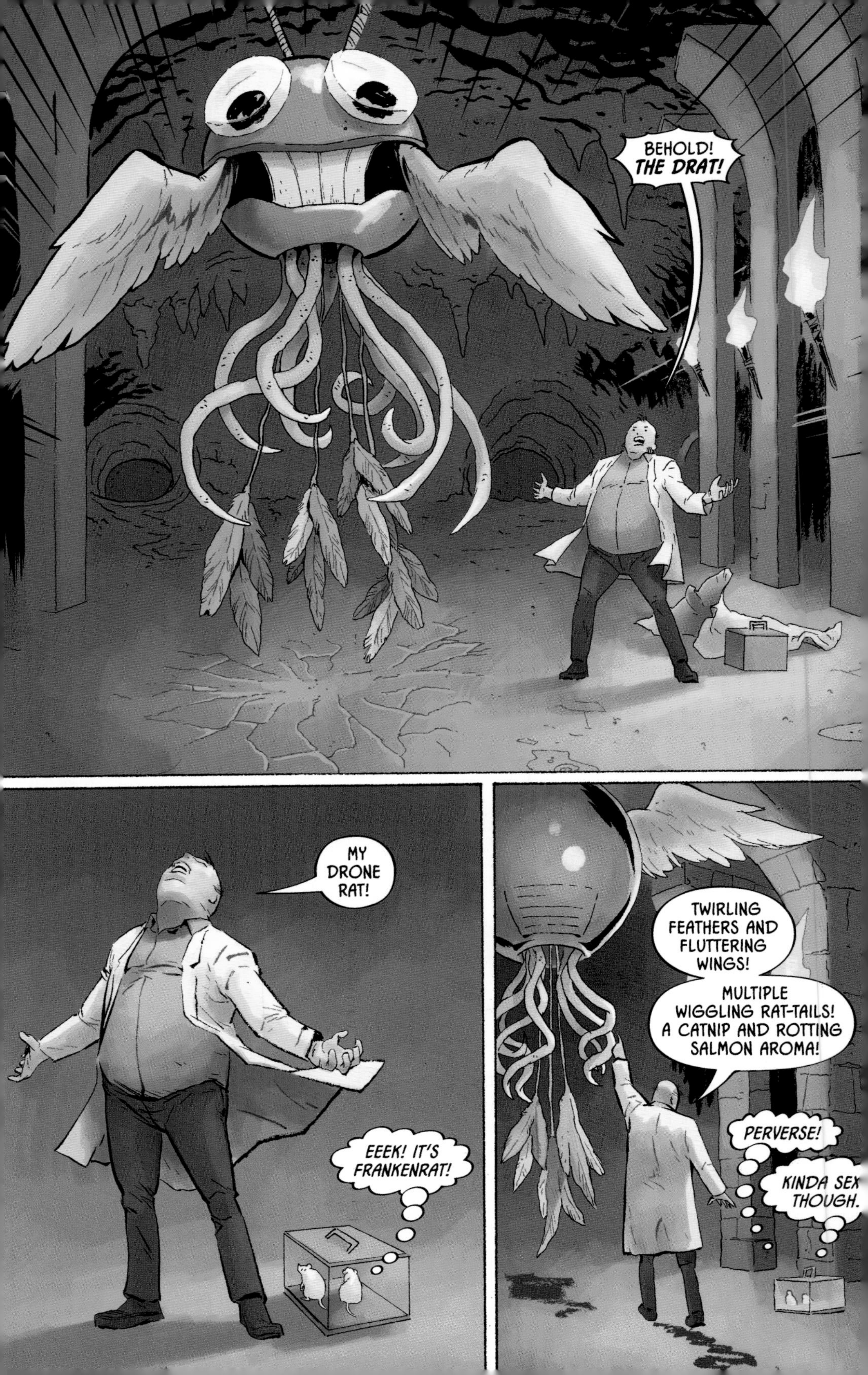
BEHOLD! **THE DRAT!**
MY DRONE RAT!
EEEK! IT'S FRANKENRAT!
TWIRLING FEATHERS AND FLUTTERING WINGS!
MULTIPLE WIGGLING RAT-TAILS! A CATNIP AND ROTTING SALMON AROMA!
PERVERSE!
KINDA SEX THOUGH.

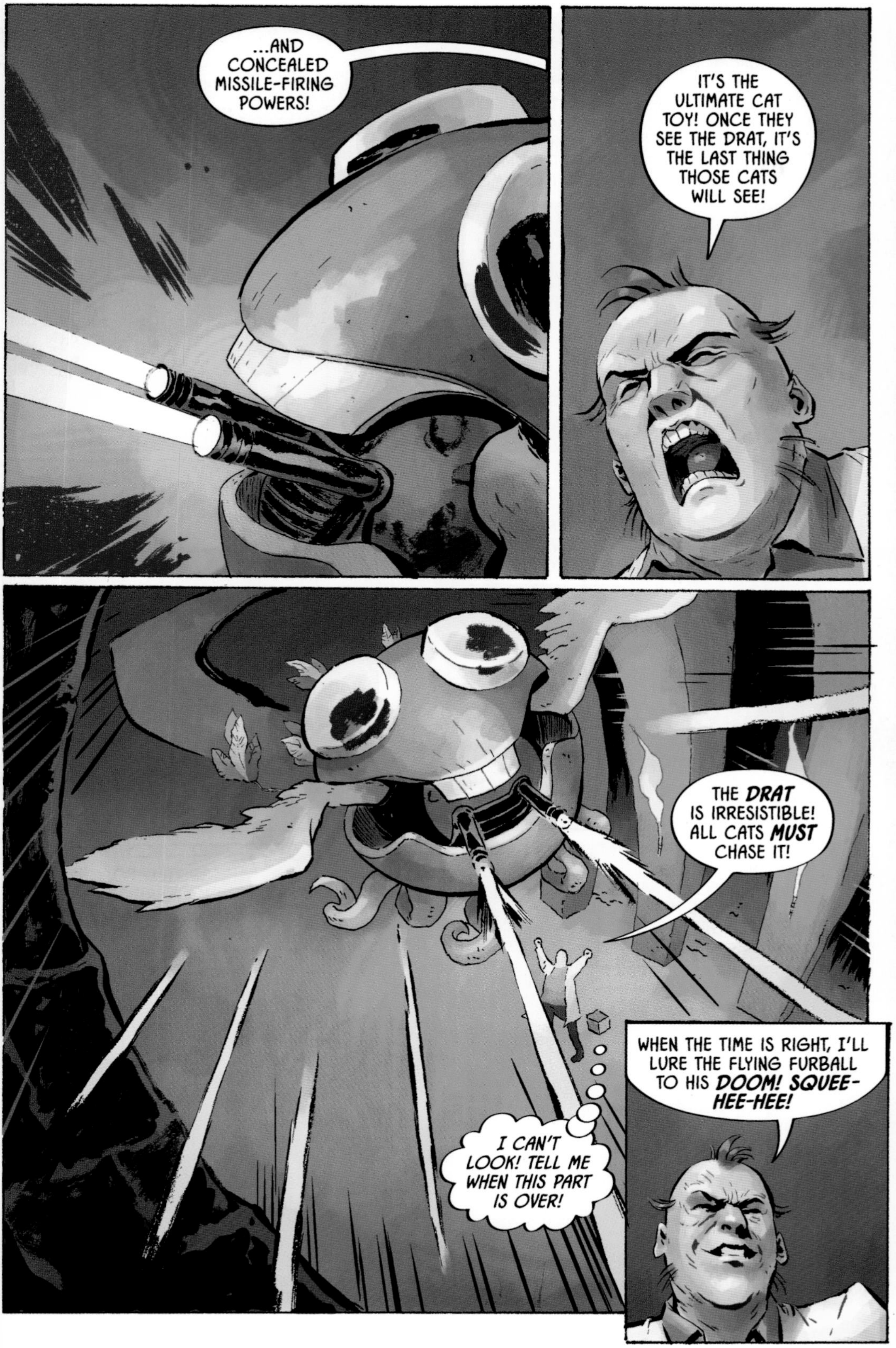
...AND CONCEALED MISSILE-FIRING POWERS!
IT'S THE ULTIMATE CAT TOY! ONCE THEY SEE THE DRAT, IT'S THE LAST THING THOSE CATS WILL SEE!
THE **DRAT** IS IRRESISTIBLE! ALL CATS **MUST** CHASE IT!
WHEN THE TIME IS RIGHT, I'LL LURE THE FLYING FURBALL TO HIS ***DOOM! SQUEE-HEE-HEE!***
I CAN'T LOOK! TELL ME WHEN THIS PART IS OVER!

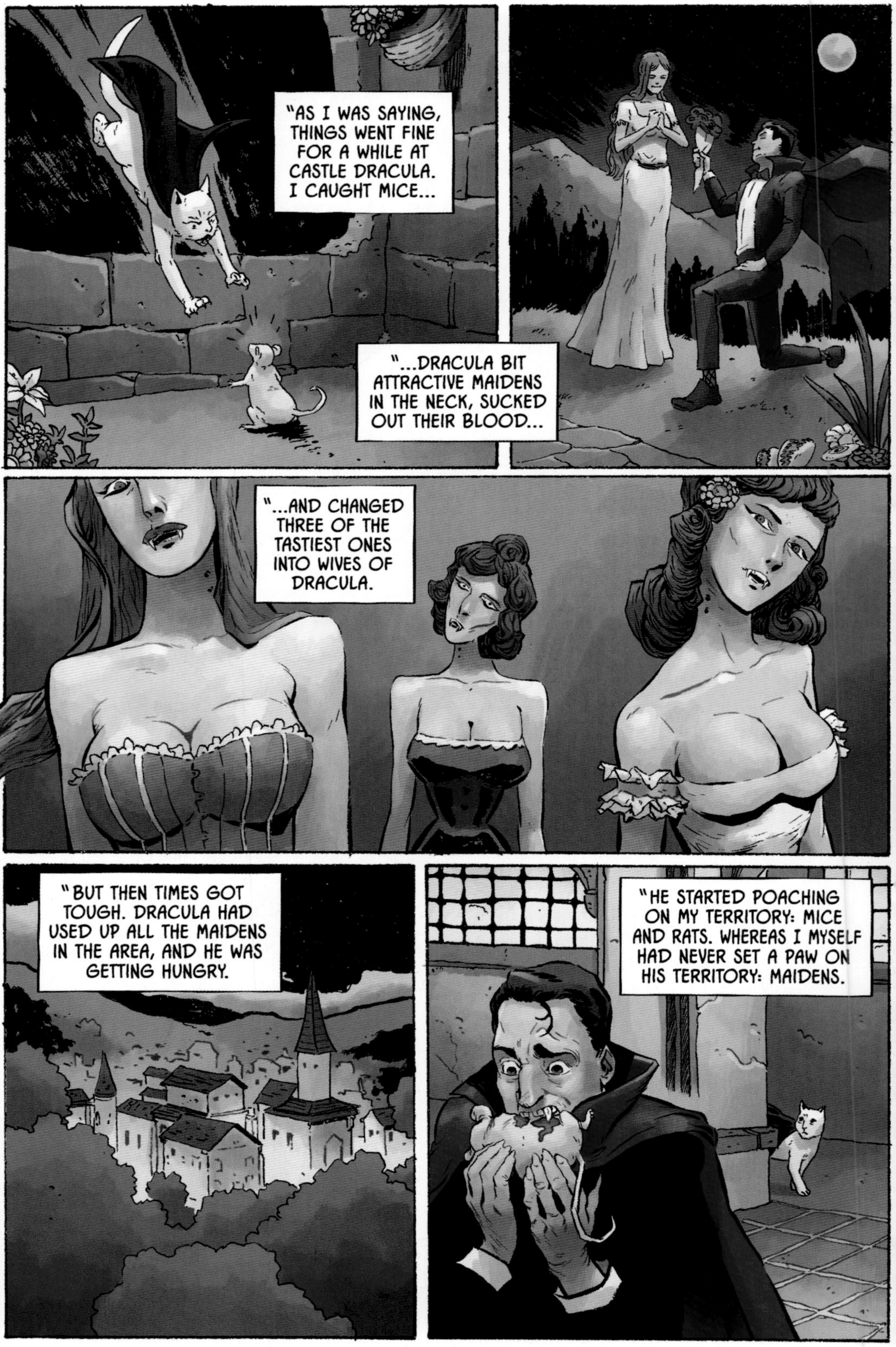
"AS I WAS SAYING, THINGS WENT FINE FOR A WHILE AT CASTLE DRACULA. I CAUGHT MICE...
"...DRACULA BIT ATTRACTIVE MAIDENS IN THE NECK, SUCKED OUT THEIR BLOOD...
"...AND CHANGED THREE OF THE TASTIEST ONES INTO WIVES OF DRACULA.
"BUT THEN TIMES GOT TOUGH. DRACULA HAD USED UP ALL THE MAIDENS IN THE AREA, AND HE WAS GETTING HUNGRY.
"HE STARTED POACHING ON MY TERRITORY: MICE AND RATS. WHEREAS I MYSELF HAD NEVER SET A PAW ON HIS TERRITORY: MAIDENS.

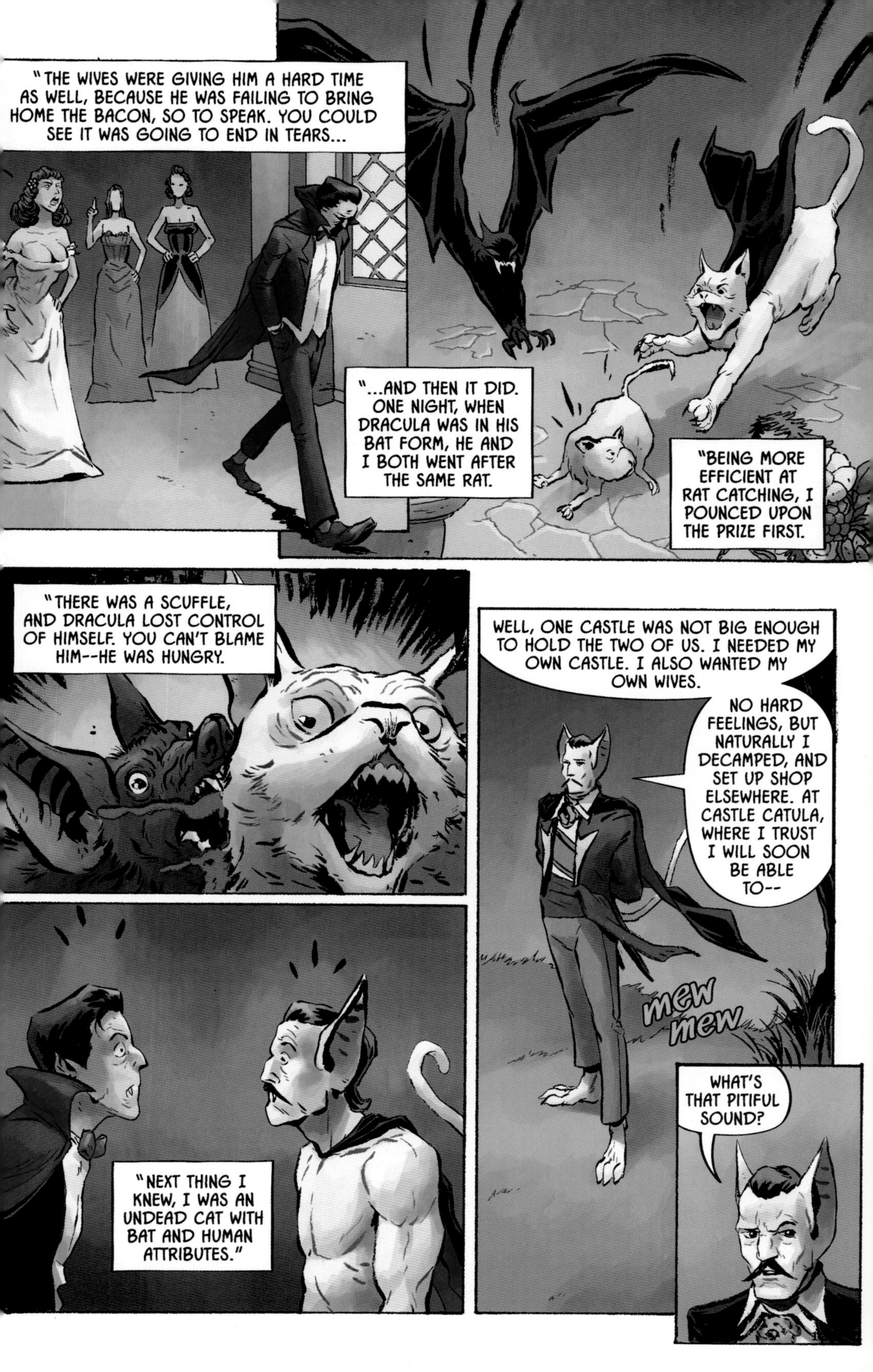
"THE WIVES WERE GIVING HIM A HARD TIME AS WELL, BECAUSE HE WAS FAILING TO BRING HOME THE BACON, SO TO SPEAK. YOU COULD SEE IT WAS GOING TO END IN TEARS...
"...AND THEN IT DID. ONE NIGHT, WHEN DRACULA WAS IN HIS BAT FORM, HE AND I BOTH WENT AFTER THE SAME RAT.
"BEING MORE EFFICIENT AT RAT CATCHING, I POUNCED UPON THE PRIZE FIRST.
"THERE WAS A SCUFFLE, AND DRACULA LOST CONTROL OF HIMSELF. YOU CAN'T BLAME HIM--HE WAS HUNGRY.
"NEXT THING I KNEW, I WAS AN UNDEAD CAT WITH BAT AND HUMAN ATTRIBUTES."
WELL, ONE CASTLE WAS NOT BIG ENOUGH TO HOLD THE TWO OF US. I NEEDED MY OWN CASTLE. I ALSO WANTED MY OWN WIVES.
NO HARD FEELINGS, BUT NATURALLY I DECAMPED, AND SET UP SHOP ELSEWHERE. AT CASTLE CATULA, WHERE I TRUST I WILL SOON BE ABLE TO--
mew mew
WHAT'S THAT PITIFUL SOUND?

mew mew BOO-HOO...
OOO LOOK, A LITTLE HALF-CAT!
WHAT ARE YOU DOING IN THE FOREST ALL BY YOURSELF?
BOO-HOO! MEW MEW! I WAS LEFT IN THE WOODS BY SOME KITTEN DUMPERS!
KITTEN DUMPERS! THEY ARE THE WORST!
KITTEN DUMPERS? WHAT ARE THOSE?
IT MAKES ME SO ANGRY!
THEY FORCE FEMALE CATS TO HAVE LITTER AFTER LITTER OF KITTENS BECAUSE THEY'RE TOO LAZY TO GET THE CATS SPAYED.
"THEN THEY TAKE THE KITTENS AND DUMP THEM IN THE FOREST!"
THAT'S WHAT THEY DID...ME AND MY FOUR BROTHERS AND SISTERS...

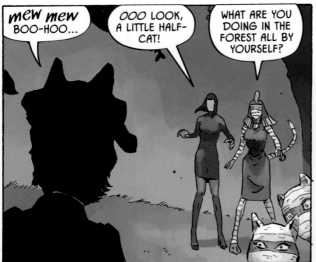

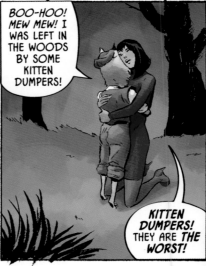

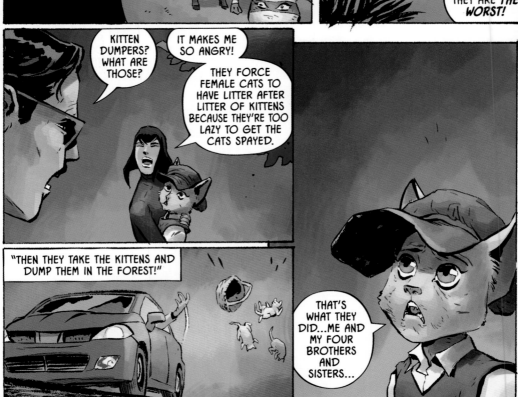

CAT ABANDON

Cats may behave with abandon, but cat abandonment is animal cruelty and contributes to the feral cat population. Abandoning an animal is illegal in Canada and most states in the US. Take any unwanted cats to a shelter, and get your new cat there, too! Read more at www.catsandbirds.ca

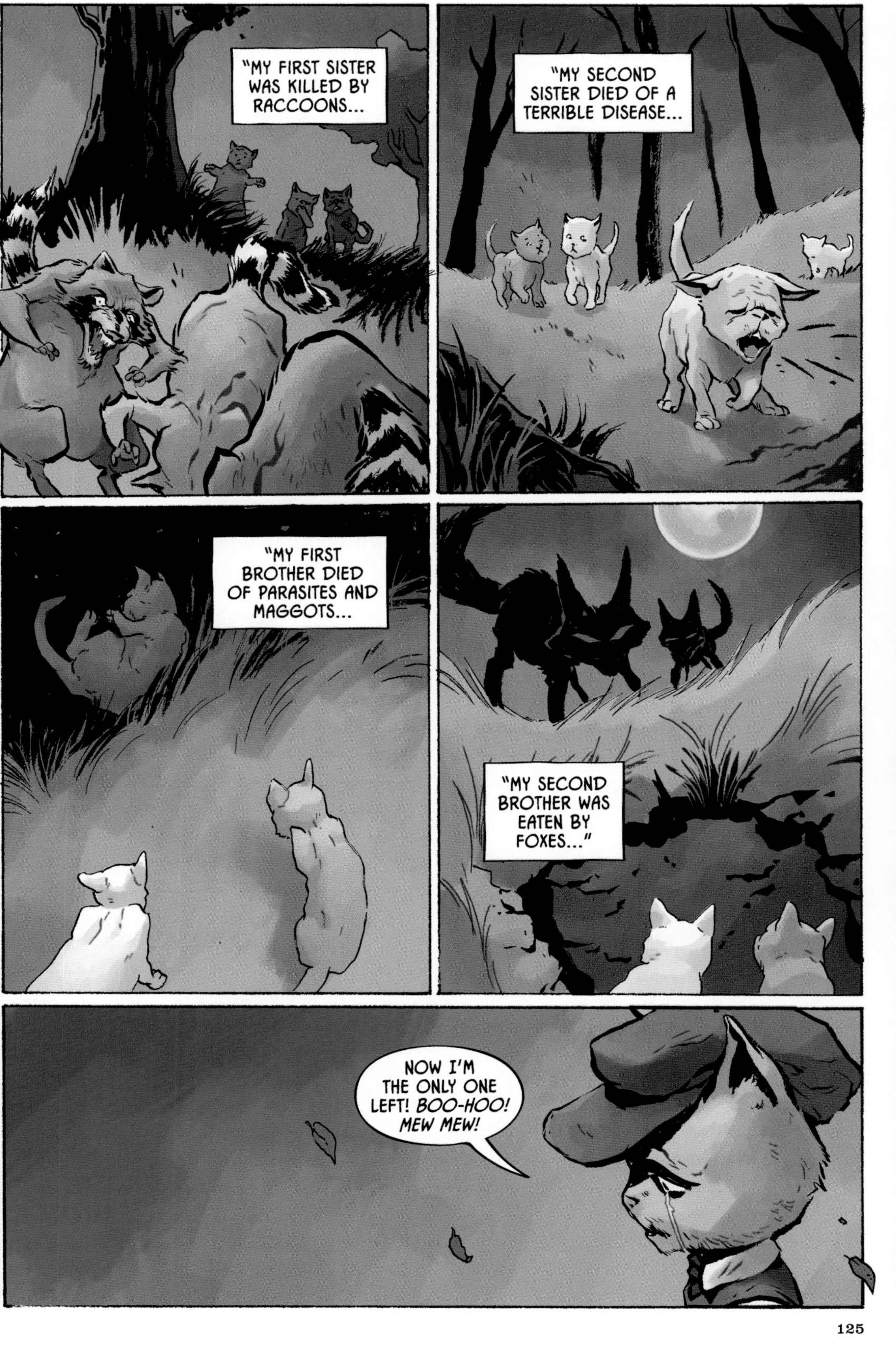
"MY FIRST SISTER WAS KILLED BY RACCOONS...
"MY SECOND SISTER DIED OF A TERRIBLE DISEASE...
"MY FIRST BROTHER DIED OF PARASITES AND MAGGOTS...
"MY SECOND BROTHER WAS EATEN BY FOXES..."
NOW I'M THE ONLY ONE LEFT! *BOO-HOO! MEW MEW!*

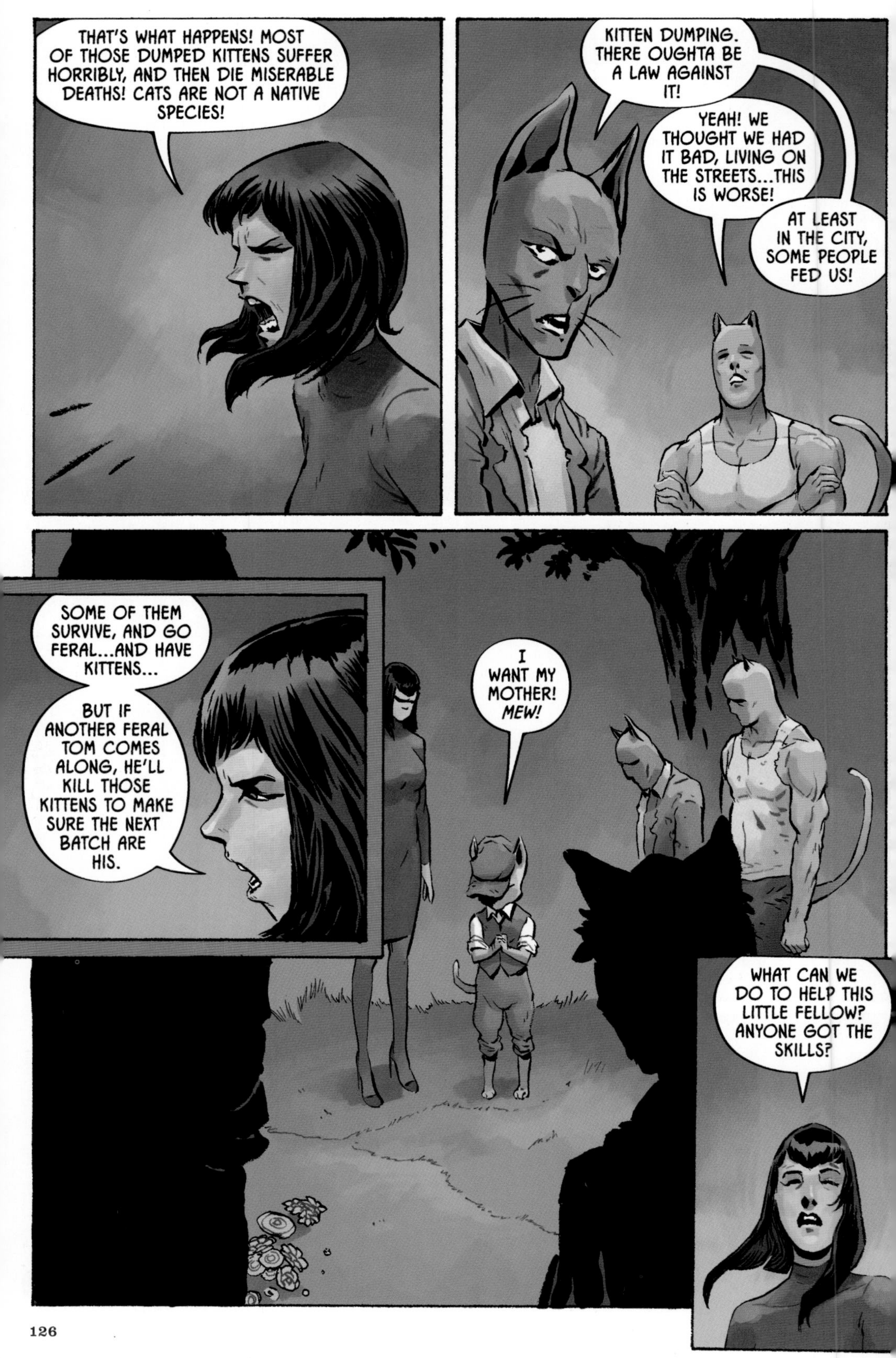
THAT'S WHAT HAPPENS! MOST OF THOSE DUMPED KITTENS SUFFER HORRIBLY, AND THEN DIE MISERABLE DEATHS! CATS ARE NOT A NATIVE SPECIES!
KITTEN DUMPING. THERE OUGHTA BE A LAW AGAINST IT!
YEAH! WE THOUGHT WE HAD IT BAD, LIVING ON THE STREETS...THIS IS WORSE!
AT LEAST IN THE CITY, SOME PEOPLE FED US!
SOME OF THEM SURVIVE, AND GO FERAL...AND HAVE KITTENS...
BUT IF ANOTHER FERAL TOM COMES ALONG, HE'LL KILL THOSE KITTENS TO MAKE SURE THE NEXT BATCH ARE HIS.
I WANT MY MOTHER! *MEW!*
WHAT CAN WE DO TO HELP THIS LITTLE FELLOW? ANYONE GOT THE SKILLS?

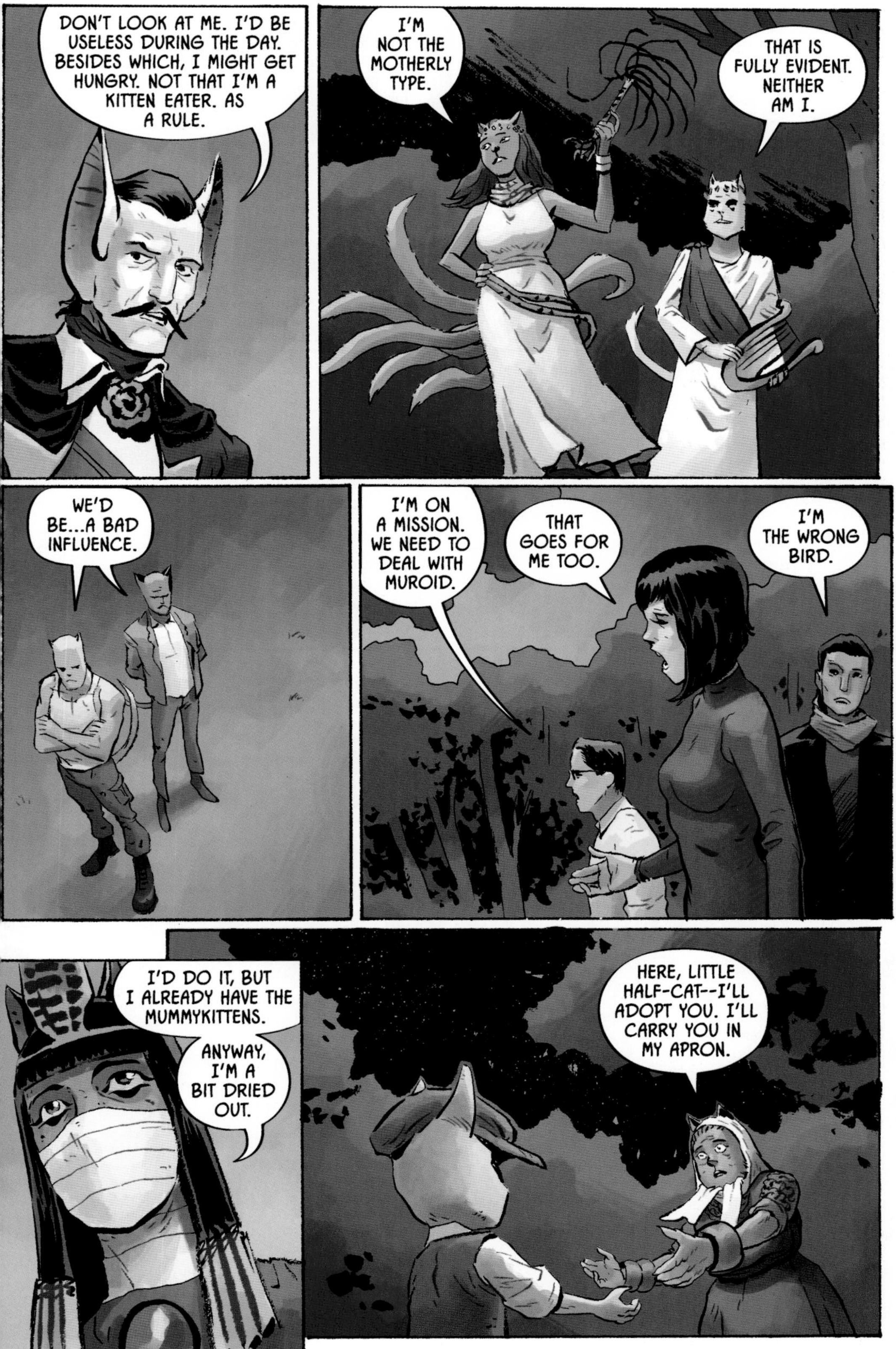
DON'T LOOK AT ME. I'D BE USELESS DURING THE DAY. BESIDES WHICH, I MIGHT GET HUNGRY. NOT THAT I'M A KITTEN EATER. AS A RULE.
I'M NOT THE MOTHERLY TYPE.
THAT IS FULLY EVIDENT. NEITHER AM I.
WE'D BE...A BAD INFLUENCE.
I'M ON A MISSION. WE NEED TO DEAL WITH MUROID.
THAT GOES FOR ME TOO.
I'M THE WRONG BIRD.
I'D DO IT, BUT I ALREADY HAVE THE MUMMYKITTENS.
ANYWAY, I'M A BIT DRIED OUT.
HERE, LITTLE HALF-CAT--I'LL ADOPT YOU. I'LL CARRY YOU IN MY APRON.

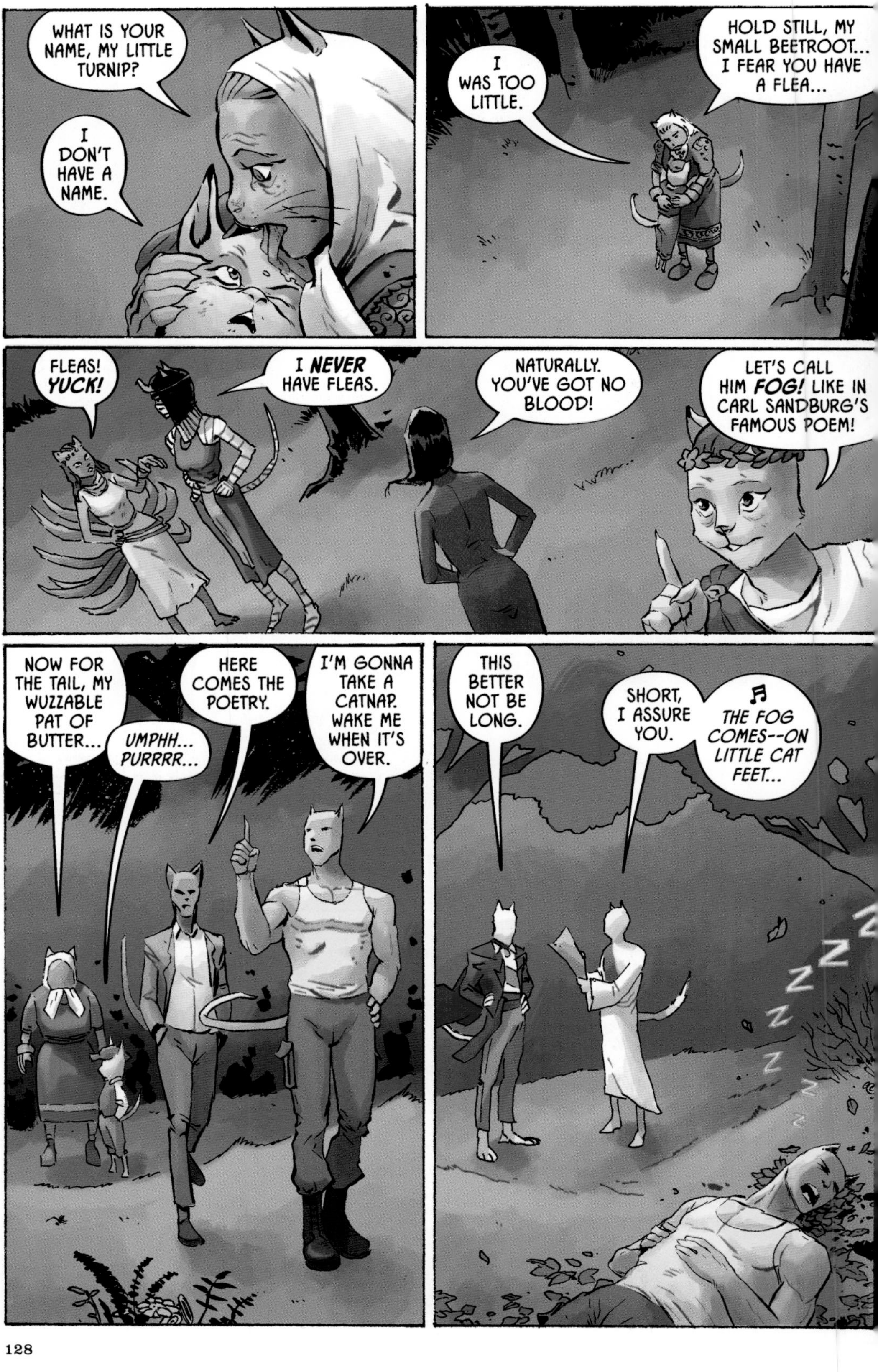
WHAT IS YOUR NAME, MY LITTLE TURNIP?
I DON'T HAVE A NAME.
I WAS TOO LITTLE.
HOLD STILL, MY SMALL BEETROOT... I FEAR YOU HAVE A FLEA...
FLEAS! ***YUCK!***
I ***NEVER*** HAVE FLEAS.
NATURALLY. YOU'VE GOT NO BLOOD!
LET'S CALL HIM ***FOG!*** LIKE IN CARL SANDBURG'S FAMOUS POEM!
NOW FOR THE TAIL, MY WUZZABLE PAT OF BUTTER...
UMPHH... PURRRR...
HERE COMES THE POETRY.
I'M GONNA TAKE A CATNAP. WAKE ME WHEN IT'S OVER.
THIS BETTER NOT BE LONG.
SHORT, I ASSURE YOU.
♬ *THE FOG COMES--ON LITTLE CAT FEET...*
Z Z Z Z Z Z Z Z

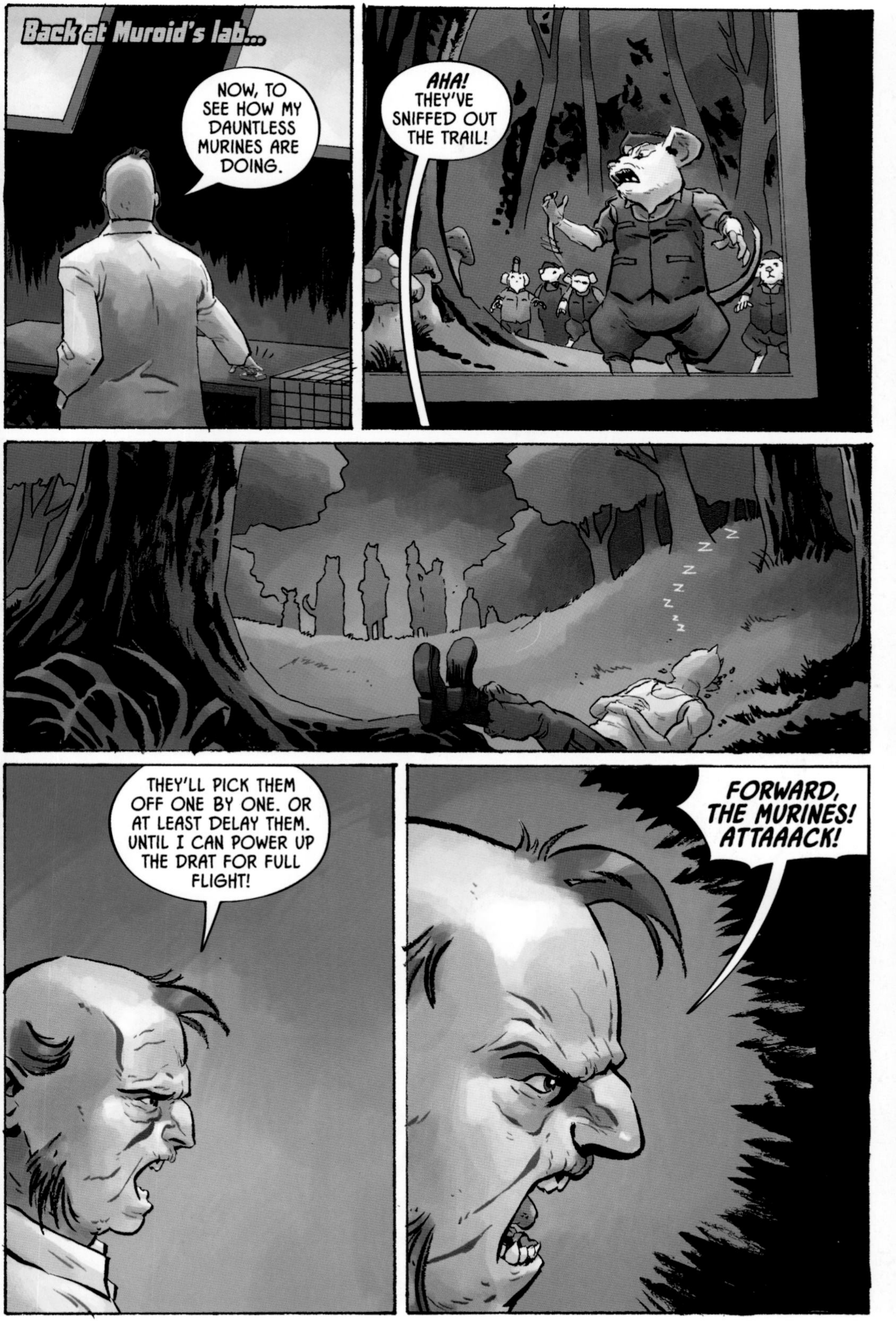
Back at Muroid's lab...
NOW, TO SEE HOW MY DAUNTLESS MURINES ARE DOING.
AHA! THEY'VE SNIFFED OUT THE TRAIL!
Z Z Z Z Z Z Z
THEY'LL PICK THEM OFF ONE BY ONE. OR AT LEAST DELAY THEM. UNTIL I CAN POWER UP THE DRAT FOR FULL FLIGHT!
FORWARD, THE MURINES! ATTAAACK!

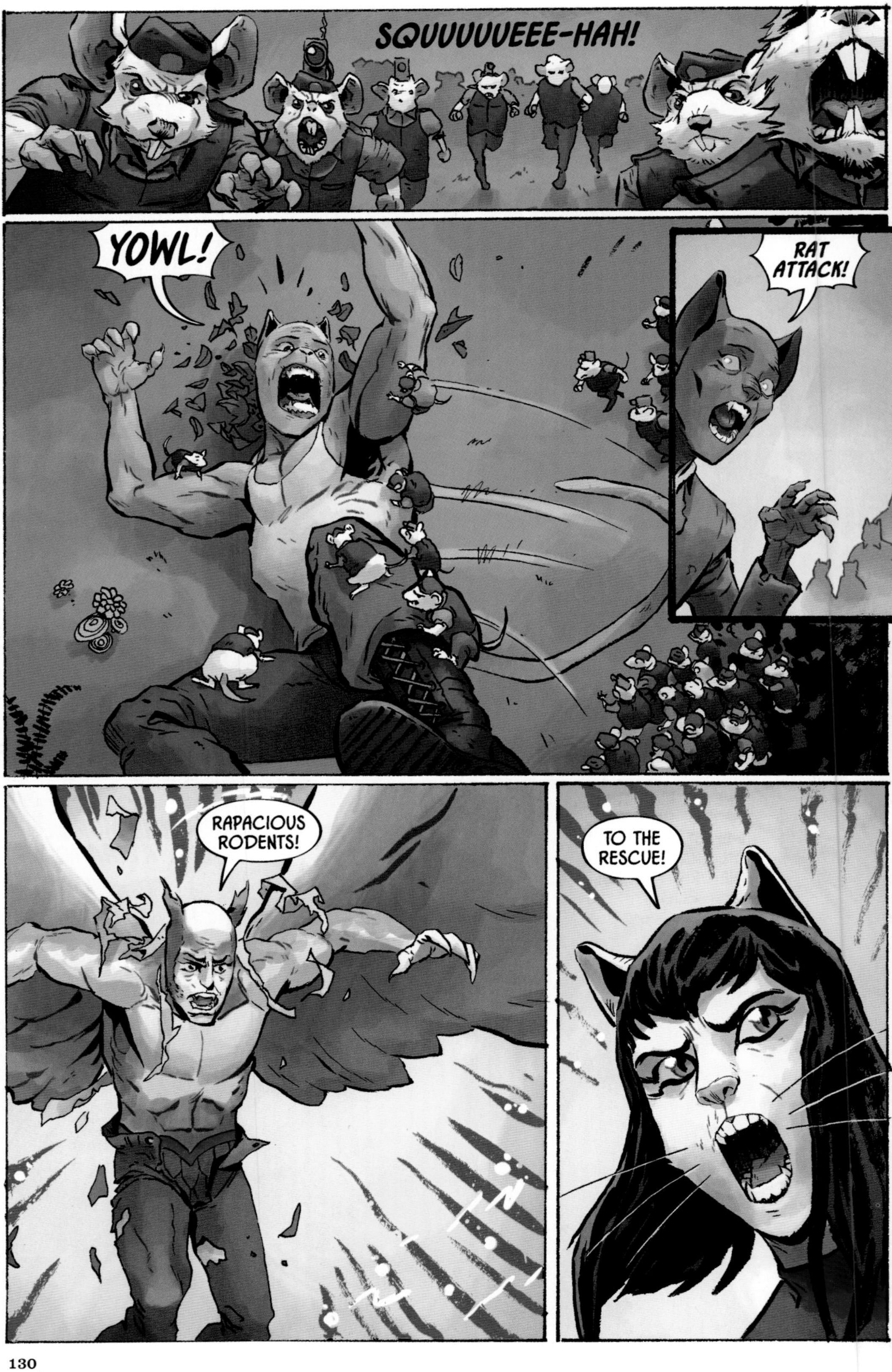
SQUUUUUEEE-HAH!
YOWL!
RAT ATTACK!
RAPACIOUS RODENTS!
TO THE RESCUE!

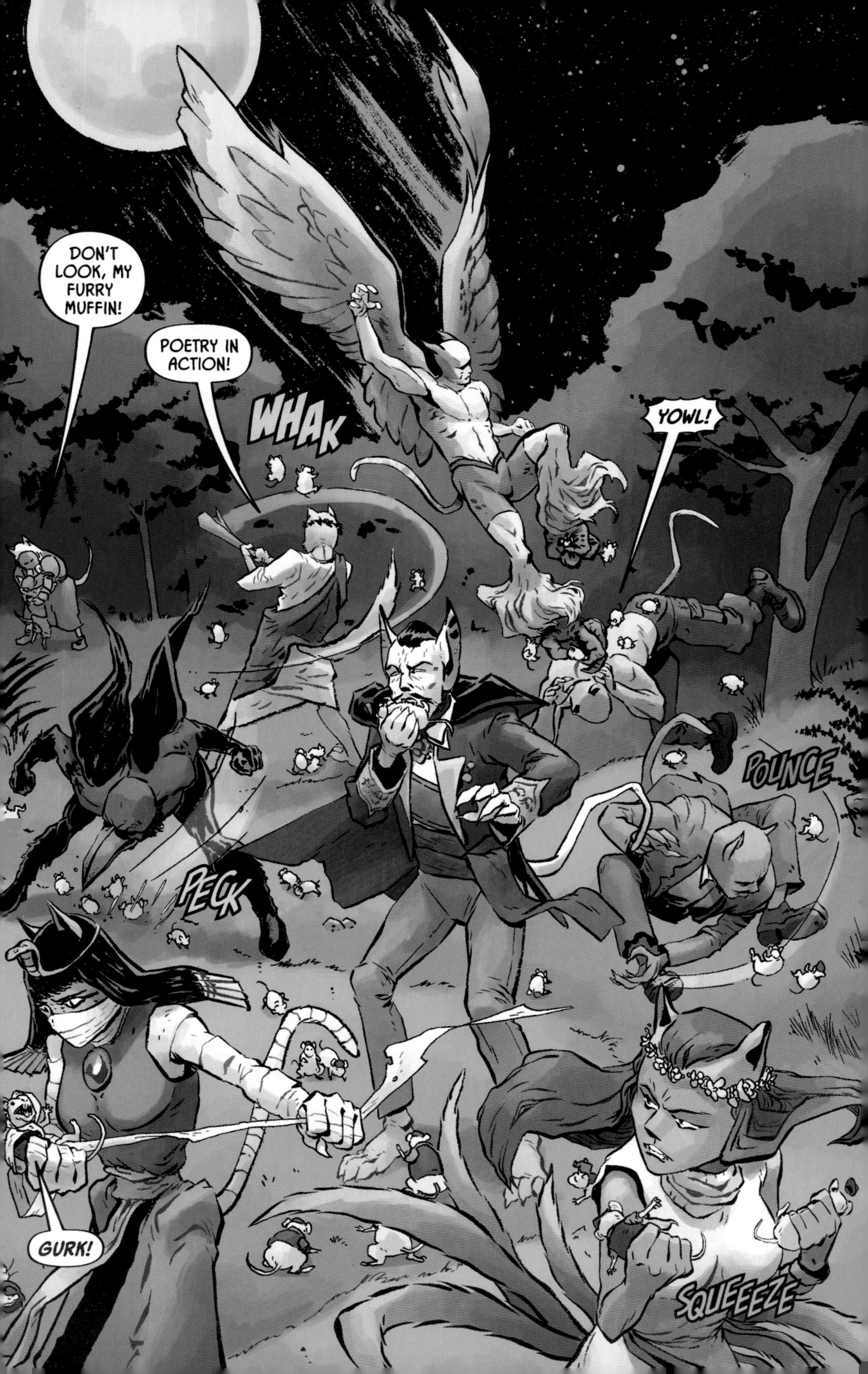
DON'T LOOK, MY FURRY MUFFIN!
POETRY IN ACTION!
WHAK
YOWL!
POUNCE
PECK
GURK!
SQUEEEZE

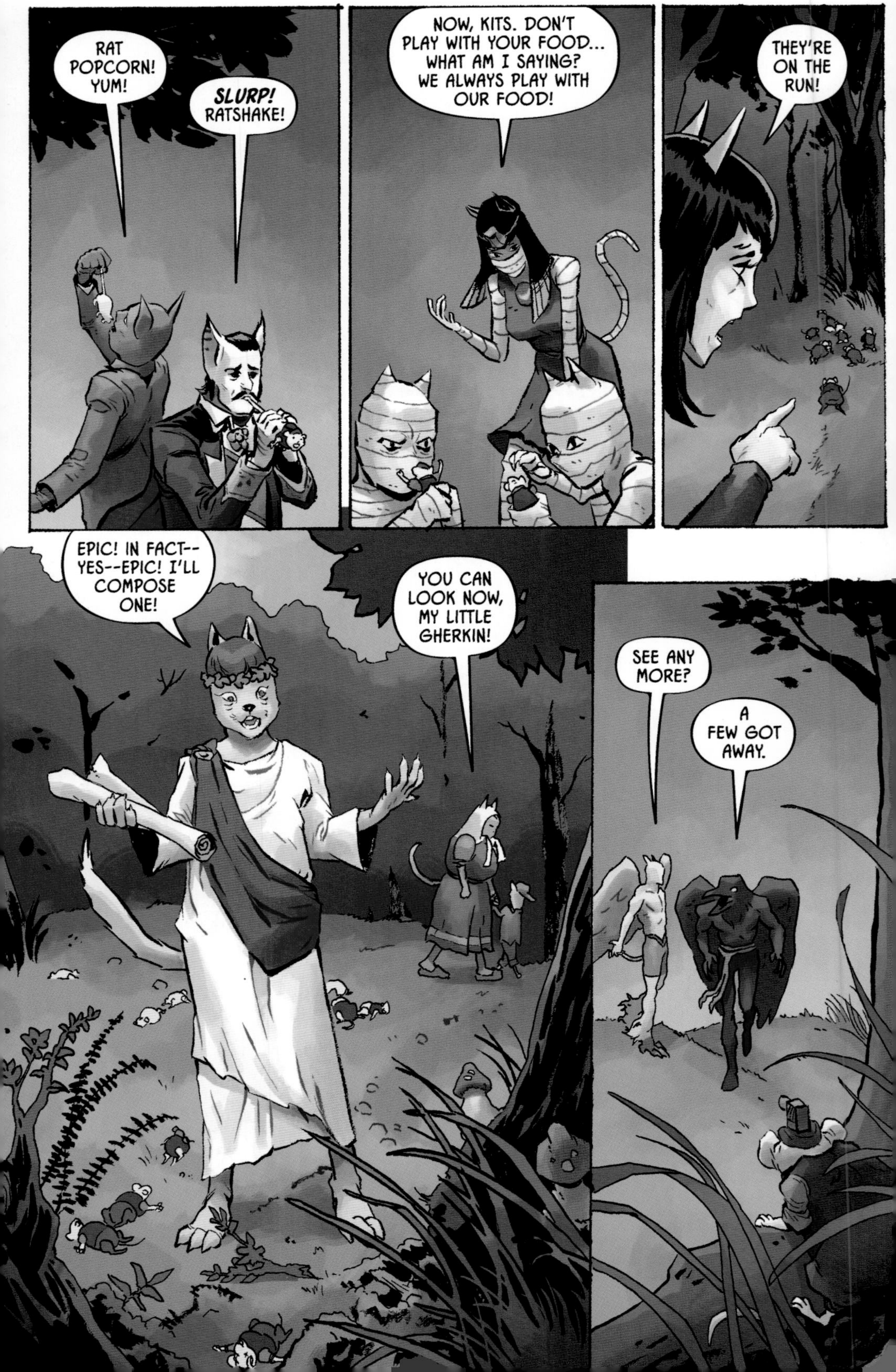
RAT POPCORN! YUM!
SLURP! RATSHAKE!
NOW, KITS. DON'T PLAY WITH YOUR FOOD... WHAT AM I SAYING? WE ALWAYS PLAY WITH OUR FOOD!
THEY'RE ON THE RUN!
EPIC! IN FACT-- YES--EPIC! I'LL COMPOSE ONE!
YOU CAN LOOK NOW, MY LITTLE GHERKIN!
SEE ANY MORE?
A FEW GOT AWAY.

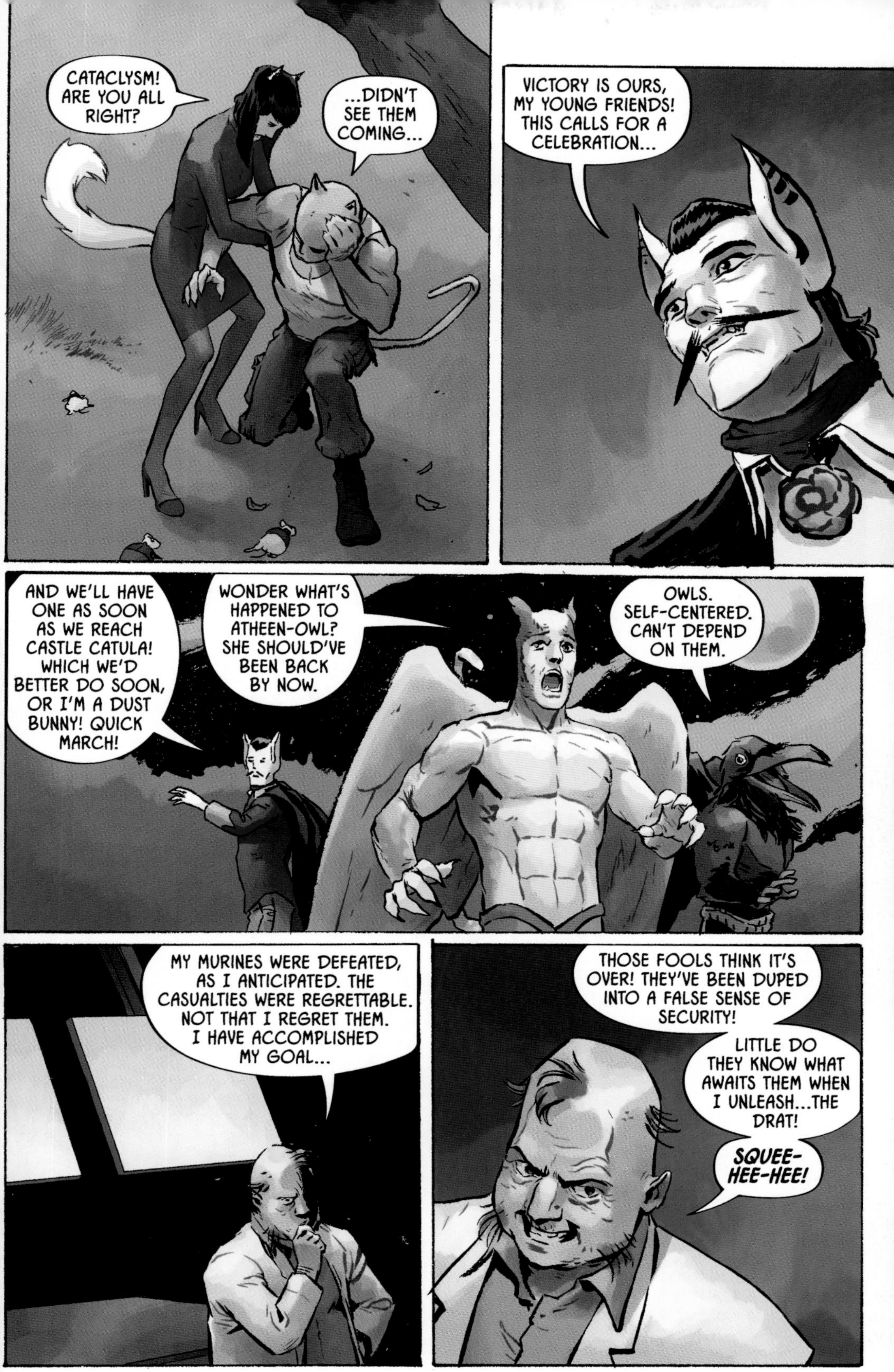

CATACLYSM! ARE YOU ALL RIGHT?
...DIDN'T SEE THEM COMING...
VICTORY IS OURS, MY YOUNG FRIENDS! THIS CALLS FOR A CELEBRATION...
AND WE'LL HAVE ONE AS SOON AS WE REACH CASTLE CATULA! WHICH WE'D BETTER DO SOON, OR I'M A DUST BUNNY! QUICK MARCH!
WONDER WHAT'S HAPPENED TO ATHEEN-OWL? SHE SHOULD'VE BEEN BACK BY NOW.
OWLS. SELF-CENTERED. CAN'T DEPEND ON THEM.
MY MURINES WERE DEFEATED, AS I ANTICIPATED. THE CASUALTIES WERE REGRETTABLE. NOT THAT I REGRET THEM. I HAVE ACCOMPLISHED MY GOAL...
THOSE FOOLS THINK IT'S OVER! THEY'VE BEEN DUPED INTO A FALSE SENSE OF SECURITY!
LITTLE DO THEY KNOW WHAT AWAITS THEM WHEN I UNLEASH...THE DRAT!
SQUEE-HEE-HEE!

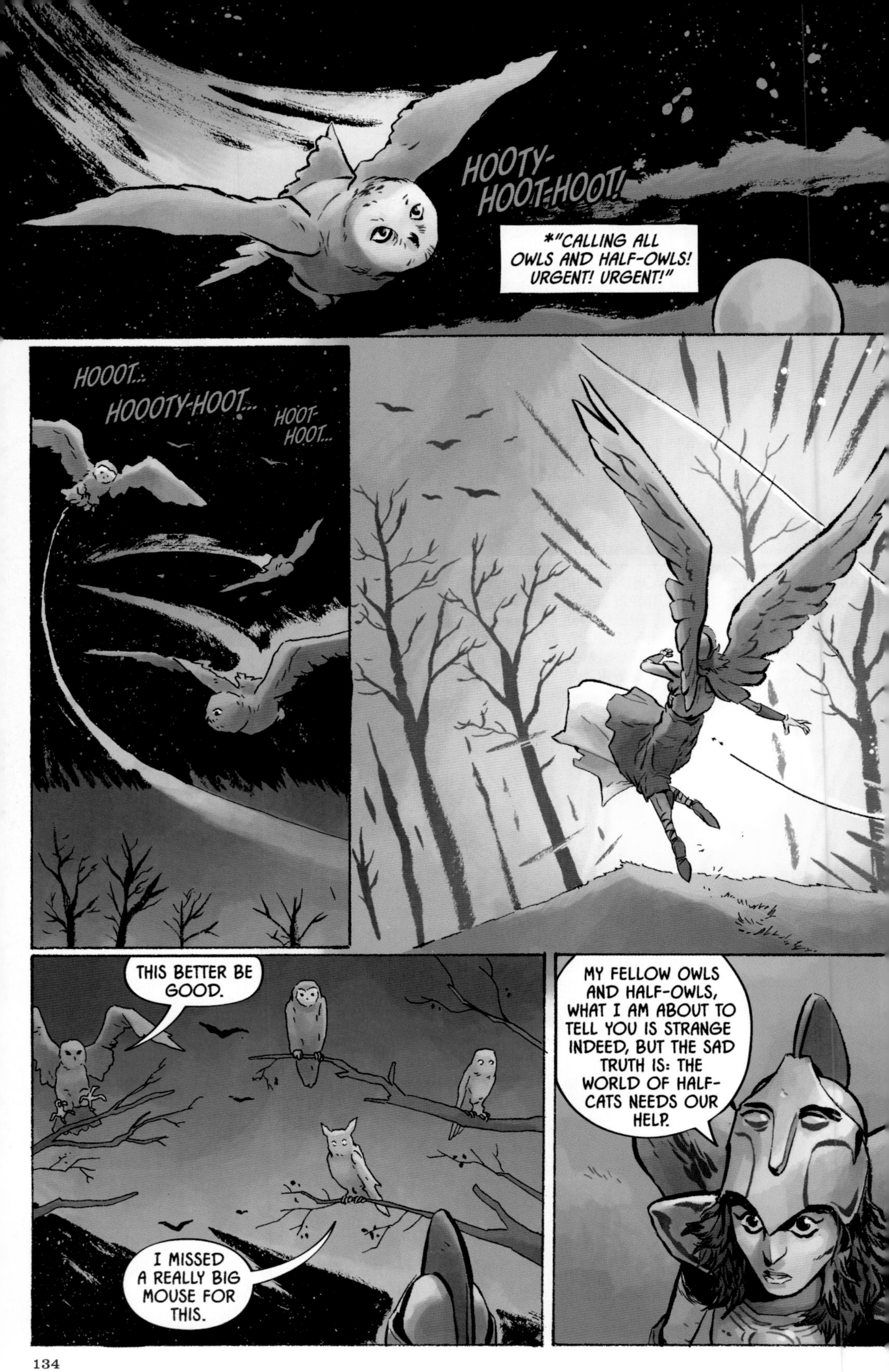
HOOTY-HOOT-HOOT!*
*"CALLING ALL OWLS AND HALF-OWLS! URGENT! URGENT!"
HOOOT...
HOOOTY-HOOT...
HOOT-HOOT...
THIS BETTER BE GOOD.
I MISSED A REALLY BIG MOUSE FOR THIS.
MY FELLOW OWLS AND HALF-OWLS, WHAT I AM ABOUT TO TELL YOU IS STRANGE INDEED, BUT THE SAD TRUTH IS: THE WORLD OF HALF-CATS NEEDS OUR HELP.

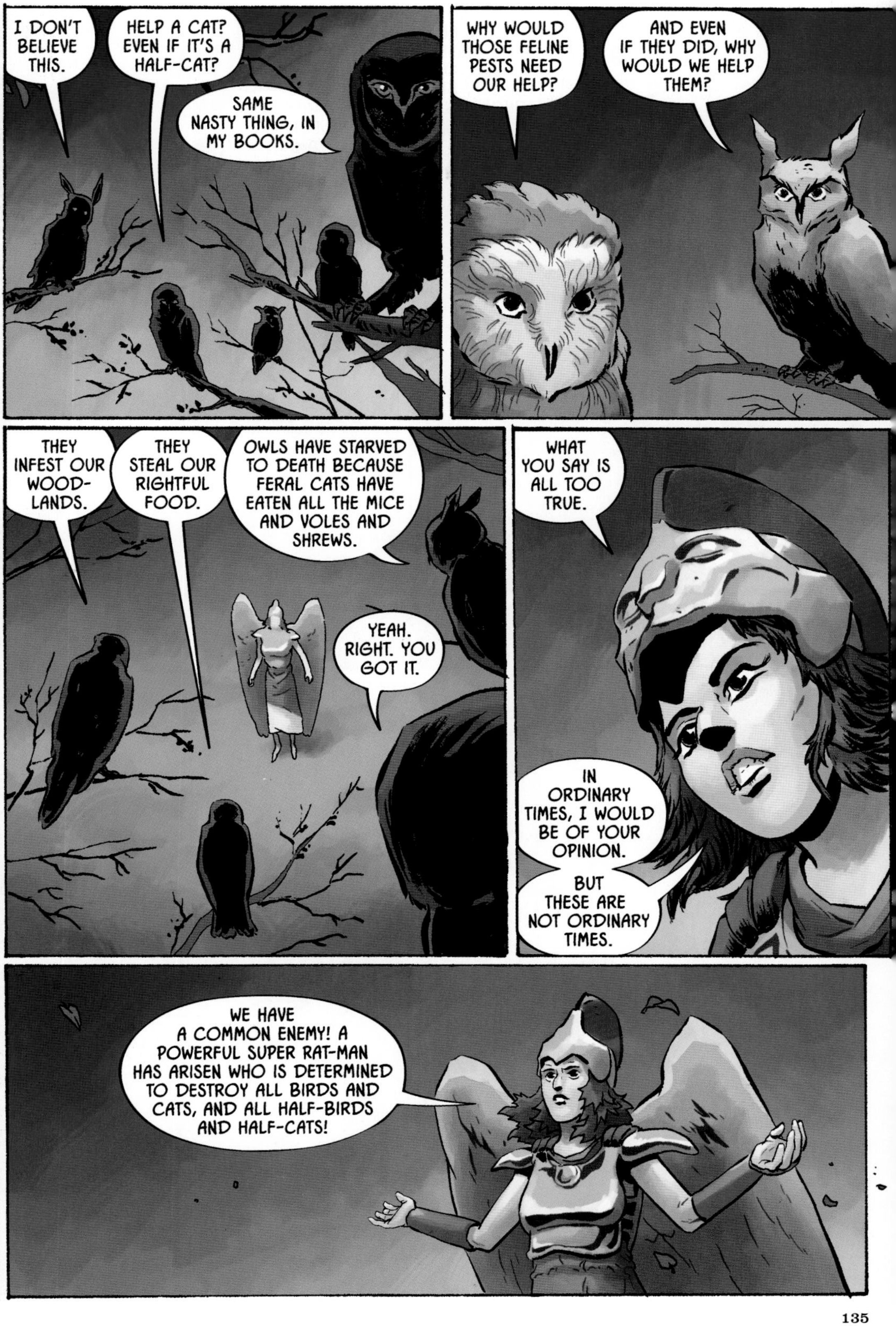
I DON'T BELIEVE THIS.
HELP A CAT? EVEN IF IT'S A HALF-CAT?
SAME NASTY THING, IN MY BOOKS.
WHY WOULD THOSE FELINE PESTS NEED OUR HELP?
AND EVEN IF THEY DID, WHY WOULD WE HELP THEM?
THEY INFEST OUR WOOD-LANDS.
THEY STEAL OUR RIGHTFUL FOOD.
OWLS HAVE STARVED TO DEATH BECAUSE FERAL CATS HAVE EATEN ALL THE MICE AND VOLES AND SHREWS.
YEAH. RIGHT. YOU GOT IT.
WHAT YOU SAY IS ALL TOO TRUE.
IN ORDINARY TIMES, I WOULD BE OF YOUR OPINION.
BUT THESE ARE NOT ORDINARY TIMES.
WE HAVE A COMMON ENEMY! A POWERFUL SUPER RAT-MAN HAS ARISEN WHO IS DETERMINED TO DESTROY ALL BIRDS AND CATS, AND ALL HALF-BIRDS AND HALF-CATS!

ATHEEN-OWL... WHAT MAGIC MOUSEROOMS HAVE YOU BEEN EATING? YOU'RE HALLUCINATING!

WE DON'T BELIEVE YOU!

DESPERATE FOR ATTENTION.

WITH HER, EVERYTHING'S A CRISIS.

NOT THAT I'M FOND OF RATS, EXCEPT AS APPETIZERS.

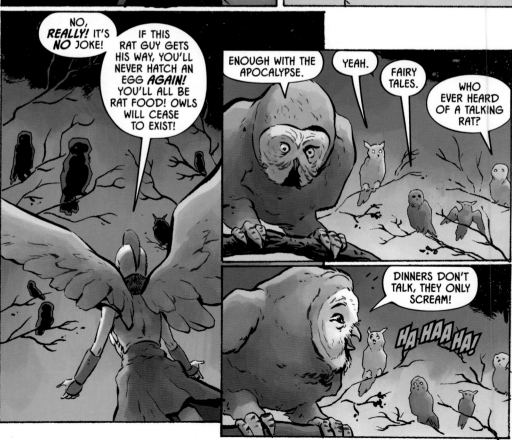

NO, *REALLY!* IT'S *NO* JOKE! IF THIS RAT GUY GETS HIS WAY, YOU'LL NEVER HATCH AN EGG *AGAIN!* YOU'LL ALL BE RAT FOOD! OWLS WILL CEASE TO EXIST!

ENOUGH WITH THE APOCALYPSE.

YEAH.

FAIRY TALES.

WHO EVER HEARD OF A TALKING RAT?

DINNERS DON'T TALK, THEY ONLY SCREAM!

HA HAA HA!

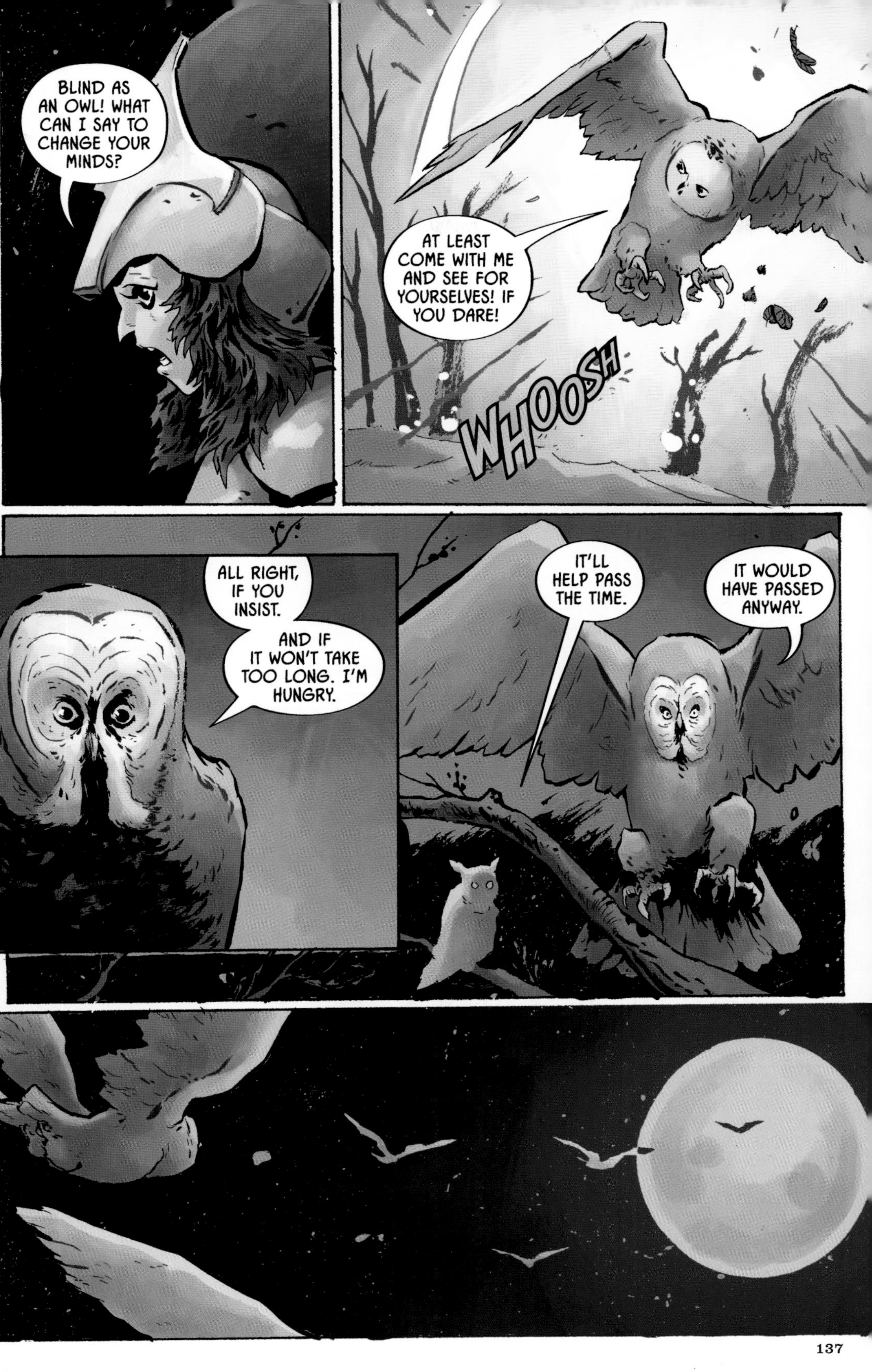
BLIND AS AN OWL! WHAT CAN I SAY TO CHANGE YOUR MINDS?
AT LEAST COME WITH ME AND SEE FOR YOURSELVES! IF YOU DARE!
WHOOSH
ALL RIGHT, IF YOU INSIST.
AND IF IT WON'T TAKE TOO LONG. I'M HUNGRY.
IT'LL HELP PASS THE TIME.
IT WOULD HAVE PASSED ANYWAY.

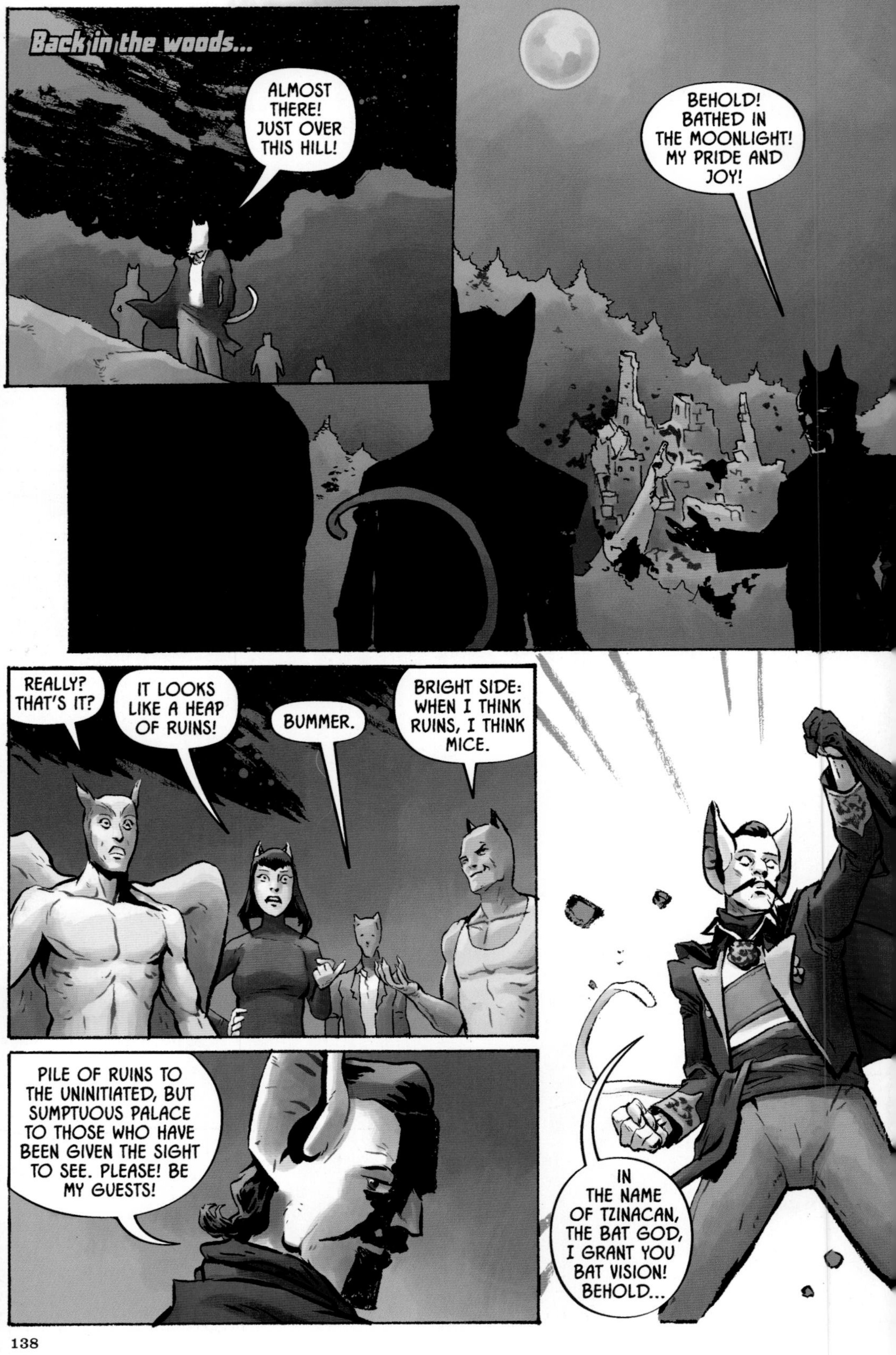
Back in the woods...
ALMOST THERE! JUST OVER THIS HILL!
BEHOLD! BATHED IN THE MOONLIGHT! MY PRIDE AND JOY!
REALLY? THAT'S IT?
IT LOOKS LIKE A HEAP OF RUINS!
BUMMER.
BRIGHT SIDE: WHEN I THINK RUINS, I THINK MICE.
PILE OF RUINS TO THE UNINITIATED, BUT SUMPTUOUS PALACE TO THOSE WHO HAVE BEEN GIVEN THE SIGHT TO SEE. PLEASE! BE MY GUESTS!
IN THE NAME OF TZINACAN, THE BAT GOD, I GRANT YOU BAT VISION! BEHOLD...

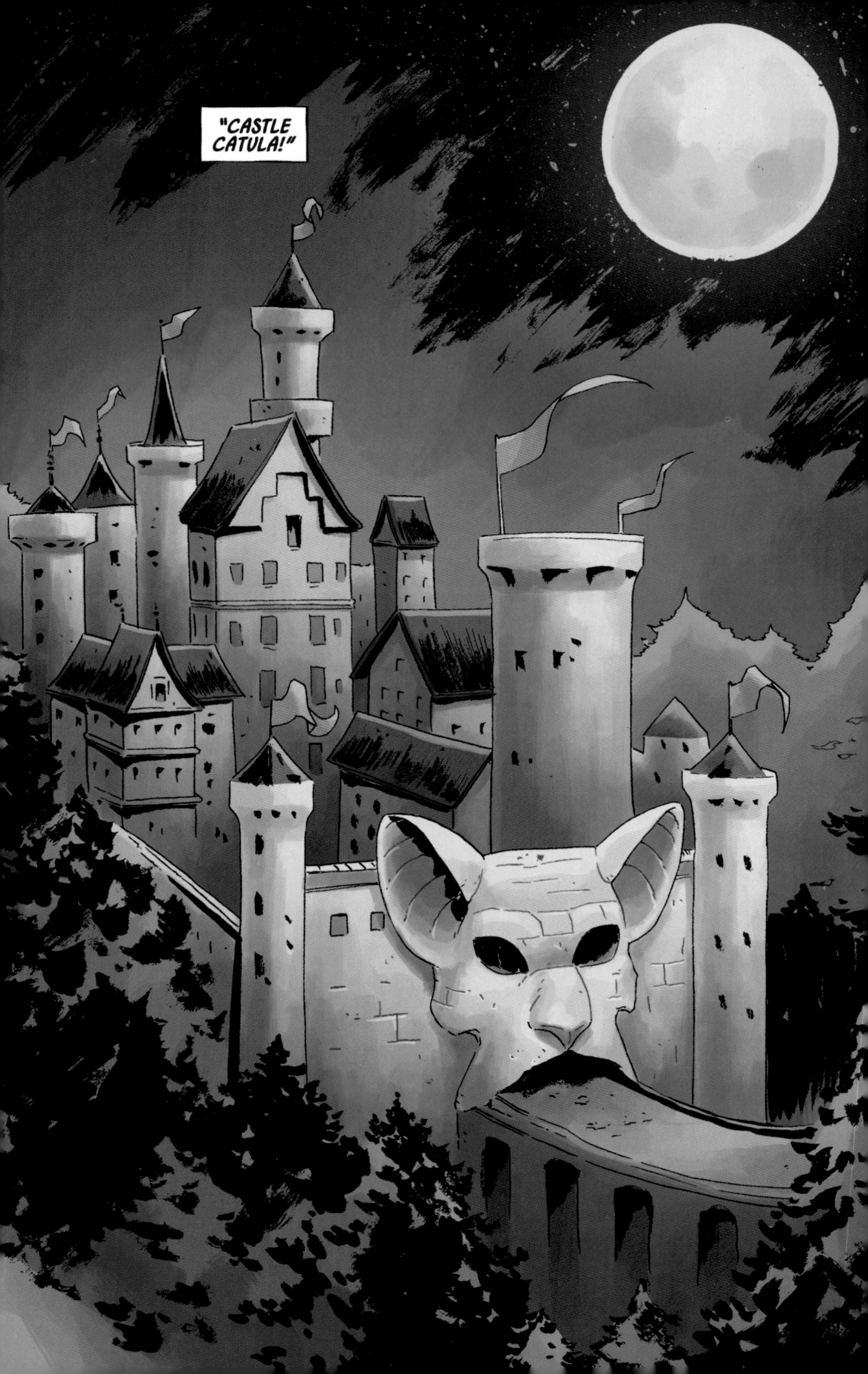
"CASTLE CATULA!"

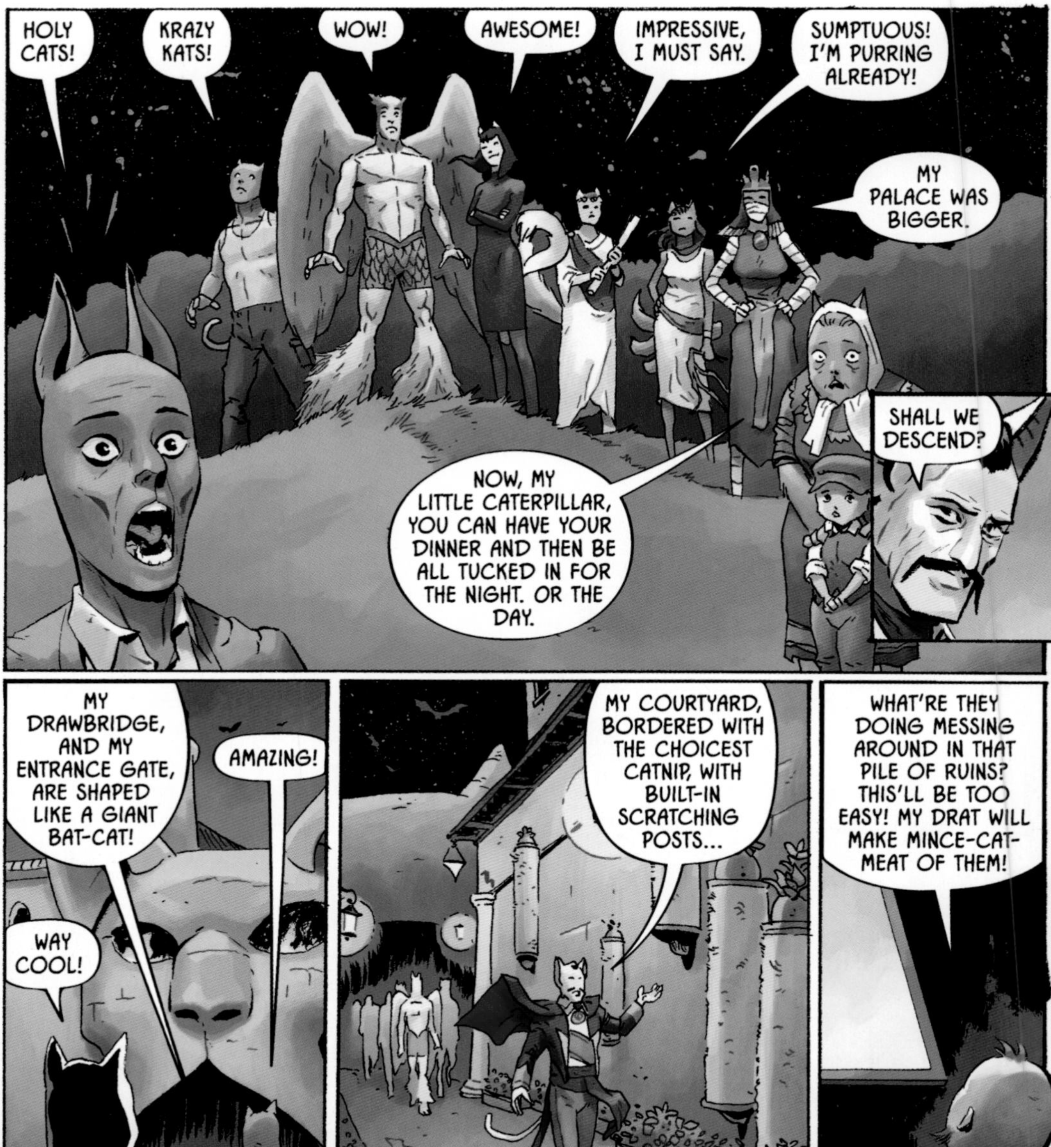
HOLY CATS!
KRAZY KATS!
WOW!
AWESOME!
IMPRESSIVE, I MUST SAY.
SUMPTUOUS! I'M PURRING ALREADY!
MY PALACE WAS BIGGER.
SHALL WE DESCEND?
NOW, MY LITTLE CATERPILLAR, YOU CAN HAVE YOUR DINNER AND THEN BE ALL TUCKED IN FOR THE NIGHT. OR THE DAY.
MY DRAWBRIDGE, AND MY ENTRANCE GATE, ARE SHAPED LIKE A GIANT BAT-CAT!
AMAZING!
WAY COOL!
MY COURTYARD, BORDERED WITH THE CHOICEST CATNIP, WITH BUILT-IN SCRATCHING POSTS...
WHAT'RE THEY DOING MESSING AROUND IN THAT PILE OF RUINS? THIS'LL BE TOO EASY! MY DRAT WILL MAKE MINCE-CAT-MEAT OF THEM!

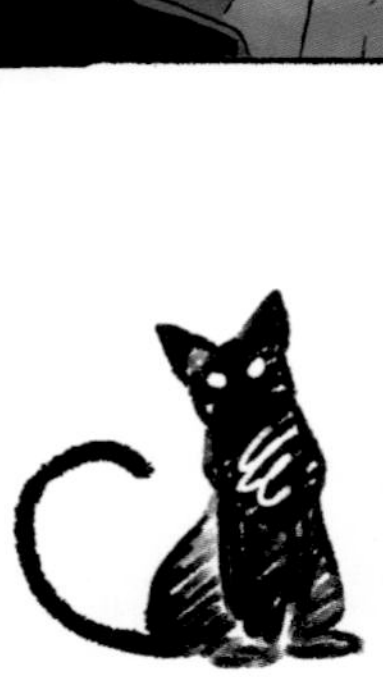

SAFE OUTDOOR CATS!

Cat enclosures, "catios," and cat walkways are all wonderful ways to let your cat enjoy the great outdoors without exposing it to the dangers of free roaming. From luxury models to DIY projects, there's a solution for every budget! Read more at www.catsandbirds.ca

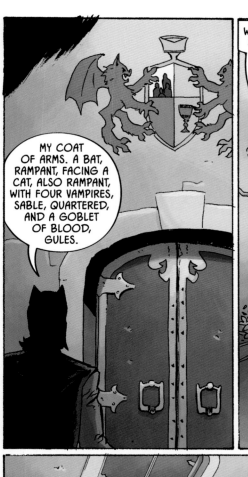

MY COAT OF ARMS. A BAT, RAMPANT, FACING A CAT, ALSO RAMPANT, WITH FOUR VAMPIRES, SABLE, QUARTERED, AND A GOBLET OF BLOOD, GULES.

WHAT'S HE SAYING?

WHO KNOWS?

OH, COUNT! YOU'RE SO... NOBLE! IN ONE OF MY LIVES I KNEW A COUNT, BUT NOT SO HANDSOME AS YOU!

THANK YOU, MY DEAR. I'M SURE HE WAS IN BLISS.

NOW I WILL HOIST THE FLAG, TO SHOW I'M IN RESIDENCE.

OOOO!

THE BAT-CAT FLIES! RIPPLING IN AN UNEARTHLY WIND!

AAAH!

SHALL WE ENTER?

CREEEAK

141

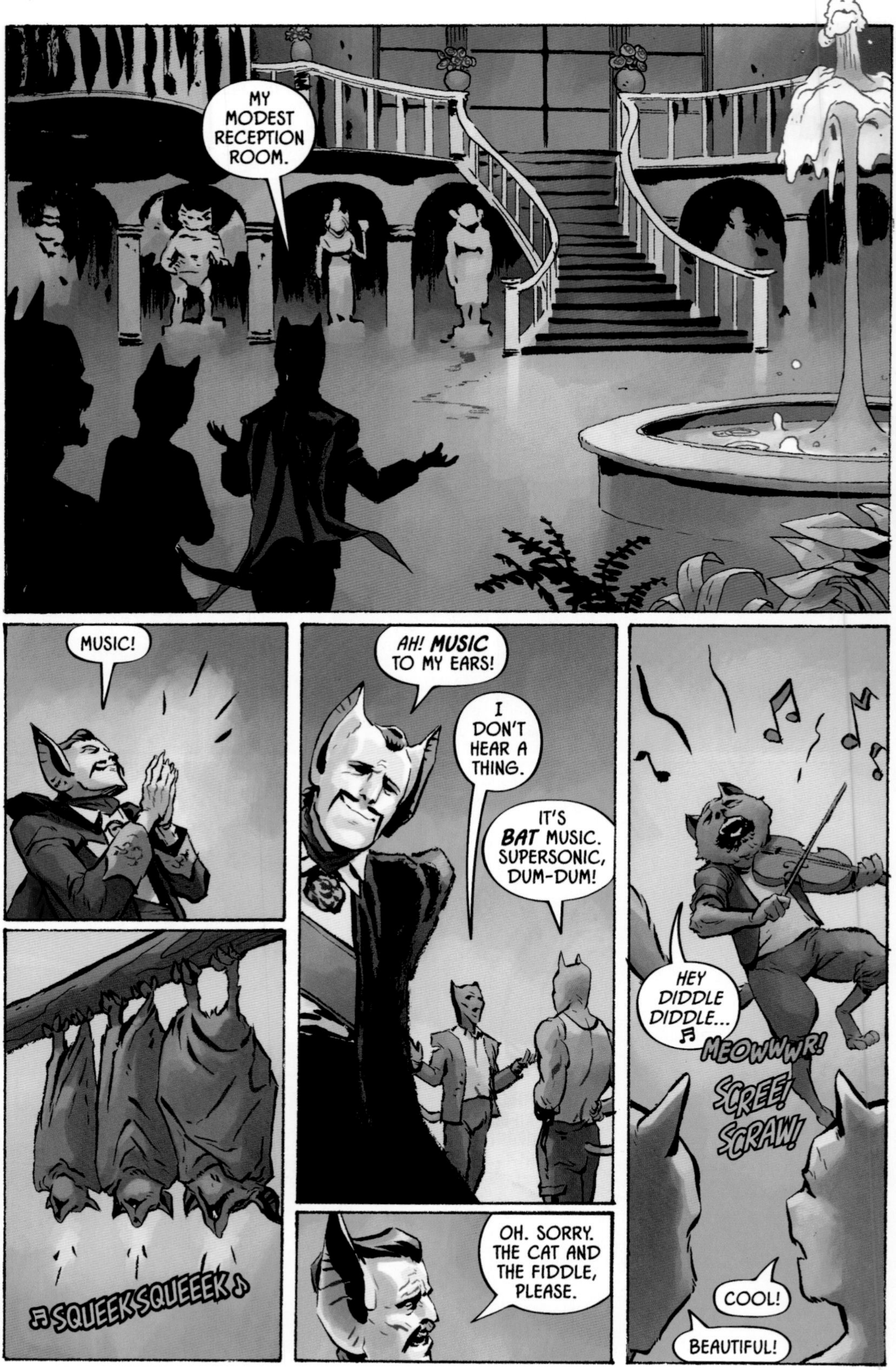
MY MODEST RECEPTION ROOM.
MUSIC!
♫SQUEEKSQUEEEK♫
AH! MUSIC TO MY EARS!
I DON'T HEAR A THING.
IT'S BAT MUSIC. SUPERSONIC, DUM-DUM!
OH. SORRY. THE CAT AND THE FIDDLE, PLEASE.
HEY DIDDLE DIDDLE... ♫
MEOWWWR!
SCREE! SCRAW!
COOL!
BEAUTIFUL!

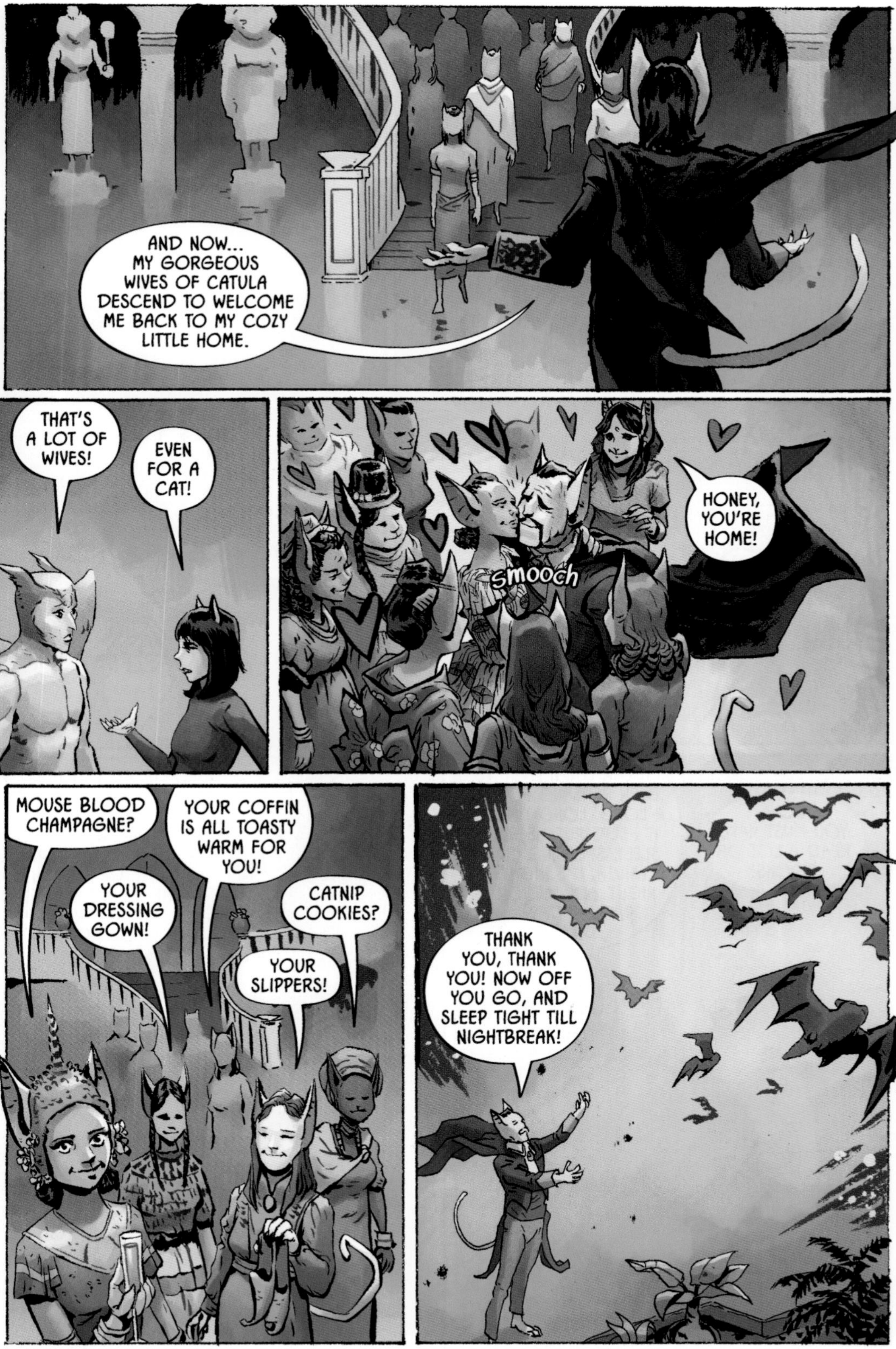
AND NOW... MY GORGEOUS WIVES OF CATULA DESCEND TO WELCOME ME BACK TO MY COZY LITTLE HOME.
THAT'S A LOT OF WIVES!
EVEN FOR A CAT!
HONEY, YOU'RE HOME!
smooch
MOUSE BLOOD CHAMPAGNE?
YOUR COFFIN IS ALL TOASTY WARM FOR YOU!
YOUR DRESSING GOWN!
CATNIP COOKIES?
YOUR SLIPPERS!
THANK YOU, THANK YOU! NOW OFF YOU GO, AND SLEEP TIGHT TILL NIGHTBREAK!

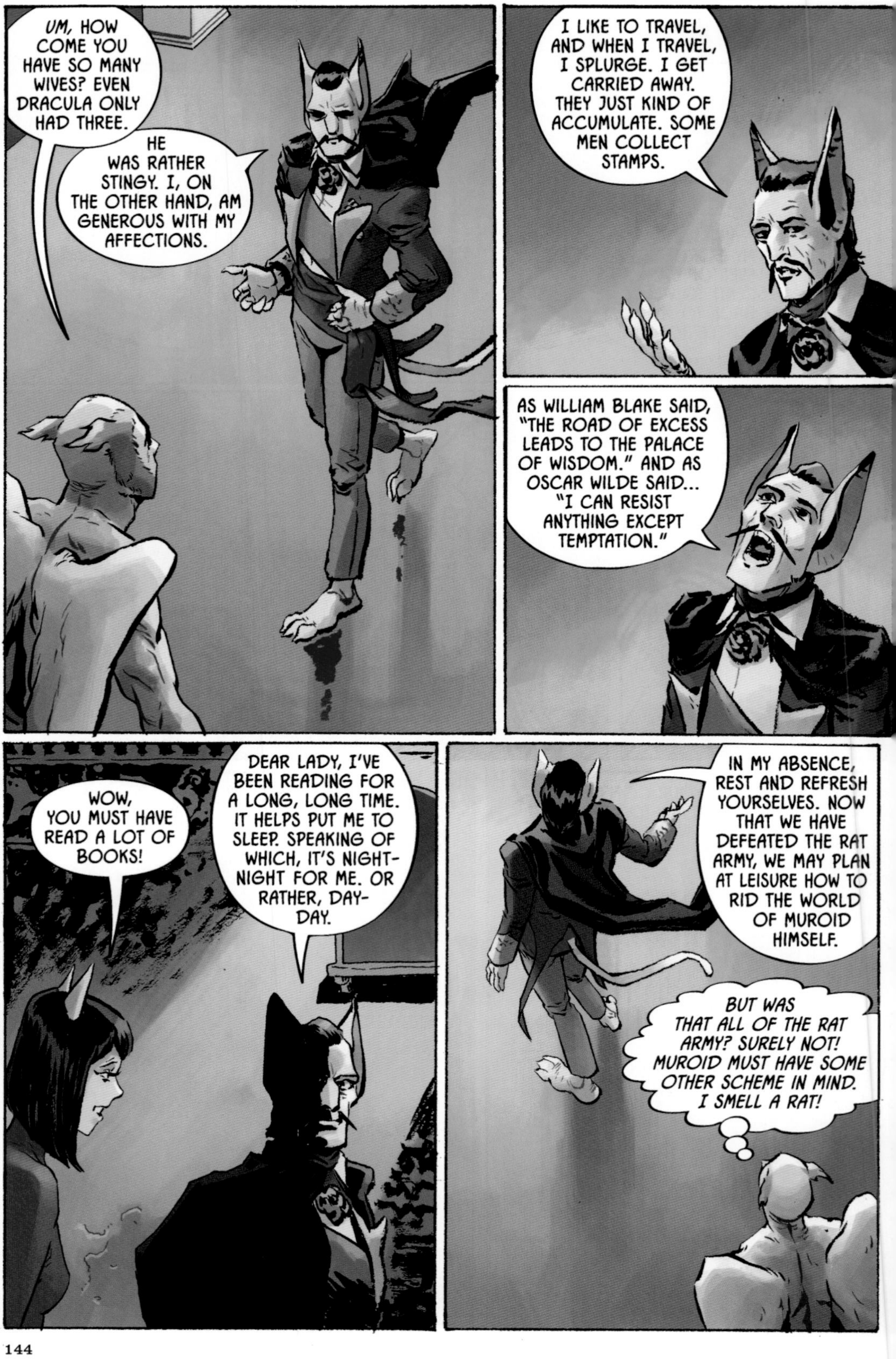

UM, HOW COME YOU HAVE SO MANY WIVES? EVEN DRACULA ONLY HAD THREE.
HE WAS RATHER STINGY. I, ON THE OTHER HAND, AM GENEROUS WITH MY AFFECTIONS.
I LIKE TO TRAVEL, AND WHEN I TRAVEL, I SPLURGE. I GET CARRIED AWAY. THEY JUST KIND OF ACCUMULATE. SOME MEN COLLECT STAMPS.
AS WILLIAM BLAKE SAID, "THE ROAD OF EXCESS LEADS TO THE PALACE OF WISDOM." AND AS OSCAR WILDE SAID... "I CAN RESIST ANYTHING EXCEPT TEMPTATION."
WOW, YOU MUST HAVE READ A LOT OF BOOKS!
DEAR LADY, I'VE BEEN READING FOR A LONG, LONG TIME. IT HELPS PUT ME TO SLEEP. SPEAKING OF WHICH, IT'S NIGHT-NIGHT FOR ME. OR RATHER, DAY-DAY.
IN MY ABSENCE, REST AND REFRESH YOURSELVES. NOW THAT WE HAVE DEFEATED THE RAT ARMY, WE MAY PLAN AT LEISURE HOW TO RID THE WORLD OF MUROID HIMSELF.
BUT WAS THAT ALL OF THE RAT ARMY? SURELY NOT! MUROID MUST HAVE SOME OTHER SCHEME IN MIND. I SMELL A RAT!

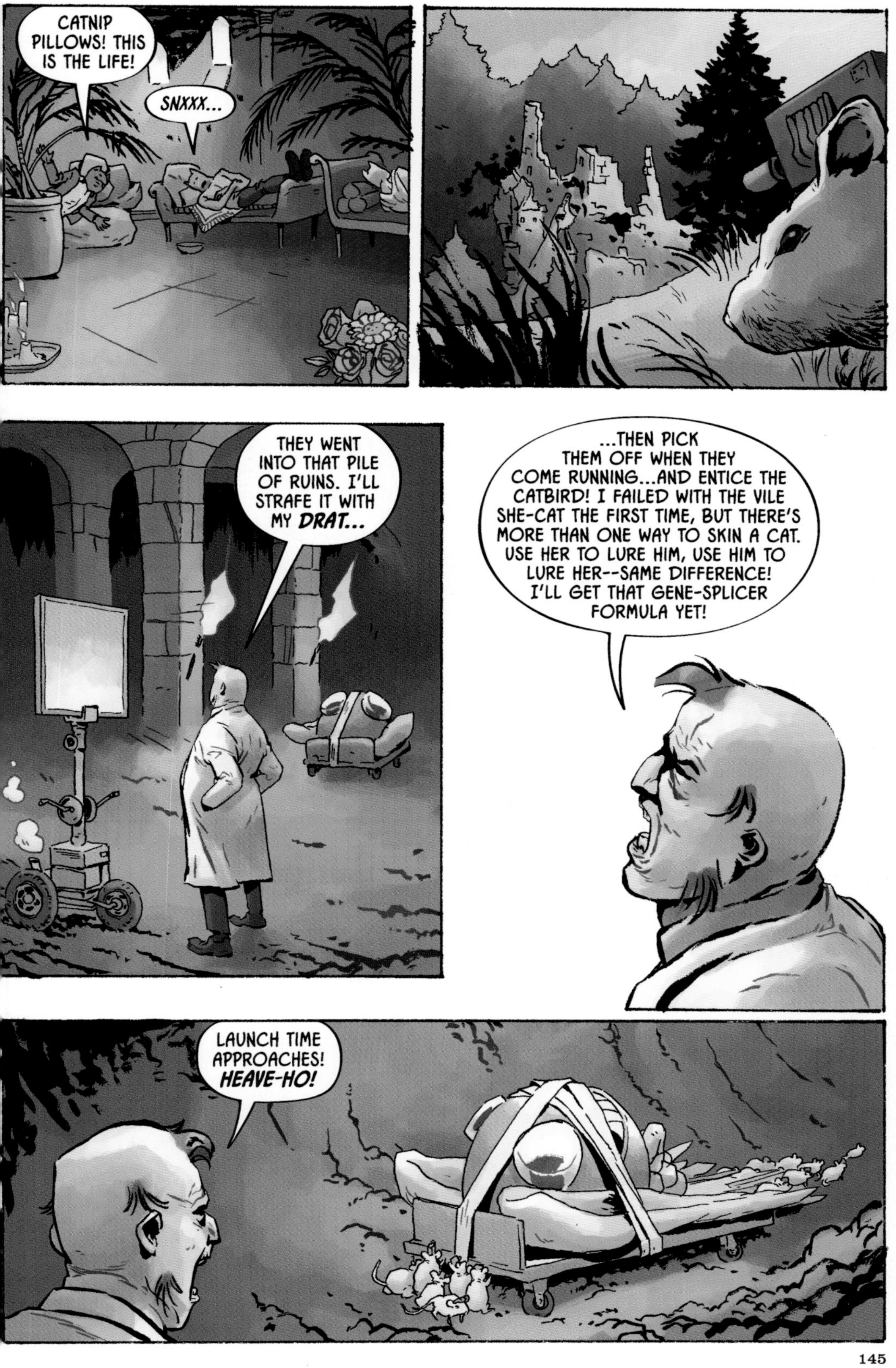
CATNIP PILLOWS! THIS IS THE LIFE!
SNXXX...
THEY WENT INTO THAT PILE OF RUINS. I'LL STRAFE IT WITH MY DRAT...
...THEN PICK THEM OFF WHEN THEY COME RUNNING...AND ENTICE THE CATBIRD! I FAILED WITH THE VILE SHE-CAT THE FIRST TIME, BUT THERE'S MORE THAN ONE WAY TO SKIN A CAT. USE HER TO LURE HIM, USE HIM TO LURE HER--SAME DIFFERENCE! I'LL GET THAT GENE-SPLICER FORMULA YET!
LAUNCH TIME APPROACHES! HEAVE-HO!

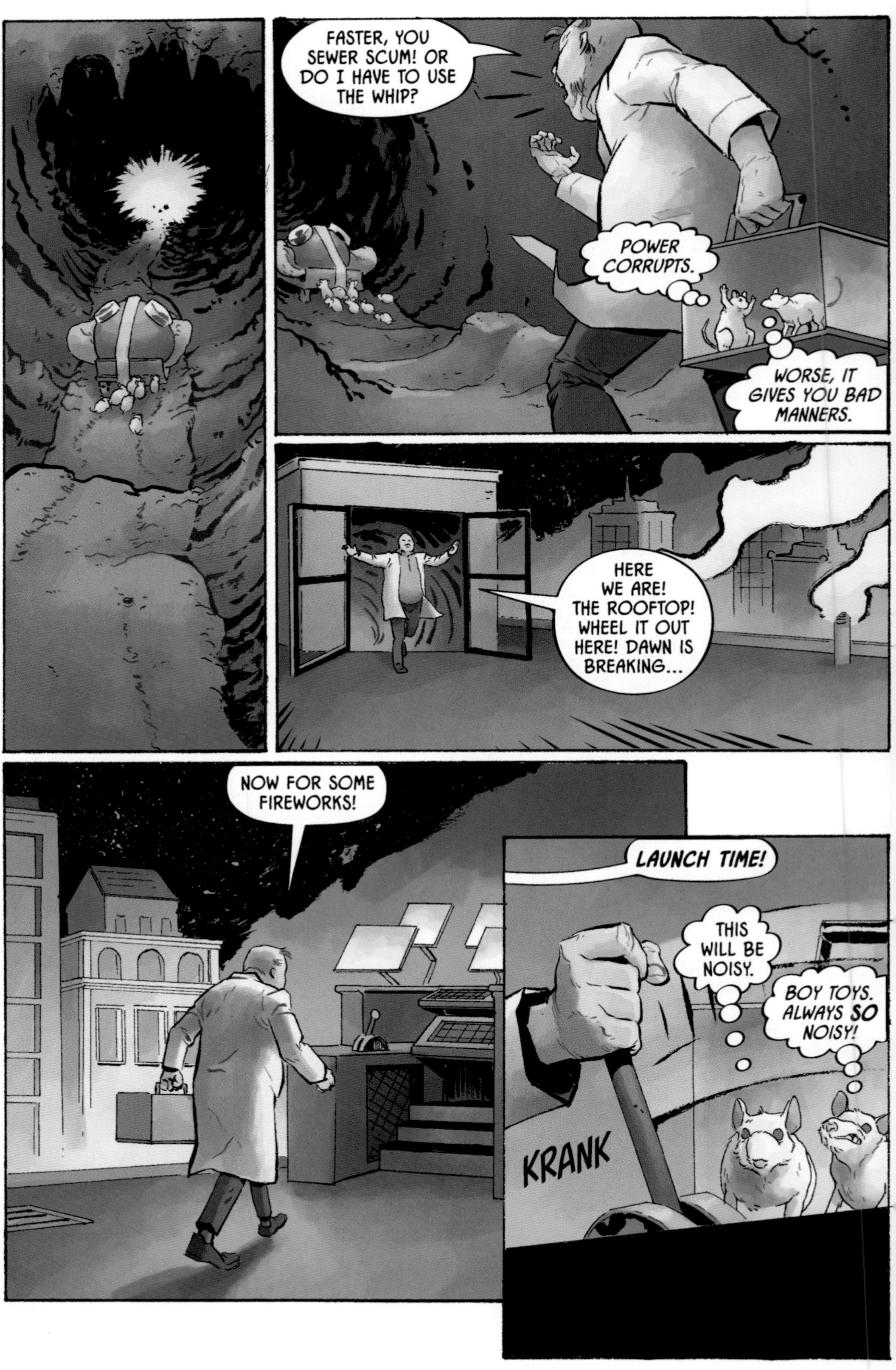
FASTER, YOU SEWER SCUM! OR DO I HAVE TO USE THE WHIP?
POWER CORRUPTS.
WORSE, IT GIVES YOU BAD MANNERS.
HERE WE ARE! THE ROOFTOP! WHEEL IT OUT HERE! DAWN IS BREAKING...
NOW FOR SOME FIREWORKS!
LAUNCH TIME!
THIS WILL BE NOISY.
BOY TOYS. ALWAYS SO NOISY!
KRANK

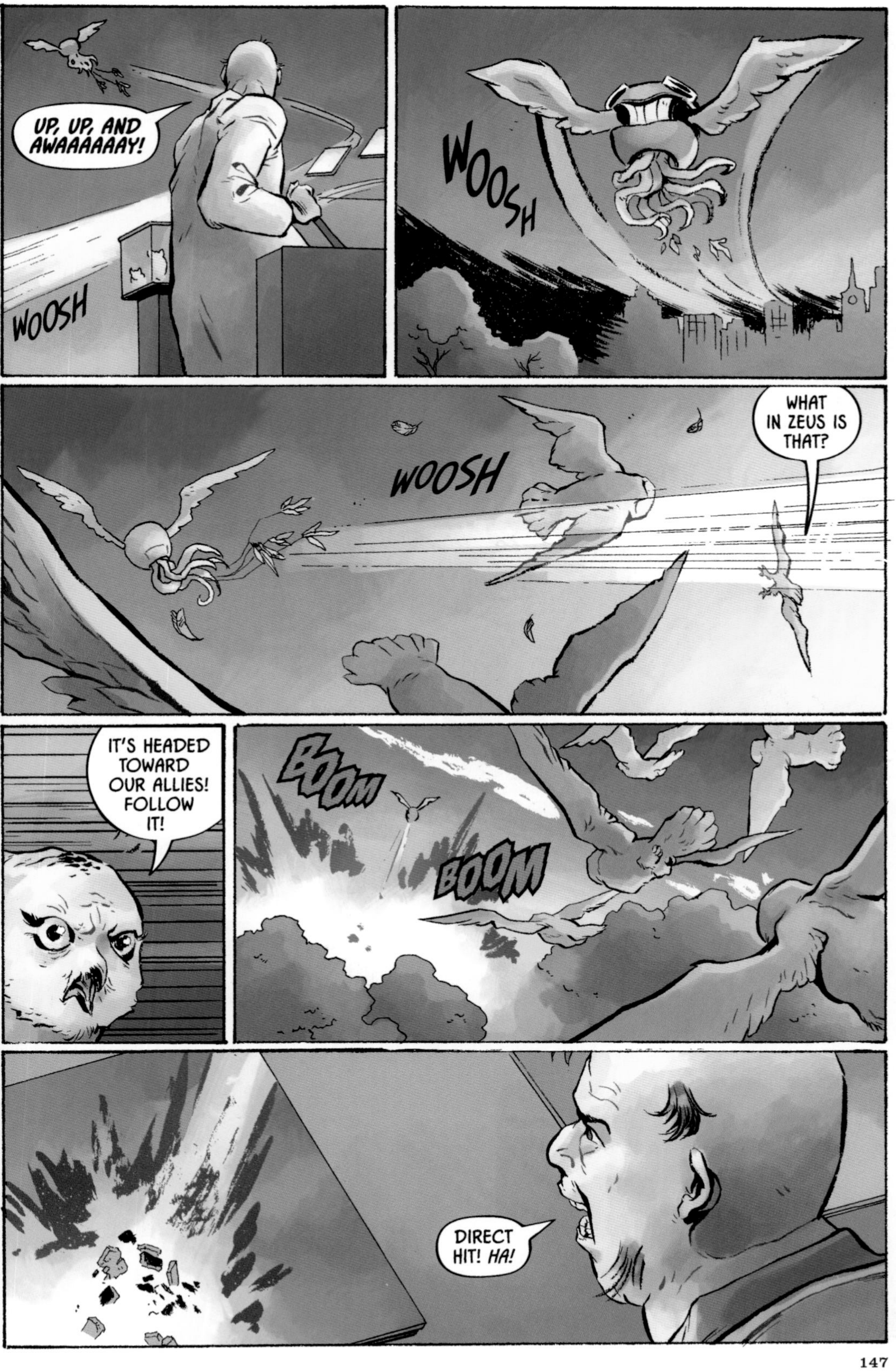
UP, UP, AND AWAAAAAAY!
WOOSH
WOOSH
WOOSH
WHAT IN ZEUS IS THAT?
IT'S HEADED TOWARD OUR ALLIES! FOLLOW IT!
BOOM
BOOM
DIRECT HIT! *HA!*

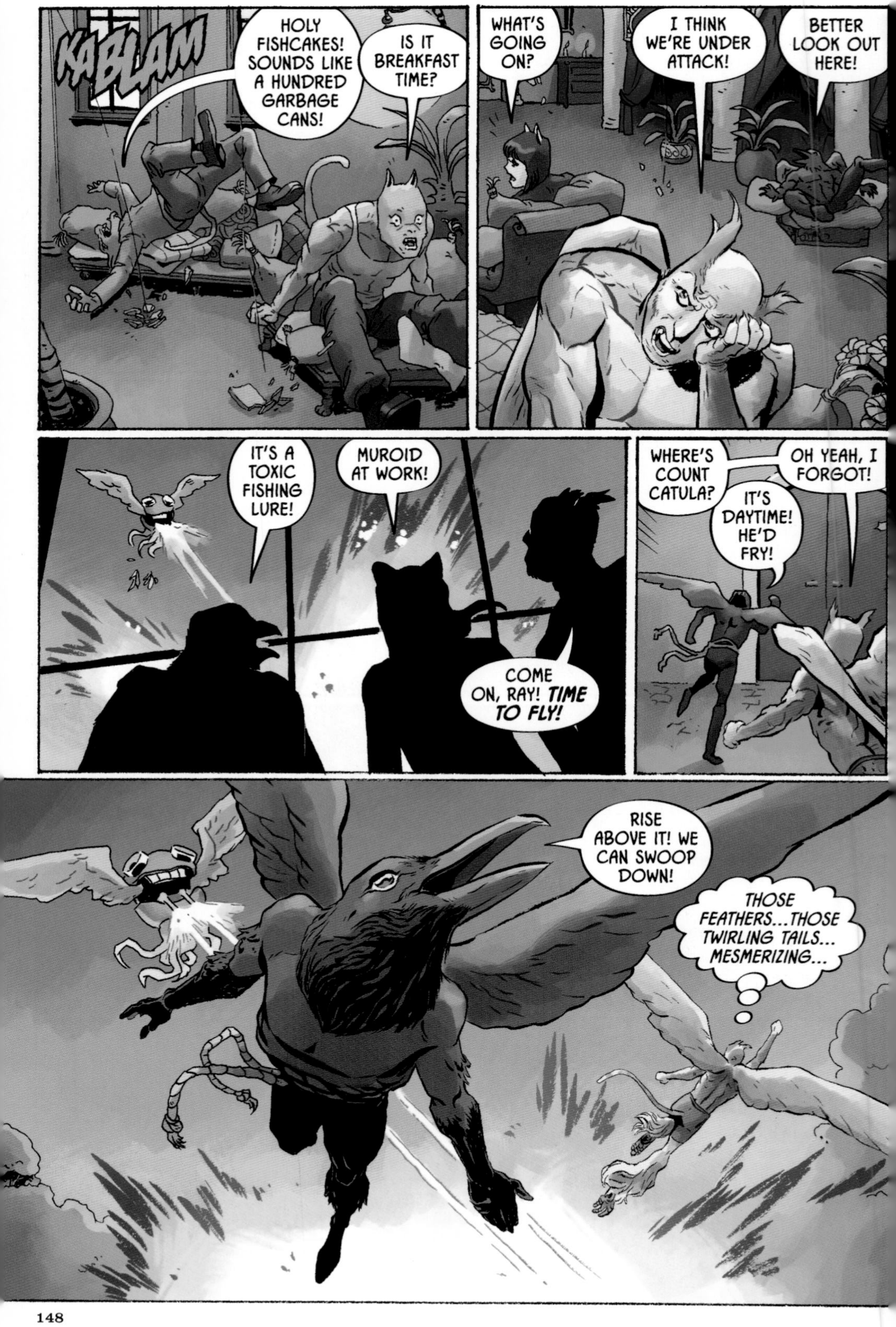
KABLAM
HOLY FISHCAKES! SOUNDS LIKE A HUNDRED GARBAGE CANS!
IS IT BREAKFAST TIME?
WHAT'S GOING ON?
I THINK WE'RE UNDER ATTACK!
BETTER LOOK OUT HERE!
IT'S A TOXIC FISHING LURE!
MUROID AT WORK!
COME ON, RAY! *TIME TO FLY!*
WHERE'S COUNT CATULA?
OH YEAH, I FORGOT!
IT'S DAYTIME! HE'D FRY!
RISE ABOVE IT! WE CAN SWOOP DOWN!
THOSE FEATHERS...THOSE TWIRLING TAILS... MESMERIZING...

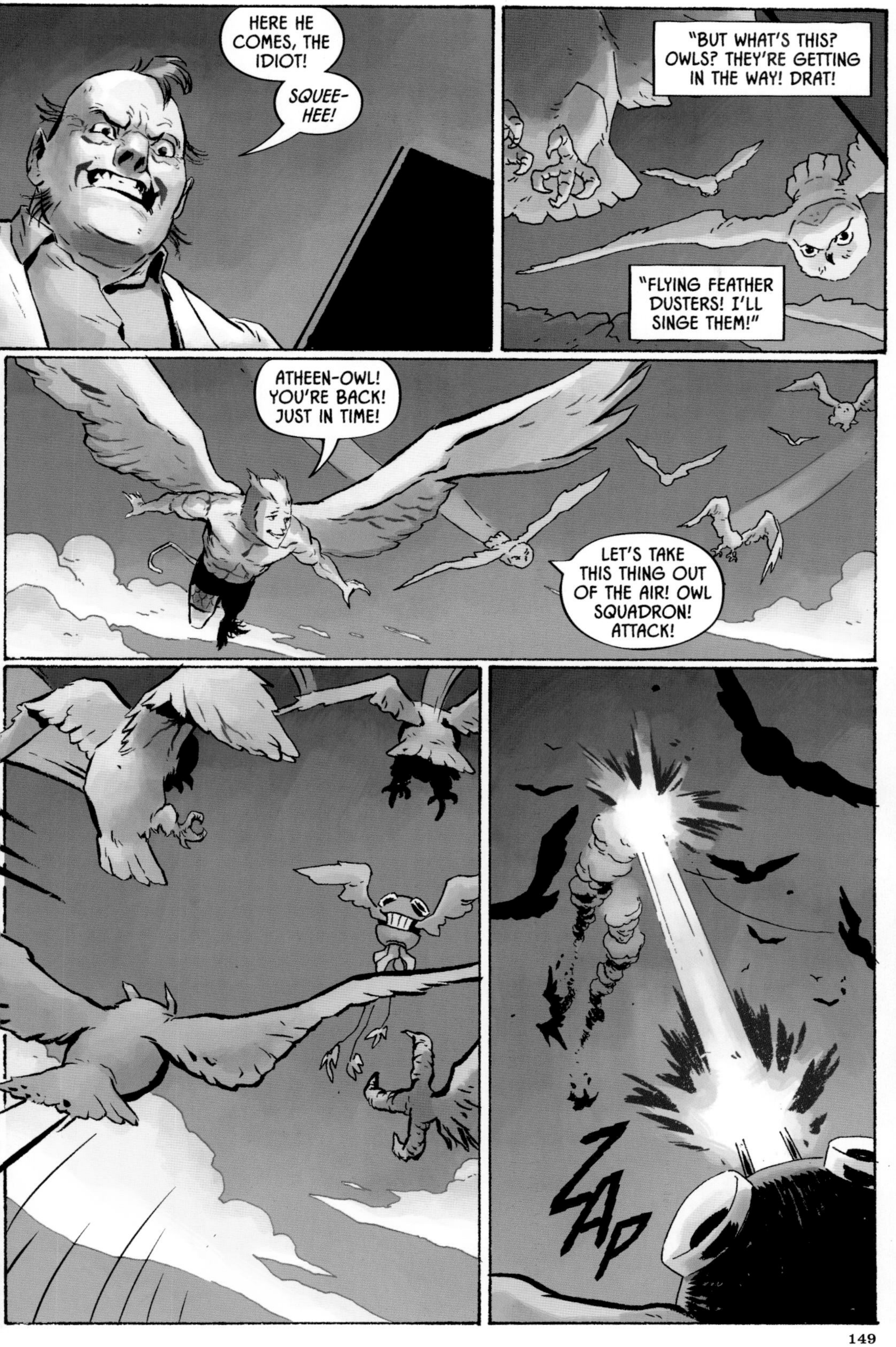

HERE HE COMES, THE IDIOT!
SQUEE-HEE!
"BUT WHAT'S THIS? OWLS? THEY'RE GETTING IN THE WAY! DRAT!
"FLYING FEATHER DUSTERS! I'LL SINGE THEM!"
ATHEEN-OWL! YOU'RE BACK! JUST IN TIME!
LET'S TAKE THIS THING OUT OF THE AIR! OWL SQUADRON! ATTACK!
ZAP

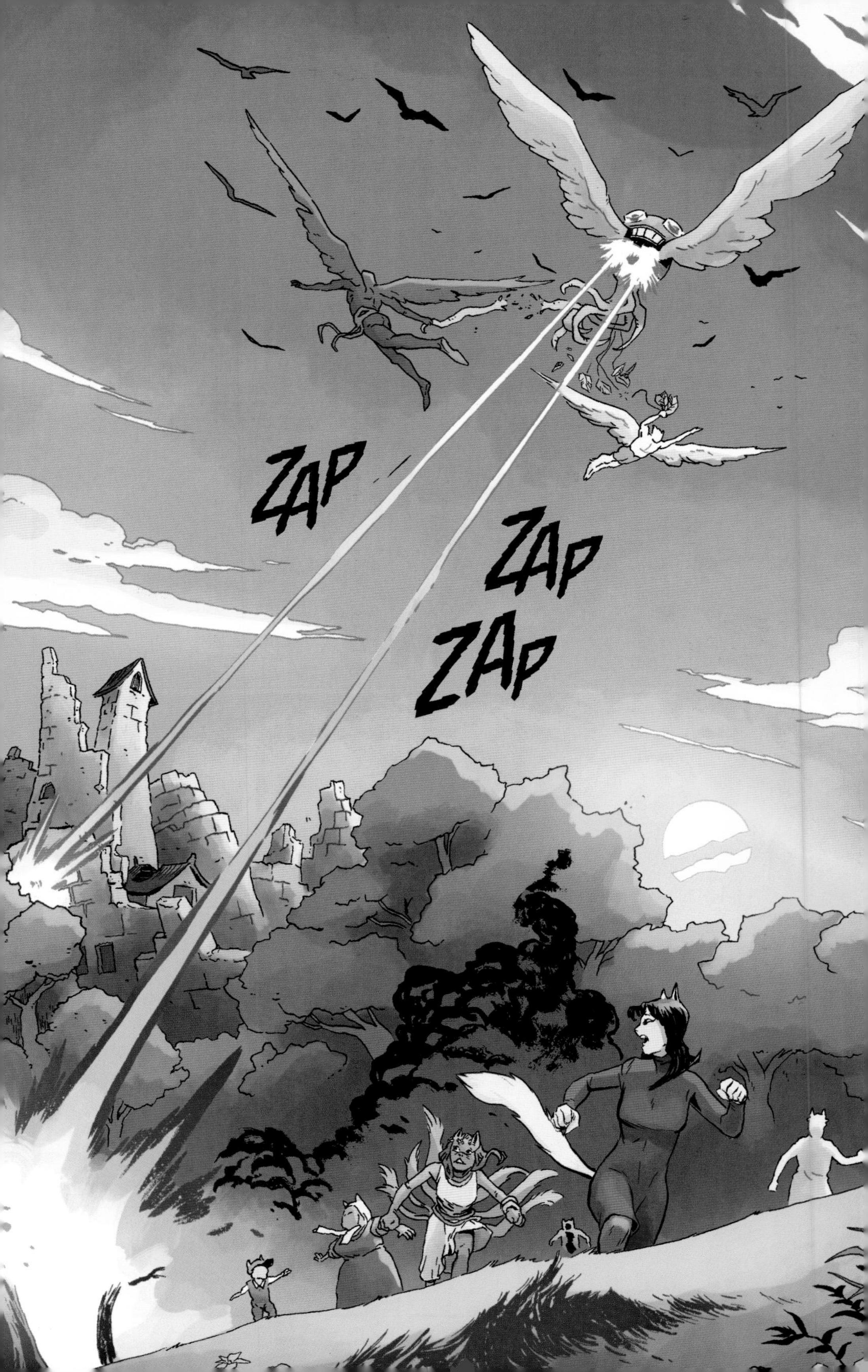
ZAP
ZAP
ZAP

THIS THING'S TRICKY!
YEAH, IT'S VERY...
...DESIRABLE! I MUST CATCH IT!
WATCH OUT FOR THE FLAME-THROWER!
WHOOSH
FWSSH
TAIL FIRE! HAVE TO BAIL!
HEAD FOR WATER!
MIDAIR POUNCE, AND THEN... CLAW! SHAKE! REND!
PREDATION AT ITS FINEST!

PLAY WITH FOOD . . . OR FOOD FOR PLAY?

Pet cats hunt for stimulation, not food. Get them toys that imitate their favorite prey and you can keep them safely entertained without the risk to local birds and wildlife! Read more at www.catsandbirds.ca

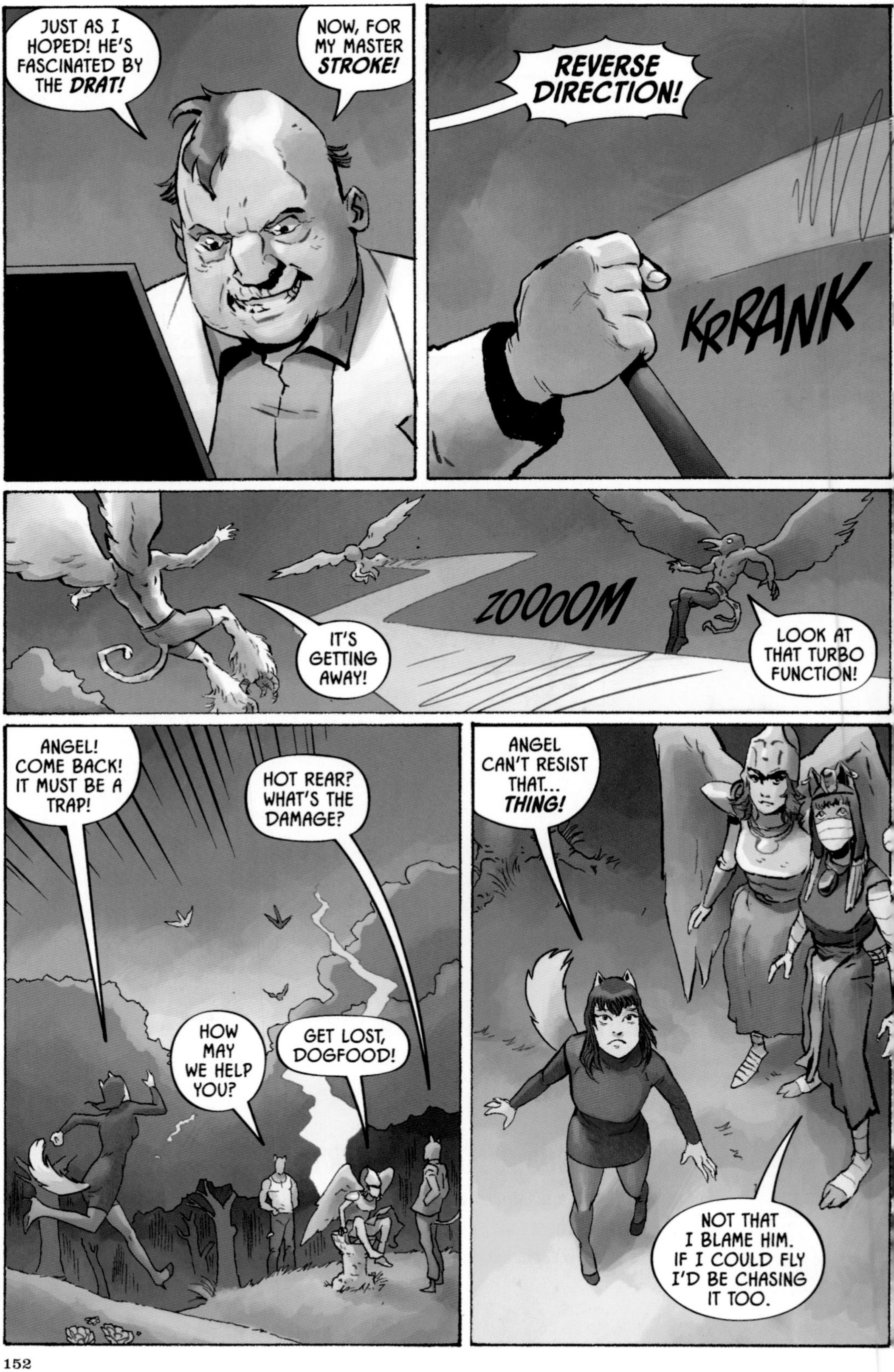
JUST AS I HOPED! HE'S FASCINATED BY THE DRAT!
NOW, FOR MY MASTER STROKE!
REVERSE DIRECTION!
KRRANK
ZOOOOM
IT'S GETTING AWAY!
LOOK AT THAT TURBO FUNCTION!
ANGEL! COME BACK! IT MUST BE A TRAP!
HOT REAR? WHAT'S THE DAMAGE?
HOW MAY WE HELP YOU?
GET LOST, DOGFOOD!
ANGEL CAN'T RESIST THAT... THING!
NOT THAT I BLAME HIM. IF I COULD FLY I'D BE CHASING IT TOO.

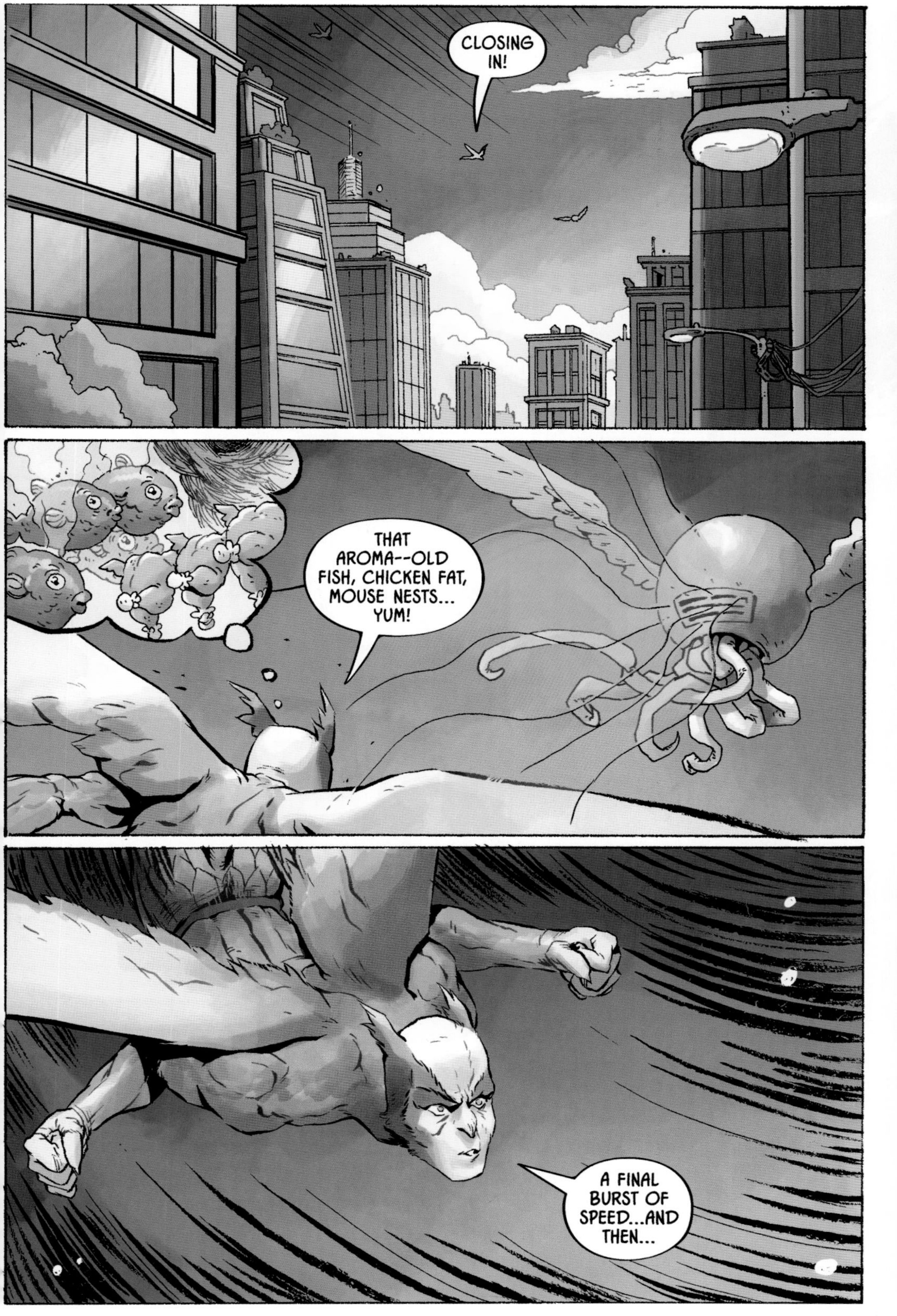
CLOSING IN!
THAT AROMA--OLD FISH, CHICKEN FAT, MOUSE NESTS... YUM!
A FINAL BURST OF SPEED...AND THEN...

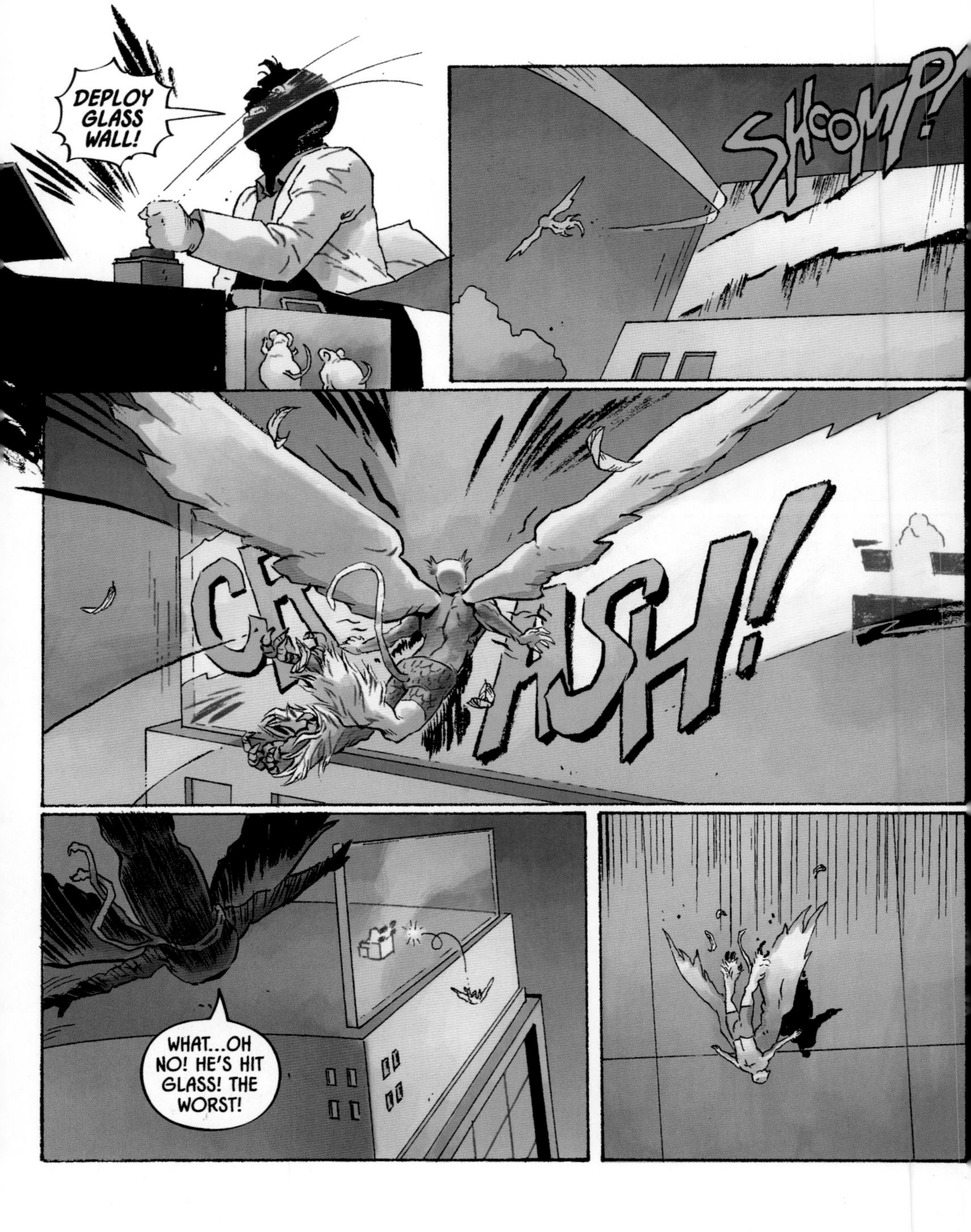
DEPLOY GLASS WALL!
SHOOMP!
CRASH!
WHAT...OH NO! HE'S HIT GLASS! THE WORST!

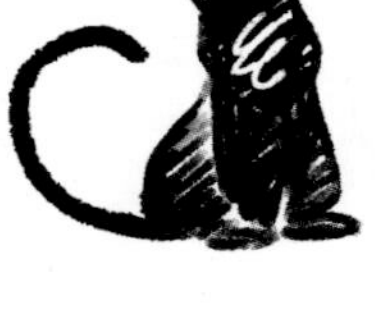

GLASS, INVISIBLE GLASS

After habitat loss, climate change, and cats, window collisions are the biggest problem people cause for birds. There are simple, low-cost solutions to make your home bird-friendly!
Read more at www.naturecanada.ca

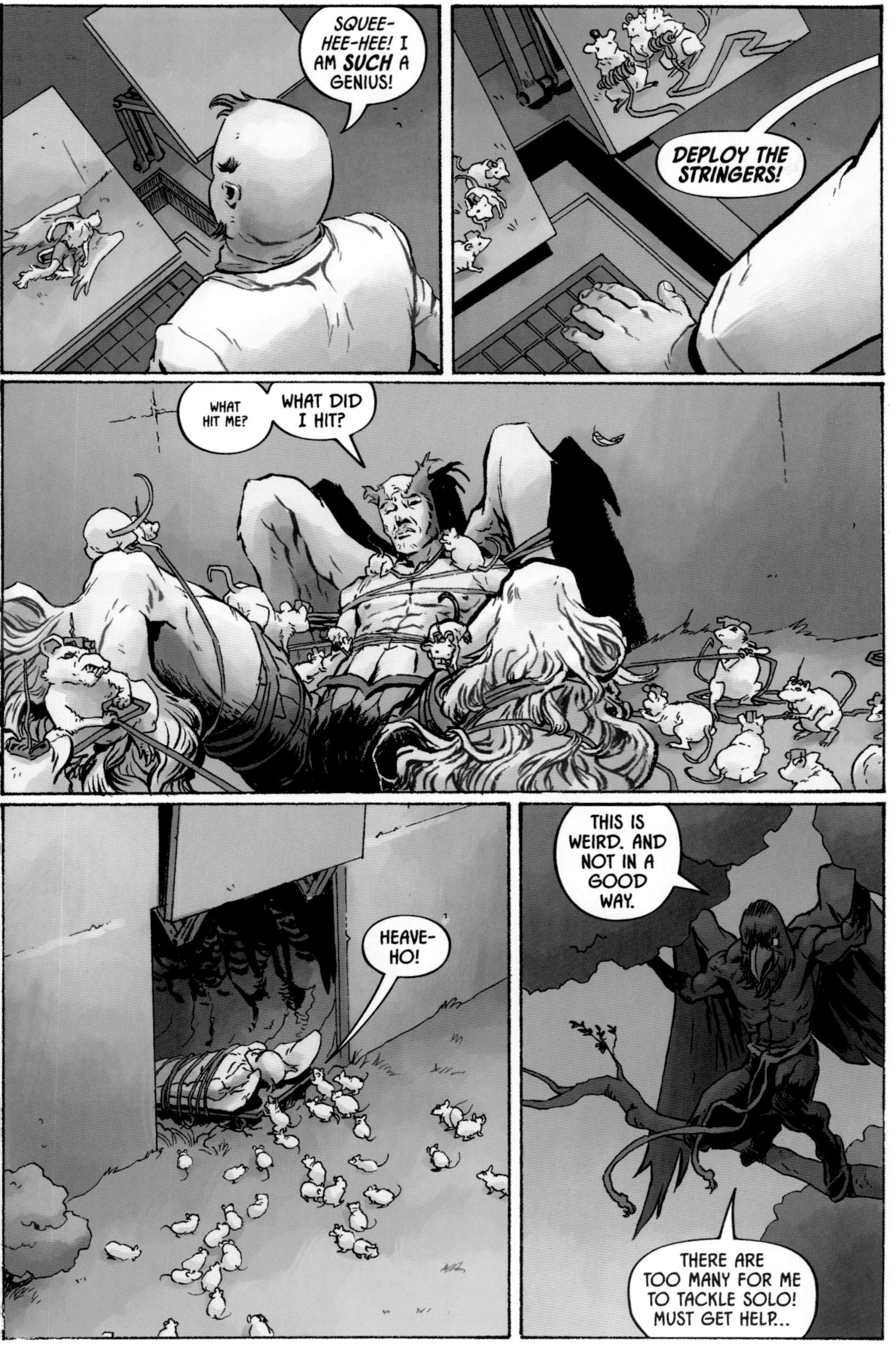
SQUEE-HEE-HEE! I AM SUCH A GENIUS!
DEPLOY THE STRINGERS!
WHAT HIT ME?
WHAT DID I HIT?
HEAVE-HO!
THIS IS WEIRD. AND NOT IN A GOOD WAY.
THERE ARE TOO MANY FOR ME TO TACKLE SOLO! MUST GET HELP...

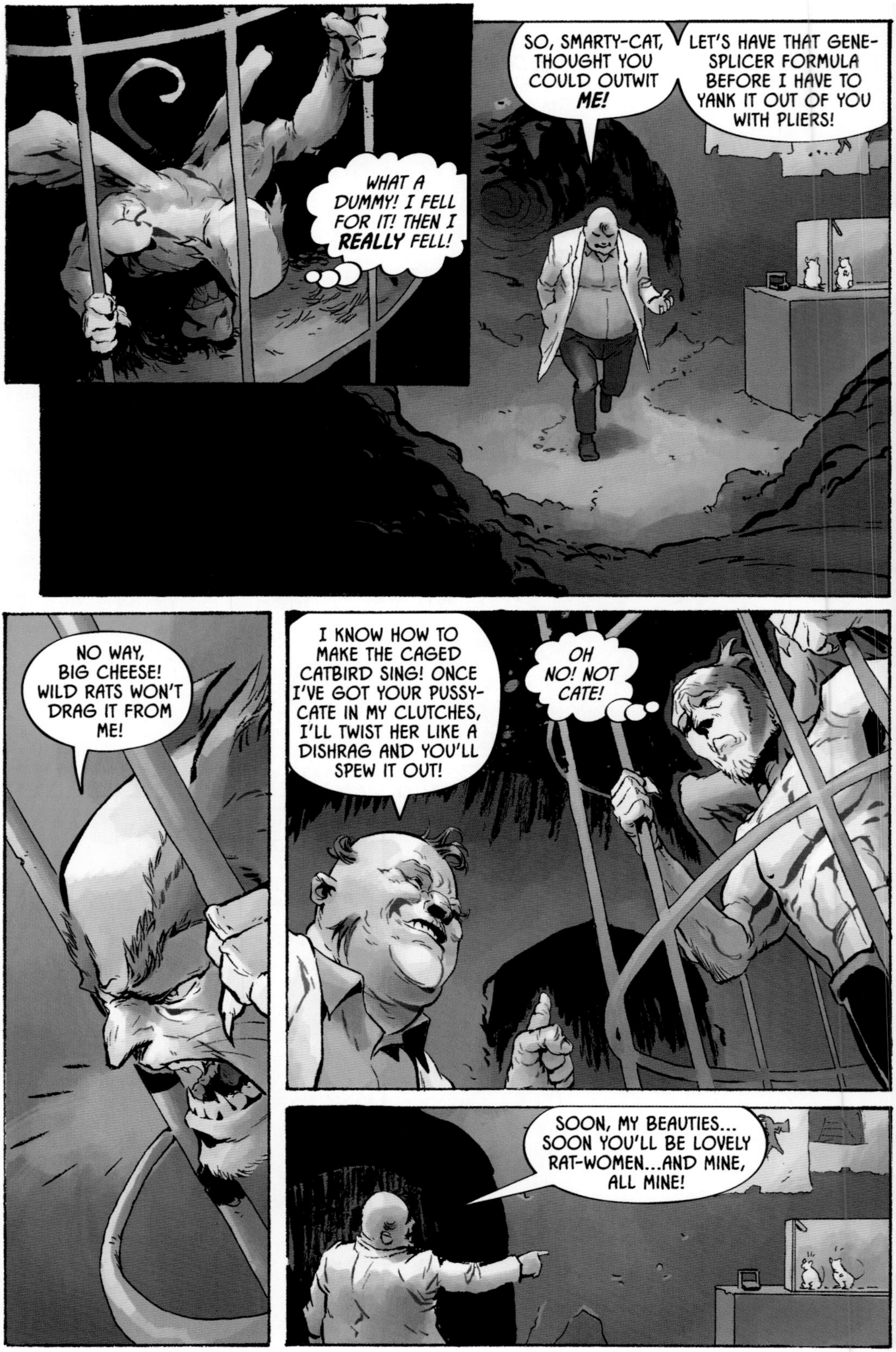
WHAT A DUMMY! I FELL FOR IT! THEN I **REALLY** FELL!
SO, SMARTY-CAT, THOUGHT YOU COULD OUTWIT **ME!**
LET'S HAVE THAT GENE-SPLICER FORMULA BEFORE I HAVE TO YANK IT OUT OF YOU WITH PLIERS!
NO WAY, BIG CHEESE! WILD RATS WON'T DRAG IT FROM ME!
I KNOW HOW TO MAKE THE CAGED CATBIRD SING! ONCE I'VE GOT YOUR PUSSY-CATE IN MY CLUTCHES, I'LL TWIST HER LIKE A DISHRAG AND YOU'LL SPEW IT OUT!
OH NO! NOT CATE!
SOON, MY BEAUTIES... SOON YOU'LL BE LOVELY RAT-WOMEN...AND MINE, ALL MINE!

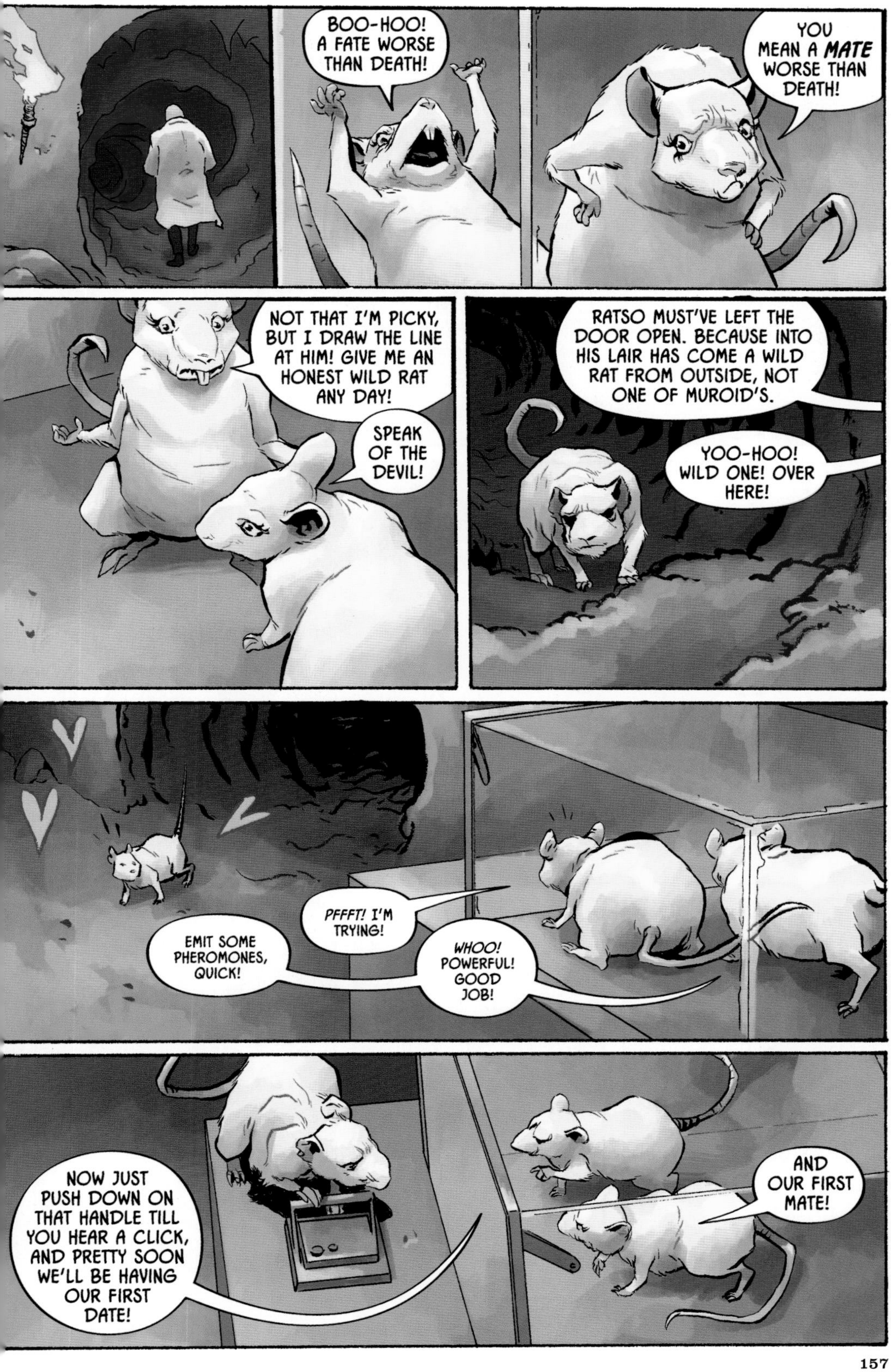
BOO-HOO! A FATE WORSE THAN DEATH!
YOU MEAN A *MATE* WORSE THAN DEATH!
NOT THAT I'M PICKY, BUT I DRAW THE LINE AT HIM! GIVE ME AN HONEST WILD RAT ANY DAY!
SPEAK OF THE DEVIL!
RATSO MUST'VE LEFT THE DOOR OPEN. BECAUSE INTO HIS LAIR HAS COME A WILD RAT FROM OUTSIDE, NOT ONE OF MUROID'S.
YOO-HOO! WILD ONE! OVER HERE!
EMIT SOME PHEROMONES, QUICK!
PFFFT! I'M TRYING!
WHOO! POWERFUL! GOOD JOB!
NOW JUST PUSH DOWN ON THAT HANDLE TILL YOU HEAR A CLICK, AND PRETTY SOON WE'LL BE HAVING OUR FIRST DATE!
AND OUR FIRST MATE!

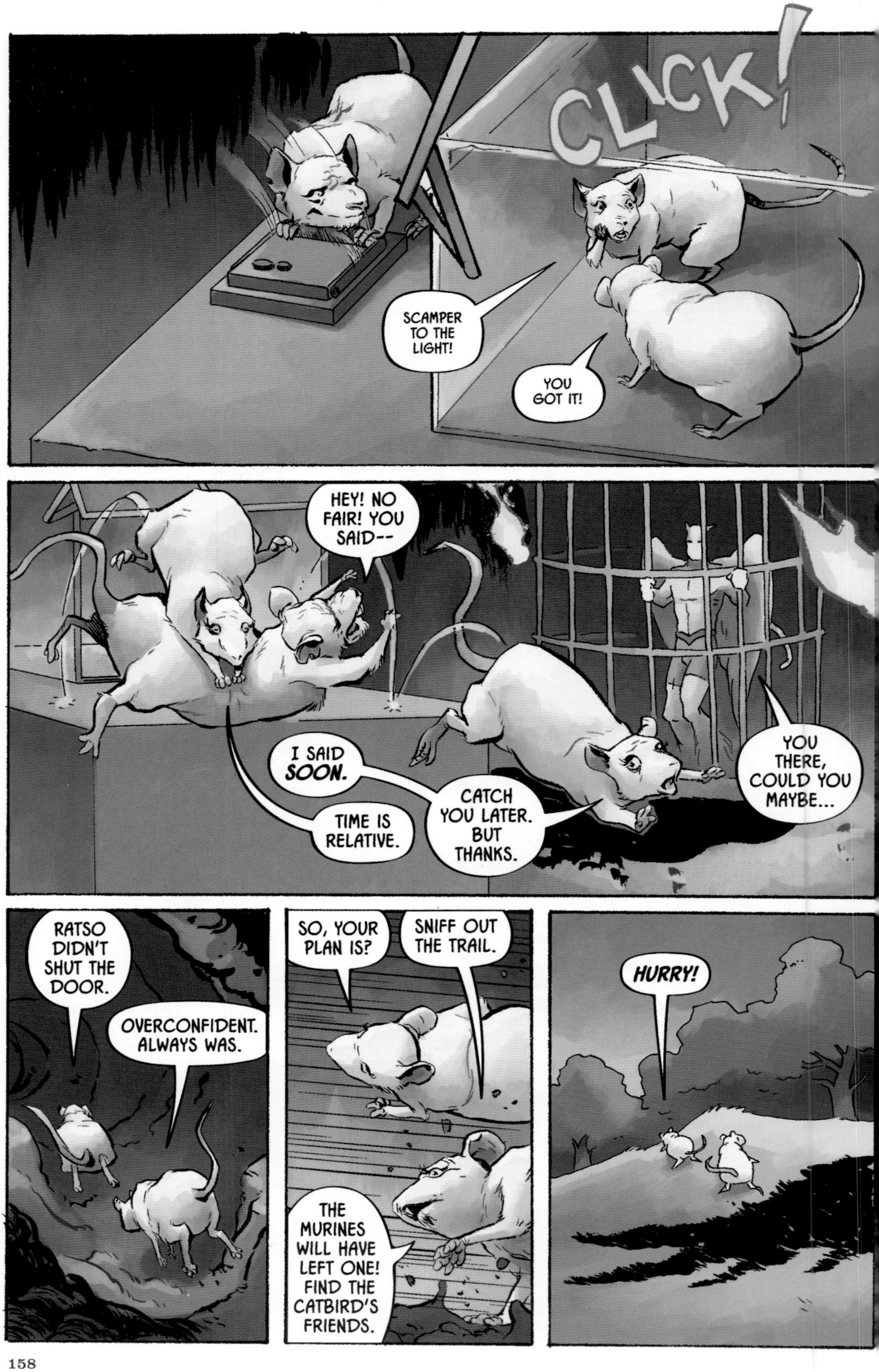
CLICK!
SCAMPER TO THE LIGHT!
YOU GOT IT!
HEY! NO FAIR! YOU SAID--
I SAID *SOON.*
TIME IS RELATIVE.
CATCH YOU LATER. BUT THANKS.
YOU THERE, COULD YOU MAYBE...
RATSO DIDN'T SHUT THE DOOR.
OVERCONFIDENT. ALWAYS WAS.
SO, YOUR PLAN IS?
SNIFF OUT THE TRAIL.
THE MURINES WILL HAVE LEFT ONE! FIND THE CATBIRD'S FRIENDS.
HURRY!

DON'T WORRY, MY PETS. I'M NOT GOING TO EAT YOU. YET.

ANGEL CRASHED. TRICK GLASS WALL. MUROID'S RATS TIED HIM UP WITH STRING.

THIS IS DIRE!

OH NO!

WE WARNED HIM!

FOUND THESE POWDER PUFFS HEADING TO THE FOREST.

MUROID'S SPIES? BUT THEY DON'T HAVE SPYCAMS...

TASTY, IN ANY CASE. SORRY. BAD MANNERS.

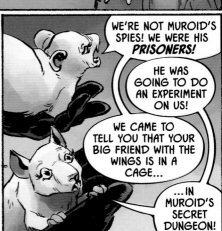

WE'RE NOT MUROID'S SPIES! WE WERE HIS **PRISONERS!**

HE WAS GOING TO DO AN EXPERIMENT ON US!

WE CAME TO TELL YOU THAT YOUR BIG FRIEND WITH THE WINGS IS IN A CAGE...

...IN MUROID'S SECRET DUNGEON!

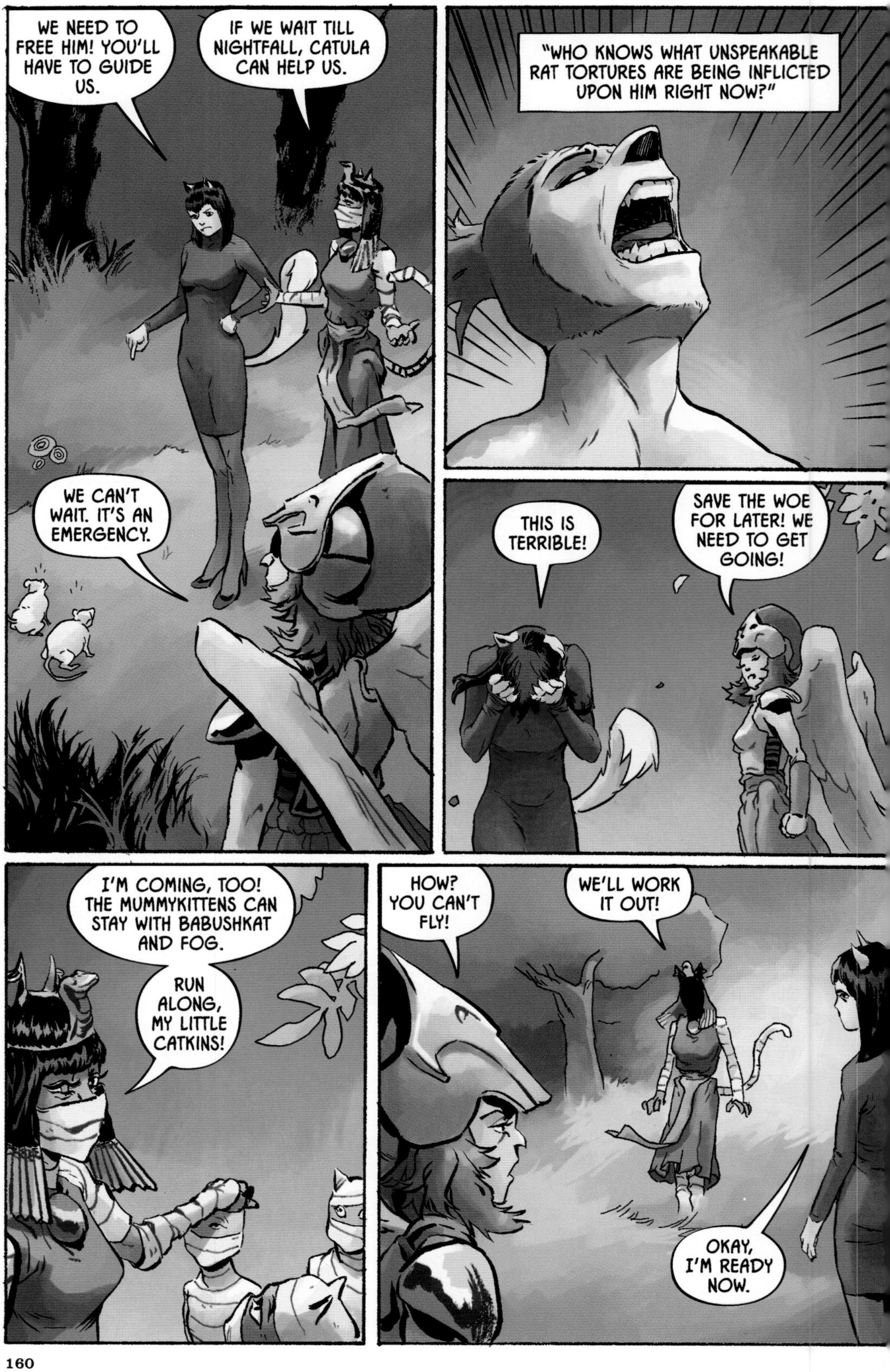
WE NEED TO FREE HIM! YOU'LL HAVE TO GUIDE US.
IF WE WAIT TILL NIGHTFALL, CATULA CAN HELP US.
WE CAN'T WAIT. IT'S AN EMERGENCY.
"WHO KNOWS WHAT UNSPEAKABLE RAT TORTURES ARE BEING INFLICTED UPON HIM RIGHT NOW?"
THIS IS TERRIBLE!
SAVE THE WOE FOR LATER! WE NEED TO GET GOING!
I'M COMING, TOO! THE MUMMYKITTENS CAN STAY WITH BABUSHKAT AND FOG.
RUN ALONG, MY LITTLE CATKINS!
HOW? YOU CAN'T FLY!
WE'LL WORK IT OUT!
OKAY, I'M READY NOW.

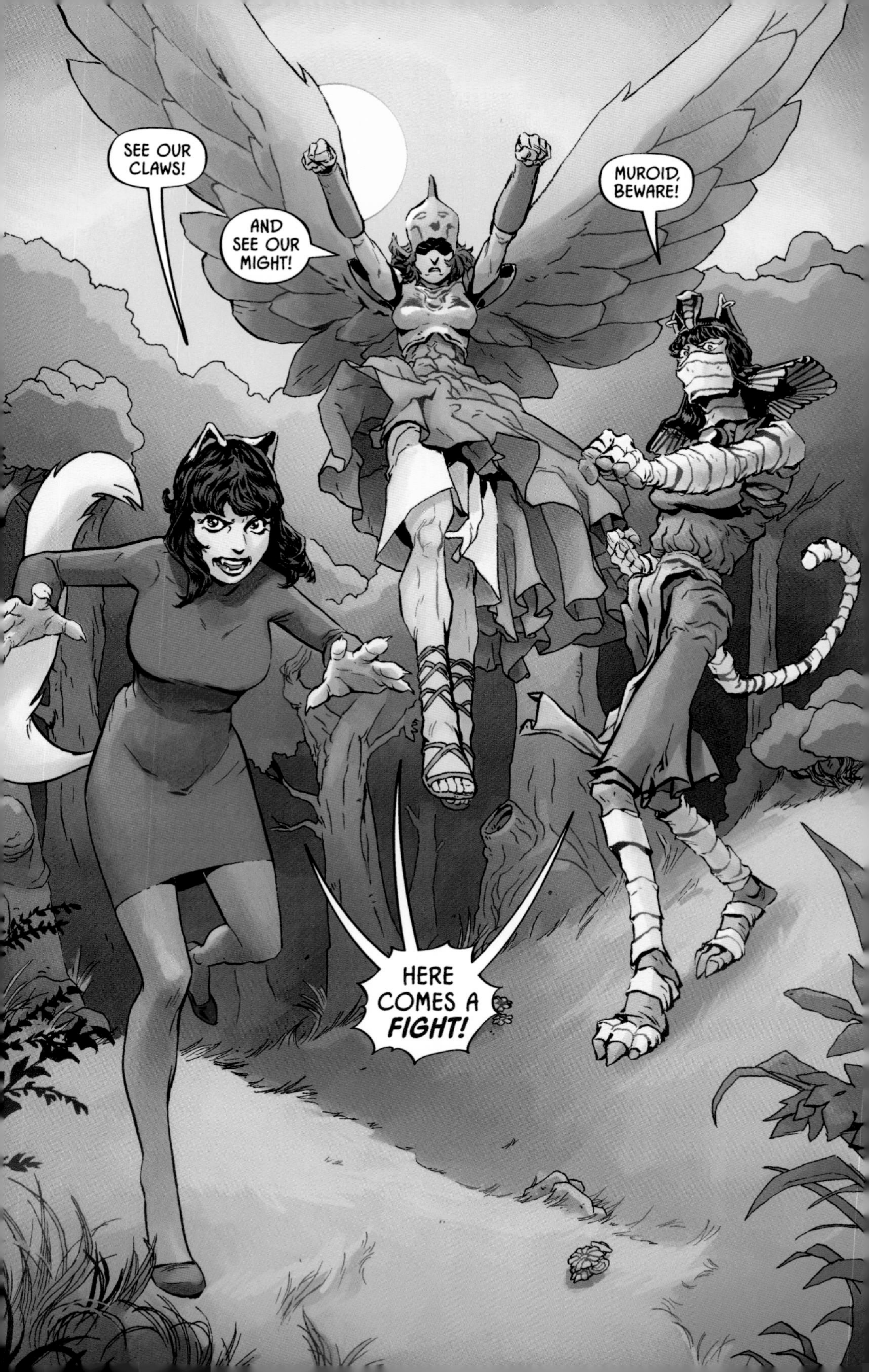
SEE OUR CLAWS!
AND SEE OUR MIGHT!
MUROID, BEWARE!
HERE COMES A *FIGHT!*

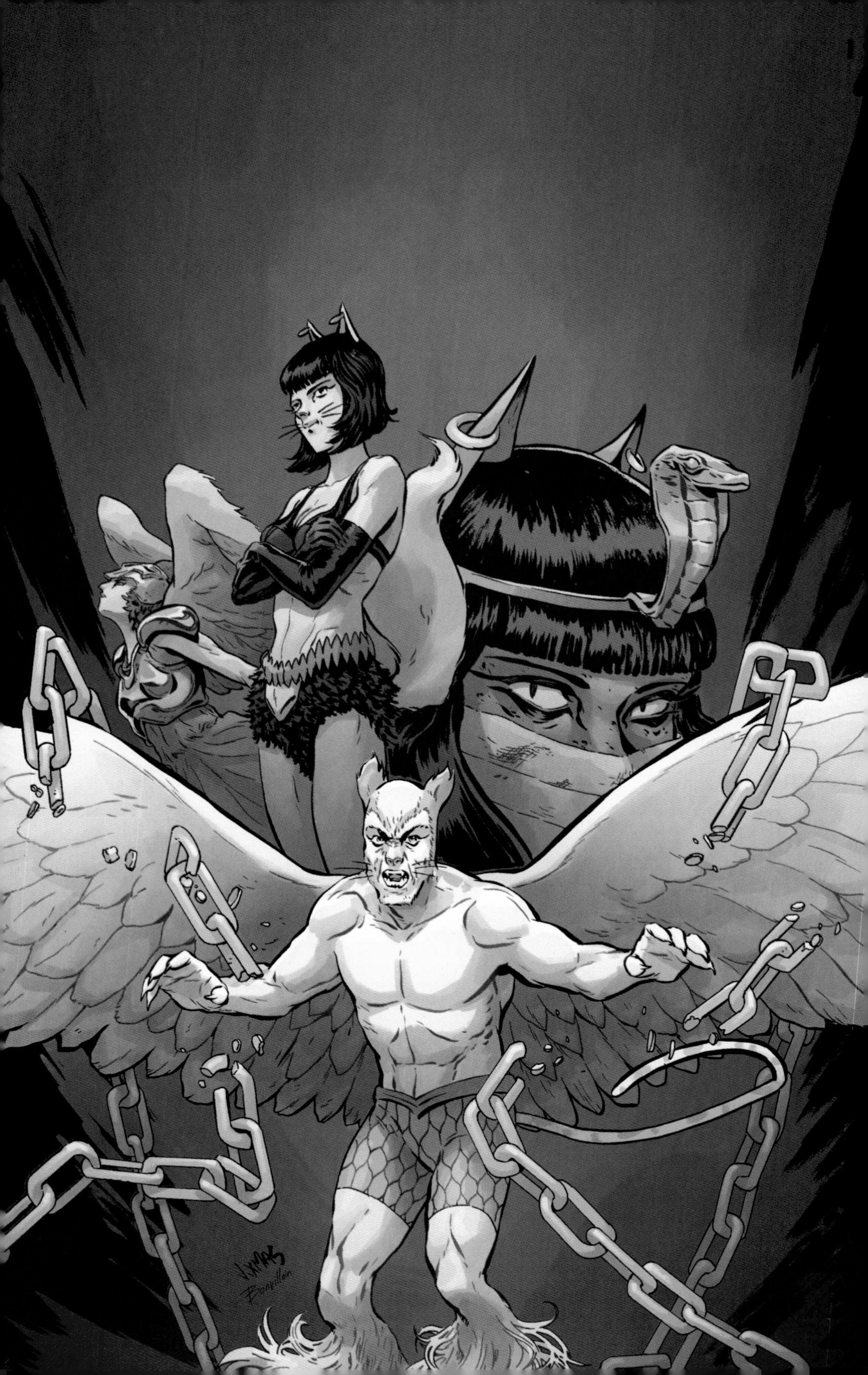

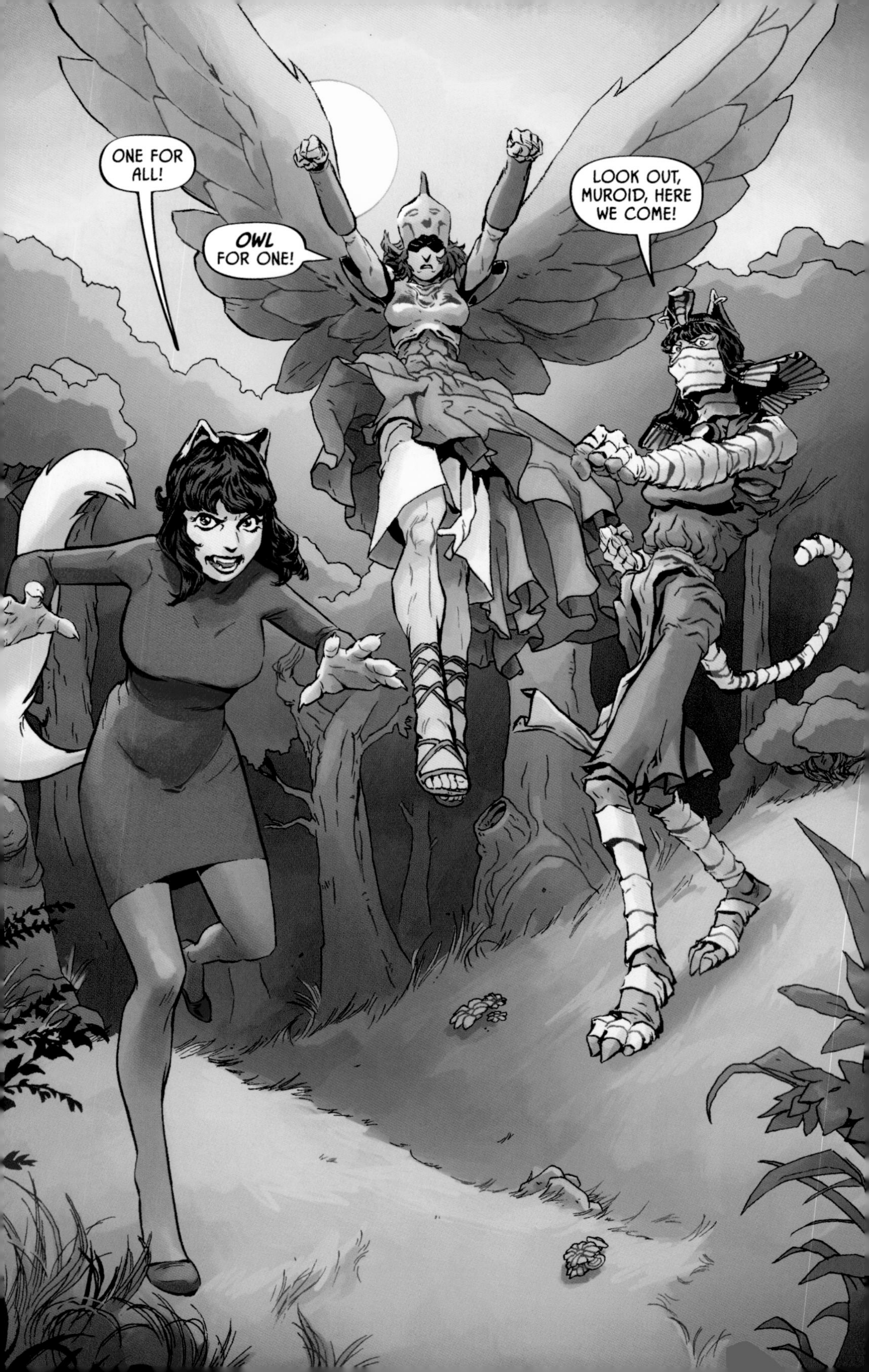
ONE FOR ALL!
OWL FOR ONE!
LOOK OUT, MUROID, HERE WE COME!

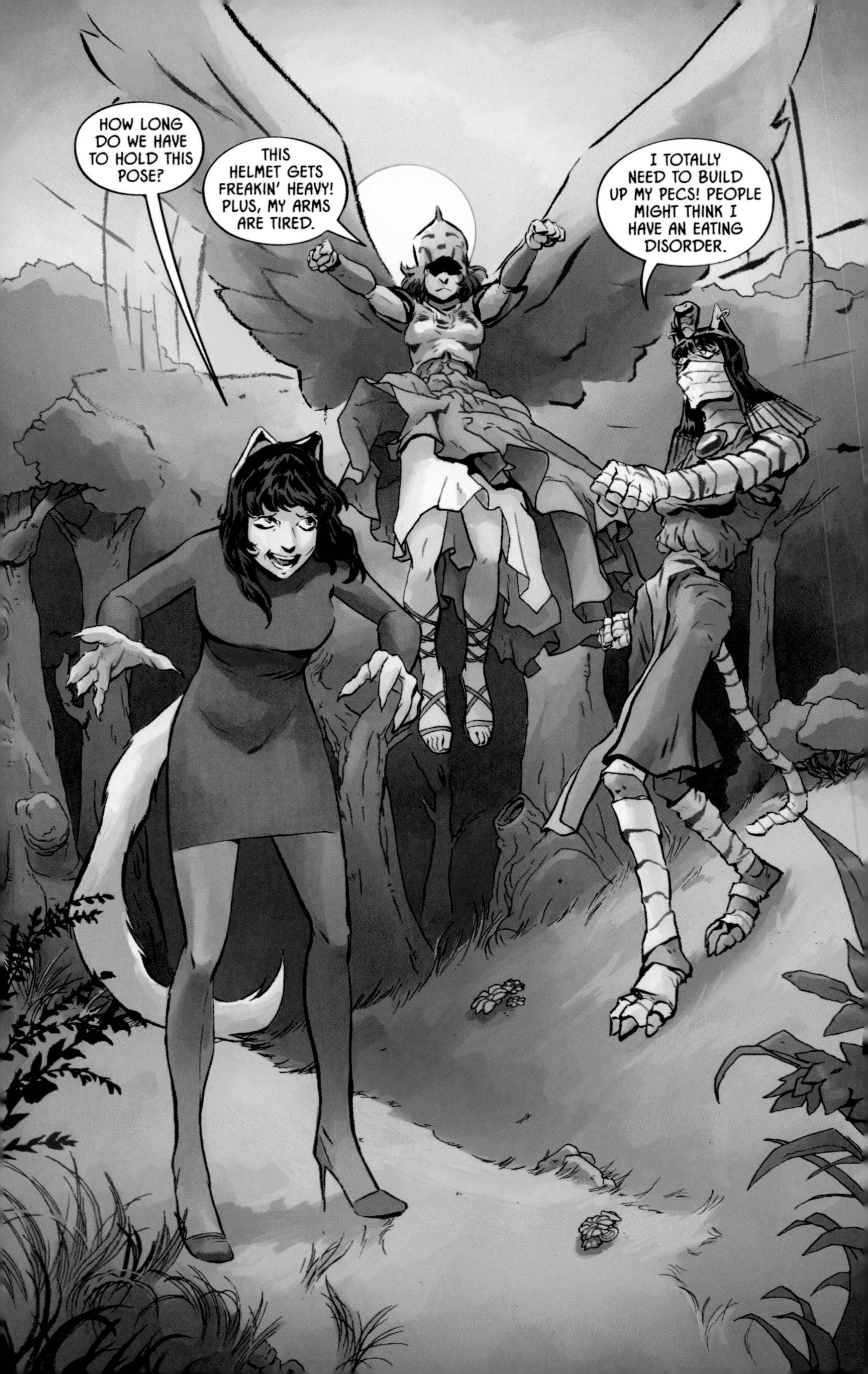
HOW LONG DO WE HAVE TO HOLD THIS POSE?
THIS HELMET GETS FREAKIN' HEAVY! PLUS, MY ARMS ARE TIRED.
I TOTALLY NEED TO BUILD UP MY PECS! PEOPLE MIGHT THINK I HAVE AN EATING DISORDER.

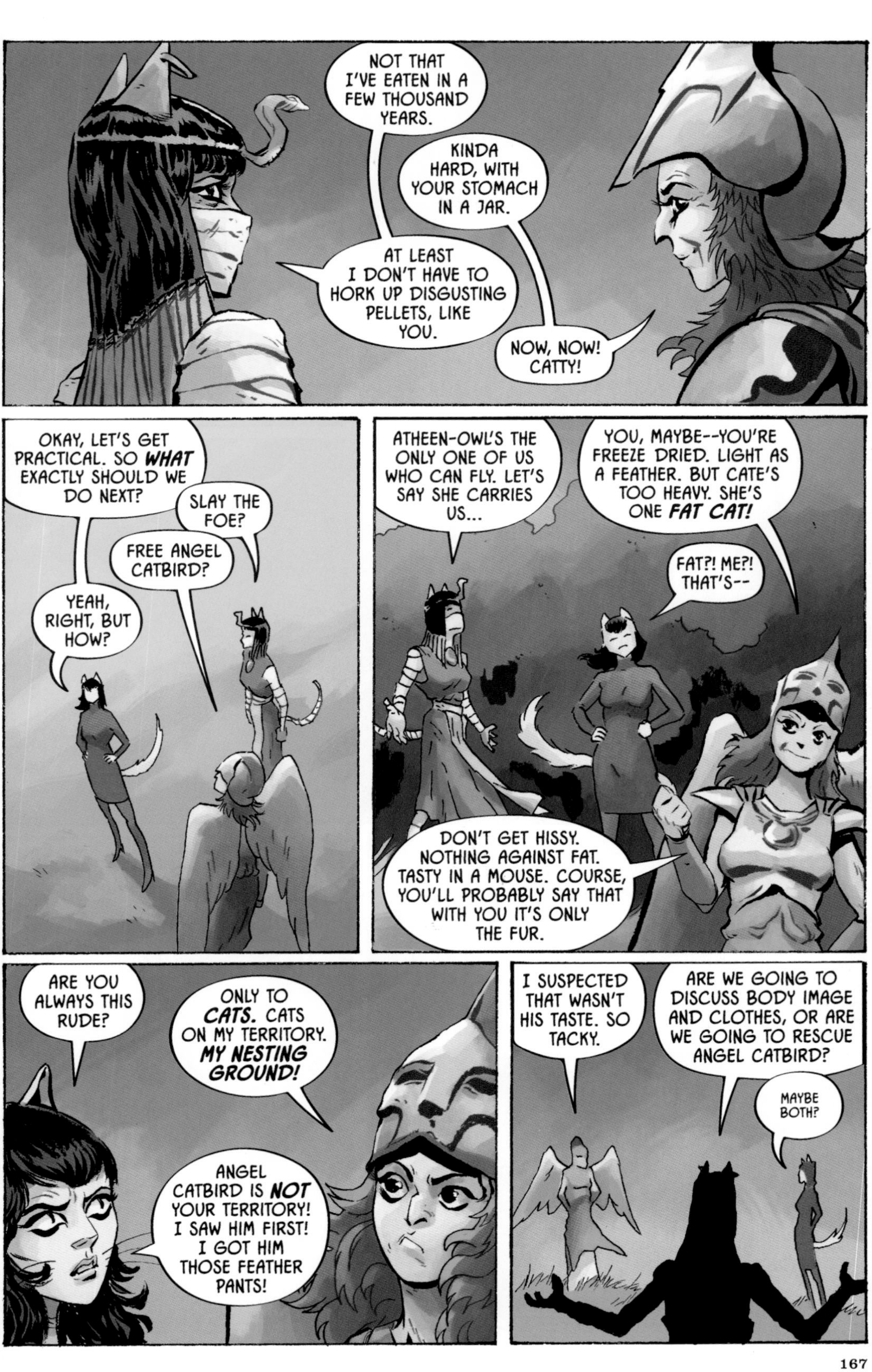
NOT THAT I'VE EATEN IN A FEW THOUSAND YEARS.
KINDA HARD, WITH YOUR STOMACH IN A JAR.
AT LEAST I DON'T HAVE TO HORK UP DISGUSTING PELLETS, LIKE YOU.
NOW, NOW! CATTY!
OKAY, LET'S GET PRACTICAL. SO WHAT EXACTLY SHOULD WE DO NEXT?
SLAY THE FOE?
FREE ANGEL CATBIRD?
YEAH, RIGHT, BUT HOW?
ATHEEN-OWL'S THE ONLY ONE OF US WHO CAN FLY. LET'S SAY SHE CARRIES US...
YOU, MAYBE--YOU'RE FREEZE DRIED. LIGHT AS A FEATHER. BUT CATE'S TOO HEAVY. SHE'S ONE FAT CAT!
FAT?! ME?! THAT'S--
DON'T GET HISSY. NOTHING AGAINST FAT. TASTY IN A MOUSE. COURSE, YOU'LL PROBABLY SAY THAT WITH YOU IT'S ONLY THE FUR.
ARE YOU ALWAYS THIS RUDE?
ONLY TO CATS. CATS ON MY TERRITORY. MY NESTING GROUND!
ANGEL CATBIRD IS NOT YOUR TERRITORY! I SAW HIM FIRST! I GOT HIM THOSE FEATHER PANTS!
I SUSPECTED THAT WASN'T HIS TASTE. SO TACKY.
ARE WE GOING TO DISCUSS BODY IMAGE AND CLOTHES, OR ARE WE GOING TO RESCUE ANGEL CATBIRD?
MAYBE BOTH?

Meanwhile, in the deepest, darkest corner of Professor Muroid's laboratory crypt...

YOU SUCKER!

HOW COULD YOU FALL FOR THAT CHEESY PIECE OF CRAP?

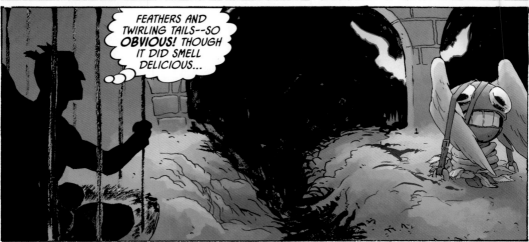

FEATHERS AND TWIRLING TAILS—SO *OBVIOUS!* THOUGH IT DID SMELL DELICIOUS...

SO NOW I'M GOOD AND TRAPPED. LOCKS, CHAINS... WHERE EVEN IS THIS PLACE?

ARROWWOHOOR!

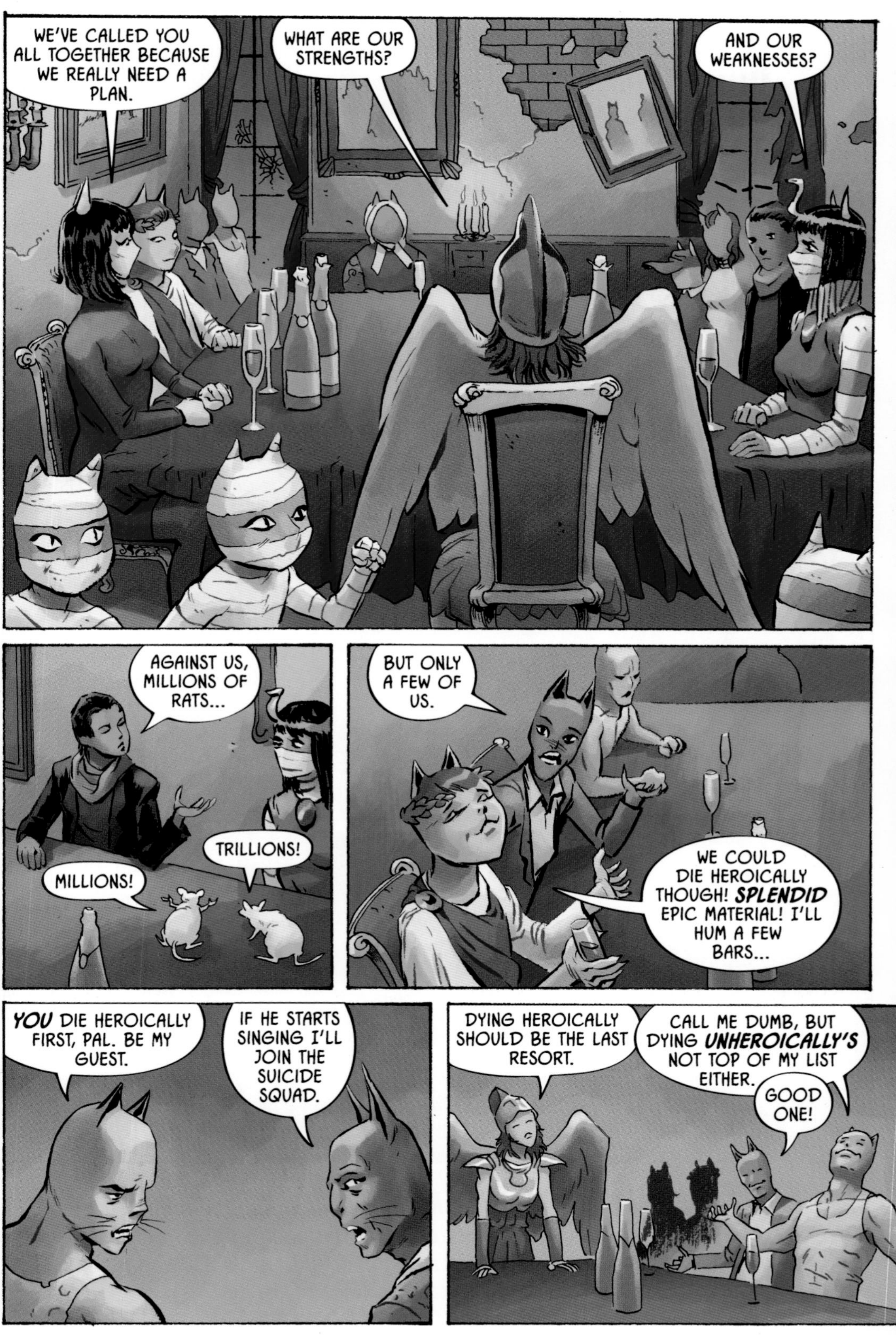
WE'VE CALLED YOU ALL TOGETHER BECAUSE WE REALLY NEED A PLAN.
WHAT ARE OUR STRENGTHS?
AND OUR WEAKNESSES?
AGAINST US, MILLIONS OF RATS...
MILLIONS!
TRILLIONS!
BUT ONLY A FEW OF US.
WE COULD DIE HEROICALLY THOUGH! SPLENDID EPIC MATERIAL! I'LL HUM A FEW BARS...
YOU DIE HEROICALLY FIRST, PAL. BE MY GUEST.
IF HE STARTS SINGING I'LL JOIN THE SUICIDE SQUAD.
DYING HEROICALLY SHOULD BE THE LAST RESORT.
CALL ME DUMB, BUT DYING UNHEROICALLY'S NOT TOP OF MY LIST EITHER.
GOOD ONE!

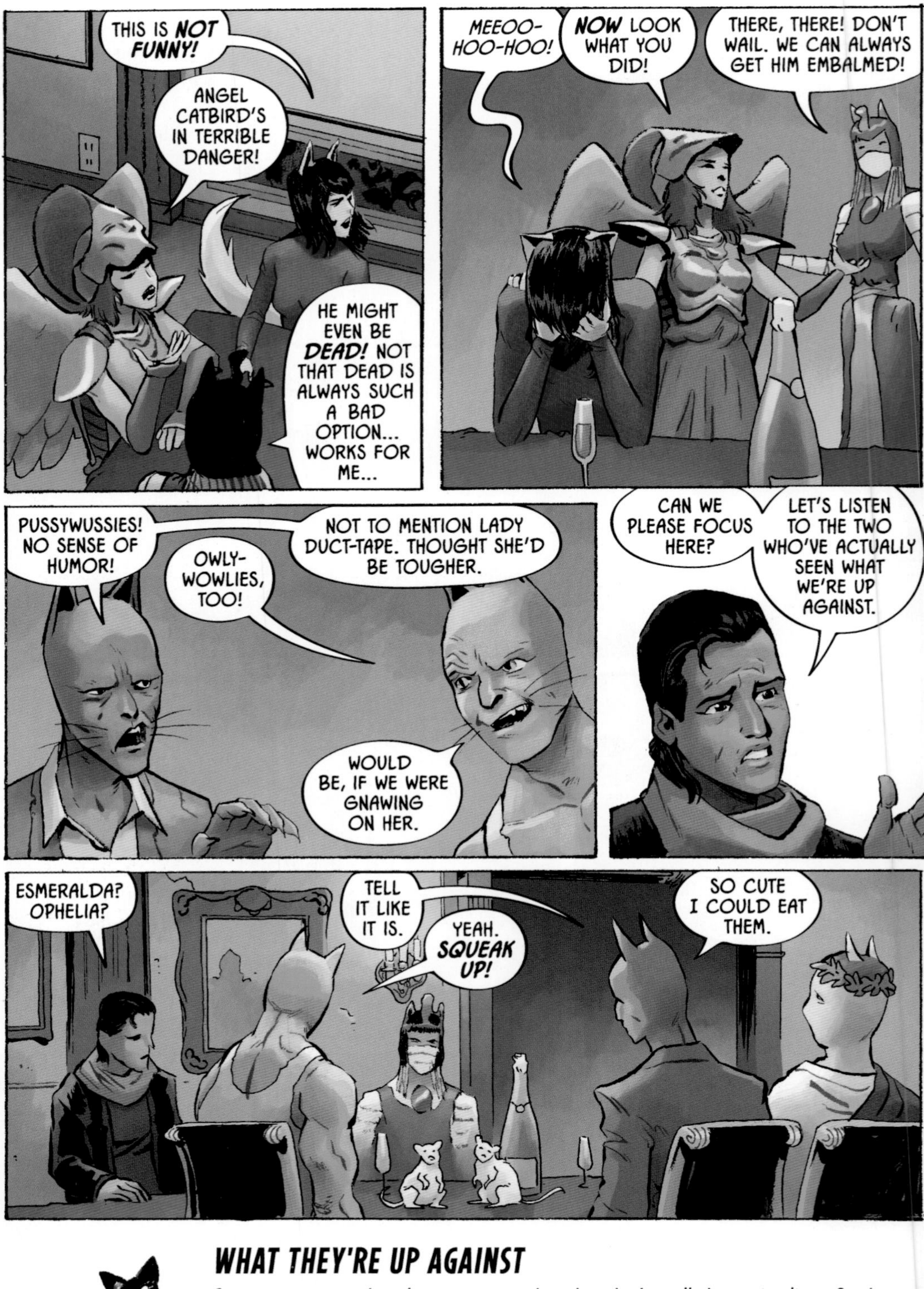
THIS IS **NOT** **FUNNY!**
ANGEL CATBIRD'S IN TERRIBLE DANGER!
HE MIGHT EVEN BE **DEAD!** NOT THAT DEAD IS ALWAYS SUCH A BAD OPTION... WORKS FOR ME...
MEEOO-HOO-HOO!
NOW LOOK WHAT YOU DID!
THERE, THERE! DON'T WAIL. WE CAN ALWAYS GET HIM EMBALMED!
PUSSYWUSSIES! NO SENSE OF HUMOR!
OWLY-WOWLIES, TOO!
NOT TO MENTION LADY DUCT-TAPE. THOUGHT SHE'D BE TOUGHER.
WOULD BE, IF WE WERE GNAWING ON HER.
CAN WE PLEASE FOCUS HERE?
LET'S LISTEN TO THE TWO WHO'VE ACTUALLY SEEN WHAT WE'RE UP AGAINST.
ESMERALDA? OPHELIA?
TELL IT LIKE IT IS.
YEAH. **SQUEAK UP!**
SO CUTE I COULD EAT THEM.

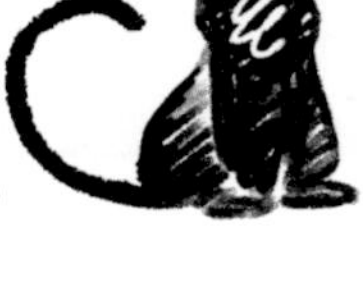

WHAT THEY'RE UP AGAINST

Cats are strong and resilient creatures, but they don't really have nine lives. Outdoor cats frequently get hit by cars and are at much higher risk of disease, getting lost, fights with wildlife and other cats, poisoning, and parasites.
Read more at www.catsandbirds.ca

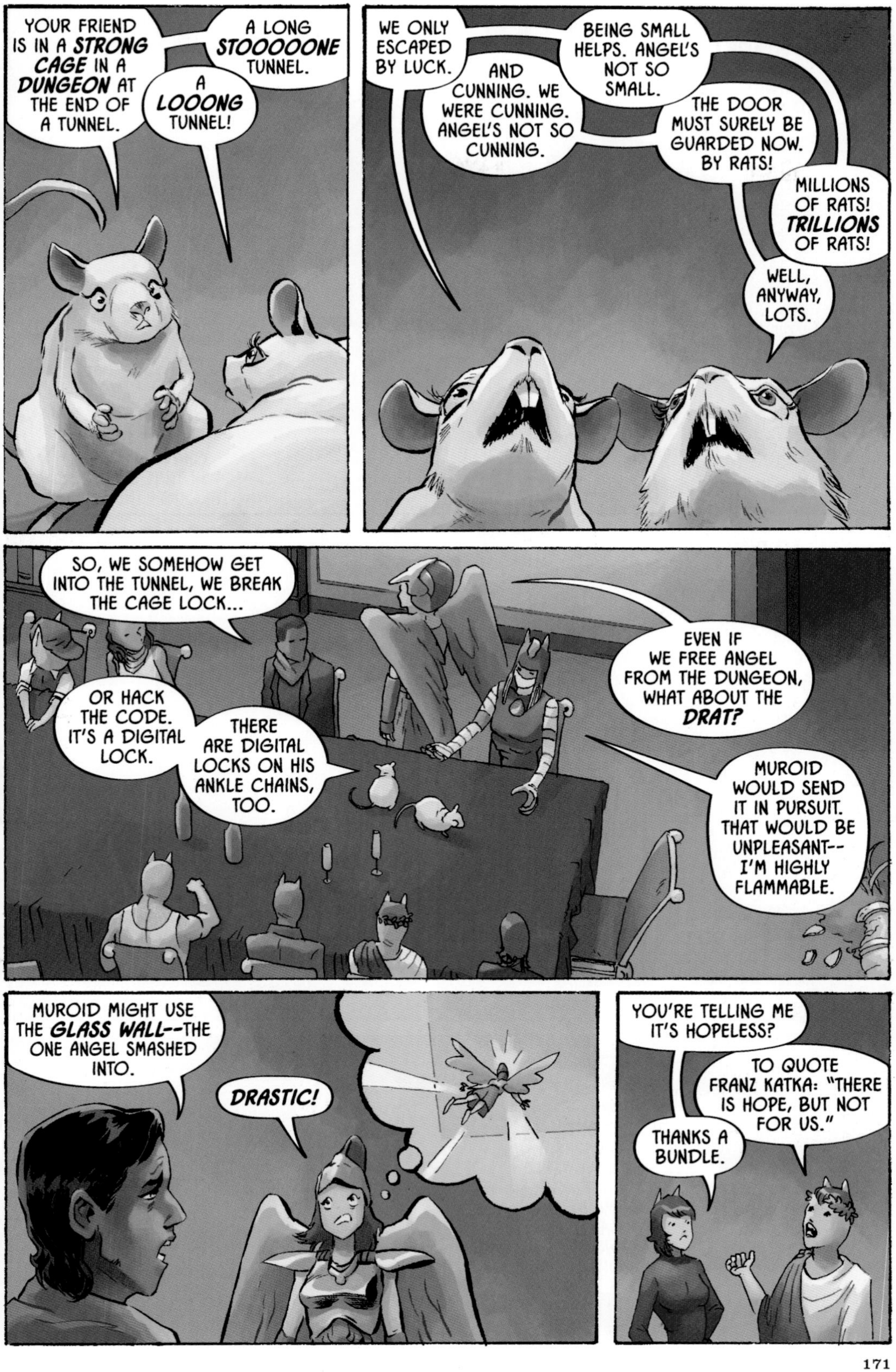
YOUR FRIEND IS IN A **STRONG CAGE** IN A **DUNGEON** AT THE END OF A TUNNEL.
A LONG **STOOOOONE** TUNNEL.
A **LOOONG** TUNNEL!
WE ONLY ESCAPED BY LUCK.
BEING SMALL HELPS. ANGEL'S NOT SO SMALL.
AND CUNNING. WE WERE CUNNING. ANGEL'S NOT SO CUNNING.
THE DOOR MUST SURELY BE GUARDED NOW. BY RATS!
MILLIONS OF RATS! **TRILLIONS** OF RATS!
WELL, ANYWAY, LOTS.
SO, WE SOMEHOW GET INTO THE TUNNEL, WE BREAK THE CAGE LOCK...
OR HACK THE CODE. IT'S A DIGITAL LOCK.
THERE ARE DIGITAL LOCKS ON HIS ANKLE CHAINS, TOO.
EVEN IF WE FREE ANGEL FROM THE DUNGEON, WHAT ABOUT THE **DRAT?**
MUROID WOULD SEND IT IN PURSUIT. THAT WOULD BE UNPLEASANT--I'M HIGHLY FLAMMABLE.
MUROID MIGHT USE THE **GLASS WALL**--THE ONE ANGEL SMASHED INTO.
DRASTIC!
YOU'RE TELLING ME IT'S HOPELESS?
TO QUOTE FRANZ KATKA: "THERE IS HOPE, BUT NOT FOR US."
THANKS A BUNDLE.

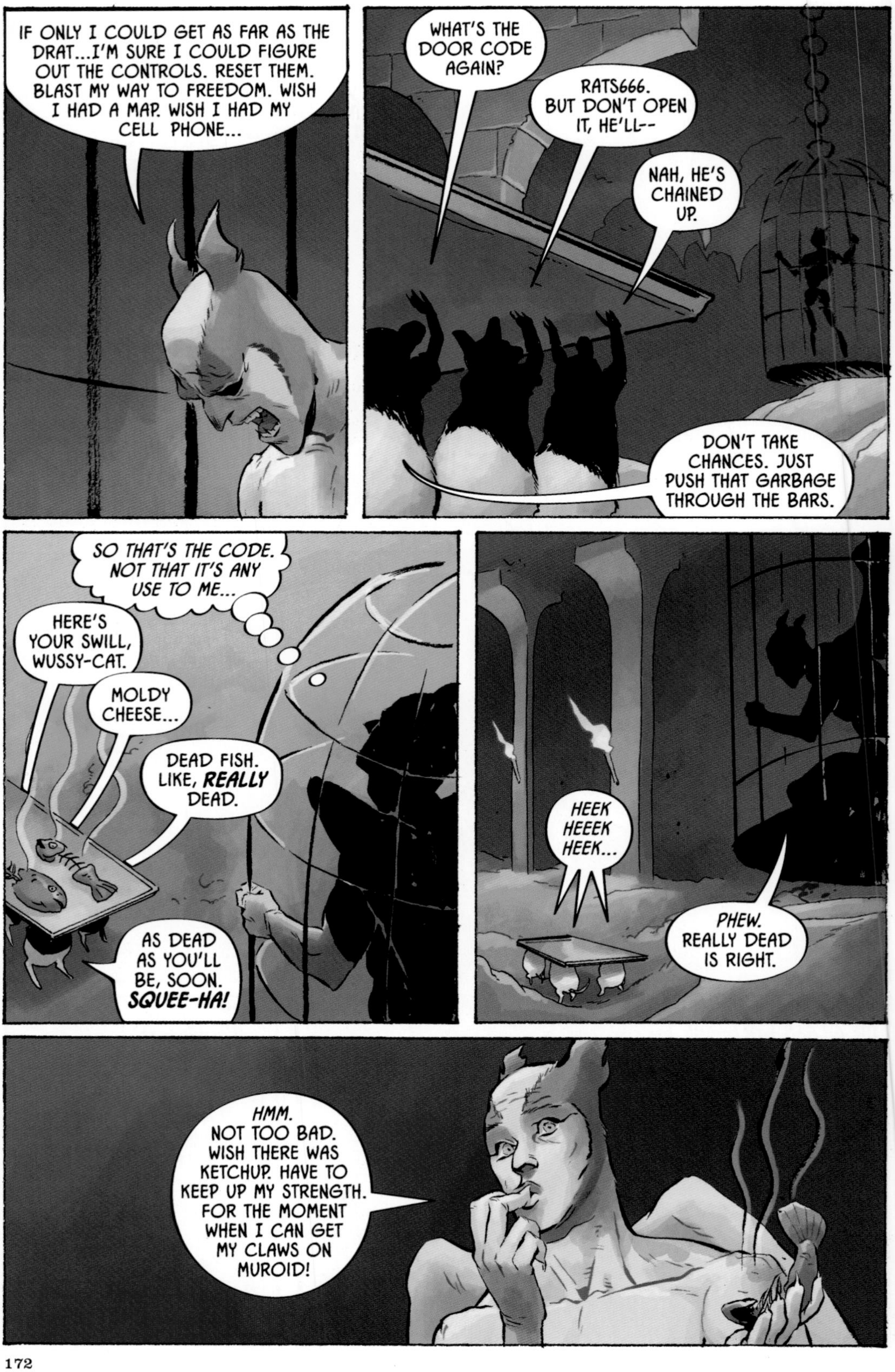

IF ONLY I COULD GET AS FAR AS THE DRAT...I'M SURE I COULD FIGURE OUT THE CONTROLS. RESET THEM. BLAST MY WAY TO FREEDOM. WISH I HAD A MAP. WISH I HAD MY CELL PHONE...
WHAT'S THE DOOR CODE AGAIN?
RATS666. BUT DON'T OPEN IT, HE'LL--
NAH, HE'S CHAINED UP.
DON'T TAKE CHANCES. JUST PUSH THAT GARBAGE THROUGH THE BARS.
SO THAT'S THE CODE. NOT THAT IT'S ANY USE TO ME...
HERE'S YOUR SWILL, WUSSY-CAT.
MOLDY CHEESE...
DEAD FISH. LIKE, REALLY DEAD.
AS DEAD AS YOU'LL BE, SOON. SQUEE-HA!
HEEK HEEEK HEEK...
PHEW. REALLY DEAD IS RIGHT.
HMM. NOT TOO BAD. WISH THERE WAS KETCHUP. HAVE TO KEEP UP MY STRENGTH. FOR THE MOMENT WHEN I CAN GET MY CLAWS ON MUROID!

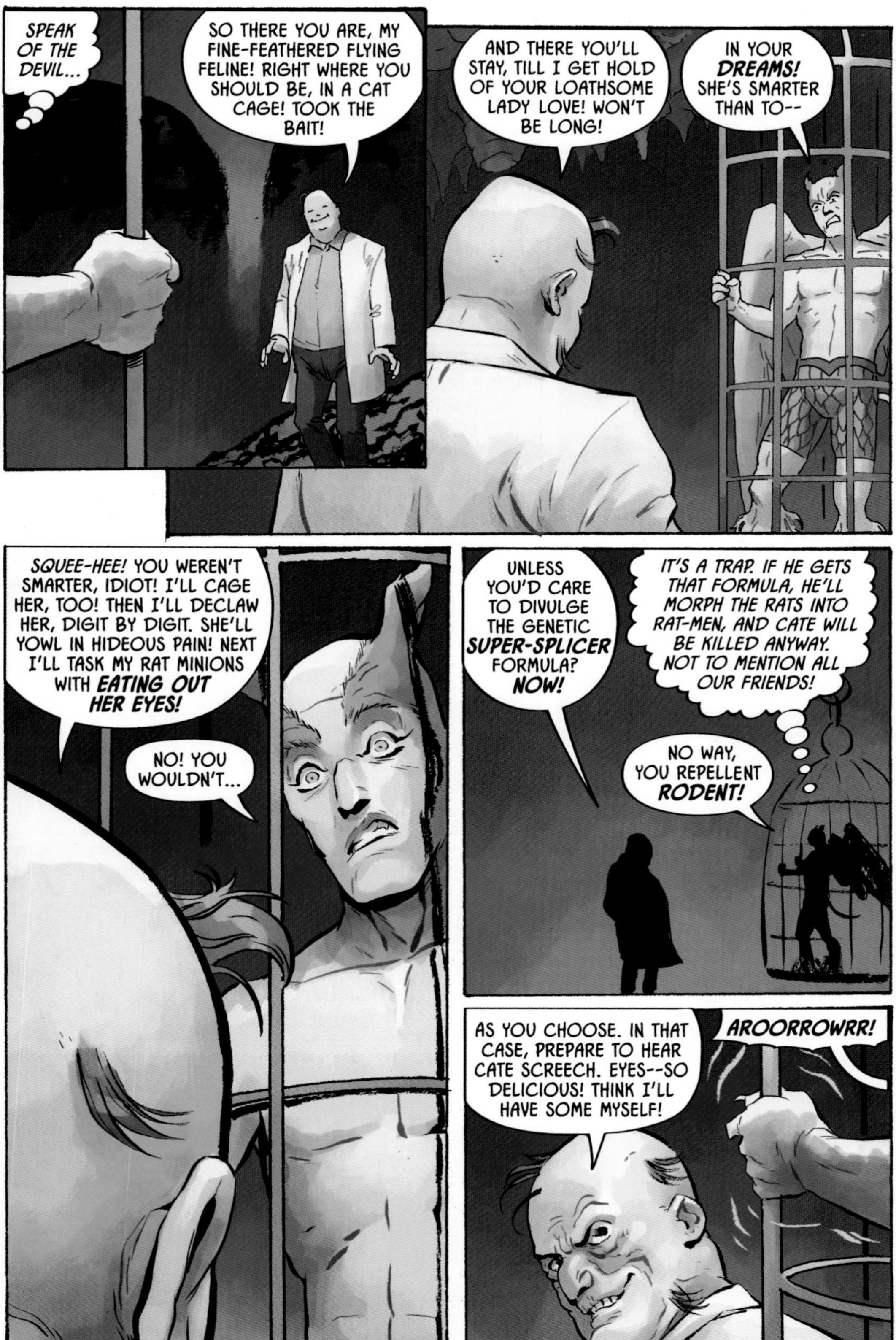
SPEAK OF THE DEVIL...
SO THERE YOU ARE, MY FINE-FEATHERED FLYING FELINE! RIGHT WHERE YOU SHOULD BE, IN A CAT CAGE! TOOK THE BAIT!
AND THERE YOU'LL STAY, TILL I GET HOLD OF YOUR LOATHSOME LADY LOVE! WON'T BE LONG!
IN YOUR DREAMS! SHE'S SMARTER THAN TO--
SQUEE-HEE! YOU WEREN'T SMARTER, IDIOT! I'LL CAGE HER, TOO! THEN I'LL DECLAW HER, DIGIT BY DIGIT. SHE'LL YOWL IN HIDEOUS PAIN! NEXT I'LL TASK MY RAT MINIONS WITH EATING OUT HER EYES!
NO! YOU WOULDN'T...
UNLESS YOU'D CARE TO DIVULGE THE GENETIC SUPER-SPLICER FORMULA? NOW!
IT'S A TRAP. IF HE GETS THAT FORMULA, HE'LL MORPH THE RATS INTO RAT-MEN, AND CATE WILL BE KILLED ANYWAY. NOT TO MENTION ALL OUR FRIENDS!
NO WAY, YOU REPELLENT RODENT!
AS YOU CHOOSE. IN THAT CASE, PREPARE TO HEAR CATE SCREECH. EYES--SO DELICIOUS! THINK I'LL HAVE SOME MYSELF!
AROORROWRR!

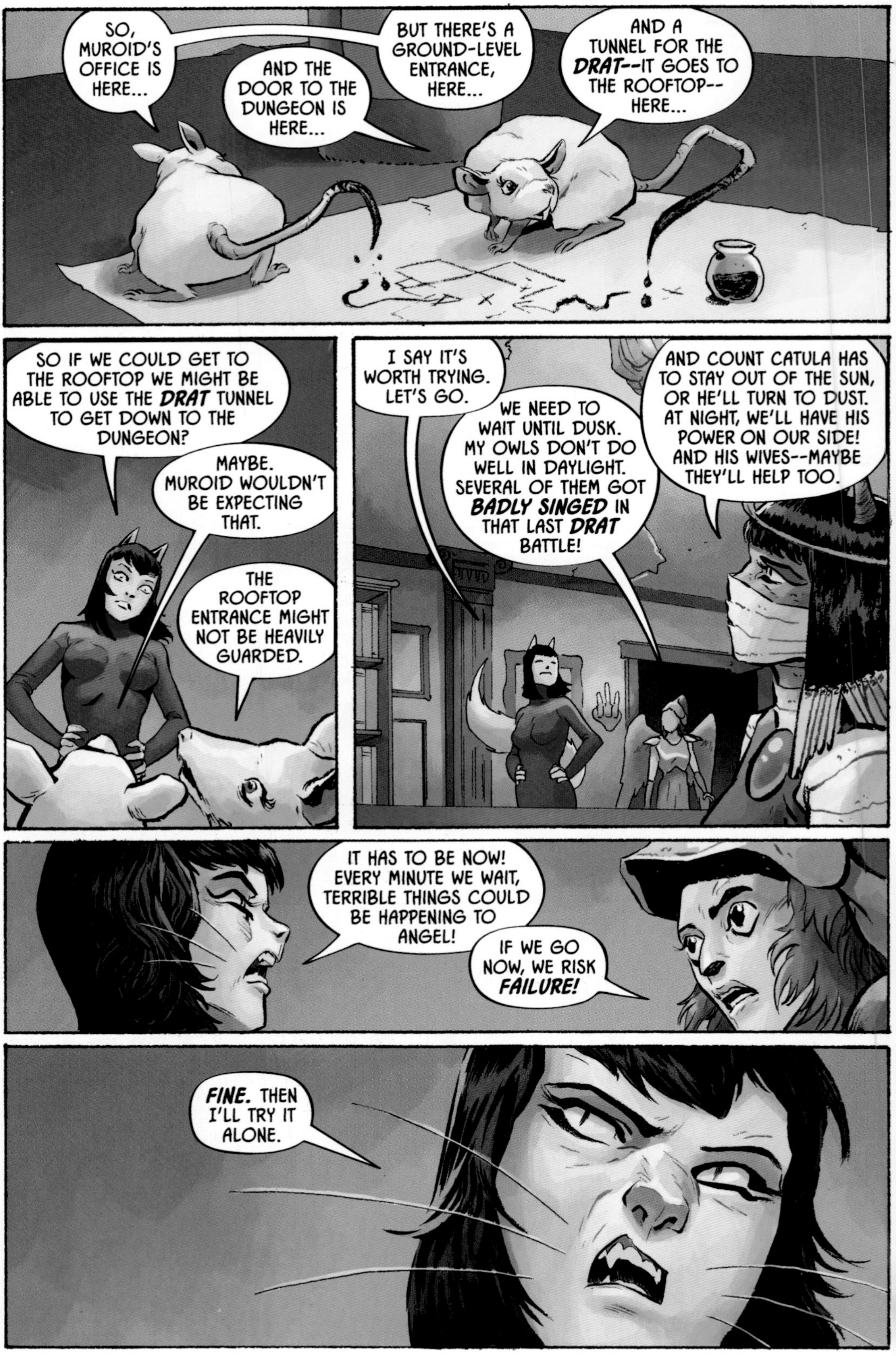
SO, MUROID'S OFFICE IS HERE...
AND THE DOOR TO THE DUNGEON IS HERE...
BUT THERE'S A GROUND-LEVEL ENTRANCE, HERE...
AND A TUNNEL FOR THE DRAT--IT GOES TO THE ROOFTOP--HERE...
SO IF WE COULD GET TO THE ROOFTOP WE MIGHT BE ABLE TO USE THE DRAT TUNNEL TO GET DOWN TO THE DUNGEON?
MAYBE. MUROID WOULDN'T BE EXPECTING THAT.
THE ROOFTOP ENTRANCE MIGHT NOT BE HEAVILY GUARDED.
I SAY IT'S WORTH TRYING. LET'S GO.
WE NEED TO WAIT UNTIL DUSK. MY OWLS DON'T DO WELL IN DAYLIGHT. SEVERAL OF THEM GOT BADLY SINGED IN THAT LAST DRAT BATTLE!
AND COUNT CATULA HAS TO STAY OUT OF THE SUN, OR HE'LL TURN TO DUST. AT NIGHT, WE'LL HAVE HIS POWER ON OUR SIDE! AND HIS WIVES--MAYBE THEY'LL HELP TOO.
IT HAS TO BE NOW! EVERY MINUTE WE WAIT, TERRIBLE THINGS COULD BE HAPPENING TO ANGEL!
IF WE GO NOW, WE RISK FAILURE!
FINE. THEN I'LL TRY IT ALONE.

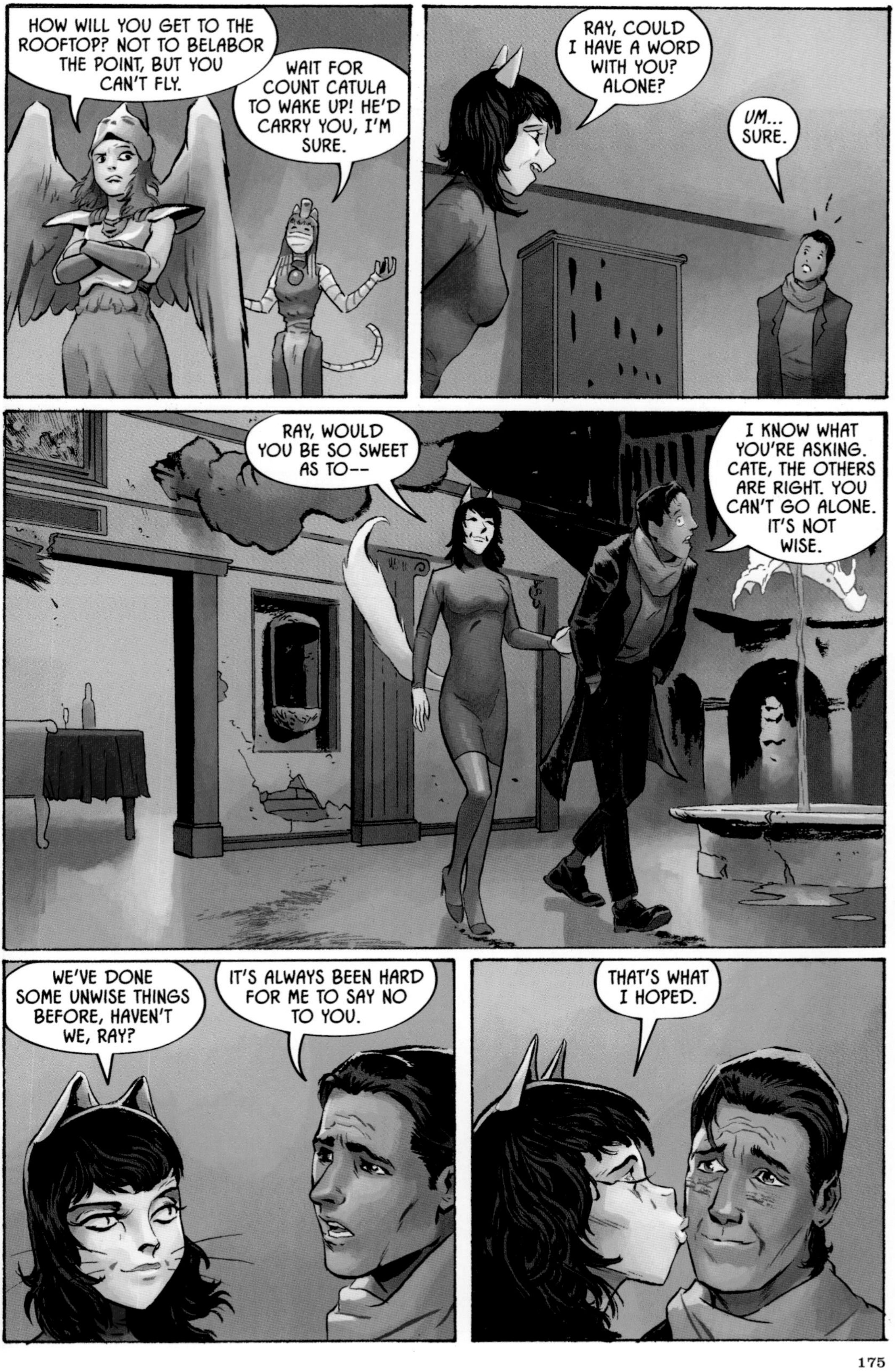
HOW WILL YOU GET TO THE ROOFTOP? NOT TO BELABOR THE POINT, BUT YOU CAN'T FLY.
WAIT FOR COUNT CATULA TO WAKE UP! HE'D CARRY YOU, I'M SURE.
RAY, COULD I HAVE A WORD WITH YOU? ALONE?
UM... SURE.
RAY, WOULD YOU BE SO SWEET AS TO--
I KNOW WHAT YOU'RE ASKING. CATE, THE OTHERS ARE RIGHT. YOU CAN'T GO ALONE. IT'S NOT WISE.
WE'VE DONE SOME UNWISE THINGS BEFORE, HAVEN'T WE, RAY?
IT'S ALWAYS BEEN HARD FOR ME TO SAY NO TO YOU.
THAT'S WHAT I HOPED.

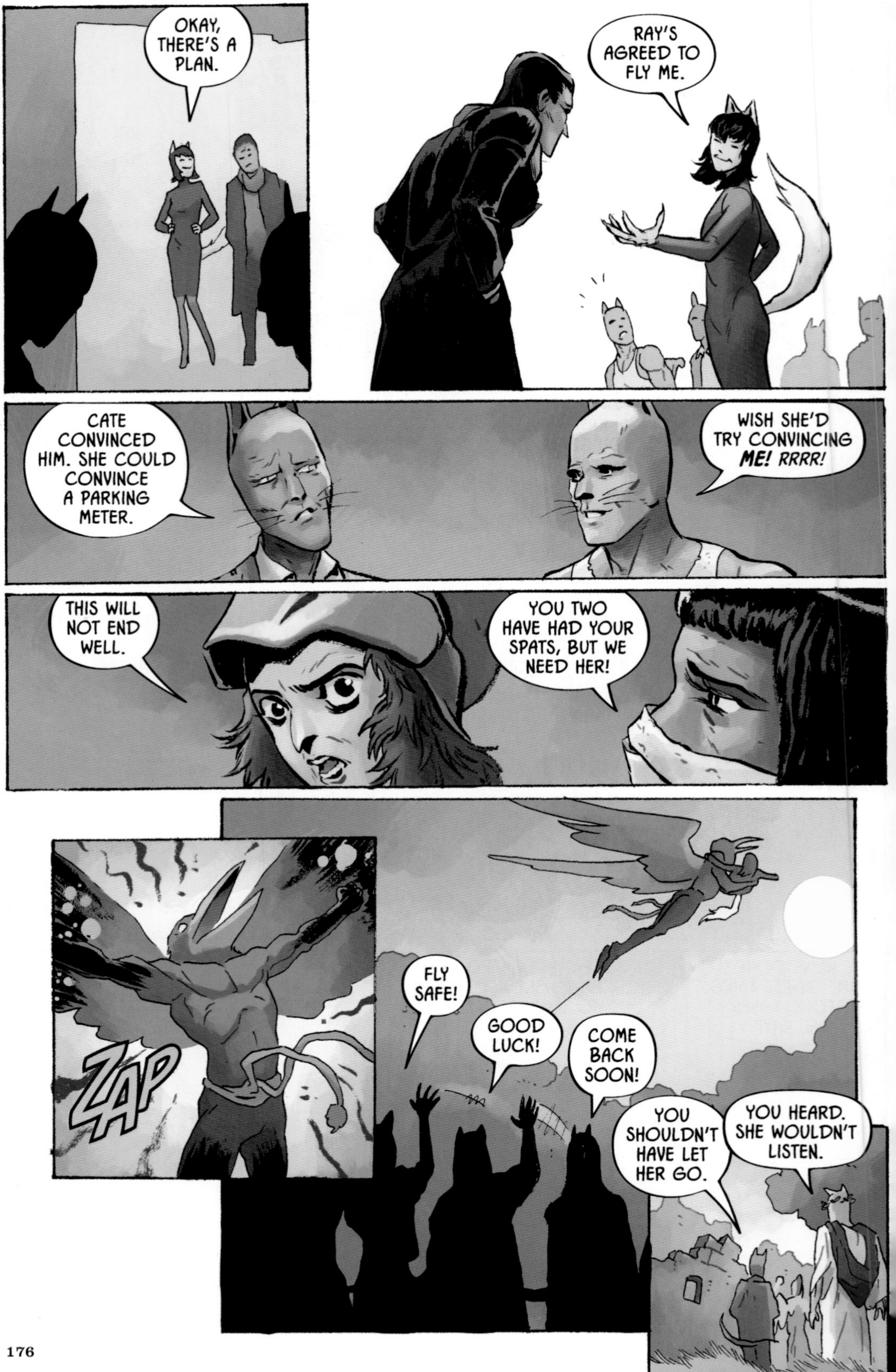
OKAY, THERE'S A PLAN.
RAY'S AGREED TO FLY ME.
CATE CONVINCED HIM. SHE COULD CONVINCE A PARKING METER.
WISH SHE'D TRY CONVINCING ME! RRRR!
THIS WILL NOT END WELL.
YOU TWO HAVE HAD YOUR SPATS, BUT WE NEED HER!
ZAP
FLY SAFE!
GOOD LUCK!
COME BACK SOON!
YOU SHOULDN'T HAVE LET HER GO.
YOU HEARD. SHE WOULDN'T LISTEN.

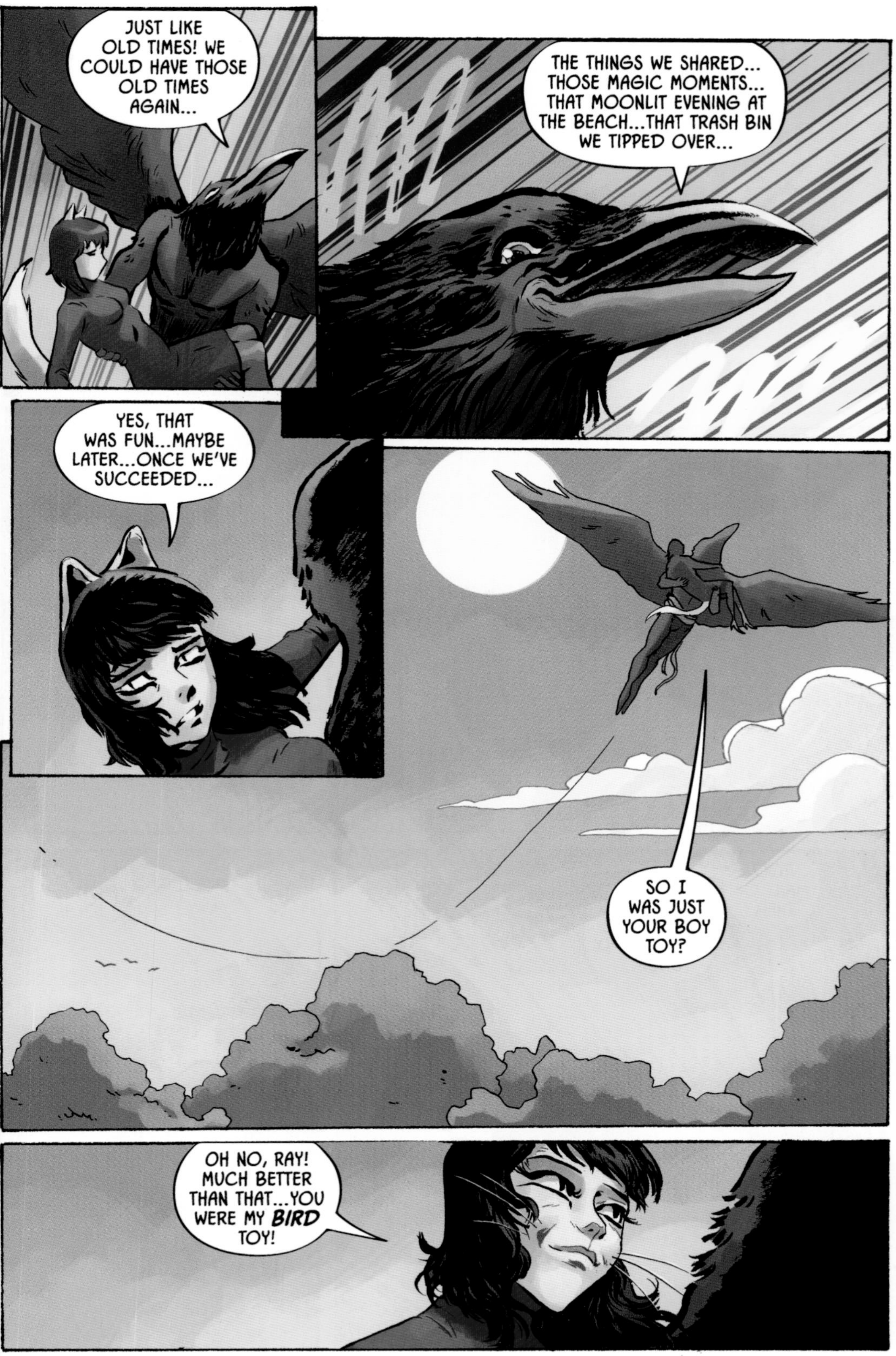
JUST LIKE OLD TIMES! WE COULD HAVE THOSE OLD TIMES AGAIN...
THE THINGS WE SHARED... THOSE MAGIC MOMENTS... THAT MOONLIT EVENING AT THE BEACH...THAT TRASH BIN WE TIPPED OVER...
YES, THAT WAS FUN...MAYBE LATER...ONCE WE'VE SUCCEEDED...
SO I WAS JUST YOUR BOY TOY?
OH NO, RAY! MUCH BETTER THAN THAT...YOU WERE MY BIRD TOY!

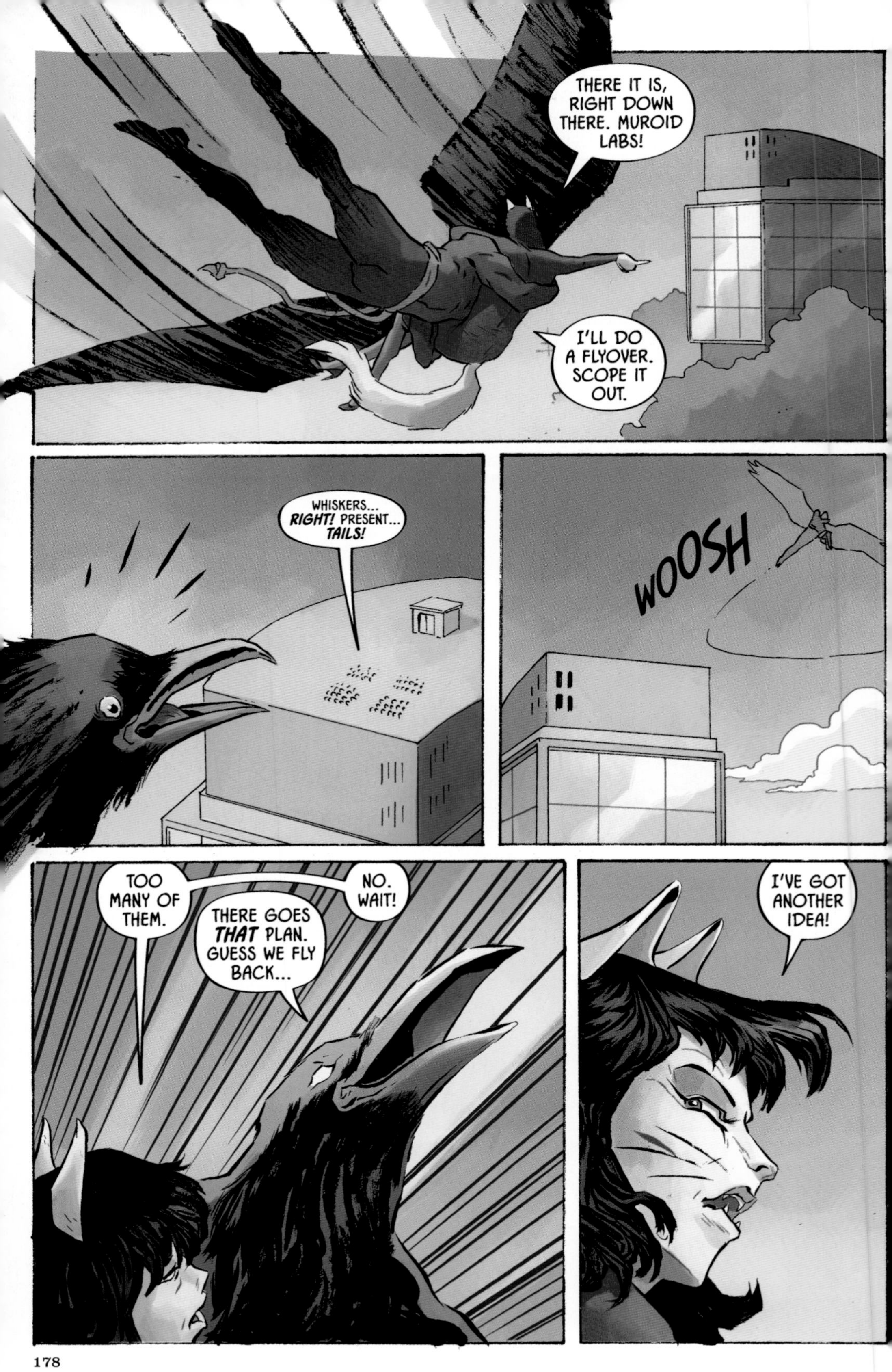
THERE IT IS, RIGHT DOWN THERE. MUROID LABS!
I'LL DO A FLYOVER. SCOPE IT OUT.
WHISKERS... RIGHT! PRESENT... TAILS!
WOOSH
TOO MANY OF THEM.
THERE GOES THAT PLAN. GUESS WE FLY BACK...
NO. WAIT!
I'VE GOT ANOTHER IDEA!

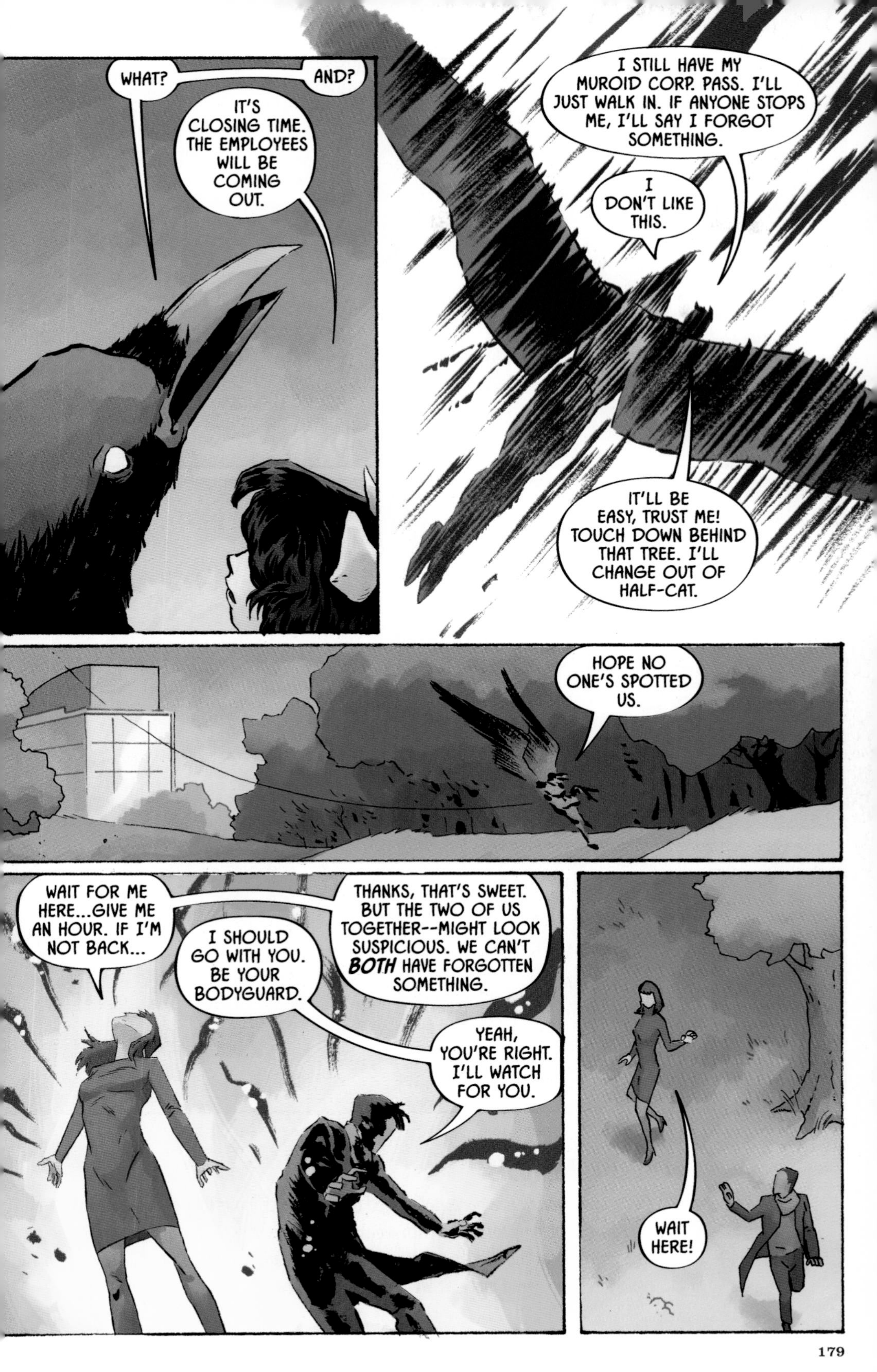
WHAT?
AND?
IT'S CLOSING TIME. THE EMPLOYEES WILL BE COMING OUT.
I STILL HAVE MY MUROID CORP. PASS. I'LL JUST WALK IN. IF ANYONE STOPS ME, I'LL SAY I FORGOT SOMETHING.
I DON'T LIKE THIS.
IT'LL BE EASY, TRUST ME! TOUCH DOWN BEHIND THAT TREE. I'LL CHANGE OUT OF HALF-CAT.
HOPE NO ONE'S SPOTTED US.
WAIT FOR ME HERE...GIVE ME AN HOUR. IF I'M NOT BACK...
I SHOULD GO WITH YOU. BE YOUR BODYGUARD.
THANKS, THAT'S SWEET. BUT THE TWO OF US TOGETHER--MIGHT LOOK SUSPICIOUS. WE CAN'T **BOTH** HAVE FORGOTTEN SOMETHING.
YEAH, YOU'RE RIGHT. I'LL WATCH FOR YOU.
WAIT HERE!

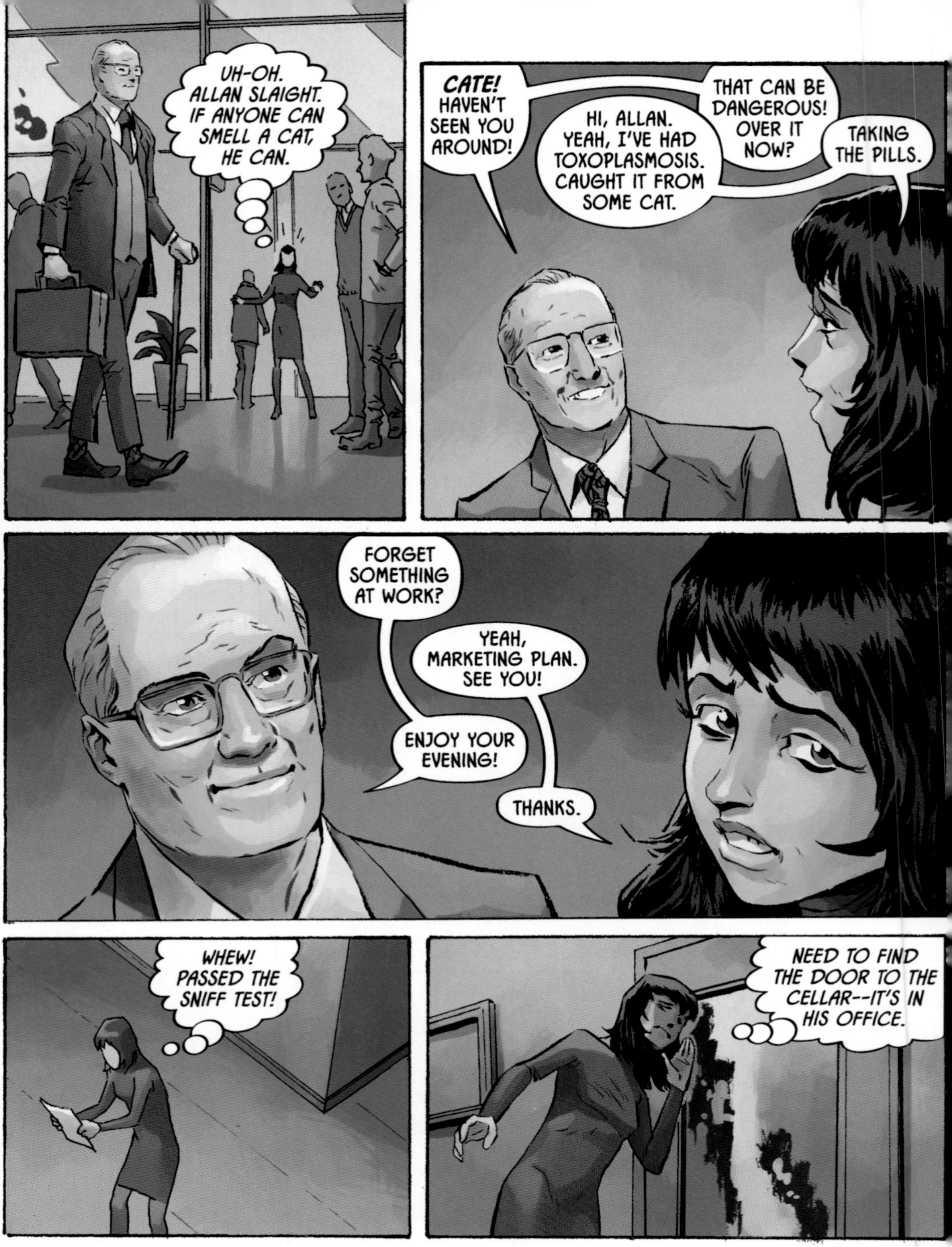
UH-OH. ALLAN SLAIGHT. IF ANYONE CAN SMELL A CAT, HE CAN.
CATE! HAVEN'T SEEN YOU AROUND!
HI, ALLAN. YEAH, I'VE HAD TOXOPLASMOSIS. CAUGHT IT FROM SOME CAT.
THAT CAN BE DANGEROUS! OVER IT NOW?
TAKING THE PILLS.
FORGET SOMETHING AT WORK?
YEAH, MARKETING PLAN. SEE YOU!
ENJOY YOUR EVENING!
THANKS.
WHEW! PASSED THE SNIFF TEST!
NEED TO FIND THE DOOR TO THE CELLAR--IT'S IN HIS OFFICE.

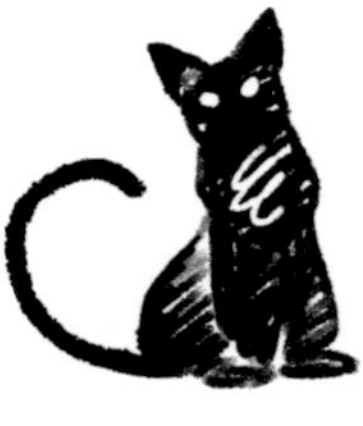

TOXOPLASMOSIS

Toxoplasma gondii is a parasite carried by cats. It has no effect on most people but can cause problems for those with weak immune systems, especially unborn babies. Keeping your cat indoors and changing the litter daily are two of the best ways to avoid infection. Read more at www.catsandbirds.ca

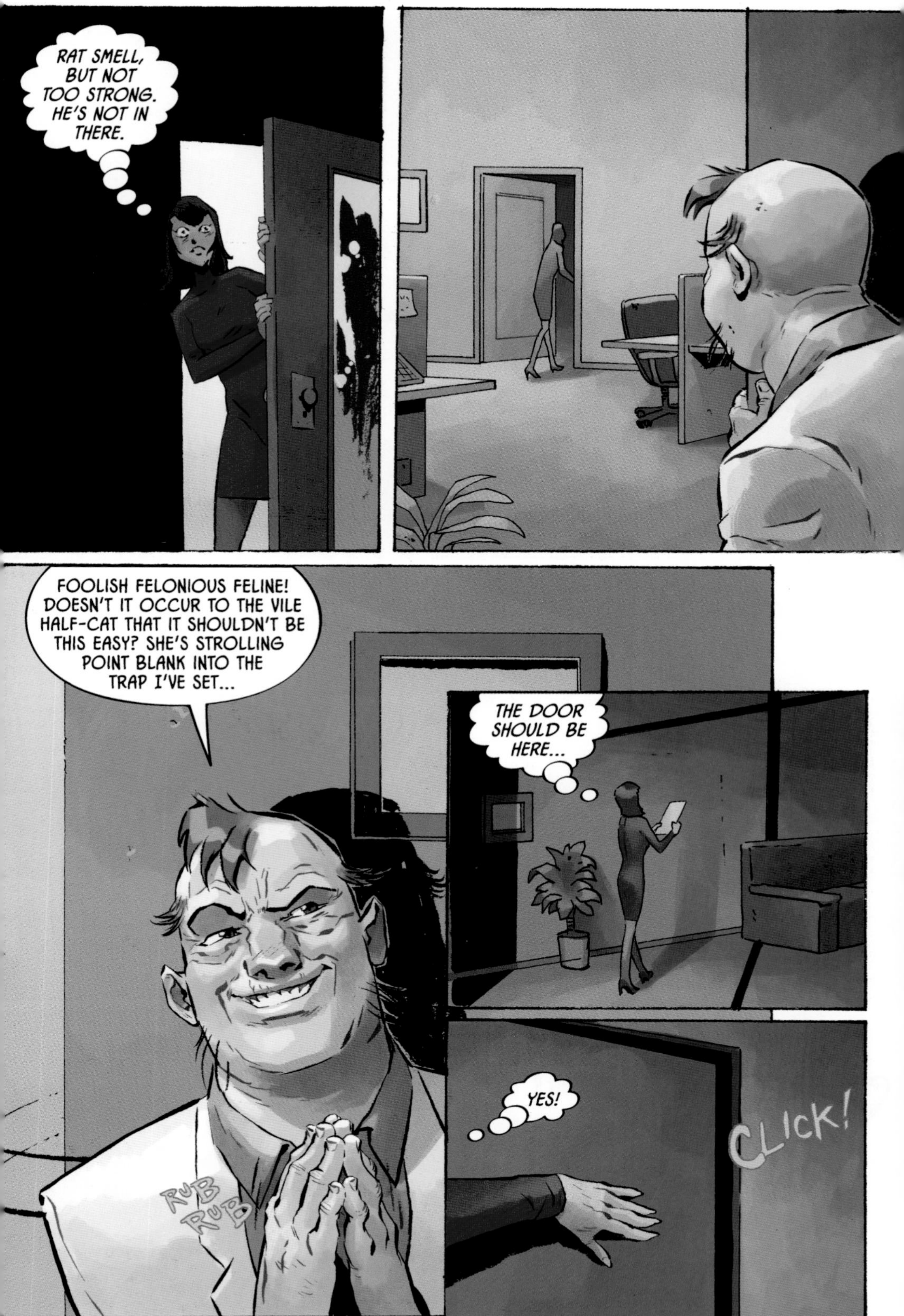
RAT SMELL, BUT NOT TOO STRONG. HE'S NOT IN THERE.
FOOLISH FELONIOUS FELINE! DOESN'T IT OCCUR TO THE VILE HALF-CAT THAT IT SHOULDN'T BE THIS EASY? SHE'S STROLLING POINT BLANK INTO THE TRAP I'VE SET...
RUB RUB
THE DOOR SHOULD BE HERE...
YES!
CLICK!

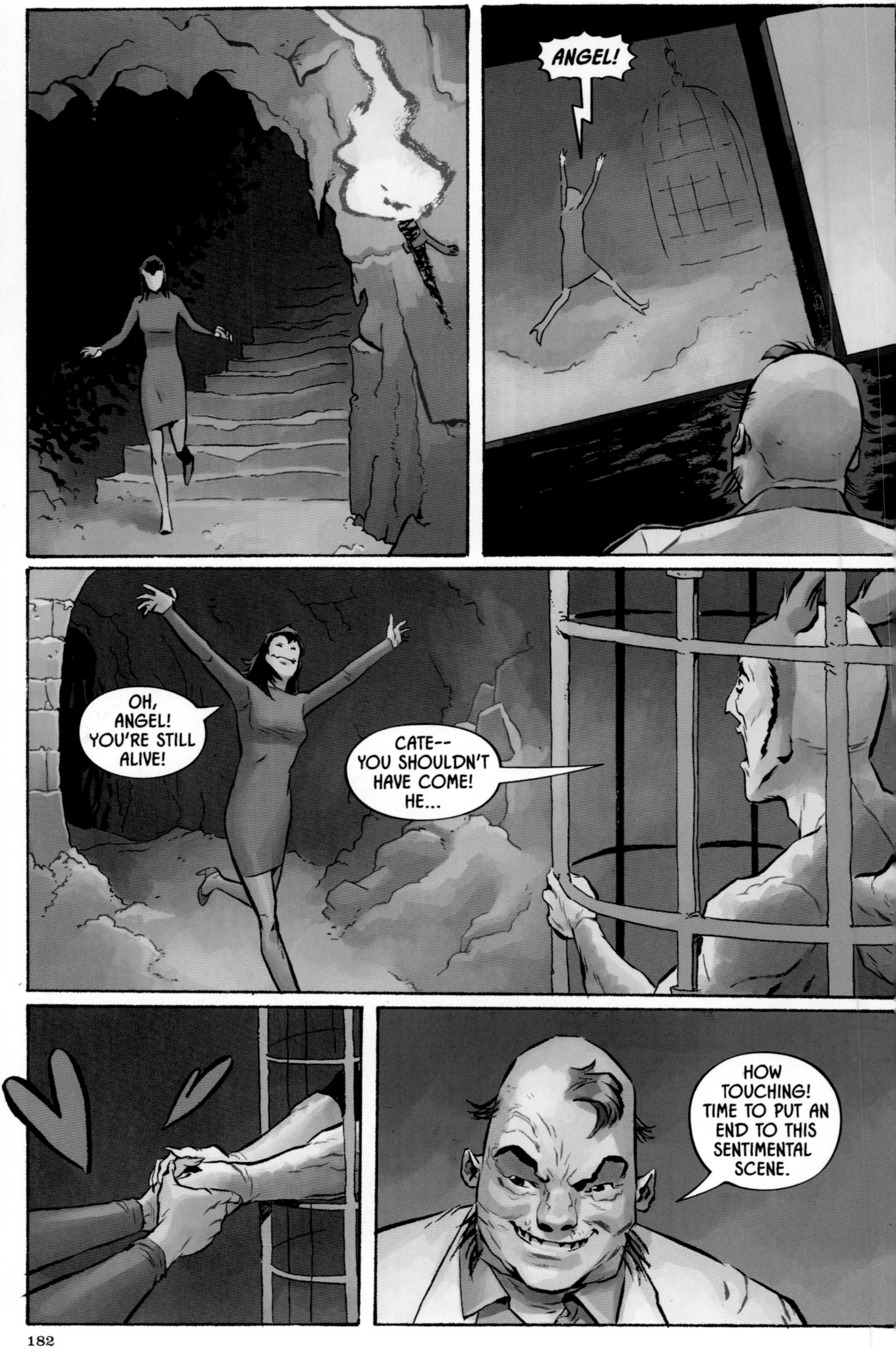
ANGEL!
OH, ANGEL! YOU'RE STILL ALIVE!
CATE-- YOU SHOULDN'T HAVE COME! HE...
HOW TOUCHING! TIME TO PUT AN END TO THIS SENTIMENTAL SCENE.

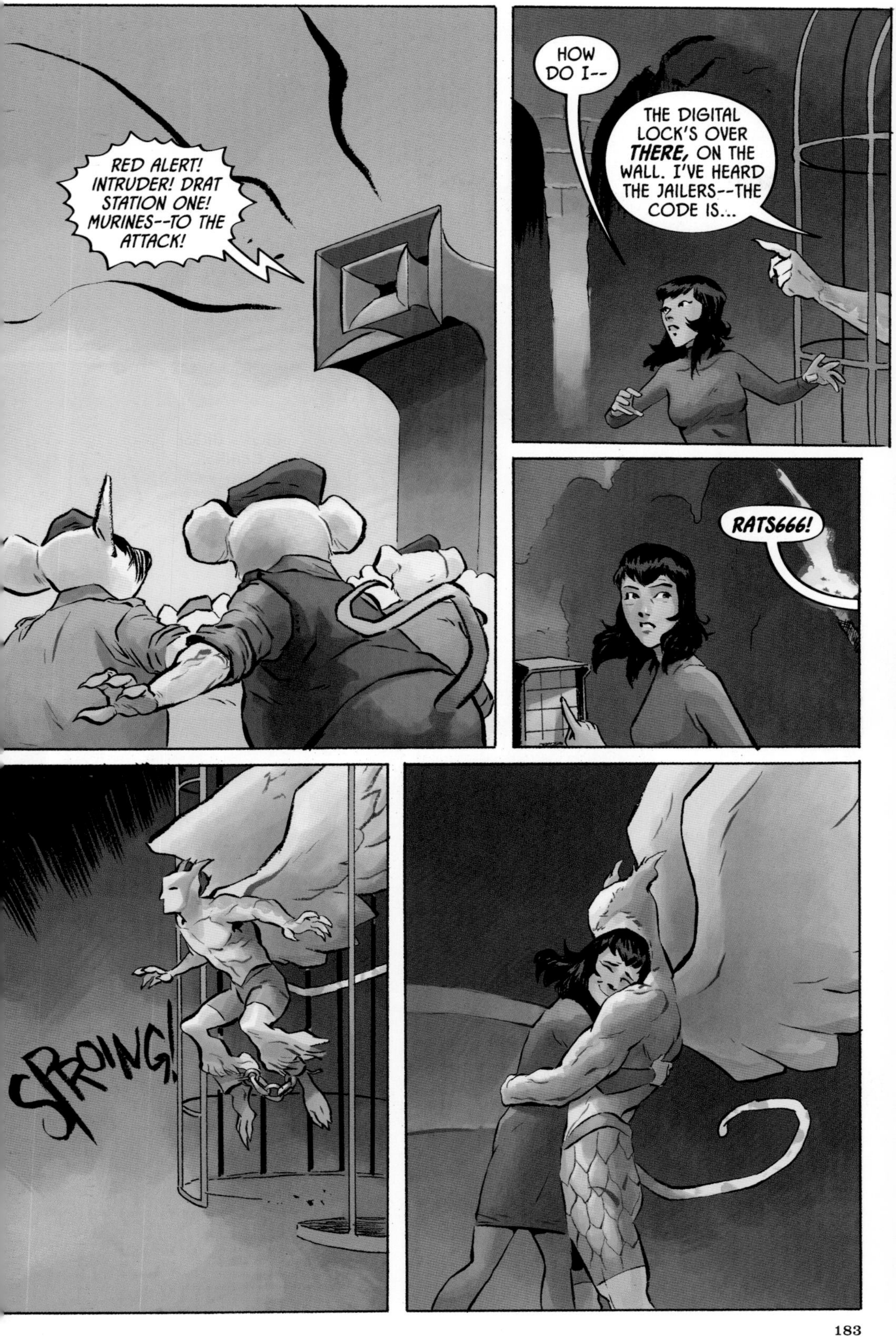
RED ALERT! INTRUDER! DRAT STATION ONE! MURINES--TO THE ATTACK!
HOW DO I--
THE DIGITAL LOCK'S OVER *THERE,* ON THE WALL. I'VE HEARD THE JAILERS--THE CODE IS...
RATS666!
SPROING!

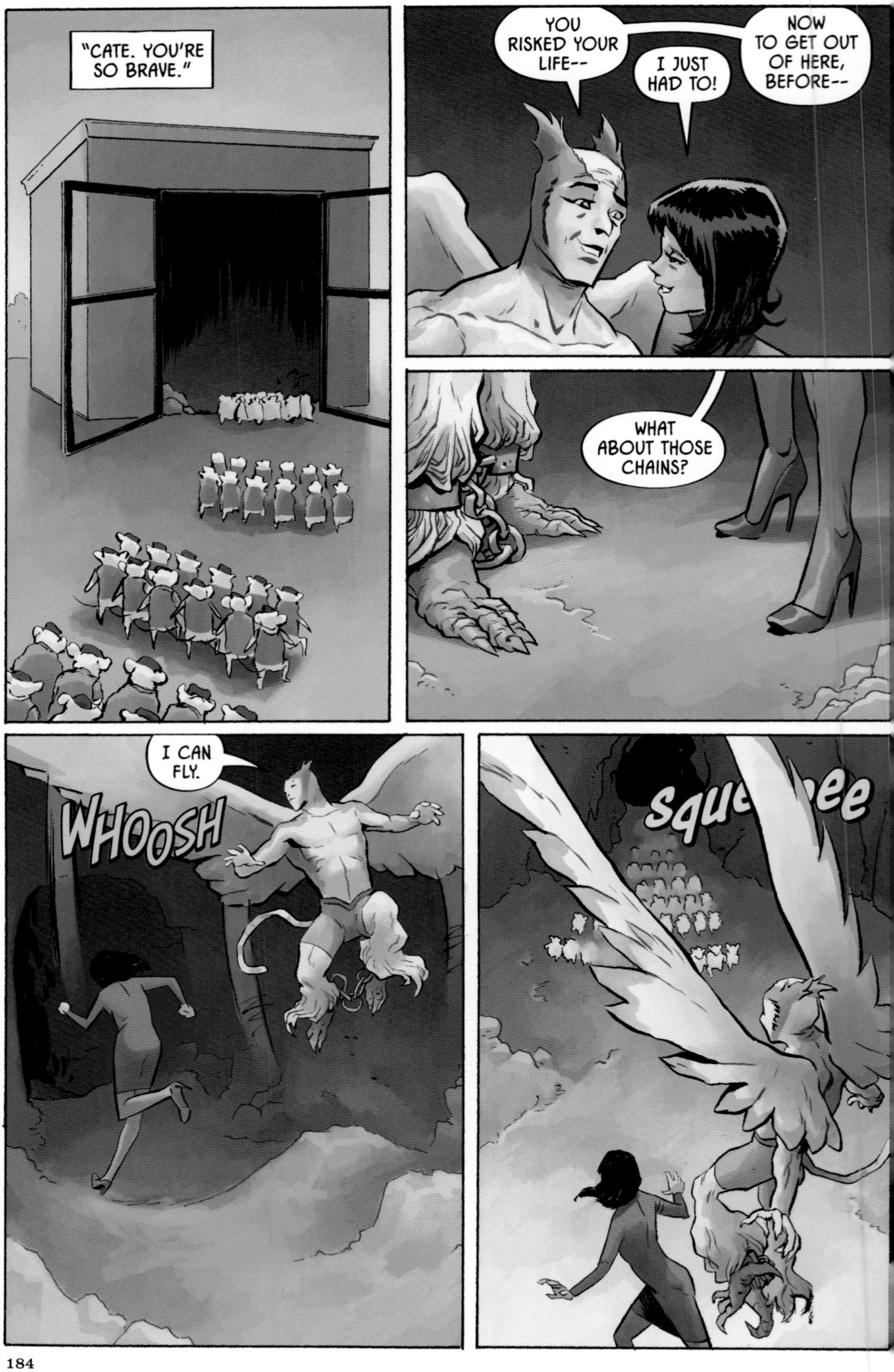
"CATE. YOU'RE SO BRAVE."
YOU RISKED YOUR LIFE--
I JUST HAD TO!
NOW TO GET OUT OF HERE, BEFORE--
WHAT ABOUT THOSE CHAINS?
I CAN FLY.
WHOOSH
Squ ee

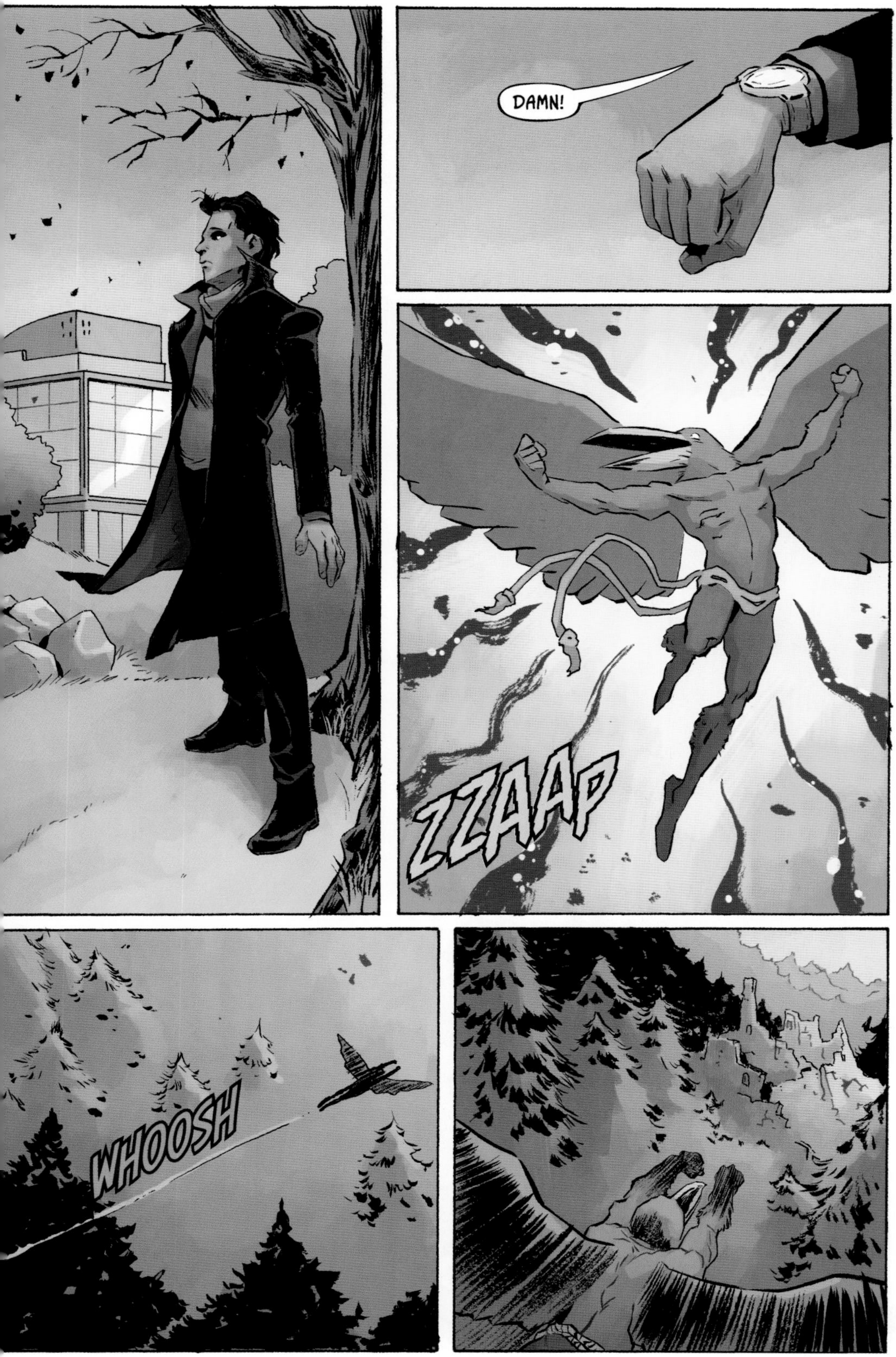
DAMN!
ZZAAP
WHOOSH

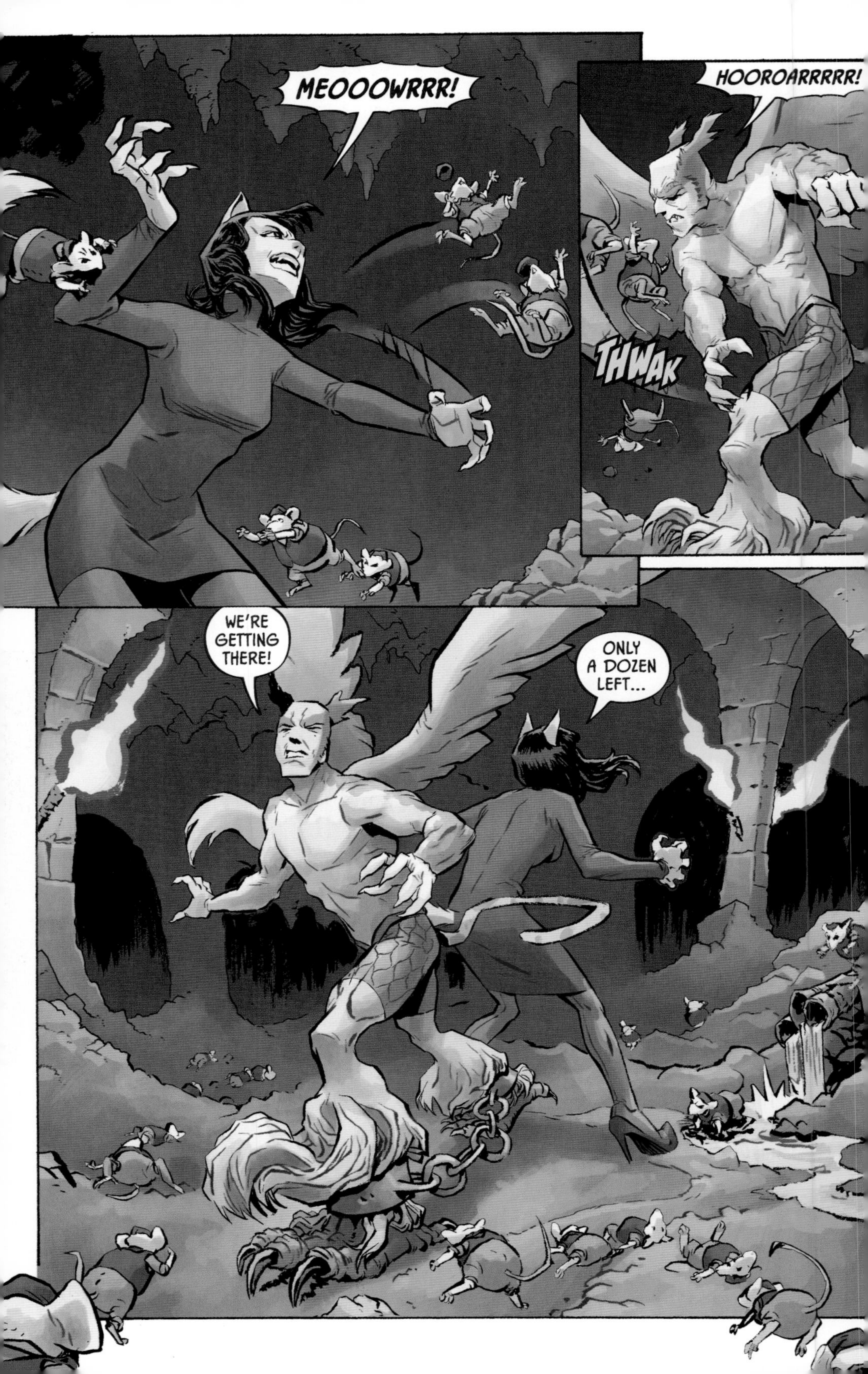
MEOOOWRRR!
HOOROARRRRR!
THWAK
WE'RE GETTING THERE!
ONLY A DOZEN LEFT...

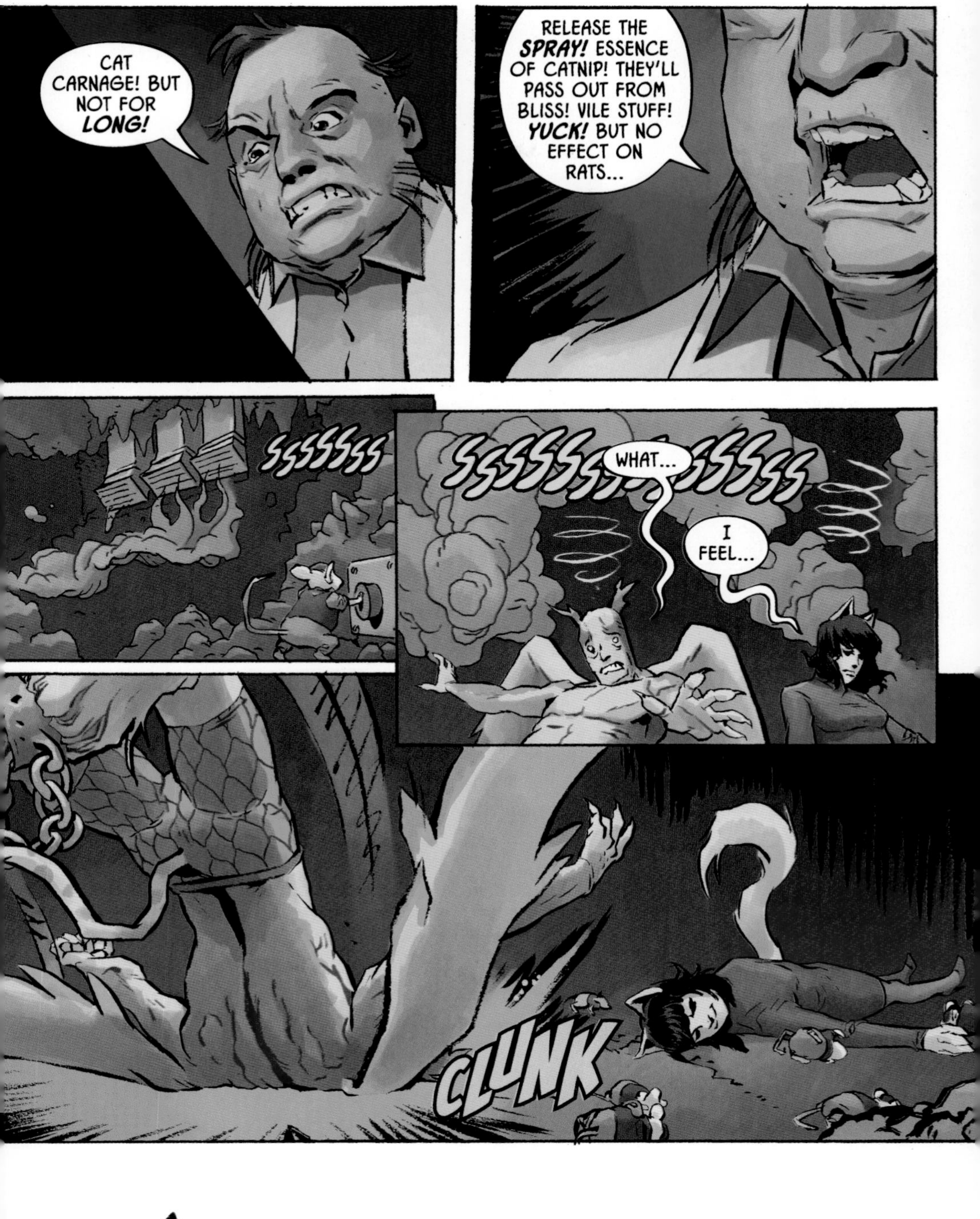
CAT CARNAGE! BUT NOT FOR LONG!
RELEASE THE SPRAY! ESSENCE OF CATNIP! THEY'LL PASS OUT FROM BLISS! VILE STUFF! YUCK! BUT NO EFFECT ON RATS...
SSSSSSS
SSSSSSSSSSSSSSS
WHAT...
I FEEL...
CLUNK

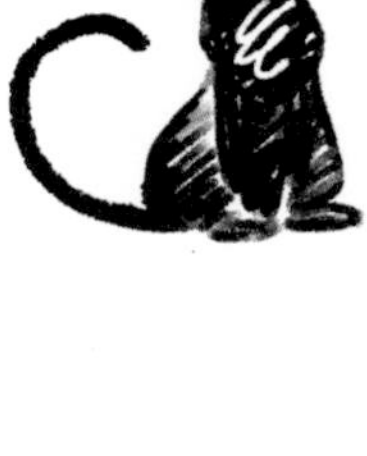

CATNIP

Catnip is a great way to keep your cat stimulated. You can use it in toys or just sprinkle it around occasionally. Cat grass is another great way to bring a little of the outdoors inside. Read more at www.catsandbirds.ca

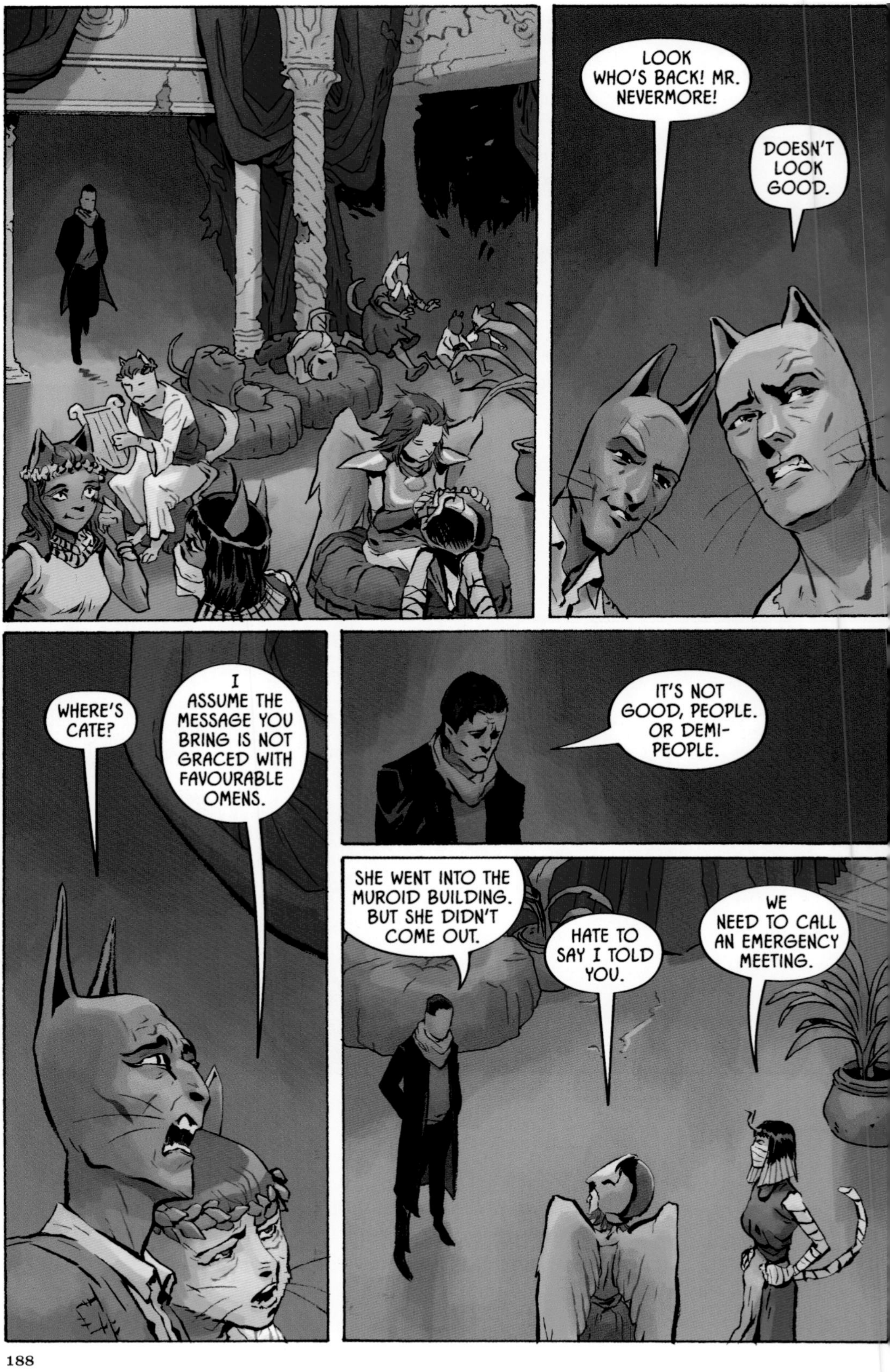

LOOK WHO'S BACK! MR. NEVERMORE!
DOESN'T LOOK GOOD.
WHERE'S CATE?
I ASSUME THE MESSAGE YOU BRING IS NOT GRACED WITH FAVOURABLE OMENS.
IT'S NOT GOOD, PEOPLE. OR DEMI-PEOPLE.
SHE WENT INTO THE MUROID BUILDING. BUT SHE DIDN'T COME OUT.
HATE TO SAY I TOLD YOU.
WE NEED TO CALL AN EMERGENCY MEETING.

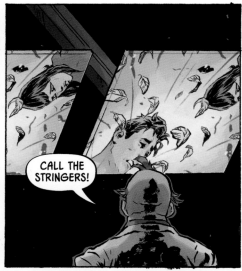

CALL THE STRINGERS!

"INTO THE CAGES WITH THEM!"

SHHHK!

SHHHHK!

CLANG!

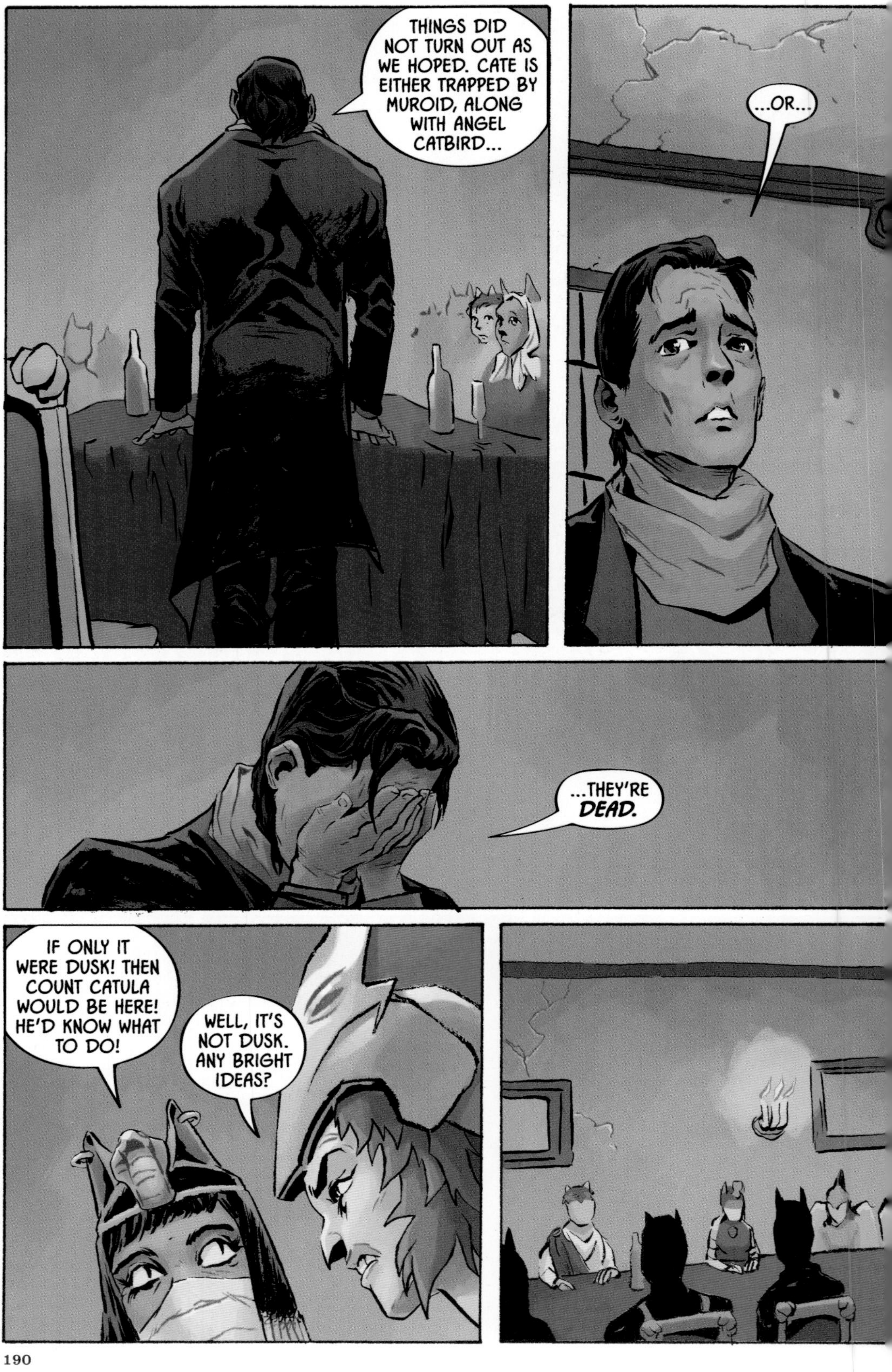
THINGS DID NOT TURN OUT AS WE HOPED. CATE IS EITHER TRAPPED BY MUROID, ALONG WITH ANGEL CATBIRD...
...OR...
...THEY'RE *DEAD.*
IF ONLY IT WERE DUSK! THEN COUNT CATULA WOULD BE HERE! HE'D KNOW WHAT TO DO!
WELL, IT'S NOT DUSK. ANY BRIGHT IDEAS?

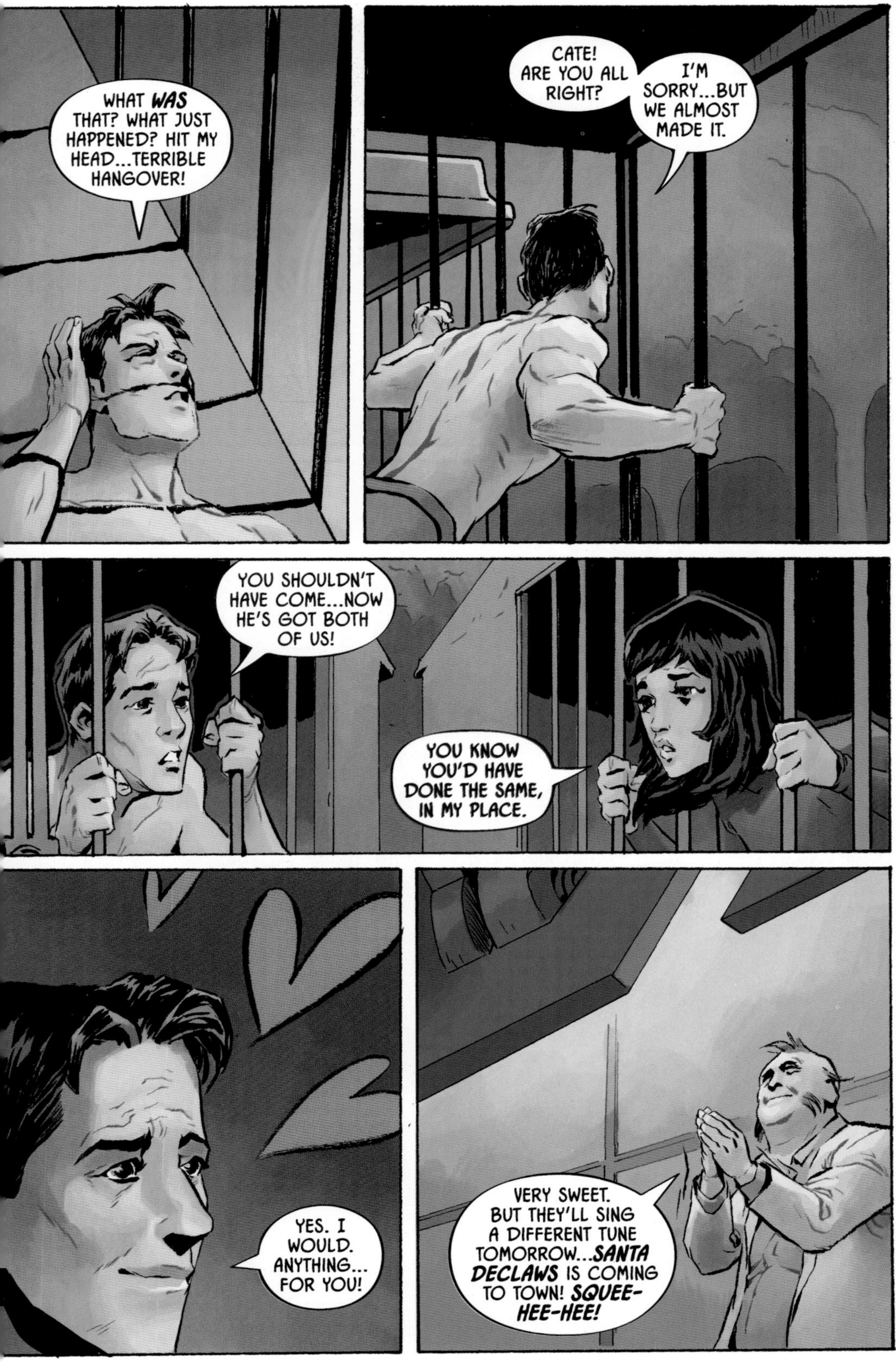

WHAT WAS THAT? WHAT JUST HAPPENED? HIT MY HEAD...TERRIBLE HANGOVER!
CATE! ARE YOU ALL RIGHT?
I'M SORRY...BUT WE ALMOST MADE IT.
YOU SHOULDN'T HAVE COME...NOW HE'S GOT BOTH OF US!
YOU KNOW YOU'D HAVE DONE THE SAME, IN MY PLACE.
YES. I WOULD. ANYTHING... FOR YOU!
VERY SWEET. BUT THEY'LL SING A DIFFERENT TUNE TOMORROW...SANTA DECLAWS IS COMING TO TOWN! SQUEE-HEE-HEE!

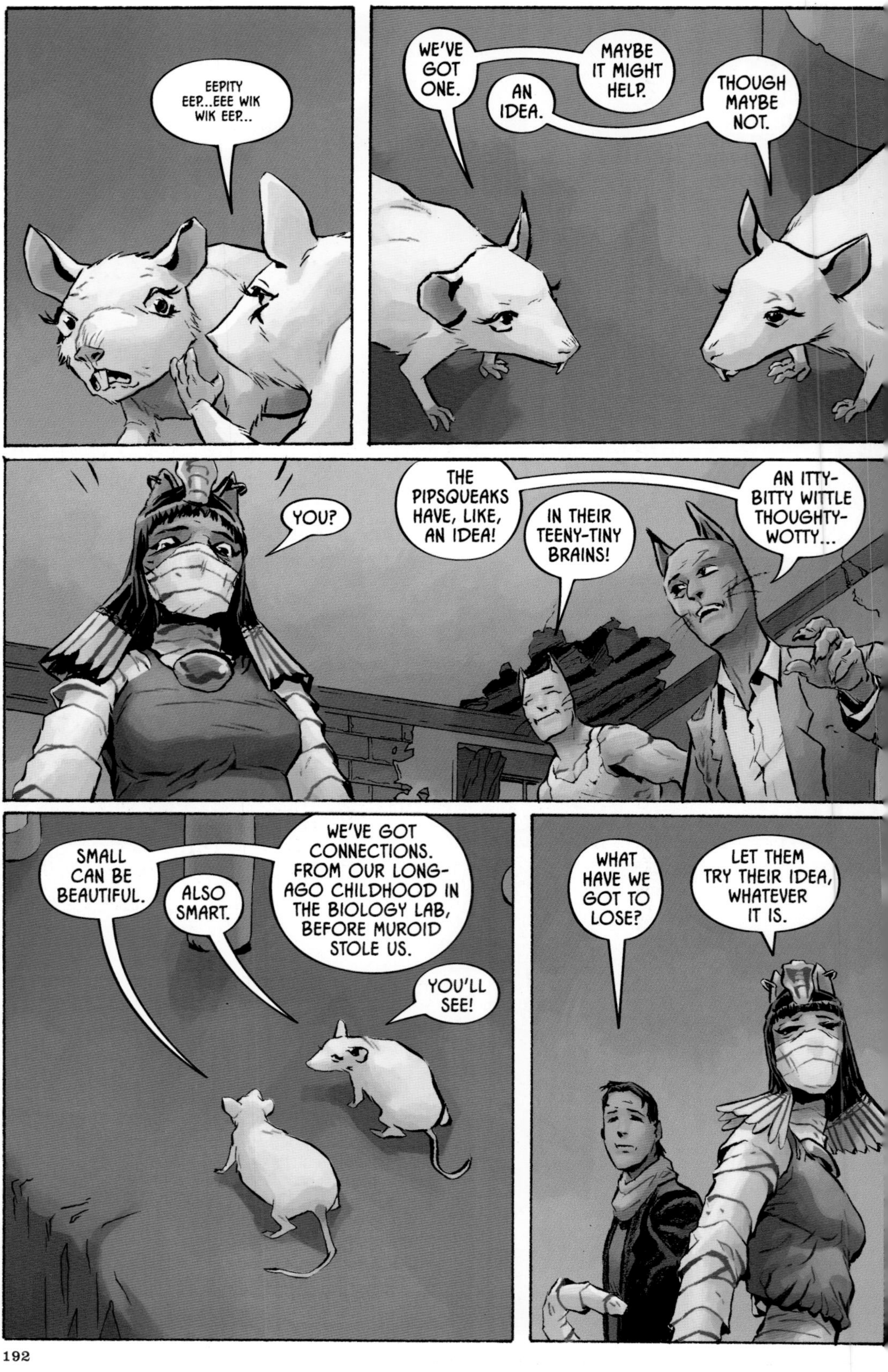
EEPITY EEP...EEE WIK WIK EEP...
WE'VE GOT ONE.
MAYBE IT MIGHT HELP.
AN IDEA.
THOUGH MAYBE NOT.
YOU?
THE PIPSQUEAKS HAVE, LIKE, AN IDEA!
IN THEIR TEENY-TINY BRAINS!
AN ITTY-BITTY WITTLE THOUGHTY-WOTTY...
SMALL CAN BE BEAUTIFUL.
ALSO SMART.
WE'VE GOT CONNECTIONS. FROM OUR LONG-AGO CHILDHOOD IN THE BIOLOGY LAB, BEFORE MUROID STOLE US.
YOU'LL SEE!
WHAT HAVE WE GOT TO LOSE?
LET THEM TRY THEIR IDEA, WHATEVER IT IS.

FIRST, HIDE THE MOUSE-BLOOD CHAMPAGNE!

REALLY?

WHY?

IT'S A PRIZE VINTAGE! THE COUNT KEEPS AN EXCELLENT CELLAR! EVEN WHEN HE'S NOT SLEEPING IN IT!

JUST DO IT. TRUST US ON THIS!

PLEASE!

WILL THIS DO?

PERFECT!

THE COUNT OF MONTE CRISTO

BLOOD WEDDING

COFFINS FOR TWO

BELFRIES I HAVE KNOWN

101 CUMMERBUNDS

DRACULA

INTERVIEW WITH THE VAMPIRE

OLD POSSUM'S BOOK OF PRACTICAL CATS

UPDATE YOUR CAPE

STYLE MAGAZINE

AROUND THE WORLD IN 80 DAYS

VAMPIRE BATS OF THE NEW WORLD

FANGS FOR THE MEMORIES

DANCING WITH WOL...

CHÂTEAUX ET RELAIS DE LA FRANCE

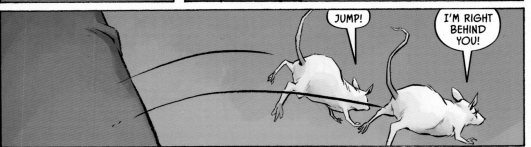

JUMP!

I'M RIGHT BEHIND YOU!

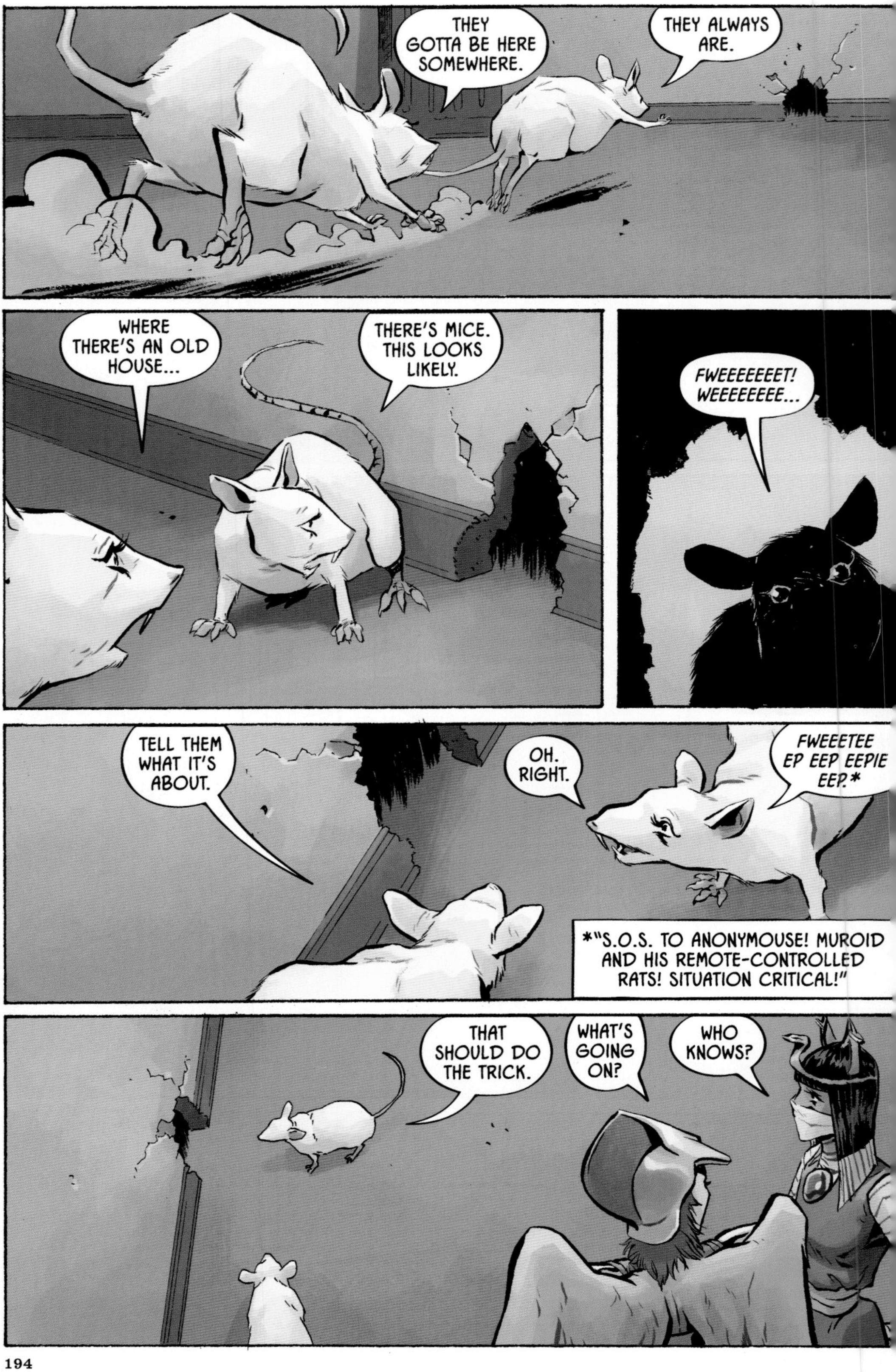
THEY GOTTA BE HERE SOMEWHERE.
THEY ALWAYS ARE.
WHERE THERE'S AN OLD HOUSE...
THERE'S MICE. THIS LOOKS LIKELY.
FWEEEEEEET! WEEEEEEEE...
TELL THEM WHAT IT'S ABOUT.
OH. RIGHT.
FWEEETEE EP EEP EEPIE EEP.*
*"S.O.S. TO ANONYMOUSE! MUROID AND HIS REMOTE-CONTROLLED RATS! SITUATION CRITICAL!"
THAT SHOULD DO THE TRICK.
WHAT'S GOING ON?
WHO KNOWS?

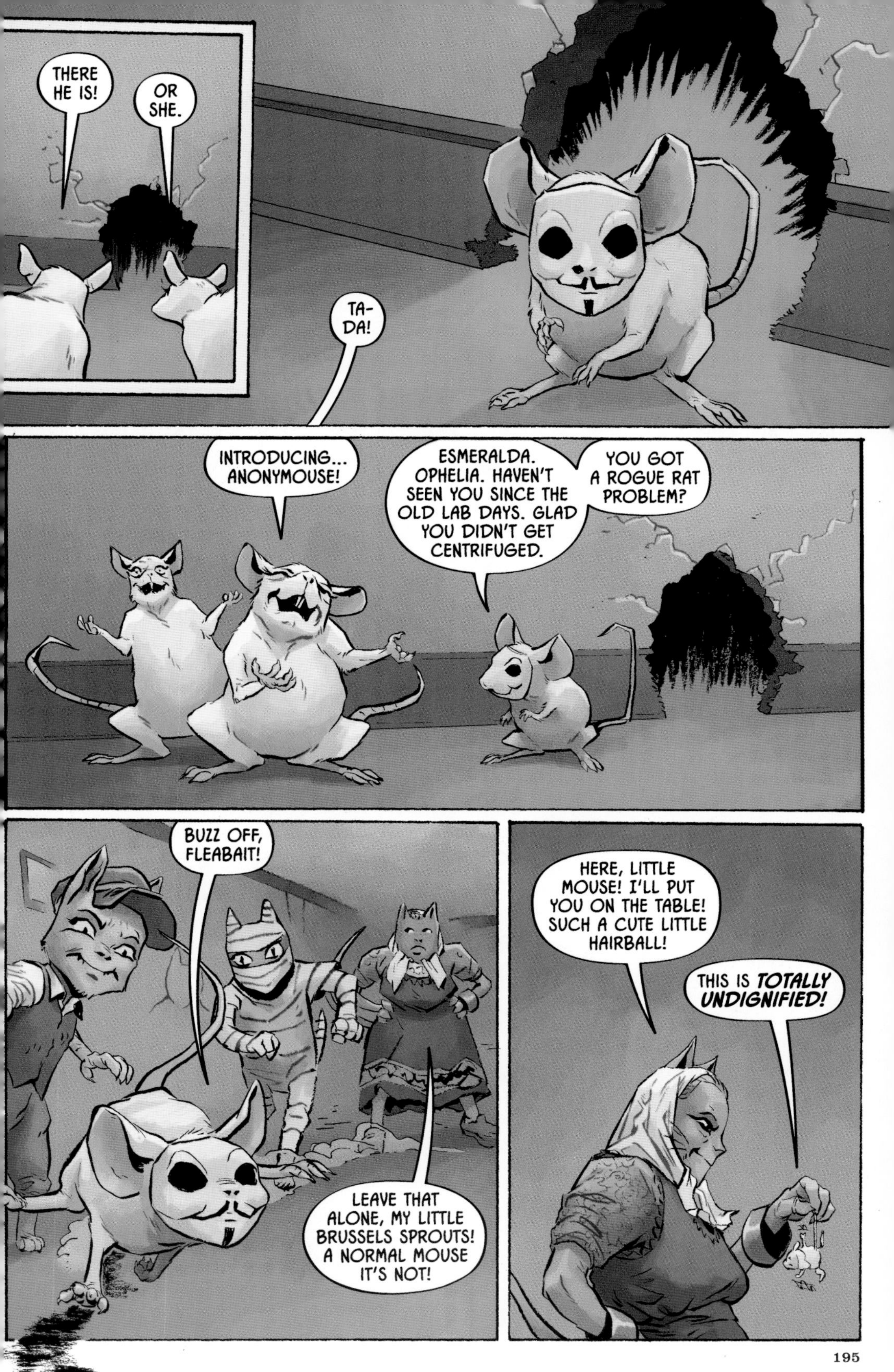
THERE HE IS!
OR SHE.
TA-DA!
INTRODUCING... ANONYMOUSE!
ESMERALDA. OPHELIA. HAVEN'T SEEN YOU SINCE THE OLD LAB DAYS. GLAD YOU DIDN'T GET CENTRIFUGED.
YOU GOT A ROGUE RAT PROBLEM?
BUZZ OFF, FLEABAIT!
LEAVE THAT ALONE, MY LITTLE BRUSSELS SPROUTS! A NORMAL MOUSE IT'S NOT!
HERE, LITTLE MOUSE! I'LL PUT YOU ON THE TABLE! SUCH A CUTE LITTLE HAIRBALL!
THIS IS *TOTALLY UNDIGNIFIED!*

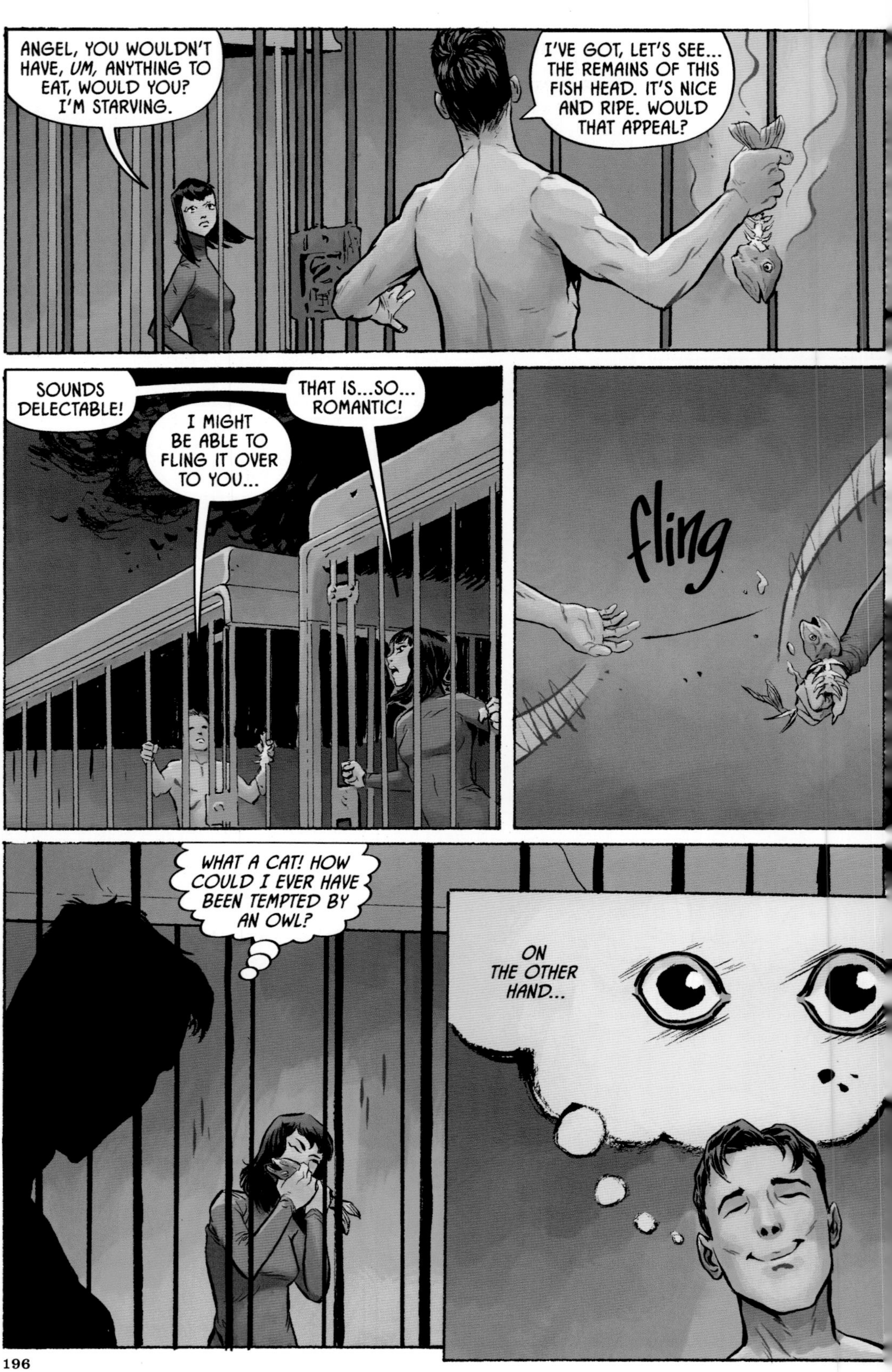
ANGEL, YOU WOULDN'T HAVE, UM, ANYTHING TO EAT, WOULD YOU? I'M STARVING.
I'VE GOT, LET'S SEE... THE REMAINS OF THIS FISH HEAD. IT'S NICE AND RIPE. WOULD THAT APPEAL?
SOUNDS DELECTABLE!
I MIGHT BE ABLE TO FLING IT OVER TO YOU...
THAT IS...SO... ROMANTIC!
fling
WHAT A CAT! HOW COULD I EVER HAVE BEEN TEMPTED BY AN OWL?
ON THE OTHER HAND...

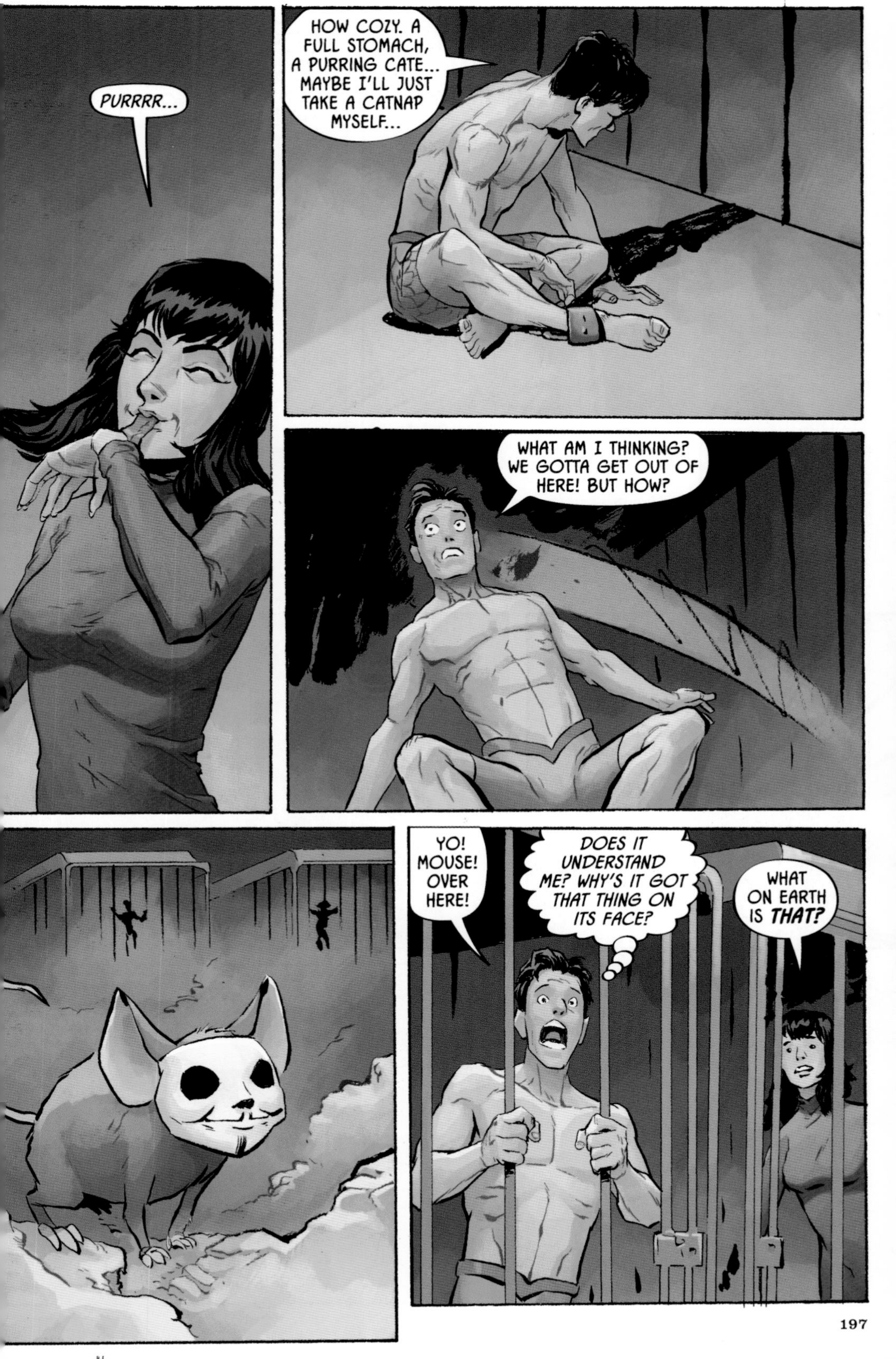
PURRRR...
HOW COZY. A FULL STOMACH, A PURRING CATE... MAYBE I'LL JUST TAKE A CATNAP MYSELF...
WHAT AM I THINKING? WE GOTTA GET OUT OF HERE! BUT HOW?
YO! MOUSE! OVER HERE!
DOES IT UNDERSTAND ME? WHY'S IT GOT THAT THING ON ITS FACE?
WHAT ON EARTH IS THAT?

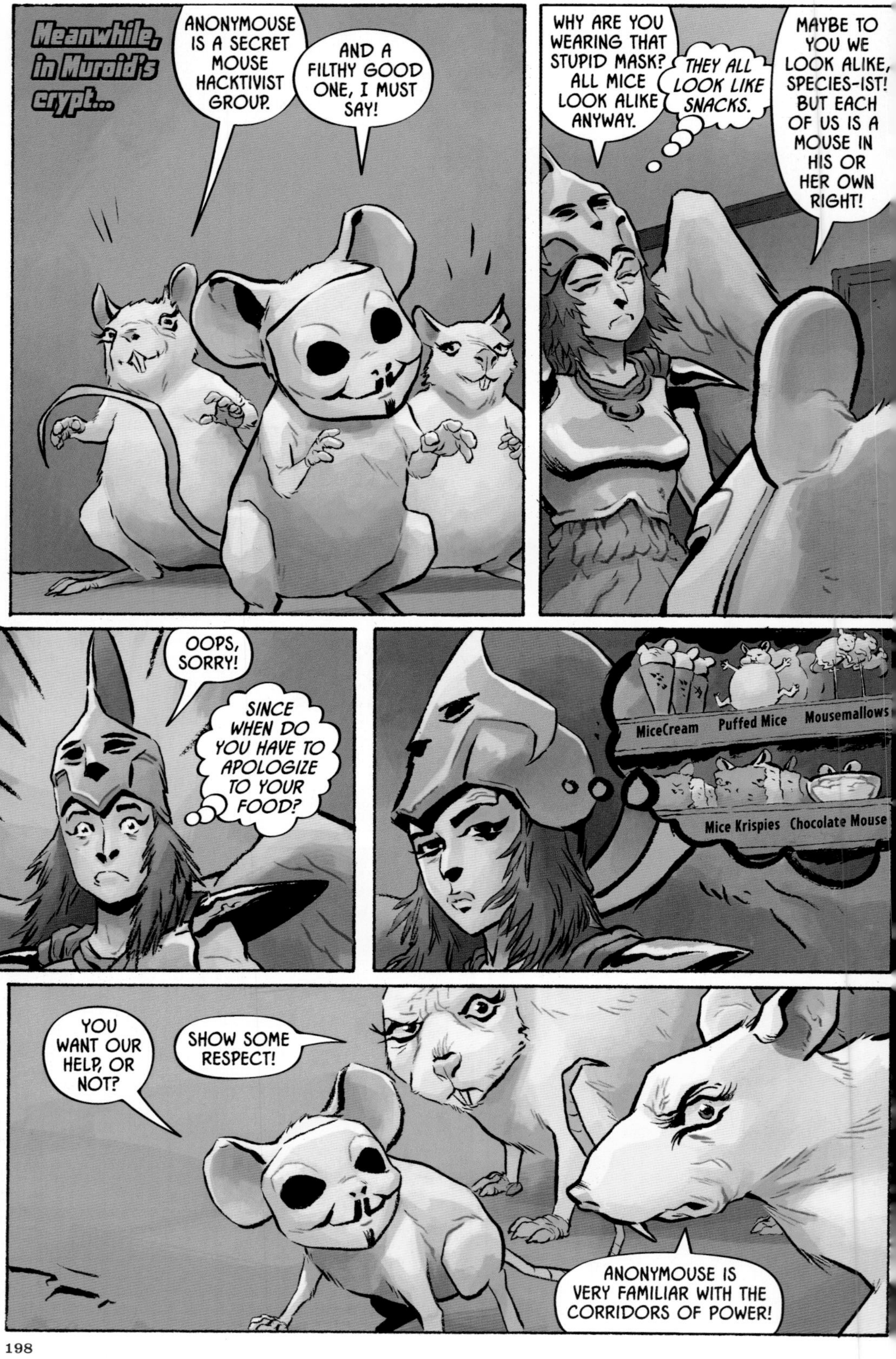
Meanwhile, in Muroid's crypt...
ANONYMOUSE IS A SECRET MOUSE HACKTIVIST GROUP.
AND A FILTHY GOOD ONE, I MUST SAY!
WHY ARE YOU WEARING THAT STUPID MASK? ALL MICE LOOK ALIKE ANYWAY.
THEY ALL LOOK LIKE SNACKS.
MAYBE TO YOU WE LOOK ALIKE, SPECIES-IST! BUT EACH OF US IS A MOUSE IN HIS OR HER OWN RIGHT!
OOPS, SORRY!
SINCE WHEN DO YOU HAVE TO APOLOGIZE TO YOUR FOOD?
MiceCream
Puffed Mice
Mousemallows
Mice Krispies
Chocolate Mouse
YOU WANT OUR HELP, OR NOT?
SHOW SOME RESPECT!
ANONYMOUSE IS VERY FAMILIAR WITH THE CORRIDORS OF POWER!

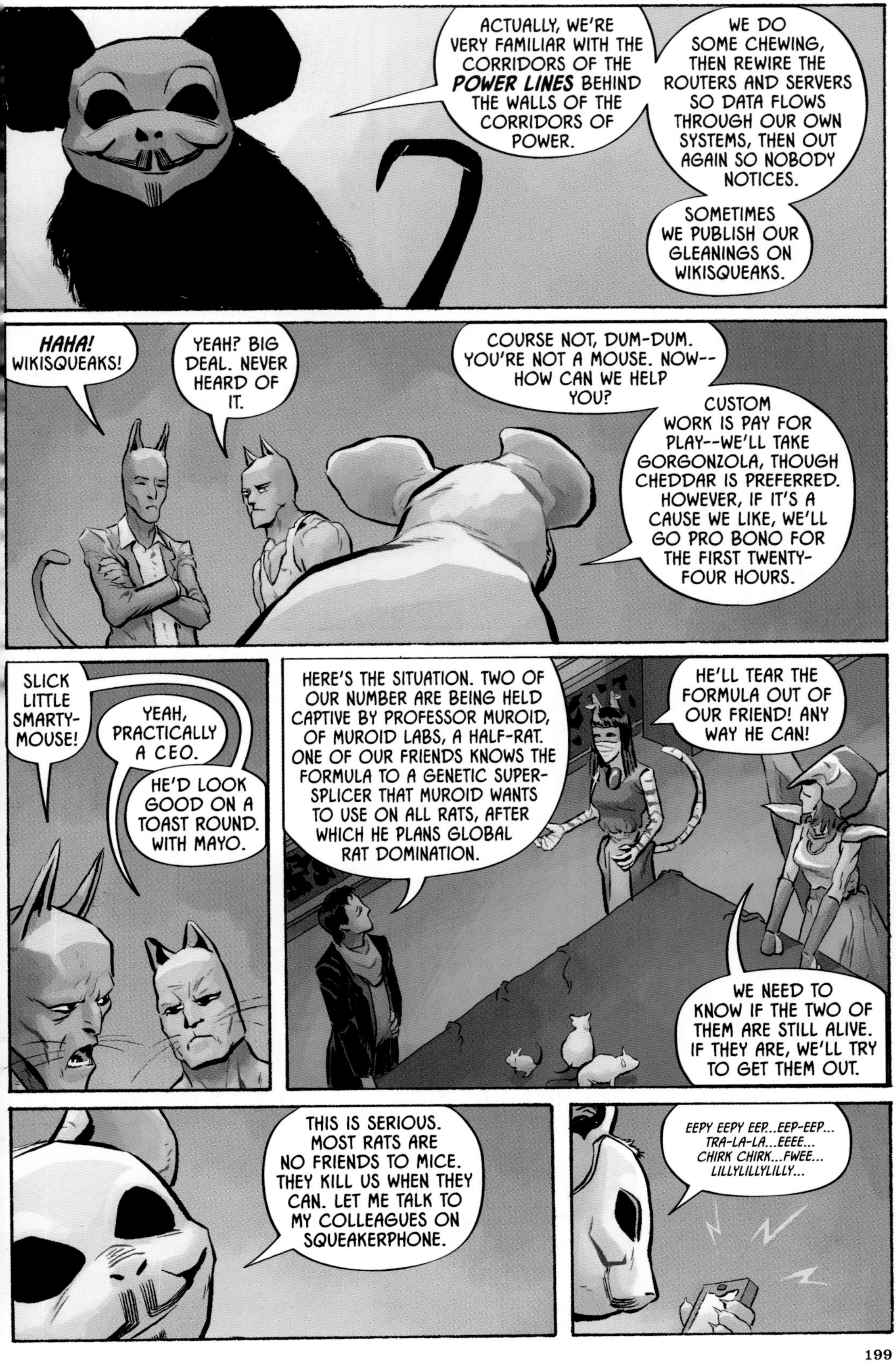
ACTUALLY, WE'RE VERY FAMILIAR WITH THE CORRIDORS OF THE POWER LINES BEHIND THE WALLS OF THE CORRIDORS OF POWER.
WE DO SOME CHEWING, THEN REWIRE THE ROUTERS AND SERVERS SO DATA FLOWS THROUGH OUR OWN SYSTEMS, THEN OUT AGAIN SO NOBODY NOTICES.
SOMETIMES WE PUBLISH OUR GLEANINGS ON WIKISQUEAKS.
HAHA! WIKISQUEAKS!
YEAH? BIG DEAL. NEVER HEARD OF IT.
COURSE NOT, DUM-DUM. YOU'RE NOT A MOUSE. NOW--HOW CAN WE HELP YOU?
CUSTOM WORK IS PAY FOR PLAY--WE'LL TAKE GORGONZOLA, THOUGH CHEDDAR IS PREFERRED. HOWEVER, IF IT'S A CAUSE WE LIKE, WE'LL GO PRO BONO FOR THE FIRST TWENTY-FOUR HOURS.
SLICK LITTLE SMARTY-MOUSE!
YEAH, PRACTICALLY A CEO.
HE'D LOOK GOOD ON A TOAST ROUND. WITH MAYO.
HERE'S THE SITUATION. TWO OF OUR NUMBER ARE BEING HELD CAPTIVE BY PROFESSOR MUROID, OF MUROID LABS, A HALF-RAT. ONE OF OUR FRIENDS KNOWS THE FORMULA TO A GENETIC SUPER-SPLICER THAT MUROID WANTS TO USE ON ALL RATS, AFTER WHICH HE PLANS GLOBAL RAT DOMINATION.
HE'LL TEAR THE FORMULA OUT OF OUR FRIEND! ANY WAY HE CAN!
WE NEED TO KNOW IF THE TWO OF THEM ARE STILL ALIVE. IF THEY ARE, WE'LL TRY TO GET THEM OUT.
THIS IS SERIOUS. MOST RATS ARE NO FRIENDS TO MICE. THEY KILL US WHEN THEY CAN. LET ME TALK TO MY COLLEAGUES ON SQUEAKERPHONE.
EEPY EEPY EEP...EEP-EEP... TRA-LA-LA...EEEE... CHIRK CHIRK...FWEE... LILLYLILLYLILLY...

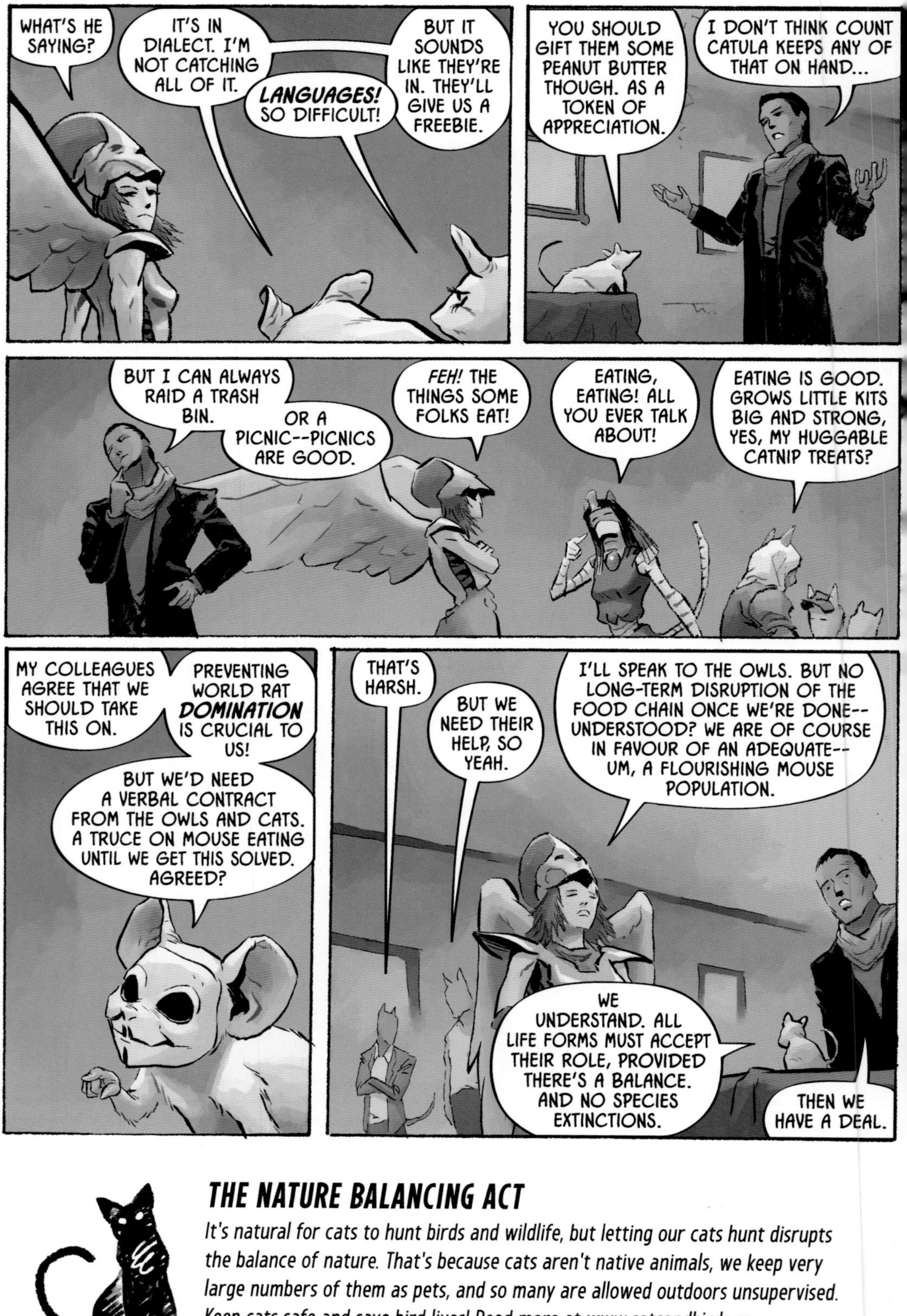
WHAT'S HE SAYING?
IT'S IN DIALECT. I'M NOT CATCHING ALL OF IT.
LANGUAGES! SO DIFFICULT!
BUT IT SOUNDS LIKE THEY'RE IN. THEY'LL GIVE US A FREEBIE.
YOU SHOULD GIFT THEM SOME PEANUT BUTTER THOUGH. AS A TOKEN OF APPRECIATION.
I DON'T THINK COUNT CATULA KEEPS ANY OF THAT ON HAND...
BUT I CAN ALWAYS RAID A TRASH BIN.
OR A PICNIC--PICNICS ARE GOOD.
FEH! THE THINGS SOME FOLKS EAT!
EATING, EATING! ALL YOU EVER TALK ABOUT!
EATING IS GOOD. GROWS LITTLE KITS BIG AND STRONG, YES, MY HUGGABLE CATNIP TREATS?
MY COLLEAGUES AGREE THAT WE SHOULD TAKE THIS ON.
PREVENTING WORLD RAT DOMINATION IS CRUCIAL TO US!
BUT WE'D NEED A VERBAL CONTRACT FROM THE OWLS AND CATS. A TRUCE ON MOUSE EATING UNTIL WE GET THIS SOLVED. AGREED?
THAT'S HARSH.
BUT WE NEED THEIR HELP, SO YEAH.
I'LL SPEAK TO THE OWLS. BUT NO LONG-TERM DISRUPTION OF THE FOOD CHAIN ONCE WE'RE DONE-- UNDERSTOOD? WE ARE OF COURSE IN FAVOUR OF AN ADEQUATE-- UM, A FLOURISHING MOUSE POPULATION.
WE UNDERSTAND. ALL LIFE FORMS MUST ACCEPT THEIR ROLE, PROVIDED THERE'S A BALANCE. AND NO SPECIES EXTINCTIONS.
THEN WE HAVE A DEAL.

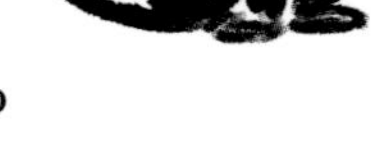

THE NATURE BALANCING ACT

It's natural for cats to hunt birds and wildlife, but letting our cats hunt disrupts the balance of nature. That's because cats aren't native animals, we keep very large numbers of them as pets, and so many are allowed outdoors unsupervised. Keep cats safe and save bird lives! Read more at www.catsandbirds.ca

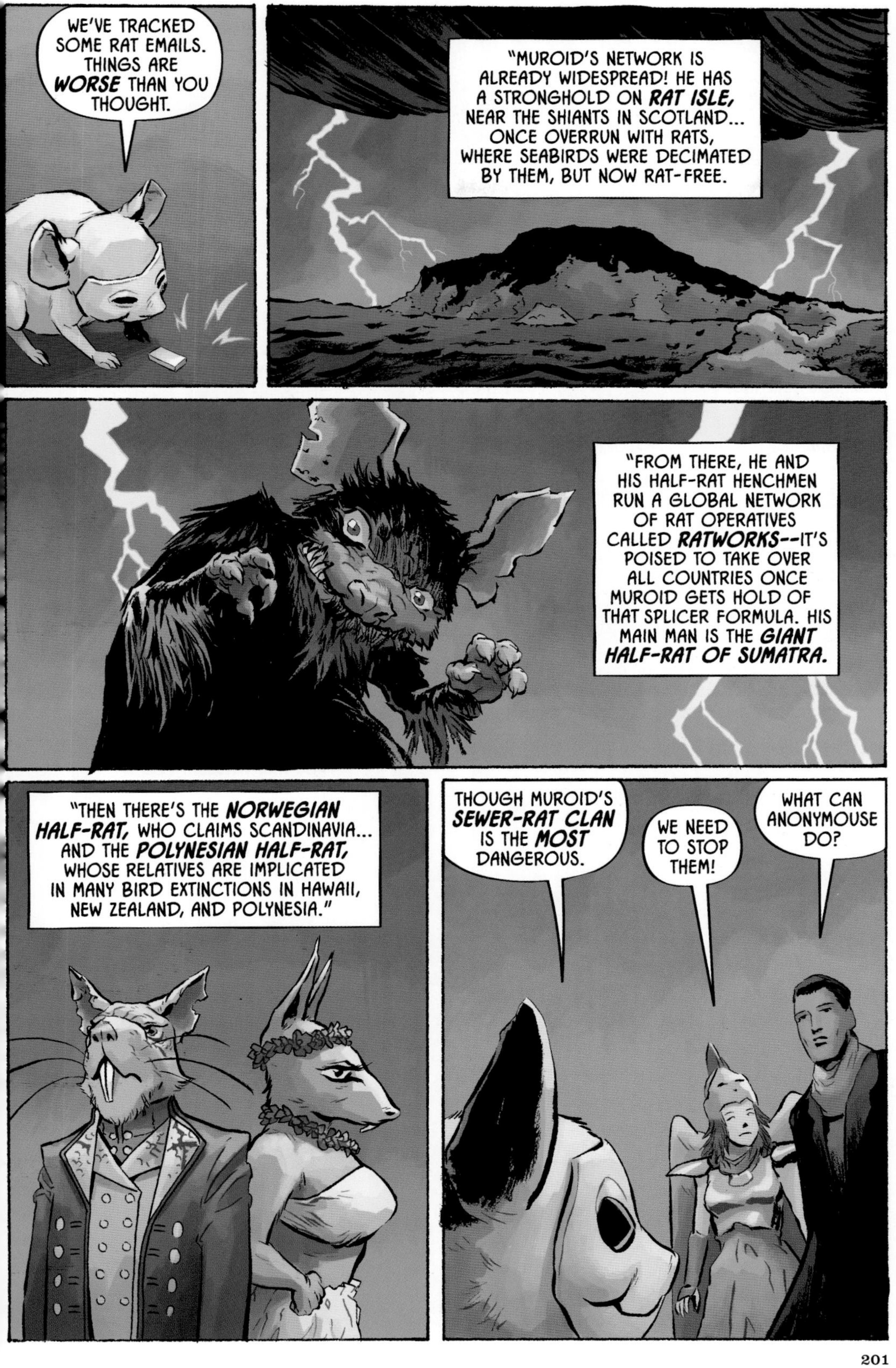
WE'VE TRACKED SOME RAT EMAILS. THINGS ARE WORSE THAN YOU THOUGHT.
"MUROID'S NETWORK IS ALREADY WIDESPREAD! HE HAS A STRONGHOLD ON RAT ISLE, NEAR THE SHIANTS IN SCOTLAND... ONCE OVERRUN WITH RATS, WHERE SEABIRDS WERE DECIMATED BY THEM, BUT NOW RAT-FREE.
"FROM THERE, HE AND HIS HALF-RAT HENCHMEN RUN A GLOBAL NETWORK OF RAT OPERATIVES CALLED RATWORKS--IT'S POISED TO TAKE OVER ALL COUNTRIES ONCE MUROID GETS HOLD OF THAT SPLICER FORMULA. HIS MAIN MAN IS THE GIANT HALF-RAT OF SUMATRA.
"THEN THERE'S THE NORWEGIAN HALF-RAT, WHO CLAIMS SCANDINAVIA... AND THE POLYNESIAN HALF-RAT, WHOSE RELATIVES ARE IMPLICATED IN MANY BIRD EXTINCTIONS IN HAWAII, NEW ZEALAND, AND POLYNESIA."
THOUGH MUROID'S SEWER-RAT CLAN IS THE MOST DANGEROUS.
WE NEED TO STOP THEM!
WHAT CAN ANONYMOUSE DO?

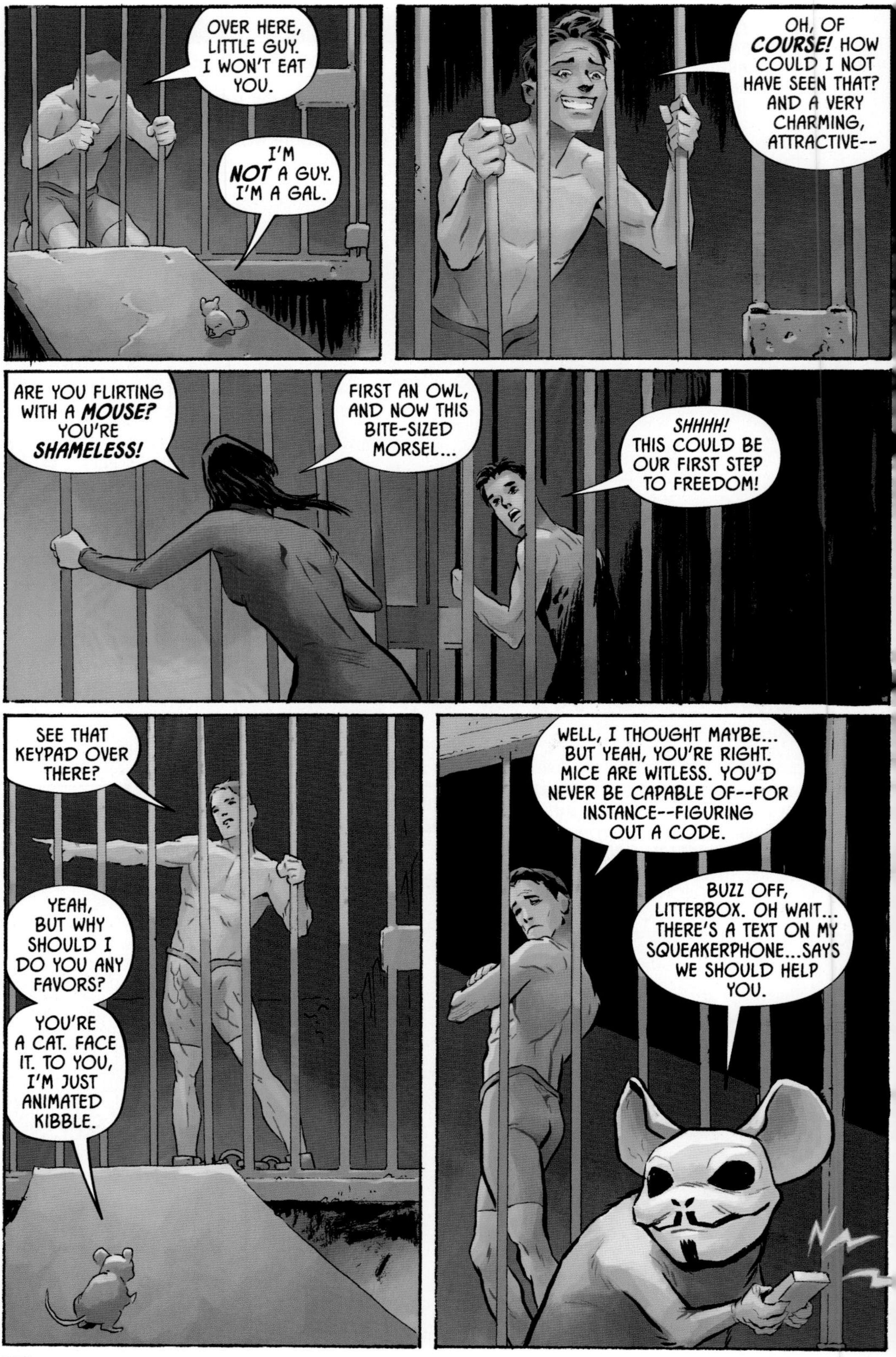
OVER HERE, LITTLE GUY. I WON'T EAT YOU.
I'M *NOT* A GUY. I'M A GAL.
OH, OF *COURSE!* HOW COULD I NOT HAVE SEEN THAT? AND A VERY CHARMING, ATTRACTIVE--
ARE YOU FLIRTING WITH A *MOUSE?* YOU'RE *SHAMELESS!*
FIRST AN OWL, AND NOW THIS BITE-SIZED MORSEL...
SHHHH! THIS COULD BE OUR FIRST STEP TO FREEDOM!
SEE THAT KEYPAD OVER THERE?
YEAH, BUT WHY SHOULD I DO YOU ANY FAVORS?
YOU'RE A CAT. FACE IT. TO YOU, I'M JUST ANIMATED KIBBLE.
WELL, I THOUGHT MAYBE... BUT YEAH, YOU'RE RIGHT. MICE ARE WITLESS. YOU'D NEVER BE CAPABLE OF--FOR INSTANCE--FIGURING OUT A CODE.
BUZZ OFF, LITTERBOX. OH WAIT... THERE'S A TEXT ON MY SQUEAKERPHONE...SAYS WE SHOULD HELP YOU.

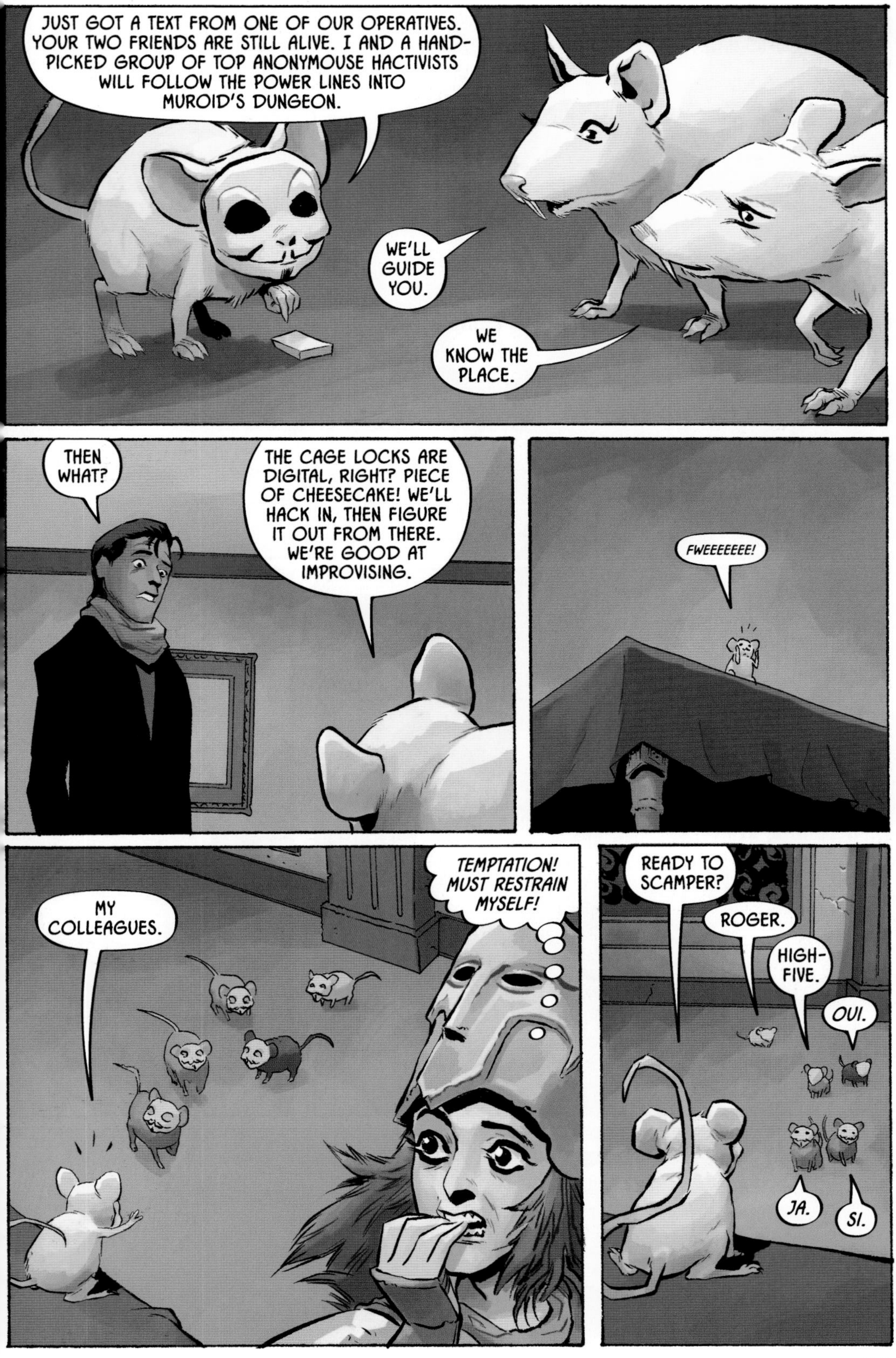
JUST GOT A TEXT FROM ONE OF OUR OPERATIVES. YOUR TWO FRIENDS ARE STILL ALIVE. I AND A HAND-PICKED GROUP OF TOP ANONYMOUSE HACTIVISTS WILL FOLLOW THE POWER LINES INTO MUROID'S DUNGEON.
WE'LL GUIDE YOU.
WE KNOW THE PLACE.
THEN WHAT?
THE CAGE LOCKS ARE DIGITAL, RIGHT? PIECE OF CHEESECAKE! WE'LL HACK IN, THEN FIGURE IT OUT FROM THERE. WE'RE GOOD AT IMPROVISING.
FWEEEEEEE!
MY COLLEAGUES.
TEMPTATION! MUST RESTRAIN MYSELF!
READY TO SCAMPER?
ROGER.
HIGH-FIVE.
OUI.
JA.
SI.

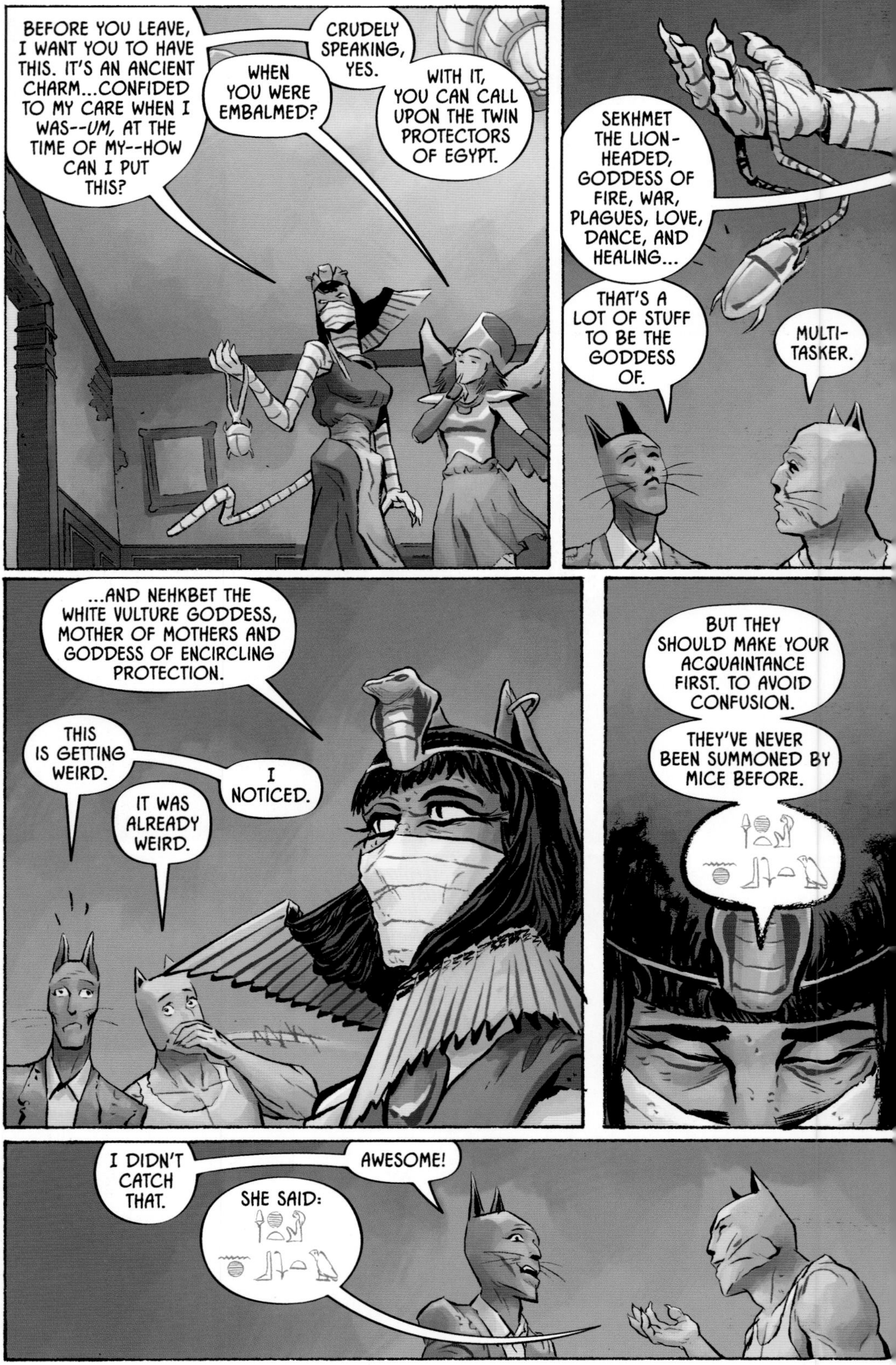
BEFORE YOU LEAVE, I WANT YOU TO HAVE THIS. IT'S AN ANCIENT CHARM...CONFIDED TO MY CARE WHEN I WAS--*UM,* AT THE TIME OF MY--HOW CAN I PUT THIS?
WHEN YOU WERE EMBALMED?
CRUDELY SPEAKING, YES.
WITH IT, YOU CAN CALL UPON THE TWIN PROTECTORS OF EGYPT.
SEKHMET THE LION-HEADED, GODDESS OF FIRE, WAR, PLAGUES, LOVE, DANCE, AND HEALING...
THAT'S A LOT OF STUFF TO BE THE GODDESS OF.
MULTI-TASKER.
...AND NEHKBET THE WHITE VULTURE GODDESS, MOTHER OF MOTHERS AND GODDESS OF ENCIRCLING PROTECTION.
THIS IS GETTING WEIRD.
I NOTICED.
IT WAS ALREADY WEIRD.
BUT THEY SHOULD MAKE YOUR ACQUAINTANCE FIRST. TO AVOID CONFUSION.
THEY'VE NEVER BEEN SUMMONED BY MICE BEFORE.
I DIDN'T CATCH THAT.
AWESOME!
SHE SAID:

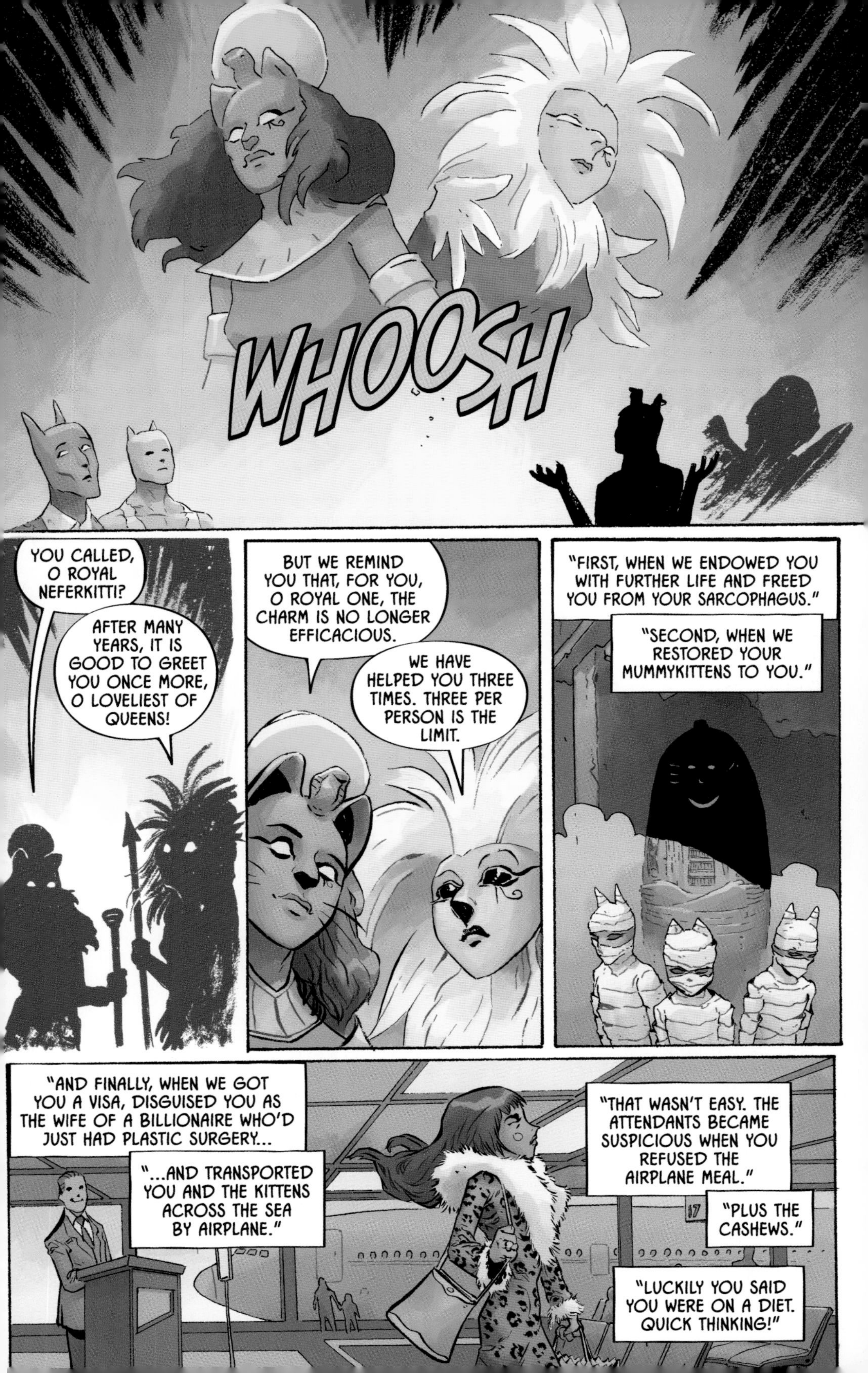
WHOOSH
YOU CALLED, O ROYAL NEFERKITTI?
AFTER MANY YEARS, IT IS GOOD TO GREET YOU ONCE MORE, O LOVELIEST OF QUEENS!
BUT WE REMIND YOU THAT, FOR YOU, O ROYAL ONE, THE CHARM IS NO LONGER EFFICACIOUS.
WE HAVE HELPED YOU THREE TIMES. THREE PER PERSON IS THE LIMIT.
"FIRST, WHEN WE ENDOWED YOU WITH FURTHER LIFE AND FREED YOU FROM YOUR SARCOPHAGUS."
"SECOND, WHEN WE RESTORED YOUR MUMMYKITTENS TO YOU."
"AND FINALLY, WHEN WE GOT YOU A VISA, DISGUISED YOU AS THE WIFE OF A BILLIONAIRE WHO'D JUST HAD PLASTIC SURGERY...
"...AND TRANSPORTED YOU AND THE KITTENS ACROSS THE SEA BY AIRPLANE."
"THAT WASN'T EASY. THE ATTENDANTS BECAME SUSPICIOUS WHEN YOU REFUSED THE AIRPLANE MEAL."
"PLUS THE CASHEWS."
"LUCKILY YOU SAID YOU WERE ON A DIET. QUICK THINKING!"

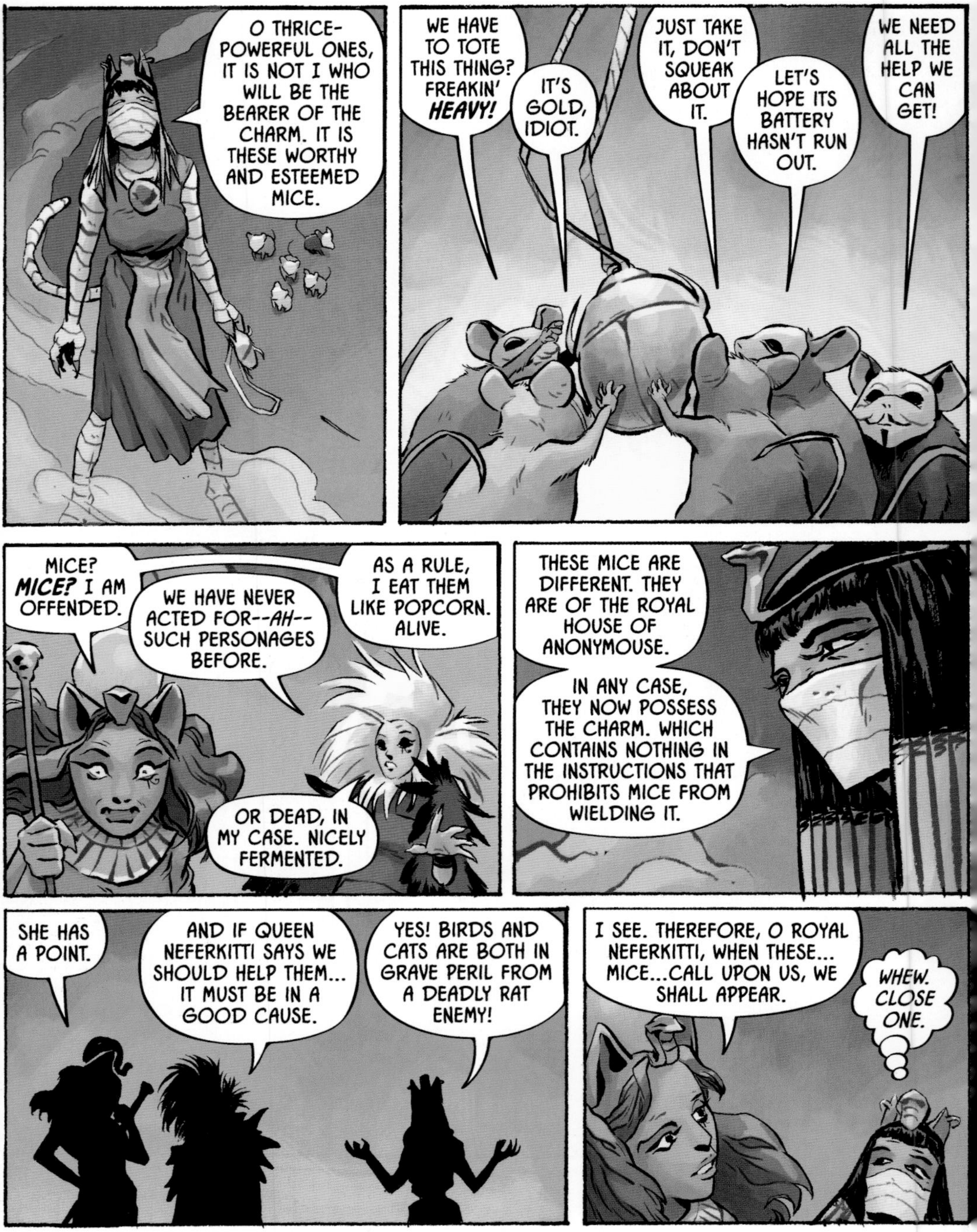
O THRICE-POWERFUL ONES, IT IS NOT I WHO WILL BE THE BEARER OF THE CHARM. IT IS THESE WORTHY AND ESTEEMED MICE.
WE HAVE TO TOTE THIS THING? FREAKIN' HEAVY!
IT'S GOLD, IDIOT.
JUST TAKE IT, DON'T SQUEAK ABOUT IT.
LET'S HOPE ITS BATTERY HASN'T RUN OUT.
WE NEED ALL THE HELP WE CAN GET!
MICE? MICE? I AM OFFENDED.
WE HAVE NEVER ACTED FOR--AH--SUCH PERSONAGES BEFORE.
AS A RULE, I EAT THEM LIKE POPCORN. ALIVE.
OR DEAD, IN MY CASE. NICELY FERMENTED.
THESE MICE ARE DIFFERENT. THEY ARE OF THE ROYAL HOUSE OF ANONYMOUSE.
IN ANY CASE, THEY NOW POSSESS THE CHARM. WHICH CONTAINS NOTHING IN THE INSTRUCTIONS THAT PROHIBITS MICE FROM WIELDING IT.
SHE HAS A POINT.
AND IF QUEEN NEFERKITTI SAYS WE SHOULD HELP THEM... IT MUST BE IN A GOOD CAUSE.
YES! BIRDS AND CATS ARE BOTH IN GRAVE PERIL FROM A DEADLY RAT ENEMY!
I SEE. THEREFORE, O ROYAL NEFERKITTI, WHEN THESE... MICE...CALL UPON US, WE SHALL APPEAR.
WHEW. CLOSE ONE.

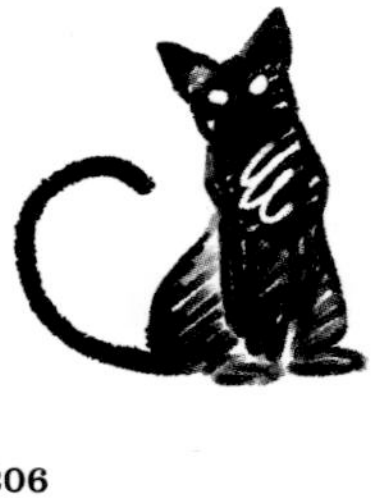

RATS

Rats are a danger to birds—they eat their eggs and young—and they're also a danger to cats. Rat bites and scratches carry a high risk of infection, and if your cat eats a rat that's eaten poison, they can be poisoned too. Keeping cats from roaming unsupervised is a great way to protect your cat from rats, not to mention other wildlife, like raccoons and coyotes. Read more at www.catsandbirds.ca

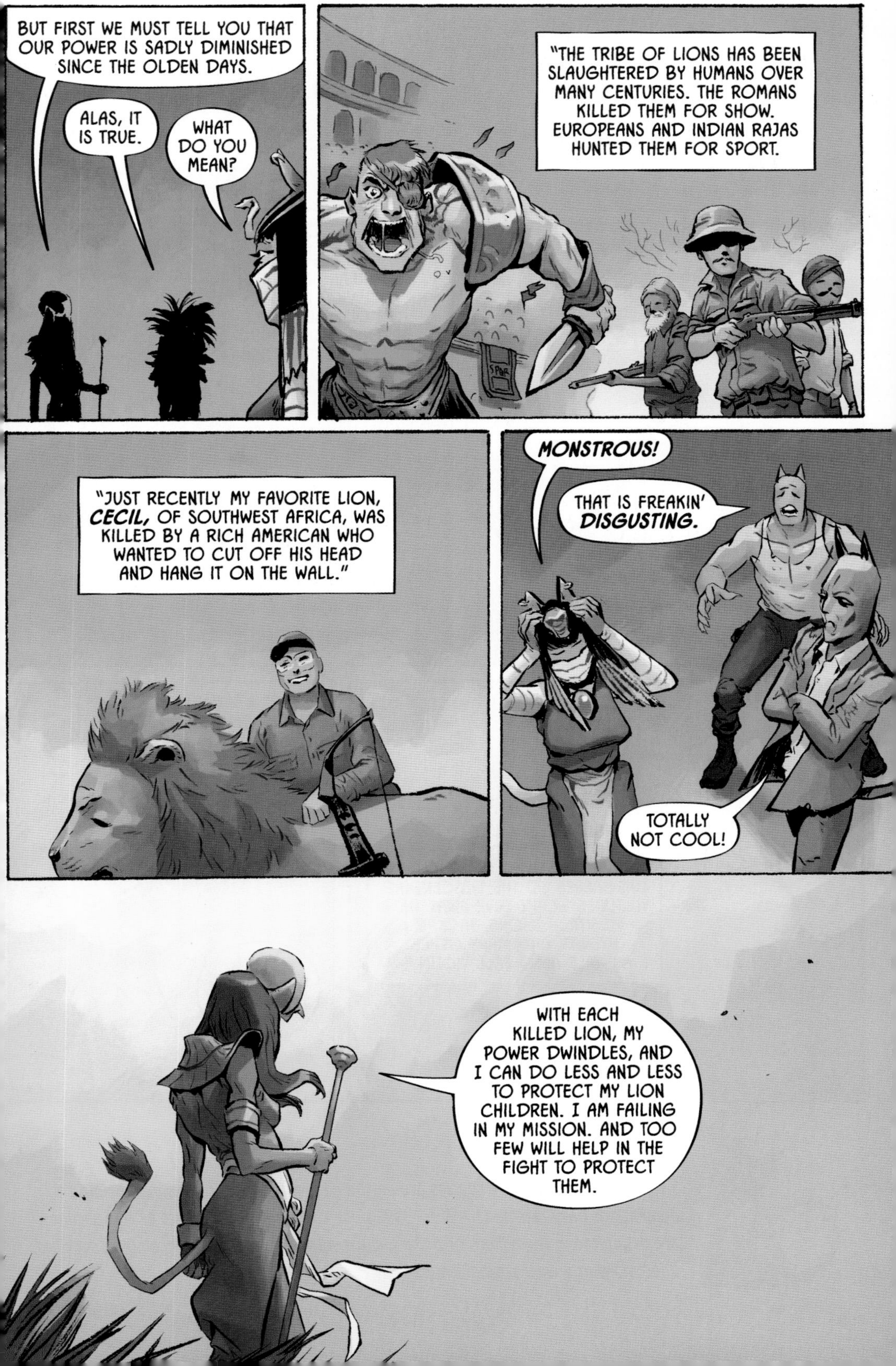
BUT FIRST WE MUST TELL YOU THAT OUR POWER IS SADLY DIMINISHED SINCE THE OLDEN DAYS.
ALAS, IT IS TRUE.
WHAT DO YOU MEAN?
"THE TRIBE OF LIONS HAS BEEN SLAUGHTERED BY HUMANS OVER MANY CENTURIES. THE ROMANS KILLED THEM FOR SHOW. EUROPEANS AND INDIAN RAJAS HUNTED THEM FOR SPORT.
SPQR
"JUST RECENTLY MY FAVORITE LION, *CECIL,* OF SOUTHWEST AFRICA, WAS KILLED BY A RICH AMERICAN WHO WANTED TO CUT OFF HIS HEAD AND HANG IT ON THE WALL."
MONSTROUS!
THAT IS FREAKIN' *DISGUSTING.*
TOTALLY NOT COOL!
WITH EACH KILLED LION, MY POWER DWINDLES, AND I CAN DO LESS AND LESS TO PROTECT MY LION CHILDREN. I AM FAILING IN MY MISSION. AND TOO FEW WILL HELP IN THE FIGHT TO PROTECT THEM.

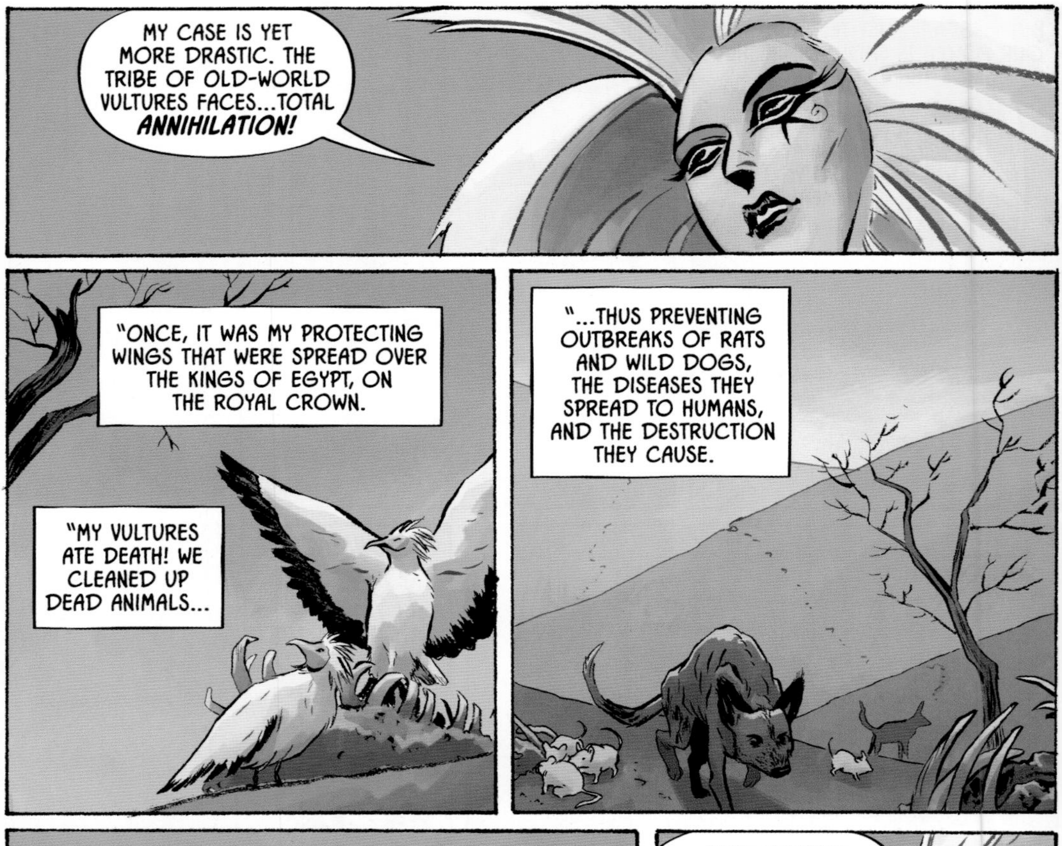
MY CASE IS YET MORE DRASTIC. THE TRIBE OF OLD-WORLD VULTURES FACES...TOTAL ANNIHILATION!
"ONCE, IT WAS MY PROTECTING WINGS THAT WERE SPREAD OVER THE KINGS OF EGYPT, ON THE ROYAL CROWN.
"MY VULTURES ATE DEATH! WE CLEANED UP DEAD ANIMALS...
"...THUS PREVENTING OUTBREAKS OF RATS AND WILD DOGS, THE DISEASES THEY SPREAD TO HUMANS, AND THE DESTRUCTION THEY CAUSE.
"IN AFRICA, VULTURES ARE BEING MURDERED BY ELEPHANT POACHERS, WHO POISON THE CARCASSES SO THE DESCENDING VULTURES WON'T GIVE AWAY THEIR POSITION. LIONS, JACKALS, HYENAS, AND MANY OTHER ANIMALS ALSO FALL VICTIM."
BUT WHATEVER POWER REMAINS TO US SHALL BE AT YOUR DISPOSAL, O EXALTED AMONG MICE.
AT YOUR CALL, WE WILL APPEAR.

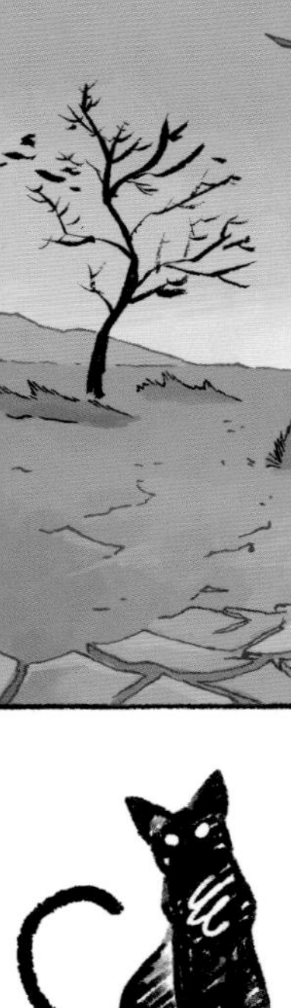

VULTURES

Six of ten African vulture species are on the edge of extinction, and Indian vulture populations have dropped by 97%–99% since the nineties. The costs of this decline are estimated in the billions of dollars, since vultures provide vital ecological services. Read more at www.catsandbirds.ca

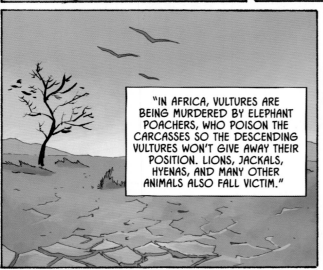

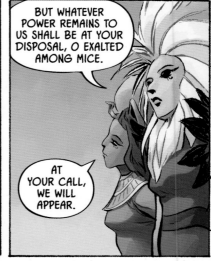

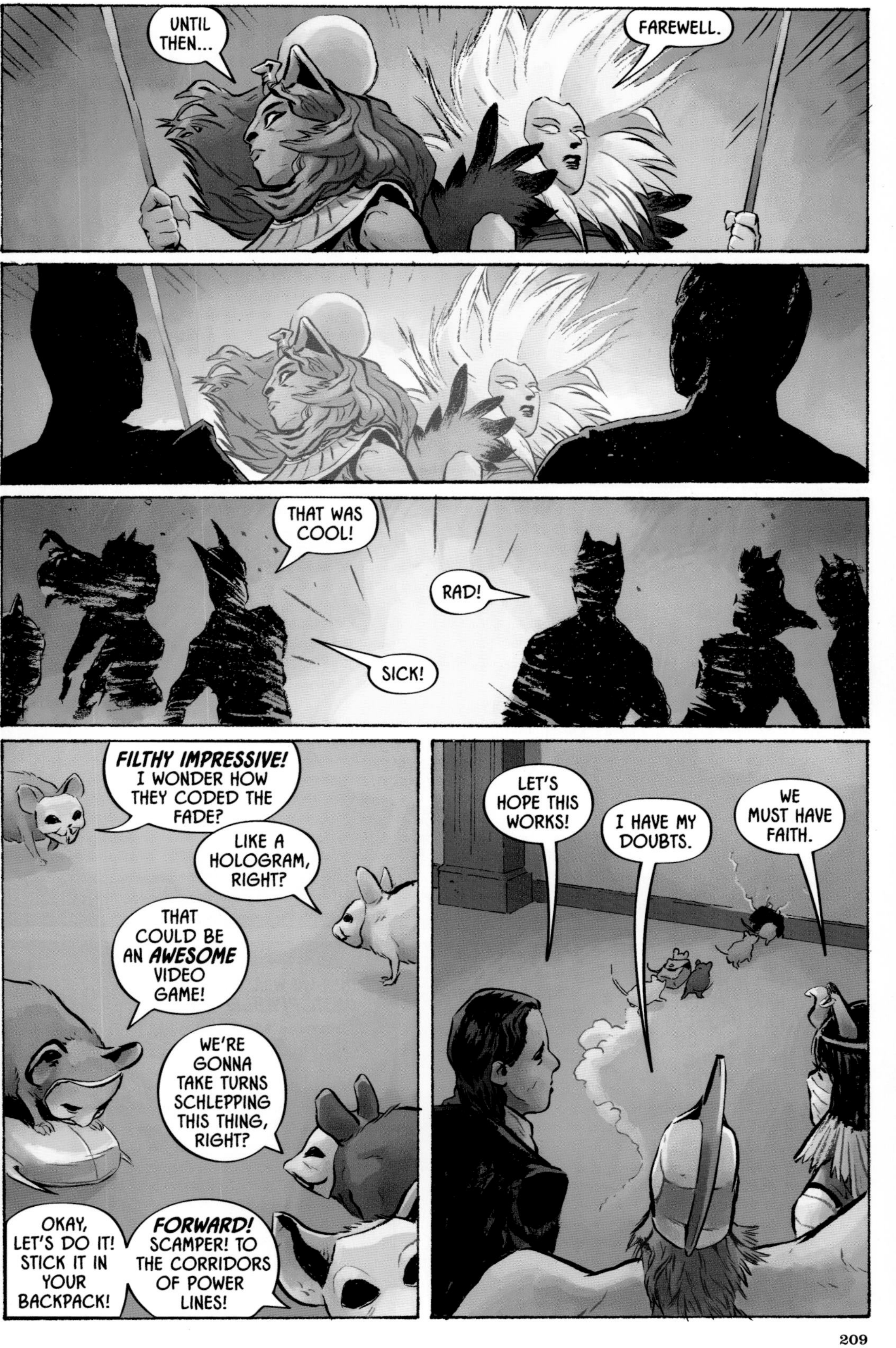
UNTIL THEN...
FAREWELL.
THAT WAS COOL!
RAD!
SICK!
FILTHY IMPRESSIVE! I WONDER HOW THEY CODED THE FADE?
LIKE A HOLOGRAM, RIGHT?
THAT COULD BE AN AWESOME VIDEO GAME!
WE'RE GONNA TAKE TURNS SCHLEPPING THIS THING, RIGHT?
OKAY, LET'S DO IT! STICK IT IN YOUR BACKPACK!
FORWARD! SCAMPER! TO THE CORRIDORS OF POWER LINES!
LET'S HOPE THIS WORKS!
I HAVE MY DOUBTS.
WE MUST HAVE FAITH.

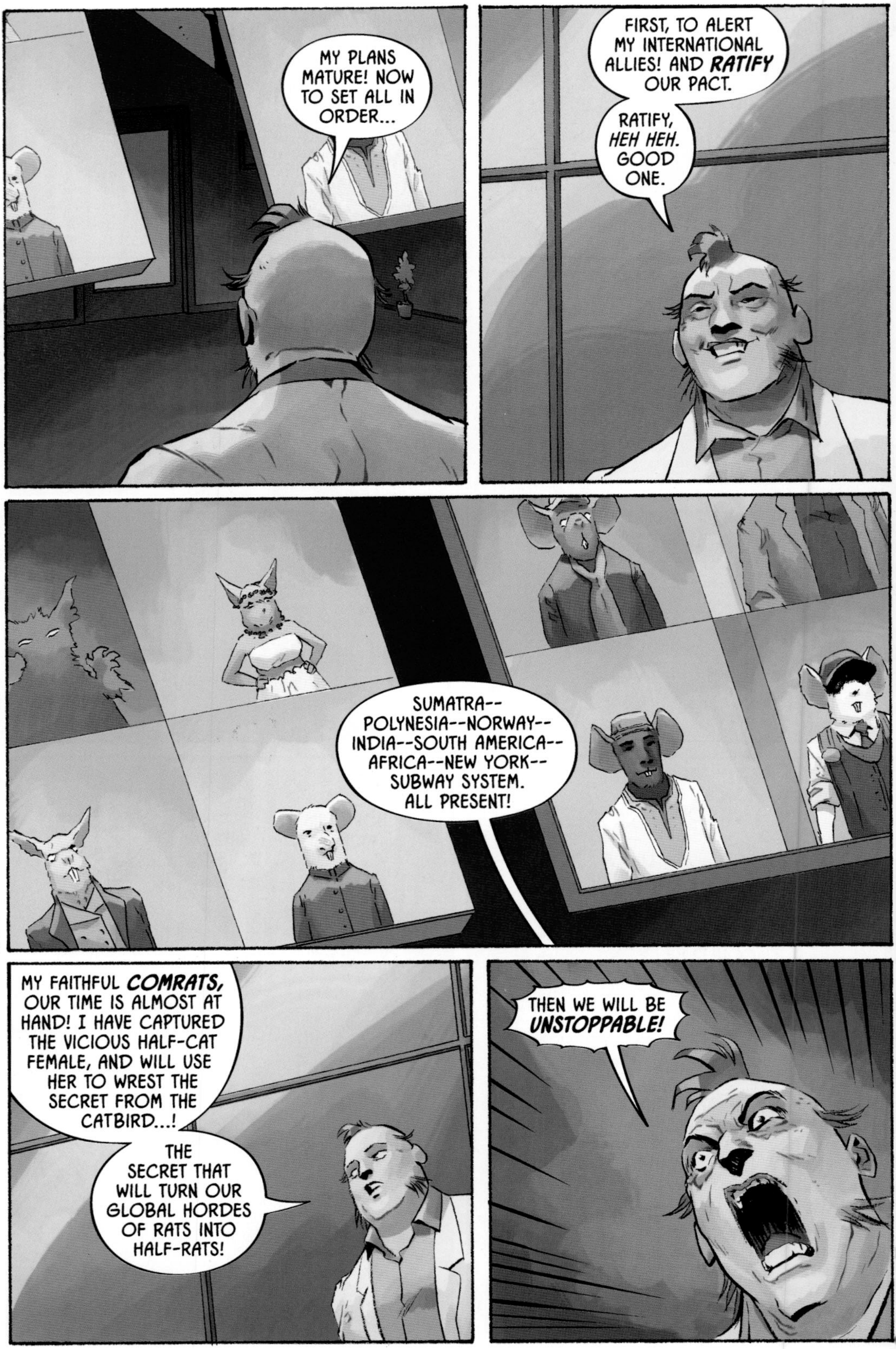
MY PLANS MATURE! NOW TO SET ALL IN ORDER...
FIRST, TO ALERT MY INTERNATIONAL ALLIES! AND *RATIFY* OUR PACT.
RATIFY, *HEH HEH.* GOOD ONE.
SUMATRA--POLYNESIA--NORWAY--INDIA--SOUTH AMERICA--AFRICA--NEW YORK--SUBWAY SYSTEM. ALL PRESENT!
MY FAITHFUL ***COMRATS,*** OUR TIME IS ALMOST AT HAND! I HAVE CAPTURED THE VICIOUS HALF-CAT FEMALE, AND WILL USE HER TO WREST THE SECRET FROM THE CATBIRD...!
THE SECRET THAT WILL TURN OUR GLOBAL HORDES OF RATS INTO HALF-RATS!
THEN WE WILL BE ***UNSTOPPABLE!***

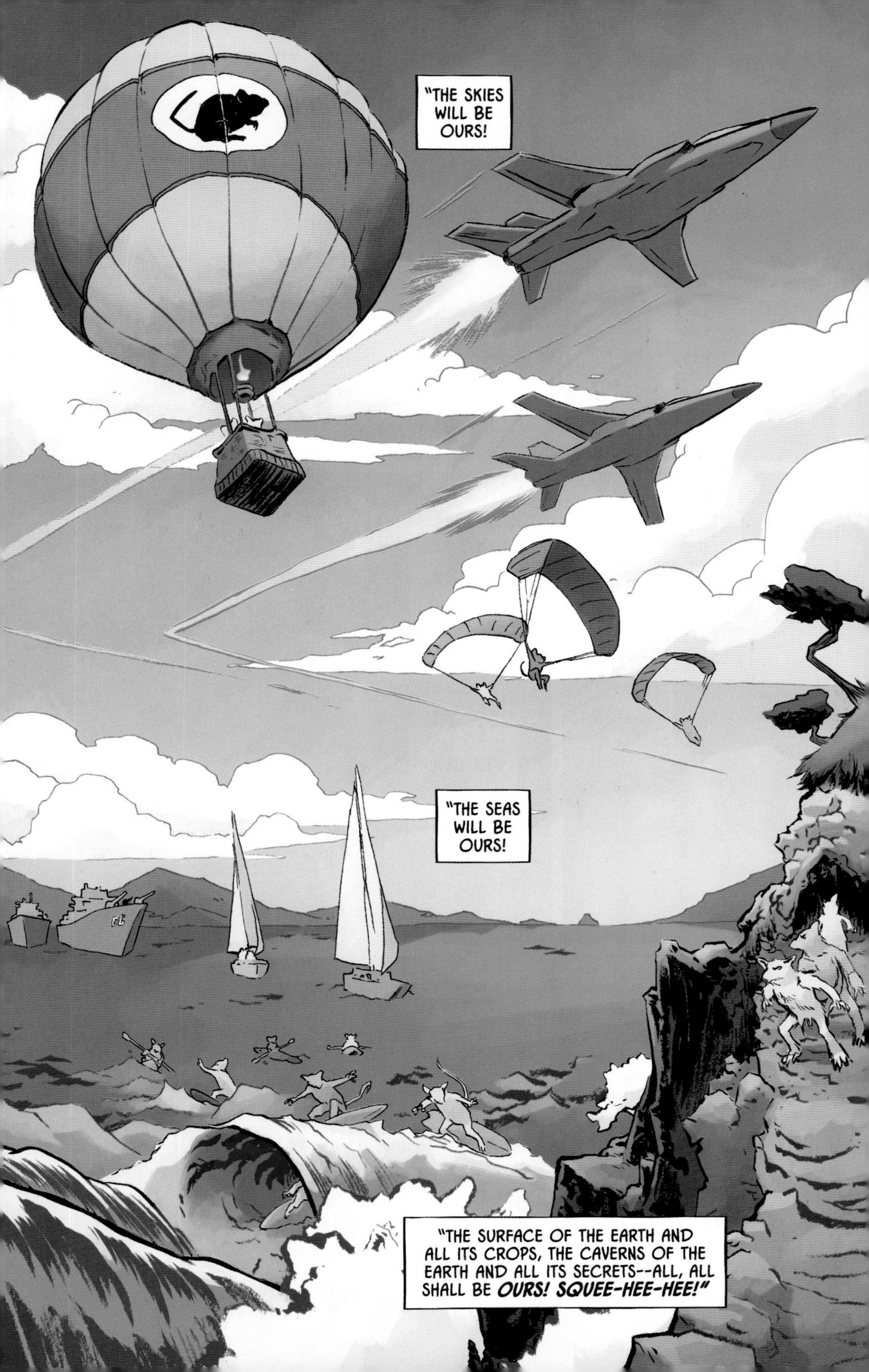
"THE SKIES WILL BE OURS!
"THE SEAS WILL BE OURS!
"THE SURFACE OF THE EARTH AND ALL ITS CROPS, THE CAVERNS OF THE EARTH AND ALL ITS SECRETS--ALL, ALL SHALL BE ***OURS! SQUEE-HEE-HEE!"***

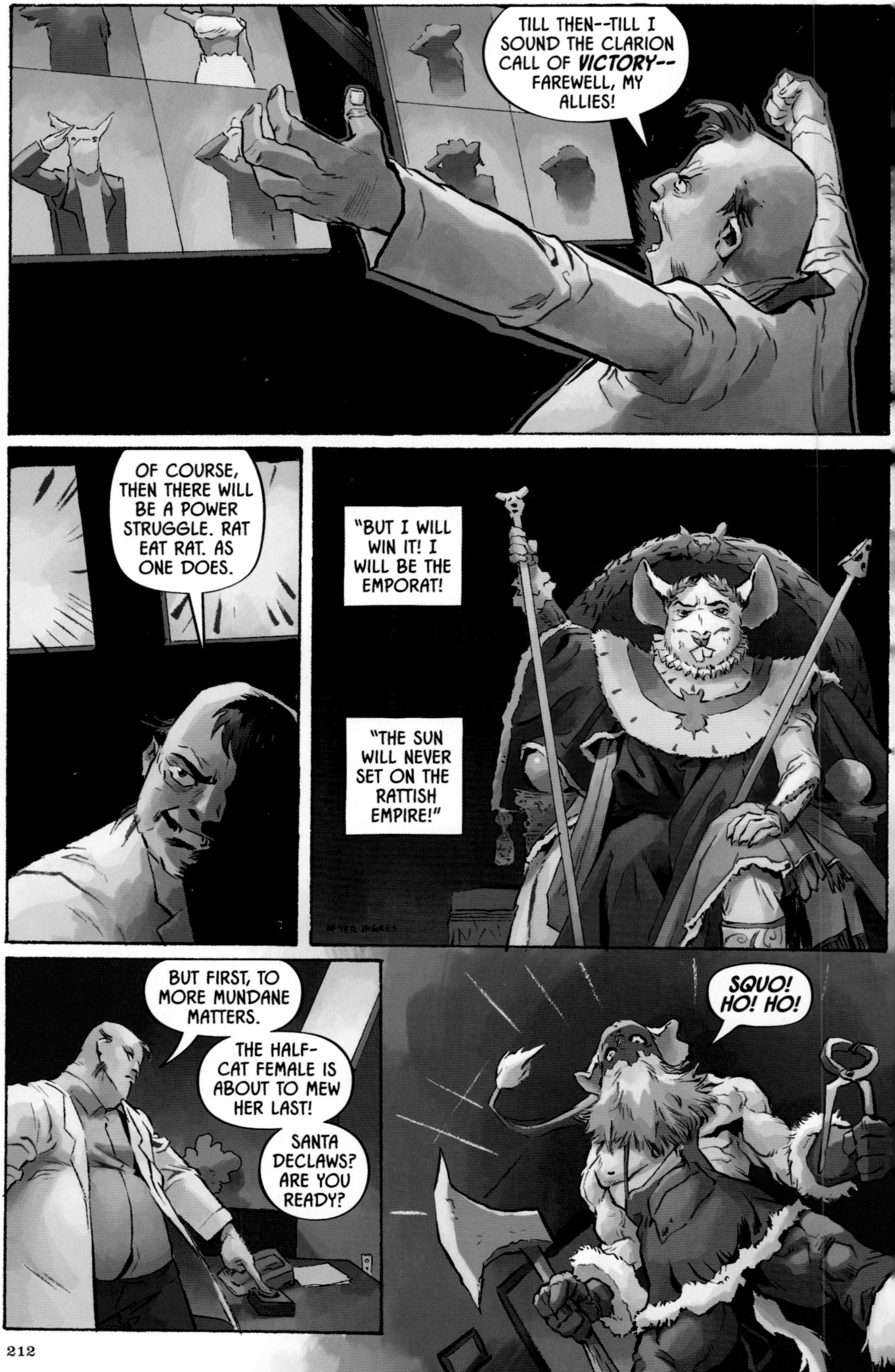
TILL THEN--TILL I SOUND THE CLARION CALL OF VICTORY-- FAREWELL, MY ALLIES!
OF COURSE, THEN THERE WILL BE A POWER STRUGGLE. RAT EAT RAT. AS ONE DOES.
"BUT I WILL WIN IT! I WILL BE THE EMPORAT!
"THE SUN WILL NEVER SET ON THE RATTISH EMPIRE!"
AFTER INGRES
BUT FIRST, TO MORE MUNDANE MATTERS.
THE HALF-CAT FEMALE IS ABOUT TO MEW HER LAST!
SANTA DECLAWS? ARE YOU READY?
SQUO! HO! HO!

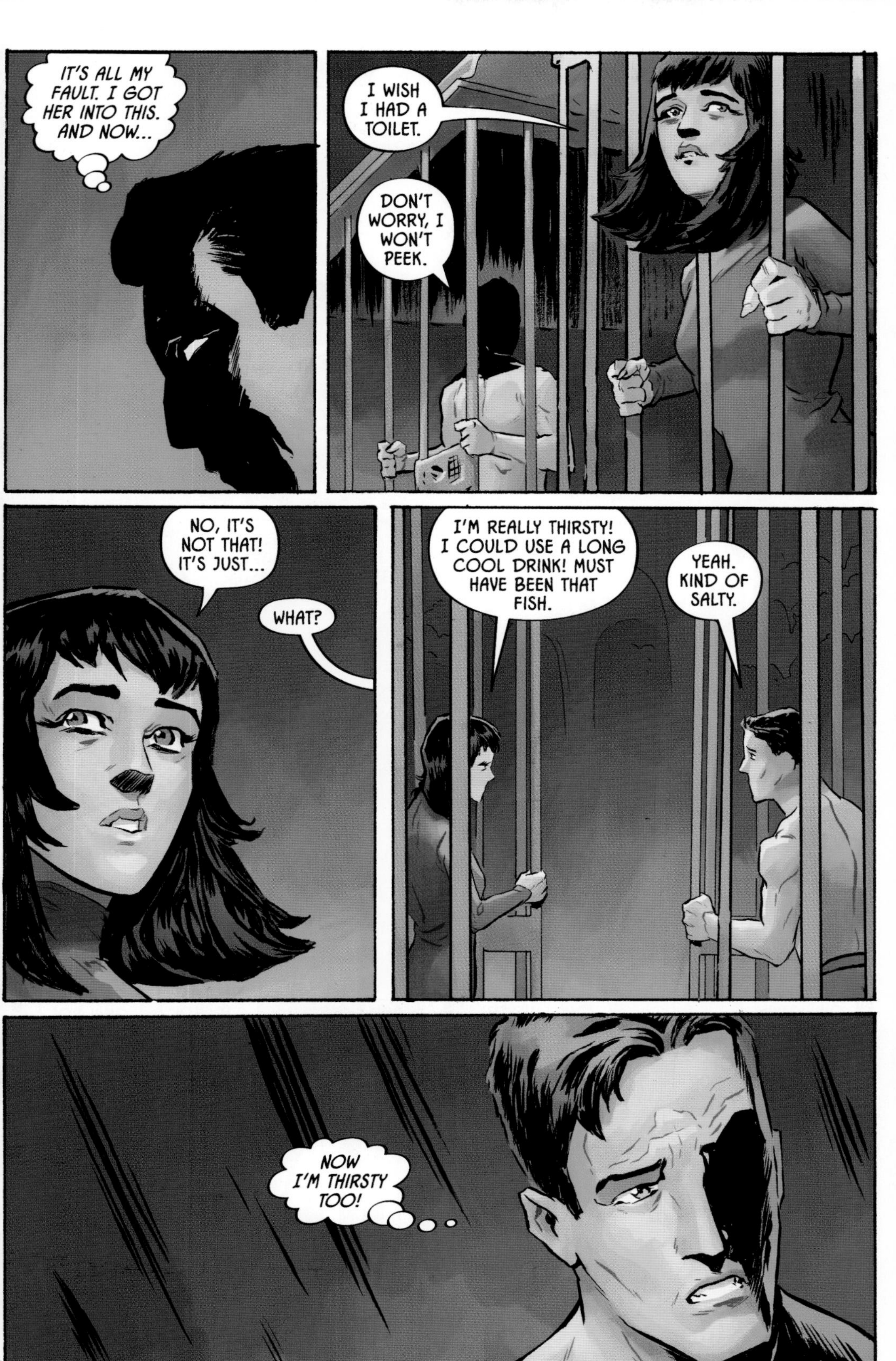
IT'S ALL MY FAULT. I GOT HER INTO THIS. AND NOW...
I WISH I HAD A TOILET.
DON'T WORRY, I WON'T PEEK.
NO, IT'S NOT THAT! IT'S JUST...
WHAT?
I'M REALLY THIRSTY! I COULD USE A LONG COOL DRINK! MUST HAVE BEEN THAT FISH.
YEAH. KIND OF SALTY.
NOW I'M THIRSTY TOO!

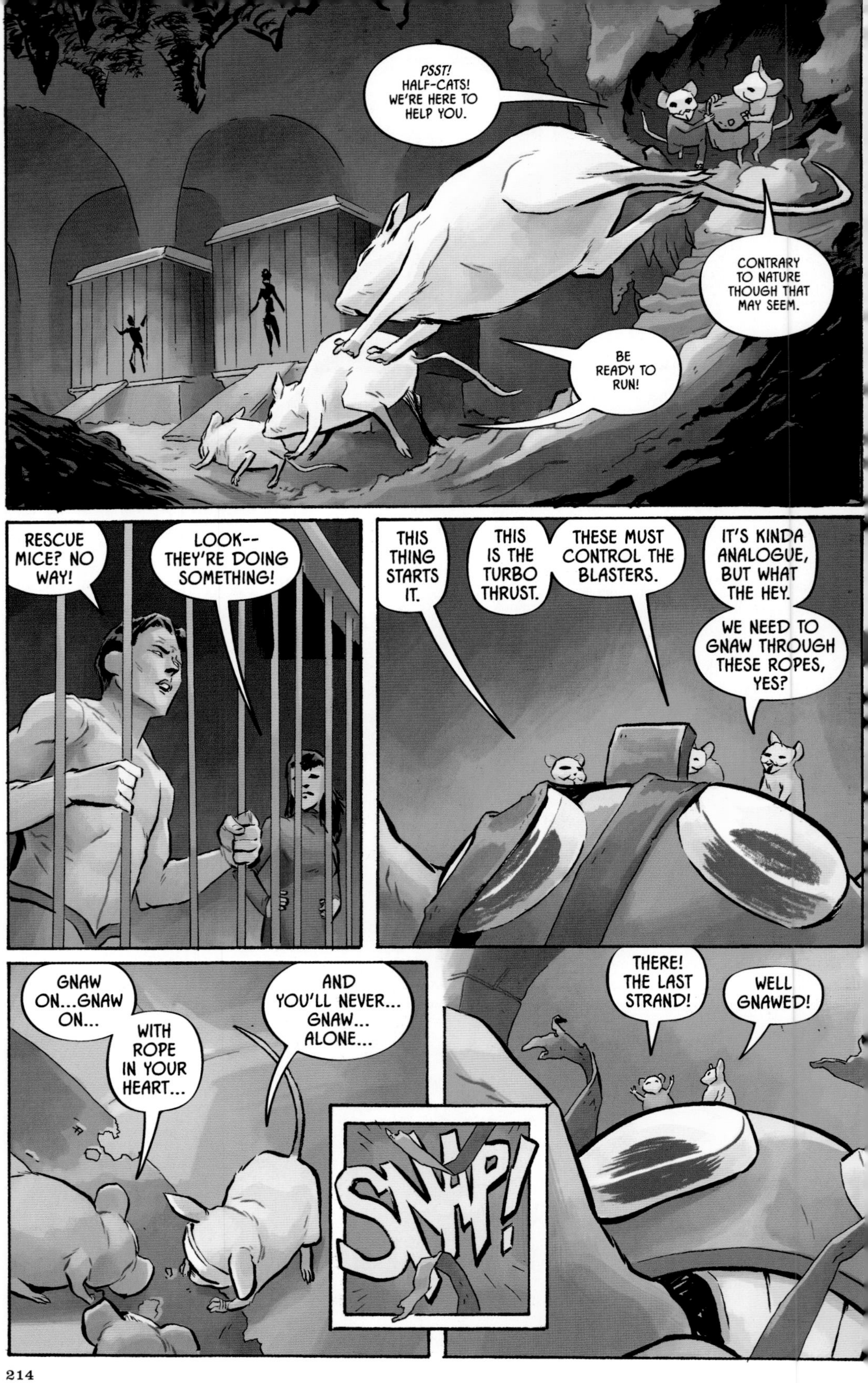
PSST! HALF-CATS! WE'RE HERE TO HELP YOU.
CONTRARY TO NATURE THOUGH THAT MAY SEEM.
BE READY TO RUN!
RESCUE MICE? NO WAY!
LOOK-- THEY'RE DOING SOMETHING!
THIS THING STARTS IT.
THIS IS THE TURBO THRUST.
THESE MUST CONTROL THE BLASTERS.
IT'S KINDA ANALOGUE, BUT WHAT THE HEY.
WE NEED TO GNAW THROUGH THESE ROPES, YES?
GNAW ON...GNAW ON...
WITH ROPE IN YOUR HEART...
AND YOU'LL NEVER... GNAW... ALONE...
SNAP!
THERE! THE LAST STRAND!
WELL GNAWED!

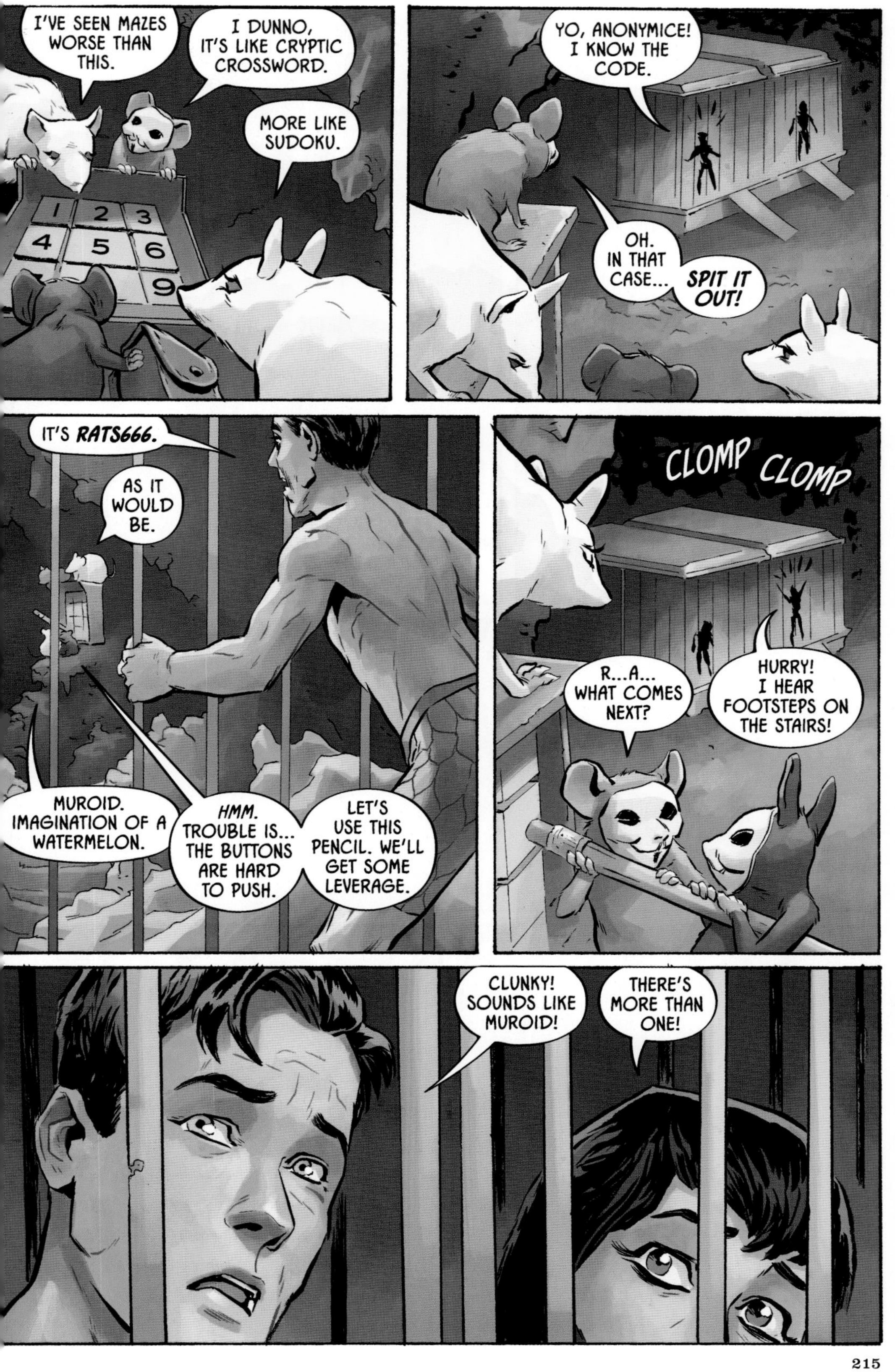
I'VE SEEN MAZES WORSE THAN THIS.
I DUNNO, IT'S LIKE CRYPTIC CROSSWORD.
MORE LIKE SUDOKU.
1 2 3
4 5 6
9
YO, ANONYMICE! I KNOW THE CODE.
OH. IN THAT CASE...
SPIT IT OUT!
IT'S RATS666.
AS IT WOULD BE.
MUROID. IMAGINATION OF A WATERMELON.
HMM. TROUBLE IS... THE BUTTONS ARE HARD TO PUSH.
LET'S USE THIS PENCIL. WE'LL GET SOME LEVERAGE.
CLOMP CLOMP
R...A... WHAT COMES NEXT?
HURRY! I HEAR FOOTSTEPS ON THE STAIRS!
CLUNKY! SOUNDS LIKE MUROID!
THERE'S MORE THAN ONE!

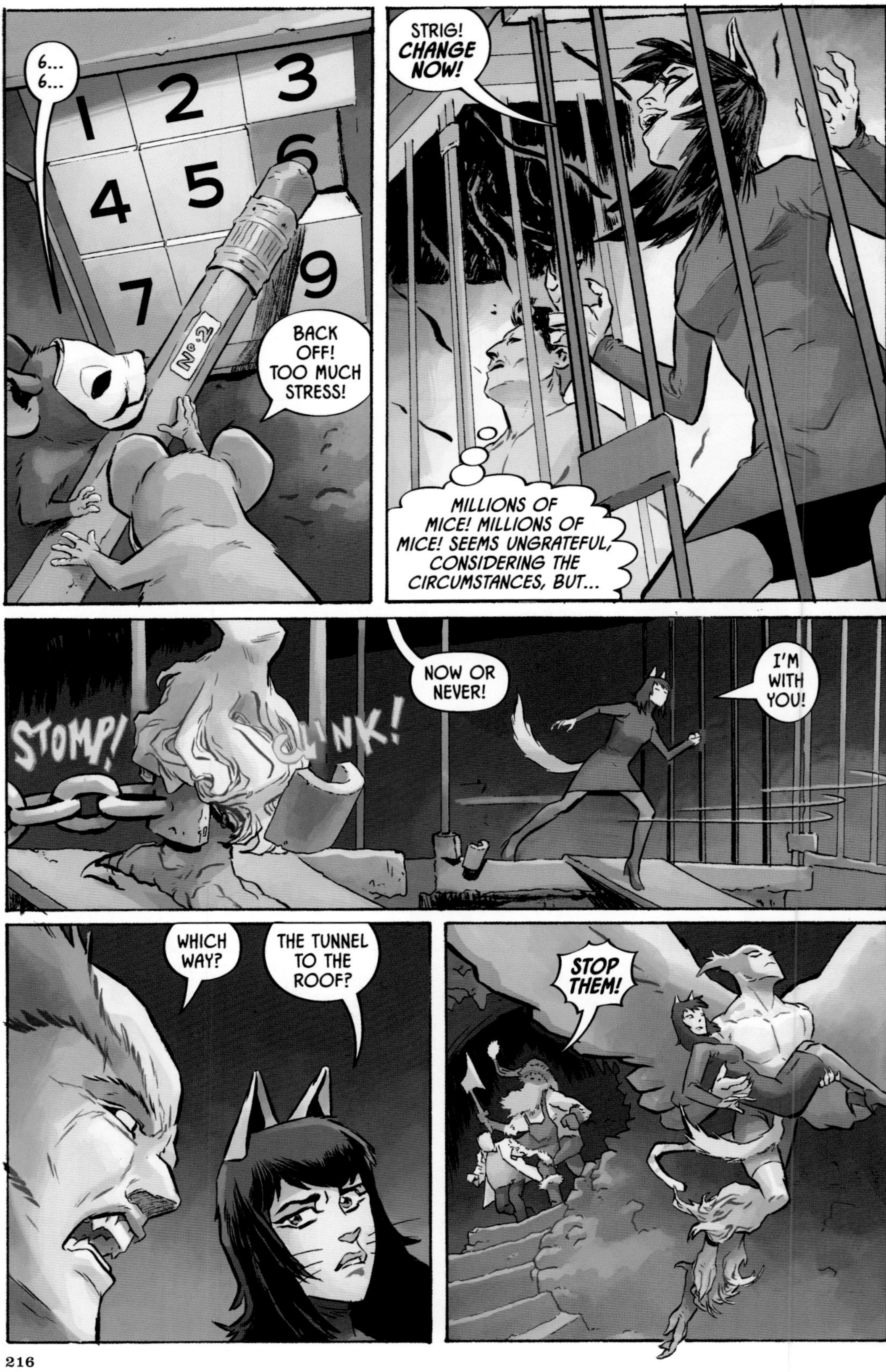

6...
6...
1
2
3
4
5
6
7
9
No. 2
BACK OFF! TOO MUCH STRESS!
STRIG! CHANGE NOW!
MILLIONS OF MICE! MILLIONS OF MICE! SEEMS UNGRATEFUL, CONSIDERING THE CIRCUMSTANCES, BUT...
STOMP!
CLINK!
NOW OR NEVER!
I'M WITH YOU!
WHICH WAY?
THE TUNNEL TO THE ROOF?
STOP THEM!

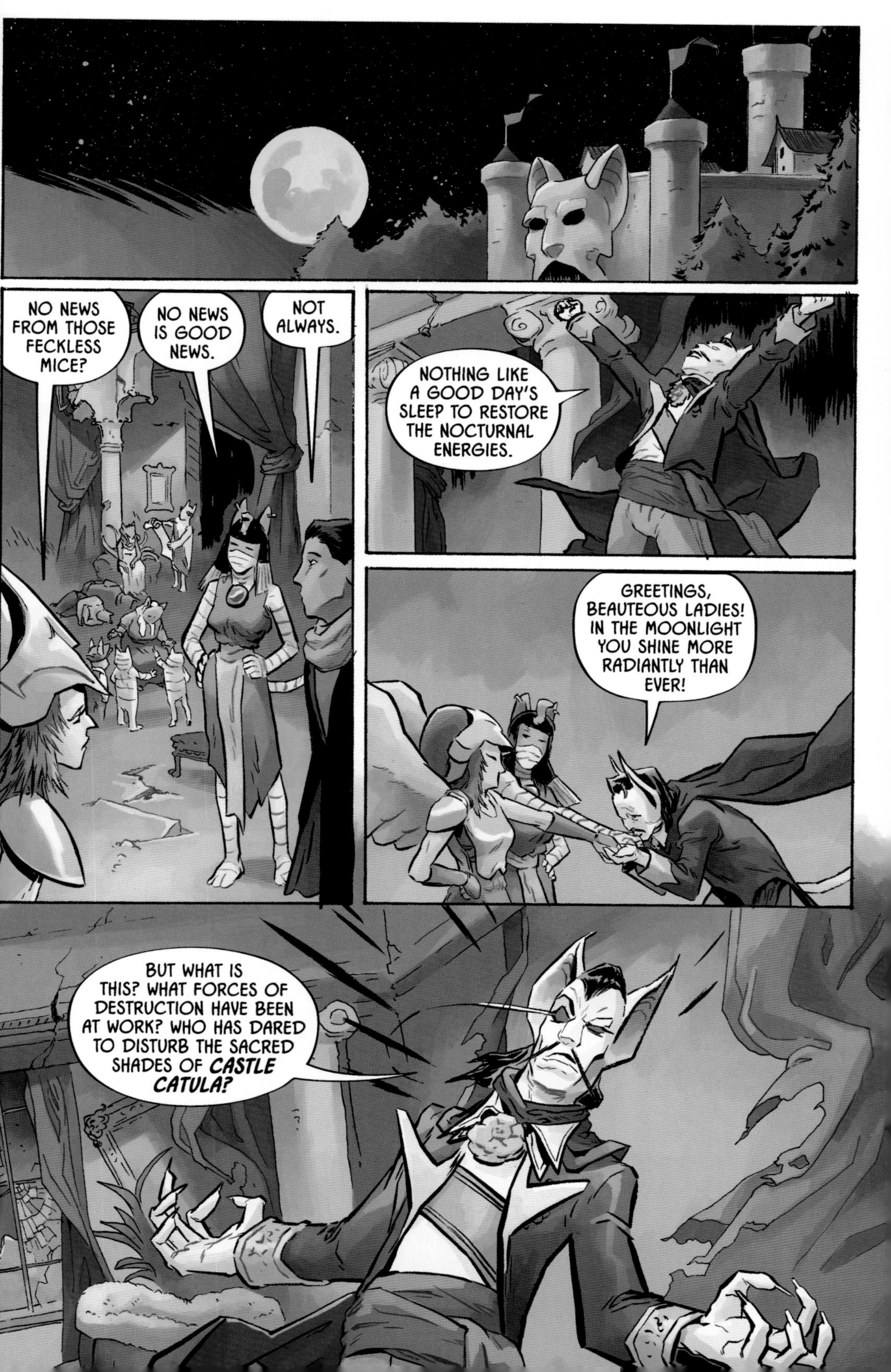
NO NEWS FROM THOSE FECKLESS MICE?
NO NEWS IS GOOD NEWS.
NOT ALWAYS.
NOTHING LIKE A GOOD DAY'S SLEEP TO RESTORE THE NOCTURNAL ENERGIES.
GREETINGS, BEAUTEOUS LADIES! IN THE MOONLIGHT YOU SHINE MORE RADIANTLY THAN EVER!
BUT WHAT IS THIS? WHAT FORCES OF DESTRUCTION HAVE BEEN AT WORK? WHO HAS DARED TO DISTURB THE SACRED SHADES OF CASTLE CATULA?

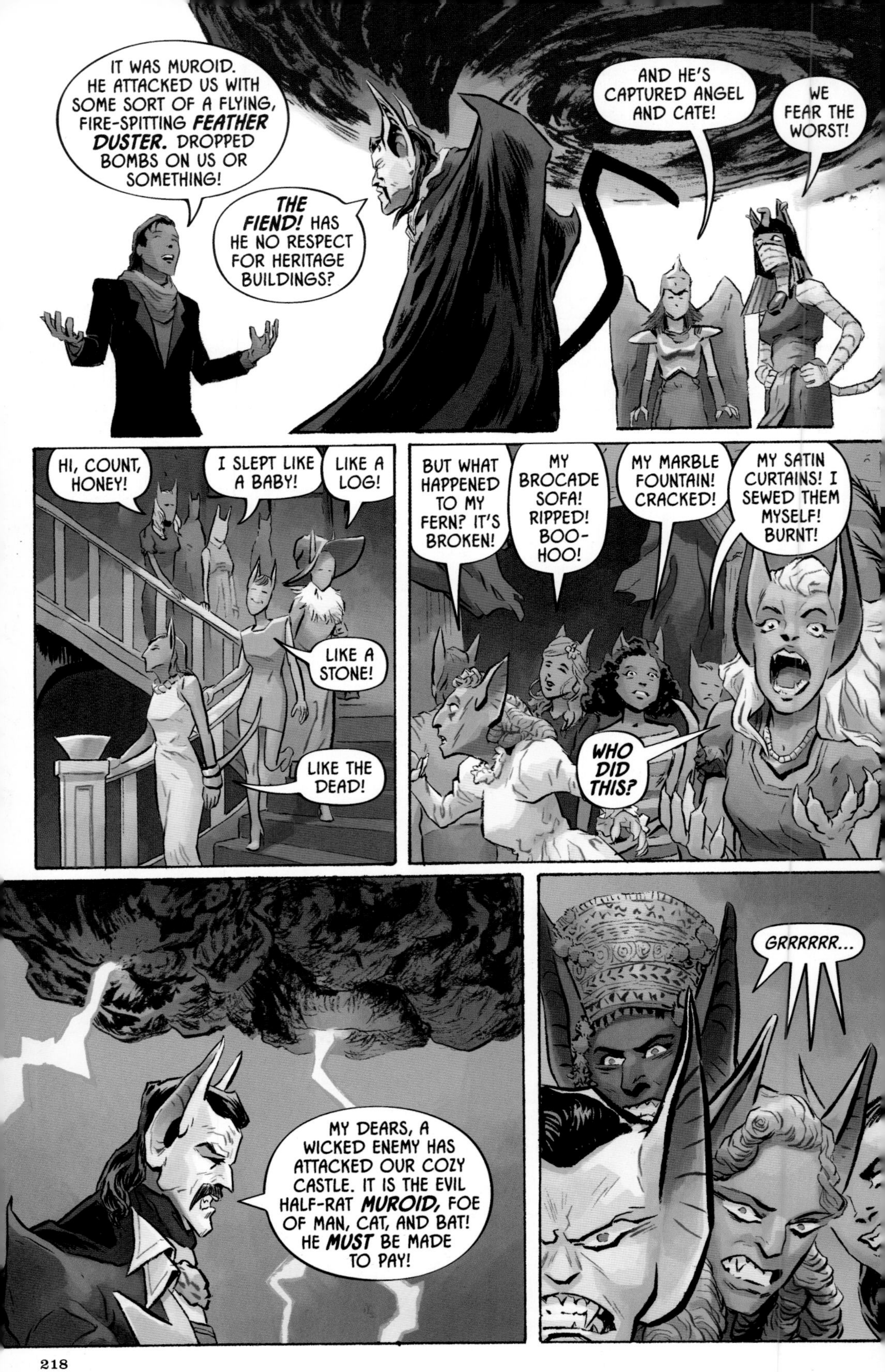
IT WAS MUROID. HE ATTACKED US WITH SOME SORT OF A FLYING, FIRE-SPITTING FEATHER DUSTER. DROPPED BOMBS ON US OR SOMETHING!
THE FIEND! HAS HE NO RESPECT FOR HERITAGE BUILDINGS?
AND HE'S CAPTURED ANGEL AND CATE!
WE FEAR THE WORST!
HI, COUNT, HONEY!
I SLEPT LIKE A BABY!
LIKE A LOG!
LIKE A STONE!
LIKE THE DEAD!
BUT WHAT HAPPENED TO MY FERN? IT'S BROKEN!
MY BROCADE SOFA! RIPPED! BOO-HOO!
MY MARBLE FOUNTAIN! CRACKED!
MY SATIN CURTAINS! I SEWED THEM MYSELF! BURNT!
WHO DID THIS?
MY DEARS, A WICKED ENEMY HAS ATTACKED OUR COZY CASTLE. IT IS THE EVIL HALF-RAT MUROID, FOE OF MAN, CAT, AND BAT! HE MUST BE MADE TO PAY!
GRRRRRR...

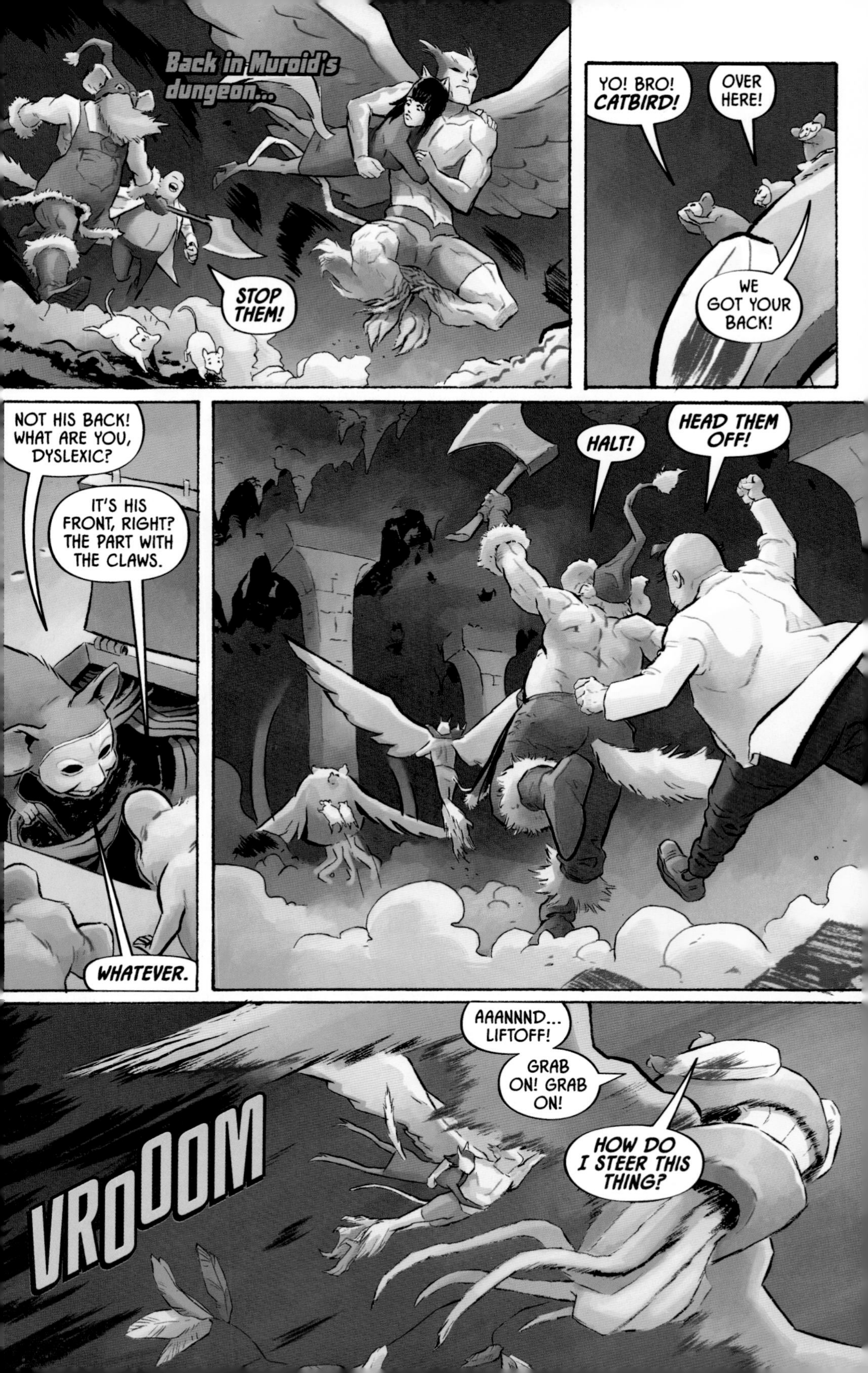

Back in Muroid's dungeon...
STOP THEM!
YO! BRO! CATBIRD!
OVER HERE!
WE GOT YOUR BACK!
NOT HIS BACK! WHAT ARE YOU, DYSLEXIC?
IT'S HIS FRONT, RIGHT? THE PART WITH THE CLAWS.
WHATEVER.
HALT!
HEAD THEM OFF!
AAANNND... LIFTOFF!
GRAB ON! GRAB ON!
HOW DO I STEER THIS THING?
VROOOM

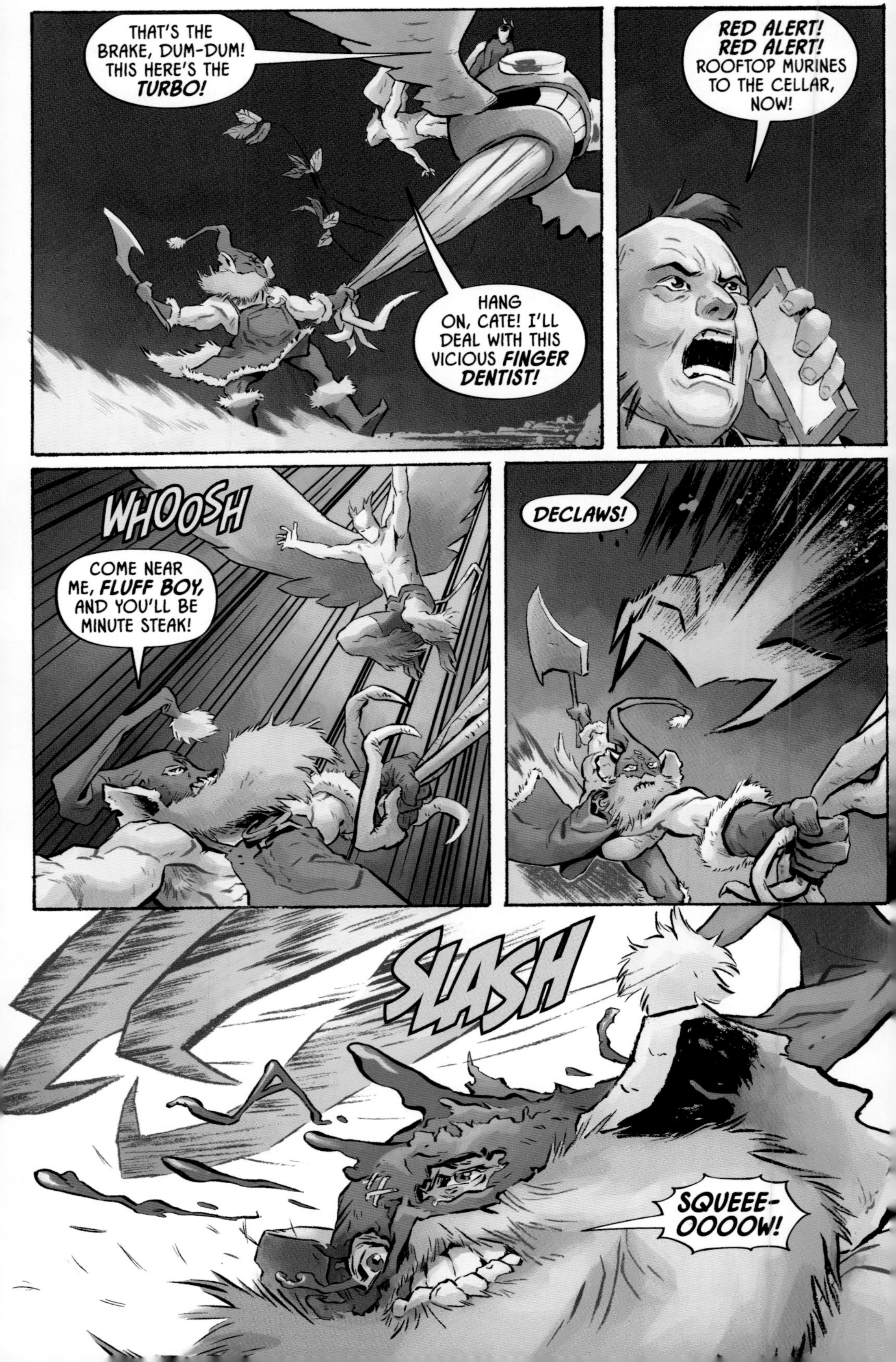
THAT'S THE BRAKE, DUM-DUM! THIS HERE'S THE TURBO!
HANG ON, CATE! I'LL DEAL WITH THIS VICIOUS FINGER DENTIST!
RED ALERT! RED ALERT! ROOFTOP MURINES TO THE CELLAR, NOW!
WHOOSH
COME NEAR ME, FLUFF BOY, AND YOU'LL BE MINUTE STEAK!
DECLAWS!
SLASH
SQUEEE-OOOOW!

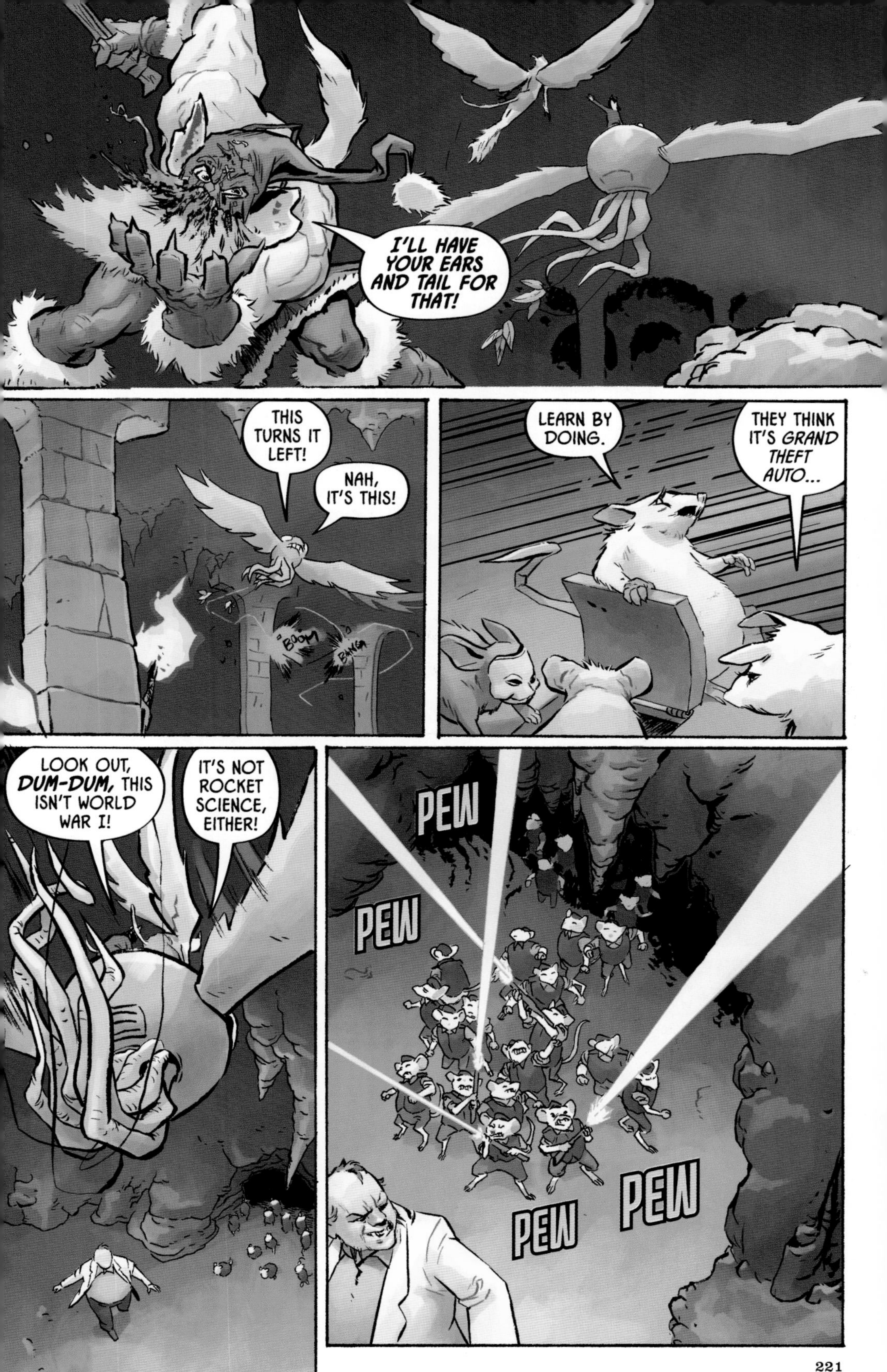
I'LL HAVE YOUR EARS AND TAIL FOR THAT!
THIS TURNS IT LEFT!
NAH, IT'S THIS!
BOOM
BANG
LEARN BY DOING.
THEY THINK IT'S GRAND THEFT AUTO...
LOOK OUT, DUM-DUM, THIS ISN'T WORLD WAR I!
IT'S NOT ROCKET SCIENCE, EITHER!
PEW
PEW
PEW
PEW

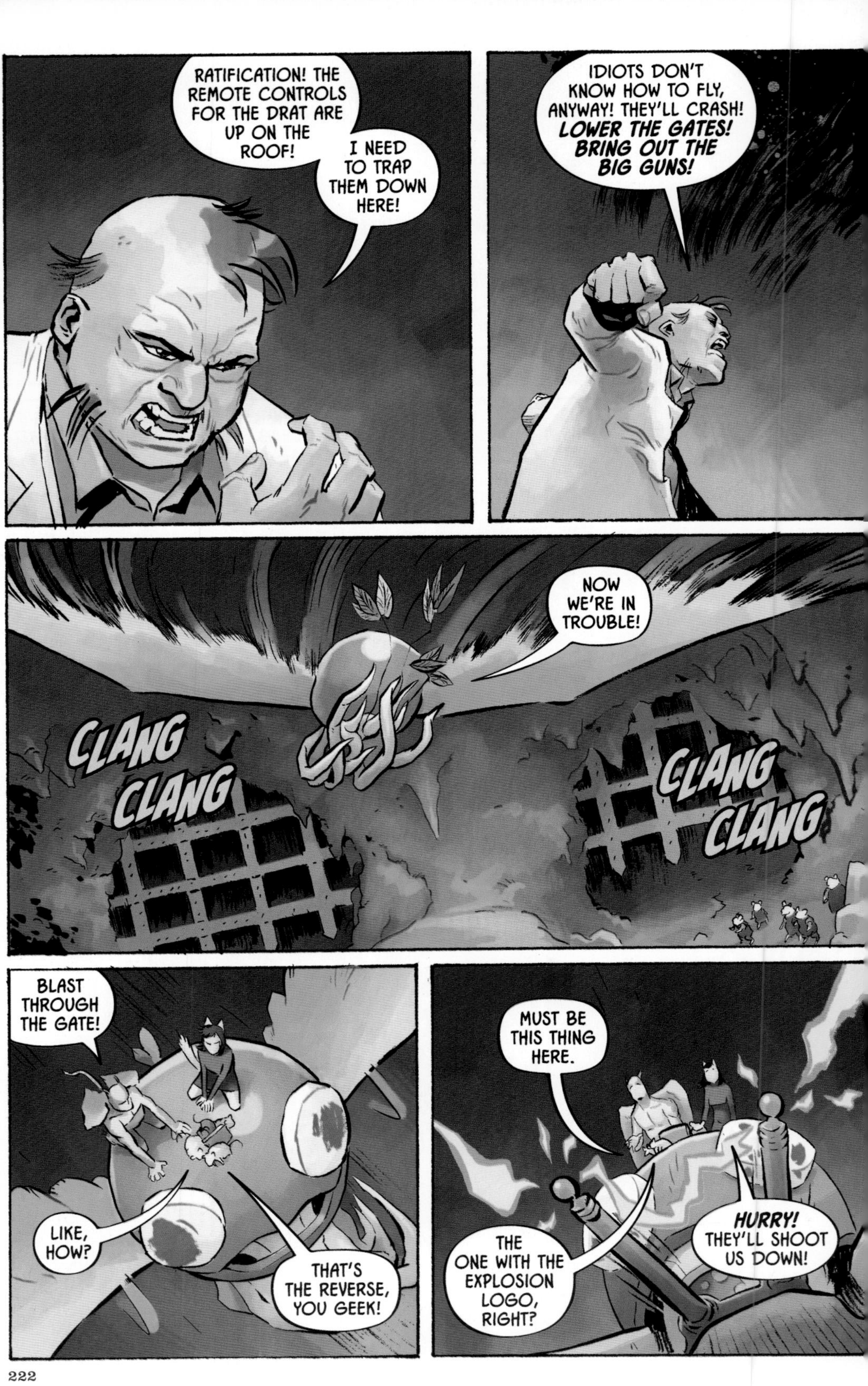
RATIFICATION! THE REMOTE CONTROLS FOR THE DRAT ARE UP ON THE ROOF!
I NEED TO TRAP THEM DOWN HERE!
IDIOTS DON'T KNOW HOW TO FLY, ANYWAY! THEY'LL CRASH! LOWER THE GATES! BRING OUT THE BIG GUNS!
NOW WE'RE IN TROUBLE!
CLANG CLANG
CLANG CLANG
BLAST THROUGH THE GATE!
LIKE, HOW?
THAT'S THE REVERSE, YOU GEEK!
MUST BE THIS THING HERE.
THE ONE WITH THE EXPLOSION LOGO, RIGHT?
HURRY! THEY'LL SHOOT US DOWN!

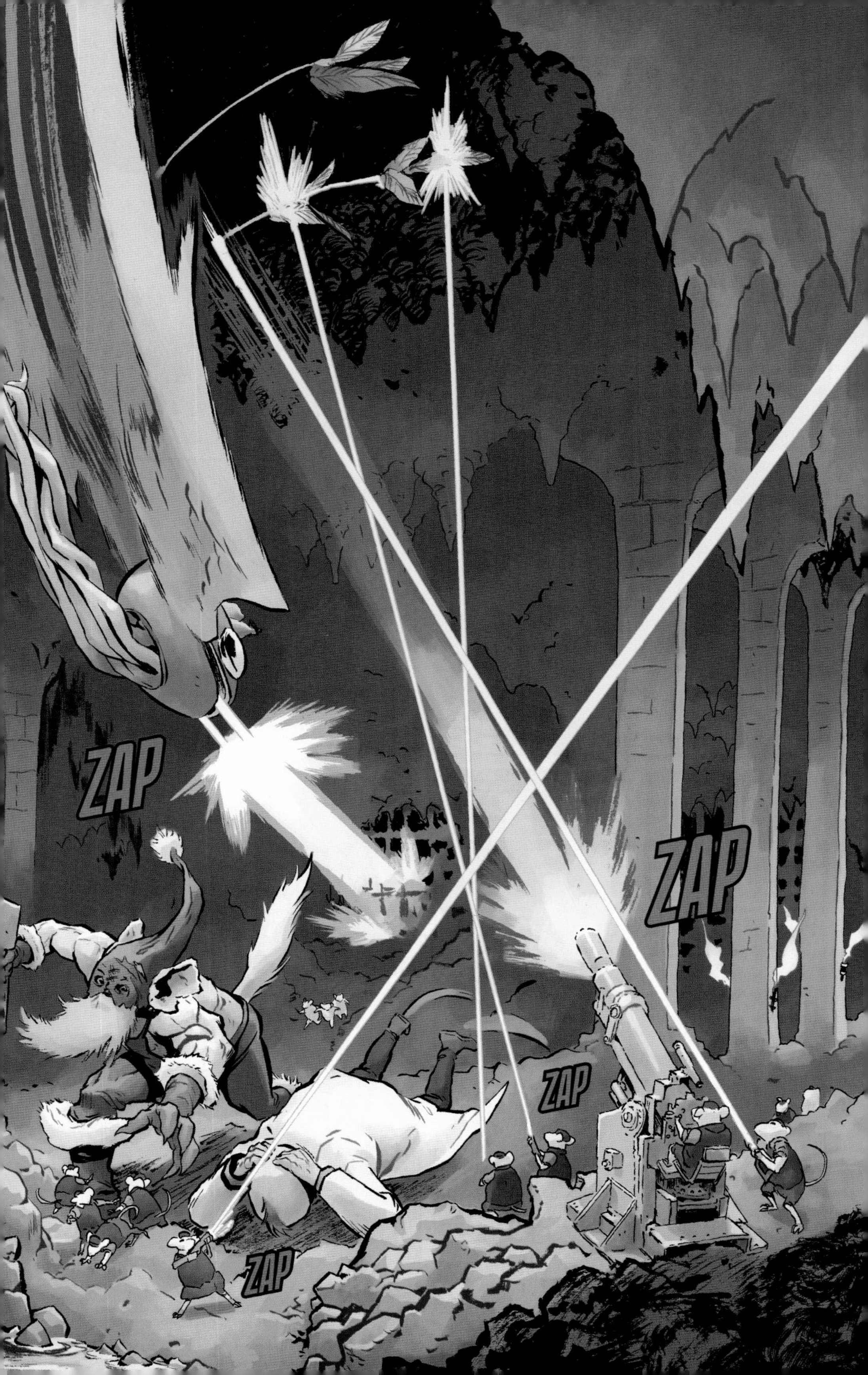
ZAP
ZAP
ZAP
ZAP

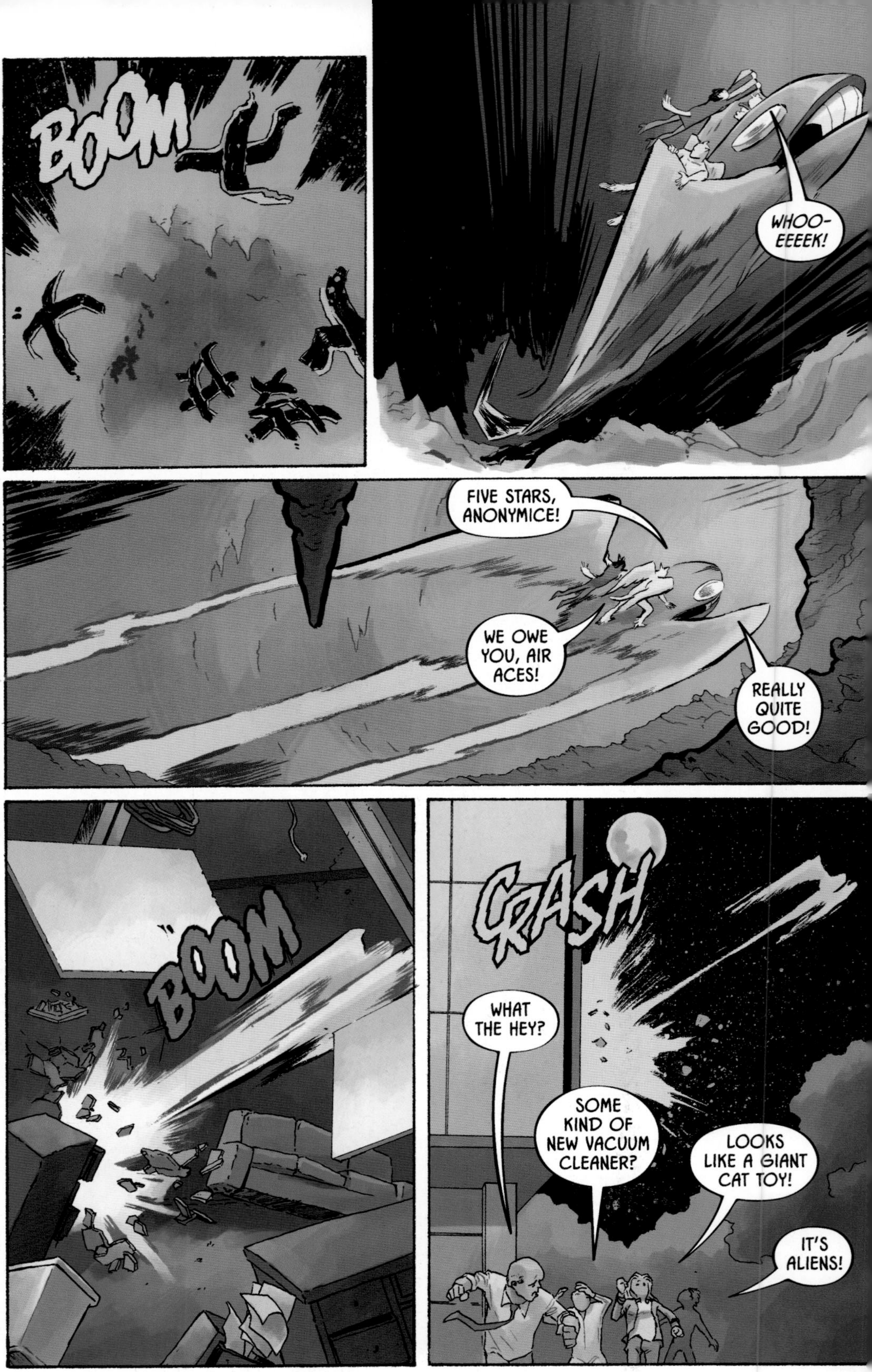
BOOM
WHOO-EEEEK!
FIVE STARS, ANONYMICE!
WE OWE YOU, AIR ACES!
REALLY QUITE GOOD!
BOOM
CRASH
WHAT THE HEY?
SOME KIND OF NEW VACUUM CLEANER?
LOOKS LIKE A GIANT CAT TOY!
IT'S ALIENS!

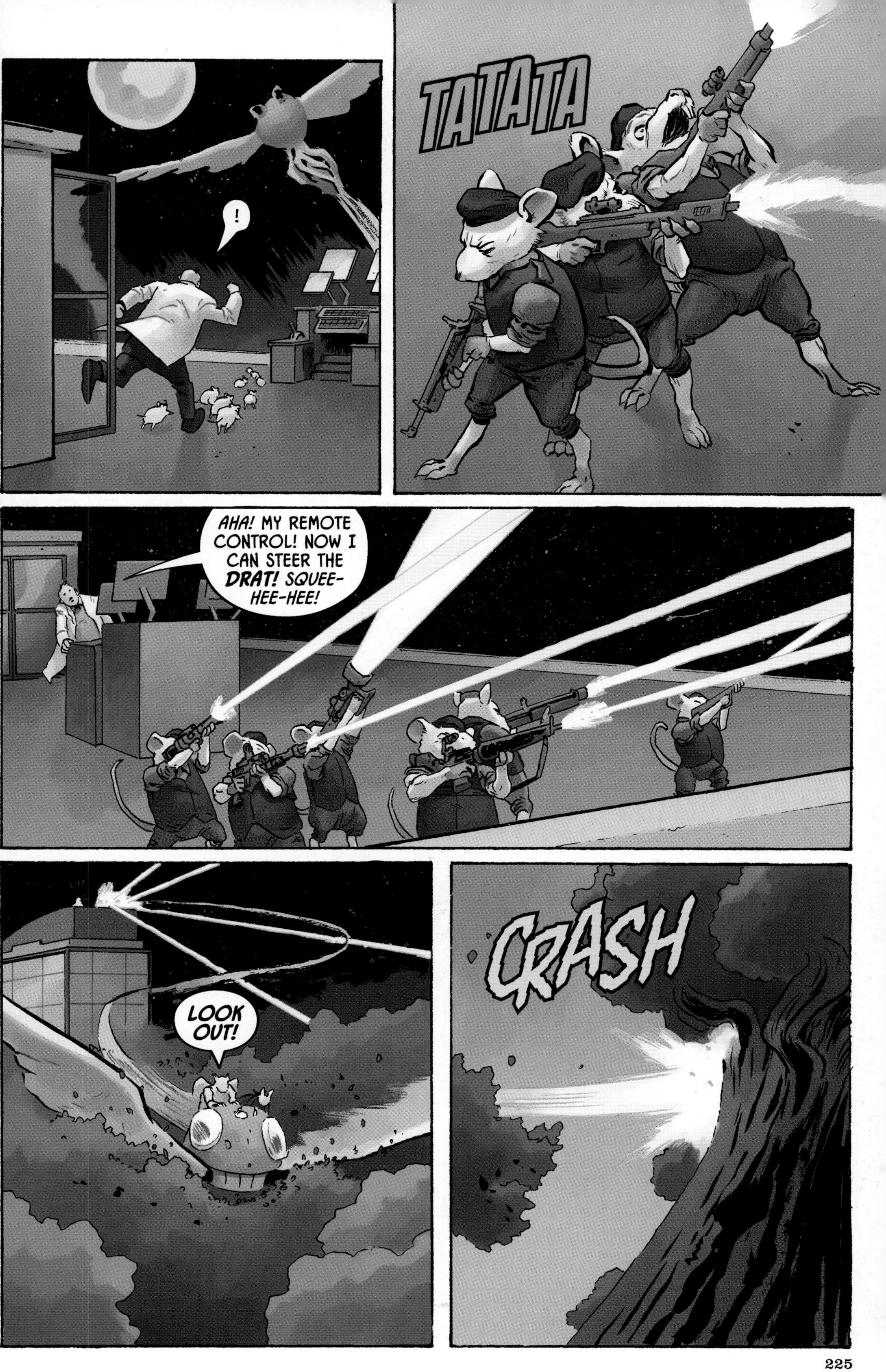
!
TATATA
AHA! MY REMOTE CONTROL! NOW I CAN STEER THE DRAT! SQUEE-HEE-HEE!
LOOK OUT!
CRASH

REEEOOOWWR!
RRRROW!
GET THEM!
WHAT HIT ME? WHAT DID I HIT?
QUICK! STRIG-- YOU'VE GOT TO CHANGE INTO CATBIRD! THEY'RE COMING-- FAST!
WE'RE TRAPPED UP HERE!
SQUEEEEEEEE!

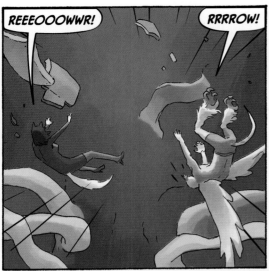

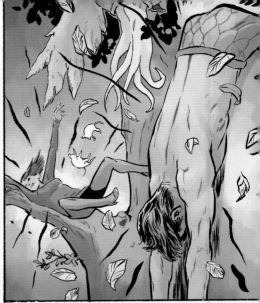

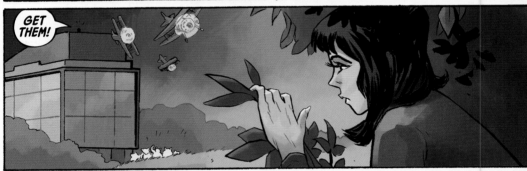

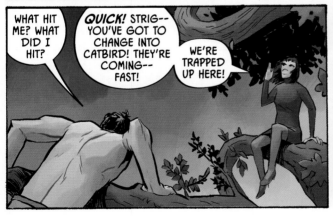

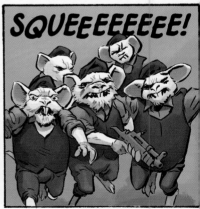

TREE CLIMBERS

Outdoor cats often climb trees, and sometimes they get stuck and can't get down. The best way to avoid having to call the fire department to rescue your cat is not to let them outside unsupervised in the first place!
Read more at www.catsandbirds.ca

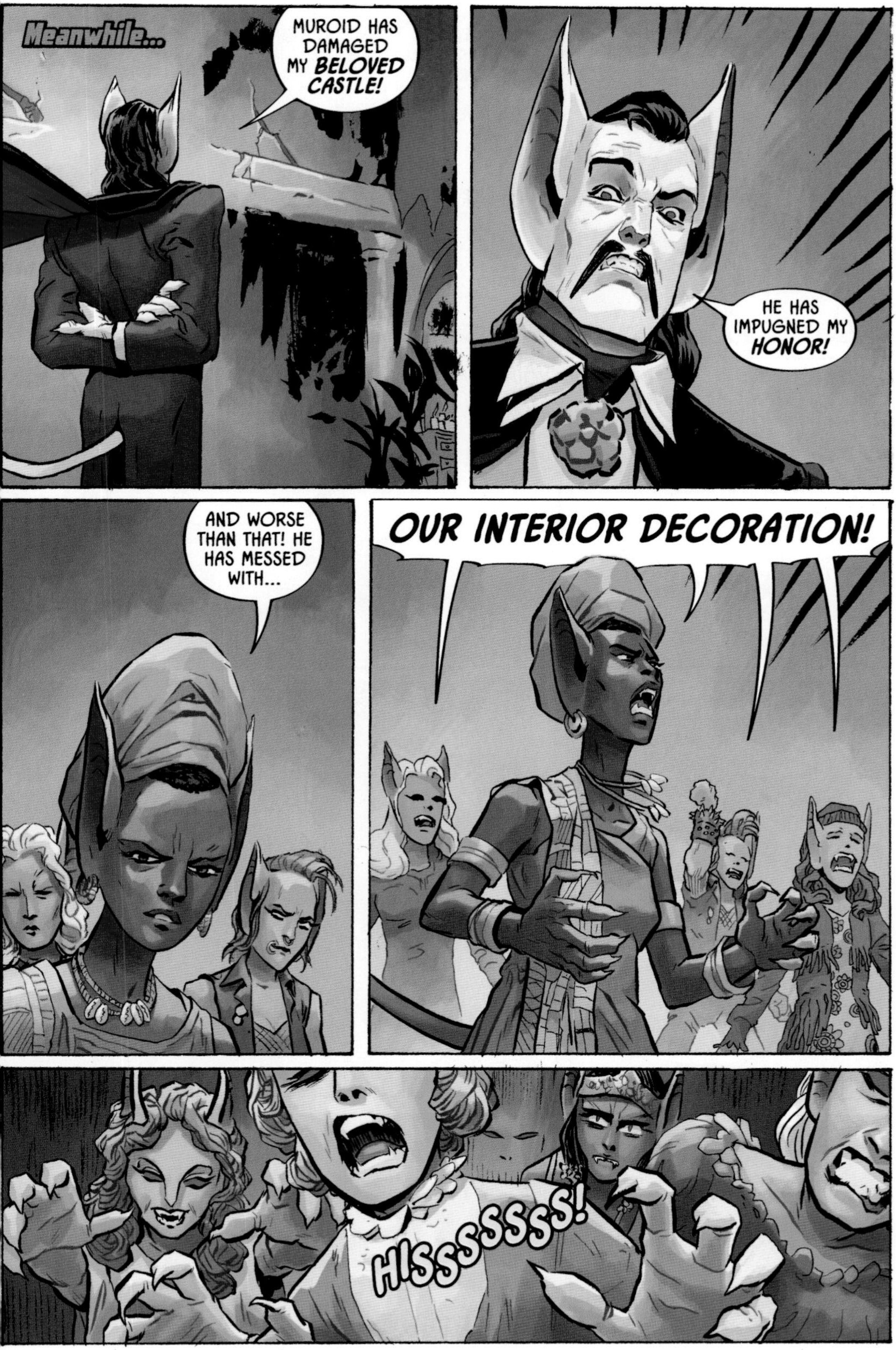
Meanwhile...
MUROID HAS DAMAGED MY BELOVED CASTLE!
HE HAS IMPUGNED MY HONOR!
AND WORSE THAN THAT! HE HAS MESSED WITH...
OUR INTERIOR DECORATION!
HISSSSSSS!

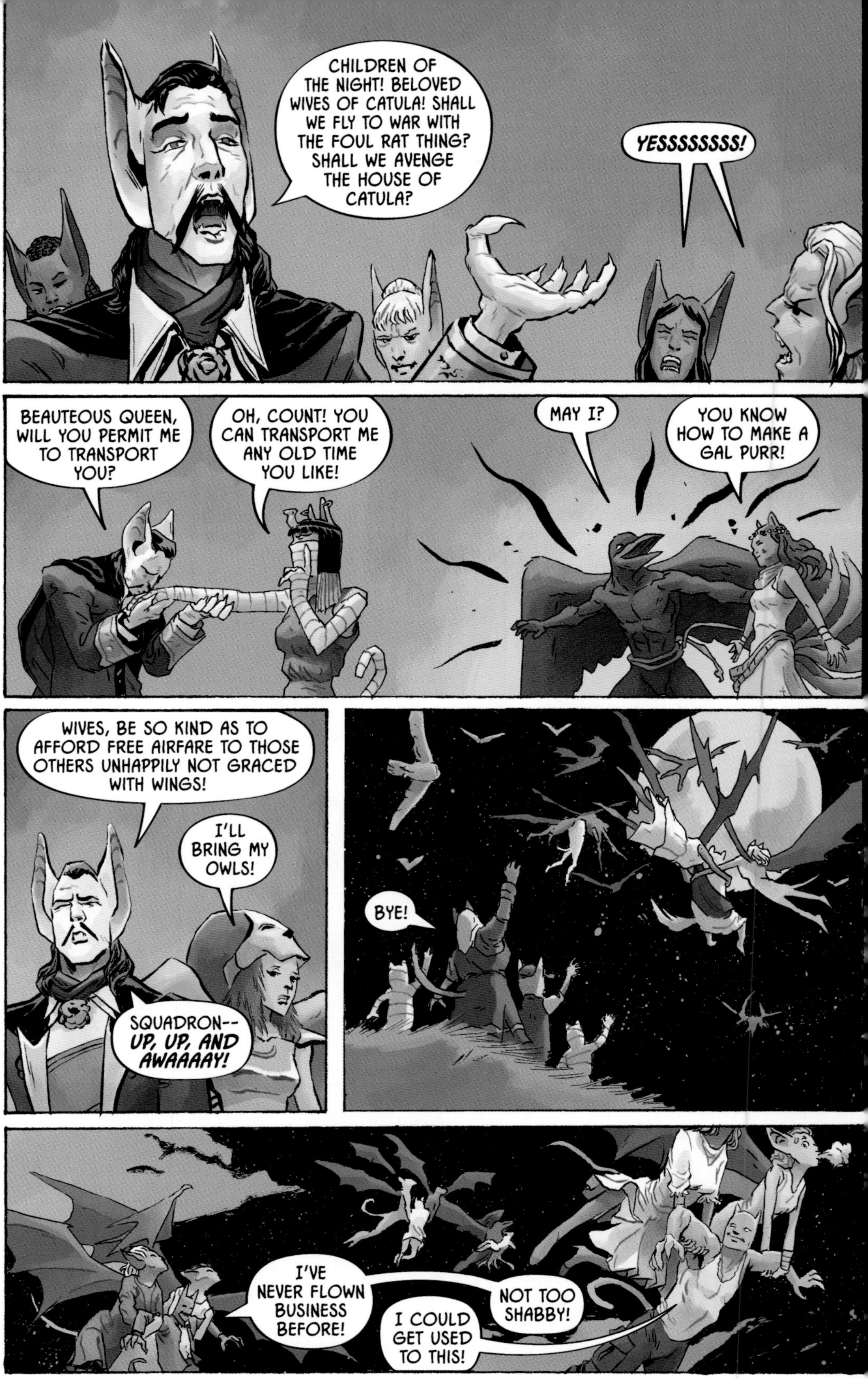
CHILDREN OF THE NIGHT! BELOVED WIVES OF CATULA! SHALL WE FLY TO WAR WITH THE FOUL RAT THING? SHALL WE AVENGE THE HOUSE OF CATULA?
YESSSSSSSS!
BEAUTEOUS QUEEN, WILL YOU PERMIT ME TO TRANSPORT YOU?
OH, COUNT! YOU CAN TRANSPORT ME ANY OLD TIME YOU LIKE!
MAY I?
YOU KNOW HOW TO MAKE A GAL PURR!
WIVES, BE SO KIND AS TO AFFORD FREE AIRFARE TO THOSE OTHERS UNHAPPILY NOT GRACED WITH WINGS!
I'LL BRING MY OWLS!
SQUADRON-- UP, UP, AND AWAAAAY!
BYE!
I'VE NEVER FLOWN BUSINESS BEFORE!
NOT TOO SHABBY!
I COULD GET USED TO THIS!

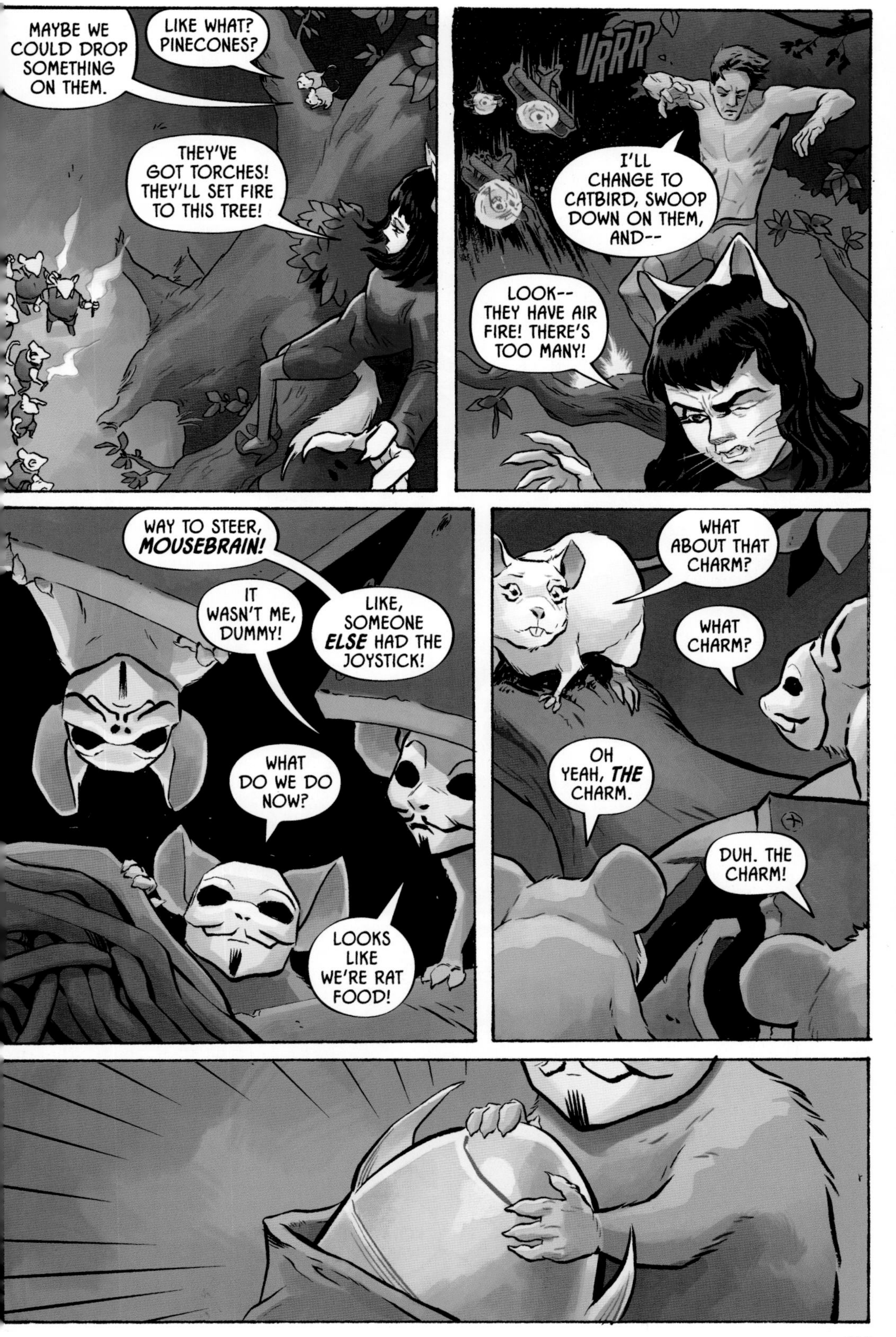
MAYBE WE COULD DROP SOMETHING ON THEM.
LIKE WHAT? PINECONES?
THEY'VE GOT TORCHES! THEY'LL SET FIRE TO THIS TREE!
VRRR
I'LL CHANGE TO CATBIRD, SWOOP DOWN ON THEM, AND--
LOOK-- THEY HAVE AIR FIRE! THERE'S TOO MANY!
WAY TO STEER, *MOUSEBRAIN!*
IT WASN'T ME, DUMMY!
LIKE, SOMEONE *ELSE* HAD THE JOYSTICK!
WHAT DO WE DO NOW?
LOOKS LIKE WE'RE RAT FOOD!
WHAT ABOUT THAT CHARM?
WHAT CHARM?
OH YEAH, *THE* CHARM.
DUH. THE CHARM!

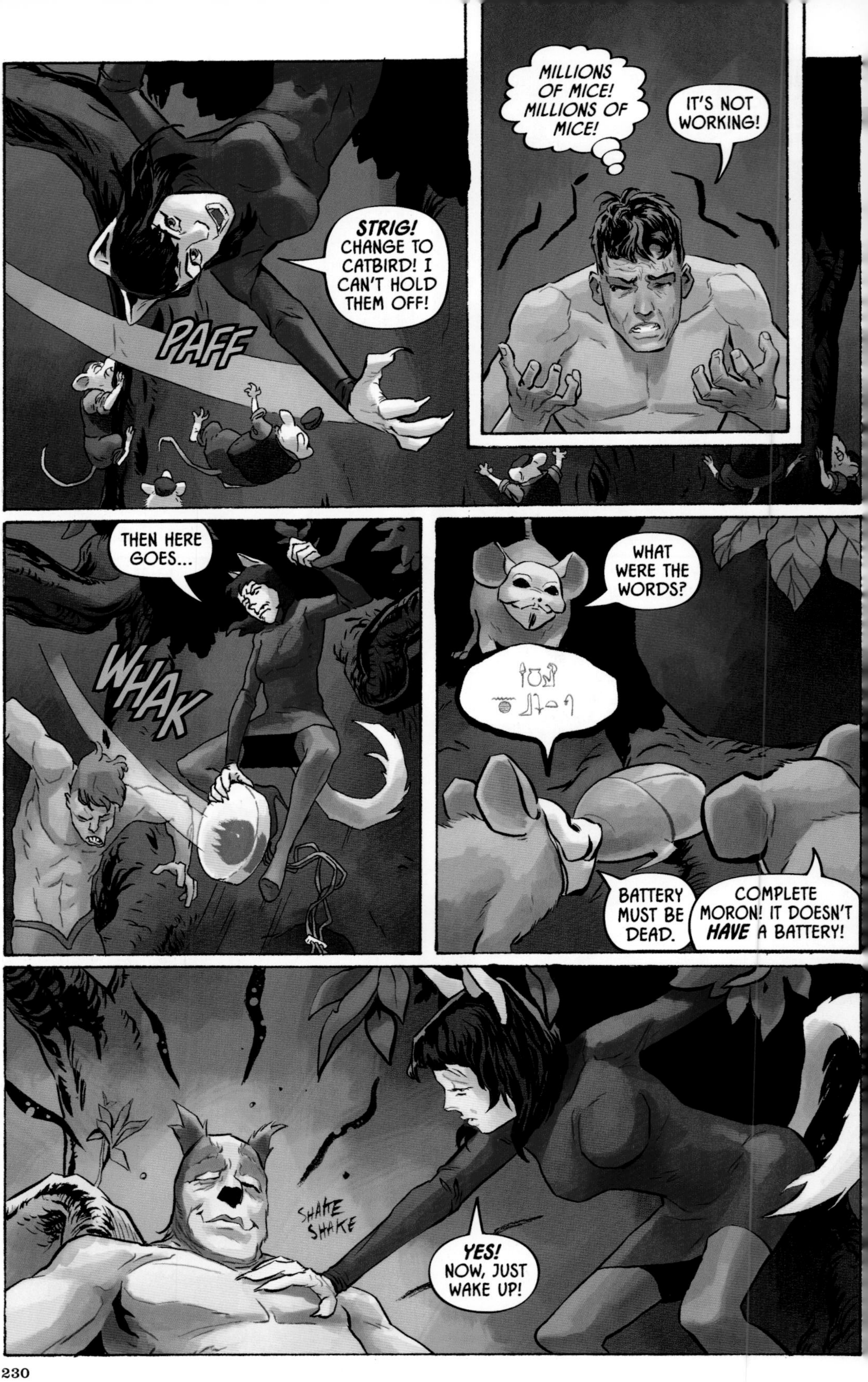
STRIG! CHANGE TO CATBIRD! I CAN'T HOLD THEM OFF!
PAFF
MILLIONS OF MICE! MILLIONS OF MICE!
IT'S NOT WORKING!
THEN HERE GOES...
WHAK
WHAT WERE THE WORDS?
BATTERY MUST BE DEAD.
COMPLETE MORON! IT DOESN'T HAVE A BATTERY!
SHAKE SHAKE
YES! NOW, JUST WAKE UP!

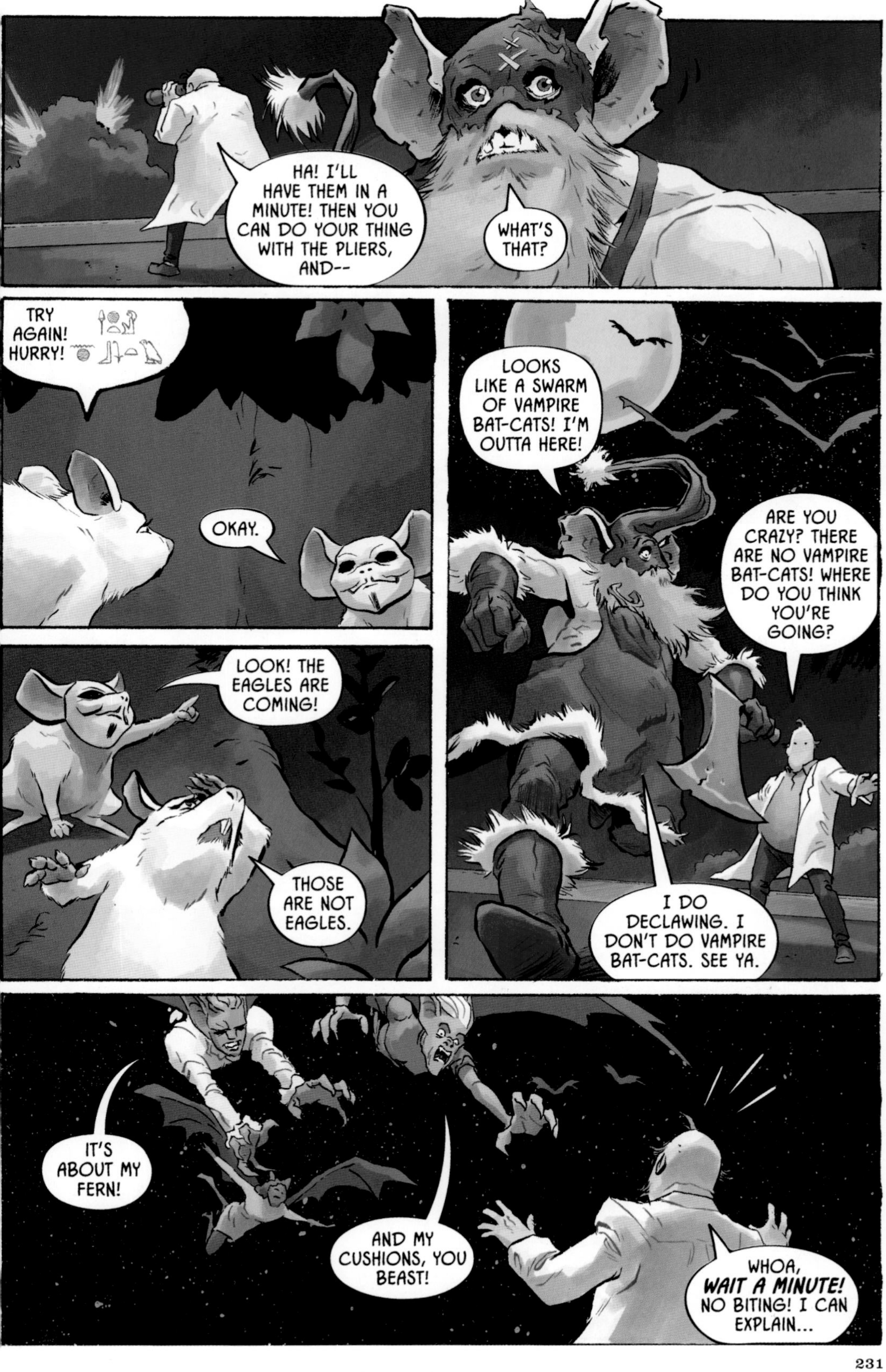
HA! I'LL HAVE THEM IN A MINUTE! THEN YOU CAN DO YOUR THING WITH THE PLIERS, AND--
WHAT'S THAT?
TRY AGAIN! HURRY!
OKAY.
LOOK! THE EAGLES ARE COMING!
THOSE ARE NOT EAGLES.
LOOKS LIKE A SWARM OF VAMPIRE BAT-CATS! I'M OUTTA HERE!
ARE YOU CRAZY? THERE ARE NO VAMPIRE BAT-CATS! WHERE DO YOU THINK YOU'RE GOING?
I DO DECLAWING. I DON'T DO VAMPIRE BAT-CATS. SEE YA.
IT'S ABOUT MY FERN!
AND MY CUSHIONS, YOU BEAST!
WHOA, *WAIT A MINUTE!* NO BITING! I CAN EXPLAIN...

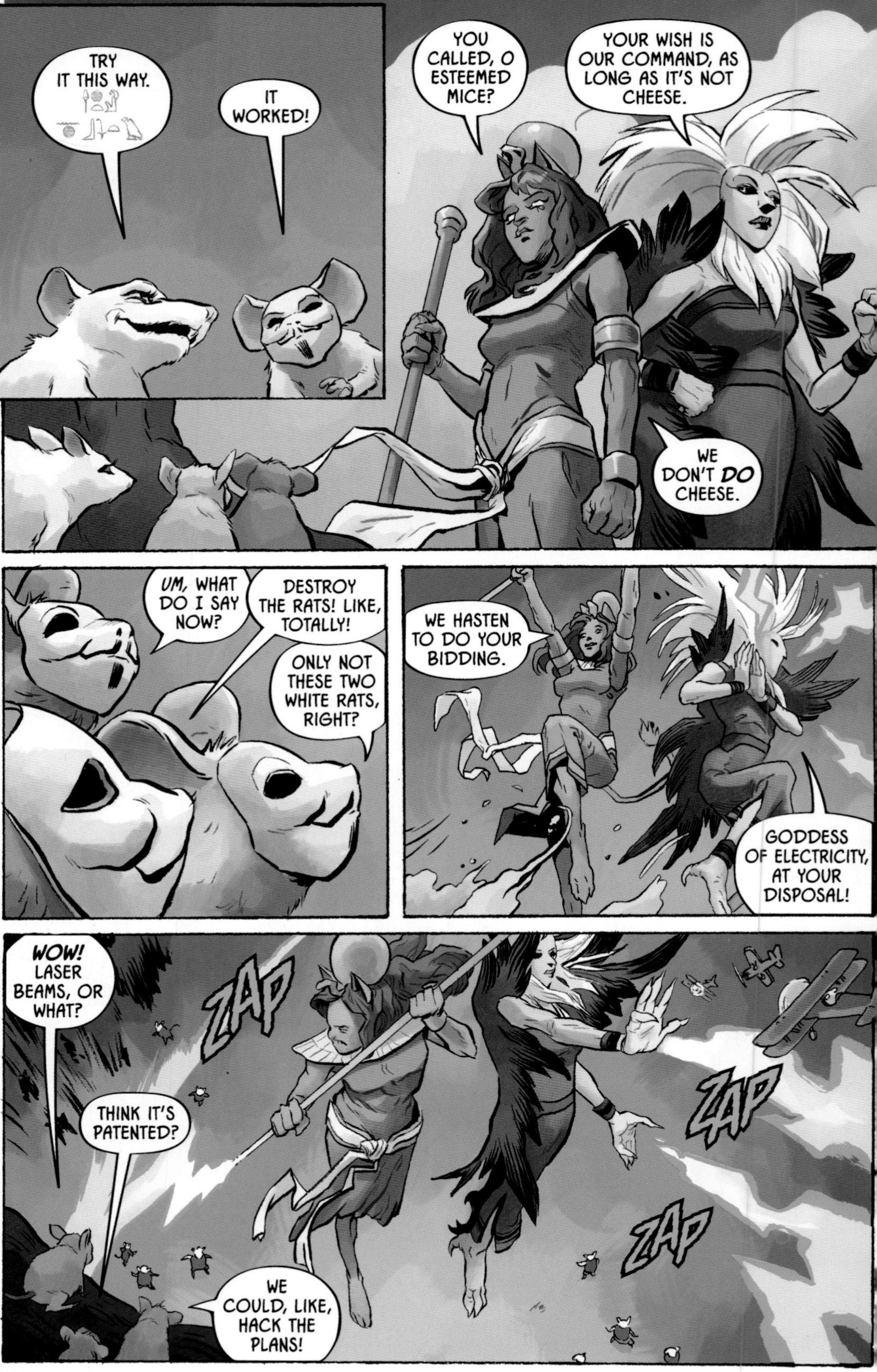
TRY IT THIS WAY.
IT WORKED!
YOU CALLED, O ESTEEMED MICE?
YOUR WISH IS OUR COMMAND, AS LONG AS IT'S NOT CHEESE.
WE DON'T *DO* CHEESE.
UM, WHAT DO I SAY NOW?
DESTROY THE RATS! LIKE, TOTALLY!
ONLY NOT THESE TWO WHITE RATS, RIGHT?
WE HASTEN TO DO YOUR BIDDING.
GODDESS OF ELECTRICITY, AT YOUR DISPOSAL!
WOW! LASER BEAMS, OR WHAT?
ZAP
THINK IT'S PATENTED?
ZAP
ZAP
WE COULD, LIKE, HACK THE PLANS!

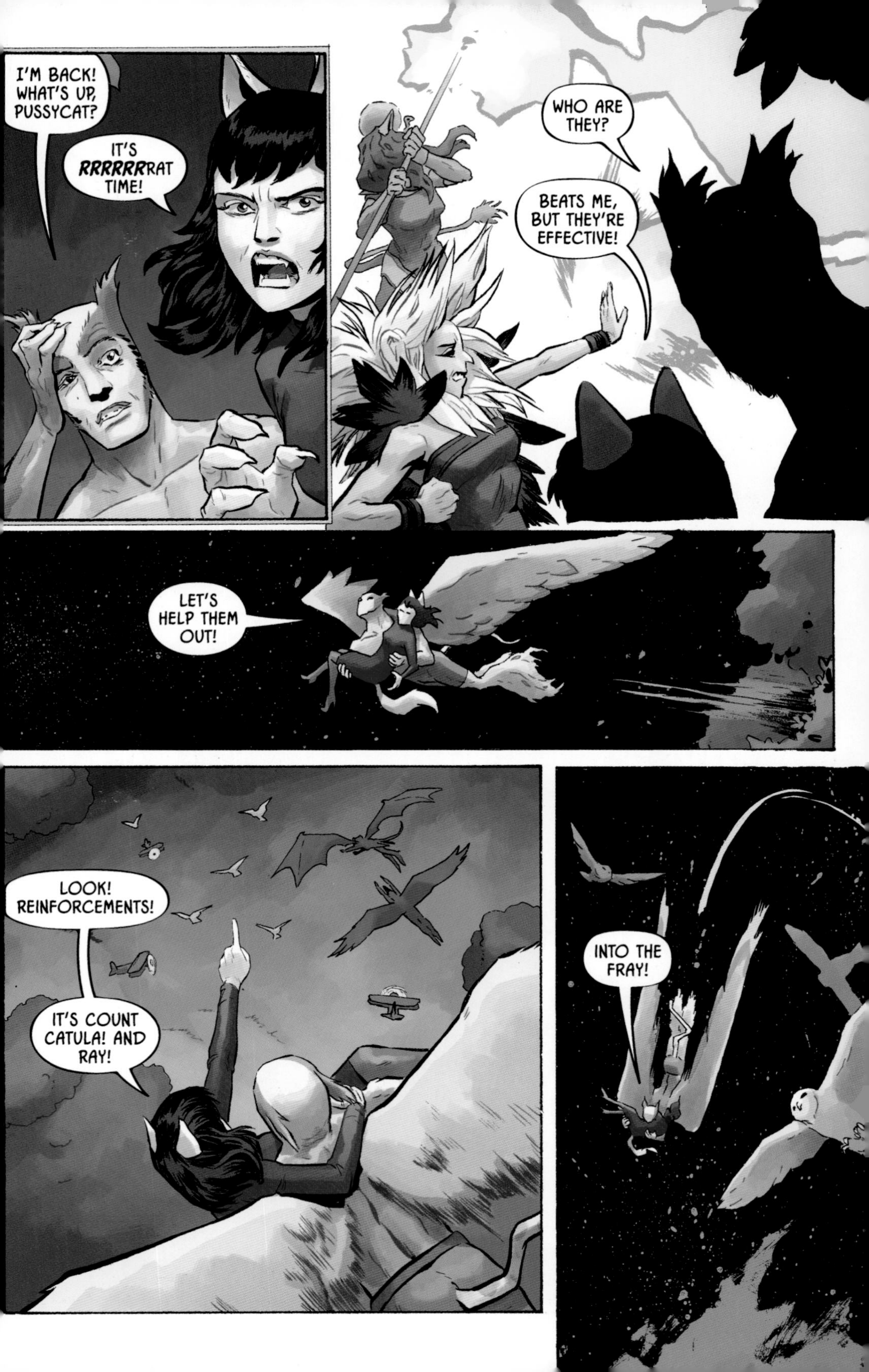
I'M BACK! WHAT'S UP, PUSSYCAT?
IT'S RRRRRRRAT TIME!
WHO ARE THEY?
BEATS ME, BUT THEY'RE EFFECTIVE!
LET'S HELP THEM OUT!
LOOK! REINFORCEMENTS!
IT'S COUNT CATULA! AND RAY!
INTO THE FRAY!

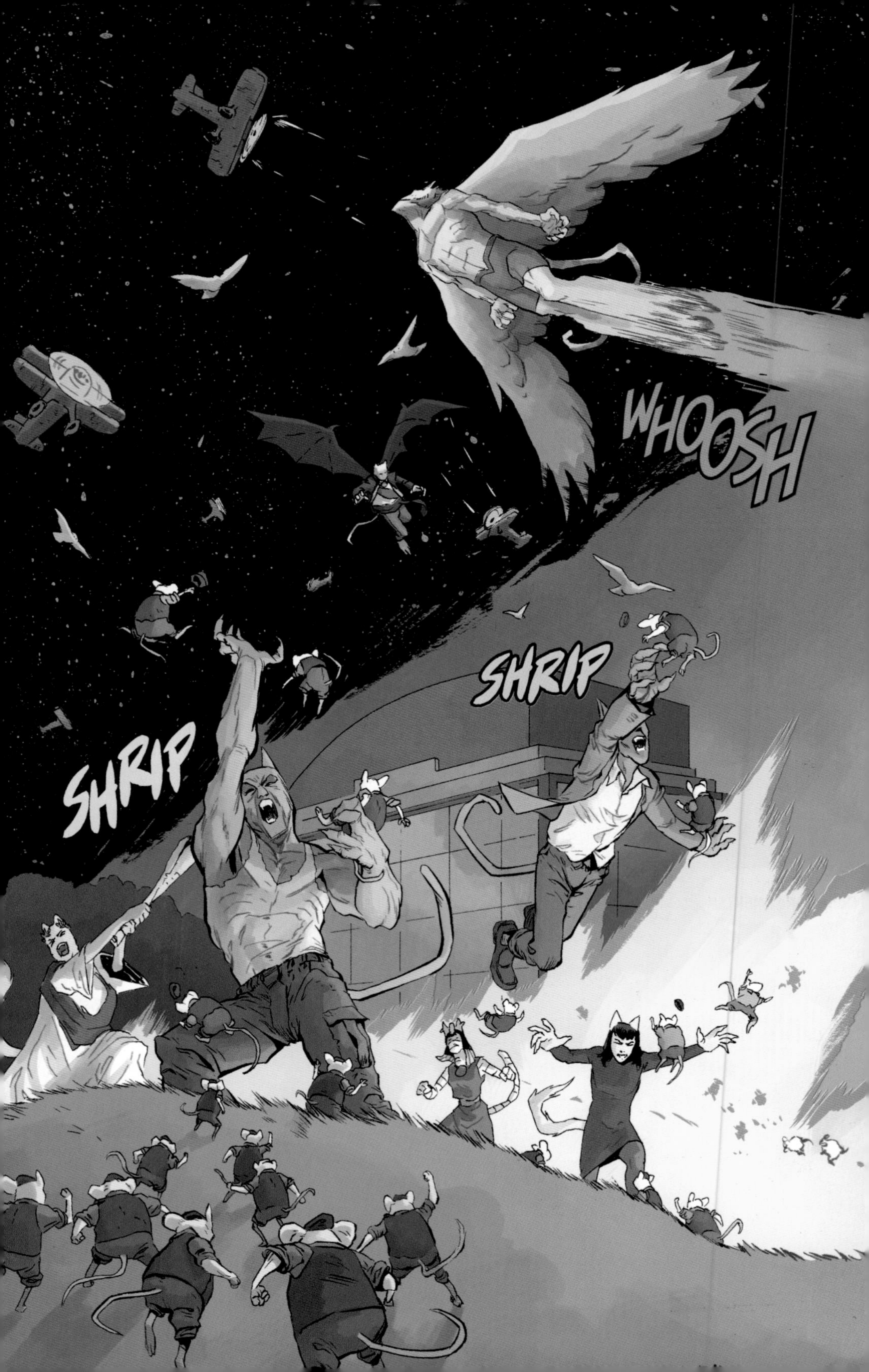
WHOOSH
SHRIP
SHRIP

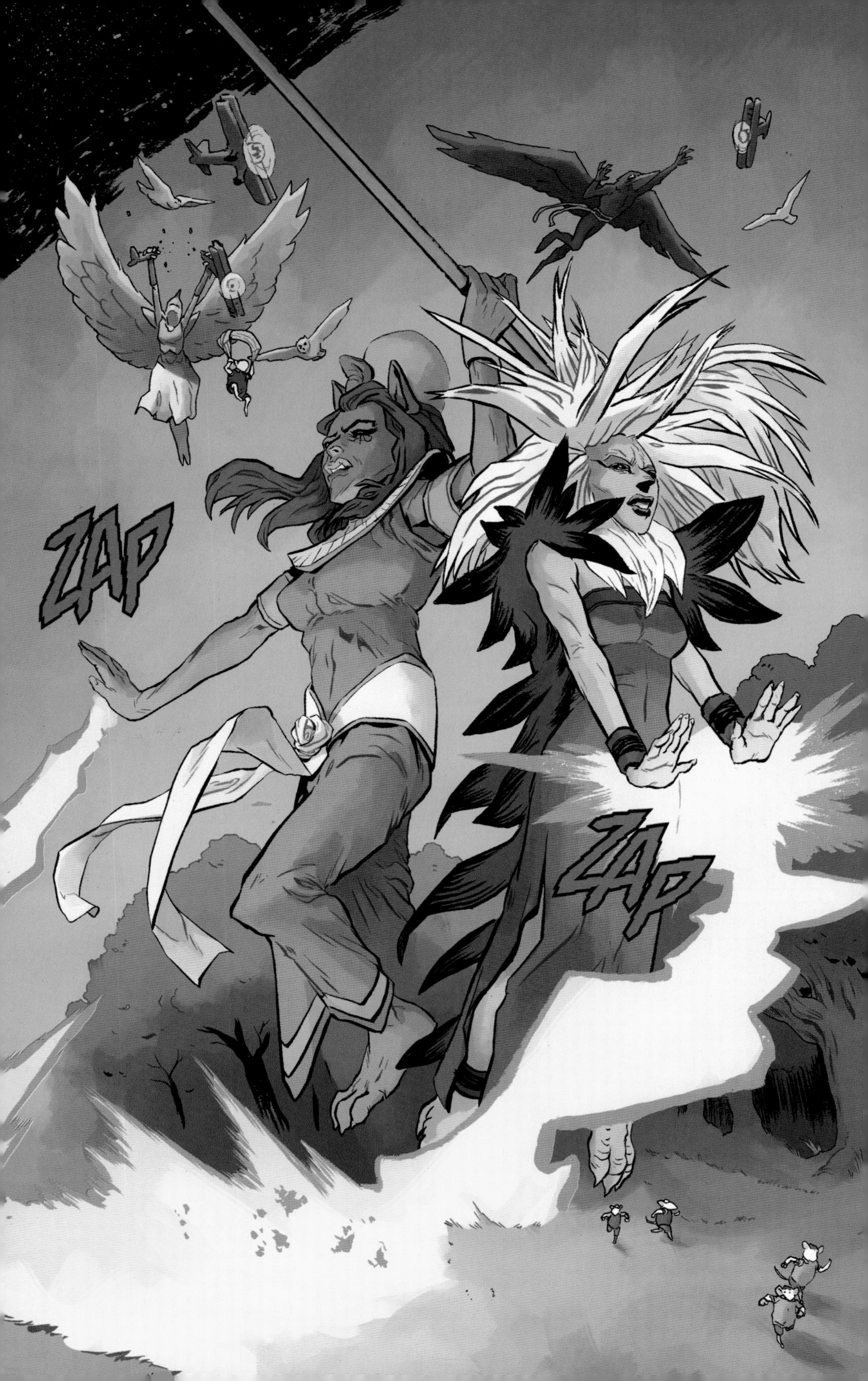
ZAP
ZAP

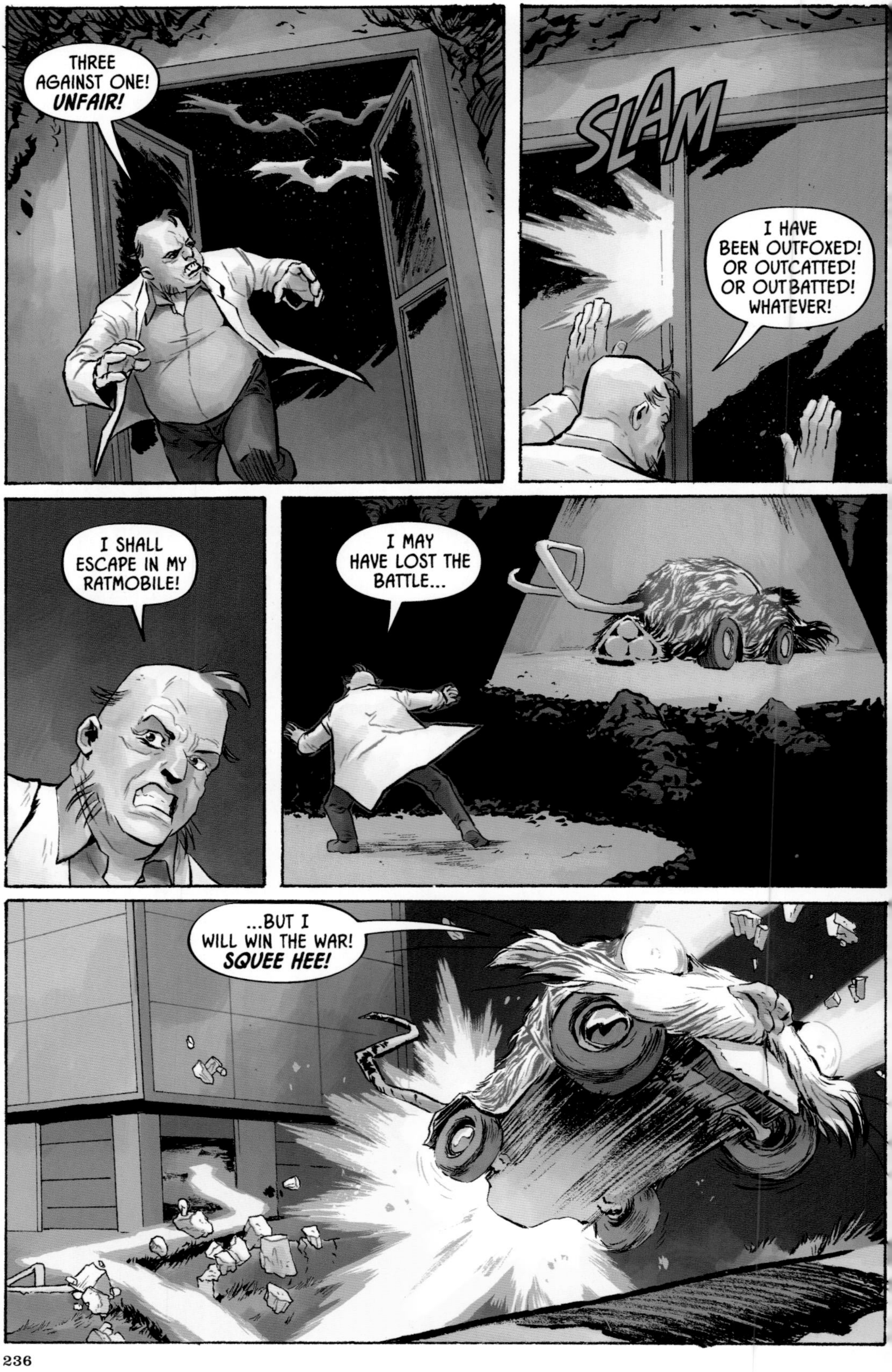
THREE AGAINST ONE! UNFAIR!
SLAM
I HAVE BEEN OUTFOXED! OR OUTCATTED! OR OUTBATTED! WHATEVER!
I SHALL ESCAPE IN MY RATMOBILE!
I MAY HAVE LOST THE BATTLE...
...BUT I WILL WIN THE WAR! SQUEE HEE!

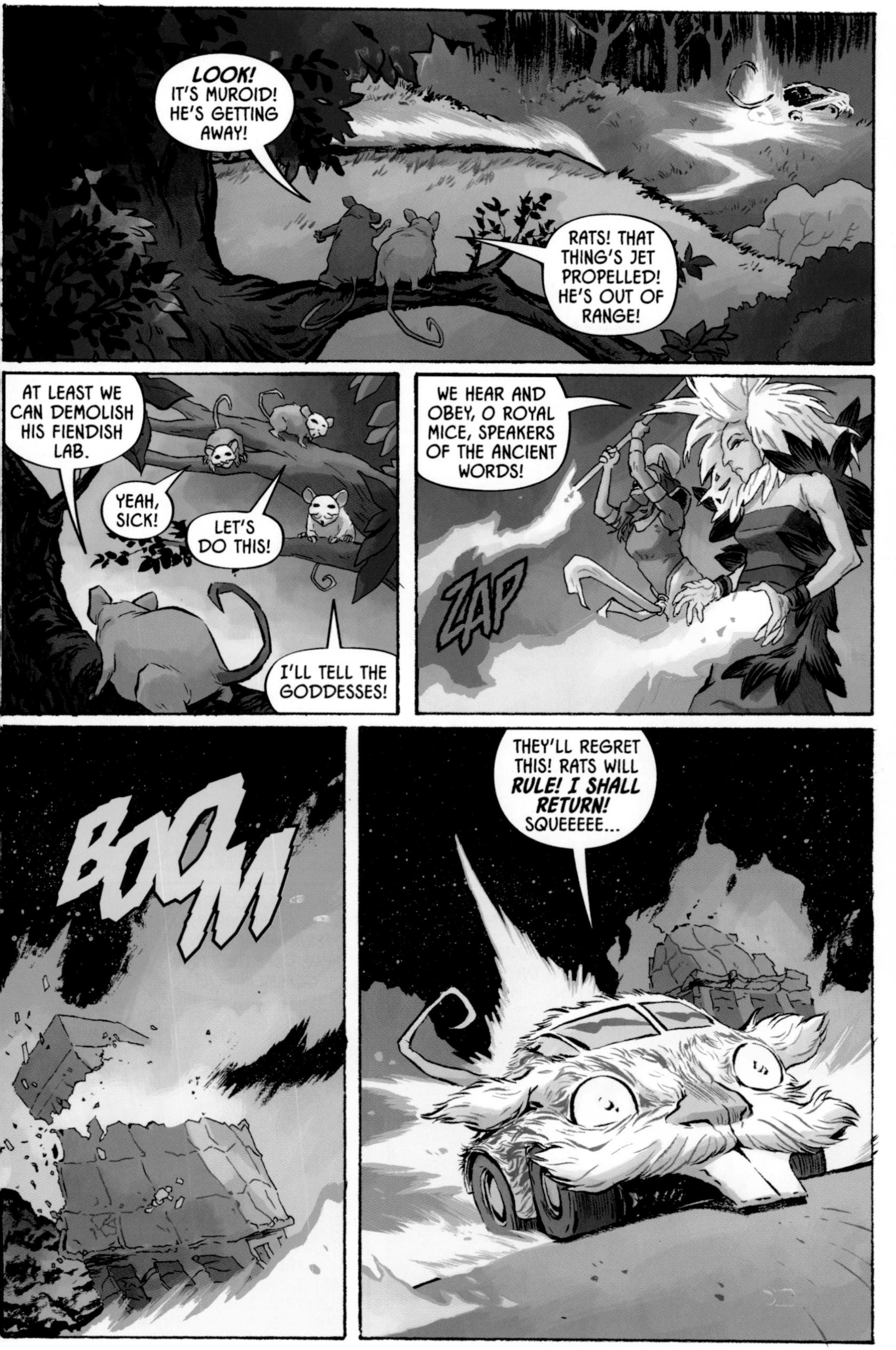
LOOK! IT'S MUROID! HE'S GETTING AWAY!
RATS! THAT THING'S JET PROPELLED! HE'S OUT OF RANGE!
AT LEAST WE CAN DEMOLISH HIS FIENDISH LAB.
YEAH, SICK!
LET'S DO THIS!
I'LL TELL THE GODDESSES!
WE HEAR AND OBEY, O ROYAL MICE, SPEAKERS OF THE ANCIENT WORDS!
ZAP
BOOM
THEY'LL REGRET THIS! RATS WILL RULE! I SHALL RETURN! SQUEEEEE...

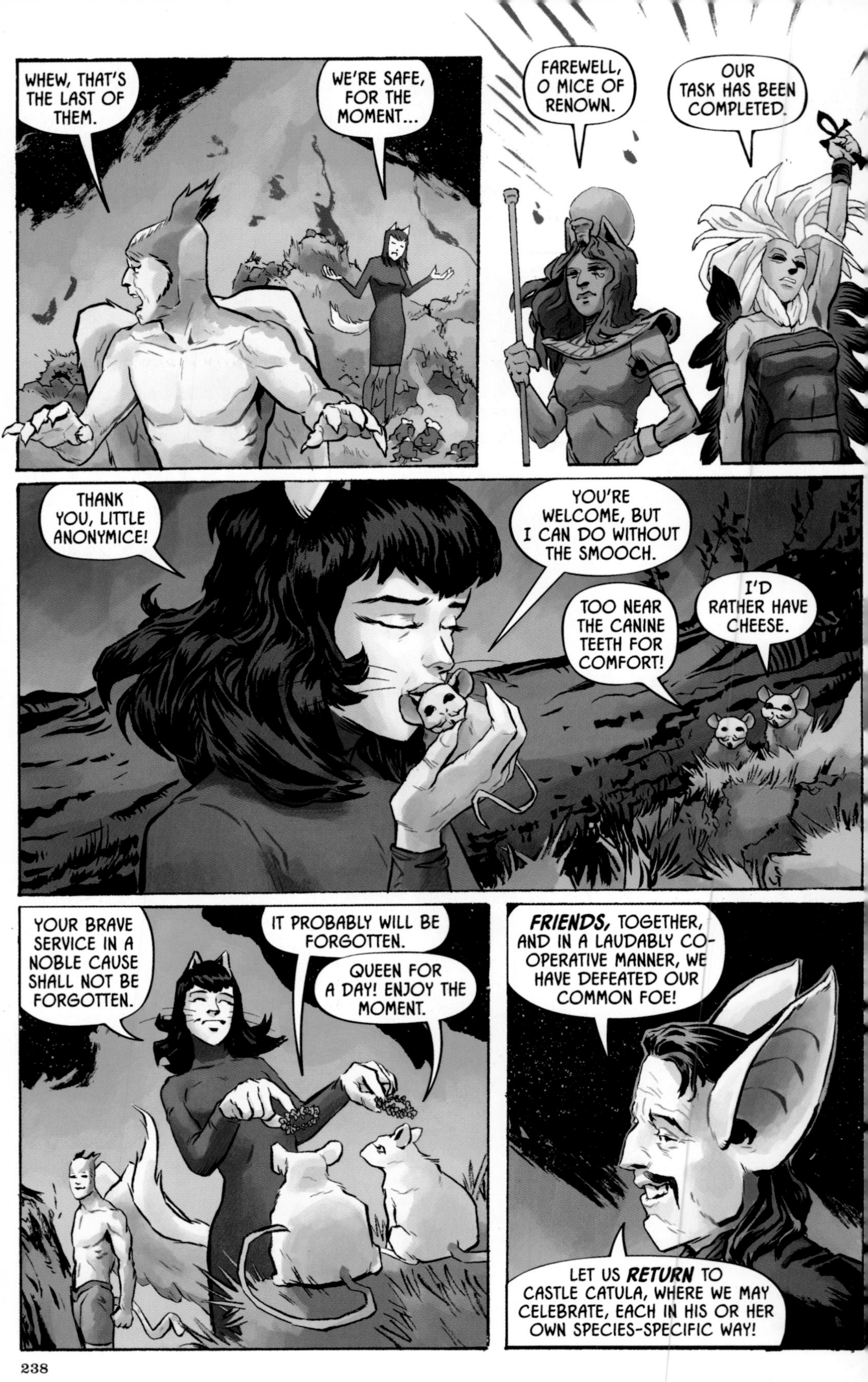
WHEW, THAT'S THE LAST OF THEM.
WE'RE SAFE, FOR THE MOMENT...
FAREWELL, O MICE OF RENOWN.
OUR TASK HAS BEEN COMPLETED.
THANK YOU, LITTLE ANONYMICE!
YOU'RE WELCOME, BUT I CAN DO WITHOUT THE SMOOCH.
TOO NEAR THE CANINE TEETH FOR COMFORT!
I'D RATHER HAVE CHEESE.
YOUR BRAVE SERVICE IN A NOBLE CAUSE SHALL NOT BE FORGOTTEN.
IT PROBABLY WILL BE FORGOTTEN.
QUEEN FOR A DAY! ENJOY THE MOMENT.
FRIENDS, TOGETHER, AND IN A LAUDABLY CO-OPERATIVE MANNER, WE HAVE DEFEATED OUR COMMON FOE!
LET US RETURN TO CASTLE CATULA, WHERE WE MAY CELEBRATE, EACH IN HIS OR HER OWN SPECIES-SPECIFIC WAY!

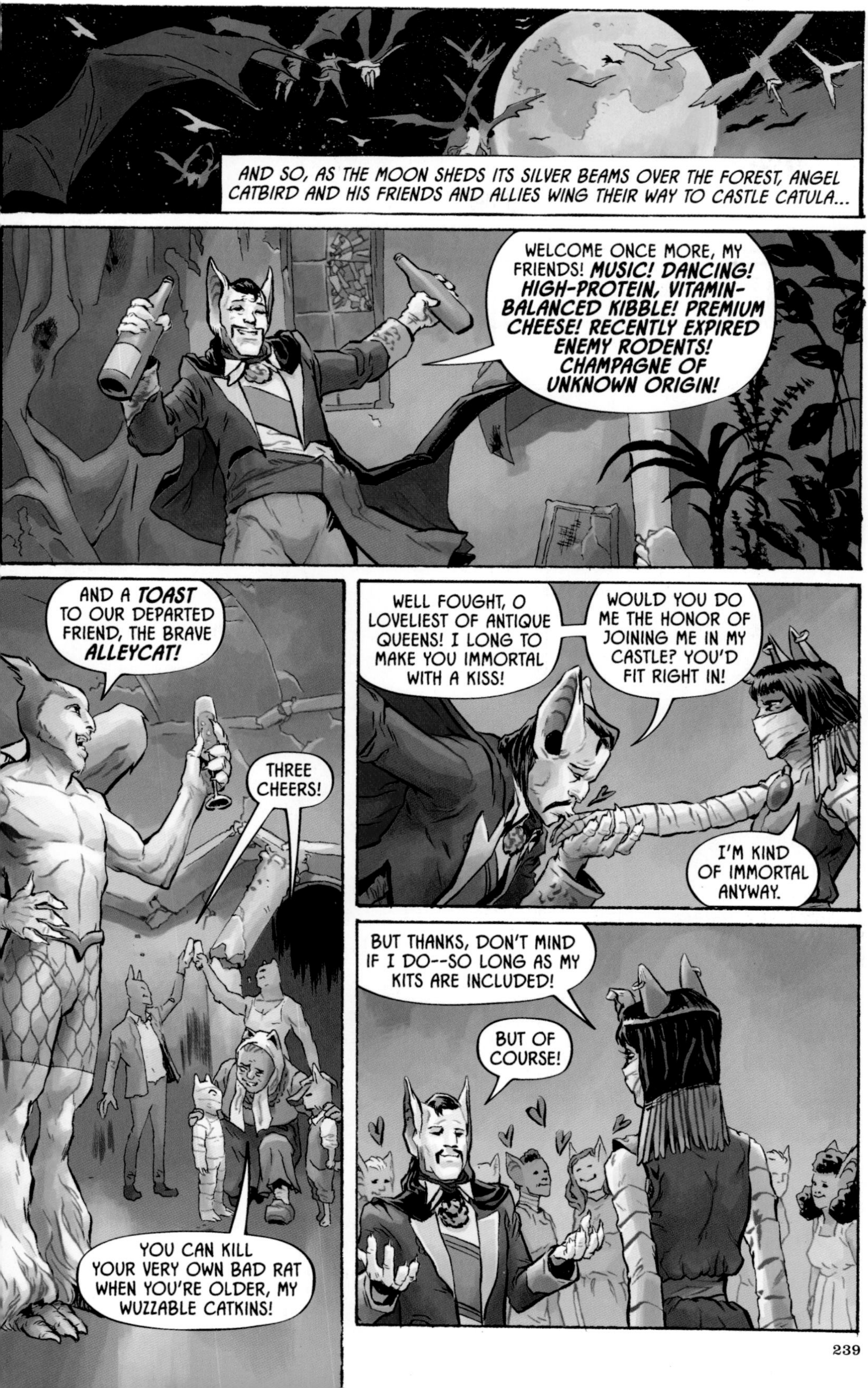
AND SO, AS THE MOON SHEDS ITS SILVER BEAMS OVER THE FOREST, ANGEL CATBIRD AND HIS FRIENDS AND ALLIES WING THEIR WAY TO CASTLE CATULA...
WELCOME ONCE MORE, MY FRIENDS! MUSIC! DANCING! HIGH-PROTEIN, VITAMIN-BALANCED KIBBLE! PREMIUM CHEESE! RECENTLY EXPIRED ENEMY RODENTS! CHAMPAGNE OF UNKNOWN ORIGIN!
AND A TOAST TO OUR DEPARTED FRIEND, THE BRAVE ALLEYCAT!
THREE CHEERS!
YOU CAN KILL YOUR VERY OWN BAD RAT WHEN YOU'RE OLDER, MY WUZZABLE CATKINS!
WELL FOUGHT, O LOVELIEST OF ANTIQUE QUEENS! I LONG TO MAKE YOU IMMORTAL WITH A KISS!
WOULD YOU DO ME THE HONOR OF JOINING ME IN MY CASTLE? YOU'D FIT RIGHT IN!
I'M KIND OF IMMORTAL ANYWAY.
BUT THANKS, DON'T MIND IF I DO--SO LONG AS MY KITS ARE INCLUDED!
BUT OF COURSE!

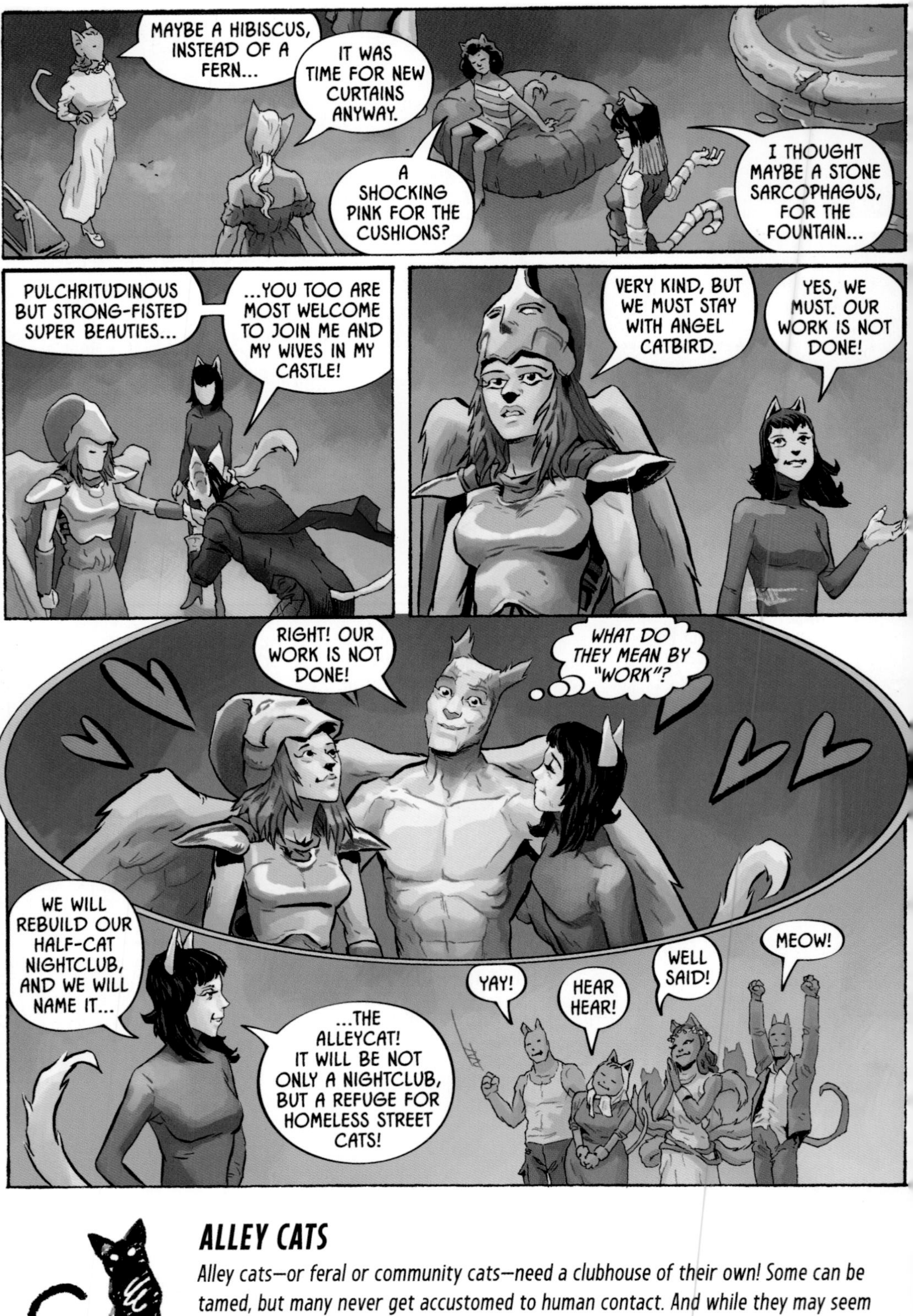
MAYBE A HIBISCUS, INSTEAD OF A FERN...
IT WAS TIME FOR NEW CURTAINS ANYWAY.
A SHOCKING PINK FOR THE CUSHIONS?
I THOUGHT MAYBE A STONE SARCOPHAGUS, FOR THE FOUNTAIN...
PULCHRITUDINOUS BUT STRONG-FISTED SUPER BEAUTIES...
...YOU TOO ARE MOST WELCOME TO JOIN ME AND MY WIVES IN MY CASTLE!
VERY KIND, BUT WE MUST STAY WITH ANGEL CATBIRD.
YES, WE MUST. OUR WORK IS NOT DONE!
RIGHT! OUR WORK IS NOT DONE!
WHAT DO THEY MEAN BY "WORK"?
WE WILL REBUILD OUR HALF-CAT NIGHTCLUB, AND WE WILL NAME IT...
...THE ALLEYCAT! IT WILL BE NOT ONLY A NIGHTCLUB, BUT A REFUGE FOR HOMELESS STREET CATS!
YAY!
HEAR HEAR!
WELL SAID!
MEOW!

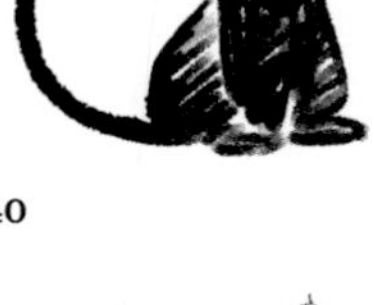

ALLEY CATS

Alley cats—or feral or community cats—need a clubhouse of their own! Some can be tamed, but many never get accustomed to human contact. And while they may seem closer to being wildlife than pets, we owe them humane treatment, just as we do any other animal. Keep alley cats and birds safe! Read more at www.catsandbirds.ca

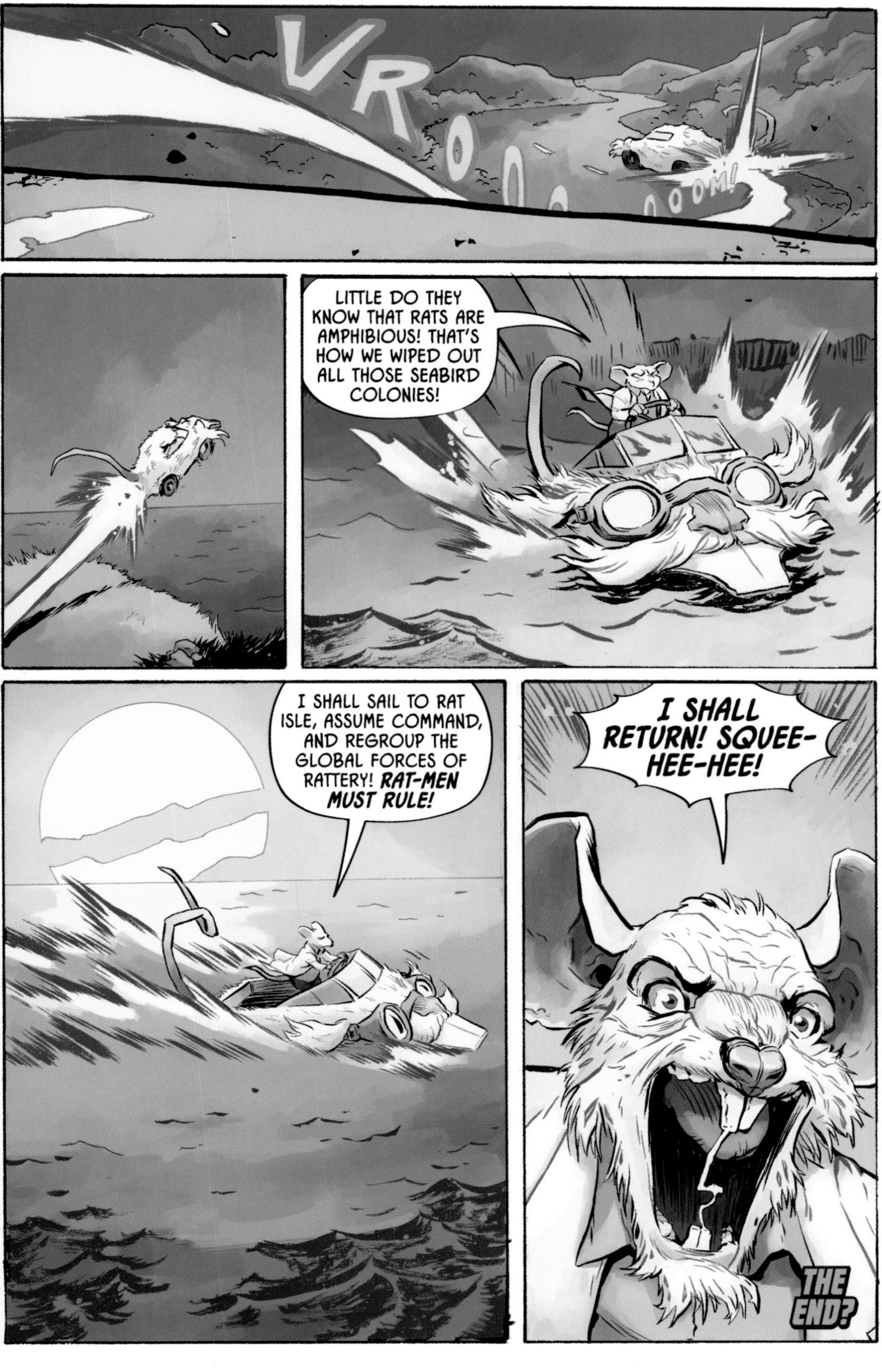
VROOOOOOOM!
LITTLE DO THEY KNOW THAT RATS ARE AMPHIBIOUS! THAT'S HOW WE WIPED OUT ALL THOSE SEABIRD COLONIES!
I SHALL SAIL TO RAT ISLE, ASSUME COMMAND, AND REGROUP THE GLOBAL FORCES OF RATTERY! RAT-MEN MUST RULE!
I SHALL RETURN! SQUEE-HEE-HEE!
THE END?

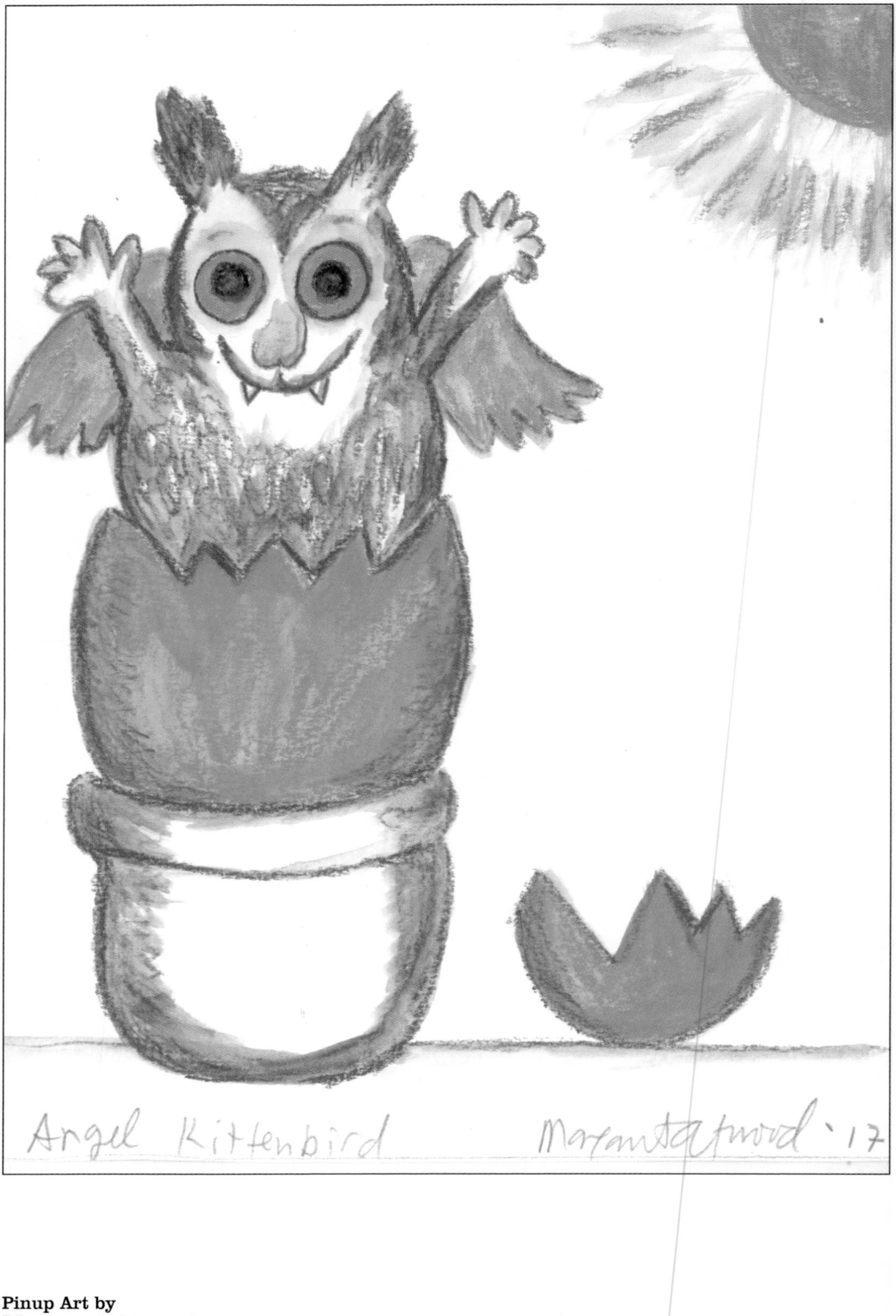
Angel Kittenbird
'17

Pinup Art by
Margaret Atwood

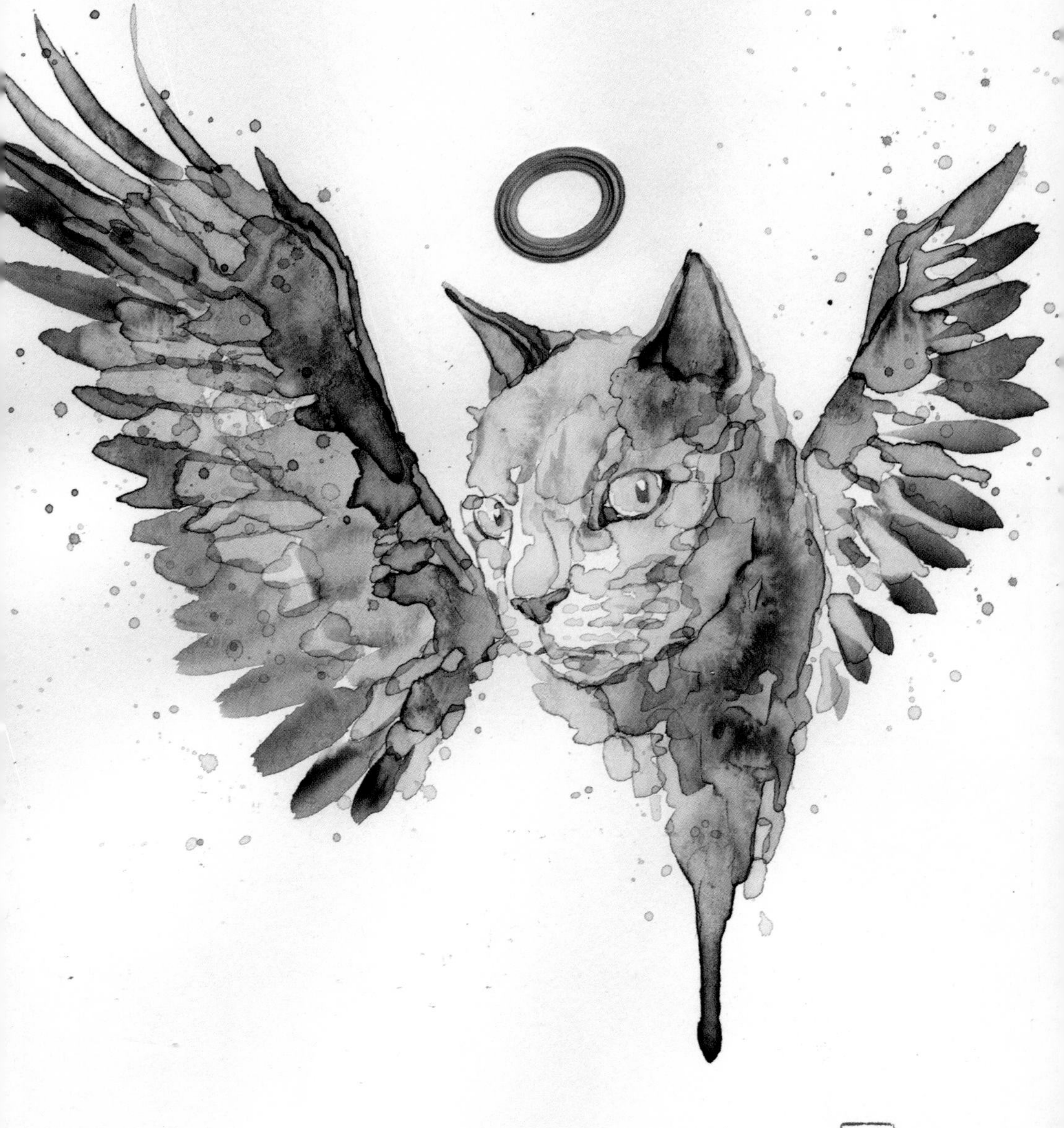
MACK

Illustration by
David Mack

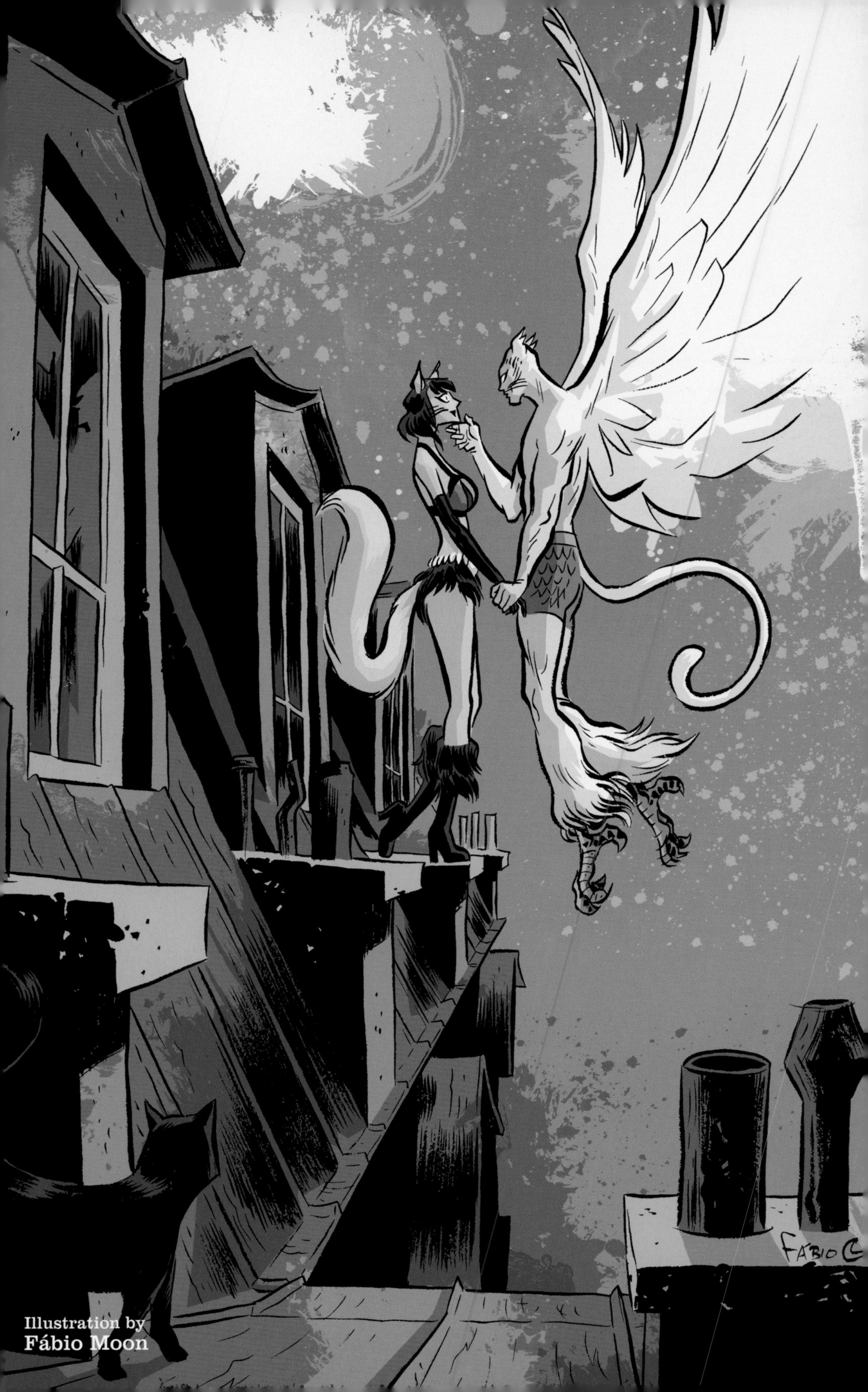
FÁBIO
Illustration by
Fábio Moon

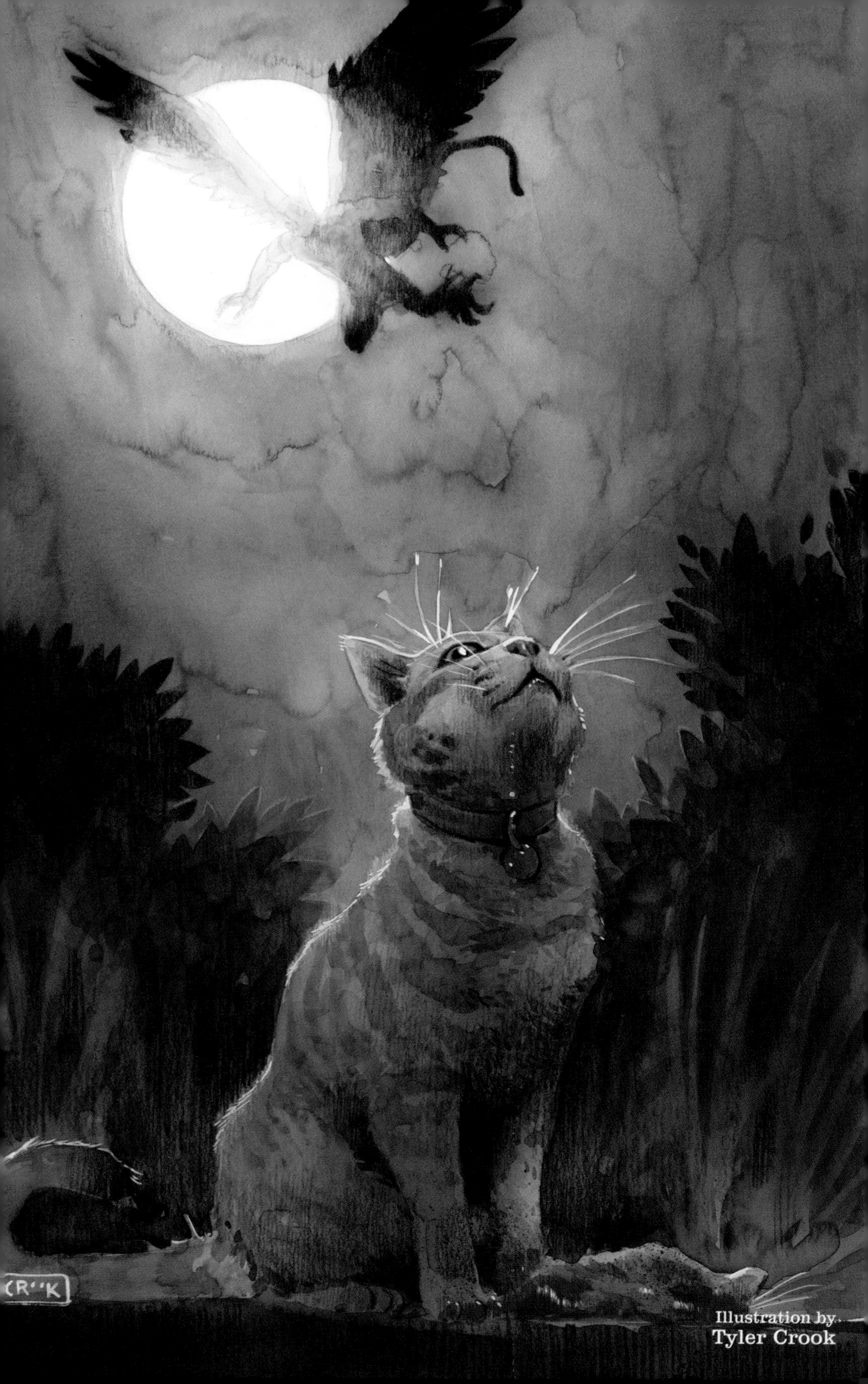

Illustration by
Tyler Crook

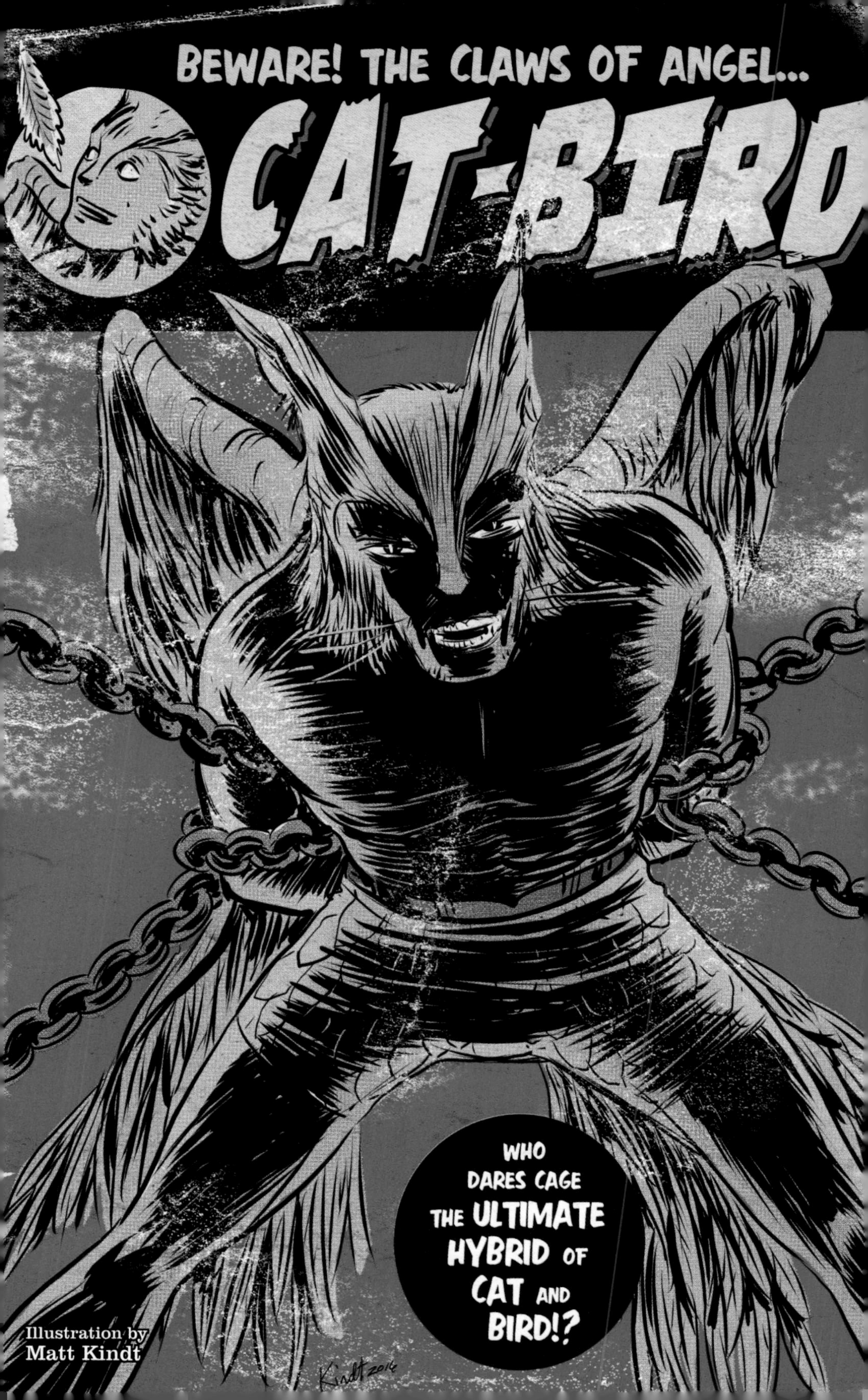

BEWARE! THE CLAWS OF ANGEL...
CAT-BIRD
WHO DARES CAGE THE ULTIMATE HYBRID OF CAT AND BIRD!?

Illustration by
Matt Kindt

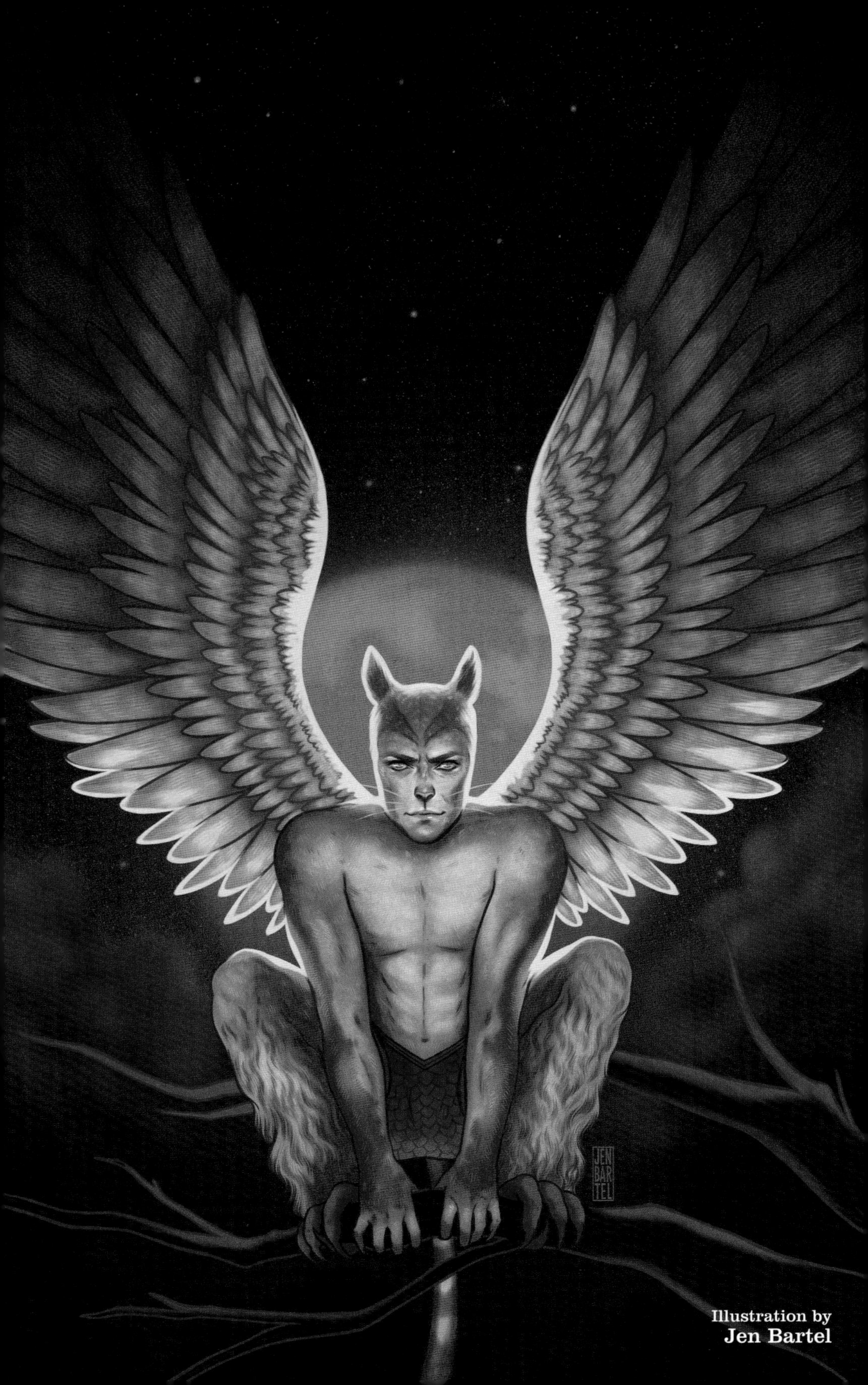
JEN BARTEL

Illustration by
Jen Bartel

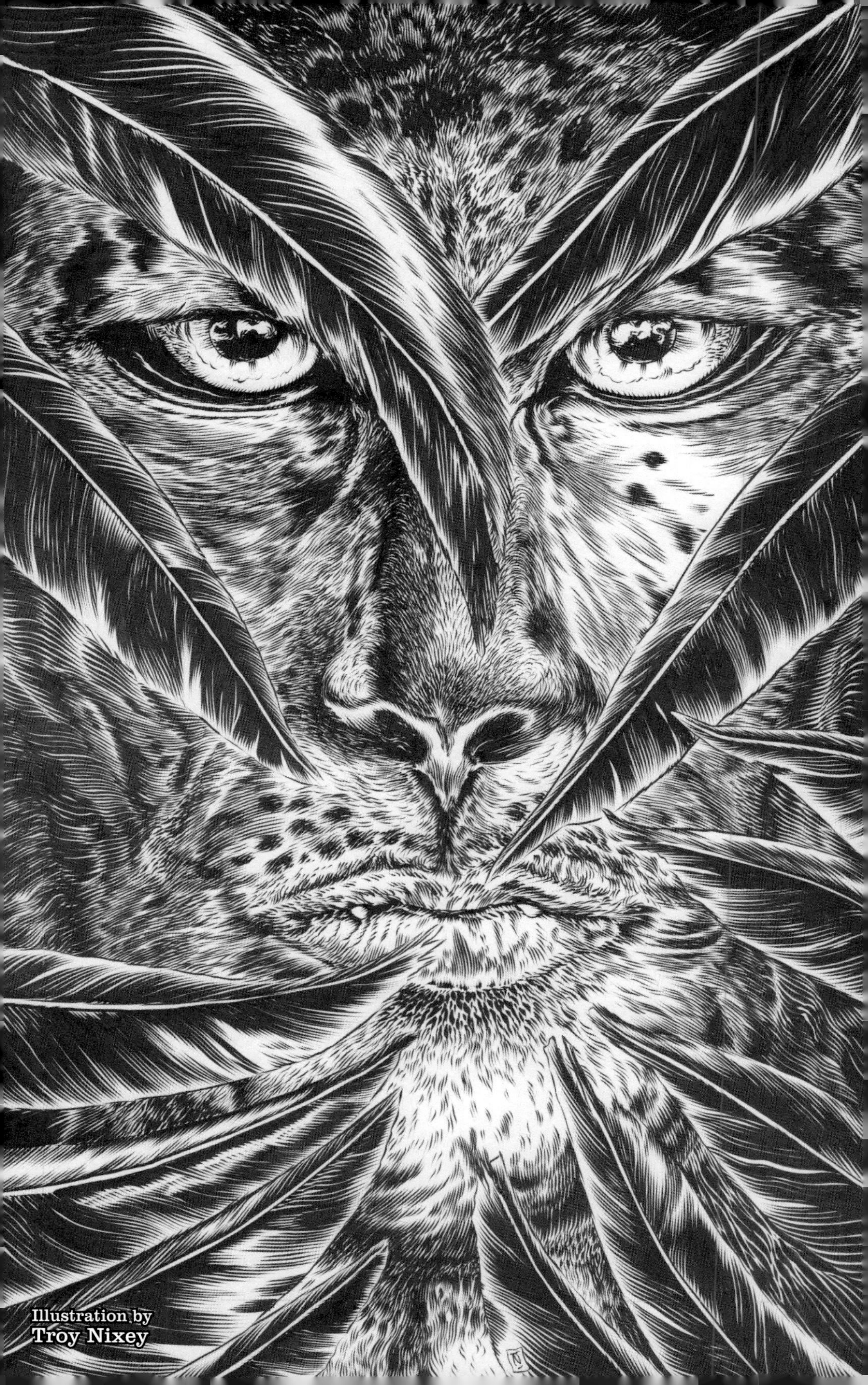

Illustration by
Troy Nixey

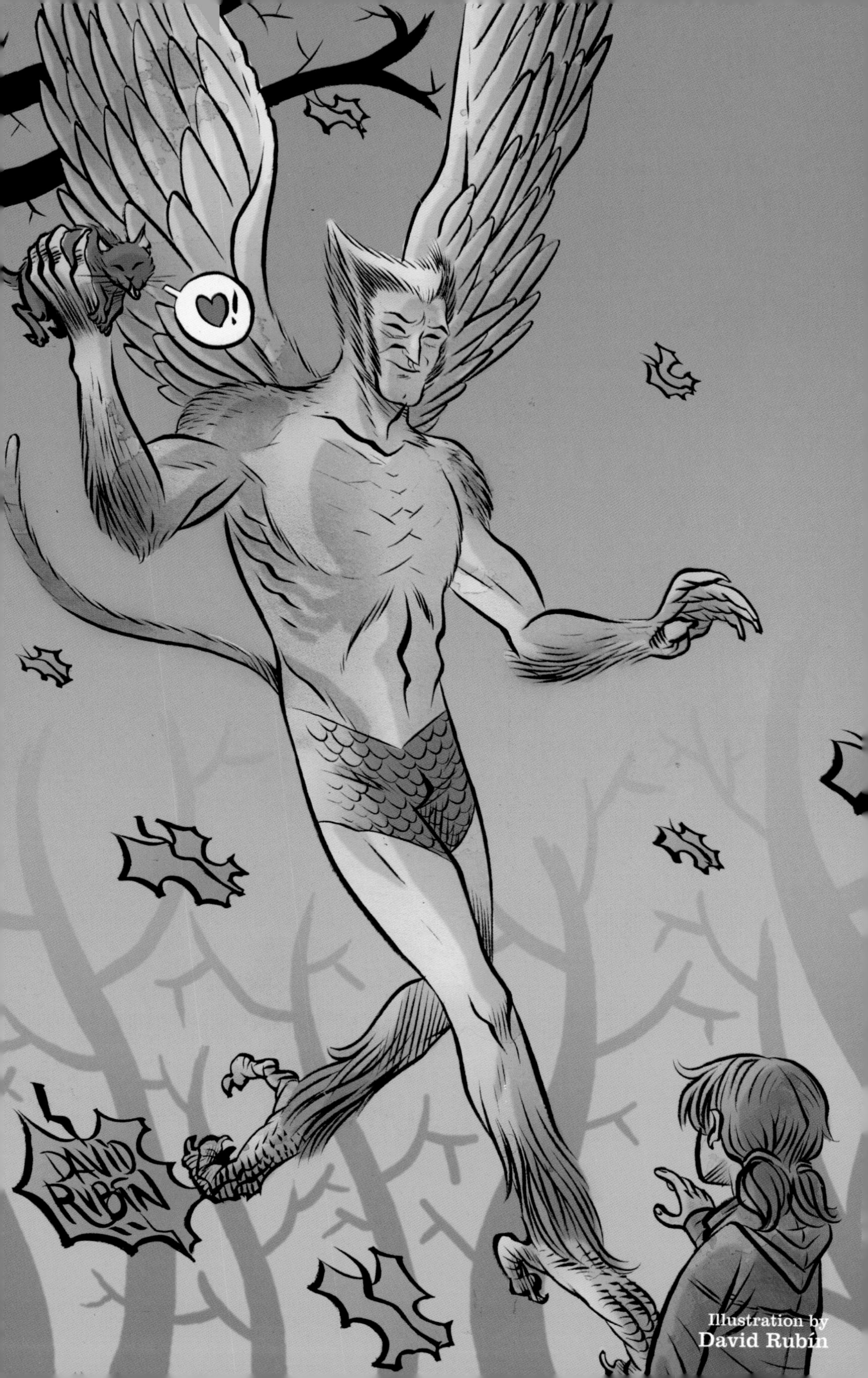

♥!
DAVID RUBÍN

Illustration by
David Rubín

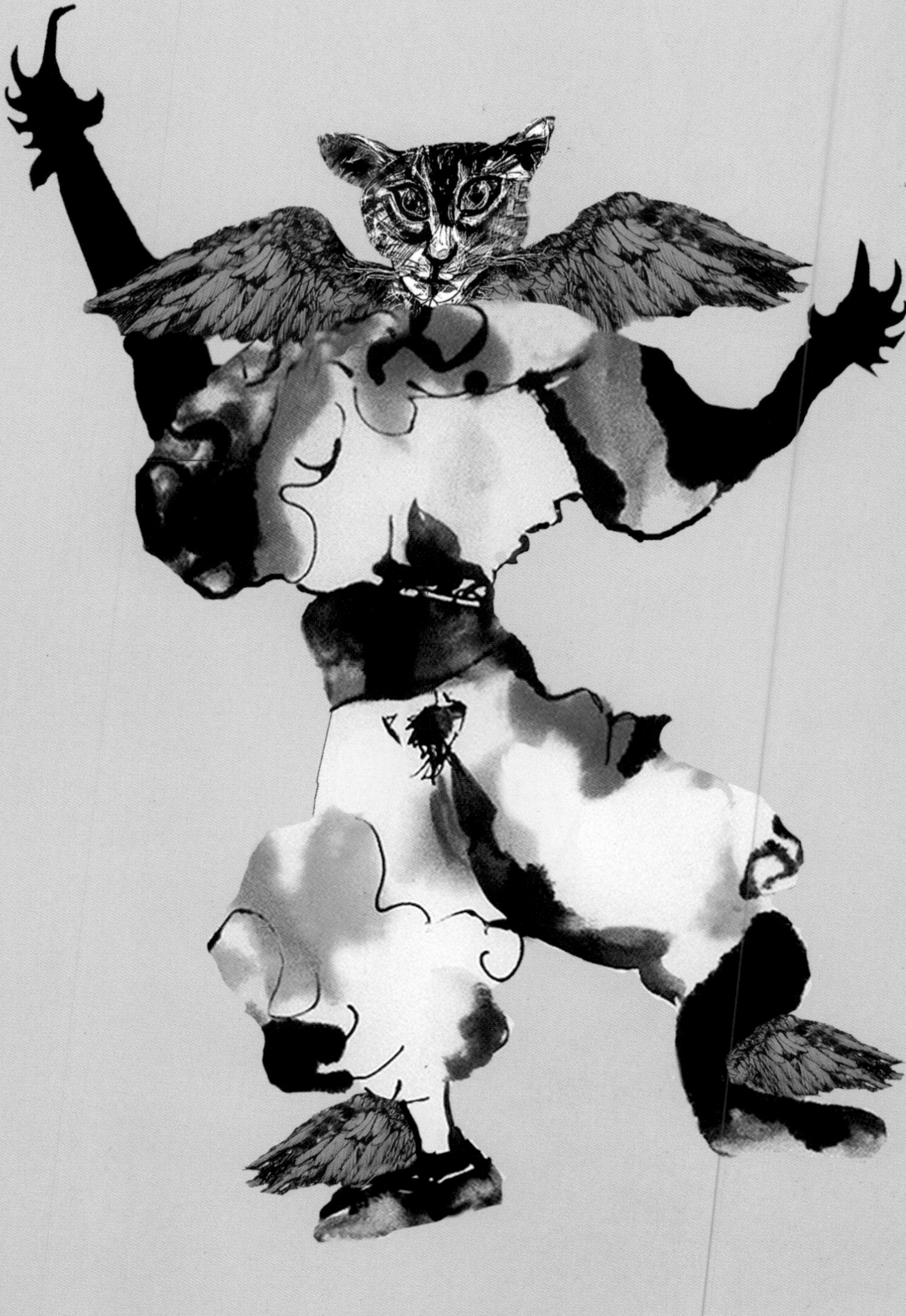

Illustration by
Charlie Patcher

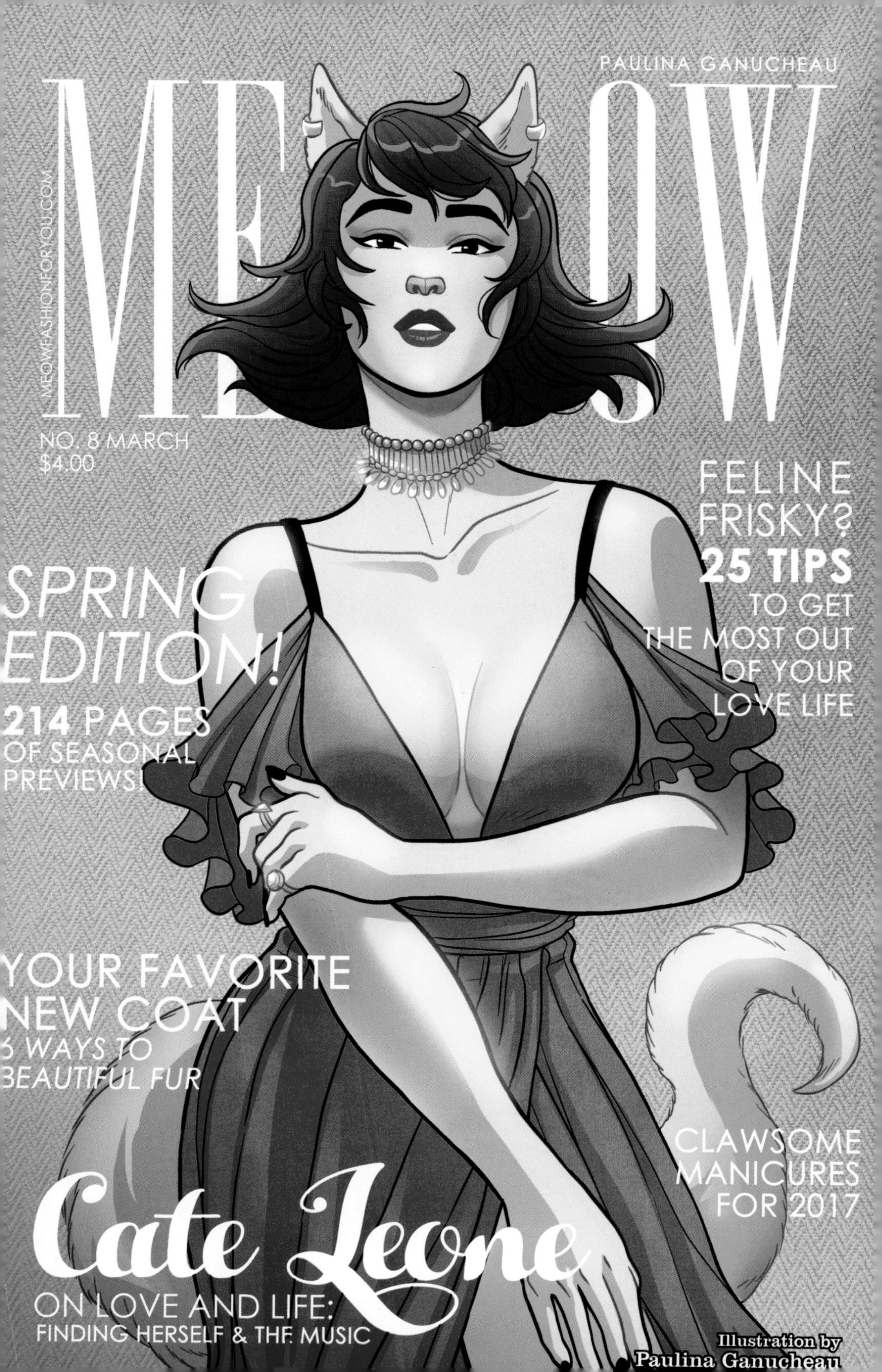
PAULINA GANUCHEAU
MEOW
MEOWFASHIONFORYOU.COM
NO. 8 MARCH
$4.00
SPRING EDITION!
214 PAGES OF SEASONAL PREVIEWS!
FELINE FRISKY? 25 TIPS TO GET THE MOST OUT OF YOUR LOVE LIFE
YOUR FAVORITE NEW COAT
6 WAYS TO BEAUTIFUL FUR
CLAWSOME MANICURES FOR 2017
Cate Leone
ON LOVE AND LIFE:
FINDING HERSELF & THE MUSIC

Illustration by Paulina Ganucheau

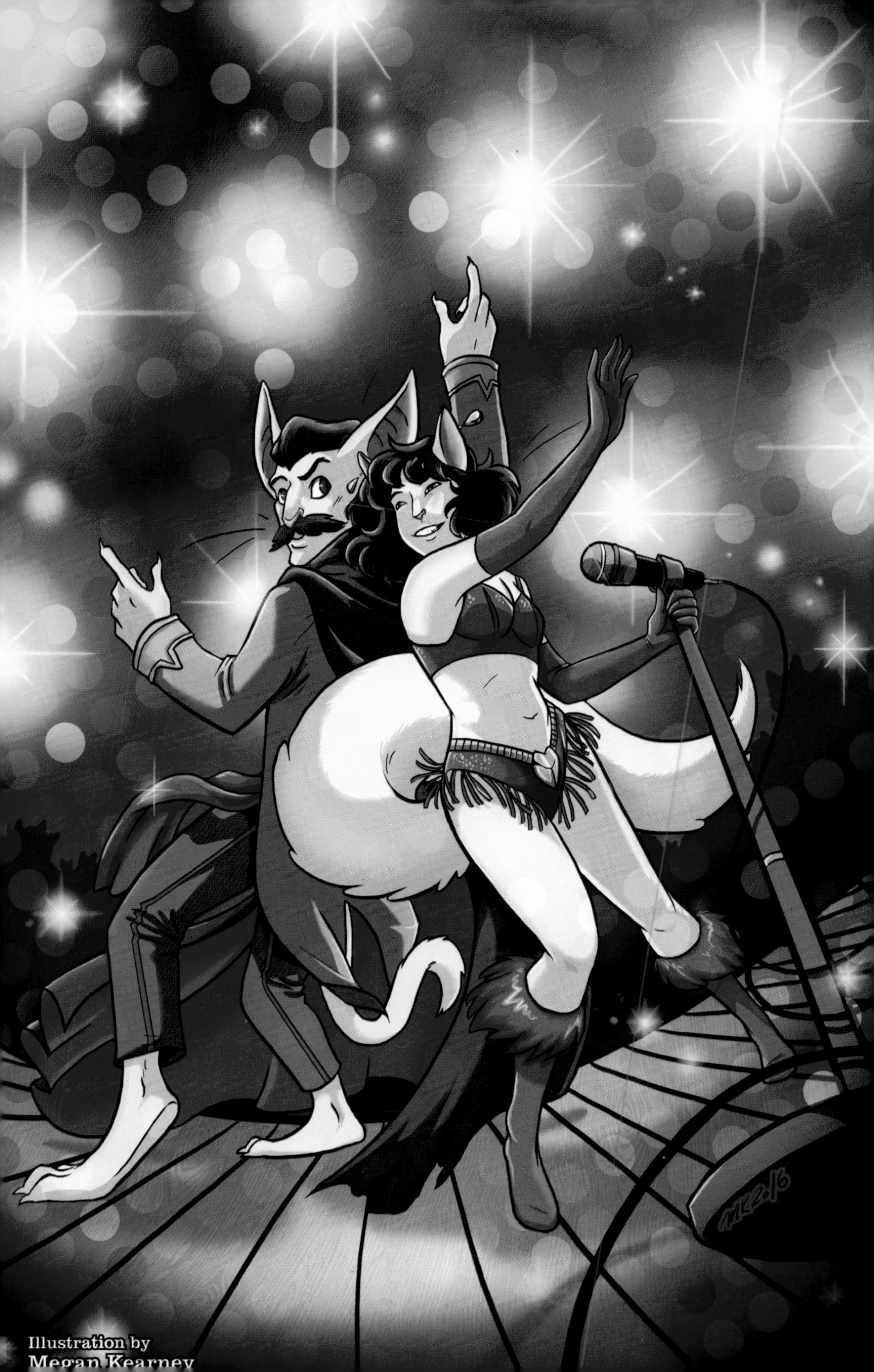

Illustration by
Megan Kearney

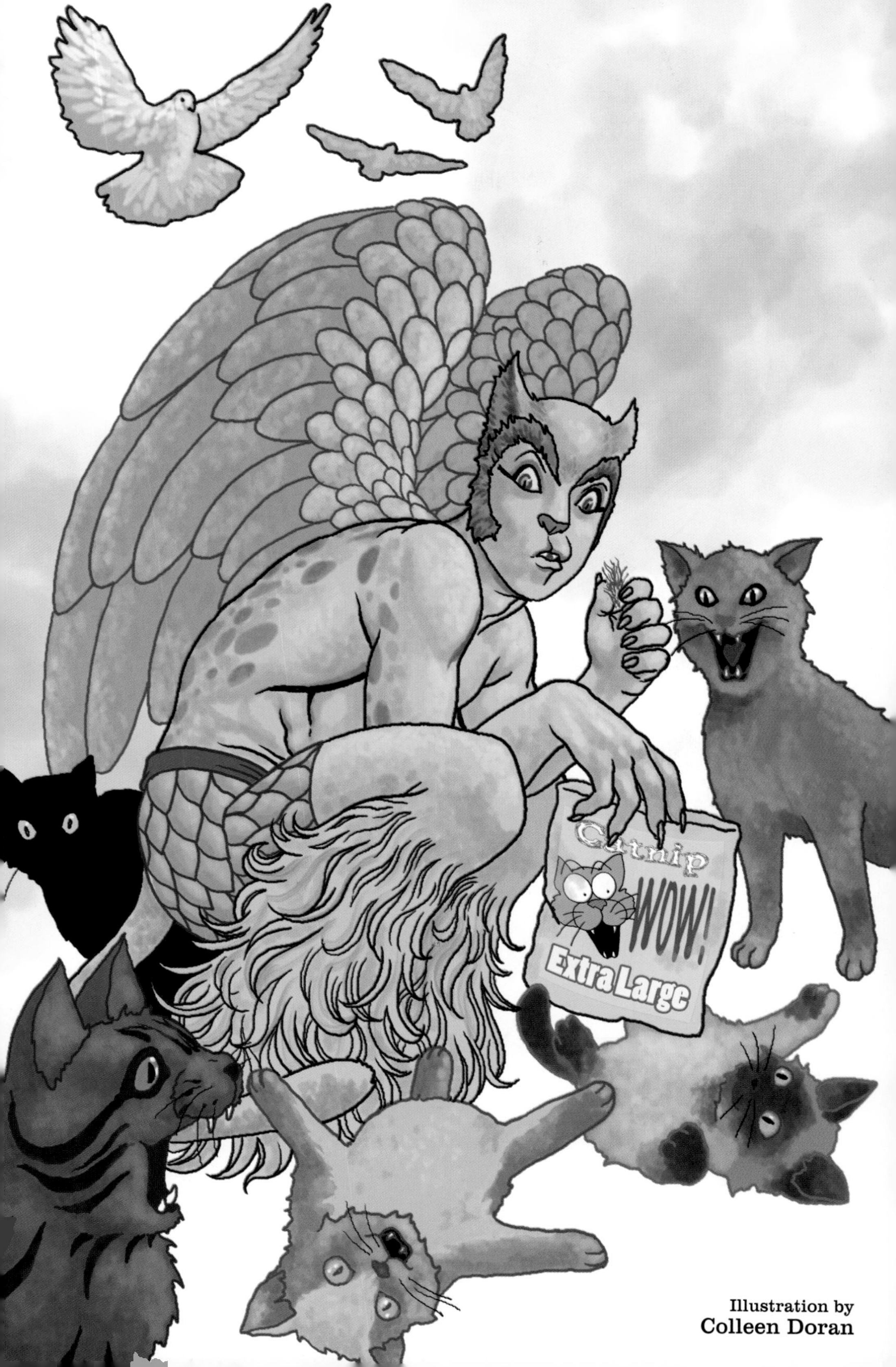
Catnip
WOW!
Extra Large

Illustration by
Colleen Doran

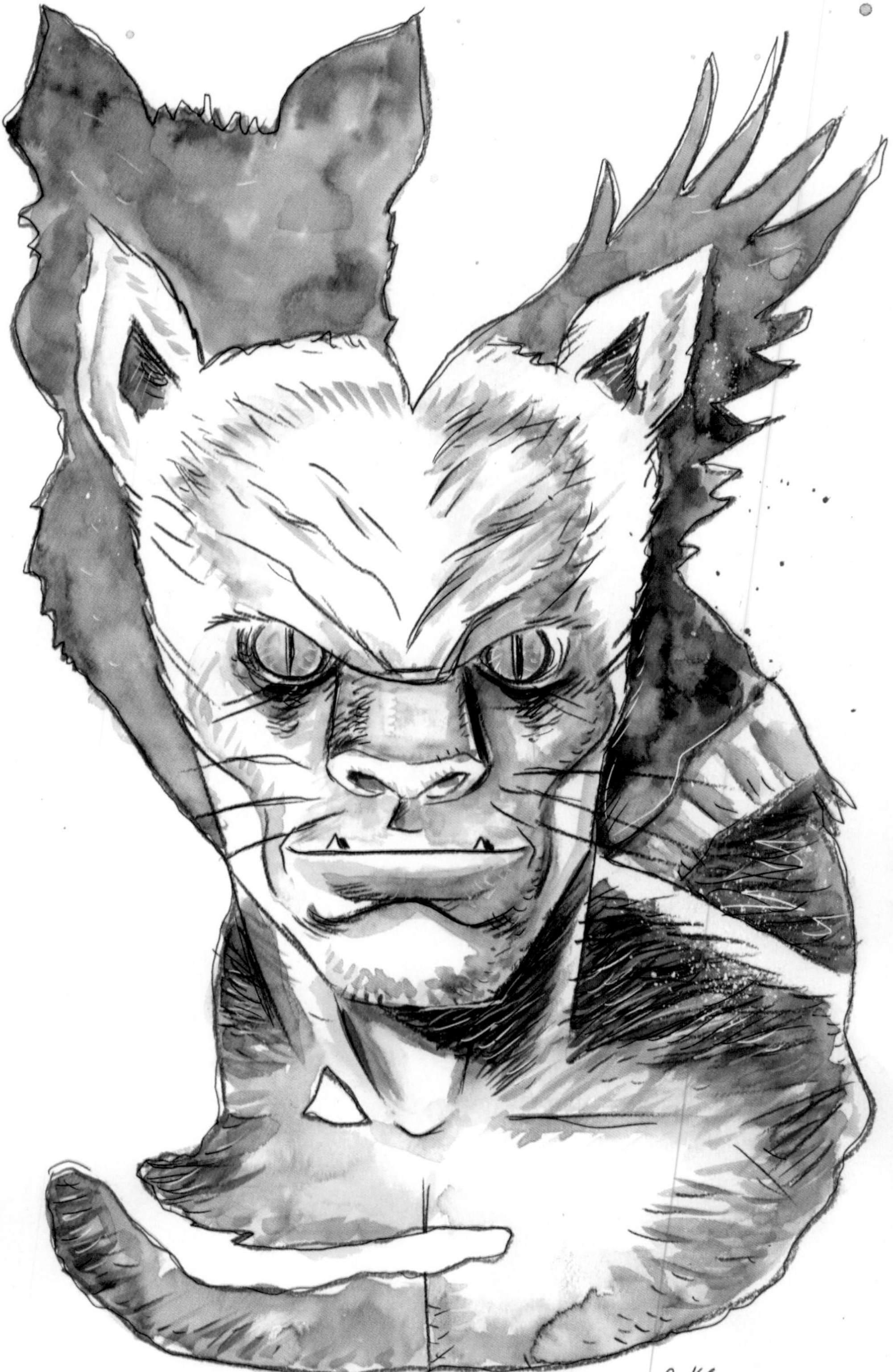

Illustration by
Jeff Lemire

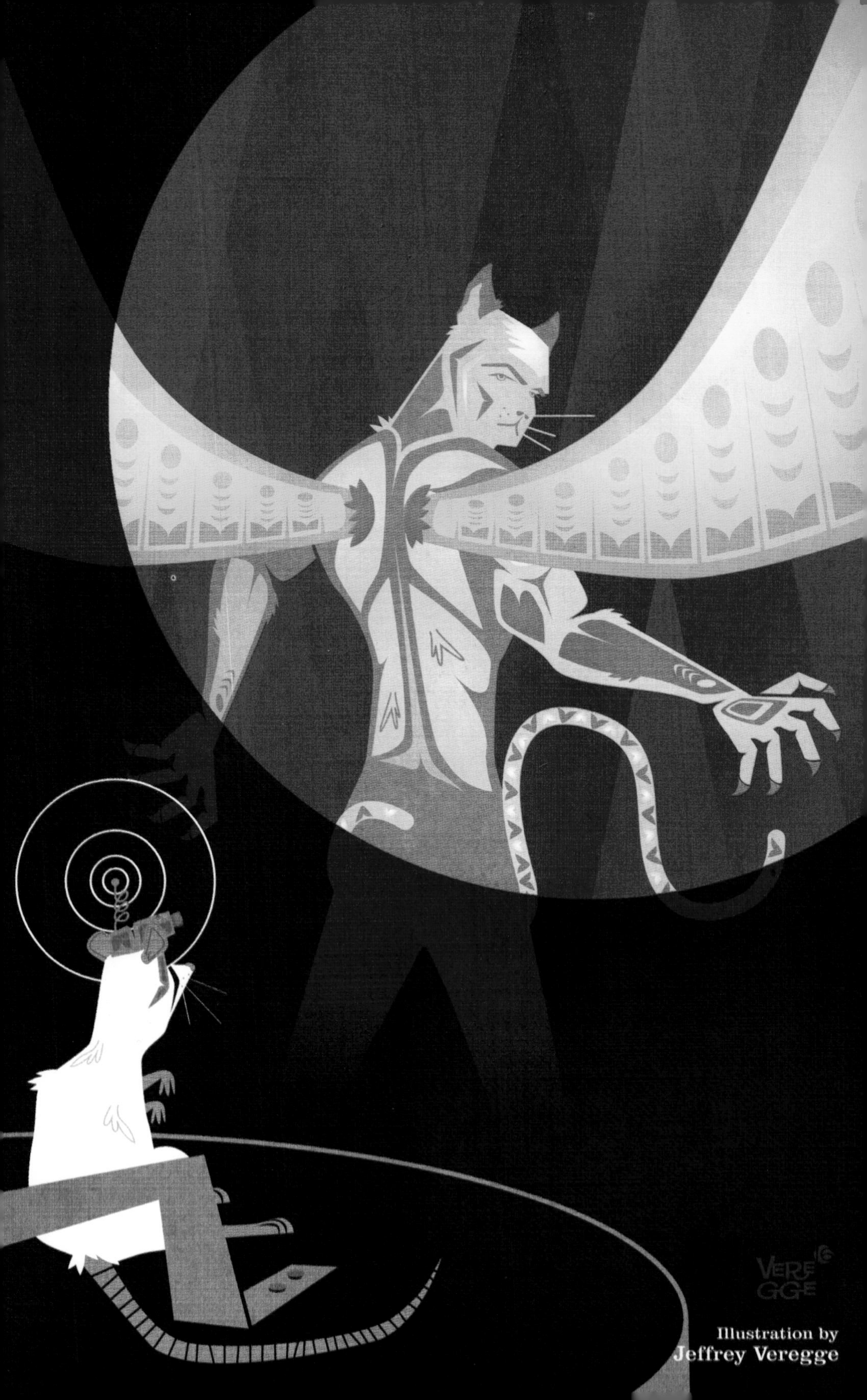
VEREGGE

Illustration by
Jeffrey Veregge

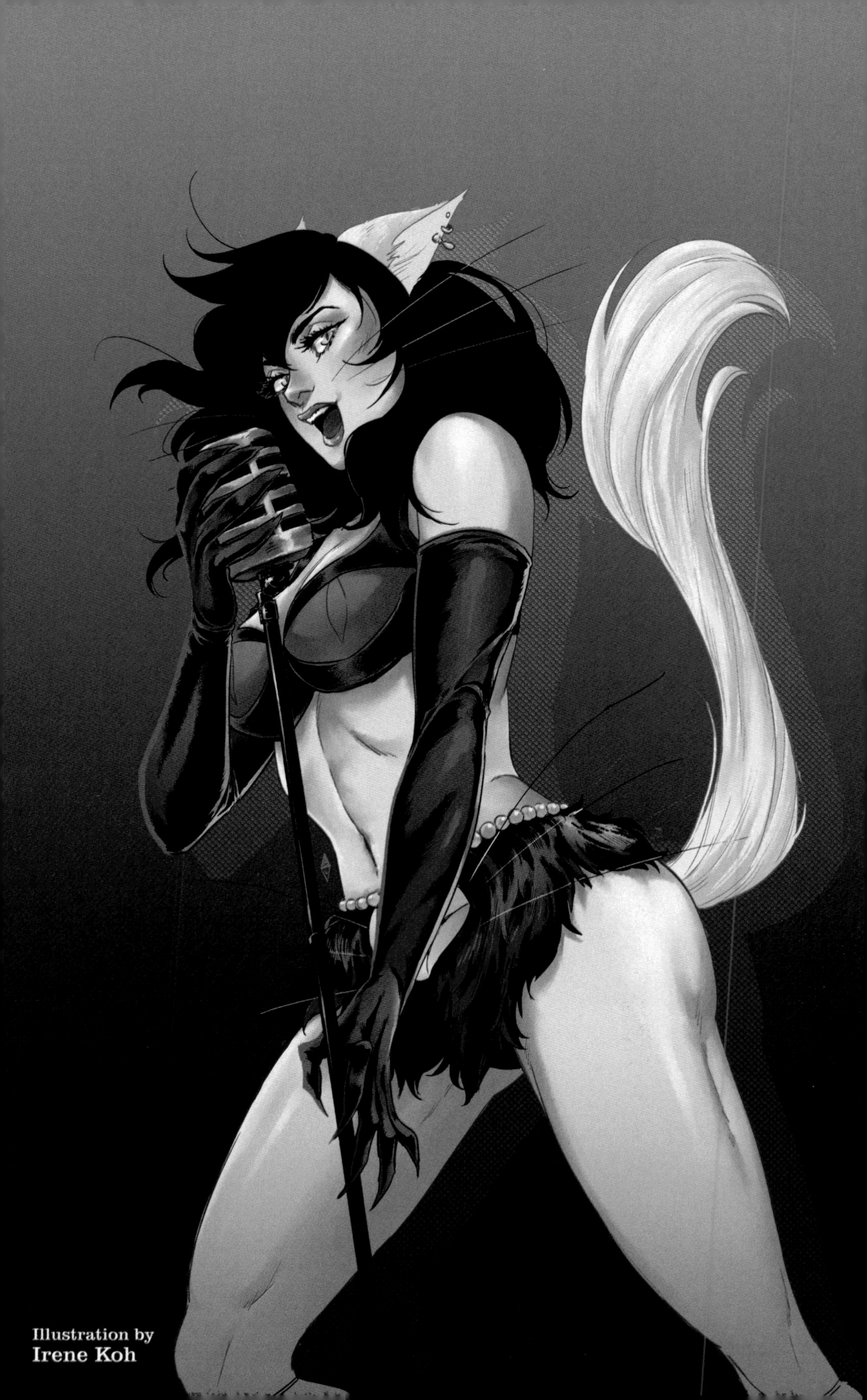

Illustration by
Irene Koh

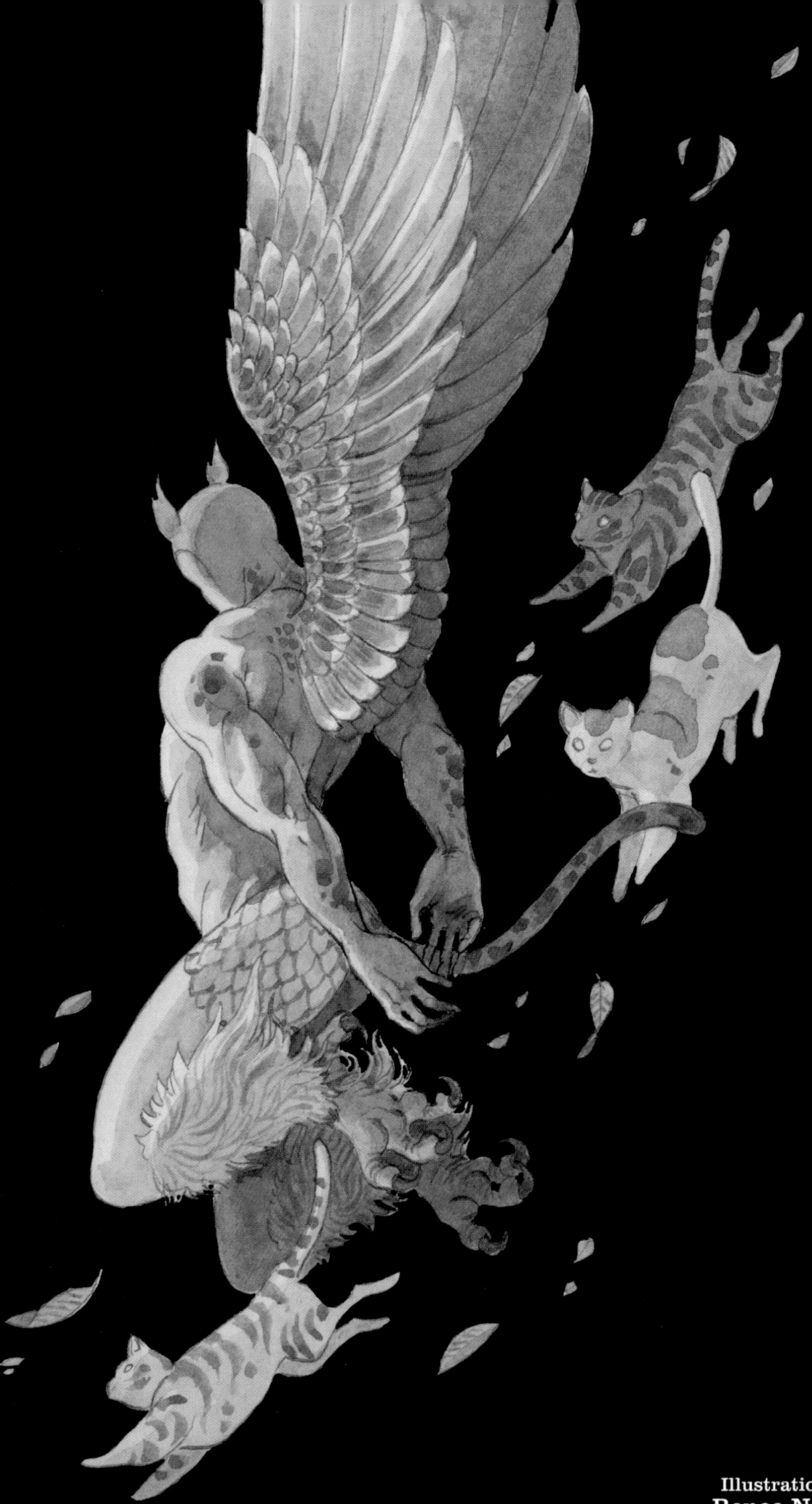

Illustration by
Renee Nault

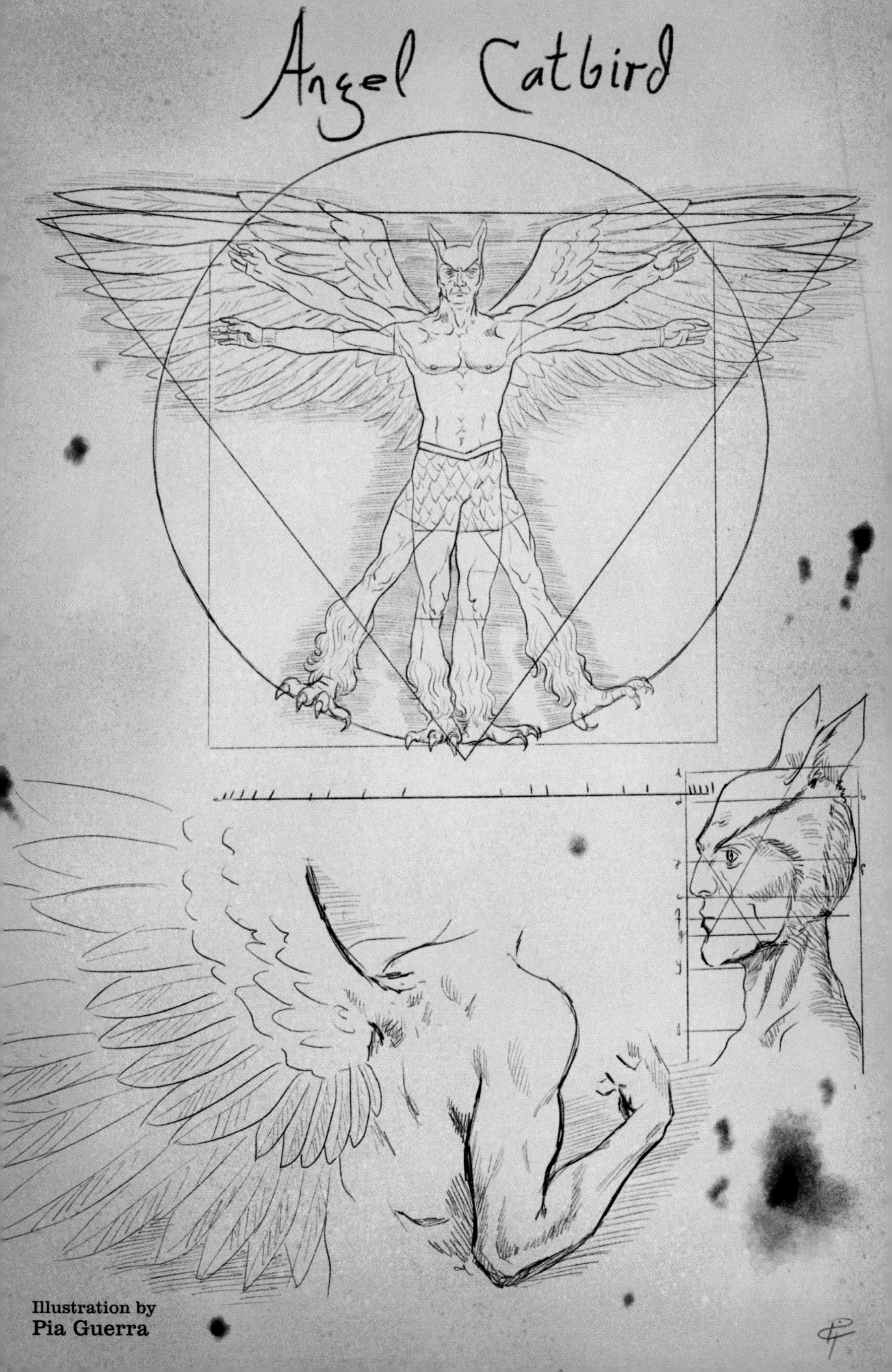
Angel Catbird

Illustration by
Pia Guerra

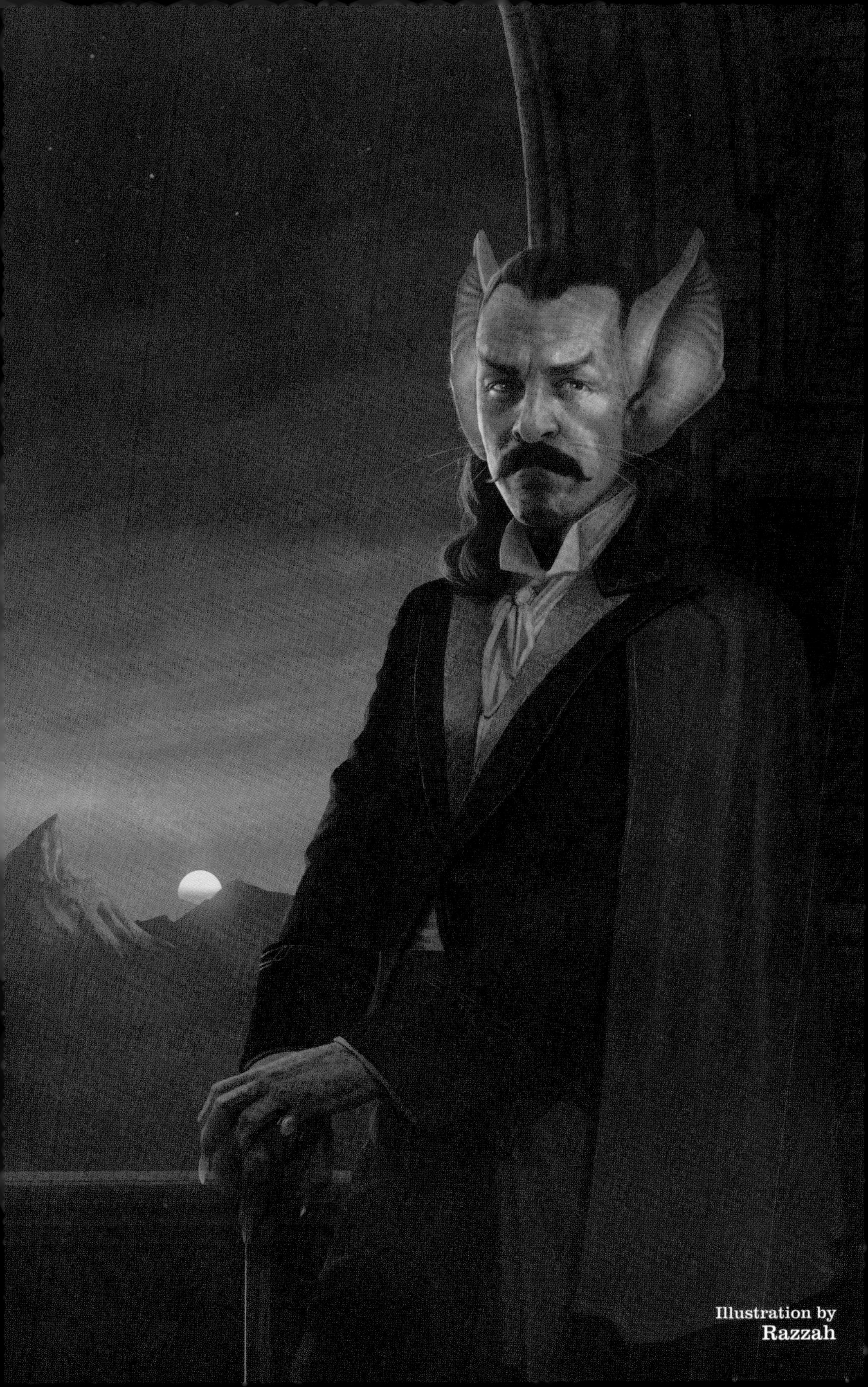

Illustration by
Razzah

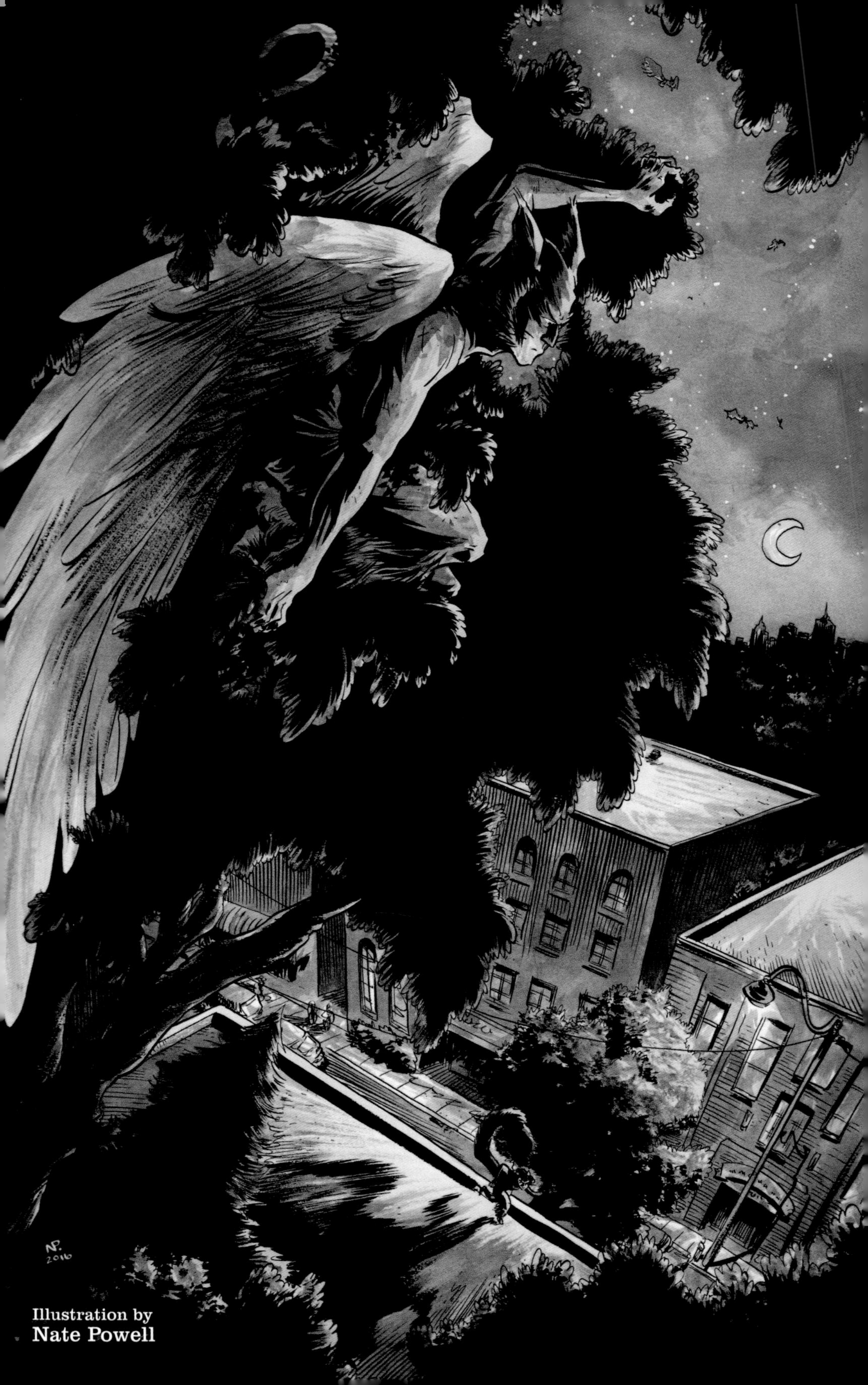
NP.
2016

Illustration by
Nate Powell

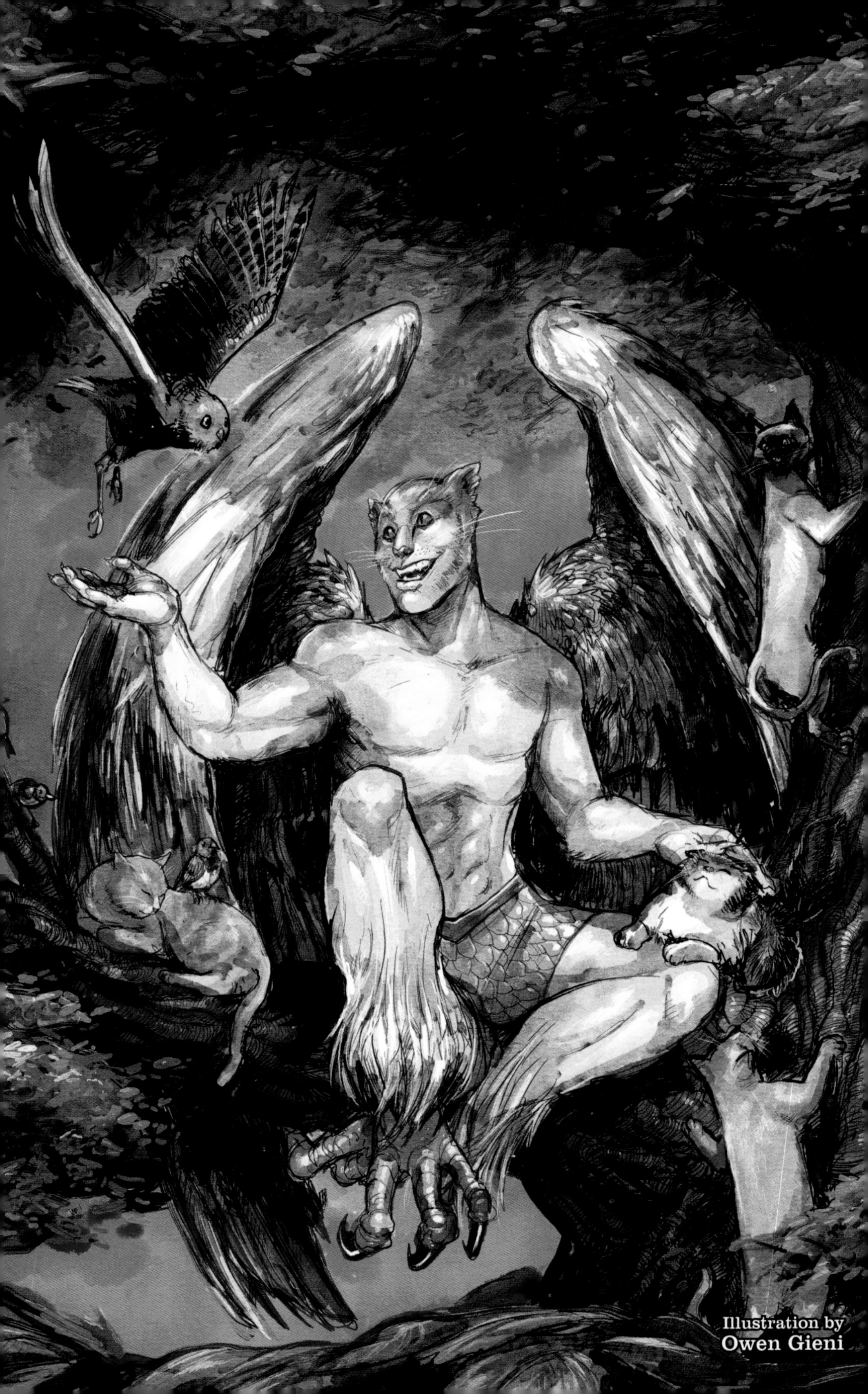
Illustration by
Owen Gieni

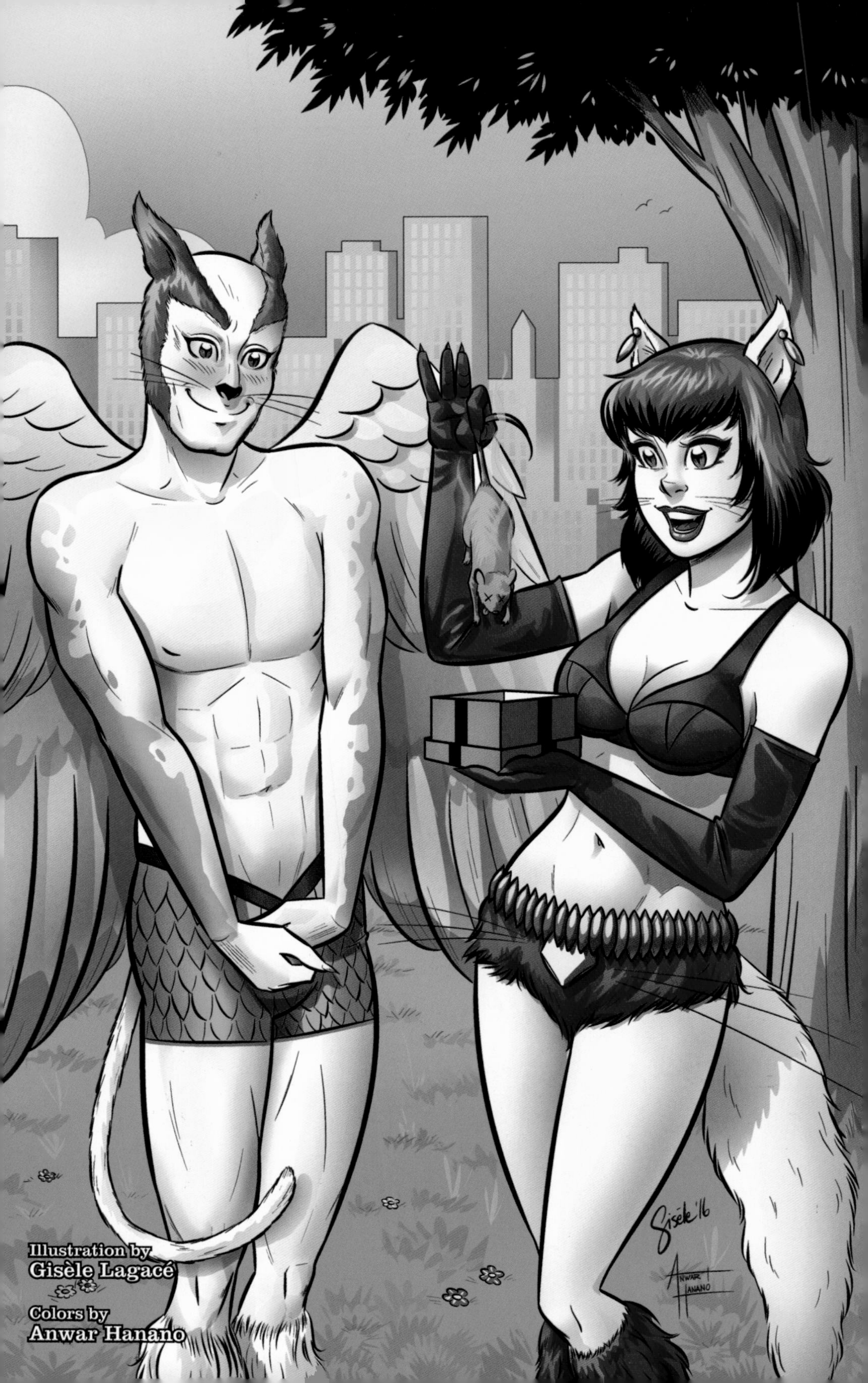
Gisèle '16
ANWAR HANANO
Illustration by
Gisèle Lagacé
Colors by
Anwar Hanano

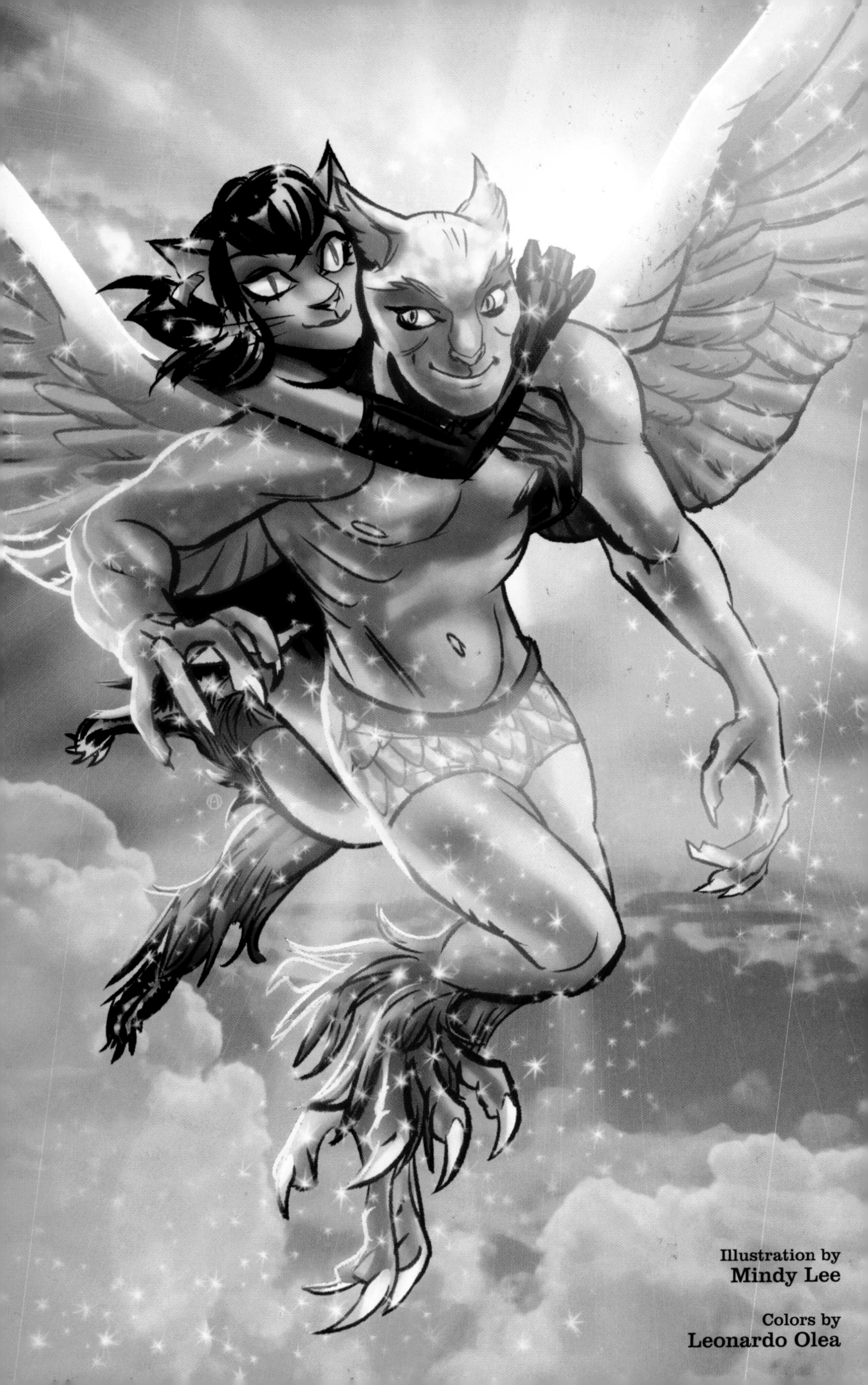

Illustration by
Mindy Lee

Colors by
Leonardo Olea

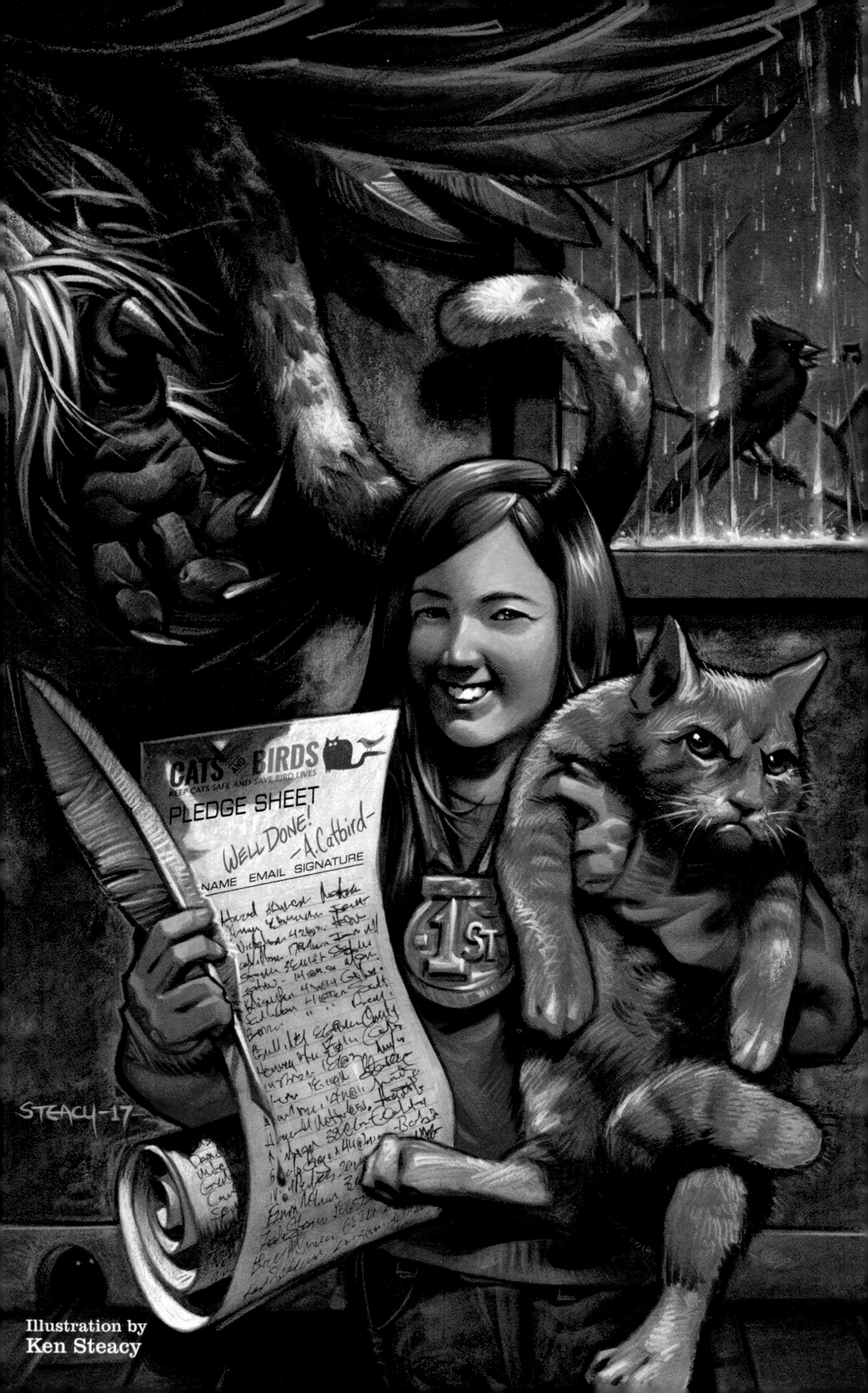
CATS AND BIRDS
KEEP CATS SAFE AND SAVE BIRD LIVES
PLEDGE SHEET
WELL DONE! -A.Catbird-
NAME EMAIL SIGNATURE
1ST
STEACY-17

Illustration by
Ken Steacy

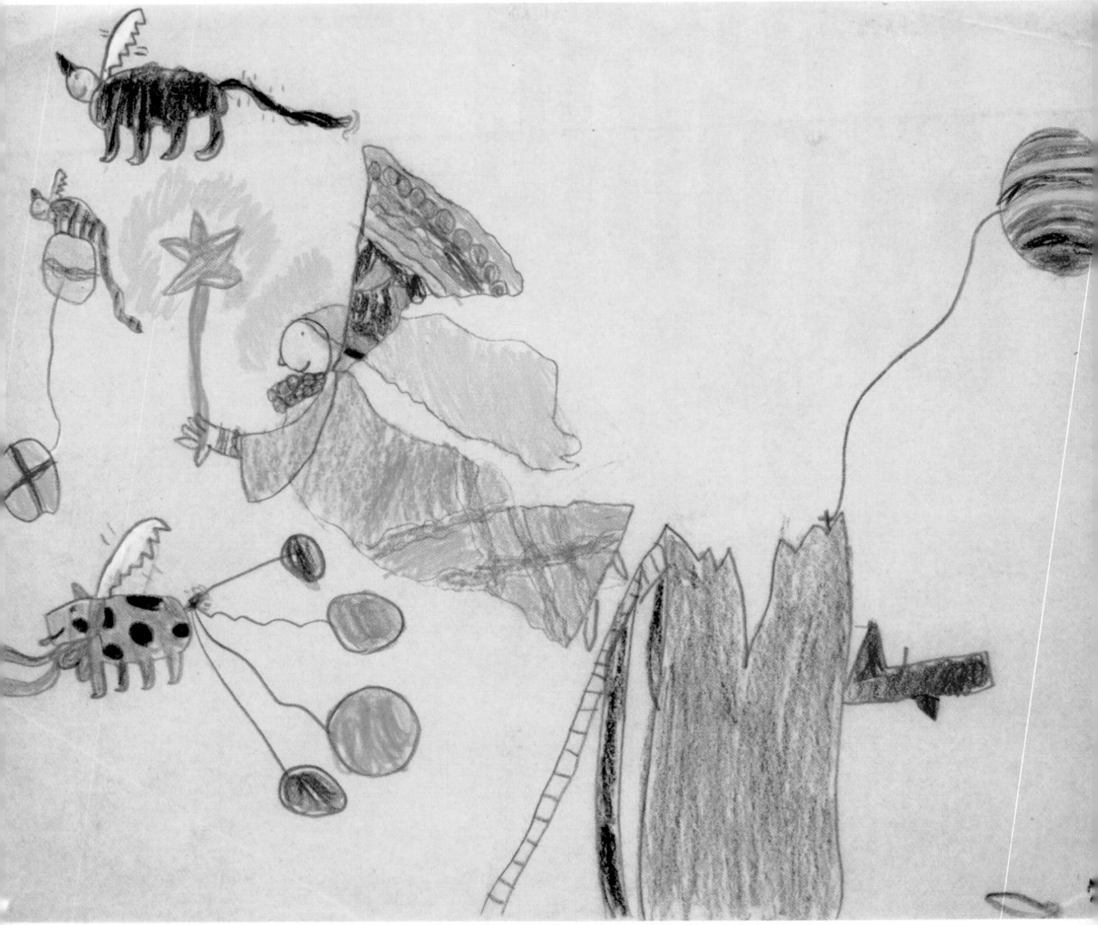

Margaret Atwood: The deep origins of Angel Catbird. Here is a drawing I did when I was six or seven, and drawing cats with wings.

ANGEL CATBIRD ™

SKETCHBOOK

Notes by
Johnnie Christmas

STRIG
(HUMAN FORM)

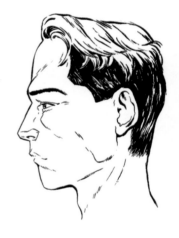

STRIG W/GLASSES

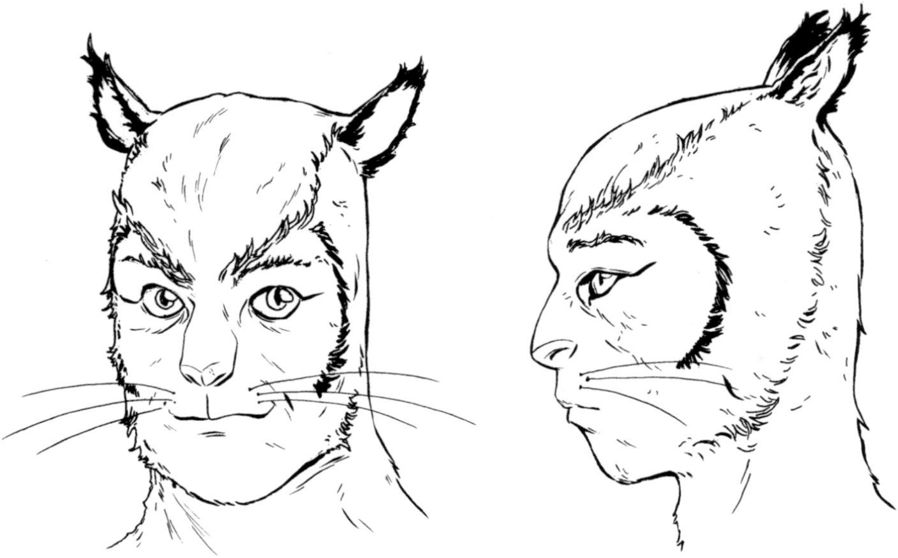

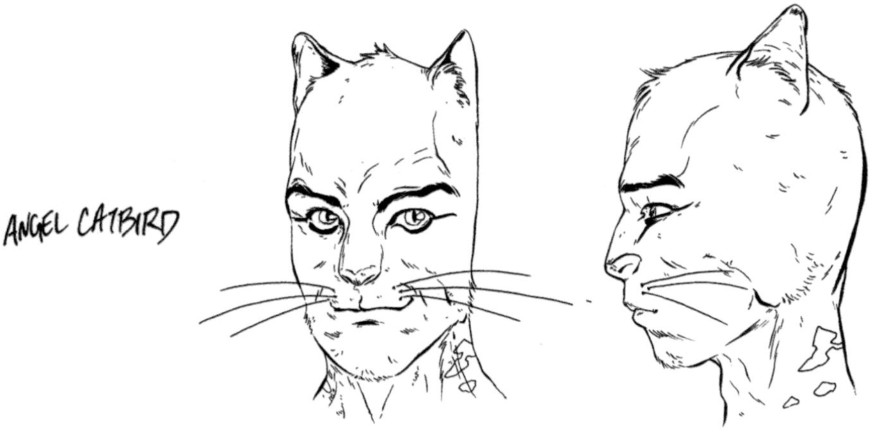
ANGEL CATBIRD

The first passes at Angel Catbird's head were too "cat" and needed a bit more "bird."

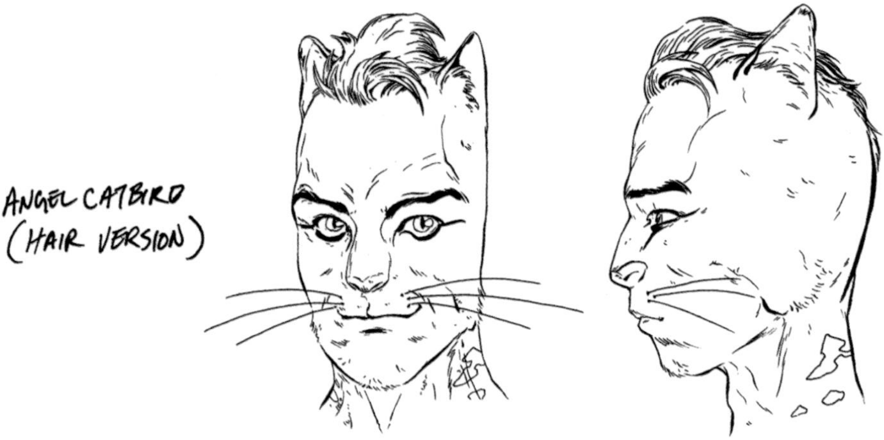
ANGEL CATBIRD
(HAIR VERSION)

I sort of like the look of Angel Catbird with a coif. But ultimately the streamlined look without human hair works best.

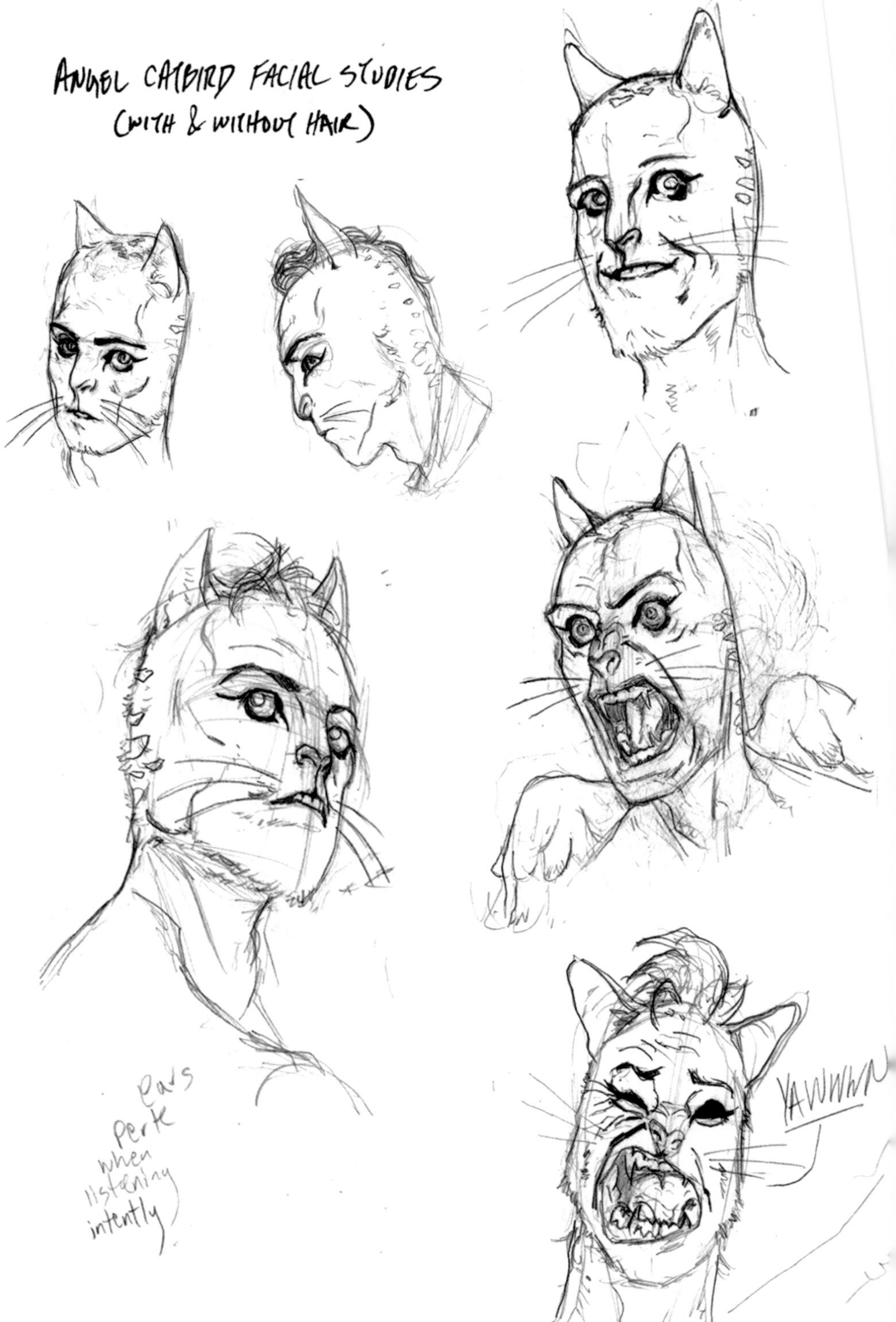
ANGEL CATBIRD FACIAL STUDIES
(WITH & WITHOUT HAIR)
ears perk when listening intently
YAWWWN

Here are some more very cat-like visuals of
Angel Catbird with different facial expressions.

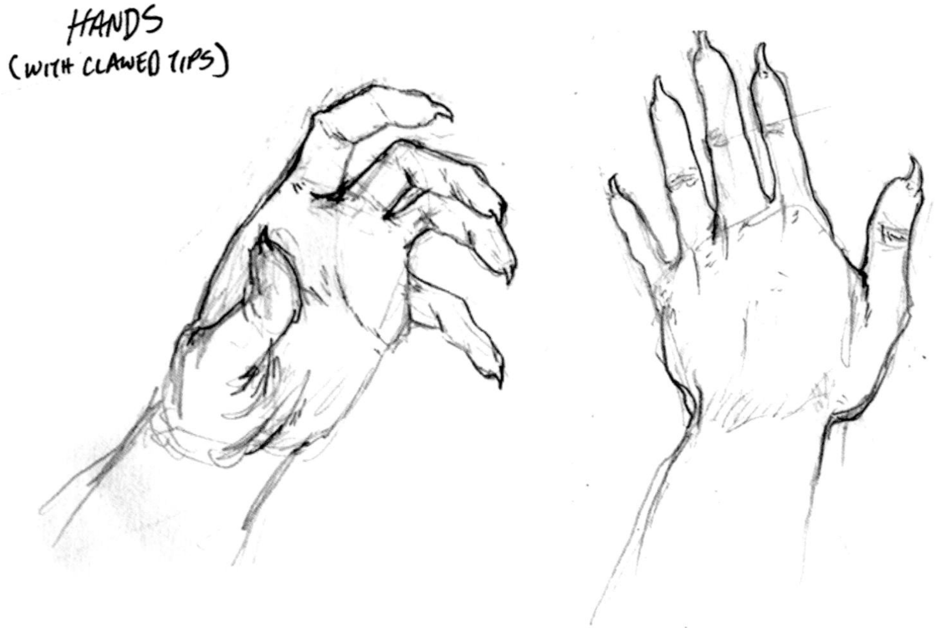
HANDS
(WITH CLAWED TIPS)

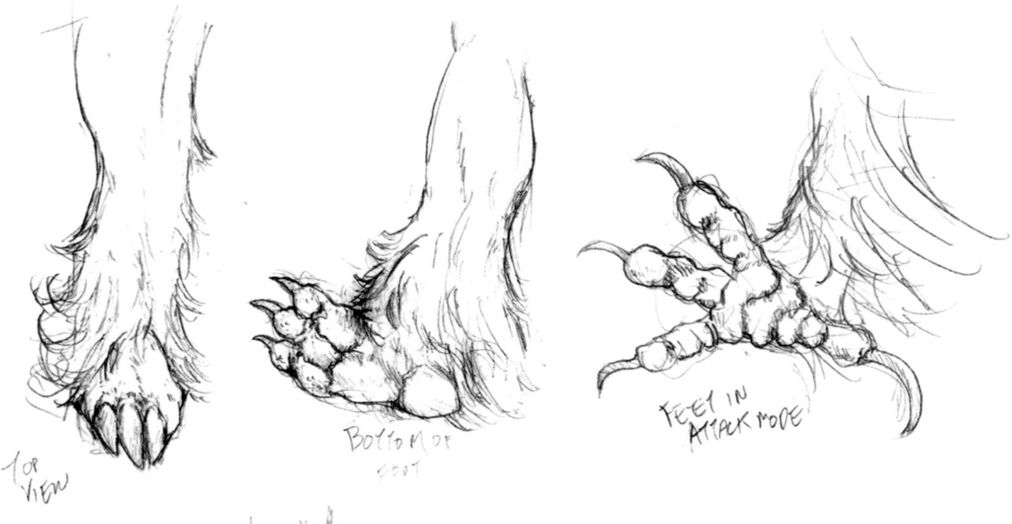
TOP VIEW
BOTTOM OF FOOT
FEET IN ATTACK MODE

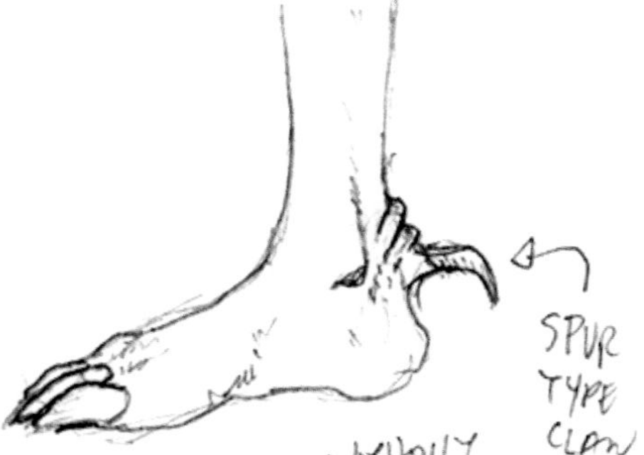
SPUR TYPE CLAW
FOOT VIEW WITHOUT FEATHERS

I wanted Angel Catbird's feet to have a friendlier aspect when he's strolling around. I like the contrast between that and the fierce appearance of his talons when he attacks.

WINGS

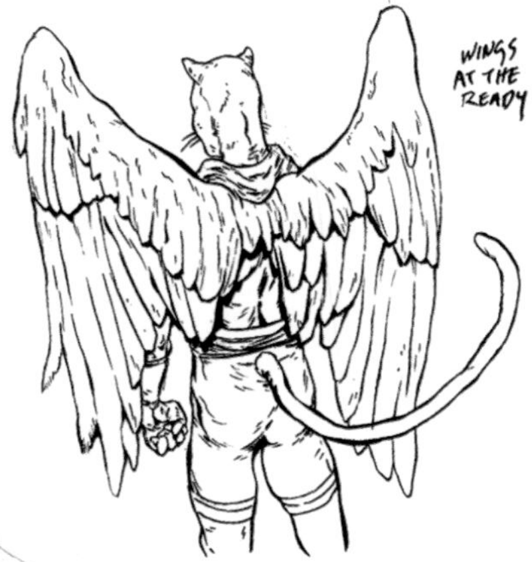
WINGS AT THE READY

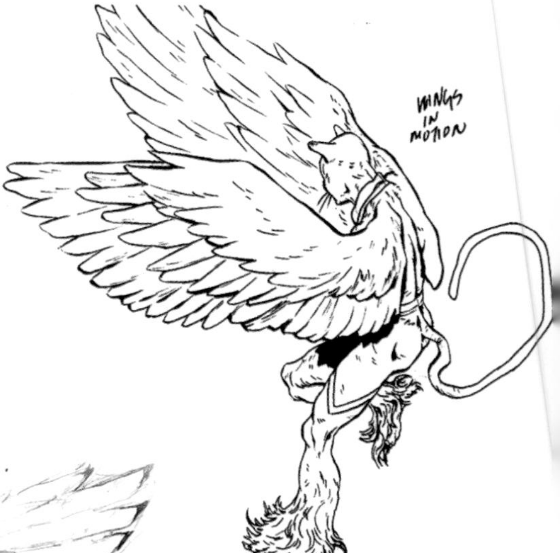
WINGS IN MOTION

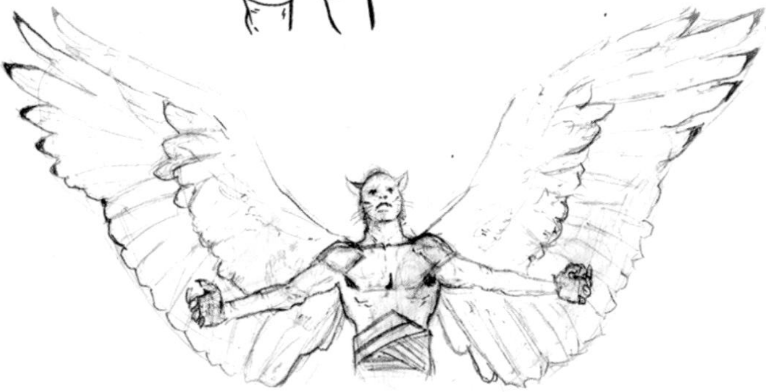

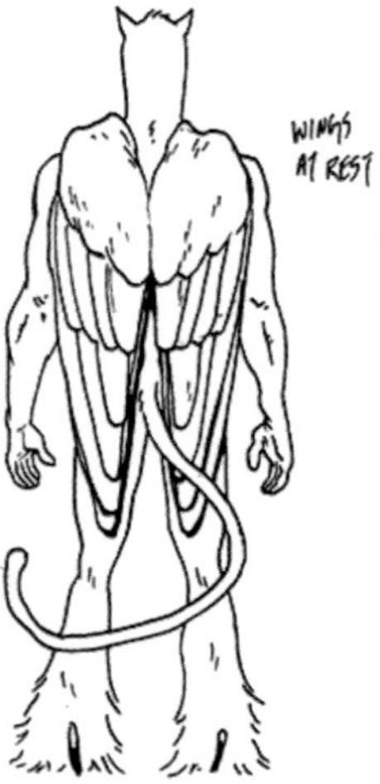
WINGS AT REST

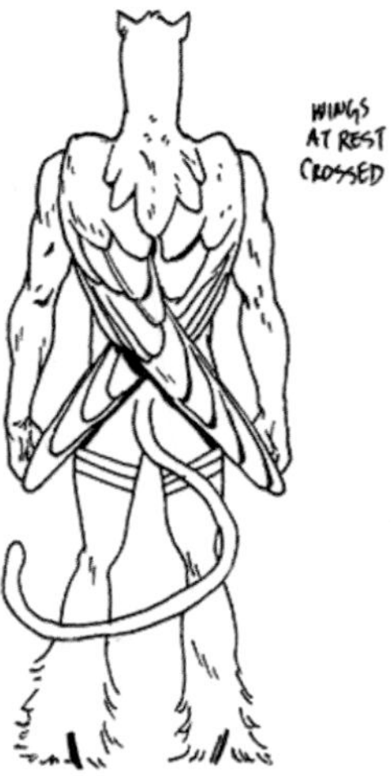
WINGS AT REST CROSSED

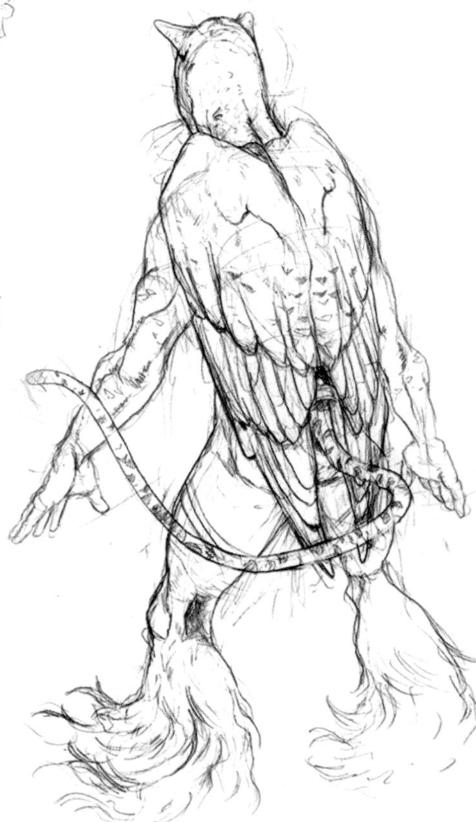

I love drawing Angel's wings.

ANGEL CATBIRD COSTUME OPTIONS

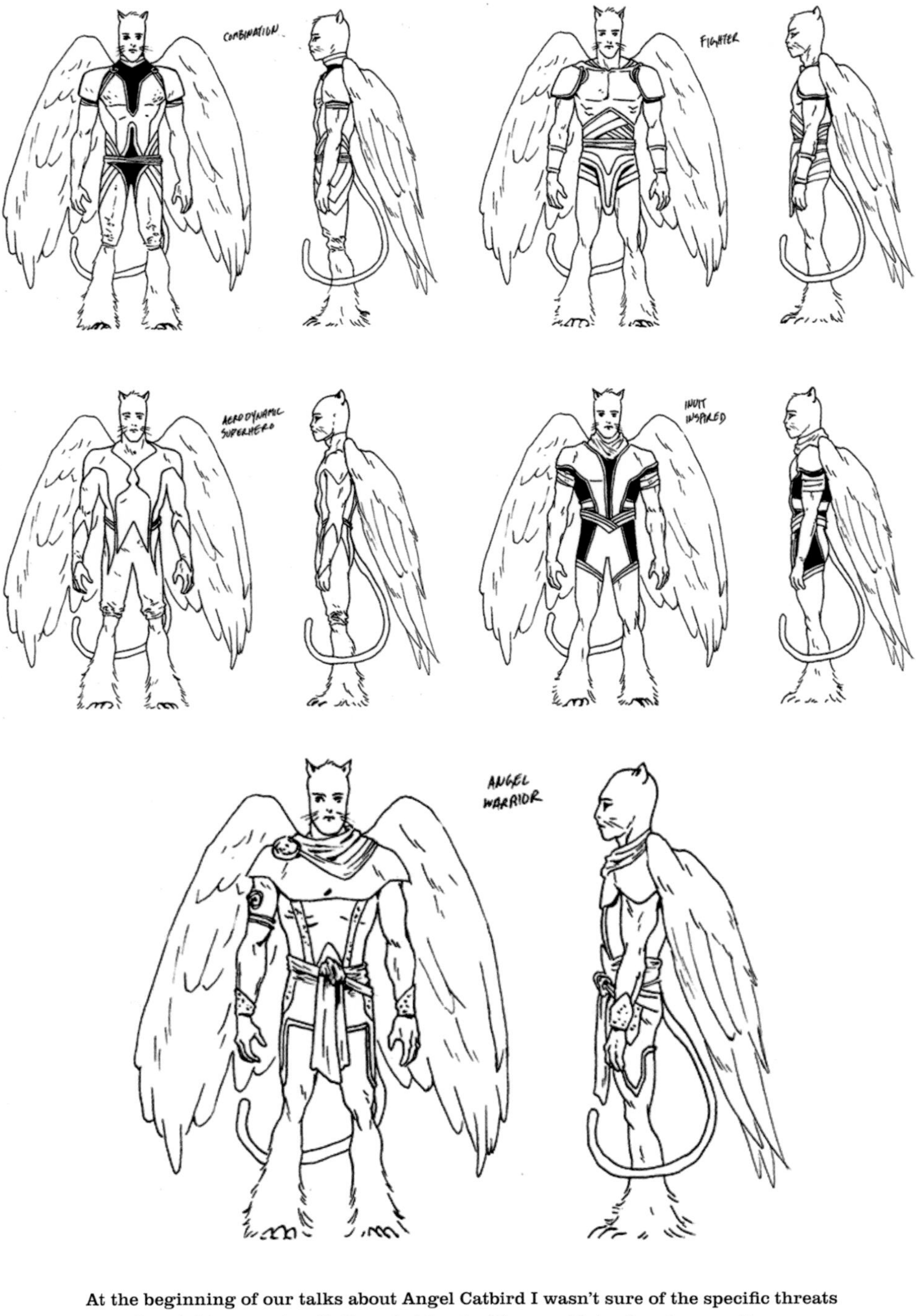
COMBINATION
FIGHTER
AERODYNAMIC SUPERHERO
INUIT INSPIRED
ANGEL WARRIOR

At the beginning of our talks about Angel Catbird I wasn't sure of the specific threats he might encounter. So I wanted to give Margaret lots of costume options.

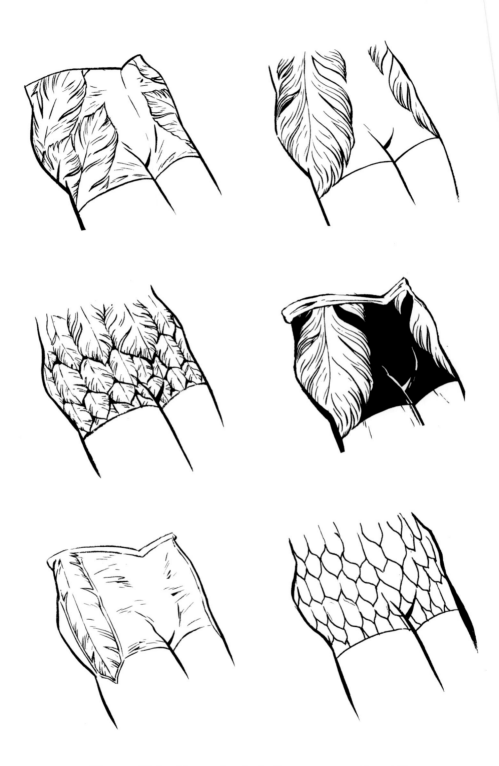

After we settled on him wearing shorts, there were more options still.
The clothes make the owl-cat-man.

SNOWY OWL PATTERN
WITH THE COLOUR OF AN ORANGE TABBY CAT

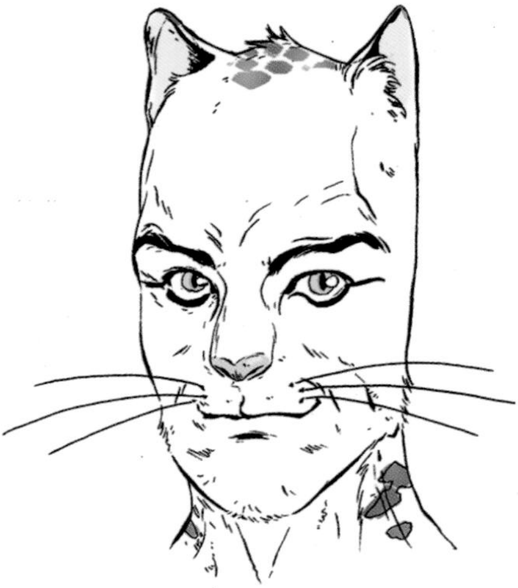

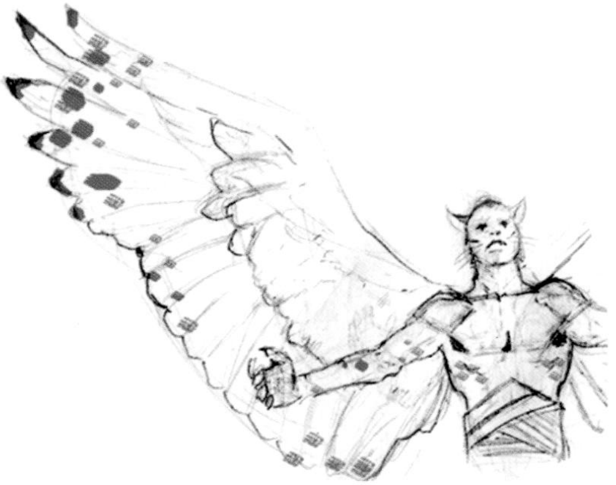

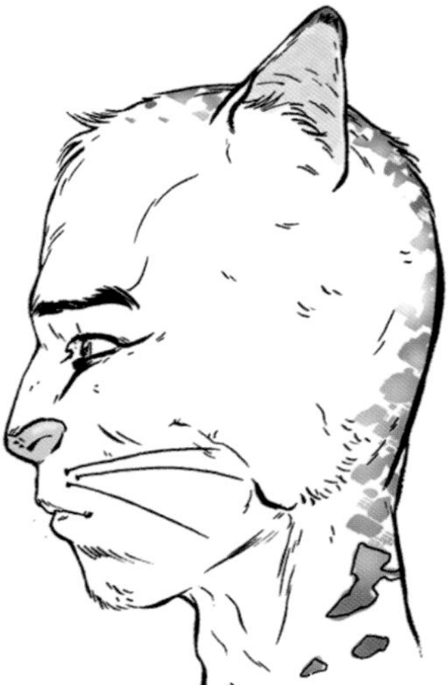

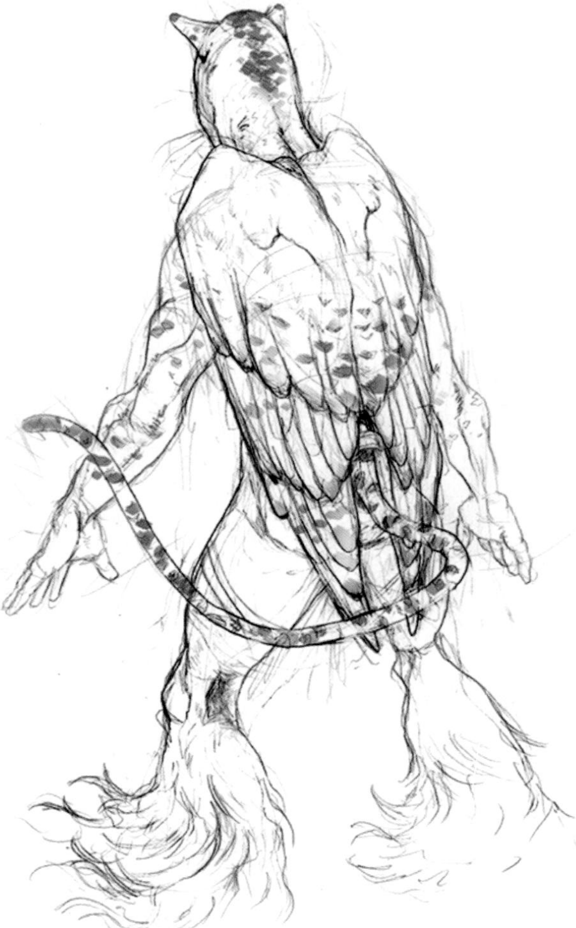

I wanted the snowy owl spots to have the coloring of Strig's cat, Ding. Another way to visually tie together Strig's mix.

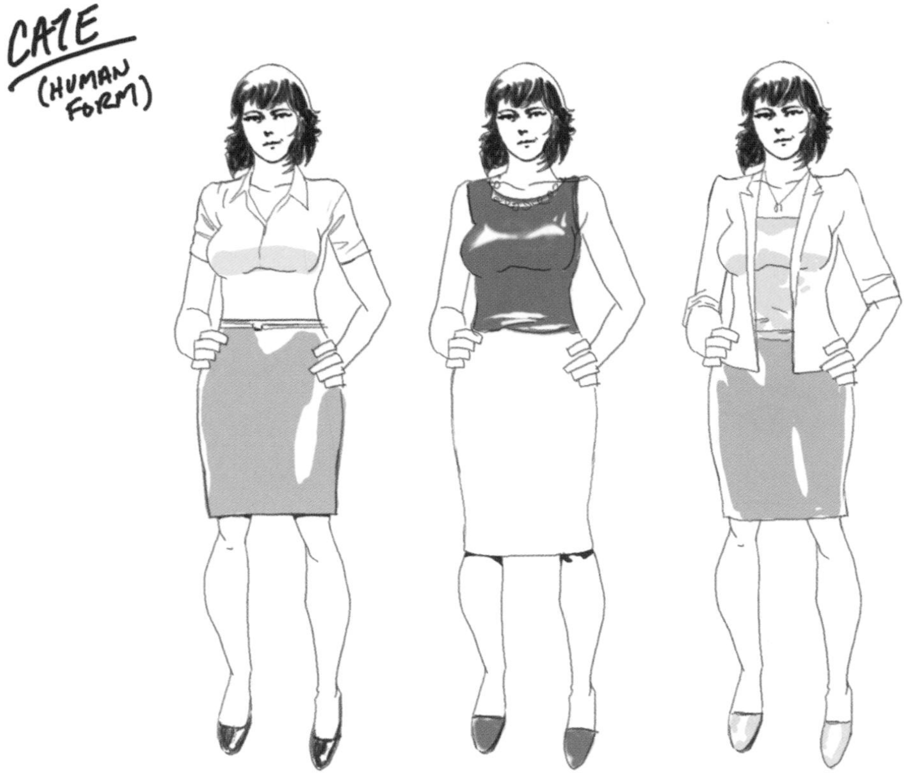
CATE
(HUMAN FORM)

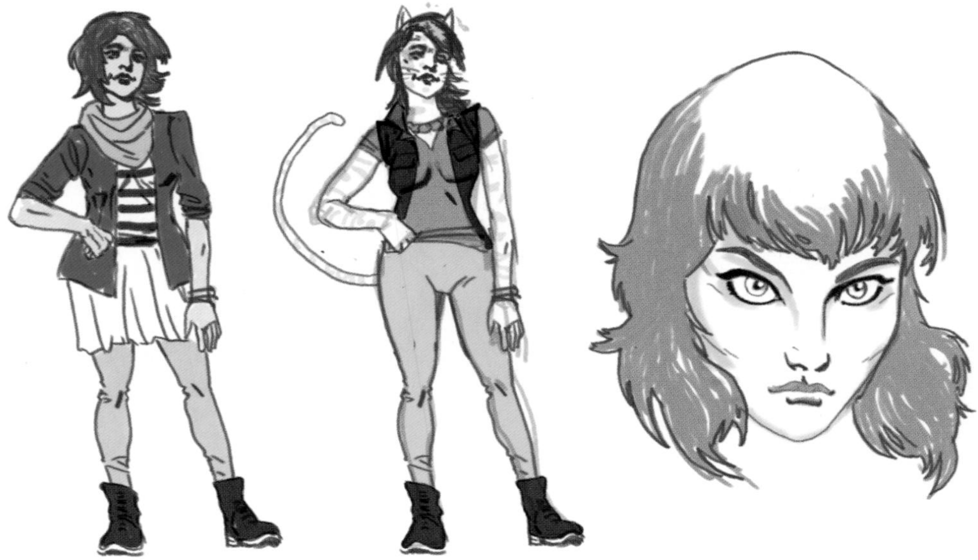

There was a longer road to finding our Cate. I haven't drawn too many characters with sex appeal in my career, so Margaret kept encouraging me to go further in trying to find a visual way to depict a primal appeal. Finally Margaret sharpened her pencil and designed Cate's nightclub outfit herself. It's really cool seeing Margaret's drawings.

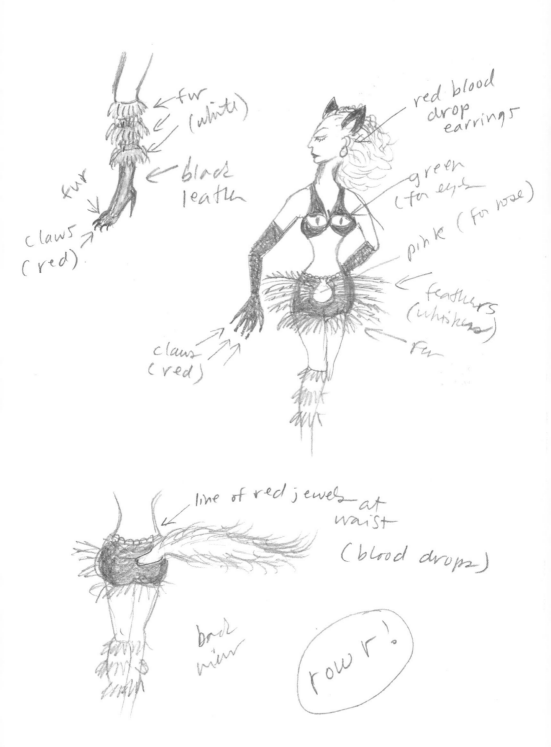

fur (white)

fur

claws (red).

black leather

claws (red)

red blood drop earrings

green (for eyes)

pink (for nose)

feathers (whiskers)

Fur

line of red jewels at waist

(blood drops)

back view

rowr!

Margaret Atwood: I designed the nightclub outfit to go with the band name: Pussies in Boots. So there are boots, of course. The tops are cat eyes, the bottoms have cat noses and whiskers. And gloves with claws that are even longer than their real claws. Blood-drop earrings. I'm kinda literal minded.

CATE
CAT FORM

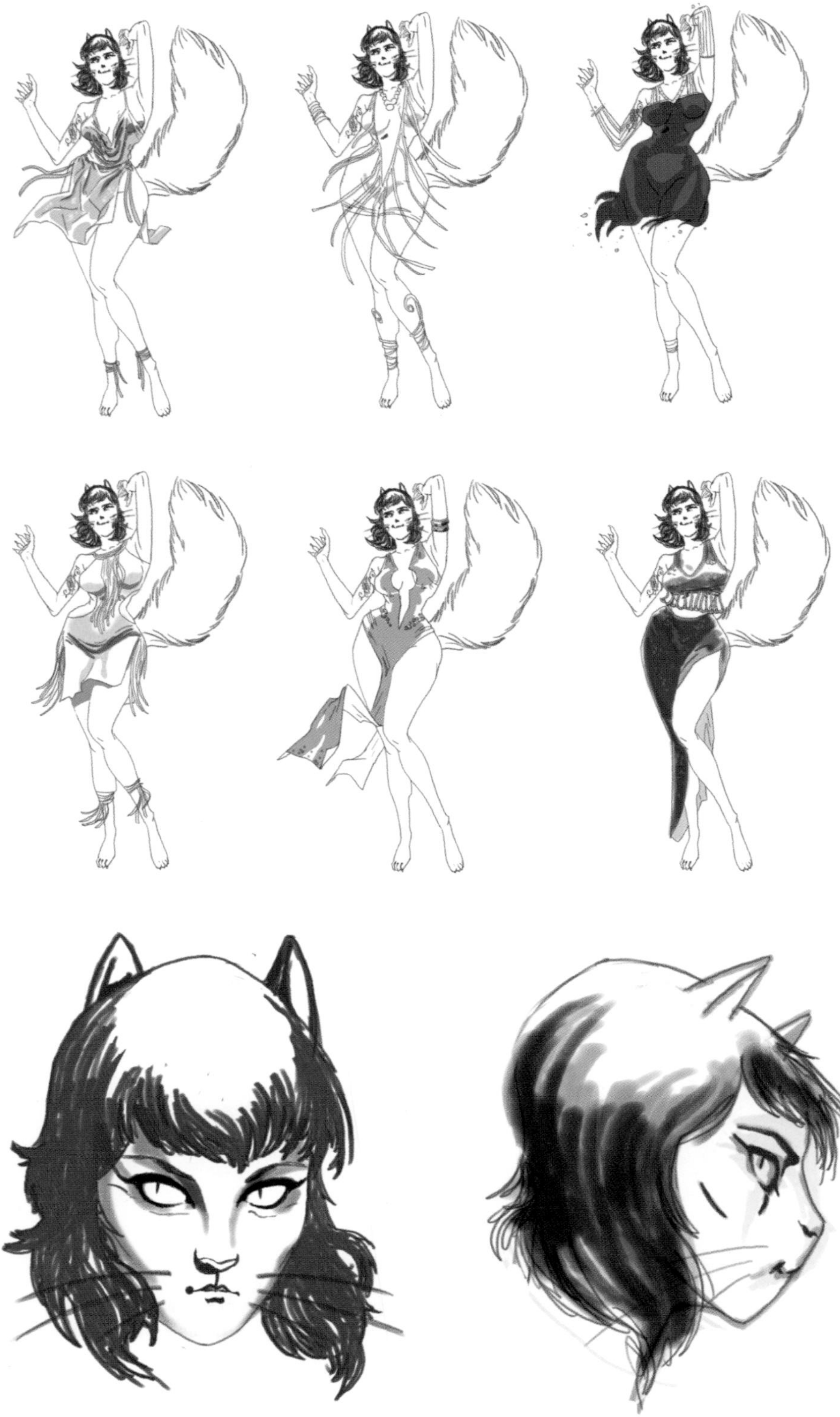

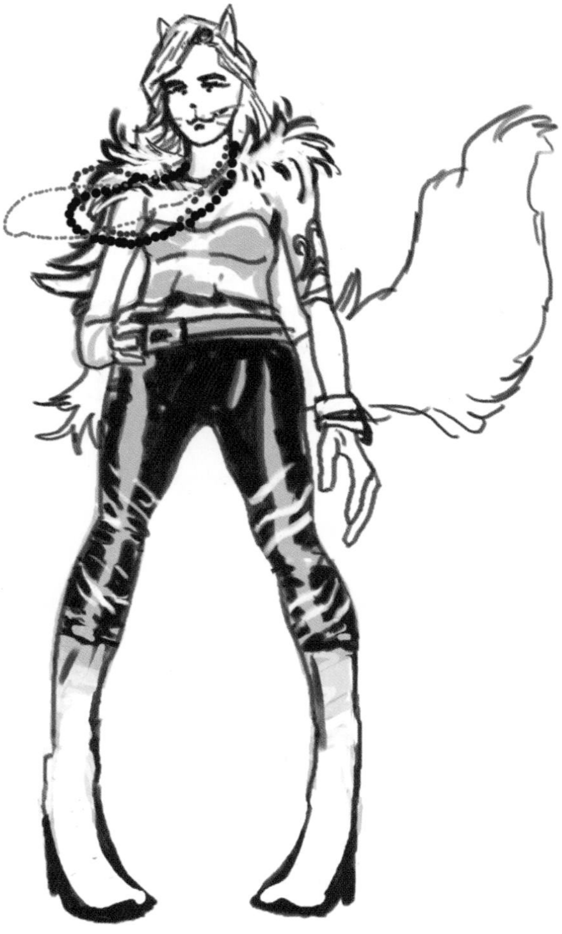

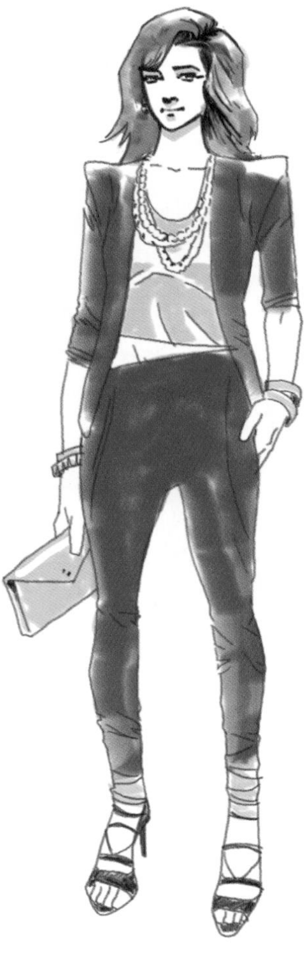

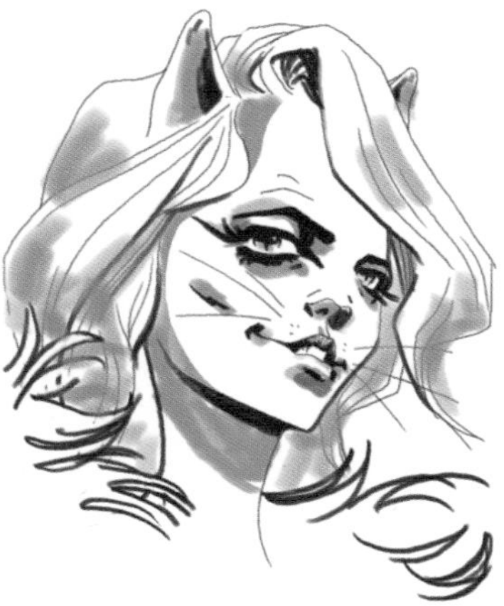

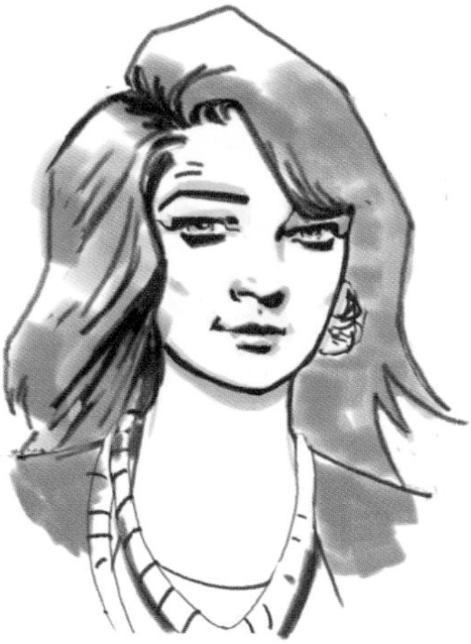

DR. MUROID

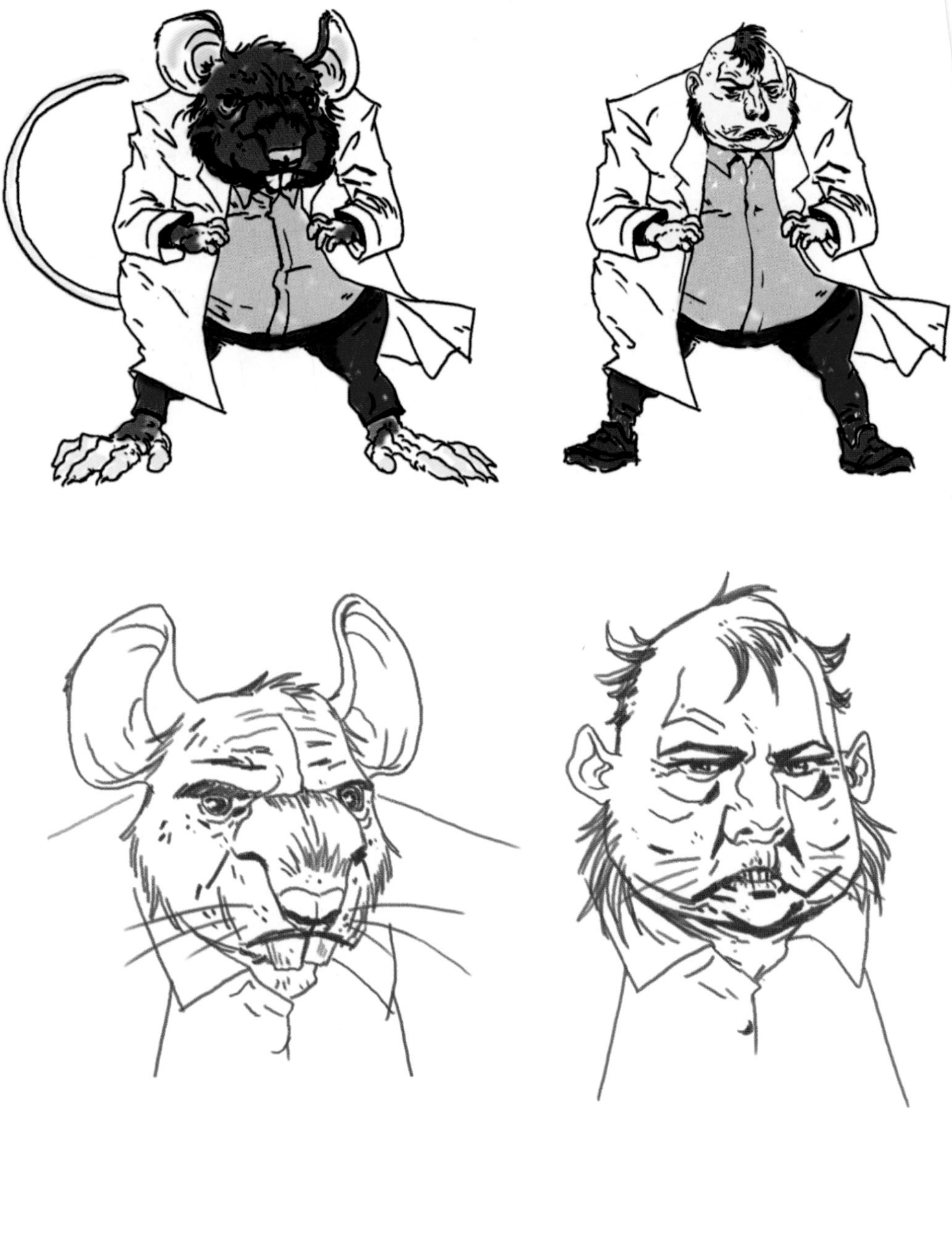

Villains are very fun to draw, and Muroid is no exception. Drawing his menacingly evil facial expressions is a highlight when I'm at the drawing board.

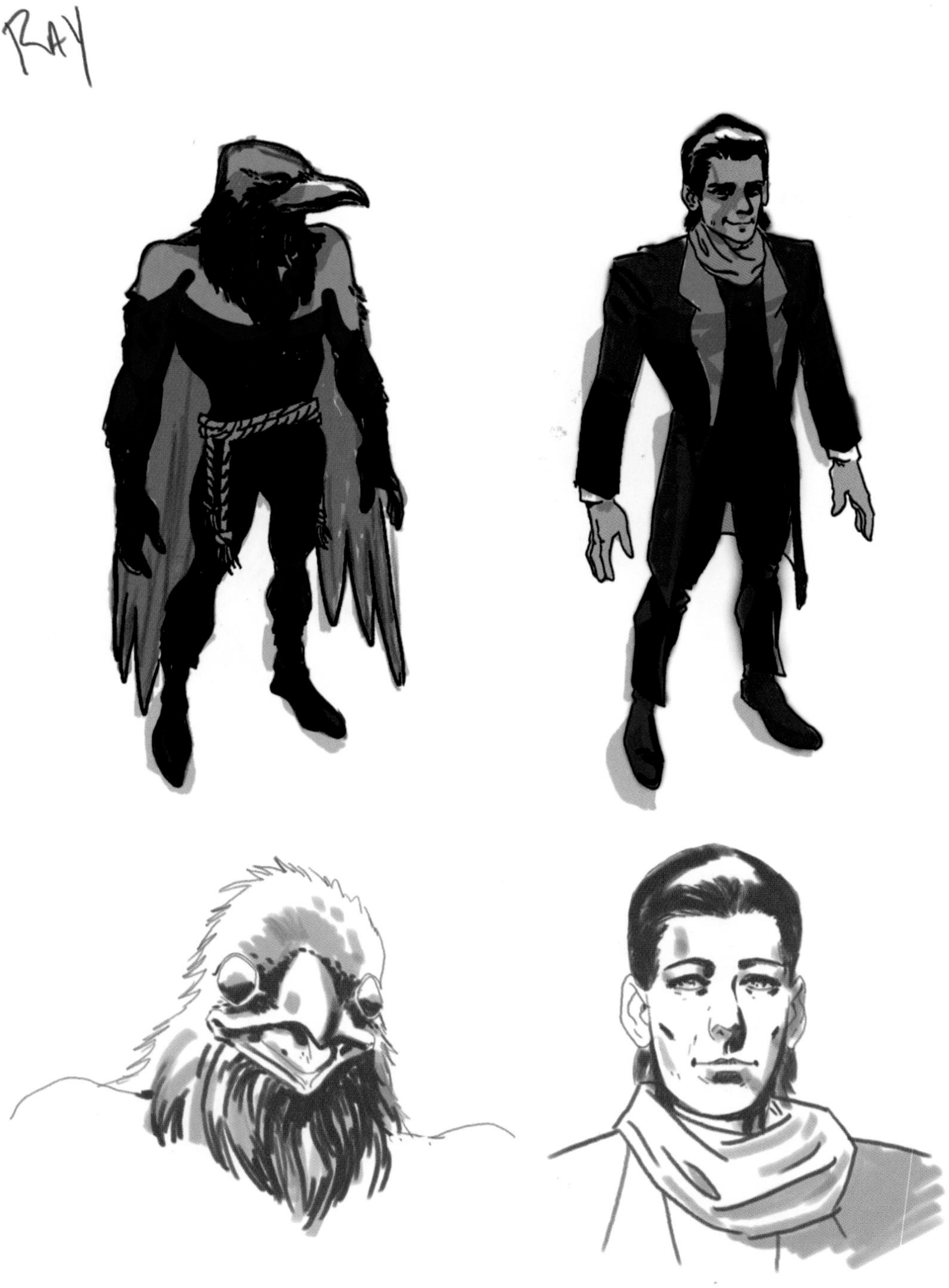
RAY

As a potential romantic rival for Cate's affections, Ray is quite fun too. He is Anishinaabe, the First Nations people of the area in which Margaret grew up.

COUNT CATULA

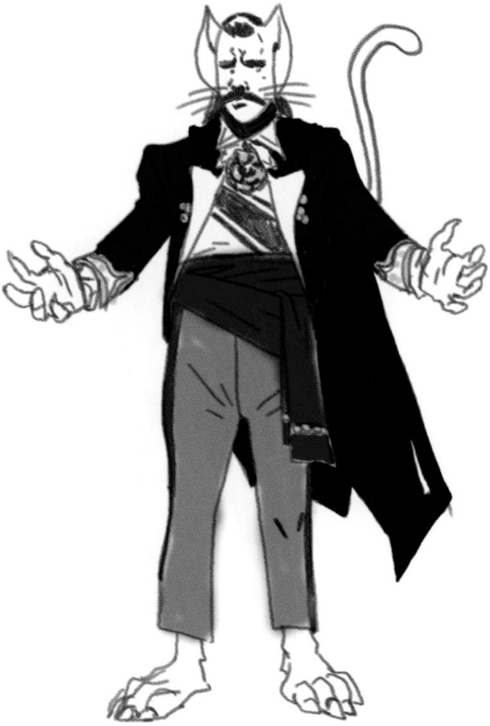

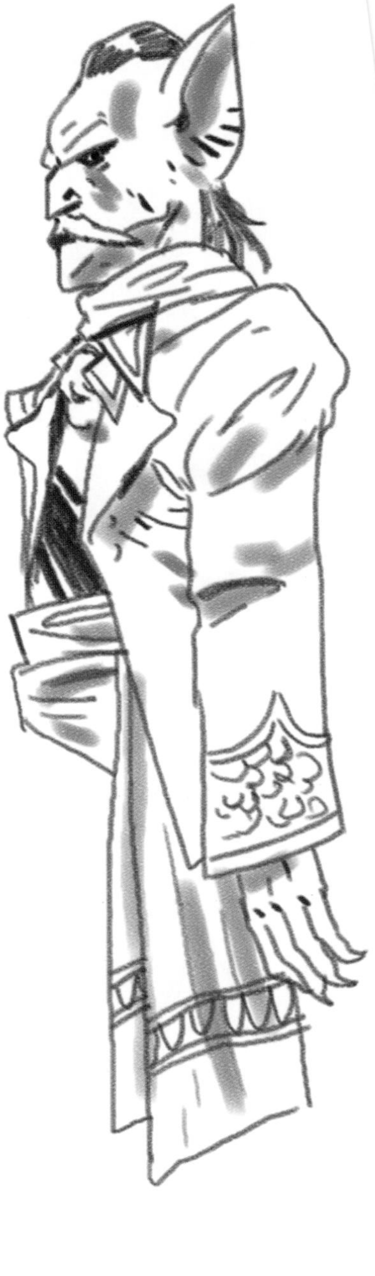

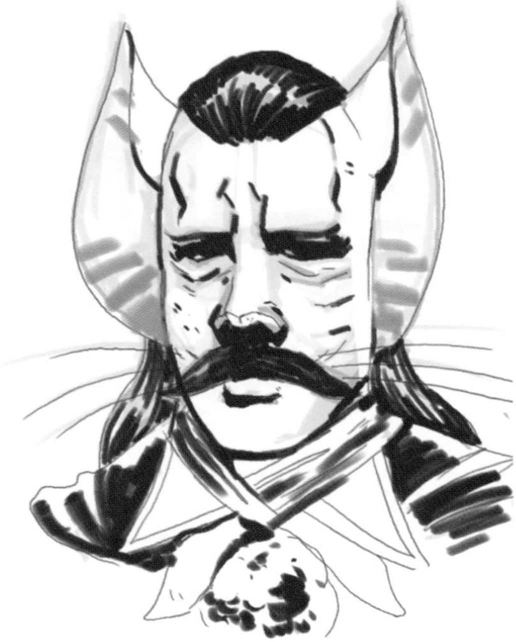

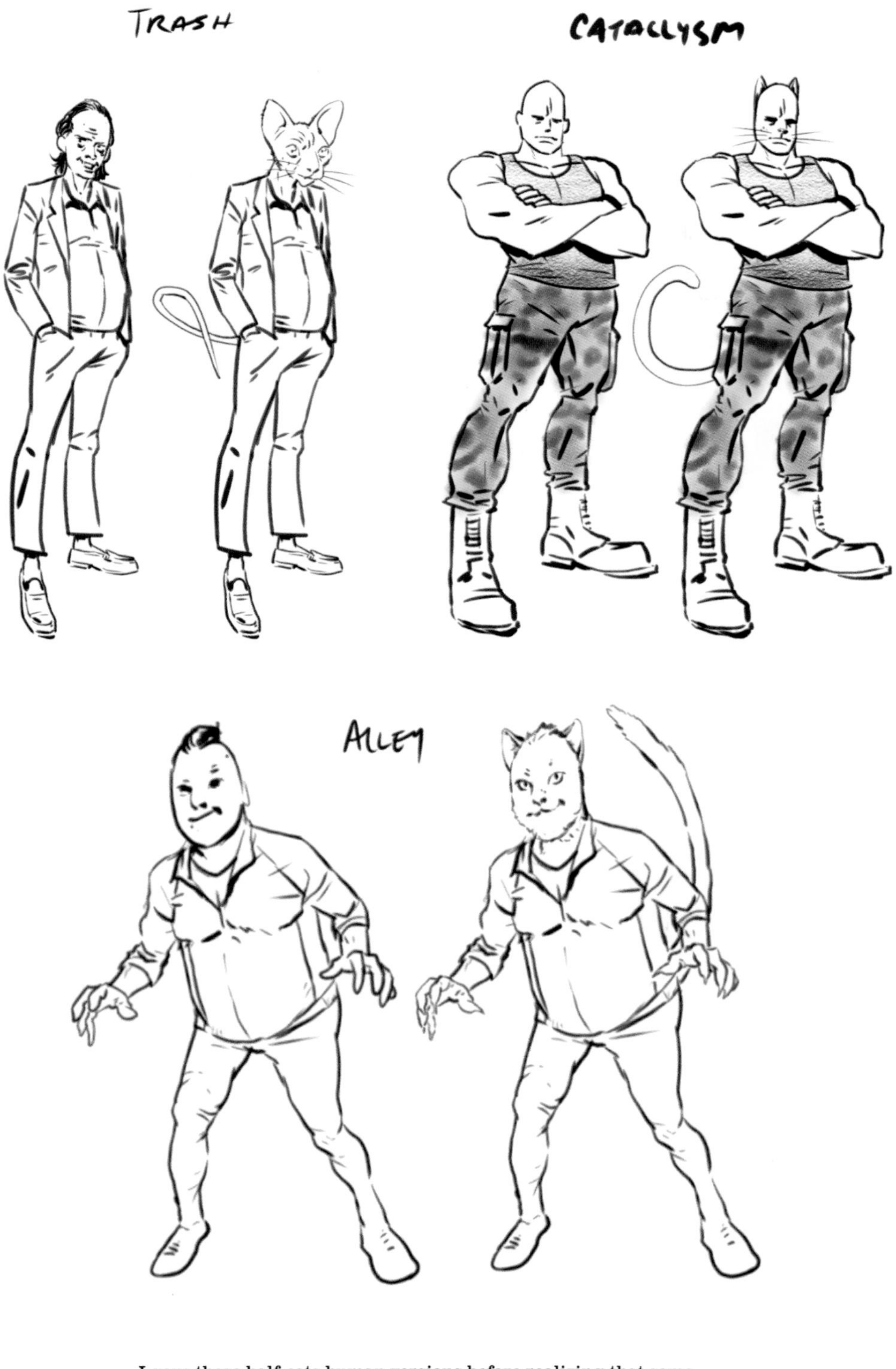
TRASH
CATACLYSM
ALLEY

I gave these half-cats human versions before realizing that some half-cats don't have human versions!

CATFISH

Bubastis

HANSEL & CATTYL

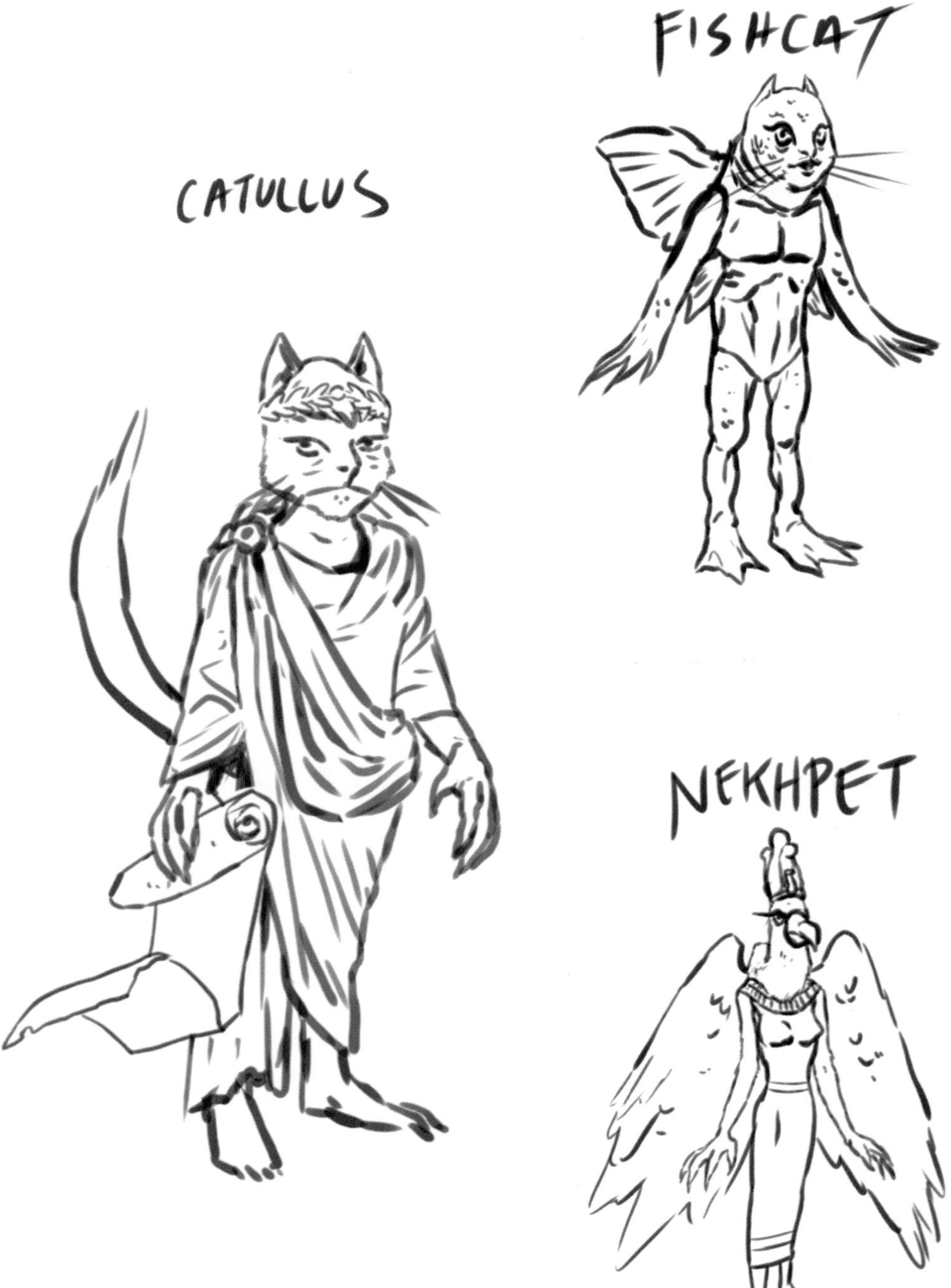
FISHCAT
CATULLUS
NEKHPET

Cats and cats and cats.

CAT O'NINETALES

BABUSHKAT

CAT O'NINETALES

OLTOPUSS

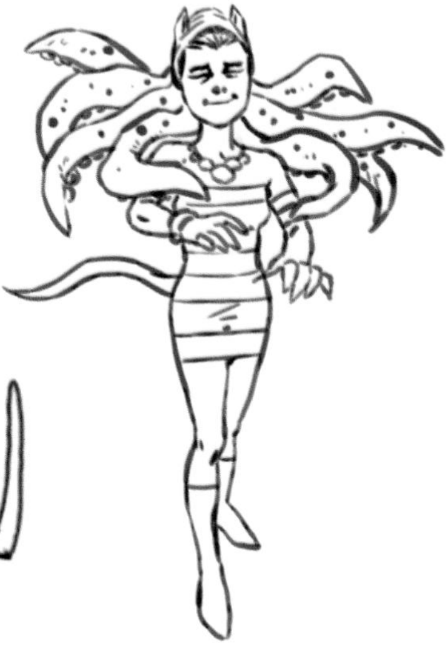

BARNBORN

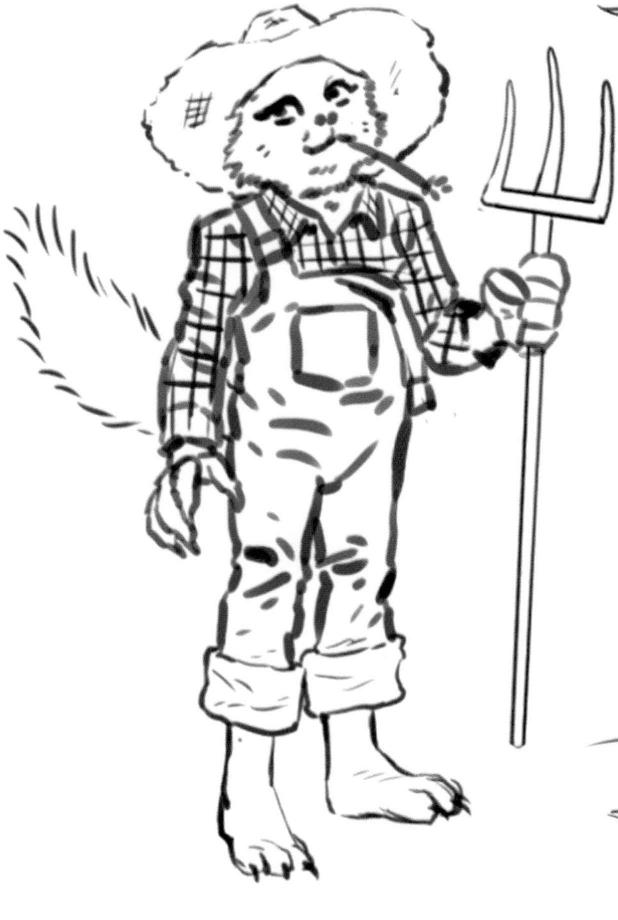

OLTOPUSS

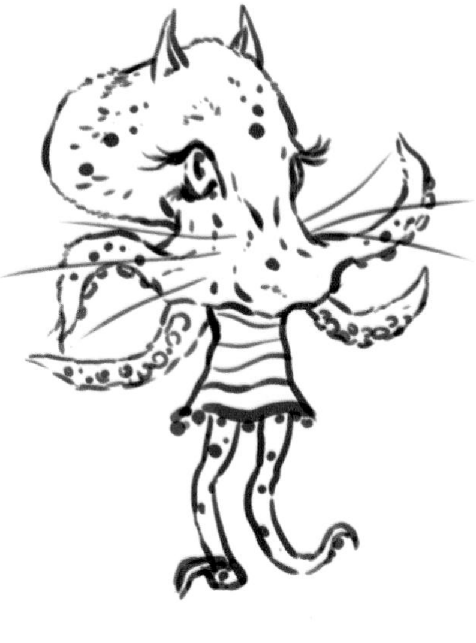

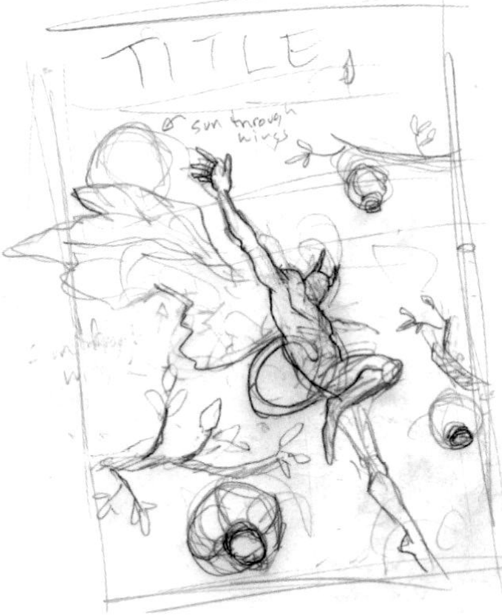
TITLE
or sun through wings

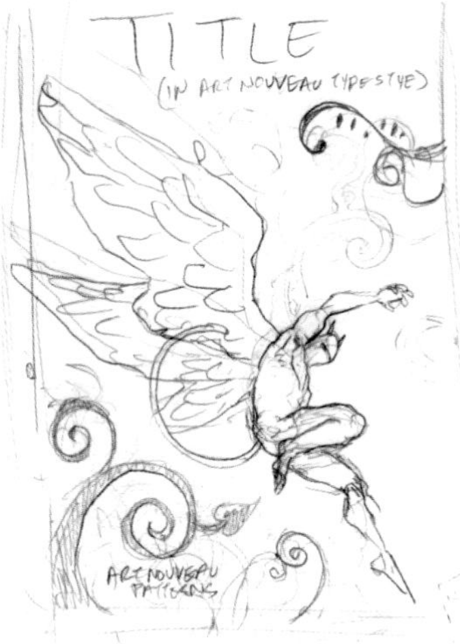
TITLE
(IN ART NOUVEAU TYPESTYE)
ART NOUVEAU PATTERNS

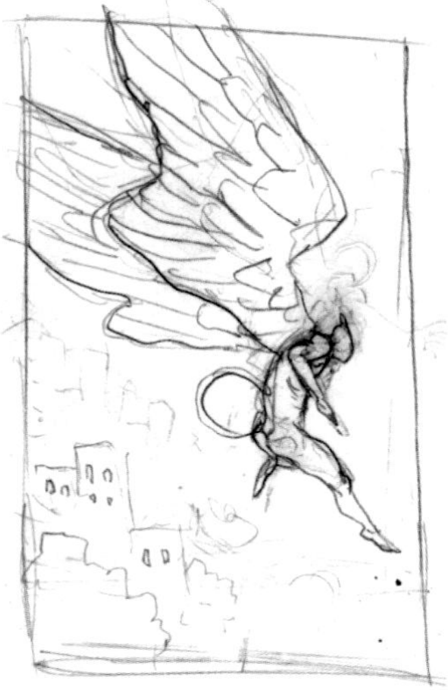

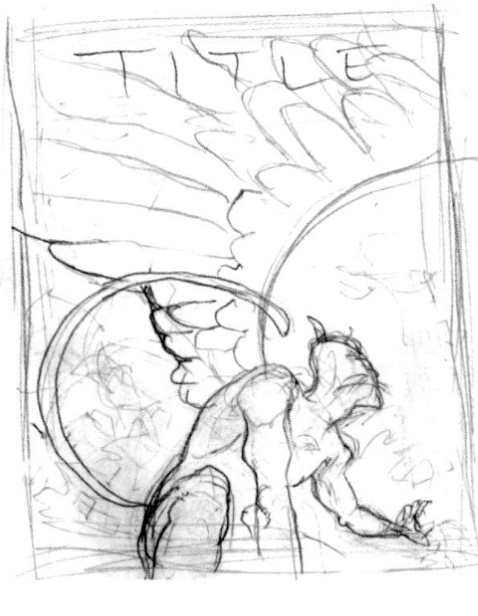
TITLE

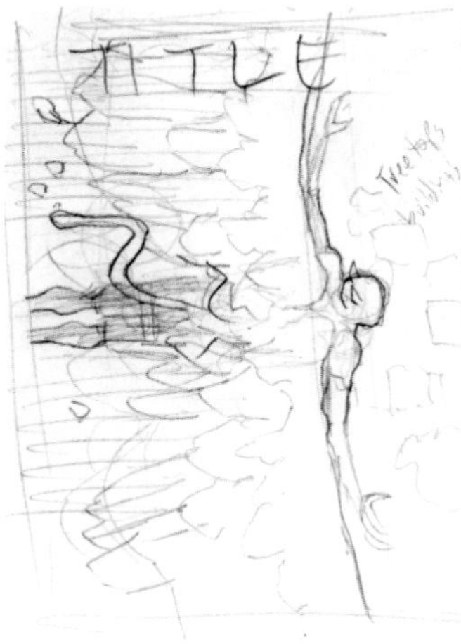
TITLE

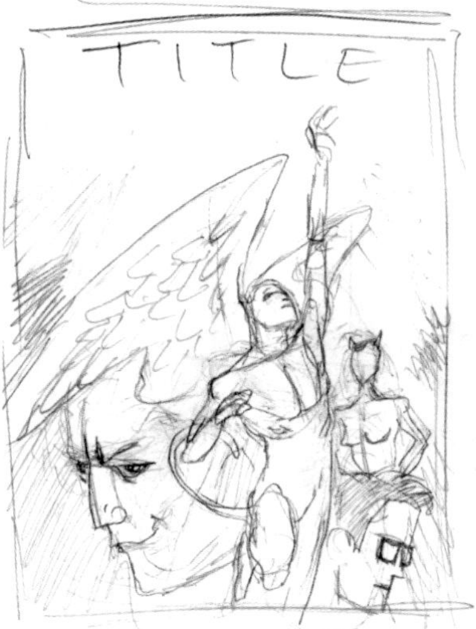
TITLE

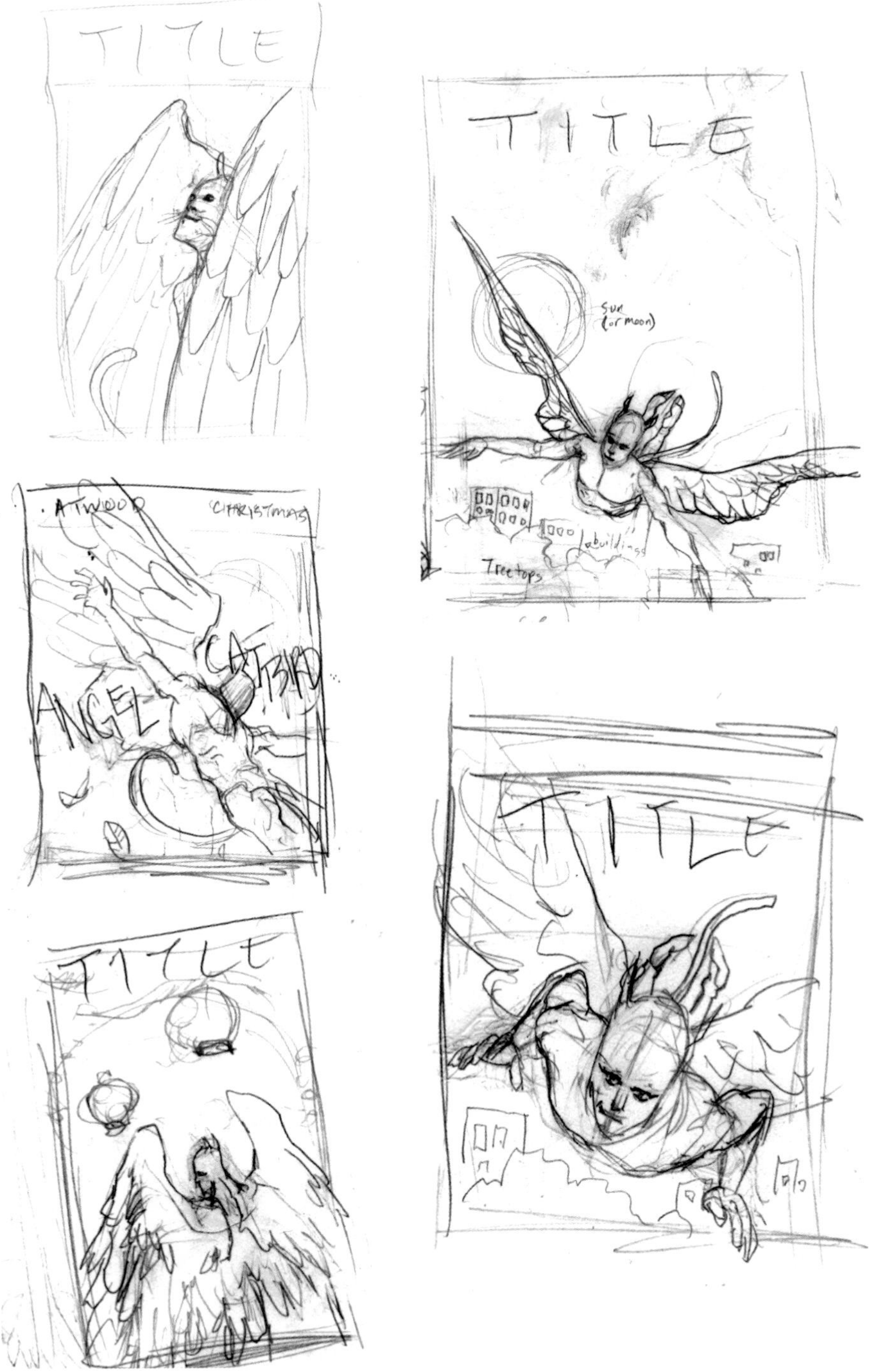
TITLE
TITLE
Sun
(or moon)
buildings
Treetops
ATWOOD
CHRISTMAS
ANGEL
CATBIRD
TITLE
TITLE

Cover thumbnails for the first volume of a book can be daunting. How does one encapsulate the feeling of a series that hasn't yet been drawn? By doing lots of versions!

COLOR PROCESS by TAMRA BONVILLAIN

1. First, I start with the black-and-white line art from Johnnie.
2. I send the pages off to a flatter. A flatter is an assistant that helps colorists by separating all the different parts of the page for easy selection. Final color choices are made by the colorist; the flats have no bearing on those decisions. These flats are by Fernando Argüello.

3. Using the flats, I adjust the colors to achieve the palette I'm going for. I do the original flats in local colors (the base color of an object, not affected by colored lighting), and then make some adjustments to help shift and/or unify things. The version shown here is after I made it a little warmer and more yellow overall.
4. Next comes the rendering. These next few rendering images are not necessarily shown in the order in which they were applied. In Photoshop, I make rendering layers that apply different effects, and I can jump between them as I'm working. These images show each layer applied one by one. Here, I'm using a saturated magenta shadow layer for the first shadow pass.

5. To tone down the shadow saturation and deepen the shadows to give things more form, I throw another shadow layer on top.
6. To bring focus to some of the areas, I apply a warmer, more saturated light layer.

7. At this stage I add the final highlights to the lit focal areas.
8. In the final few steps I blend the harsh edges that can't be easily defined from the flatting stage, colorize some of the line art subtly, and then make a small adjustment over everything to increase the contrast a touch.

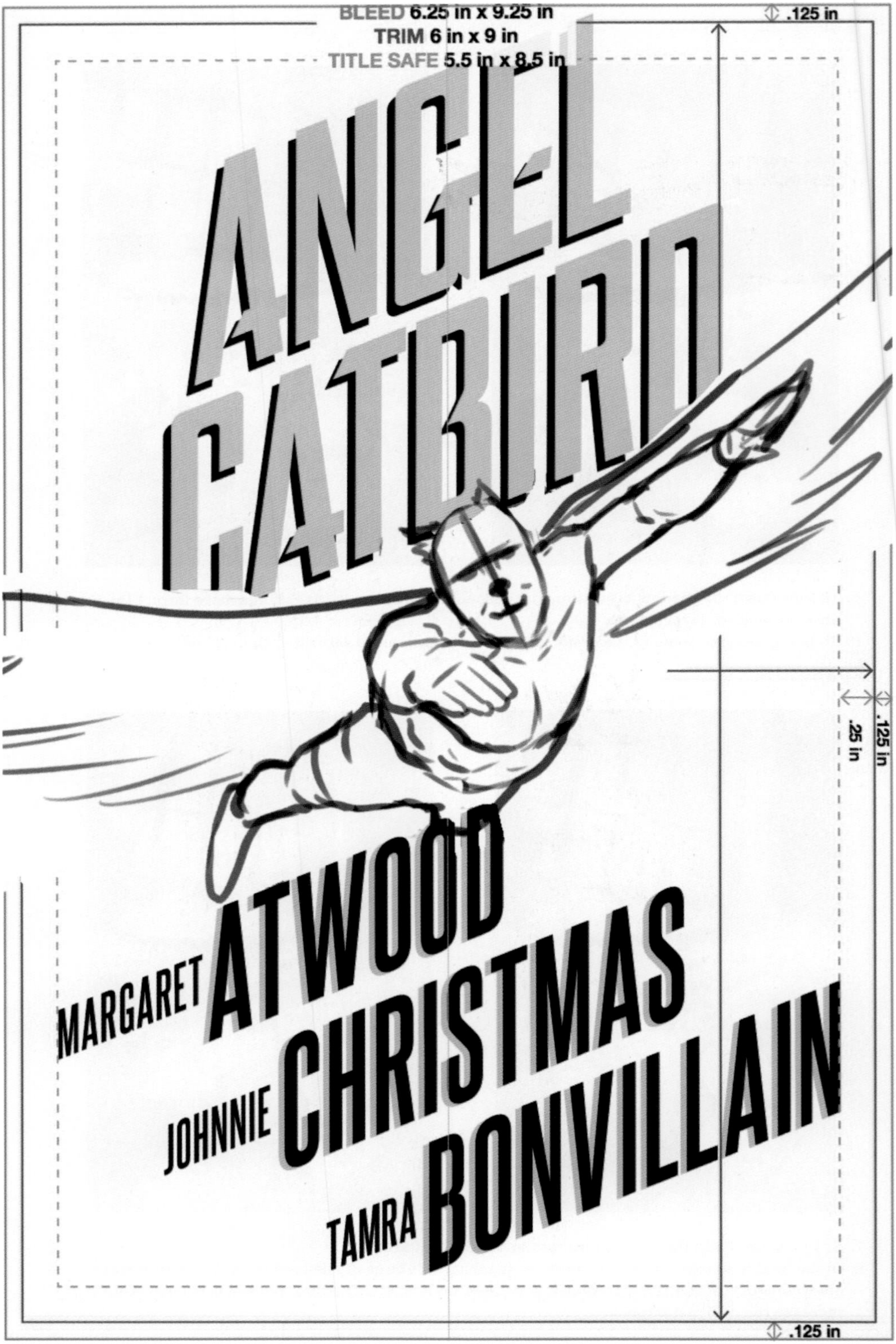
BLEED 6.25 in x 9.25 in
TRIM 6 in x 9 in
TITLE SAFE 5.5 in x 8.5 in
.125 in
ANGEL
CATBIRD
.25 in
.125 in
MARGARET ATWOOD
JOHNNIE CHRISTMAS
TAMRA BONVILLAIN
.125 in

Sketches for the *Complete Angel Catbird* cover.

Character design for volume 2's fierce
new warrior, Atheen-Owl.

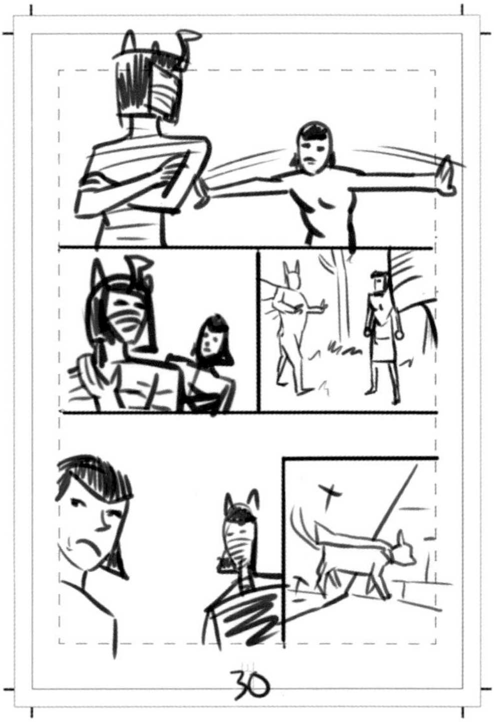
30
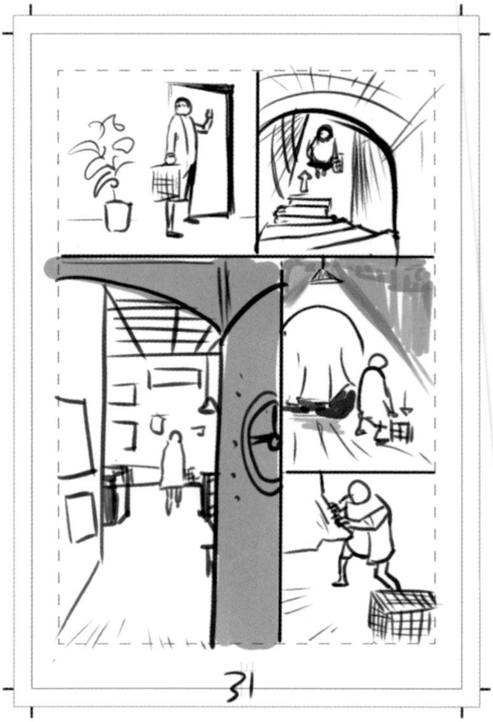
31
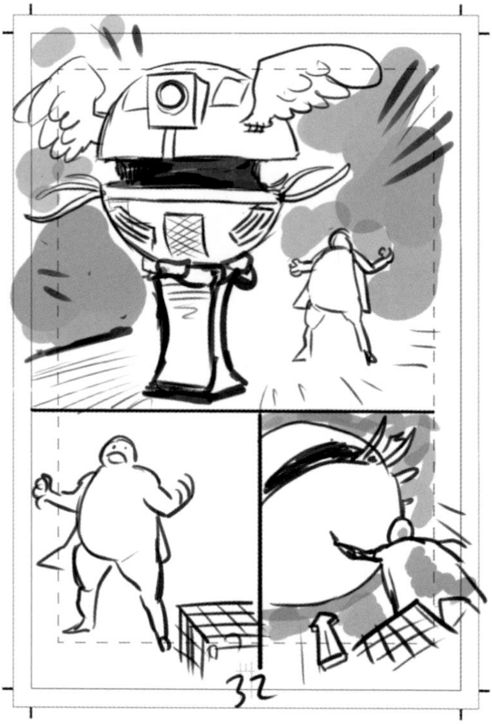
32
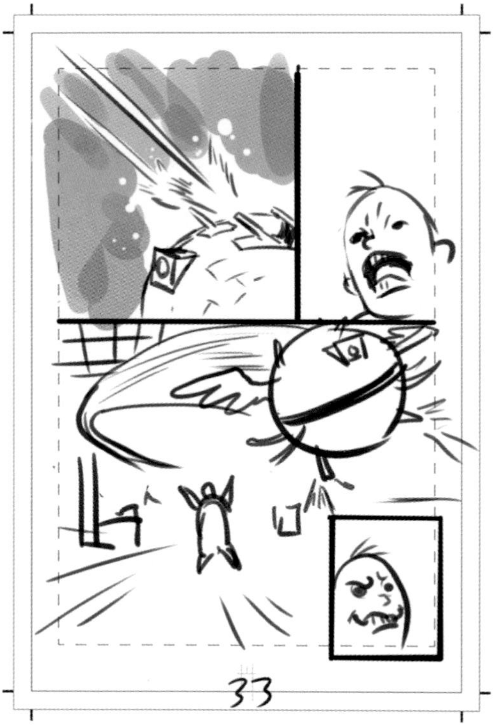
33

Here is a look into my part of the process of bringing *Angel Catbird* from script to page. I start with thumbnail drawings that show placement and page composition. I send these over to Margaret and our editors, Daniel and Hope, for feedback.

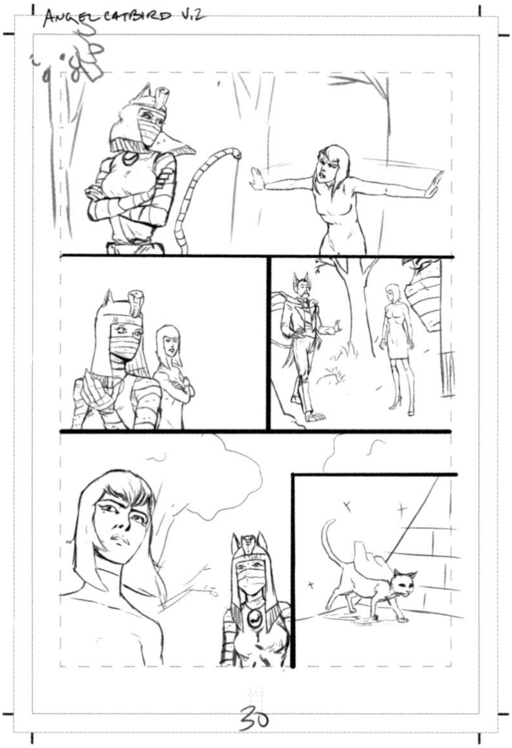
ANGELCATBIRD V.2
30

Pencils are then drawn digitally and . . .

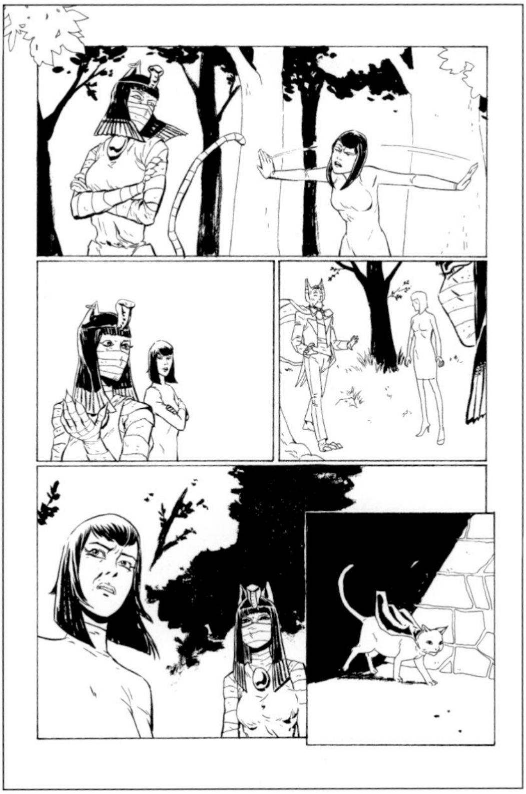

. . . final drawings are done in ink, with a watercolor brush. Details are added, and the drawings are clarified.

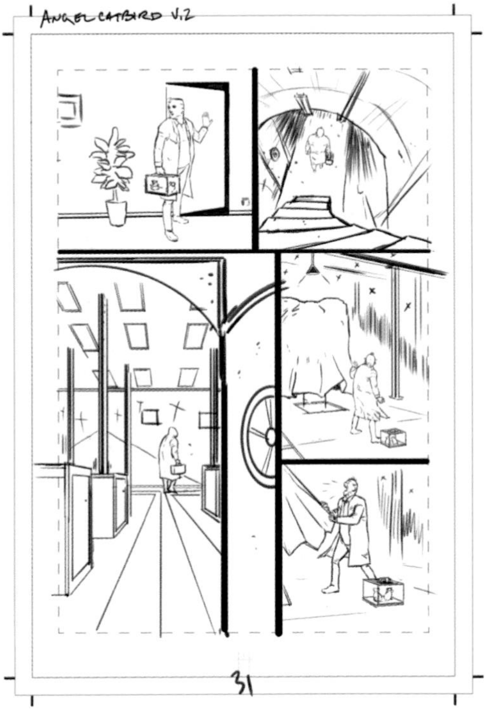
ANGEL CATBIRD V.2
31

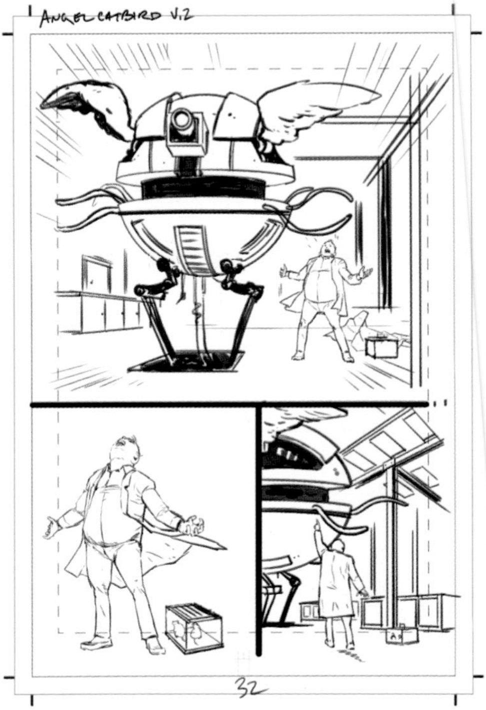
ANGEL CATBIRD V.2
32

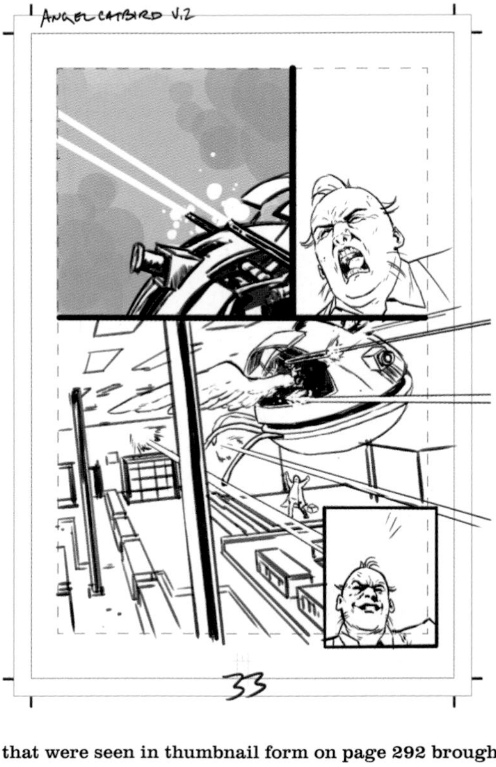
ANGEL CATBIRD V.2
33

Here we see the pages that were seen in thumbnail form on page 292 brought to the pencils stage. These pages didn't make it into the book in this form. Margaret wanted Muroid's lair to look more like a rat's underground nest than a science lab—a great idea. Also, the DRAT in this version is more sleek and mean. Margaret wanted it to look more like an actual cat toy . . . with laser beams!

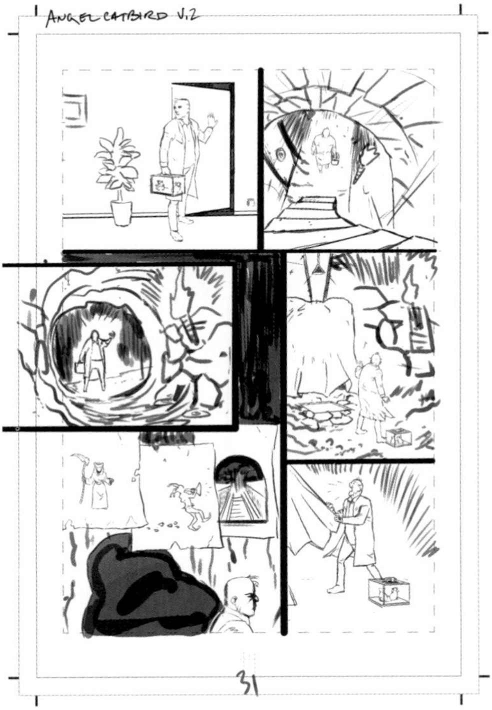
ANGEL CATBIRD V.2
31

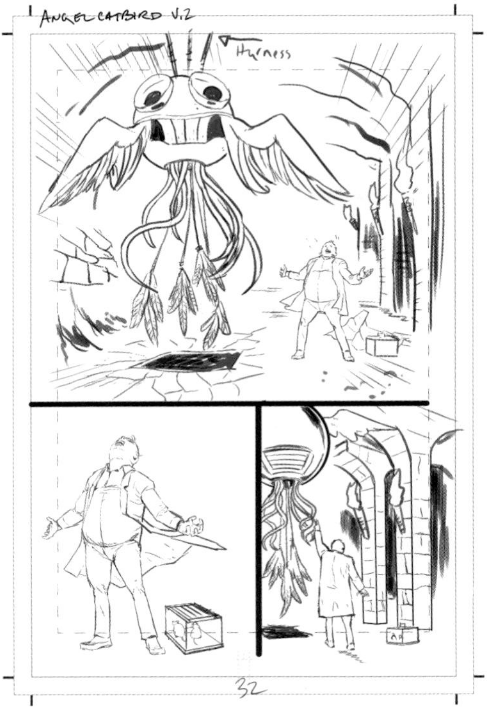
ANGEL CATBIRD V.2
Harness
32

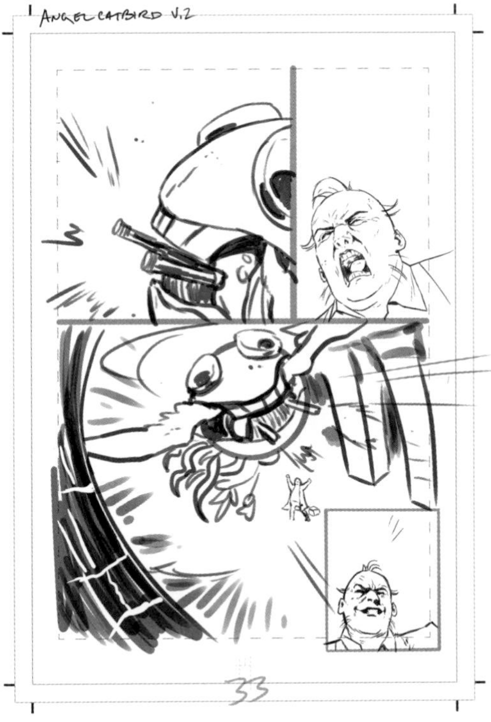
ANGEL CATBIRD V.2
33

Revised pencils for lair and DRAT.

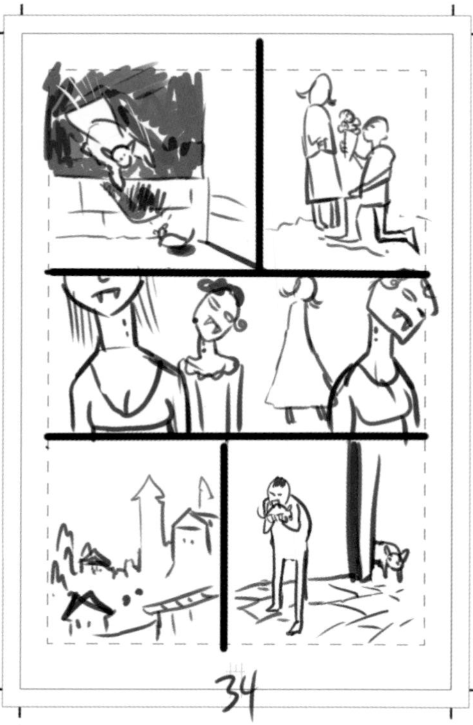
34

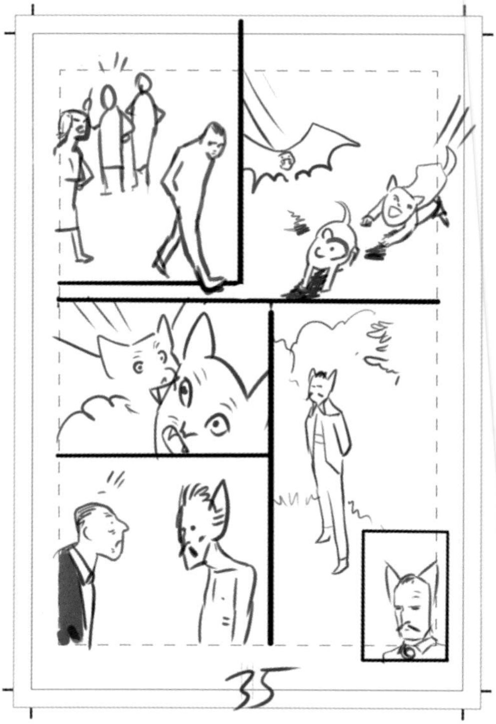
35

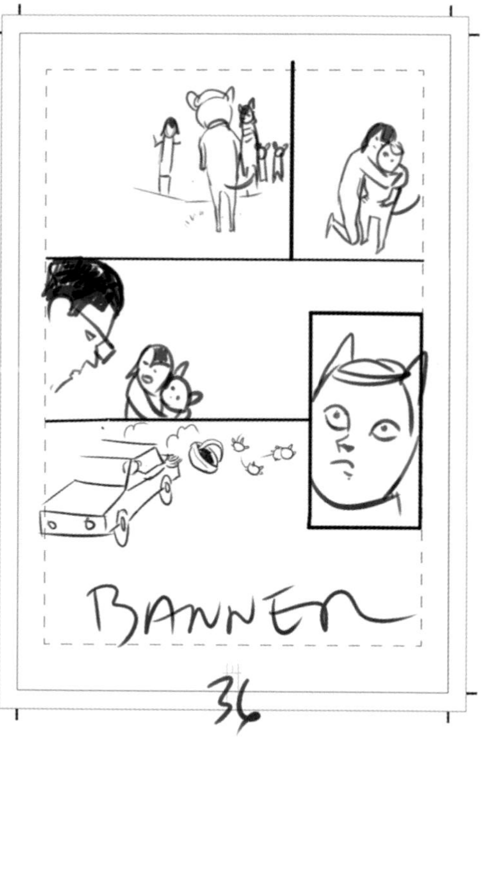
BANNER
36

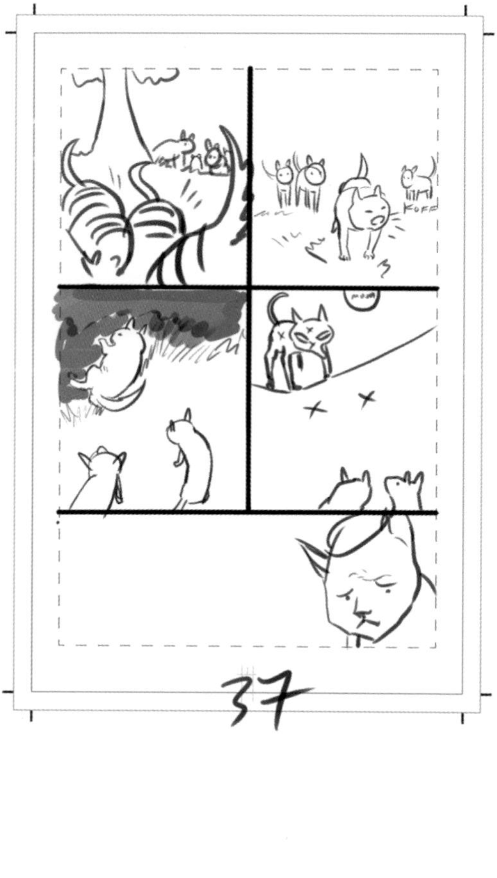
KOFF
37

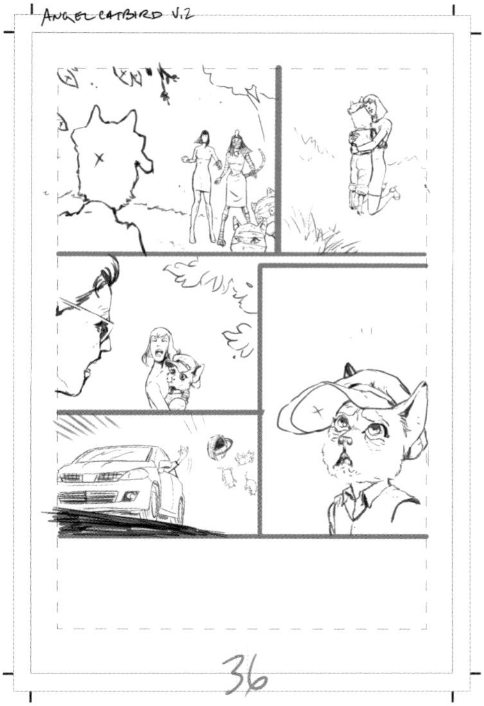
ANGEL CATBIRD V.2
36

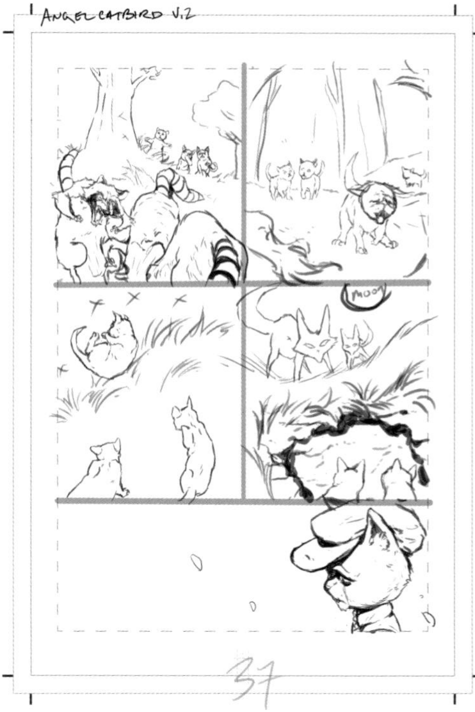
ANGEL CATBIRD V.2
37

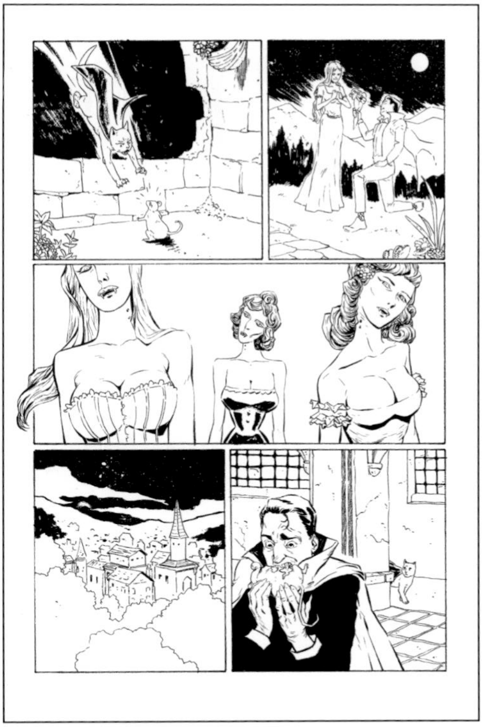

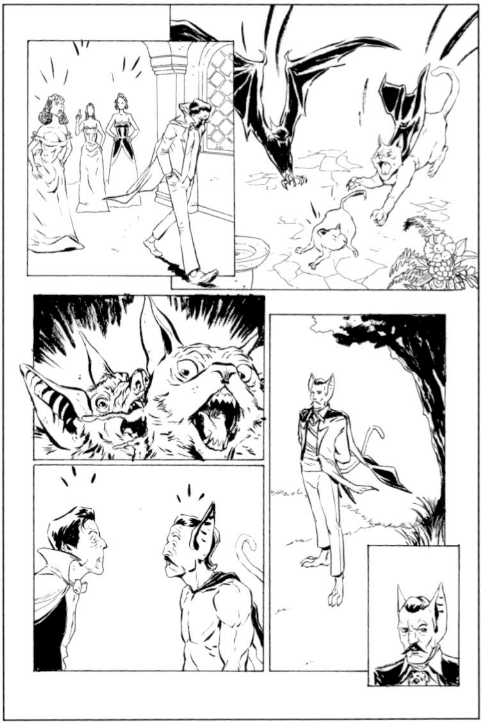

The origin of Count Catula, from thumbs to inks. I really enjoyed this sequence. Dracula seems so hapless.

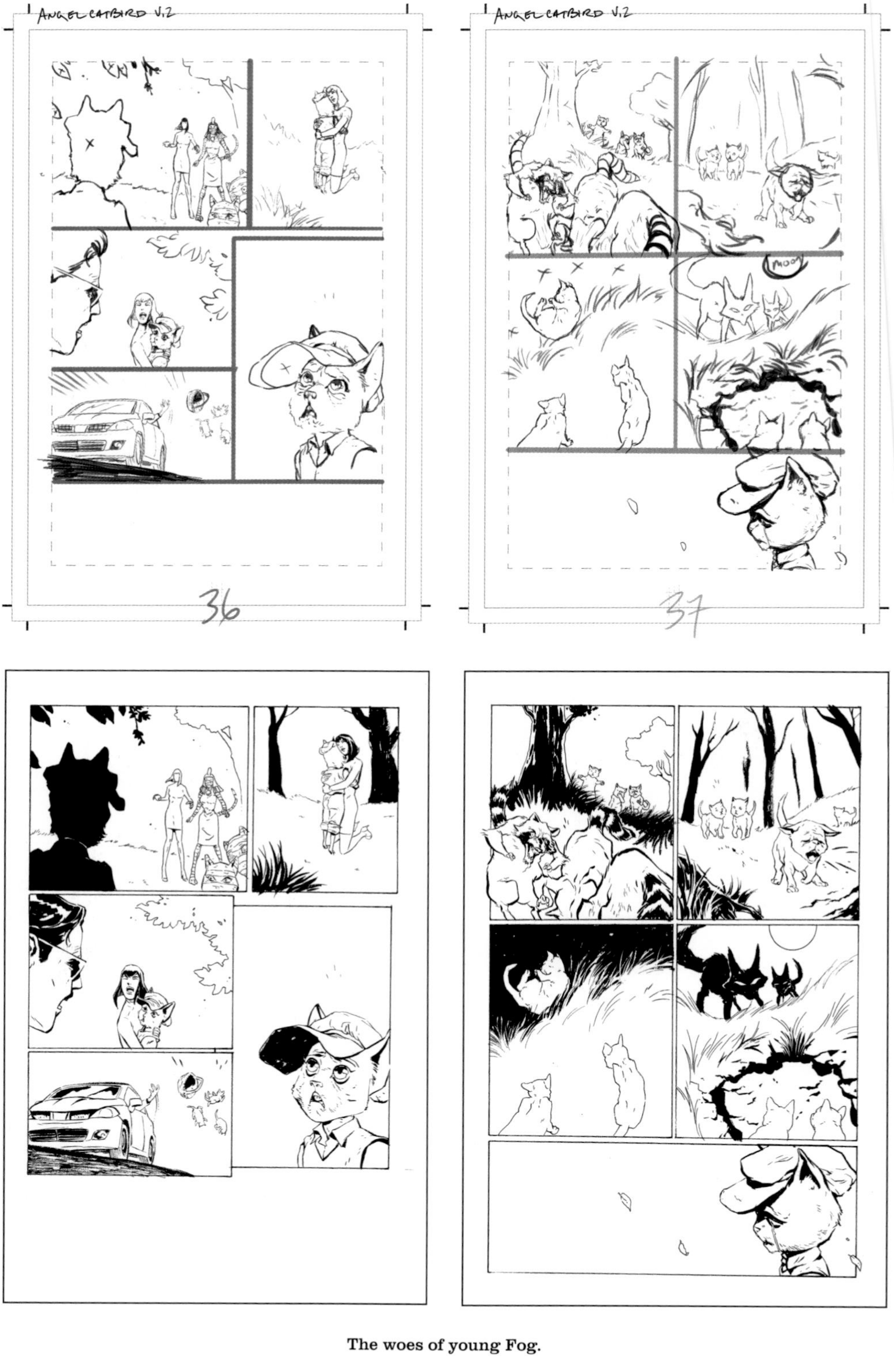
ANGELCATBIRD V.2
ANGELCATBIRD V.2
36
37

The woes of young Fog.

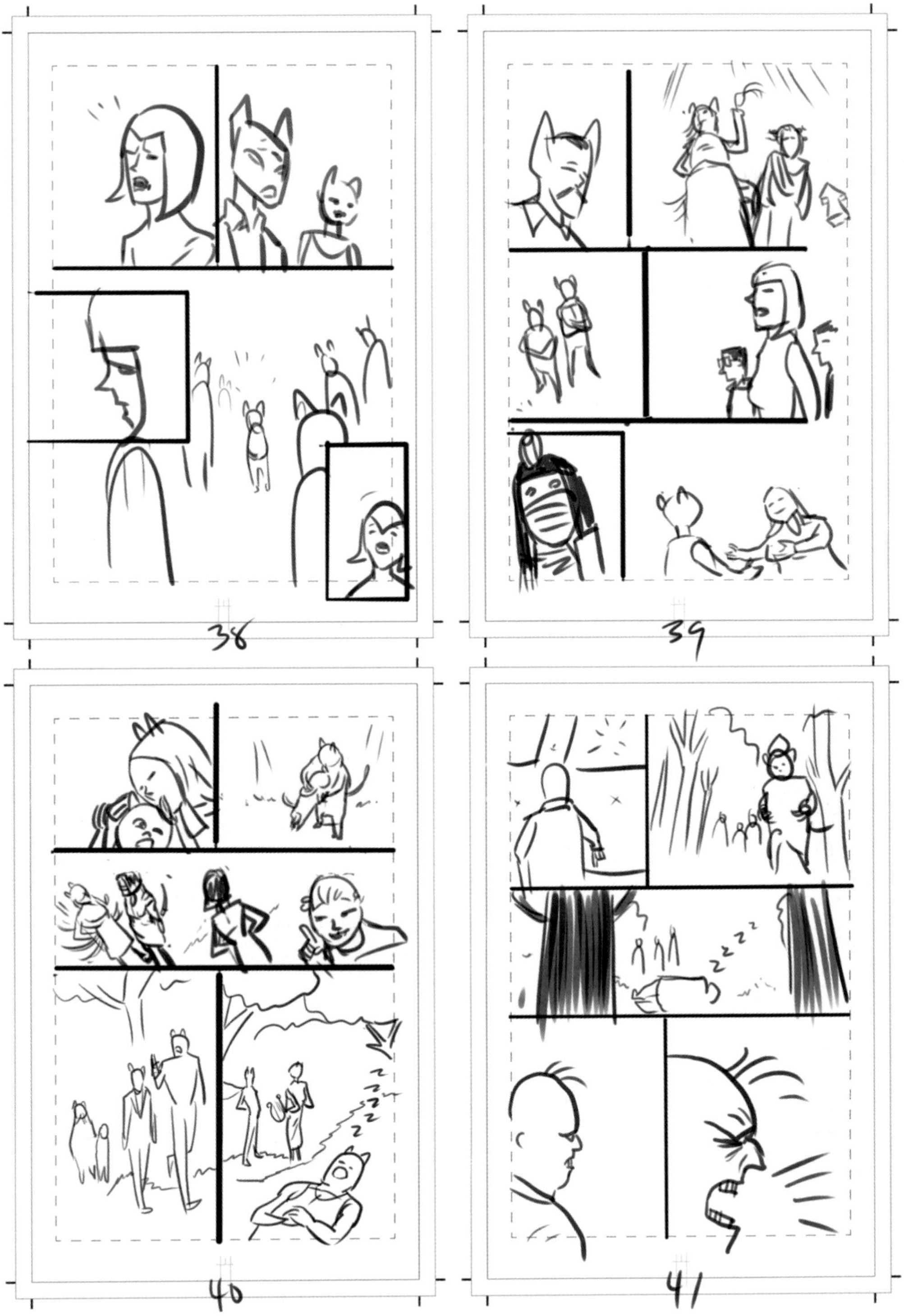
38
39
40
41

More thumbs.

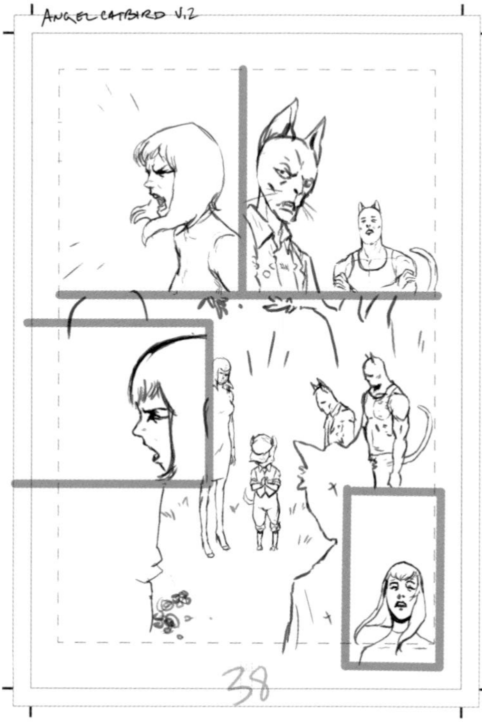
ANGEL CATBIRD V.2
38

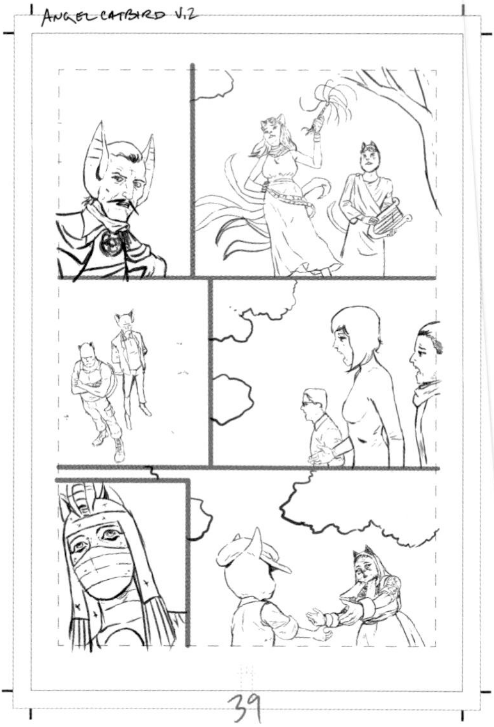
ANGEL CATBIRD V.2
39

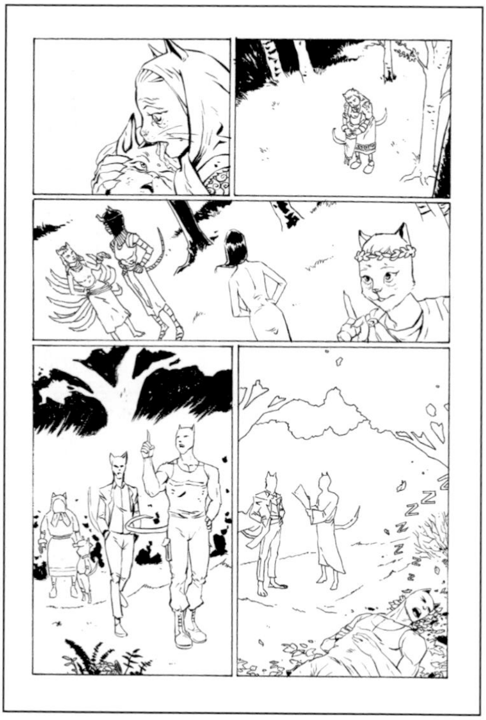

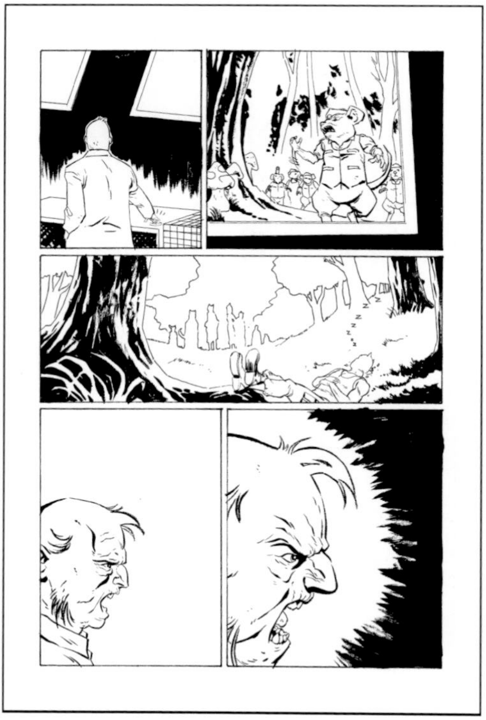

One of the unique challenges of drawing *Angel Catbird* is the many speaking roles on a given page. I need to find ways to position the characters in respect to their speaking order—in comics that are read from left to right, the person who speaks first is preferably on the left side of the panel.

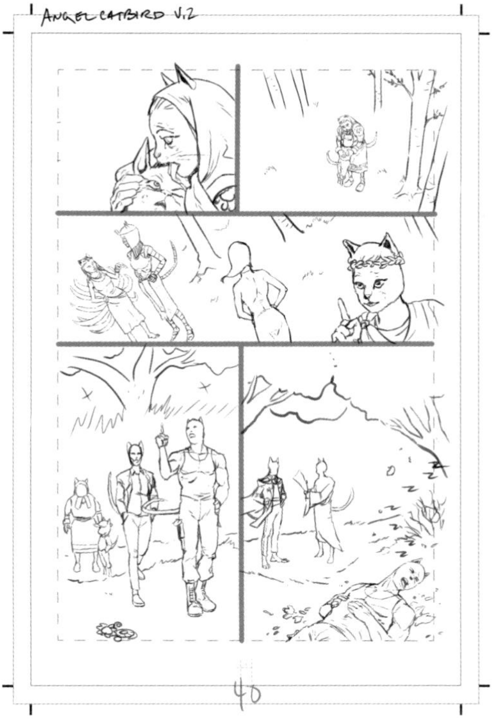
ANGEL CATBIRD V.2
40
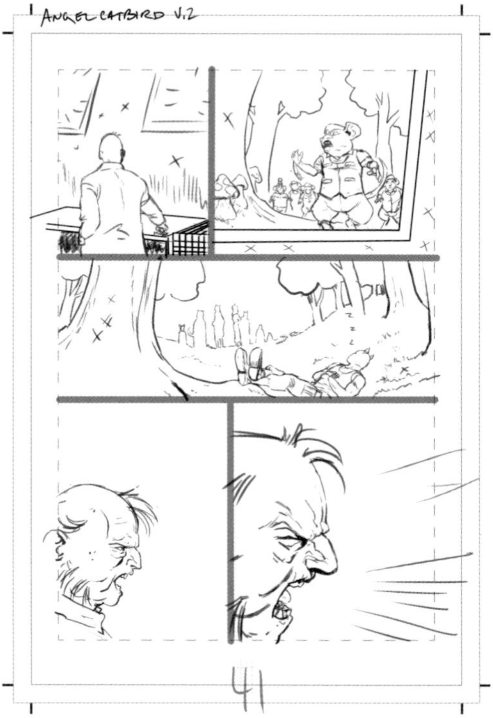
ANGEL CATBIRD V.2
41
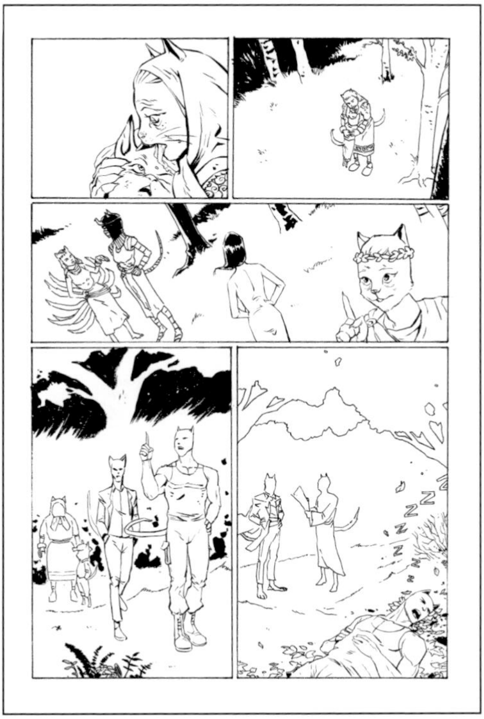
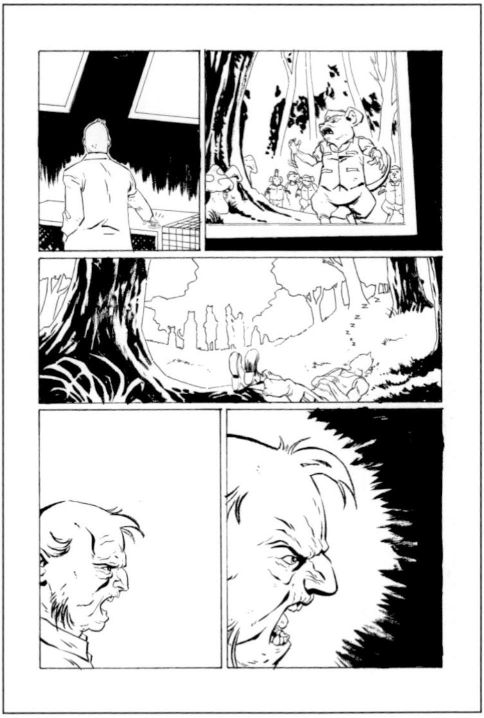

One of my favorite things to draw is Muroid emoting. He's always wound up.
That makes for fun villainy.

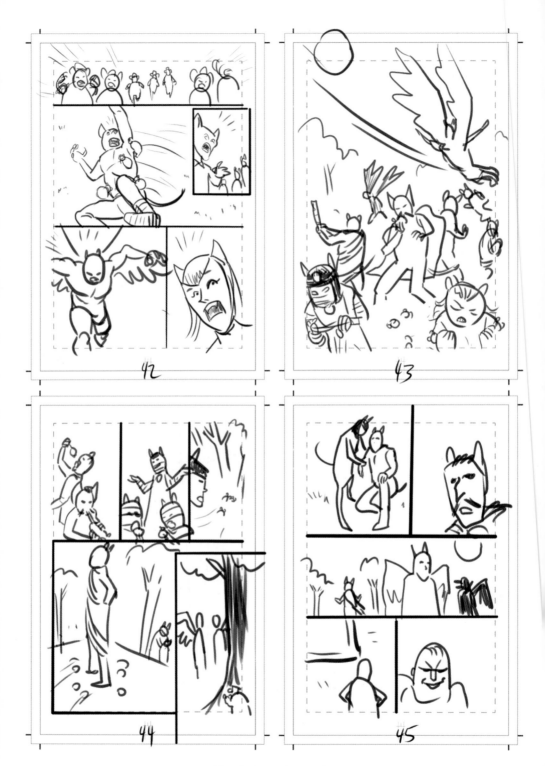

Thumbs for the big battle.

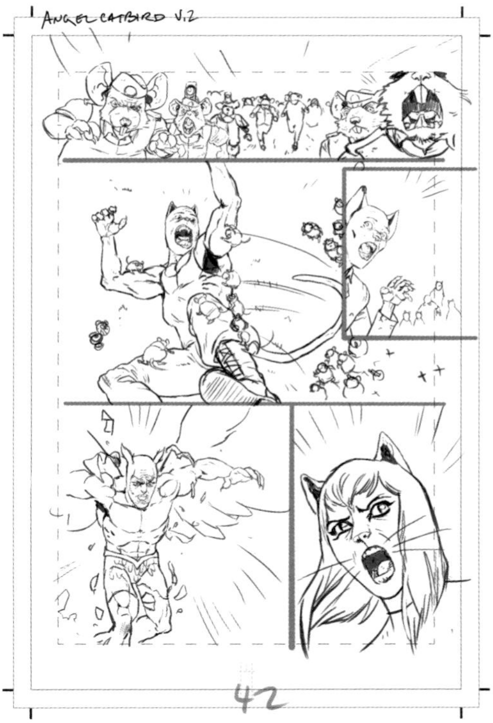
ANGEL CATBIRD V.2
42
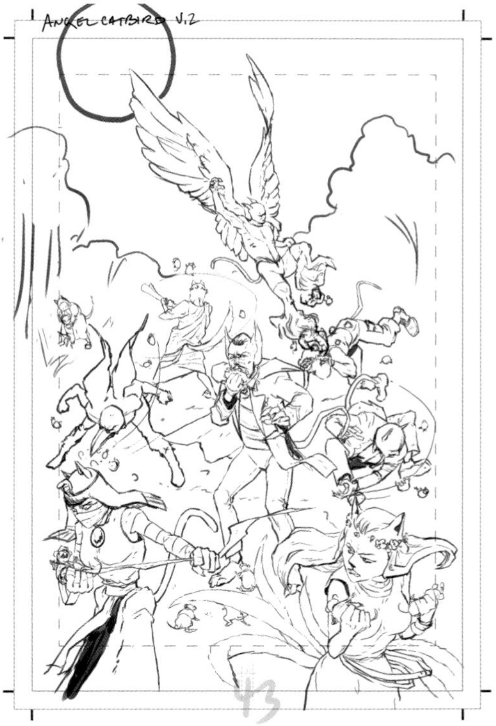
ANGEL CATBIRD V.2
43
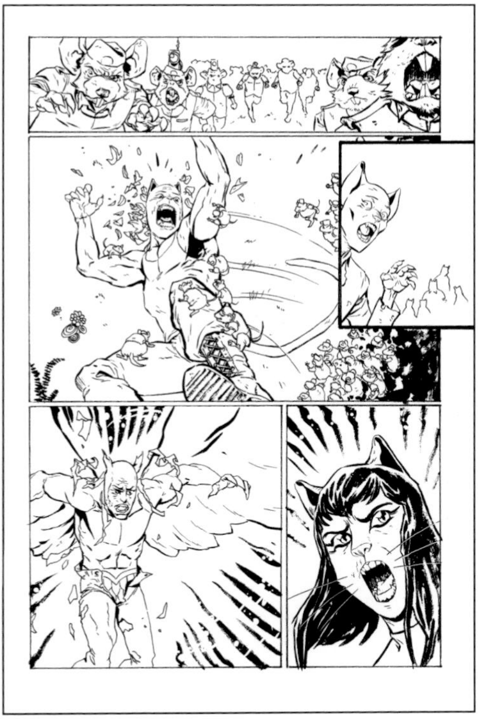

This fight scene was a favorite. Our heroes springing into action and giving the Murines what for.

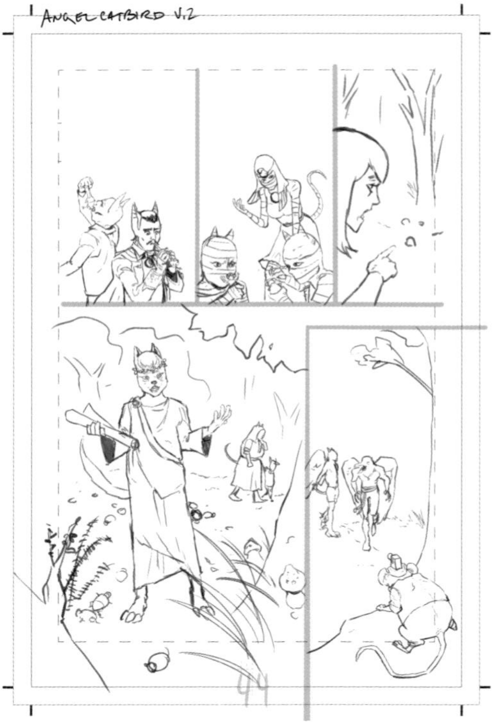
ANGELCATBIRD V.2
44
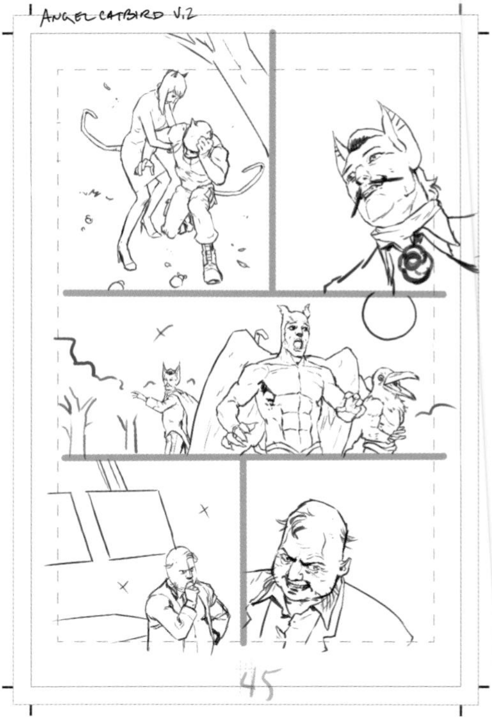
ANGELCATBIRD V.2
45
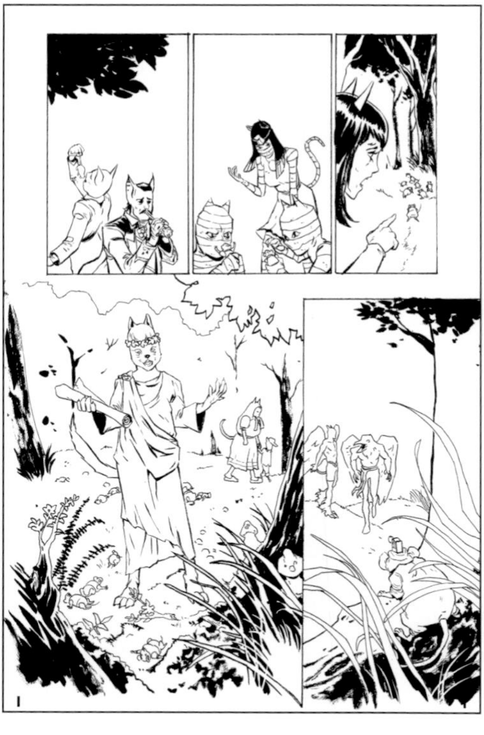
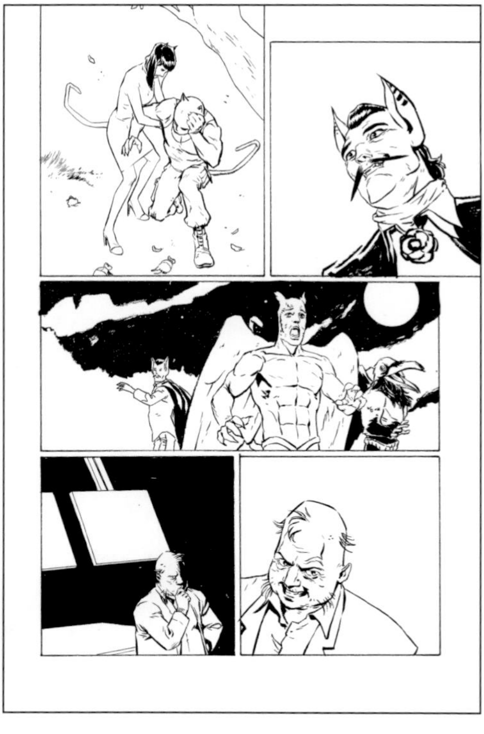

After inks are approved, they're sent off to Tamra. She then adds another dimension to the project with her coloring.

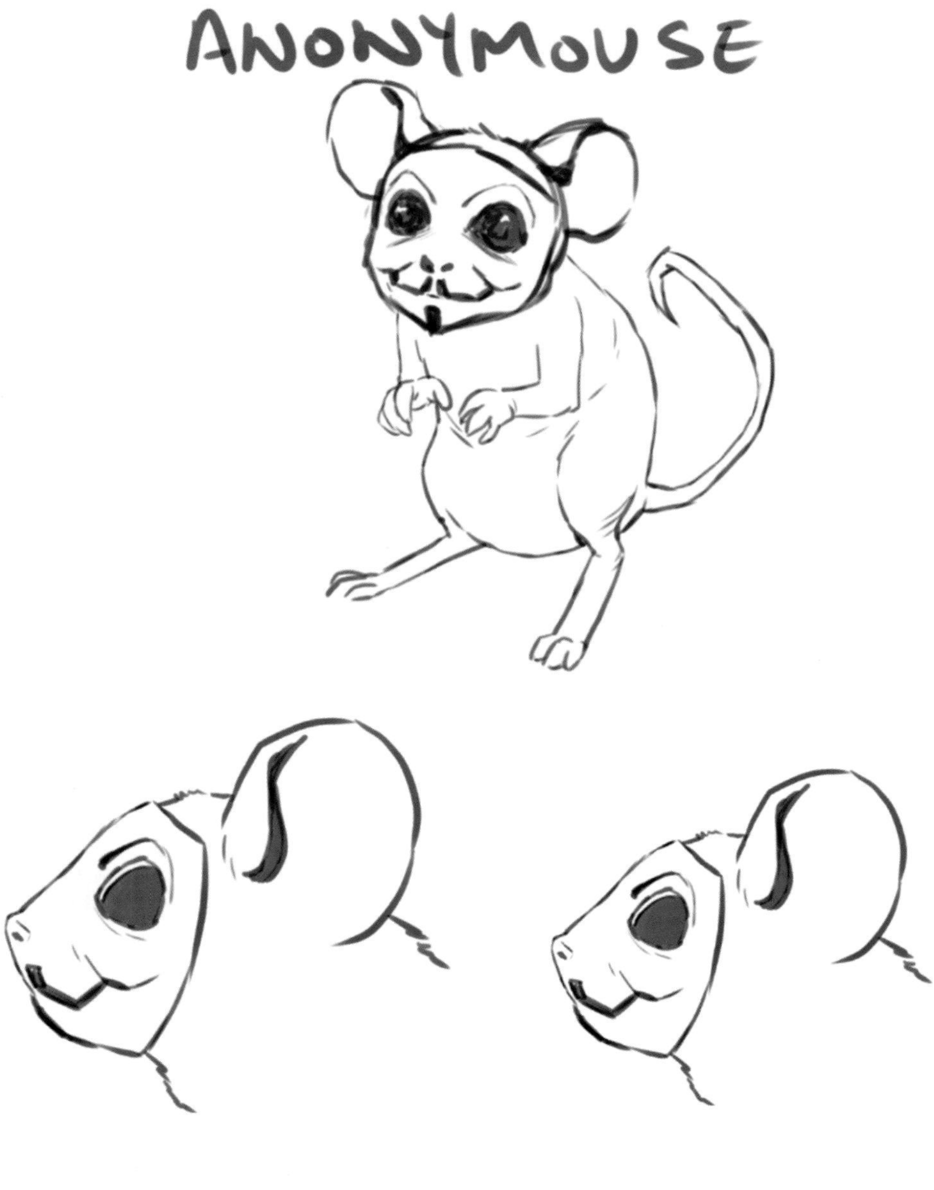
ANONYMOUSE

The Anonymice are one of my favorite additions to the series!

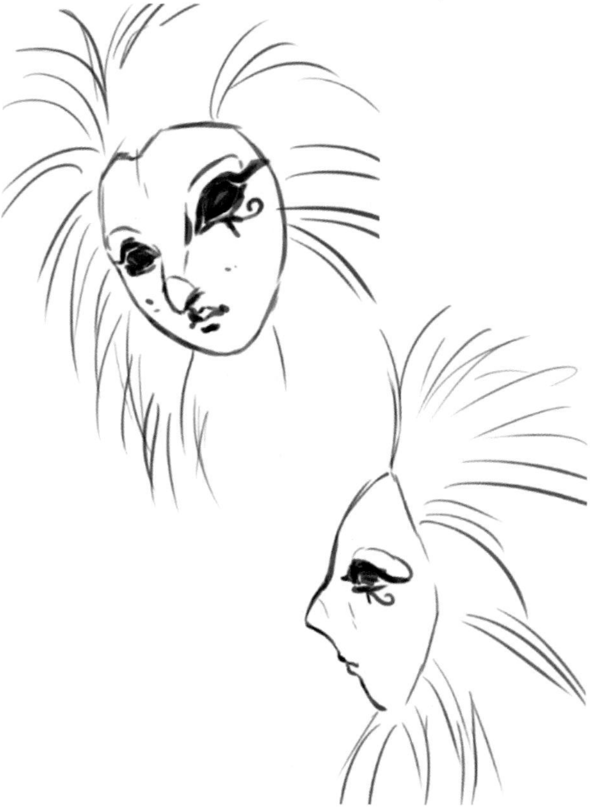

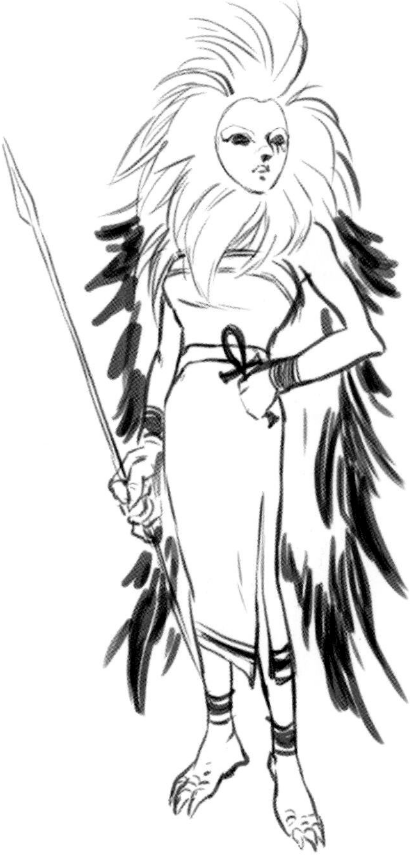

For volume 3, we reworked Nekhbet. Margaret wanted to bring in the punky, spiked plumage of real-life Egyptian white vultures, as well as the suggestion of a beak and their miraculously dark eyes.

SEKHMET V2

SEKHMET

Sekhmet is one of my favorite characters to draw.
I cheated a bit and gave her a male lion's mane. I
thought it would make for a more dramatic
character design, so I went with it.

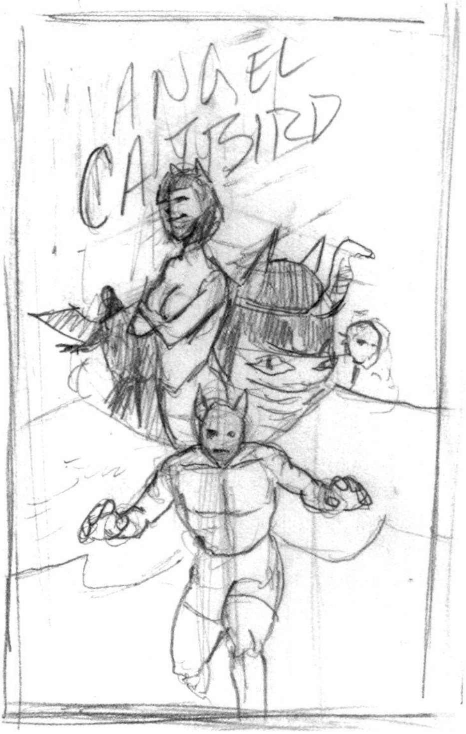
ANGEL
CATBIRD

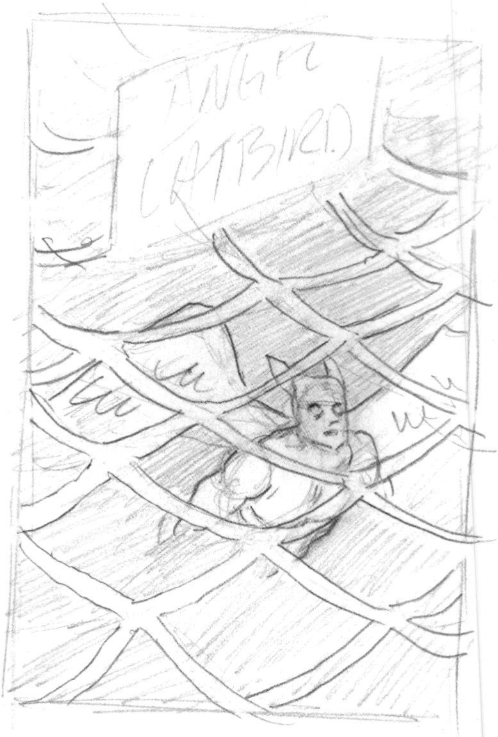
CATBIRD

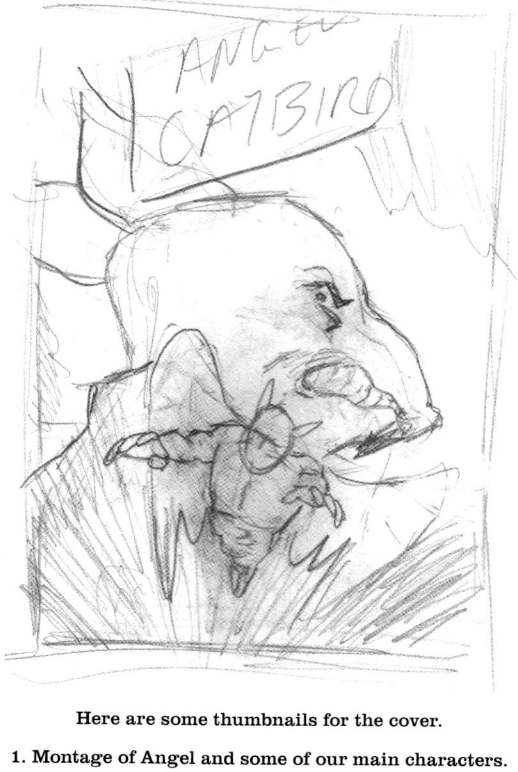
CATBIRD

Here are some thumbnails for the cover.

1. Montage of Angel and some of our main characters.
2. Angel emerging from the dark, captured but unbroken.
3. And a final-showdown-style cover with Angel in the foreground flying headlong into the fray. Muroid looks over, ominously baring his teeth.

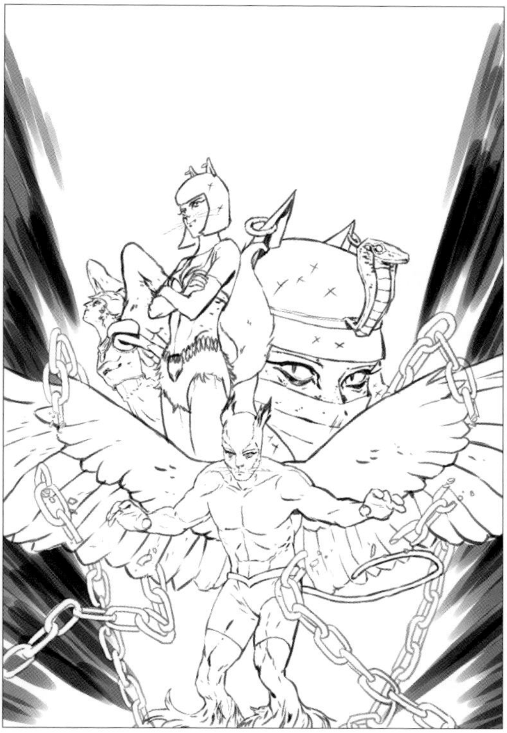

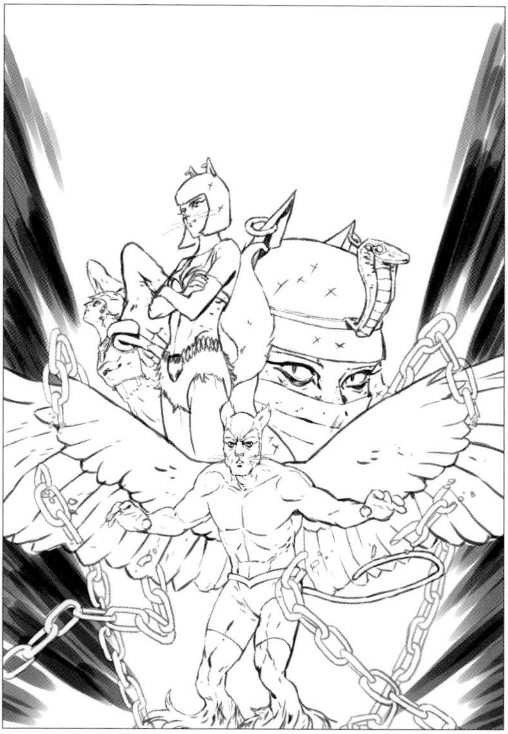

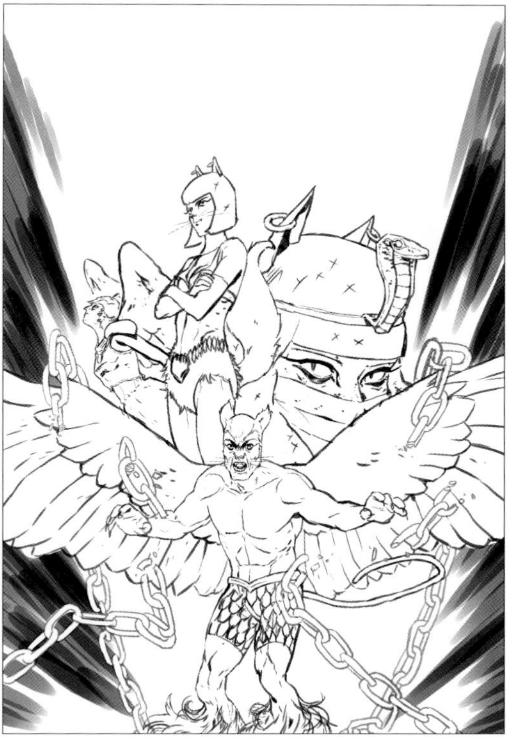

We went with the montage version. There were a few changes to Angel's facial expression along the way and the addition of chains.

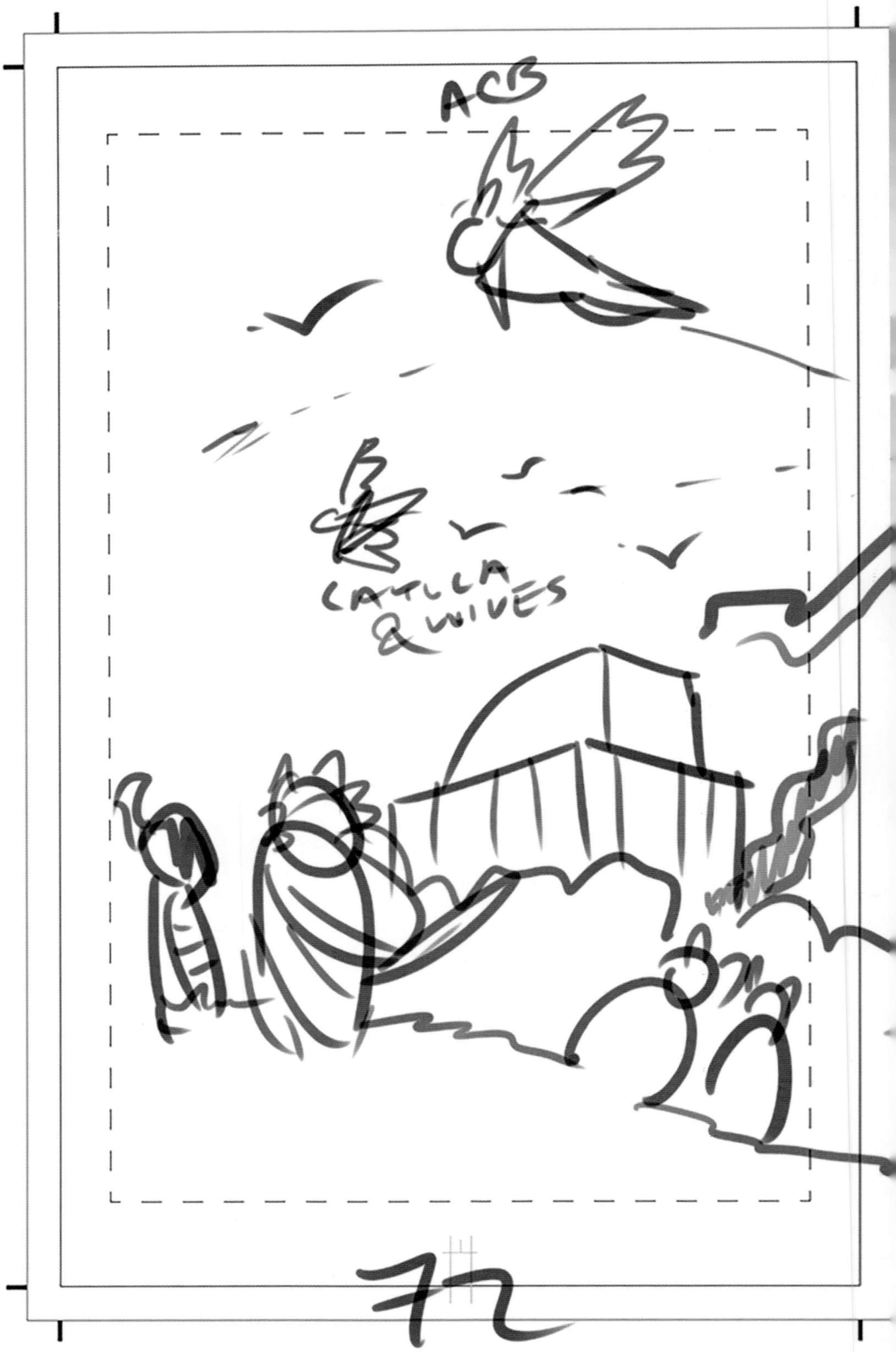
ACB
CATLLA
& WIVES
72

Here's a thumbnail of our big action fight spread. It's important to nail down the composition and action of the page at this stage.

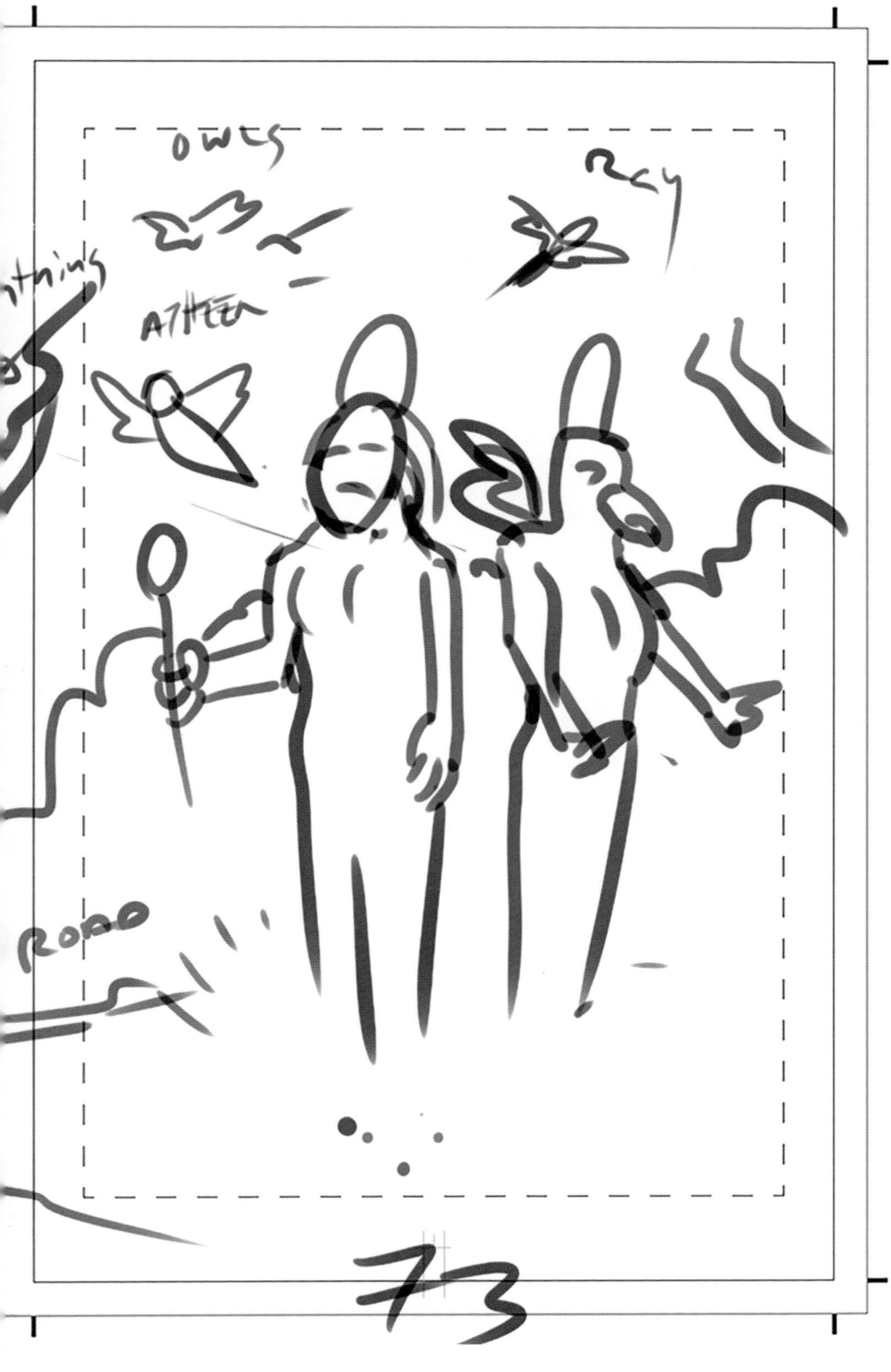
OWLS
ROAD
73

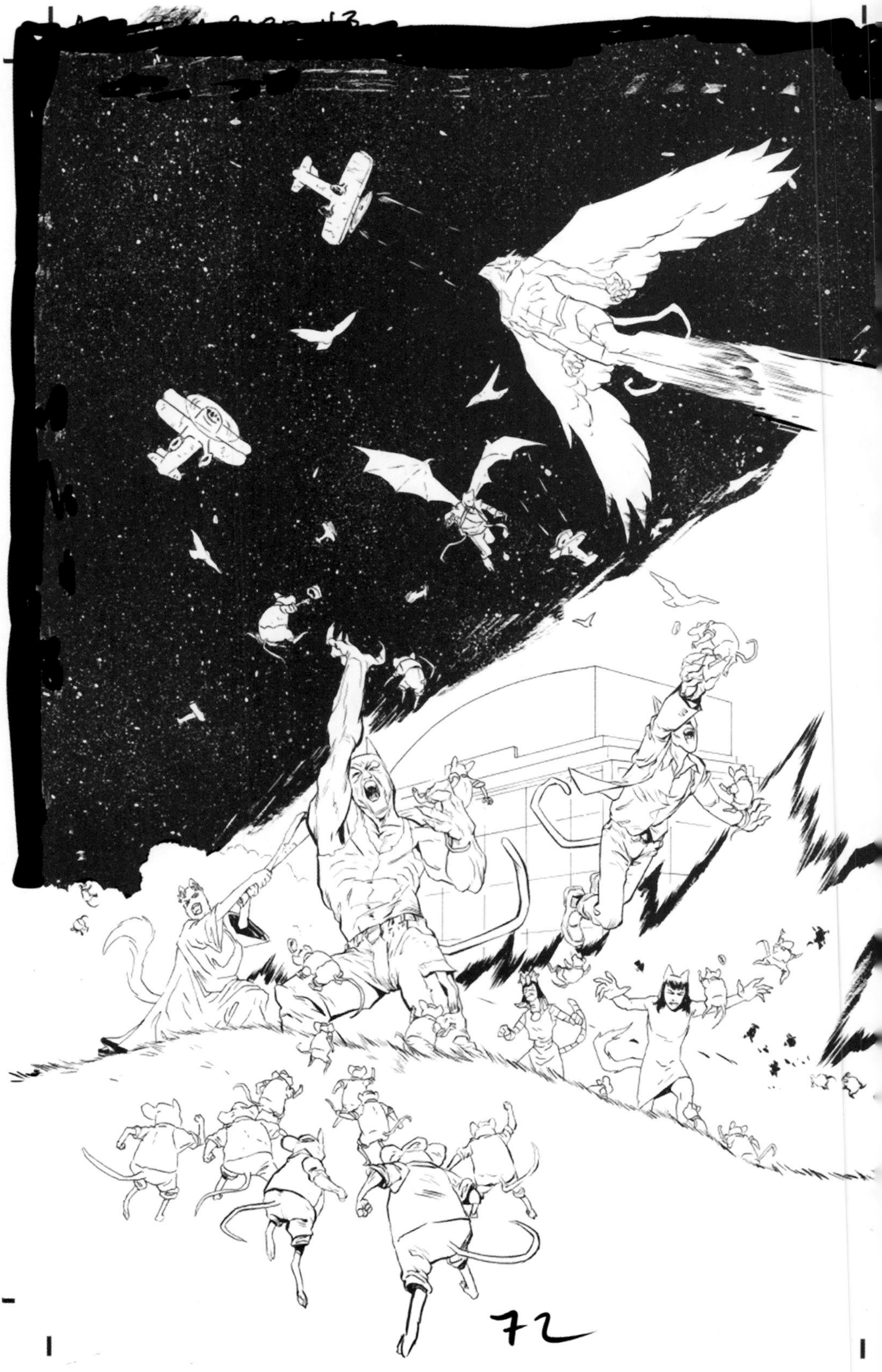
72

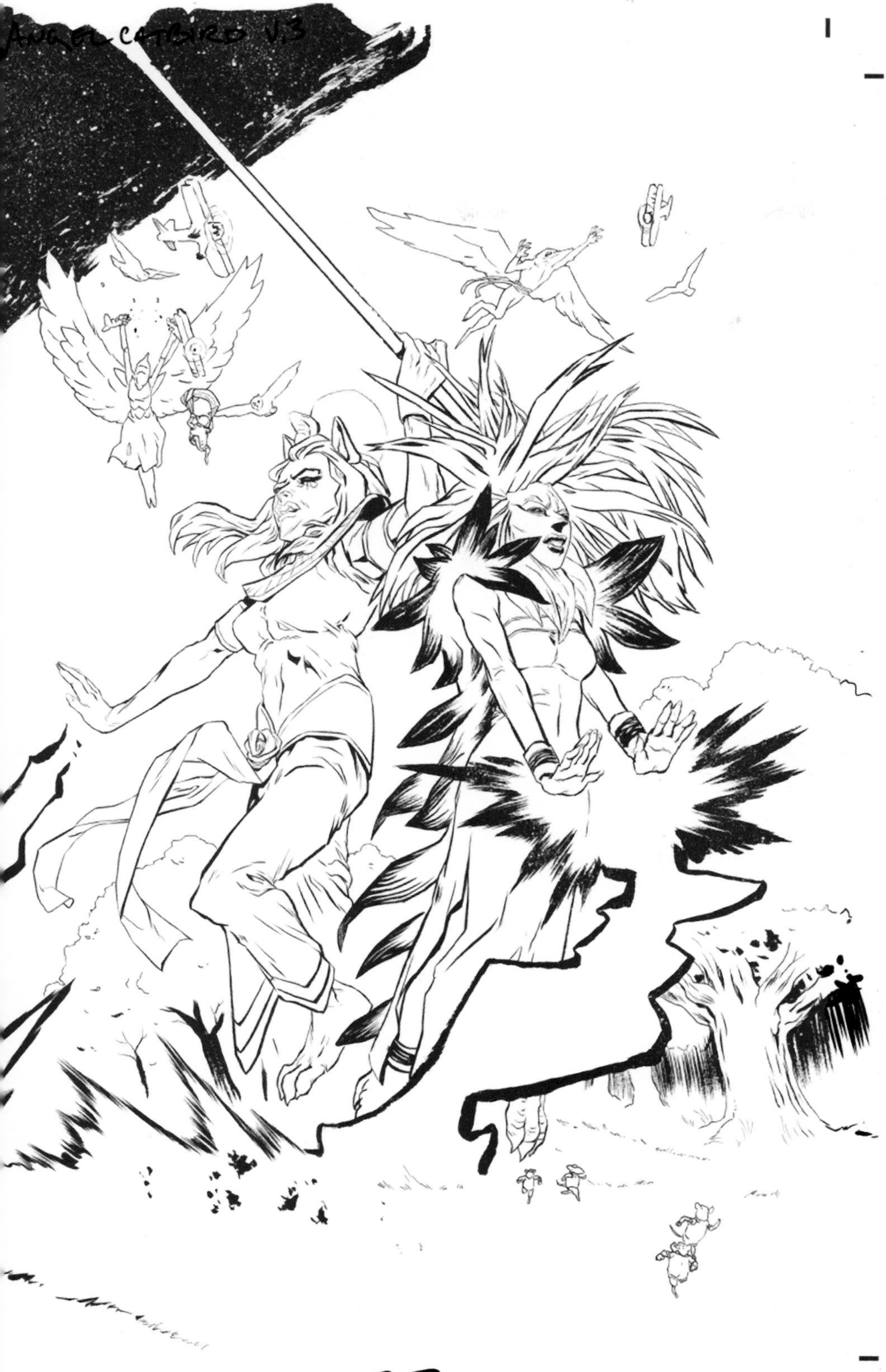
ANGEL CATBIRD V.3
73

And here's the same spread, but with final inks. At this point I handed it off to Tamra to work her wonderful color magic on the page.

MARGARET ATWOOD

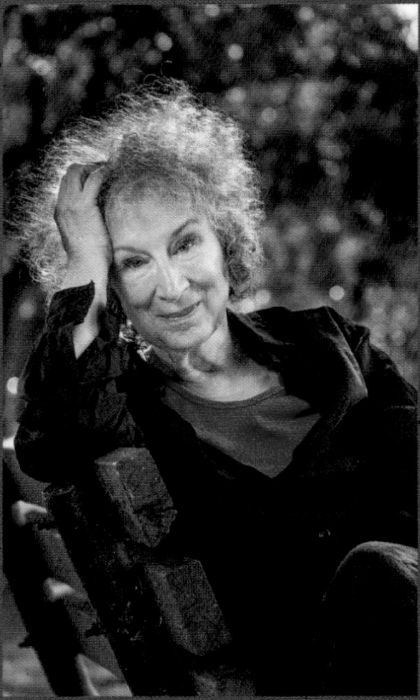

Photograph by LIAM SHARP

Margaret Atwood was born in 1939 in Ottawa and grew up in northern Ontario, Quebec, and Toronto. She received her undergraduate degree from Victoria College at the University of Toronto and her master's degree from Radcliffe College.

Atwood is the author of more than forty volumes of poetry, children's literature, fiction, and nonfiction, but is best known for her novels, which include *The Edible Woman* (1969), *The Handmaid's Tale* (1985), *The Robber Bride* (1993), *Alias Grace* (1996), and *The Blind Assassin*, which won the prestigious Man Booker Prize in 2000. Her latest work is a book of short stories called *Stone Mattress: Nine Tales* (2014). Her newest novel, *MaddAddam* (2013), is the final volume in a three-book series that began with the Man Booker Prize–nominated *Oryx and Crake* (2003) and continued with *The Year of the Flood* (2009). *The Tent* (mini-fictions) and *Moral Disorder* (short fiction) both appeared in 2006. Her most recent volume of poetry, *The Door*, was published in 2007. *In Other Worlds: SF and the Human Imagination*, a collection of nonfiction essays, appeared in 2011. Her nonfiction book *Payback: Debt and the Shadow Side of Wealth* was adapted for the screen in 2012. Ms. Atwood's work has been published in more than forty languages, including Farsi, Japanese, Turkish, Finnish, Korean, Icelandic, and Estonian.

JOHNNIE CHRISTMAS

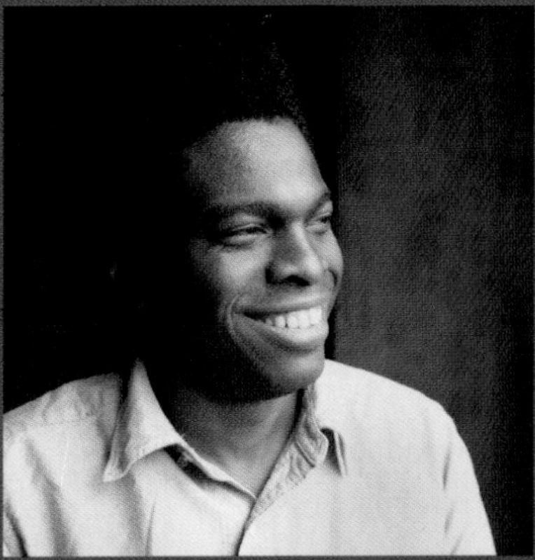

Photograph by AVALON MOTT

Johnnie Christmas was born in Río Piedras, Puerto Rico, and raised in Miami, Florida. He attended the Center for Media Arts magnet program at South Miami Senior High School and received a BFA from Pratt Institute in Brooklyn, New York, before going on to a career in graphic design and art direction. In 2013 he entered the world of comics as cocreator of the critically acclaimed Image Comics series *Sheltered*. He's also the creator, writer, and artist of *Firebug*, serialized in *Island*, also published by Image Comics. His work has been translated into multiple languages.

Johnnie makes Vancouver, BC, his home.

TAMRA BONVILLAIN

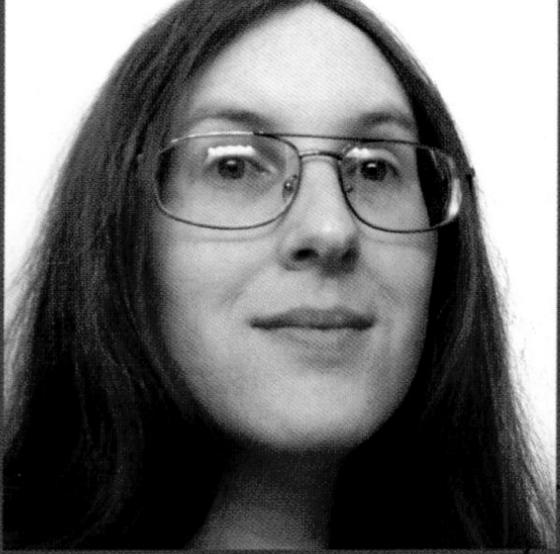

Tamra Bonvillain is originally from Augusta, Georgia, and took an interest in art and comics at a young age. After graduating from the local Davidson Fine Arts Magnet School in 2000, she majored in art at Augusta State University. She later attended the Joe Kubert School, and upon graduating in 2009, she began working full time as an assistant and designer for Greg Hildebrandt and Jean Scrocco's company, Spiderwebart. During this time, she also began to take on work as a comics colorist, eventually leaving the company to pursue a career in the comics industry full time. In the years since, she has worked for many major comic publishers, including Dark Horse, Dynamite, Boom, Image, and Marvel. She is currently the colorist for *Rat Queens*, *Wayward*, and several other titles.

AS SEEN ON

A daily dose of fantasy is better than reality.

As cat owners, we can provide our cats with engaging entertainment options that have a positive plot-line. Keeping cats from roaming freely outdoors protects both our cats and the birds they love to watch.

By keeping your cat safe, you've taken an important first step. Celebrate by joining our growing movement.

Learn more & take the pledge at www.catsandbirds.ca

Keep Cats Safe & Save Bird Lives

It seems so very unlikely, but experts agree: Cats can be trained to walk with a harness. Your neighbours will get used to the sight!

Cats allowed to roam freely are exposed to risks from cars, diseases, parasites, fights with other cats, dogs and wildlife and malicious humans, not to mention getting lost.

Learn more & take the pledge to keep your cat safe & save bird lives at: **www.catsandbirds.ca**

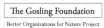

Keep Cats Safe
& Save Bird Lives

Catios are a great way to give your cats the benefits of the outdoors without the risks to them and local birds and wildlife!

Cats allowed to roam freely are exposed to risks from cars, diseases, parasites, fights with other cats, dogs, and wildlife, and malicious humans, not to mention getting lost.

Learn more and take the pledge to keep your cat safe and save bird lives at: **www.catsandbirds.ca**

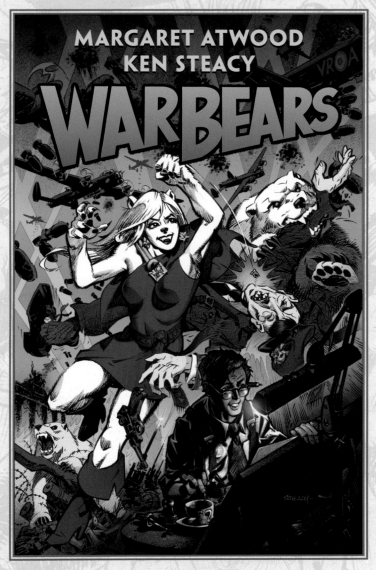

MILK AND CHEESE: DAIRY PRODUCTS GONE BAD

Evan Dorkin

The Eisner Award–winning dairy duo returns in this deluxe hardcover collecting every *Milk and Cheese* comic from 1989 to 2010 and a staggering array of extras, supplements, and bonuses.

ISBN 978-1-59582-805-7 | $19.99

RESET

Peter Bagge

If you could relive major events in your life, would you try to make things better—even if your best attempts only make things worse? Or would you set your most twisted fantasies into motion? A hilarious new hardcover graphic novel from Harvey Award–winning writer/artist Peter Bagge!

ISBN 978-1-61655-003-5 | $15.99

CHIMICHANGA

Eric Powell

When Wrinkle's Traveling Circus's adorable little bearded girl trades a lock of her magic beard hair for a witch's strange egg, she stumbles upon what could be the saving grace for her ailing freak show—the savory-named beast Chimichanga!

ISBN 978-1-59582-755-5 | $14.99

BUCKO

Jeff Parker and Erika Moen

After discovering a body in an office bathroom, Rich "Bucko" Richardson becomes suspected of the murder. A quest to find the real killer becomes a romp through the wilds of Portland, Oregon. After taking the Internet by storm, Jeff Parker and Erika Moen's dirty, funny murder mystery is now a hilarious hardcover book!

ISBN 978-1-59582-973-3 | $19.99

THE MIGHTY SKULLBOY ARMY

Jacob Chabot

Skullboy stars in two volumes of manic fun, and the robotic, rascally Unit 1 and super-smart, simian Unit 2 await his orders. Are you ready for necktie-wearing bears in thinking caps, ninjas in tuxedos, police chases, giant squid battles, time-travel showdowns, not-so-evil duplicates, vengeful pigeons, flying dogs, wrestlers, jungle commando clashes, and more?

Volume 1 (2nd Edition) ISBN 978-1-61655-734-8 | $14.99
Volume 2 ISBN 978-1-59582-872-9 | $14.99

RECESS PIECES

Bob Fingerman

When a science project goes wrong, only the prepubescent children are spared the fate of zombification—which doesn't mean they're immune from being eaten alive! Bob Fingerman (*Beg the Question*, *You Deserved It*) dishes up a grisly combination of Hal Roach's *Our Gang* and zombies.

ISBN 978-1-59307-450-0 | $14.99

THE BOOK OF GRICKLE

Graham Annable

As befits his classically trained animation background, Graham Annable's fluid art pulses with life, in stories that practically jump off the page. Alternately poetic and hilarious, *Grickle* presents a strange twist on the everyday with heart and humor.

ISBN 978-1-59582-430-1 | $17.99